THE

Alan Pauls was born in Buenos Aires in 1959. He has worked as a university lecturer, scriptwriter, film critic and, more recently, as a journalist. He has published four novels, including the much-praised *Wasabi*. *The Past* has been published in several foreign languages, and it was the unanimously acclaimed winner of the 2003 Herralde Prize.

ALAN PAULS

The Past

TRANSLATED FROM THE SPANISH BY
Nick Caistor

VINTAGE BOOKS
London

Published by Vintage 2008

2 4 6 8 10 9 7 5 3 1

Copyright © Alan Pauls 2003

English translation copyright © Nick Caistor 2007

Alan Pauls has asserted his right under the Copyright, Designs and
Patents Act 1988 to be identified as the author of this work

First published with the title *El pasado* in 2003 by
Editorial Anagrama, Barcelona

First published in Great Britain by Harvill Secker in 2007

Vintage
Random House, 20 Vauxhall Bridge Road,
London SW1V 2SA

www.vintage-books.co.uk

Addresses for companies within The Random House Group Limited
can be found at: www.randomhouse.co.uk/offices.htm

The Random House Group Limited Reg. No. 954009

A CIP catalogue record for this book
is available from the British Library

ISBN 9780099481270

The Random House Group Limited makes every effort to ensure that
the papers used in its books are made from trees that have been
legally sourced from well-managed and credibly certified forests.
Our paper procurement policy can be found at:
www.rbooks.co.uk/environment

Mixed Sources
Product group from well-managed
forests and other controlled sources
www.fsc.org Cert no. TT-COC-2139
© 1996 Forest Stewardship Council
FSC

Printed in the UK by CPI Bookmarque, Croydon, CR0 4TD

For some time now, I have grown used to being dead.

JENSEN, *Gradiva*

PART ONE

CHAPTER 1

Rimini was taking a shower when the entry-phone buzzed. He went out wrapped in a hand towel – the only one he could find in that bazaar of perfumes, shower caps, creams, salts, lotions, remedies and massage oils into which Vera had converted the bathroom – and a trail of obedient drops followed him into the kitchen. 'Postman,' he heard a voice say between the roar of two lorries. Rimini asked him to push the letter under the door, then all of a sudden, as if surprised by the shadow of an intruder in a room he had thought was empty, he caught sight of himself, naked and shivering, in a glass door panel blown open by a sudden gust of wind. The classic image of confusion: trivial, precise, too obvious. The wisps of steam from the bathroom – he had left the shower running as if this might shorten the interruption – made him feel somehow nauseous. 'You have to sign for it,' came the shout through the intercom. Snorting, Rimini pressed the buzzer to open the door, and looked on helplessly as the vistas of his happiness collapsed around him.

A morning at home; the pleasure of the sun's rays caressing his face while he showered, the renewed enthusiasm he had felt, as though setting out on a journey, when he woke up and found himself alone; his first befuddled, innocent gestures that ended the silence of the night; the life-giving although slightly naïve sense of combativeness he experienced after strenuous bouts of love-making with Vera – all of this was crumbling about him. Although perhaps . . . Rimini tucked the receiver in the palm of his hand and stood for a few moments hunched over the hall table, as if trying to make himself invisible. But the buzzer rang again and the last glass panes of his morning happiness slowly crashed to the floor, as though in a scene from a silent film. Rimini, who most of all hated the way that the world sometimes seemed determined to imitate his private mishaps, did not feel plagiarised this time. He was in danger. He was not the victim

3

of a marginal note, but of a plot. And yet he resigned himself to his fate and opened the door. While he was staring down at his feet – a giant's feet, around which spread two tiny human oceans – he heard what he had been afraid of hearing from the start: the street door was locked.

Rimini ran down the three interminable flights of stairs that he cursed every day ('Fantastic! I *hate* lifts!' Vera had exclaimed the first time they had visited the apartment and she had seen the dark spiral of the staircase) and opened the front door, but could not see a soul. He felt so angry he thought he was going to explode. How was it possible? A battered old truck passed by in slow motion, a tangle of tanned forearms sticking out of the windows. The horn sounded repeatedly. 'Sweetheart!' a mocking voice shouted from somewhere among the throng of arms. Rimini looked down again at his feet (his left sandal was on his right foot, the right was on the left: a typical morning mix-up), at the pink towel just covering his thighs, like the garment of a Roman gladiator, and the raincoat getting soaked across his shoulders – but for some reason did not take the comment personally. He was about to step back inside when a smiling face popped up from behind the nearby newspaper kiosk and stopped him. It was a young man as gaunt as a fakir, with the kind of knotted, skinny body that rock musicians had stolen from Egon Schiele. But he was not tall, and was not wearing a uniform. 'Remini?' he asked, waving an envelope in the air. Rimini was about to correct him, but preferred to cut things short: 'Where do I sign?' The other man handed him the letter and a crumpled form covered with boxes with scrawled signatures and ID numbers. Rimini waited: a biro, a pencil, something. But the postman just stood there staring at Rimini's toenails glinting in the sun while he produced strange gurgling sounds from a chewed plastic straw in an empty can. 'Have you got something to write with?' asked Rimini. 'No, I haven't. Daft, isn't it?' the other man replied, as if by showing his amazement he would be excused his imbecility.

Ten minutes later, by now in a thoroughly black mood (Rimini had asked the man in the newspaper kiosk to lend him a pen, but the man would only sell him one, so Rimini – whose emergency attire did not include a wallet – had to promise to pay him later; then Rimini claimed his missive, but the postman-fakir would not hand it over until he agreed to buy a Christmas raffle ticket, and when Rimini protested that he had no money on him, winked and suggested he use the same credit line he had just called on to buy his pen with), Rimini collapsed on to a chair and for the first time was able to look at the letter properly. He felt a sense of infinite relief, as if this tiny oblong envelope he now held in close-up were the only talisman capable of exorcising his nightmare morning.

What caught his attention was not so much the shape of the letter as the paper it was made from. It was shiny and soft as silk, and it was a pale sky-blue colour which when bought might have been lavender. As if observing a ritual common among recipients of such old-fashioned letters, Rimini lifted the envelope to his nose. Its perfume (a mixture of petrol, nicotine and strawberry or cherry chewing gum) seemed to match the postman's fingers rather than the paper and its delicate colour: there were traces of his prints in one corner. There was no sender's address, and the handwriting did not mean much to Rimini. His name and address were written in printed capitals that looked too impersonal to be spontaneous (dictated not by the heart but by strategy, he thought, suddenly finding himself in the middle of a libertine novel): no clue either that could be explained by chance or a lack of familiarity with writing letters. What did seem strange to him was the way the address was scrunched into one corner of the envelope, as if the person who sent the letter had been reserving the rest of the space for a message they never managed to write, or had changed their mind about. There was something there, that he hoped could be salvaged from the destruction of his morning happiness. He glanced at the postmark: 'London'. Multiplied three times, an insolent, emaciated face wearing a wig stared out at him from the stamps. The figures of the date of posting formed a straggly moustache on one of the faces. With some difficulty, he managed to decipher it: a month and a half, he calculated. In a split second, Rimini saw the adventures on the letter's tortuous journey, overcoming strikes, drunken postmen, wrong letter-boxes. He felt that six weeks was far too long a time for a letter sent to someone who was not used to receiving them.

The truth was that Rimini did not even know how to open them.

He tried to tear a corner, but something resisted. He used his teeth, like a terrier, and when he spat out the piece of envelope, he realised he had also destroyed part of the contents. Inside was a colour photo: in the centre a red rose lay on a modest black stand in a glass case; beneath it on a white plaque in small but legible letters he could read: 'In Memoriam Jeremy Riltse, 1917–1995'. He was shaken by an obscure sense of foreboding: the damp, the dust, the sordid alchemy starting to seep under a door. Another chunk of his innocence fell away. When Rimini, who somehow knew what he would find, turned the photograph over, he was less young than he had been ten seconds earlier.

Indelible dark-blue ink, microscopic handwriting sloping to the right. And that old compulsion of putting everything in brackets at the slightest excuse. He read: *'In London (just like six years ago), except that now the window of the flat (rented from a Chinese woman who has a patch over one eye) looks out on to a yard with no flowers where dogs (the same ones, I think) rip open the refuse sacks every night and growl at each other over a few sad bones. (You should see the sight that greets me every morning when I wake up.) Two nights ago I awoke from a long, sweet dream: I can't remember much, but you were in it, worked up as usual over something that wasn't in the least bit important. At the same exact moment as I was having this dream (I learnt later) J.R. was killing himself. Things happen; they happen because they have to, without anyone putting them up to it. You can do what you like with this. (I've changed, Rimini, so much that you wouldn't recognise me any more.) This paper seems to have been specially made for you: everything written on it can be rubbed out with your finger without leaving a trace. It may even be that these lines have disappeared before they reach you. But the photo and J.R. are not to blame. If you had been in my place (and you were, my dream tells me so) you would have taken the photo too. The only difference is that I have the guts to send it you. I hope young Vera does not get jealous over a poor dead painter. I hope you know how to be happy. S.'*

Rimini turned the photo back over and studied it. He recognised the art gallery and then, at the right-hand edge, the outline of one of Riltse's paintings that he had not noticed the first time. The glass case looked clouded, as if it were a double image. He brought the photograph closer and on the glass shielding the rose he could see the reflection of the flash, the small automatic camera, and finally, like a crown of shining light, the great blonde halo of Sofia's hair.

CHAPTER 2

Why was he so surprised? The last time he had heard from her, six months earlier and a year and a half after they had separated, it had also been via a written message. It had not been a whole sheet of paper, but only half of one – torn off by hand, with that little piece left from the top half that a hasty or angry tug leaves above the line traced with a thumb-nail – from a yellow sheet at the foot of which there was an address in the Belgrano neighbourhood.

It had been Rimini's birthday. Yet again, he had decided not to celebrate it, beyond enjoying the solitary pleasure of making a list of the friends who throughout the day left him congratulations on his answering-machine. But Vera, who interpreted his reticence as a form of male coquettishness (and Vera was right), sneaked the list of proven telephonic loyalties from him in an unguarded moment, counted them, and reserved a table for twelve at a restaurant in the city centre. (Only ten years separated her frank attitude to life and Rimini's hysteria: he had been born with the Cuban Revolution; she with the landing of man on the moon.) Victor had been the first to arrive. Rimini saw him come in, scan the restaurant rapidly, then cross the empty room with his upper body tilted forward in that typically unstable balance of his, something Rimini put down to his feet being far too small compared to the rest of him. He sensed he would also be the first to leave. Victor sat down next to him, but did not wish him happy birthday. Something was on his mind. 'Where's Vera?' he whispered. Rimini gestured towards the bar, where Vera stood rubbing the back of one calf with her other foot as she went through the evening's menu with the maître d. 'I bumped into Sofia this afternoon,' Victor said. All of a sudden Rimini felt something pressing against his ribs, as if he were being held up. He looked down, and Victor's fist opened: a delicate, carnivorous flower with slender petals and varnished nails. In his palm Rimini saw a piece of paper, uncurling as though released from prison. After a quick glance over at the bar (Vera was already coming towards them) he made it disappear as if by magic. 'I'm sorry,' said Victor with relief, as he stood up to greet Vera: 'but as soon as she heard I was going to see you, there was nothing I could do to stop her.'

It was not until three hours later that Rimini remembered this secret time-bomb. He was in the restaurant bathroom, trying to clear his head by staring at himself in the mirror while rummaging for a coin to buy a tablet of soap. His fingertips brushed against his keys, the top of a biro which at that very moment, uncovered, was staining some pocket or other of his jacket, the indented rim of an Underground token and finally, the edge of the piece of paper. Just touching it gave him a shock, as if by merely opening it he might unleash a whole torrent of catastrophes. But it was now or never. So he unfolded the paper and read it in front of the mirror, swaying to and fro against the washbasins to catch the flickering light. '*Happy birthday, beast. How can you carry on having birthdays without me? I woke up early this morning, too early (I'm not sure in fact I even slept), and it was only when I was out in the street (coat over my nightdress, woollen stockings, slippers) that I realised why. Another 14th August! I bought something for you (I swear I couldn't help it). It's nothing, I've still got it with me. I'm not giving it to Victor because I feel a bit ashamed of it (and you know I would never want to embarrass you in front of my successor. I'm sure I'll regret it as soon as he's gone (look after him, and make sure Vera does too, remind him to take his pills); but by then it'll be too late. Call me if you want. I'm at the usual address. S. (Don't worry, this message will self-destruct in fifteen seconds.)*'

Someone pushed the door open. Rimini felt a blow in the small of his back and, fearing he had been found out, turned on a tap. The scrap of paper slipped from his fingers and landed in the bottom of the basin, where it was baptised by three tiny streams of water. 'Bastard,' he heard a voice he recognised say behind him. Rimini half-turned towards the intruder, as Sofia's handwriting was slowly washed away in whirls of pale ink. It was Sergio, one of his guests. 'You've done the lot?' Rimini smiled: 'I had every right to. It was a birthday present.'

CHAPTER 3

Her writing compulsion was nothing new to him. How often had he suffered from it in the past? How often in the long period since he had been apart from Sofia, and how often *during* the nigh-on twelve years he had spent with her? In opera, characters who have reached an emotional limit, a point of no return where imperious passion demands that they change register, stop talking and start to sing. Actors in musicals stop walking around and start to dance. Sofia *wrote*. As a young girl (she was the typical schoolgirl overwhelmed with a long list of extra-curricular activities, always half-asleep, always contented) she had studied singing, and later as part of her 'corporal research' – as she called all the different classes and workshops she put herself through when no longer an adolescent – on more than one occasion she had come across the discipline of dance. But when love was too much for her, when one of its accidents, either the happiest or the most wretched (when she was in ecstasy, for example, or in despair) somehow crossed the threshold where love renders words or gestures invalid, Sofia fell silent and withdrew, as though she had to disappear in order to move on. An hour, a day, sometimes a week later, when the economy of love had regained its daily balance and the 'incident', as Rimini had privately baptised those episodes of aphasia, seemed to have spontaneously healed, he would suddenly find a message, a letter of three cramped lines or whole pages of confessional renunciation that Sofia had written all alone, in the strange intervals when she existed without Rimini but entirely for him: shut in a room or bar, elbow-deep in small paper napkins, or sleepless in the early hours and seated at the kitchen table, while Rimini took advantage of her absence and sprawled diagonally across the bed, his legs spread in a perfect 4. Or two romantic lines, slipped as if by accident into a shopping list for groceries or cleaning products, would suddenly leap out at him. He would open his wallet at the bus-stop and in between two dog-eared bank-notes would

10

discover the unexpected tip of an envelope, his initials traced on it by a loving hand. Inside, he would find the fruits of her passionate reflections crammed on to a medical prescription. Sofia's messages lay in wait for him in the bathroom cabinet, stuffed at the bottom of a jacket pocket, on the notepad next to the phone, between the pages of the document he had to translate (where Sofia sprinkled them like hidden signposts) or even in the fridge, where they waited long hours for him to notice them, frozen but stoic, propped against a milk carton or pot of yoghurt.

In the beginning, Rimini saw them as love offerings and felt flattered. Written as though they were cries for help or secret messages on the back of already-used scraps of paper, they seemed to him like domestic gems, possessing the enchantment of a sentimental, loving craftsmanship, as moving as much for the gaps in them as for their insights ... As if in a belated echo of the urgency with which Sofia had composed them, Rimini felt compelled to read all the messages the moment he found them. In his desire to savour the untimely phrase he was known to have turned on the gas on the stove and have forgotten to light it, to have dropped whatever work he was doing, or come to a halt in the midst of crossing a busy avenue, or with that rudeness so typical of people in love, to have left a question asked him floating in mid-air. Every message was a balm, a shot of happiness, the tiny dose with which the ultimate drug – his love for Sofia – confirmed his addiction when he was least expecting it, or when habit – and Sofia's momentary absence – had led him to think he might be able to do without her. He was moved not so much by finding them, as by the fact that they unerringly found him. Like suicide messengers, they crossed and overcame obstacles that the world threw up between him and Sofia. He read them immediately, in even the most hazardous circumstances, when the slightest distraction could harm or endanger him. Somehow, they made him feel invulnerable: the letters – and above all the delicious fog they conjured up around him – were his armour and his antidote. And after he had read them, almost always whispering the words to himself in the hope that this would mean his voice and Sofia's were in dialogue, Rimini went back to whatever he had been doing when the letters had interrupted him. He returned to work, to talking, to crossing the street like a robotic sleepwalker, still clutching them like a secret talisman. And then, when they met again at nightfall, Sofia did not even need to ask him if he had read them, because Rimini would leap in first and collapse in her arms, euphoric and vanquished at the same time. Before even greeting her, overwhelmed by the pleasure of finally being able to respond to the love-token she had offered him, he would smother her in kisses, and rush to carry on with the message from the very point she had decided to bring it to a close. They had been apart for scarcely eight or ten hours, sometimes even less, but the simple intervention of the letter – which Rimini, despite being familiar with the system, was always surprised and somewhat taken aback by, as if it were a chance occurrence – seemed to prolong their separation unbearably and to increase the distance between the worlds in which, throughout all those hours, each of them had gone on existing without the other. (Once Rimini, startled by a message while travelling on the Underground, almost fainted when his eyes lit upon Sofia's handwriting: he found himself thinking that Sofia was dead, had been dead for years, while at the same time he was horrified to discover that these few lines slipped stealthily into a page of his diary like a voice from Beyond or an unexpected sign of life, destroyed this possibility at the same moment as he was injecting himself with it.) It was this strange *rebirth* of love – doubtless the fruit more of a retrospective hope than of love itself – which explained the deep, almost desperate trance-like state Rimini and Sofia fell into whenever they met again. They embraced more like victims than lovers, victims who at last had won their freedom, and the almost inaudible words of love they whispered as they kissed did not so much speak of the fatal distancing brought by daily life, but celebrated a reprieve from a sentence that would have kept them apart for all eternity.

As time went by, Rimini built up a vast collection of these messages. He kept them in secret hiding-places that he changed every so often out of fear that Sofia might discover them. He never re-read the notes: it was enough for him to possess them; but few things excited him, especially when he could hear Sofia's footsteps approaching, as much as sniffing in an old shoe-box, a book, or in the pocket of a jacket he no longer wore, to add a new item to his hoard. (Rimini, who did not condemn adultery but saw it as something completely alien, something as outlandish and unlikely as levitating, astrology or drug addiction, had nevertheless found a way of practising it: he deceived his beloved with the love-tokens she herself had sent him.) He collected them in the same way that others keep photographs, locks of hair, beer mats, theatre tickets, boarding passes or postcards from foreign countries, relics that lovers contemplate from time to time in order to remember the historic dimensions of an everyday passion or to revivify it, to stoke up the flames whenever, stuck in some sluggish backwater, it runs the risk of turning into sterile repetition.

One day – a day like any other, with no portent or sign – Rimini found a message, and for the first time ever postponed the moment of reading it. He was late for something. He was charging down the Underground steps three at a time, pushing his way through a sleepy crowd, when he heard the sound of a train pulling up at the platform. He rummaged in his pocket for a token: his blind fingers had to rescue it from where it was hidden between the folds of a piece of paper. He rushed through the turnstile, skirted a line of travellers who had decided against getting on, and stopped the doors closing by forcing half his body into the carriage. Ashamed at his own daring, he travelled two stations without looking up, and when he thrust his hands in his pockets – to make himself smaller, as if this polite gesture, which no one noticed, could help redeem the rudeness of his barging in – he touched the letter again. At first he thought that to read it there, in such an extreme situation, squashed up against doors of the carriage, would be an irrefutable proof of love, but then he thought better of it and, after stroking the edges of the paper as though to silence this mute voice calling out to him, he let it lie in his pocket. But then, suffering from that strange knock-on effect which an initial lack of punctuality often triggers, he kept on arriving late, so that although it was only just beginning, he spent the whole of the rest of the day trying to recover the ten or twelve minutes he had lost at the start. He did not succeed. Every decision he made was wrong: he confused the times and places he had arranged to meet people, he caused incidents in the street, his lunch and his work went badly. He was tense, and got upset over the slightest thing (he read an eight instead of a three on his bill, and thought he had been swindled; he heatedly defended a footnote in a translation that was indefensible). And he completely forgot Sofia's message.

Over dinner two days later, Sofia asked him if he had read it. Rimini's head whirled, as if a sudden squall had blown up in the pit of his stomach. 'Yes,' he managed to say, 'of course I did.' For a few minutes, they went on eating in silence, avoiding each other's gaze. Everything was white in front of Rimini's eyes: that endless, dull, guilty white that often floods the memory of a student sitting down to an exam. He played with his food for a while, then, almost without realising it, crossed his knife and fork on the plate. Later, they fell asleep in bed watching an old Argentine film on TV. Rimini found himself struggling to keep his eyes open; he could hear the sound of the film like an indistinct background rumour, a sort of scummy foam over which the ripples of Sofia's breathing came and went. He did not dare look at her. All his attention was fixed on her breathing, the tiniest movements of her body, the way in which her arm, flung across his chest, seemed to be getting heavier or lighter. At that moment it seemed to him that his whole life depended on which of the two of them would give in to sleep first, and that this key moment, usually eagerly awaited by them as a loving proof, the threshold of night where the weaker of the two finally entrusted themself to the other's care, was on this occasion a battle to decide an undeclared war.

With her back to the camera, a young woman was undressing under a lascivious sculptor's gaze. At the same time, she was writhing in ecstasy, dying of poison. In his dream, Rimini saw an image (a hand as white as ivory, its fingers slowly opening and letting slip a tiny phial of poison). He woke up. He was alone. It was morning, probably after eleven. As he started to dress, he saw the pair of trousers Sofia had rescued from the laundry the previous evening hanging from the wardrobe door. He decided to put them on. He put his hand into one of the pockets and at the bottom his fingers came into contact with a piece of stiff, rough paper, which crumbled beneath his touch.

CHAPTER 4

To say they liked Riltse would have been an insult – the worst, most miserable, most philistine insult imaginable. They *adored* him. They had always adored him, from the moment they had become adults, a time that had begun, they told both themselves and any disbelieving observer who happened to be listening, the day they discovered that they loved each other. Rimini was sixteen; Sofia was seven months older – a gap Rimini could never get used to, and which he saw as equally distressing as the few, decisive metres separating Achilles and the tortoise. They adored Riltse and loved Tanguy, Fauxpass and Aubrey Beardsley, the dubious family of artists that students in the know – those experts in naïvety and petulance – stuck on their folder covers to humiliate their enemies, who put film or rock stars on theirs. It was not long before they changed their minds. Two or three years later, deliquescent objects, stalactites in the shape of loving couples, old-fashioned beds, eyes and hats floating in clear blue skies, the whole gamut of artistic tricks they had once worshipped as the height of imagination, now seemed completely fraudulent, and only produced a sense of rejection. They had discovered (although they only realised it later on, when they were living together in a carpeted den in Belgrano R, and their former schoolmates, in a typical outburst of sarcastic admiration, had started referring to them as the 'young fogeys') that youth does not adore artists and their works, but simply different kinds of families, and that beyond their indiscriminate adoration, equally indiscriminate disappointments lay in wait. To discover this was painful. They felt complete and utter idiots, because anything one is proud of that is later found to be ridiculous is twice as painful, while in this now aching wound they realised that a small but real part of their youth had vanished. It was this sensible self-criticism that saved them. It saved them from the scorn of their friends and the rest of the world, always the first to detect any lapse in taste; and it saved Riltse from the disdainful fury with which Rimini and Sofia rid themselves of the gang of swindlers they had previously worshipped.

They made short work of Tanguy. The painter rewarded them by scattering the last few ashes of his glory while the dew still glistened on the grass. They burnt all Fauxpass in an afternoon, in the fly-filled jungle which one of Sofia's grandmothers had behind her house in City Bell. They did not even waste any time watching how the flames purified their betrayed hearts. Max Brauner took even less time: they had very few reproductions of his work. They only knew of it at second-hand, thanks to the exalted descriptions in the autobiography by an astute contemporary, a failed painter who forty years later, when Brauner himself had been rotting in a Polish graveyard for some thirty years, became the Soviet Union's richest and most elusive *marchand*. They also destroyed the autobiography.

Then it was Riltse's turn. Sofia gathered up the posters. By now an accomplished arsonist, Rimini got the kerosene and the matches. Until that moment, less out of rancour than superstition, they had denied the condemned artists that last look of farewell rather than forgiveness which softens the walk to the gallows. But when it came to Riltse, Sofia hesitated, as if the shadow of committing an irreparable error had flitted across her mind. The posters dangled for a second above the flames. Rimini, whose fingers were already being singed, dropped them. Sofia pushed them away from the fire and, like someone searching through piles of identical-looking papers to find the safe-conduct that will permit them to cross a frontier, she rummaged among them for one in particular. Rimini was about to protest. He was stubborn: there was nothing he hated more than breaking rules he had set himself. He allowed his anger to simmer while he looked at the fire for a few moments, and then, when the length of time he had mentally given Sofia to change her mind was over, he turned back to her. She was sitting on the grass with her back to him; her shoulders were gently shaking. He went over and asked what was wrong. Sofia was crying silently: between her legs, three reproductions from Riltse's series *The Tortures* lay cradled like tiny corpses. Rimini cast another glance at the round platforms, the bodies hanging like sides of beef, their long white ribcages, the dress suits hanging neatly from the portable clothes racks, and smiled. Riltse survived.

Their first trip to Europe had simply been an excuse to see the originals of Riltse's work. Sofia had already travelled there with her parents, and so she used this second slight advantage of hers to oblige Rimini's father – one of the sponsors of the journey – to base their itinerary on the rather old-fashioned but unforgettable path traced on her previous one, which Sofia's parents had in turn inherited from a couple who were friends 'with the whole world' and who liked sportswear (Rimini swore they had been the pioneers of *jogging* – the clothes, the sport and the militant attitude – in Belgrano and perhaps the whole of Argentina), glass miniatures and Spanish art part-works. Out of the seventy days for the half-a-dozen countries their trip covered, fifteen were reserved for Austria. Rimini thought this rather exaggerated: not that he had anything against Austria, but a glance at a map of Central Europe, an estimation of how big Austria was and how complete his lack of German, compared to the length of the fortnight to be spent there, made him realise he was missing some essential element to help him understand what was going on. It was only on the flight out that Sofia, emboldened by the little bottle of wine she had with her meal, confessed that the married couple her parents were friendly with were Austrian.

Rimini saw this simply as another of her lovable quirks, one of the many that gave his relationship with Sofia that slightly old-fashioned eccentricity which won both respect and ridicule from his closest friends. That same year, more than half the class they had finished secondary school with travelled to Europe, but apart from César Lichter, whose glasses Rimini thought he saw glinting behind a sports-car magazine in the station they had alighted at to change trains, they never met any of their former schoolmates. The fact was that the Europes they were roaming round were the same continent only for tourist guides and travel agents' maps. Fels and Matheu zigzagged their way around Amsterdam laden with drugs, scarves, and pornographic miniatures. Catania went back to his native Turin and joined a group of 'theoretical debate' – the intellectual embryo, it later transpired, of the first *Brigate Rosse* cells. Bialobroda and his legendary two canine teeth – one broken, the other made of gold – put an end to two decades of dissolute living by hanging himself with a belt in the Hôtel du Vieux Paris, two blocks from the Seine, in a room that was never paid for.

Maure slept rough in Ibiza and Nepper, blond, skinny as a rake and extremely good-looking, was arrested in the toilets of a bar in Barcelona's Chinese Quarter. While all this was going on, Rimini and Sofia, insulated by the asbestos of a parallel, more Alpine and less disturbing Europe, collected medieval villages, snow-capped mountains, squares as clean as clinics, traditional costumes, trams, stifling eiderdowns, beer festivals and folk songs celebrating nightingales, hills, harvests and hearts, all of which after half a dozen energetically downed *steins* of beer, somehow turned into raucous battle hymns.

More than once, as Rimini changed trains, marvelling at the promiscuous punctuality of his Railpass, struggling with their suitcases and his heavy suede overcoat – his mother's last-minute contribution – which made him look like a stiff snowman as he walked along, he suspected he might be making the wrong journey. There was not much for him to object to: the trains were comfortable, the service efficient; the locals compensated in a friendly way for the difficulties he found in communicating; the cafés had newspapers from all over the world waiting for him on charming wooden poles; and the cakes were irresistible. Almost unrecognisable due to the amount of clothes she was wearing, Sofia dragged him down blind alleys she claimed to remember, rather vaguely, from her previous trip and was keen to verify according to what she said she had written in her diary. 'Wait . . . down here there was an in-cred-ible lace shop . . . I've got it written down . . . Here it is: lace! "at the far end of Blacksmiths' Court" . . . that's where we are, isn't it? "Beyond the Grillpärzer pastryshop" . . . There, that's Grillpär . . . It must be down here . . . they had wonderful strudel, we can have one afterwards . . . There! That's it, I remember now! The window was all white . . .' 'It's a music shop, Sofia.' 'Don't be so negative. Let's cross over and look.' 'Can't you see? It says old instruments.' 'It must be wrong.' 'You came two years ago, Sofia: things change here as well.' 'Look at that lute, isn't it beautiful?' No, the problem for Rimini was not the lace (most of which was to be found, naturally enough, on Lacemakers' Street), nor the strudel in Grillpärzer (delicious), nor the lutes (although as soon as they had entered the shop, the owner had asked them to put their cigarettes out, shake their boots off outside and not to talk so loudly), nor anything else he encountered. The problem was everything he did *not* encounter, the kind of negative

18

journey that persistently troubled him, like an unpaid debt, and caused him secret regrets. Shouldn't we be a bit dirtier? Shouldn't we have lost our passports? Shouldn't we quarrel more? Shouldn't the police look at us suspiciously, stop us, demand to see our passports? Where had the discos got to, where were other youngsters like us, the youth hostels, the syringes?

These were only fleeting doubts – the wingbeat of a distracted bird, too fleeting, thought Rimini, to do any real harm – and they left no traces. Besides, every new destination seemed to belie the suspicions aroused by the previous one. Salzburg made up for Innsbruck's blind spots, Vienna compensated for those of Salzburg, and so on. And it was in Vienna, once Sofia had emerged beautiful and gaunt from the flu ordeal that had kept her in bed for five days, that the paintings by Klimt, Egon Schiele and Kokoschka were like a foretaste of the ecstasy he dreamt of finding in London when he came face to face with Riltse's works, so that he finally came to terms with the trip. Before this, Rimini had sat watch over the bed where Sofia raged with fever. The first day, he found it impossible to tell when she was asleep or awake. She threw off the covers as if they were burning her, then five minutes later, shivering with cold, searched desperately for them in the darkened room. In the middle of the night, she sat bolt upright, her pale lips mouthing words in an unknown language. Rimini searched for the hotel doctor; he spoke to the woman at reception, the night porter, the maître d in the restaurant, and finally the hotel manager. By the time he had exhausted the list of possible English-speakers and exhausted himself along the way, he thought he had understood that 'for the first time in twenty years, Doctor Kleber had called in sick'. But they did not abandon him. They sent up aspirins, tepid soups (there were six floors between the kitchen and the room they were in) sets of towels with another hotel's monogram on them, an abnormally slow thermometer, some back copies of the Austrian airline magazine. Rimini was on the go the whole time; he had never opened the same door so often, or felt so discouraged when he closed it again. Whenever Sofia lay quietly for ten minutes at a time, he was so happy he felt rejuvenated; barefoot, he would tiptoe over to the window and celebrate the miracle by watching the slow, stupid snowflakes falling through an impossibly red night.

The next day, the fever had gone down slightly. Sofia had already begun to notice some old-fashioned features in the room when Rimini, sleepless but lucid, picked up the telephone directory and found the address of the British Hospital. A short while after they got there, a young doctor attended them. He seemed very distinguished, and wore a white coat that was so crisp it crackled. In order to gain their confidence, or perhaps just to practise, he spoke a few words with a distinct Spanish lisp – Rimini deduced that he must go to Spain for holidays – then prescribed them antibiotics – he spoke to them both, as if Rimini was as ill as Sofia – and had the courtesy to suggest a pharmacy where English was spoken. The two of them left the hospital and hugged each other. Overcome with gratitude, each of them thought that it was the other who was on the point of bursting into tears. Sofia suggested they go and buy the medicines and, when they were back in the hotel, that they write the doctor a thank-you letter. They had to tell him, she said, all he had done for them: it was an opportunity they could not miss. Yet again, Rimini talked her out of it. Throughout their journey he had sabotaged half a dozen similar epistolary urges, all of them aimed at repaying the generosity of gondoliers, taxi-drivers, museum attendants, waiters or bank clerks – anonymous saviours whose merits often consisted in little more than helping them spell a street name properly, asking them where they were from, smiling vaguely, or even simply not raising their voices to them.

Sofia got better. She was starting to get her appetite back: after polishing off her own plate, she would tuck into the mounds of *spätzle* that Rimini had left untouched. By the fifth day, when Rimini no longer needed to stand by the window to describe everything that was going on around the street corner visible from their room, Sofia suggested he go out for a while. Rimini protested. 'Just for a while,' she insisted, 'an hour won't make any difference.' Rimini decided to go and visit the Freud museum, an idea which, according to the visitors' book, had occurred to at least three and a half dozen Argentines in the previous six weeks. He read through the list quite carefully, but did not spot any names he knew. And yet, no sooner had he added his signature at the bottom – without adding any comment, just his first and family names, rendered unrecognisable by the speed of his signing, plus the date – than something made him look elsewhere on the page: an 'irregularity', something indefinable that seemed to be lurking just outside his visual field, which suddenly seemed to be waving like the dark branch of a tree. Rimini scanned the list of visitors again, and his eyes lit on an almost illegible one – Ezequiel, Rafael, Gabriel – written in flowery curlicues, but he immediately dismissed it. By the time he left the museum it was half-past five. Night had fallen. It was not snowing, the air was clear, and there were none of the usual patches of mist around the street-lamps.

Rimini felt strange. After an hour without Sofia, he had the not unusual sensation that he was the only living being in the entire city. He was desperately lonely: at the very moment when Sofia was returning to life, their journey seemed to him completely ridiculous. He decided to call Buenos Aires and ask his father why he had included Vienna in their itinerary. The cold was so piercing he wanted to ignore the traffic light and run across the deserted avenue, but was dissuaded by the barking of a dachshund whose owner, a hunched, trembling woman, had just positioned it next to a tree. Ten or twelve blocks further on, a public telephone refused to allow him to make a reverse charges call, but did accept the two extras coins he had inserted from fear of being cut off. At the far end of the line, a new maid, who repeated the name Rimini several times in a dubious way, told him somewhat suspiciously that his father had gone to Villa Gesell for the weekend.

Two days later (two days which Vienna, in the final reckoning, would end up having stolen from London), when they entered the Klimt rooms in the Österreichische Galerie – Rimini on his guard, Sofia weak and adorable, wrapped in a poncho like some wintry Bedouin, both of them enlivening the warm air inside the gallery with little white clouds of breath they brought in from the street – Rimini felt safe and protected like someone who has returned home after long, sad years in exile. He drifted through the rooms, lulled by the soft yellow lighting, gazing at the paintings with a happy detachment, as though he were so distant from everything that not even their beauty could disturb his sense of well-being. The two of them came to a halt in front of *The Kiss*. They wrapped their arms around each other, in an act of mimetism lovers invariably indulge in when confronted by an image they have always imagined to be looking and speaking directly to them. 'The worst is over,' thought Rimini, and when he tried to decide what 'the worst' meant, what came to mind was not Vienna and their problems with the language, not Sofia's fever, not even the money and time that what he had begun to call 'the Austrian mistake' had robbed them of, but the simple possibility, which he saw as something from the past rather than the future, that Sofia, that small, solid ball of warmth he could feel pressing against him, might have disappeared for ever from his life. Like a survivor who each night before falling asleep relives the accident that almost killed him, and only after going over all the details realises that on that particular day nothing had distracted him, there were no slippery pavements or fatal cars, and that even so the accident which never happened had stolen part of his future, tearing a gaping wound in his soul, Rimini again saw himself far from Sofia, saw himself without her, and this orphaned, bereft figure chilled him to the bone. He had just had a glimpse of what is left of a man when the woman he loves is subtracted from the sum of everything he is or believes himself to be.

The membranes of love are fragile: it takes only the most casual touch to tear them. If they had been torn by Rimini's doubts, exposing them to the infection always lying in ambush for the person in love who is trying to lead a different life, this flirtation with catastrophe was enough to regenerate them. And perhaps this was the true function of those unlikely tragedies, which existed only in a world and time created by the backward glance of the imagination: to drown him in horror and immediately rescue him; to crush him and then save him; to minimise almost to the point of ridiculousness the unwelcome eventualities which might cloud his love at some distant point in the future. Sofia had not disappeared or died, she was with him and still loved him: what did the rest – *any* of the rest – matter?

CHAPTER 5

Rimini had already spent three years cultivating this mixture of humility and superstition; since it had begun six months after he had met Sofia, it was natural for him to think it was part and parcel of their relationship. Excited, in a kind of trance, Rimini had just told her about the conversation he had had that afternoon with a friend. They had been talking, he said, about 'commitment in love'. His friend was completely against monogamous relationships. As a precocious expert in dissolute living, he was taken aback by Rimini's attitude to love – his strange constancy, the depth of his feelings, his laborious faithfulness, like that of a goldsmith. Six months with the same woman? He could hardly bear to see the light of day on the face of the woman he had spent the night with. How was it possible? Didn't Rimini desire other women? Didn't he need others? Rimini realised that beyond this bewilderment lay a theory, but he never tried to refute it. That afternoon, as on several previous occasions, Rimini turned his back on his friend and, like the extra who goes unnoticed on stage for almost three acts and then finally gets to the speech that will make it all worthwhile, that will imprint his unremarkable face on the mind of even the least attentive spectator, launched into a monologue about trust and the spontaneous and therefore somehow magical way in which that trust, if it were mutual, could suspend – Rimini corrected himself, he had wanted to say *abolish*, but the word resisted, sneaked away and would not come back to him – even the most apparently natural of needs.

This was the defence of love that Rimini had repeated to Sofia, standing in front of her as she sat on the bed – a clumsy, passionate monologue throbbing with intensity as if he were delivering it at last to the person for whom it was really intended. But when he finally fell silent, moved by his own emotions, Sofia said nothing, and Rimini could see a dark cloud flit across her face. 'Trust' . . . 'mutual feelings' . . . as though in a dream, Rimini thought he could hear his own voice fading away, being torn to shreds. 'Rimini,' Sofia said very quickly, 'I slept with Rafael.' For a split second, Rimini looked on as a procession of conflicting emotions fought over his poor, stunned and betrayed body. He was going to die. Or to be sick. He was going to trash his room, hurting – accidentally of course – Sofia in the process. He would never speak again. A blood clot would strike him down. Someone was coming into the room, and he had to hide his feelings. He contemplated all these possibilities, but they slipped away from him, as though more interested in someone else. So instead he opened his mouth and burst into tears. Then somebody with less trembling lips than his spoke in his place and demanded the most trivial, sordid and yet voluptuous of satisfactions: he wanted to know the details. Sofia pretended not to have heard him. 'You know,' she said, 'that it was something I had to do. If I hadn't got it out of the way, I couldn't have continued with you.' She stood up. Rimini was leaning against the window-frame, looking down through a veil of tears at the fountain in the garden three floors below. He could feel Sofia's fingertips close to his face, then stroking his cheek, less in order to comfort him than to get him to look at her. He felt a deep sense of shame. As if by magic, his tears dried up. Sofia was examining him closely. It was then that Rimini realised it would take more than another man or woman for him to stop loving her: it would have to be something inhuman and blind like a disaster, a plane crash or an earthquake. Only something like that could tear her from his side and expunge her from his soul. But Sofia was not exactly looking at him, and was certainly not looking him in the eye; in fact her almost lascivious curiosity was fixed on a point just below one of them. Turning back to the window, Rimini stared at his own reflection in it. He saw a dark spot, like a beauty mark, the scab of a tiny wound he could not even remember having done to himself. For another few seconds, Sofia seemed completely absorbed by it, but then she snapped out of it, blushed, and stroked his face again very gently with one hand. 'Give me a call. I'll be at home,' she said.

CHAPTER 6

Even Riltse's most devoted fans admit it: *Spectre's Portrait* is not one of his best. It is a small painting (Riltse always shone in large formats) and dark (the maestro was still painting *against* Cézanne's light), and seems to be pulling in two opposite directions at the same time: while formally it demonstrates the painter's expressionist fervour, his spirit seems to be tiptoeing out by the side-door. It is a typical transitional work, in which the voices of the past refuse to die, whereas the future, with all its outpourings of light and cruelty, is still stated with bewildered hesitancy. When he painted it, Riltse wanted to go back to London. He had gambling debts, he hated the sun, and the first signs of illness were becoming evident: he had two purple blotches on his legs, felt dizzy in the mornings, and had some difficulty remembering what had happened in the previous half-hour. It was only his relationship with Pierre-Gilles, by then in its final stages, that kept him in Aix-en-Provence. To kill him or kill himself? Kill him and kill himself? Not a day or hour went by without Riltse fleetingly considering these alternatives. His only reason for going out in the countryside to paint was to get away from his lover, although perhaps he also hoped that a new painting or the effects of sunstroke would once and for all remove this thorn from his tormented heart. In its childish way, *Spectre's Portrait* shows the failure of these attempts. Despite the fact that Riltse coated it with layer upon layer of muddy violet, and replaced the noonday sun with cave-like gloom, the landscape in the picture is still recognisably the countryside, with its unmoving air, its relentless horizon, its trees which, although unrecognisable, are still weighed down with fruit. It is as though Riltse had painted the countryside *through their eyes*, through the eyes of that fruit, not in the state they were in when he was studying them at the start of spring, but in their final moments, in the state of rapid putrefaction Riltse seems to wish on them. In the foreground there are two patches of colour, two lighter touches that break the monotony of the painting as a whole. At first sight, these could be confused with the halos of light around two street-lamps, or two glow-worms whose size is exaggerated by their closeness. On further inspection, however, this overall sense of luminosity vanishes, or becomes more precisely situated: the two patches have the same internal structure made up of the thinnest of concentric circles which, like the trunks of trees, seem to radiate out from a dark central core. The effect is forced, but after a few moments, it takes hold: the dark centre is an open mouth screaming with terror, and the patches become the faces created by the reverberation of this horror. Another step closer makes everything clear, like the veins of a leaf brought into focus under a microscope: inside the dark circle of the mouth there are teeth and a tongue; above them the outline of a nose; the eyes repeat the mouth's terror: they are wild and stare *directly* at the viewer of the picture, who by this time, if the spell has worked, will have his face pressed right up against the canvas. The viewer understands, or thinks he does, that the figures are calling for help, and feels sorry for them. But then if he looks down at the bronze plaque and reads the work's title, he realises both how wrong he was, and the artist's secret intention. *Spectre's Portrait*. It is his own face which is terrifying the patches. Riltse has portrayed himself as the spectre.

Myopic in their enthusiasm, they stared at the painting from so close that they began to steam up the glass with their breath. For a second, two damp circles obscured the two patches staring in terror out of the canvas. Who could have criticised such devoted insolence? After all, it was at this distance that the painter had wanted his work to be studied. *Spectre's Portrait* was the *only* Riltse on show. Somebody – an Argentine tourist, one of those bearers of bad tidings whom Argentines love to represent whenever they meet a fellow countryman abroad – had told them as much when they were climbing the museum staircase, intoxicated with anticipation: the rest of his work (the diptychs, triptychs, the retouched photographs, even the monumental *The Middle of the Event*, brought back home after a quarter of a century of ignominious German captivity) had been transferred to an official warehouse on the outskirts of London, where it would slumber throughout the three months needed by the State to refurbish the museum.

While Sofia was trying to confirm the news at the information desk,

Rimini spent twenty minutes outside, protesting out loud and deliberately getting in the way of the workmen moving to and fro among their scaffolding. What was the purpose of their journey now . . . ? What right did they have . . . ? Shouldn't they at least have been warned . . . ? He searched for reasons, for some comfort; all he could think of were reprisals. All at once he thought he had found the worst, the most wounding of all: to leave without even going in. 'Fuck them . . .' 'Are you sure?' replied Sofia, worried she would have to spend the whole night calming his desperate regrets: 'We're here now, Rimini. One is better than nothing at all; we may as well go in.' They went in. To show he was not convinced, Rimini dragged his feet as noisily as he could, like a reluctant pilgrim. Sofia suggested they stop off first at the cafeteria: perhaps a drink would lessen their disappointment. But this interlude only served to increase Rimini's annoyance. Like the rest of the museum, only half or even a quarter of the café was open; flimsy partitions separated the part they could use, with its dozen tables, flickering lights and floor covered with double newspaper sheets, from the work area, out of which issued the regular thud of hammers and delicate little clouds of white dust. Sofia, who never shirked her responsibility for a mistake, offered to queue for their drinks. Strangely, Rimini agreed. (Expecting him to refuse, as he usually did whenever she offered to sacrifice herself for him, Sofia was somewhat taken aback, and for a split second stood rooted to the spot, as though frozen at the exact point at which the two situations – one virtual, the other real – had overlapped.) Rimini had in fact felt the urge to behave like a gentleman, but was so exhausted – disappointment always affected him much more on a physical than a moral or psychological level – that all he could think of was to get rid of the immense weight of his body by sitting down. Five minutes later, by which time the palms of his hands, his forearms and even his left cheek (which he had rested on the table for a moment) were already covered in a film of white dust from the building works, Sofia reappeared carrying a tray with two polystyrene cups of coffee and a plastic plate with two brownies on it. Close behind her came a tall, thin man who had that air of precarious dignity – held together with bits of thread, adhesive tape, clips, metal clasps – typical of people who have not washed in weeks. A bottle of beer dangled from his hand. Sofia sat down. As he went past their table, the man bowed to her in a rather old-fashioned way. 'Who's that?' Rimini asked, slightly stunned by the foul smell the stranger had left in his wake. 'I don't know. He was in the queue. He was asking for change so he could buy himself something. But you know what English people are like: you should have seen how they looked at him. Or rather, didn't look at him. That would have been something, at least.' 'Did you give him money?' 'Yes.' 'Hadn't you decided to stop giving to beggars?' 'This is different. I'm sure he's *someone*. Mmm . . . try these brownies, they're excellent.' 'Someone?' Rimini was growing impatient. 'How do you know?' 'I know. I can *see* these things.' 'You ought to try smelling them as well.' 'I still have a bit of a cold from Vienna.' Sofia suddenly leaned forward and sniffed at her plate and the steaming coffee cups. 'Is something off? Shall we ask them to change it?' 'Anyway, everyone is someone: isn't that a bit of a weak excuse to help a stranger?' 'Don't be silly. I mean *someone* important.' 'The museum director for example,' scoffed Rimini. Sofia looked over his shoulder and smiled into the distance as she chewed, then covered her mouth with the back of her hand. 'Don't turn round, but I'm almost certain that . . .' Rimini saw she was blushing. 'That what?' 'No, it's crazy.' 'What is it you're certain of?' 'Nothing, nothing; don't pay any attention. Do you want some cream?'

They went into the gallery separately, without speaking. Rimini was the only one aware of what was going on. As always when something caused a rift between them, it was Rimini whose behaviour remained bogged down in the episode that had caused the tension, circling round it like a useless, childish and slightly ridiculous planet. Sofia, on the other hand, appeared to forget the incident at once, so that everything she did subsequently – everything which, for Rimini, was the sad, sterile consequence of their quarrel – was born of different causes and interests, which might not be important but were at least new. Whereas for Rimini life had become stuck at this one painful moment which could not be resolved, for Sofia life just went on. But it was only Rimini who noticed this difference, and only he could see the abyss opening between them. As always when he wanted to appear indifferent, his body had become a mass of hostile impulses. He felt hot, but there were no more clothes he could take off. He spotted a few crumbs of chocolate on his sleeve, and brushed them away as if they were poisonous. Someone – someone exactly the same height as him –

obscured his view while he was looking at a Turner. Responding with a fluency he had not known he was capable of, Rimini unleashed a long stream of silent Argentine curses at the back of the man's neck.

All this changed when he saw the Riltse. He caught sight of it all of a sudden, at exactly the same moment that Sofia had spotted it too, which made him think with sly satisfaction that this coincidence would put a stop to the insulting autonomy that Sofia had shown ever since the incident in the café. So, when she turned towards him with the obvious intention of inviting him to look at the picture together, he looked the other way and, pretending to be staring at something else, left her on her own in front of the picture. Only then, with her facing the other way, did Rimini deign to examine it as well.

Hanging in amongst huge paintings by others, it looked too modest, or too intimidated. Rimini did not know the painting. The few visitors to the gallery – a group of tourists, a dozen or so sleepy schoolkids, a couple who went, or rather jumped from painting to painting with their arms round each other and their legs intertwined like a pair of obscene gymnasts – walked past it as though they had not noticed it. Rimini felt an unknown fervour that was so intense it troubled him: this was ecstasy, the messianic joy an idolater feels when in a crisis his idol decides to honour him, entrusting him with the hardest, most crucial task of all: to redeem him. Rimini was not one of the damned, he was one of the chosen, and *Spectre's Portrait* was not his solace but his privilege. He went round the entire gallery as slowly and thoroughly as possible, stopping in front of insipid pictures, listening to every word the museum guides had to say, even helping a couple of lost, snivelling schoolboys to join up again with their party before the teacher noticed they were missing. Although it cost him a great effort, Rimini was killing two birds with one stone: it postponed the pleasure of finally finding himself in front of the Riltse picture with Sofia, and at the same time made it look as if they were coming together there by chance.

Spellbound, Sofia was already drawing close to the painting when Rimini came to a halt beside her. They did not look or speak to each other, but Rimini could feel the charmed circle into which the picture was drawing them. He forgot his resentment and surrendered too. That is how they were, their heads close together as they leaned forward at almost ninety degrees and their red noses almost pressed against the glass, when they were startled by a voice behind them: 'I wouldn't get so close if I were you.' Thinking it was an attendant, they instinctively raised their arms to prove their innocence, as they had grown used to doing every time they were leaving a store and the alarm went off, and stepped back a couple of paces. Rimini lifted his eyes slightly and peered at the blinking red eye of the security sensor. 'No,' the man said with a disdainful laugh, 'that's not the problem.' Rimini got the feeling that the voice was closer still, and all at once he caught a dreadful smell, like badly rinsed clothes, a mixture of bleach and dampness: the same smell that had dazed him half an hour earlier. He turned his head circumspectly; he did not want to look at the man directly (he was too intimidated by the brutality with which the other person had burst into their lives), but was content merely to include him in a corner of his field of vision and establish a quick, overall impression of him, to get an idea of who he was to replace the fleeting blur he had seen in the café. The intruder stepped in front of him. 'I'm responsible for that horror,' he said, pointing to the Riltse picture. His English had a disgruntled tone to it, as if he were only speaking it because he had no other choice. 'What did I tell you? I *see* these things, Rimini,' Sofia whispered to him. Taken by surprise, Rimini found himself forced to study the man. He was tall, with misshapen shoulders, and seemed all skin and bone under a suit that would have been out-of-date twenty years earlier. He had long hair, that bore traces of having been dyed at some point, and now lay flat under a layer of dirt. His cheeks were covered with a scrawny beard from not shaving for several weeks, and he kept his hands, which were so pale that the blue veins shone through as if they had been drawn there, raised in front of his face both before and after any gesture he made. The fingers wavered and trembled for a moment: Rimini managed to catch a glimpse of his lips, as red and shiny as a drunkard's, moving as if in silent prayer. The man looked back at him, as if astounded. 'I am . . .' he started to say, as if introducing himself. 'You, me: all of us,' Rimini interrupted him, 'that's the idea behind the painting, isn't it?' The man waved his hand in the air, then closed and screwed up his eyes. There were dried white flakes of skin on his eyelids, his forehead, and the area around his hairline. One of them on the bridge of his nose had started to bleed. 'The idea behind the painting?' he murmured, staring at Rimini. Rimini felt a tug at his elbow and saw Sofia standing next to him, her mouth clamped as if by an invisible gag, pointing her chin at something on the floor. 'The idea behind the painting?' Rimini heard him repeat, but the tone now had changed from one of astonishment to one of annoyance. He looked down and saw two left-footed ski-boots with no laces. The tongues were pushed forward with what seemed like calculated nonchalance, and behind them Rimini could make out the skin, the skin of his instep, which was also covered in the same shiny flakes, that disappeared up under the end of his trouser-legs. When Rimini looked up again, the man was so close he was practically engulfing them in his fetid cloud. 'You've no right,' he threatened Rimini, but his voice betrayed a strange sense of sorrow. 'I'm the only one who has the right to look at that picture and say: "I". I'm the thing that those two horrified faces are looking at. Me, me, me. Forty-two years ago. I'm the thing, the cause. I was there. A beautiful spot. I milked cows standing with shit up to my ankles while the sun . . . You have to know how to look . . . It's all there. The countryside, the washing on the line, the hammock, the rotten, bird-pecked fruit . . . The bastard put it all in, except for my face. Why? Touch me. Go on, touch me, I'm no monster. I've returned, that's all. Condemned to return. According to the law, I can't come within a hundred metres. I'm from the country: "metres" doesn't mean anything to me. 45 by 45. But the law doesn't say anything about this painting. Or does it? I'm from the country, I don't know anything about paintings. Love, miss. *Love is a rushing torrent.* You know what I mean. Hold this for me, will you? It's my turn. It will only take one second.'

It was longer than that, of course, but who could begrudge a slight miscalculation in someone whose heart has been torn apart for more than forty years? Besides, nobody takes *one* second to fulfil the dream of a lifetime, especially when that dream consists of taking an axe to the only painting by Jeremy Riltse on show in the most security-conscious museum in London. In fact it took three minutes, counting from the moment when poor Pierre-Gilles (alias Douglas Durban, alias Stephen Stacy, alias Richard Right, alias another half-dozen fake identities – all of them faithful to the cinematic belief, doubtless inculcated by Riltse, that repeating the first letter in each name is bound to lead to glory – assumed by Pierre-Gilles in the forty years since his separation from Riltse to throw the British immigration officials off the scent and launch a two-pronged assault on his former lover: Riltse – broken-hearted but unbending Riltse – time and again rejecting the loving accusations, British justice rejecting the absolutely ludicrous legal ones) handed Sofia his purse, got out the small axe (the same instrument, he later declared, that Riltse had almost used to end one of the sterile arguments that characterised their siestas in the south of France, and the same one with which he, Pierre-Gilles, fulfilling a time-honoured threat, had employed to chop the end off his penis on the carpenter's bench in the studio, after reading Riltse's letter explaining why he was leaving him for ever) from an inside pocket and smashed the glass protecting the painting, to the moment when the slow but bulky security guards succeeded in disarming him and pinning him to the floor, surrounded by shards of broken glass, strips of painted canvas, bits of picture-frame and plaster.

CHAPTER 7

They believed in their way of loving, and that belief was stronger than anything else, any sign from the world seeking to prove they were wrong or ridiculous. They were arrogant but modest, proud of themselves but extremely polite about it. They never shared their problems with anyone – there was an air of the mafia, of *esprit de corps* and an unswerving discretion, born out of love but reinforced by a sort of fear of catastrophe, about the way in which they avoided any revelations of this kind – and yet their apartment in Belgrano R soon became a kind of emotional clinic, open twenty-four hours a day, where almost all their friends ended up at one time or other. All of them: those who each first of January secretly decreed their relationship would end, those who desperately tried to copy them, those in between, who approved of the marvel but every so often expressed their 'reserves' about it. Their parents too came to see them, anxious to discover the clarity and wisdom apparently lacking in their own marriages. Rimini and Sofia never judged: they listened. They were broad-minded, tolerant, unfailingly even-handed. This was perhaps the only thing of which in private, once the 'sessions' had finished, they allowed themselves to feel proud: although they themselves were monogamous, conservative, and believed in a loving discipline which needed daily watering, air and light, they had no problem understanding those friends who were actively engaged in the opposite – fleeting passions, unbridled desire, fickleness, unfaithfulness – even though the advice they offered was entirely one-way. Apart from Sofia's one indiscretion with Rafael – something which was so quickly absorbed as part of the mystique of the essential sincerity of their love that it soon became not a threat but a healthy challenge, an opportunity to grow, to surpass themselves and so to consolidate the idea which at first sight it had seemed to shatter: that love was a fortress – neither of them had any experience of deceit, betrayals, or love triangles. And yet, however

33

distant this world seemed to them, it was as though they knew all about it. They understood the mechanisms of passion, the logic of betrayal, the secret workings of domination and contempt, all the manoeuvring that provoked, excited, and sometimes destroyed other people's lives. They located the problem precisely; their diagnoses were rarely wrong; and when they offered advice – which they rarely did, except in the most serious or urgent of cases, so reluctant were they to indulge in anything that might smack of emotional manipulation – they took great care to avoid any weaknesses, impulses or inclinations that could make their words seem partial. They dealt with close friends whose suffering made them suffer too, whose misfortunes made them feel equally misfortunate, and whose passions they accepted whole-heartedly; but, far from predisposing them to any sense of complicity, in their 'sessions' this closeness appeared on the contrary merely to reinforce their policy of a sobriety bordering on indifference. They always behaved in a disinterested way, and this allowed them to proffer the starkest truths without risking offence. It was simple: they did not feel they had to be faithful to their friends, or even to their feelings: what they owed their loyalty to was the situation, and the ideals involved: love, trust, intimacy, respect, deeply felt emotions – those absolutes for which they were willing to suffer, to go to battle, to sacrifice everything.

They seemed hardly human. But they were human – at least Rimini was. How often, while busy letting some fresh air into their living-room, emptying the ashtrays of cigarette butts still damp from tears, or tearing off sheets from the notebook by the phone where their friends had doodled, in a fit of Cubist automatism, the typical squares, triangles, and spirals of their tormented hearts, how often had he noticed the unmerited weariness in his legs, how often – as had happened more than once during his trip to Europe – had it occurred to him to wonder whether all this: their willingness to listen, their impartiality, their air of supreme existential integrity, combining as it did the self-sacrifice of a public hospital and the remote wisdom of a pair of gurus, might not be hiding something completely different at the very bottom, an obscure, unknown presence he would prob-ably recoil from in horror if he ever caught proper sight of it. They lived in that nirvana where all those who feel they are experiencing something unique live, or lived the unique experience of those who feel they are living in a nirvana unattainable by the great majority of mortals. They had no idea how they themselves had got there. If they had known, they would probably never have made it. So much so that they had destroyed all traces of ever having arrived. They liked to imagine that they had *always* been there, that he might have been born in a clinic in Banfield and she in one in Caballito, but that they had been born *together* in their fairy kingdom, from where they could allow themselves the luxury of understanding everything without ever having to go through it. Occasionally, Rimini faltered. He wavered, ran away from Sofia. He was enraged at his own weakness.

He had once been contracted to do a rush job translating an Argentine film that was being presented at a European film festival. He spent two days almost without sleeping, peering at a pair of video screens and spelling out for an editor with a haircut like the letter 'b' and joined-up eyebrows ways of saying things like '*avisá, che*' or '*aguantá que es un minuto*' in French. By the end they were reeling from coffee, cigarettes, and the extravagant sweets she went out to buy in the middle of the night, when the only thing disturbing the silence in the studio was the nightwatchman's snores. When they parted at the front door in the early morning, stepping over the waves of water that a woman neighbour was creating as she washed the pavement in front of her house, laughing when they realised they had used the two worst lines in the film to say goodbye with, and she, who was called Maria or Mirna or something else that Rimini always managed to get wrong, leaned on his arm and kissed him on the corner of his mouth in a casual, gentle way (not so much intentionally as clumsily, because it was so early and she was so tired) Rimini felt his heart was literally turned upside down, and he had a brief, merciful glimpse of what might happen to him if, like the nightwatchman in the studio, he allowed his vigilance to slip for a moment, and let his weariness get the upper hand.

Sofia was strong. She might not have been aware of the shocks that Rimini's heart suffered every once in a while, but she sensed intuitively what was going on. She even went so far as to welcome them, convinced like all true believers that the faith she embraced would not be worthy of that description until it had emerged intact, or even strengthened, from the trials it had to overcome along the way. She did not need to know: she already knew. It was as if the sixteen, twenty, twenty-five, twenty-eight years – all the ages that Rimini had known her at – were merely the official, visible tokens of a measureless, timeless lifetime, a lifetime during which she had learnt all there was to know. So Rimini was transparent. Sofia could see through him as if he were a pane of glass, or perhaps even more clearly – because glass, which was only inert matter, simply offered no resistance to her gaze, whereas Rimini, who could not avoid rebelling against this situation, outdid himself in producing firework displays, smoke screens, diversionary manoeuvres, anything that might make himself a little more opaque. Not only did Sofia let him do so, but she celebrated his efforts without a word, as if she were a spectator at an impromptu magic show. She knew every-thing, and it is highly likely that part of that everything was the fact that Rimini would never take his threats any further than offering his cheek to the editor in the studio doorway, and then a short while later, when he got home exhausted, refuse Sofia's invitation to take his clothes off and get into bed with her, as though afraid that when she saw him naked, Sofia would spot the tell-tale signs of the betrayal that had *not* taken place. Apart from one uncalled for and unnecessarily sarcastic reference to the editor that was obviously a cover-up: 'a stupid girl', he had called her, without Sofia even asking him anything: so stupid they had taken 'two days over something they could have finished in one at most', Rimini had not said a word. But Sofia could picture the scene down to the tiniest detail: the pale light of dawn, the chilly air, their weary bodies over-sensitive from lack of sleep drawing closer to each other despite themselves, the illusory but real sense of intimacy that Rimini had shared with the editor ... No, it was not an agreeable feeling (Sofia felt a stab of pain) but her certainty that she was seeing the events exactly as they had happened – indeed, that she had seen them even before they had happened, and was now simply confirming them – somehow softened and sweetened the pain until it became one of those complicated, confused but exciting physical sensations that are the price we have to pay for satisfaction on some higher level.

For them, love was that higher level. Rimini imagined it as a small, well-heated room, carpeted and with the walls lined with books, a place where the upheavals of the world outside only filtered through in the gentle accents of the local dialect. Apart from one or two oriental touches

– carpets on the walls as well, spirals of perfumed smoke rising from a corner, curtains hiding other rooms beyond, a general atmosphere of decadent clutter – which were more pronounced in his daydreams, he imagined it exactly like the living-room in the apartment he shared with Sofia. It was not that he lacked imagination, more that he accepted the efficacy of the real world. Why imagine the level where love existed any differently if he was already living in it, was immersed by it, if it was his everyday environment, which he could describe from memory down to the minutest detail, without the slightest error. And yet, was it real? That was the question with which his most sceptical friends always ended up challenging him. Rimini would stand there blinking at them in a perplexed fashion, as if their question somehow immediately turned him into a creature from some kind of exotic species. All he could find to reply was to ask: 'Are you being serious?' What on earth could they be thinking? That it was all an illusion? That the kind of love they professed was simply a façade? That Sofia and he were going around sleepwalking, or were under the influence of some mind-bending drug? This was in the mid-seventies. Rimini had come to the conclusion that these words of caution were less the fruit of any observation of, or impressions created by, his relationship with Sofia, than the result of one of the most fashionable political theories of the time, one which said that any ideology was necessarily the inversion of what existence was really about, and that to escape from its illusory effects, what was needed was to turn the initial process of inversion on its head, and to stand upright everything that ideology had turned upside down: righting the upturned. In their own way, and without even being aware of it (they had no need to be, it was in the air at the time, like the flu virus in winter, or treacherous pollen particles in spring), Rimini's questioners were also Althusserian, but had widened their field of enquiry from the traditional areas of ideology, religion, or art, to a sphere which until then had not seemed susceptible to political analysis: that of love. Consequently, in the same way that they rejoiced in and encouraged any social conflict or breakdown that posed a threat to bourgeois institutions, any crack through which the real, deep, invisible order of things could spread its obscure dissonances to the surface, and celebrated just as much when the turmoil worked against them as when it turned in their favour, so they were prepared to welcome any uncertainty that might undermine Rimini and Sofia and expose their weaknesses, or even to encourage, fortified by a kind of moral hygiene, any opportunity that might lead them from the path of mutual righteousness that they had chosen.

All to no avail. The cracks were never wide enough, or the membrane protecting them was too resistant, or (the greatest scandal of all) time, that traditional enemy of every effort to make love permanent, seemed in this case to be extraordinarily well disposed to them, to the extent that its famous poisons – erosion, habit, the tedium of a familiarity with no hidden compartments – had only to come into contact with them to change completely, and become elixirs, strange brews that when mixed with their love made it all the more patient, solid, and invulnerable. Time was on their side. That was the secret. As the years went by, their friends, whether supporters or detractors, gave up the struggle: they remained close, their friendships did not diminish, but they gave up hope of obtaining any fragment of the secret that only Rimini and Sofia seemed to possess, even that tiny but vital part which could help them destroy that higher level they lived in, or to steal it and adapt it to their own needs, so that their love, no longer either admired or envied or detested, but simply always there, eternal like a rock that sun, wind and water polish and sculpt until it glows a little more with each passing day, went on through time, piling up the years and falling out of fashion, as though the membrane which protected it was also a preserving fluid keeping it intact, separate from everything else, untouched yet ancient, somehow defeated, like those characters in science-fiction movies who manage to reach atomic shelters a split second before the catastrophe and spend years cut off there, speculating on the privilege of being the only survivors, only to return finally to the surface once they think that the danger has passed and the world has returned to normal, and find that the catastrophe never happened, that if they had never been aware of this it was due directly to being hermetically sealed in the depths of their bunker, and that the world now, many years since they had last formed part of it, was unrecognisable, disfigured and indifferent, and looked on them with the sort of amused bewilderment with which in only a few years from now the world's children will look upon all of today's icons.

CHAPTER 8

Years later, only seventy-two days (exactly the length of time it took Riltse to paint the first of his three extraordinary *Half-length Portraits of Pierre-Gilles*) away from their twelfth anniversary, Rimini and Sofia split up. They had beaten all the records of conjugal longevity they knew of. Despite the fact that they were sensitive enough to let people know gradually, in a carefully graduated fashion – starting with their newest acquaintances, then single friends, followed by couples, then his family, who were pioneer divorcees, and finally her parents, who had just celebrated their silver wedding – when their break-up became official, everyone was shaken, as though there had been an earth tremor, or a clap of thunder had broken a centuries-long silence. It was not possible. A few – those rare people who still prided themselves on having seen it coming – received the news with melancholy satisfaction, as if they lamented the passing of a decrepit but much-loved institution, which no one ever visited any more but felt was part of their cultural heritage. Others were completely taken aback, and commented on it as if it were an extraordinary event, as though Rimini and Sofia were Siamese twins who had finally and perhaps fatally been separated by surgeons. A third group felt itself betrayed. They despised Rimini and Sofia; refused to speak to them on the phone, and even stopped seeing them for several months, until the period of convalescence was over and a certain normality returned. 'It's as if from one day to the next, I don't know . . . we changed the currency!' someone suggested in one of the numerous private discussions that their friends devoted to the miracle, fate, catastrophe. Given the lack of stability in the Argentine economy at that time, the comparison could have seemed almost cynical, but it must have been accurate, because no one protested.

They were very odd days, filled with frantic activity. They were engulfed by waves of revisionism about the case-study into which time had turned them – twelve years of love! Those twelve years! – which

39

sought to explain the sequence leading up to the conclusion. It no longer mattered whether they had been reactionary or avant-garde, hypocrites or idiots, fogeys or pioneers. What was important was the logic of events which suddenly began to join up to form a secret pattern in which a trail of tiny prophecies, ignored at the time through either blindness or stupidity, pointed to the fact that the separation was not such a surprise after all. It was obvious it must have started at some point. But when? When they moved? With the trip to Brazil? That was possible. Right up to the last moment, Rimini had resisted. He gave in only when he saw there was no way out, but still tried to change San Salvador de Bahía – its *feijoadas,* nights of macumba on the beach, the *pelourinho,* all the delightful tortures Sofia was trying to tempt him with – for Rio de Janeiro. This risible demand, formulated as it was after giving way on the main point at issue (Brazil itself), buzzed for a moment in Sofia's ear like an insect that might sting badly but was not insistent. When they got back, they had changed. Sofia was pregnant; Rimini was practically unrecognisable due to the effects of a sudden allergy and from the natural products (jojoba, mango, aloe vera) which Sofia swore that Bahía, the same Bahía that had caused his illness, would provide to cure it.

They had an abortion. They spoke of it in the plural in the hope that this might ease the pain. One Saturday morning Sofia's mother accompanied them to Vicente López and sat in the roofed-over patio that served as a waiting-room for the hour and a half that the whole thing lasted, clasping one of Rimini's hands in hers (to warm him up, she said) while the rain beat on the sheets of corrugated iron on the roof, and a nurse in slippers watered the straggly plants from a kettle. The abortion brought them to a halt, but did not separate them. Their ever-adaptable 'higher level' yet again found a way to absorb the event. Hadn't they taken the decision together? The distinction was subtle but significant: it incorporated the exterior accident and its violence into the structure of their love, and by assimilating them and so reducing them to an internal function, helped neutralise their most dangerous effects. Two months later, when Rimini and Sofia were still making love fearfully, the abortion already figured in the annals of their relationship as a dreadful battle that had been won.

Perhaps then the famous 'turning point' had been the temporary separation that took place more or less eight years into their relationship and which neither of them had tried to blame on any particular event. On the contrary: while it was taking place, they seemed certain it would only be temporary. The separation lasted eight months: one for each year they had been together – even in that they were consistent. Sofia stayed in the comfortable apartment that had replaced their den in Belgrano R. Rimini, helped by one of those new, persuasive friends often washed up on the shore of separated people, moved to a depressing former consulting-room near the Faculty of Medicine. He did not pay much rent, and killed time by stripping off bits of the ancient wallpaper, or cheated his anxiety by staring at the orthopaedic legs or dentists' chairs displayed in the windows of the local stores. Each of them had two new passionate but inconsequential love affairs. They called each other on the phone every day. They gave each other presents. Of the dozen letters she wrote, Sofia sent him eight; she read the other four out loud to him once they had got back together again. They saw each other between once and three times every fortnight, almost always at Sofia's place. These meetings, distinguished by that strange kind of amorality which comes from betraying a lover of a few days with a partner of years, ended in lengthy confessional outbursts (Rimini cried at last) or in volcanic bouts of love-making which they used to show each other the new tricks they had learnt while apart.

There were no fissures. Nothing had faded. While it was true they spent long periods without making love, not even then did the word 'deterioration' seem appropriate: sex had never been that important to them. One night they were in bed: Sofia was already dozing off – Rimini was looking for passages in a book with the aid of a torch-pen she had given him – when Sofia turned on her pillow and, as though with her last waking breath before she succumbed to sleep, stared at him through eyes like slits and smiled sadly (with the kind of sadness that comes from contemplating something very beautiful but completely useless), and when he wanted an explanation (shining the torch-pen on to her) she turned her back to him, snuggled on to her pillow like an animal settling, then murmured as though she were dreaming out loud: 'We're a work of art.'

A couple of evenings later they went to the cinema to see *Rocco and his Brothers*, a film they fought over with fierce rivalry. How many

41

times had they seen it before? Twelve? Seventeen? A few seconds prior to the scene where Annie Girardot and Alain Delon are on the cathedral roof – a scene where Rimini always lost his self-control and cried like a baby – Sofia glanced at him as though she were searching him out in the darkness, and before Rimini could dissolve in tears, she held her open hand to the back of his neck and kept it there for a moment, letting it give off heat, like one of those healers who does not need to touch a body to effect a cure. Prevention had replaced compassion. The scene finished: Annie Girardot ran off along the roof, Delon chased after her, Sofia's fingers barely trembled behind Rimini's head, and Rimini of course did not cry. He did not cry then, and never cried again. *Rocco* was swallowed up in that dreadful night. They had attained a rare kind of perfection. They lived in the interior of an interior, one of those ecosystems artificially created, within four walls and behind a huge screen of glass, so that visitors can admire the realism, the temperature, the humidity and pressure, the fauna and flora of an exotic environment. There was no point on their bubble that was not enclosed by the membrane. Rimini and Sofia breathed normally, but the outside world was already coming to seem slightly blurred, misted up by their exhalations on the glass walls.

They had done everything. They had deflowered and kidnapped each other from their own families; they had lived and travelled together; had survived adolescence and then youth together, and had raised their heads together into the adult world; they had been parents together and had wept over the tiny dead creature they had never seen; they had known teachers, friends, languages, jobs, pleasures, summer holiday lets, disillusionment, habits, strange meals, illnesses together – every attraction that a prudent but varied version of the surprises and fleetingness normally known as life could offer, and they had kept something of each and every one of them, that defining characteristic which allowed them to remember it and to once more become, if only for a moment, those same people who had experienced it. And to complete their collection, to make it truly complete, they added the final touch: they split up. As with everything else, they planned it together, with the scrupulousness, the dedication, the loving attention to detail they had employed to create all their trophies. For the month and a half it took them to organise it, nothing, not the slightest hint of spite or thoughtlessness was allowed to obscure the purity with which they had decided to part. Separation was not the opposite of love: it was its frontier, its culmination, the interior wall of their confinement; if it went as they had lovingly planned it, it would be what allowed their love to know a noble death; in other words, as they said, to be able to carry on its existence without them inside the bubble that they had created.

They agreed Rimini would move out. Every morning, he looked for an apartment in the classified ads, and read out the most promising candidates. While she prepared breakfast, Sofia listened carefully and occasionally made a telling remark: 'Are you sure you'd like the centre of the city?' or 'Mmm . . . I can't really see you in an *unusual* apartment,' or 'Call and ask how old the building is'. These comments invariably forced him to think or revise his opinion about what he was really looking for. As was to be expected, the task of trying to decipher the jargon of the ads soon completely took them over; they could spend hours reading between the lines, scornfully picturing the turquoise carpets, wooden panels, or fake tiles that might be hidden behind the word 'jewel', the gold-plated taps hinted at by the expression 'everything brand new'. It was as though the torn fabric of their love reconstituted itself at an amazing speed, on its own, and the threads, remembering by heart the original pattern, closed up in such a way that soon all trace of the tear had disappeared. One afternoon in the Institute library, while Rimini was checking a bibliography for a translation he was working on, as though thinking aloud he commented to himself that he was looking for an apartment to rent. An ex-university colleague, someone he did not know at all, with whom he had only exchanged perhaps ten words during the five years of his degree poked his head between two rows of books and said with a broad smile that he was just about to move in with his girlfriend, who was giving up a 'fantastic' apartment only three blocks from Colegiales station.

It was odd for Sofia to call him at the Institute, but that afternoon she did. She had nothing special to say to him, she simply wanted 'to talk'. No sooner had she said that than they both fell silent. Eventually, slightly embarrassed, Rimini confessed he was on his way to see an apartment. 'That's quick,' she said almost involuntarily, then checked herself, and Rimini could almost see her moving the handset away from her face so as not to betray her emotion. Then, once she had recovered, she helped him run through the list of requirements the new apartment would have to fulfil. Of course, the girlfriend's 'fantastic' place did not meet any of them: it was dark, noisy, and if you stuck your hand out of the window, it was already inside the apartment opposite. The walls sweated under a flowery wallpaper that the girl peeled with a long fingernail as she was showing it him, to prove how 'easily it came off'. Then they gave him a cup of cold tea and mentioned the expenses, which were either very high or ludicrous. The street air brought Rimini round. He knew there was no going back.

He returned home in a cheerful mood. He found himself telling Sofia all the place's defects in extraordinary detail, as if his memory had lingered on things his eyes had never seen. But Sofia was not listening. When she had put down the phone that afternoon, she had come to a decision herself: she would move too. 'There's no way I could stay here,' she said, 'surrounded by all these things.' Rimini said nothing. He felt weak, suddenly robbed of strength. It was not Sofia's decision which affected him so much as the purely strategic consideration (because it is with separations, when the tide of love is out, that the true balance of forces in a relationship is exposed to view, like a bed of razor-sharp shells) that suddenly, no sooner had Rimini shown every sign of wanting to change his life, than Sofia, who up to that point had been playing the role of the person left behind, had snatched the initiative from him.

Very early the next morning, when Rimini opened the front door, the newspaper was not on the mat. That seemed to him a bad sign. He roamed the apartment calling Sofia's name. The newspaper was in the kitchen next to the coffee pot, but the classified ads had been pulled out. He found three of them ringed in red, and three in blue, and under a cup discovered this note: '*The red ones are mine; the blue ones, yours. (I don't want us to meet trying to rent the same place. You know how I hate estate agency people.) If I were you, I'd try the one in Las Heras first, the one with two and a half rooms. It looks promising. And if I rent the one on Cerviño we'd be neighbours, and who knows . . . (I think I made the coffee a bit weak again).*'

But Sofia did not rent the apartment on Cerviño. 'Too done up.' She did not want to be hasty. She would stay on in Belgrano and wait

44

calmly for her chance. This meant she had plenty of spare time, so she went with Rimini to look at Las Heras. She was in raptures at the scent of the lime trees in the street, loved the balcony giving on to the garden in the centre of the block, discussed the rent with the estate agent, a pale woman full of nervous tics who accompanied them from room to room with a notebook in her hand and seemed completely flummoxed. 'You have to take it,' Sofia told him when they were out in the street again, 'if you lived here I wouldn't mind visiting you.' As he was paying the deposit, Rimini remembered those two remarks, and for a split second a horrible suspicion paralysed him. What if Las Heras, the caretaker at Las Heras, the owner of Las Heras, the new neighbourhood, the new habits, in short everything which he, with the clumsy and spontaneous enthusiasm born of his lengthy virginity, liked to call 'my new life', were not in fact his conquests, or symbols of his newfound independence, but the first steps taken by Sofia to ensure that she kept control? What if, instead of leaving her behind, he was only getting more deeply involved with her? But he paid the deposit, and a week later, after making up all kinds of excuses to prevent Sofia coming with him, he signed the rental contract. Rimini had the impression that this simple legal ceremony, carried out in the gloom of a vulgar office by a solicitor who read as though he were praying, was obliging him to cross a threshold. It was depositing him a long way off, leaving him (truly, and this time Rimini felt it was for ever) out of Sofia's reach.

Contrary to Rimini's expectations, they had no problem dividing up their furniture. They had always chosen and bought the pieces together, and their sentimental value had often come to eclipse completely their functional or aesthetic worth. That was precisely why he had thought it would be impossible to share them out. Rimini wondered, if they were all fruits of their love, if each piece of furniture was in some way a monument commemorating an episode in their sentimental journey, what sort of life could they have once that was over? And yet, without Rimini ever being aware of it, over the twelve years they had been together Sofia had succeeded in working out the secret affinities that each of them had established with their possessions. Now therefore, Sofia was able to defuse the violence implicit in the split thanks to a spontaneous, natural law born out of the everyday complicities that only she could see, and which enabled her to know who each object should go to without the slightest hesitation, with that same degree of certainty that she used to identify where a scratch on a wooden table, or a nip in a chair cover had come from.

Rimini did not protest: he could not think of any suitable way to divide things up, and Sofia's method was beyond reproach. Despite his freedom, however, Rimini began to feel a certain cloying sensation, as though their separation was so civilised that it gave off the sickly perfume of an over-ripe fruit. It was strange: the loss of love only served to increase the ways, the cares and atmospheres of love. Although there was no argument over who should have what piece of furniture, throughout the morning Rimini spent in Belgrano carrying it out, he could sense he was sweating more than usual, and felt his heart skipping a beat, or as if he were about to faint. They went from room to room like a pair of effusive valuers. Sofia would come to a halt next to a particular object and with photographic accuracy recall when and where they had bought it, how long it had taken them to find it, how much they had paid for it, where they had gone afterwards to celebrate, and all the marks that the years and their love had left on it. Was it possible for her to remember so much so well? Was she making it up? No, no, she was right about everything. Even though he could not imagine how she did it, as soon as Sofia reconstructed their histories, Rimini could not help agreeing, concurring, and following their tracks back into the past. The oak furniture store in Escobar, the lunch at a roadside grill, the cane-bottomed rocking-chair, the mirror for the portmanteau in which their triumphal, absurdly happy faces was reflected . . . The sharing out of their possessions was like a concentrate, an essence of love, a love with no story, one crystallised in a series of unmoving points. Sofia was right: that was how it had been, it was all true – but those blocks of existence, those miniatures of love, the intact trophies of an obsessive collector, seemed to descend and weigh on Rimini like heavy, hypnotic clouds. He wanted it over with, everything over and done with for once and for all. The bedside tables, the bamboo curtains, the sound system cabinet, the paintings – if he had to take one more wicker basket he would collapse. As had happened during his first trip to Europe, he felt that there was something missing: there should have been arguments, misunderstandings, a certain amount of bad feeling, shouts, something to disturb this tranquil, protective ever-present sweetness . . . Suddenly, Rimini said he had to go. 'But . . .' Sofia protested, alarmed. 'I've got things to do. The removal van is downstairs,' he said, stumbling over his words. 'Everything is labelled anyway. You don't need me.' Sofia could detect the quaver of fear in his voice, and quickly replied: 'What about the photos? What are we going to do with them?' Rimini had the image of a huge cardboard box, slanting away from him – it was so big he could only see it in miniature – in which millions of faces, places, moments from the past, pets, seaside resorts, cars, t-shirts, haircuts, relatives, roads all raised their tiny orphaned arms towards him, begging him (in that half-language the past speaks) not to forget them.

'Some other day. I have things to do,' said Rimini, as stubborn as a little boy, although his only certainty was that he did not want to slip and be drowned in all that sea of photographic obscenities. 'Fine, but don't leave it too long,' Sofia said. 'No,' he replied. He started putting on his jacket, measuring the distance between him and the door. 'You'll call me, won't you?' she said, helping him put one arm into the proper sleeve of his coat. 'Yes, yes,' but by then Sofia was up close to him, stroking his cheeks, determined to give their farewell the emotional intensity that twelve years of love demanded. The bell rang. Rimini gave her a quick, nonchalant kiss on the corner of the mouth; Sofia wanted to prolong their contact, and pushed her lips out as he was drawing away from her. She grabbed at him, and implored: 'You will ring me, won't you?' 'Of course,' Rimini said, opening the door and rushing out. He almost bumped into the removal men, who as always were sweaty and exhausted before they began.

Rimini flung himself into a taxi – the first that came along, a Dodge 1500 with an exhaust fuming in the cold afternoon, and gave vague directions ('to the centre') as if to tell the driver that all he wanted was to get away from there as far and as fast as possible. He had just made a mistake, the kind of foolish error which when it happens on the cinema screen gives even the most phlegmatic viewer a frisson of fear and anticipation, and causes him to scream in a way he can only remember ever having done at a distant childhood puppet show.

Yet Rimini was no cynic; nobody as frightened as he was has the time to be cynical: refusing to go through the photos (because postponing it was simply to mask something more definitive – a refusal) had not been so much calculated as a question of survival. He was fleeing. Some people flee a volcano, an earthquake, a fateful plague. In his own foolish, double-dealing, detached and even ridiculous way, Rimini was fleeing something as conventional and domestic as this sharing out of memories: but to see them sitting cross-legged on the floor, bent over the box of photos, digging up images she remembered with exactly the same precision as he had forgotten them, so that what to her were well-known faces were for him puzzling mysteries – even that 'friendly' vision of the scene did not make it any the less catastrophic, and if Rimini was fleeing it was because in that mound of photos he could no longer recognise anything of himself, nothing which might prove he had once existed and been happy, but on the other hand he could sense a sentimental weight he found it physically impossible to bear.

Yet it had been a mistake, and if he could have scanned the horizon that his running away had opened up in his life, Rimini would have jumped out of the speeding taxi and run back to the apartment where the removal men were already denting the walls with the corners of the furniture. He would have accepted the anxiety, the agonies of tenderness, the sterile intimacy of this funeral rite and even its possible immediate consequences: the tremulous maelstrom of comforting caresses, the puffy lips and tears that so often end with a bitter, reluctant release on the carpet, clothes strewn all around and photos stuck to their buttocks, the remains of an obscene bed of withered leaves. It is never furniture which causes a problem in separations. However imbued the different pieces may be with meaning, they are always useful, and that usefulness somehow allows them to go on living, to remake their lives in new conditions and surroundings. But photographs, like the majority of the symbolic knick-knacks that couples accumulate over time, lose everything when the surroundings that gave them their meaning disappear: they are literally no use for anything, they have no after-life. In some way, they can have only two destinies: either destruction (Rimini had thought of that, but lost heart when he imagined himself striding triumphantly across a field carpeted with burnt photographs, like a conjugal Attila) or a sharing out. Rimini's mistake had been not to choose between them, to have simply run away. The result was that the photos were still there, marooned in indecision, like magic charms which, being no longer in circulation, have nothing better to do than store up energy and meaning.

CHAPTER 9

The world shone like a gleaming new object, and Rimini, tired but content like a traveller who has landed after an interminable journey in an unknown foreign city, was too caught up in being part of it to want to waste time on the past. He did not think of Sofia. Sometimes when he returned to Las Heras at two or three in the morning and collapsed into bed, he realised the whole day had gone by without him so much as giving her or anything related to her a single thought. He could scarcely believe it. It was as if she had been cut out of him. He even began to think that someone at some moment – one of those lengths of time that a machine or a mad scientist steals from a sequence and then, once they have worked on it and inserted all kinds of fresh material, replaces in the sequence as if nothing had happened – had wiped his mind clean, had given him the latest, absolutely perfect kind of brain-washing, so perfect that it also included secondary and apparently irrelevant organs such as the heart, stomach and skin. But it was enough to realise that Sofia had disappeared from his life for him to start thinking of her, and within half an hour – the final half-hour he spent awake, without even getting undressed, tossing and turning on his bed – he was trying to repair the damage caused by his lack of consideration. Like a prisoner trying to earn remission by doing voluntary work, Rimini went through memories, thoughts, imaginary episodes in which Sofia was present, and made sure he accompanied every recollection with the kind of emotion that would have gone with it had it appeared spontaneously. And so every night, with one foot in the waking world and the other in sleep, Rimini felt sad, afraid, nostalgic or repentant; he loathed, distorted and reconciled himself with the past, and every night, just as others say a prayer, so he offered his tribute to dead love. Then came dawn, and as the first breeze blew in through the window he had forgotten to shut, caressing his cheek, Rimini half-opened his eyes and saw without seeing the red stripe in the sky, the cold herald of a hot day. He was shivering a little. As he finally got undressed, an almost painful shudder of pleasure ran over his body as though when he touched it with his fingers he was scraping it, and once he was in bed, intoxicated by the cool sensation of the sheets round his legs and almost asleep once more, he would masturbate slowly and languidly.

A few days after he had moved out, Sofia called and asked him – trying to avoid any possibility of reproach – if he had called her. She said her answering-machine was broken, and thought that perhaps Rimini had left her a message, but it had not been recorded, and ... Rimini for his part thought of taking advantage of the situation and lying. No, he said, he had not called her. After that, neither of them said anything for a while. 'Isn't that what we agreed?' she said eventually. 'Yes,' he said, and started making excuses, giving details of all the things he had been obliged to do. Sofia asked him where he had put the furniture in his apartment. She could recall perfectly the size and distribution of each room, and most of the changes she made over the phone, without even seeing how he had distributed everything, were just right. It was as though their conversation had two levels: the first was completely technical, and was taken up with problems and the solution of details, and the anecdotal aspects of their new lives (an expression which between them only she used, and then specifically to refer to his life); the other involved feelings, and hung like a huge, dim and distant roar in the background, or like the shabby underside of a tablecloth used only one way up. 'What about you? Have you found somewhere to live?' Rimini would ask, trying desperately to cling to the technical details. No. She had stopped looking. She wasn't in the mood. Besides, where would she find an apartment better than the one she was already in? 'No,' said Rimini, 'it's just that you said ...' 'Yes,' she would reply, her tone of voice switching from apathetic to close to furious, 'but this is my home, this is where I wanted to live. Why should I leave? Who is trying to get rid of me?' 'I don't know ... to make a change, perhaps?' 'I don't want to change. Things have changed enough already. Something has to stay the same, doesn't it? It's true that it's all a bit much, but so what? I made it that way. You and I made it that way. Why should I have to leave?' That was the problem with details – they never lasted long enough. The supermarket, the local bars, the

Underground station nearby, the caretaker's limp, the twins in the apartment next door, the woman in the laundrette reading Mallea: Rimini searched for these anecdotal gems, he collected them and told her all about them with boundless enthusiasm, as though trying to show her that by simply existing they proved that nothing was over between them. But there was something fragile about them, something too short-lived or unconvincing, or perhaps it was some sort of chemical reaction when they came into contact with Sofia, or when Sofia or something within Sofia – a certain belief in density, the idea that anything that was not dense in this way was a betrayal of experience – contrasted them with the other level of their conversation, that made them disappear like shooting stars. Rimini watched them climb quickly to their summit, then vanish into thin air, swept away by the depths of night. By the time Sofia really got going (comforted by the victory of the essential over the anecdotal): 'We have to learn to live with what we once were, Rimini: that's the best lesson our love can teach us', all Rimini could think was: hang up. But they went on talking for a while, until each word became a tiny island, drifting in a sea of silence and awkward voice clearing, and Rimini, almost numb from embarrassment, ended by inventing some urgent task in order to hasten their goodbyes. 'I'm sorry, there's someone at the door.' 'I didn't hear anything. Where are you talking from?' 'From the bedroom.' Another silence. Then something crackled in Sofia's voice: 'Is it a girl?' 'I don't know,' said Rimini with a laugh, 'I doubt it.' 'Will you call me?' 'Of course. By next week I should be . . .' 'Remember, you owe me something.' 'I owe you something . . . ?' 'You owe *us* something. The photos. I was looking at them yesterday: I don't know, there must be at least a thousand or fifteen hundred of them.'

Rimini never rang, so a week later Sofia called him again. She was happy: she was going to Chile for a fortnight with Frida Breitenbach, her teacher. She was going to help with a seminar for artists with motor disabilities. They had called Rimini's father to arrange the air tickets. 'That's not a problem, is it?' she said, a sarcastic fellow-conspirator, 'we may be separated, but I still think he's the best father-in-law in the world.' To Rimini she sounded so pleased, so little threatened, that he thought that if he had seen her like this he might have fallen in love with her all over again. He suggested they meet when she got back. He felt relaxed about it: he calculated that the details of her trip would prevent the conversation falling into any great emotional outbursts. 'That's great,' she said, 'and I'll be able to see how your place looks.' 'There's nothing new for you to see,' he said, drawing back, 'it would be better if we meet in that bar on Canning and Cabello.' 'The one with the chrome chairs?' 'Yes.' 'Have you forgotten how I hate chrome? There's a better one, with everything in wood, on the corner of Paunero and Cerviño.' Rimini agreed, although he had been there once or twice on his way home, and could clearly remember the strange smell – a stale mixture of rancid cheese and disinfectant – it had greeted him with.

As if he had spent the whole night stewing over it, one morning a couple of days later he woke up with his mind made up: he would have a haircut. He decided to get it cut short, really short, and since this meant putting an end to fifteen years with long hair, a dogma his father (who rejoiced in the sixties' new freedom in hairstyles, but whose baldness prevented him from putting into practice himself) had inculcated in him from his early years, and which Sofia had not only approved but celebrated, Rimini spent the whole day finding arguments he could use to stifle any protest he was sure they would make. He hesitated. Decided he could not go through with it, and felt miserable. To lighten the burden, he reduced it to an on-the-spur-of-the-moment thing, and plunged into a small salon in the arcade near his Las Heras apartment, a hairdresser's he never passed without wondering who could be stupid enough to go into it. He sat in a chair – the only one not shaped like a plane or canoe or elephant – and caught sight of his terrified face in a mirror covered in children's stickers. When the hairdresser arrived, clacking his pair of scissors next to Rimini's head, all he could say was: 'Nice and short.' For the rest of the time – the half-hour he spent sweating beneath a huge check gown, his eyes aching from the blazing lights in the salon – he bitterly regretted his decision. Every so often he glanced outside, and stared in amazement at the people looking at him in amazement: he could not believe that with him tied up captive like that, gradually having his head shrunken by a hairdresser who insisted on speaking to him in diminutives, other people were simply walking by, peering into shop windows, leading their normal lives. All at once, among the amazed faces, he saw one staring at him too insistently, as though trying to provoke him. A couple of seconds later, he recognised the face: it was Victor. As he was being dusted with talc, Rimini signalled to him to wait outside, as though by dissuading him from coming in he was saving himself any further humiliation. He refused the hand mirror and the sweets he was offered, paid, and resolved for the next ten hours at least not to contemplate the disaster they had made of his image in the mirror. 'Wow!' said Victor, before Rimini could even tell him of his plan. 'What a change.' They gave each other a hug. They had not seen each other for some time. In the schism that the separation had caused among their friends, Victor had stayed on Sofia's side. This was only logical: they had gone out together when they were twelve or thirteen, and it was thanks to her that Rimini had met him. But Victor, although he had no problem telling Rimini whose side he was on, at the same time displayed an odd kind of impartiality, a judicious mix of concern and distance, of commitment and fair-mindedness, that Rimini found only rarely in other friends. Standing in the arcade – the separation was too recent for them to go and have a drink together – while Rimini watched as the hairdresser swept up the heaps of his hair with a broom and Victor examined the near-disaster the scissors had left on Rimini's scalp, they talked of Sofia. Rimini told him they were going to meet when she got back from her trip. 'Yes, she told me before she left,' Victor said. With exaggerated enthusiasm, Rimini said he had been surprised that Frida put so much responsibility on to Sofia. He thought it must be some kind of 'promotion'. 'You think so?' Victor said. 'Well, how many students does she have? A hundred, two hundred? She could have chosen any of them.' 'Yes, any of them willing to accept that kind of job.' 'It's not so bad: they're all used to working with handicapped people.' Victor looked at him with some astonishment. Rimini insisted: 'You mean because it's work with actors who have difficulties, don't you?' Embarrassed, Victor smiled, but before long the smile became a worried look. 'Frida's the one who has difficulties,' he said, 'she had a hip operation two months ago. Sofia is not going for the seminar: she's going as her therapeutic assistant. As her crutch.'

Sofia came back a week earlier than planned. 'I wasn't interested: it was all too basic,' she told Rimini on the phone. There was an emphatic tension in her voice, as though she was trying to convince herself of something by using her interlocutor as a test bed. They brought their rendezvous forward. Rimini wanted to suggest that they change the venue. 'I brought you something,' Sofia said, with that blind sense of opportunity that despair brings. They almost did not recognise each other. Sofia had dark lines under her eyes, but was very tanned from the Chilean sun (the skiers' winter sun that seems to spread a kind of orange sheen on people's skin) and had a cold sore on her lip that disfigured half her mouth. She spent the first ten minutes of their meeting staring at Rimini's head, without even daring to touch it – she stretched out a hand, but her fingers drew back before they could reach him, as though they had received an electric shock – constantly playing with the pottery figure covered in tiny coloured ribbons and bits of thread in her hands. None of Rimini's lengthy explanation, with his apocryphal request: 'Not too short, please', his exhaustive, mean-spirited description of the hairdresser and his equally apocryphal decision to get revenge by not paying him, seemed even to reach her ears. In the end, with the last ounce of her strength, like someone placing all they have on one last bet before they go off into the desert, she pushed the figure towards Rimini. 'It's a kind of Chilean Ekeko,' she said. 'They say it brings good lu . . .' she broke off and burst into tears. 'Never again. Never again', she repeated between sobs. 'I beg you, please, Rimini: the next time I say . . . Don't let me . . . Don't listen to what I . . . Just don't let me. No, never again. My God! And now I've got this monstrosity on my lips . . . No, please don't look at me!'

It had been a nightmare week. Frida was in constant pain. Their hotel room – only one for the two of them, with only one bed – was on the third floor, and there was no lift. The hotel was full, all its five floors occupied by a Cuban volley-ball team who never went to bed before half-past four in the morning. Forewarned by one of those malicious rumours so typical of Buenos Aires, Frida had refused from the outset to eat any seafood or fish. 'These Chileans are not going to poison me,' she said. All she ate were boiled potatoes. As the days went by, she started to swell up, to find it impossible to sleep, and to mistreat her students. There were five of them. Two of them dropped out on the third day, after presenting a formal complaint to the management of the centre where the seminar was being held: they described the visiting teacher as a 'professional psycopath'. She had almost forced a third, a young man with epilepsy who only spoke in a whisper and had once been a star on Chilean TV, to undergo a rebirthing exercise that Sofia said was one of the hardest she had ever seen: when he came out of it, he had to be rushed off to hospital in the middle of a convulsive fit. The seminar was suspended. They took advantage of this to go and spend a day sunbathing up in the mountains, and it was that same night that Sofia felt the first tingling on her lip. Frida was furious and criticised her for being so weak. How was it possible for any disciple of Frida Breitenbach to have such low defences? She threatened her: if the herpes spread, as soon as they got back to Buenos Aires she would make her change groups. She would have to start the fourth year again, from the beginning. If necessary, she would go back to third year. The seminar never restarted; the centre paid only for the days when there had been a class, and Frida, blaming 'reasons beyond her control' took Sofia off her list of expenses. That night they were thrown out of the hotel after the volley-ball team trainer complained that Frida (or her nocturnal double, whom he described, to a pair of intrigued Chilean policemen, as 'a great panting monster, covered in freckles and with hair standing on end as if from an electric shock, coming towards me spouting obscenities in some diabolical language') had harassed him sexually and threatened him with her stick in a particularly dark section of the staircase between the second and third floors. 'I should have trusted my intuition,' Frida told Sofia on the flight back to Buenos Aires as she stroked her face condescendingly: 'You're too young and innocent: you're not ready for this level of experience.'

'Well, it's all over now,' said Rimini, reaching out and ruffling her hair. It was an odd gesture: calculated and affectionate, but somehow too professional, as though he were a nurse. But as soon as she felt the caress, Sofia, who had hidden her head in her hands, raised it and offered him a full view of her distress: her irritated eyes, smeared mascara, red drippy nose, the strange purplish caterpillar stuck to her bottom lip. Then, as though she were performing a karate chop (a loving karate, designed to win back a former lover) Sofia caught Rimini's hand in mid-air as he was withdrawing it, lifted it to her lips and kissed it: once on the palm, twice on the edge, three times on the back. She turned it over, forced it open (because the hand had curled up like a hedgehog) and kissed the centre of the palm once more, as though in adoration. Rimini had frozen. He felt as if he was being subjected to some sort of vaguely esoteric treatment by which a mouth with a cold sore could somehow cure a healthy hand by applying a specific number of kisses. 'But it wasn't all bad,' Sofia said, smiling for the first time, while Rimini extracted his hand with the excuse of calling the waiter. She looked at him. She stared at him levelly, calmly, with immortal aplomb, as if a disastrous week in Santiago with Frida Breitenbach, converted to the metric system of her emotions, somehow stretched into a centuries-long experience and invested her with the authority of an Egyptian goddess. 'You see, it gave me time to think,' she said. 'I thought a lot about us, and what happened to us . . .' Rimini nodded automatically. Sofia smiled again and looked at him inquisitively, as if inviting him to speak. 'What?' he said, 'What's wrong?' 'You,' she said, 'did you think of anything?' Rimini searched and searched and searched, but the room was completely dark. 'It's all too recent,' he said. 'Come on,' Sofia replied, leaning towards him as though trying to discover his centre, 'you must have thought something.' 'I don't know, I wouldn't know what to say.' 'Hey, this is me, Sofia. Nothing's going to happen to you, is it?' They sat for a few moments in silence, without moving. She was very close to him, looking up, still waiting, while he pretended to be gazing at the shadows which every so often crossed the burnt-out street corner. Some secret length of time must have elapsed, because with a sigh Sofia bent down, opened her bag and said: 'I wrote you a letter.'

CHAPTER 10

It's ten past three in the morning. The Witch has finally gone to sleep, and I've come down to the bar with your old copy of Ada *(don't look for it any more, it was at my place, you either forgot to take it or you didn't have the heart to ask me for it, now it's mine and you've no right to protest), the postcard with Riltse's spectre on it and my Gloria exercise book. It's almost completely dark, but I want to write you a letter to tell you all I would have said to you if you had just once stopped trying to escape and we were in Buenos Aires together, you and I, Rimini, Rimini and Sofia, together. (I can't see very well, my handwriting's a disgrace: I promise to write it all out again tomorrow.) Ever since you left I've been filling up notebook after notebook with things that occur to me: memories, phrases, things I read ('Forgetting is a play we put on every night', Ada p. 263). It really helps me to write, Rimini. I don't know why, but as I'm writing I feel you close by, watching me, and often I find myself doing what I used to do at school, raising the cover of my notebook so that stupid Venanzi girl couldn't copy. You're not forgetting me, are you? Please tell me you aren't, Rimini. I couldn't bear that. Tell me you hate me, that you want to hit me, to make me bleed, that you fell in love with another woman, that you're going to live abroad, but please don't tell me you're forgetting me. That would be criminal. Twelve years, Rimini. (Almost half our lives!) Nobody (you can't see it, because my biro is running out, but I underlined 'nobody' twice) can forget twelve years just like that, from one day to the next. You can try, if you like (I tried, Rimini, don't think I didn't, but I couldn't – that's all there is to it), you can try as hard as you like, but it doesn't make sense. You won't be able to. The hotel is full of Cuban volley-ball players. I saw them playing in the street today outside the hotel, and I remembered. No, I didn't remember: I saw you, Rimini. I saw you jumping beside a volley-ball net on a beach, blond and skinny, looking so young I wanted to cry. (I'm sorry. I don't think Ada is good for me. Riltse isn't good for me. Nothing is good for me.)*

CHAPTER 11

But Rimini did not read the letter. He folded the envelope in two and put it in his pocket, just as he did each time Sofia handed him something she had written, and each time Sofia looked at Rimini with sad disappointment when he deprived her of her greatest pleasure: to watch his face while he read what she had written without him, far from him, just for him. He did not read the letter she had written him in Chile in front of her, nor the one she wrote some time later in her homeopath's waiting-room ('*We've made our minds up, Rimini: we're going to get to the bottom of this herpes thing*'), nor the one she decided to write, when her whole bottom lip had disappeared beneath the purple caterpillar and she was stuck for twenty minutes between stations in an Underground train on the way to a dermatologist who was a fervent believer in hydro-cortisone ('*Where are you, my love? You tell me I can count on you, but where are you now, when I need you?*'), nor the one she started to write in her mind at Frida's house the night the teacher and her disciple made it up, with the blessing of an English documentary on the language of the deaf ('*I place my hand on my heart and then on yours: the Witch says that two people like us cannot separate*'), nor even the ten thirsty, utterly despairing lines, the blue ink of half a dozen words blurred by teardrops, which Sofia swore she had written almost fifteen years earlier for him, after she had told him she had slept with Rafael, and which she had kept in the same jewel box where she had put a lock of the six-year-old Rimini's hair.

One afternoon they met in the street by chance. It was pouring with rain. Sofia offered him shelter under her umbrella, and suggested they went for a drink. Yet again, Rimini noted in puzzled admiration the way that she always seemed to have nothing to do; it was as if, following their separation, Sofia could devote all her time to love. He made his excuses: he was late getting somewhere. Yet as always when he was busy, he was very friendly, and peered closely at the tiny piece of gauze and plaster that had replaced the herpes on Sofia's lip. She had had an operation. 'Can you have an operation for cold sores?' he wanted to know. Now that he was sure he had to go, an inexplicable but genuine curiosity kept him with her. Sofia gazed at him sadly: 'Did you read my letter?' she asked. 'Yes, of course,' Rimini said, then asked: 'Local or general anaesthetic?' 'Did you read my letter?' she insisted. 'Yes, I just told you I did. Did they give you stitches?' 'So why are you asking me everything I already told you in my letter?' They argued about it in the rain, pressed together within the narrow radius of protection offered by the umbrella. Rimini waved his arms about and hit her on the chin, right next to her wound, so he said he was sorry. Two men running along with briefcases over their heads had to step down into the street to get round them. Over the sound of the rain, Rimini heard one of those insults tinged with envy often used to condemn a romantic scene considered out of place: as if the inclement setting – a downpour, wind, narrow pavement, or city centre – somehow made the exhibitionism of a man and woman allowing themselves to be seen so close to each other in public seem absolutely intolerable. They ended up standing at the bar of a gloomy café, with vaguely yellow walls, surrounded by cadets and office workers who were glancing all around them as they ate and drank, as if on the run from some robbery. Raising her voice above the hissing of the coffee machine, Sofia reminded him that the question of the photos still had to be resolved, and gave him an ultimatum. As the tip of the umbrella dripped on to the top of his shoe, Rimini came clean and confessed that he simply could not face it. He had thought of the task in front of them, and it seemed to him literally impossible. Not because there were fifteen hundred photos. Paradoxically, that made it easier. No, all he had to do was think of *one*, a single photograph, not even one of the most meaningful, just any one of them, those that usually disappear without trace, to feel that the whole thing was crazy, that the past was one huge block that could not be split up – you either had to accept it as it was, whole, or reject it. Neither of them spoke. The umbrella had stopped dripping. Rimini thought he was about to start crying, and quickly looked away. It was a reflex action; he was well aware he did not stand the slightest chance of hiding his emotion: when it came to demonstrations of love – and by love, Sofia also included everything that came before and after it, everything that went with it, everything it left behind, everything that floated like a cloud around it, as well as all that love had displaced and all that had displaced love: *everything* – Sofia's eyes were as rapid and accurate as those of a croupier scanning the alphabet of hands, numbers and colours with which the baize cloths of roulette tables are written every night. Deeply moved, Sofia stretched out her hand to his, and tried to intercept his gaze – Rimini felt a pulling sensation at his neck, as if some tiny but tenacious creature were burrowing underneath his skin up to his face – then she slid two fingers into the gap between his shirt sleeve and wrist. 'I know,' Sofia said. 'Do you think I don't feel the same?' Rimini was relieved. He turned his head back slightly and started to examine her, as if to familiarise himself slowly with what he might see. 'But we have to do something, Rimini. You couldn't do it on your own; nor could I. We *both* have to do it. Even if it's the last thing we do together. Please. Don't leave me on my own with this corpse. I'll go mad.'

CHAPTER 12

'It's me. It's half-past six: you should have been here an hour ago. I'm worried, Rimini. Hello? Hello? You're not there . . . Well, I don't know. I'm waiting for you. Call me, please. No matter what time. I'm staying in the studio . . .' Rimini stretched out a hand to lower the volume on his answering-machine, and as he did so, carried away by a kind of storm raging inside him, he bumped into the corner of his desk and knocked over a bottle of mineral water, an acrylic pencil-box, and a pile of books. Sofia's voice faded until it died away completely, as though it had disappeared down a deep well. As he was putting right the disaster – the third of the day, and inconsequential compared to the other two – Rimini had the sensation that he was feeling something like guilt, but it felt remote and deadened by distance, in the same way that after it has been anaesthetised, the pain of an incision feels like a superficial tickling to the skin. In fact he registered the fact more than he felt it. Cocaine had turned him into an ubiquitous, ever-vigilant recorder, like a radar or one of those closed-circuit television cameras which are trained for days on a car park without seeing anything. If he imagined a feeling of guilt it was almost a reflex action, simply being faithful to experience rather than because he recognised its moral consequences in him. He thought of it as an idea, an intellectual construction, as though he were staring at something out of reach, behind a wall of glass, in a museum, completely stripped of any possibility of affecting him.

He had not meant at all to stand Sofia up. But he no longer needed to mean to do anything. And now, when he finally discovered he had done so, he thought to himself: 'Of course. How could I have got there?' Everything seemed separate and pre-determined, as if written in a book he had not read, and that sense of pre-determination was the soft, comfortable bed on which he had learnt to rest his poor, painful body. Everything that happened – everything that did not matter to him, in other words everything apart from translating and, for the last ten days, receiving visits from Vera – happened on another plane, a parallel world complete with padded walls and soundproofing, a world in which events did not so much take place as were acted out lackadaisically before a bored audience. Rimini would enter this deserted little theatre, pretend to sniff about a bit, then leave. When he returned to his books and his work, even this fleeting concession to the world of facts seemed like an unforgivable distraction to him.

He had only been taking drugs for less than a week, but life already seemed to him like a mortal combat. All he wanted to do was translate. The rest – brushing his teeth, eating, going out, talking on the phone, getting dressed, meeting people, opening the door to the pest control man – were mere obstacles, things that got in the way, attempts at sabotage. In that week, as if his encounter with drugs had not been a novelty, the start of something, but rather the culmination of a long but almost imperceptible process, Rimini had learnt almost all there was to know. He spoke freely to his dealer, in the flat, neutral manner of business transactions, avoiding the kind of slang that those who are not really part of the drugs world use to convince themselves and others that they are experts. He would call and say: 'Hi, this is Rimini. Can I come round?' That was all. He would never dream of mentioning cocaine on the phone, although this was an irresistible temptation for those newcomers who are more excited by the sense of danger than by the cocaine itself, and who multiply the synonyms and aliases in order both to impress their dealers and at the same time confuse any police who might possibly be listening. Rimini was discreet and to the point. He paid for exactly as much as he bought. His one rule was: don't get into debt. The first time he bought cocaine, he ground the crystals and made the lines with professional skill. He paused only for a moment as he was peering over the glass to snort the first line when he saw first some patches of colour, then skin tones and something that looked like a mouth, a face trying desperately to come together beneath his own, a face reflected in the glass. He finally realised that the tray he had used to make the lines of coke was a framed photo of Sofia: the only portrait that had managed to escape the complete closure of his borders. It was eleven in the morning, and Rimini was still sober, but the simultaneous appearance of Sofia's photo at the moment of his initiation into drugs, bought with his own money from a dealer who had just added him to his list of regular clients – this fortuitous occurrence, which at some other time might have led to him think of things from a sentimental, psychological or simply historical point of view – now seemed directly related to the logic of drugs itself, which divided the fact into two halves, dismissing one, its meaning, as irrelevant, and retaining the other, the fact itself, because of its simple existence as fact: the sheet of glass was big, clean, perfect: it offered plenty of room for six lines.

Everything had happened so quickly: Vera appearing, the drugs, the translations: in the space of a fortnight, the myriad possibilities that Rimini's life had become since his separation from Sofia had precipitated into a dense, compact, extraordinarily concentrated deposit, in which all the promises he had previously thought he recognised as offered by the future had been translated into the self-absorbed language of a present that seemed eternal. A fortnight earlier he used to go out into the street in a state of great excitement, like someone entering a fairground anxious to try all the stalls at once, and whatever the day actually offered, he fed, and almost choked, on this enthusiasm for hours, until he returned to Las Heras and shut himself in to go over not everything that had happened to him, because this varied from day to day, but everything that might have happened to him. This was necessarily an infinite and therefore essential list, which he had allowed himself the luxury of passing him by. But none of that was possible now: everything was of the moment. He took one or sometimes two hits of cocaine a day. He saw Vera every other day. He was translating three books at the same time, for three different publishers: he managed forty pages a day. He was no longer choking: he was a happy workman.

By contrast, Vera was young and wild. The first time he saw her, one Friday afternoon twenty-four hours before he took up drugs, she was on her own, talking into a cordless phone held between cheek and shoulder as she strode up and down on the other side of the glass window of the shop where she worked. An animal, thought Rimini: an animal cooped up in a glass cage, an animal recently captured from a jungle she will never return to, an animal trying to breathe an unaccustomed atmosphere. He went closer to the shop window, pretending to be interested in a hideous shell bracelet, and took the opportunity to study her for several minutes, his nosed pressed up against the glass, while his prophetic imagination ran through the stages of a completely impossible scene: he, Rimini, humiliated before he even began, going into the shop, making his way awkwardly across the ten square metres of carpet, dichroic lamps and fake marble tops, debating what his first words would be, and then in what was almost a panic attack, trying desperately to work out what she would say back to him, resulting in nothing more satisfying than a trivial dialogue and a stupid purchase, at the end of which the girl would dial the same number she had been talking to before, and Rimini would disappear in a puff of smoke, his pockets empty and with a disgusting golden packet – the only reward for his daring – in his hand, the rhodocrosite ring, the onyx egg, or the pewter treble clef that a beggar would later rummage and find in the arcade's rubbish.

He had never committed the folly of talking to a woman he knew nothing about. Before he made any advance he needed some sort of prologue, a minimum stock of shared past, some context that could prepare and protect him. But the pewter, the rhodocrosite and the onyx egg all melded into a big blind patch, Rimini raised his eyes a little and looked at her – Vera was turning first one way, then the other, as though avoiding blows or throwing punches, with the phone still stuck between shoulder and ear – and at some point, one of the few moments when he got a clear view of her, he discovered the tiny V her hair drew on her forehead and decided to go in. Everything seemed hostile to him: the heat, the proximity of everything, the strange way the hand-icrafts welcomed him (the ridged back of a glass dinosaur almost severed one of his fingers, and when he tried to save an endangered seahorse he almost knocked a Peruvian ceramic hut to the floor) and above all, his own failure to seize the opportunity. Vera was still talking on the phone, or rather was arguing on the phone with someone whose name reached Rimini's ears mangled beyond recognition. She lowered her voice, then raised it again in sudden exclamations of outrage; she hunched over as though to protect her private quarrel from Rimini's gaze; she gesticulated, and every so often opened a parenthesis of icy lucidity, demanding the details of a confused incident, wanting to know times, places, the names of witnesses, how long it had lasted, angrily repeating every reply she was given, as if hearing the words in her own mouth would convince her they were untrue. Just once, interrupted by a man coming in to offer her a coffee, she gazed rapidly around the shop. When her eyes lighted on Rimini's intimidated face, she looked straight through him as if he had been made of glass. Rimini thought her eyes were green, and clung on. He walked round the shop again, hesitating between a stone ashtray and a cane pencil-box – why did everything he could see have to have a double name? 'Do you think I'm a fool?' Vera was shouting on the phone. 'That I don't have eyes, that I don't see or hear?' Rimini wondered why he was still there. To humiliate her? Not knowing what to do, he looked out of the shop: leaning in the doorway of the Indian clothes shop opposite, a woman was looking at him suspiciously while she filed her nails. 'More proof?' he heard. 'What, you want me to have you followed? You want photos, like in the movies? Photos of you fucking? With that little cunt?' Behind his back, Rimini could hear her gasping for air. 'Bastard. You're a bastard. Get out of my life. I'd like to see you dead.' Vera was in tears. 'No,' she added, 'not even that: I don't ever want to see you again. Not even dead.' Rimini spun round when he heard a dull thud on the carpet. He saw the phone on the floor, its tiny green light still flashing. He saw Vera standing there silently crying, like a film image without the sound. As he walked towards her, Rimini could see two red patches flaring on her pale cheeks. She looked so beautiful he was on the point of bursting into tears as well. 'How much . . . how much is this?' Vera took her eyes from his chest level and stared at the pencil-box. She immediately stopped crying; Rimini could have sworn that the tears rolled back up her cheeks into the tear ducts, as if the whole sequence were being projected backwards. 'Nothing: it's free,' she said. 'You can have it.' She opened a drawer in the counter, took out a handful of small notes, stuffed them into a transparent bag and said as she went out: 'You can take whatever you like.'

Ten minutes later, in the bar where he discovered her sitting at the least inviting table, her back to the world as though she had been made to sit in a corner, Rimini came to a halt and handed her the bunch of keys he had used to lock the shop door. 'You left them in the lock,' he explained, as though excusing himself. She scraped the keys across the table and dropped them in her bag. Then she gulped down her drink – cognac, he thought, or one of those anonymous spirits that only appear when all the others have been finished, and serve to get desperate people drunk – 'But . . .' she said, as if this followed on from some previous paragraph that Rimini had not witnessed but which as far as he could tell had been maturing for days, months, or even years in silence inside her head, and then immediately started to speak, and went on without stopping for half an hour. Rimini listened to her in silence, first of all standing next to her table, shifting from foot to foot, and then, taking advantage of the pause during which, in a feeble, begging voice she asked for her glass to be refilled, sitting next to her, staring down at how white her childish hands were, with their chewed cuticles. He listened as she reconstructed her dreadful calvary as though in a dream: the repeated warning signs she had missed, the evidence she had like an idiot ignored and which she now referred to and displayed once again like someone spreading out the pieces of a game on a cloth, a game whose rules she did not know, but played all the same, and which now it no longer held any secrets she displayed once again, apparently for the sole purpose of demonstrating to herself that she had been right, that everything was lost from the start. Rimini was there, right next to her (the casual contact of their two forearms had given him gooseflesh) but he had no illusions: Vera was not talking *to* him, she was talking *in front of* him, as if he were the abstract, ideal instance before which a lawyer speaking in court appeared. In the precision with which she recalled every detail from the past there was not so much indignation as a kind of stubborn, incorruptible objectivity that smacked more of the legal than the sentimental. She was extraordinarily lucid. She remembered everything: late arrivals, changes of clothes, marks on the neck, contradictory explanations, the smell of a recent bath, arrangements cancelled at the last minute, new names pronounced in a casual voice, pages torn from a diary; and with all these clues, recalled without any show of emotion, she built her spider's web, closed in on the scoundrel who had given them away and enfolded him in them, forcing him to face the naked truth of his betrayal. Rimini felt giddy, as if he suddenly found himself in mid-air, hanging from a gossamer thread; he struggled or forced himself to struggle for a few moments, and as soon as her attention strayed, leapt in and suggested they meet up that same night. She stopped speaking and stared at him, blinking rapidly, as though the veil covering her eyes had suddenly lifted and she was seeing him properly for the first time. He saw her smile. It seemed to him as though Vera had become younger and was once more timid, shivering, scared. 'Excuse me for a minute,' she said all at once, then leaned forward and held her head in her hands. Rimini looked away, as though refusing to eavesdrop on another private scene. A few seconds later, when he wanted to look at her again, he was taken by surprise, as if during that brief moment of modesty some kind of subtle but undeniable optical illusion had been corrected. He did not know what to do, or what to blame his bewilderment on. Nothing had visibly altered, and yet everything was different, just as in the science-fiction series that had given him nightmares as a child. But he conquered his fear and looked at her steadily, and at almost the same instant that he noticed the tiny lens glinting on the tip of one of her fingers, he realised that the green iris of her right eye was no longer green but amber-coloured.

But the V-shape on her forehead was real. Apart from that, Rimini had succumbed to something much less easy to fake than the colour of her eyes: being trapped, imprisoned, the delicious and almost erotic torment of jealousy. What wouldn't he have given to be the one who aroused such an insomniac passion, to be the target of all these avalanches of fury? What wouldn't he have given to be in the centre of the web, watching the shadow of Vera slowly drawing near to exact her revenge. That night at Sergio's, while Vera searched desperately for him like a shipwrecked sailor in the midst of a noisy gaggle of natives, Rimini rather unsteadily shut himself in the bathroom and with unusual dexterity for a beginner who was in addition quite drunk, a dexterity learnt in part from all the versions of the scene that he had seen in films, and in part from the surreptitious schooling that desires we do not know we have offer us, injecting us bit by bit with knowledge we will only put into practice at a much later date, when they finally come to the surface, firmly snorted the two lines of coke that someone had just made on the black marble top of the washbasins. Rimini straightened up abruptly, propelled by this last inhalation: he could feel his whole body spreading, as though all of a sudden more blood were coursing through his veins. It was only afterwards, when the flash of lucidity that had blinded him had passed, that he looked around and saw that in addition to the man who had made the lines of coke there was a girl in the bathroom. It seemed to him as though either the room was too small or they were too large for any of them to be able to move without bumping into each other. They were so close to each other that while the girl was bending over the marble to snort her share, Rimini could see the tiny round scar the size of a teardrop that shone between two strands of hair at the nape of her neck. Rimini could not get over it. This intimacy with strangers that at another moment would have been unbearable to him, now offered only a sense of protection and calm. He was as open as before, he thought, but these nameless faces in front of him were also his furthest limit, a kind of smaller, more portable horizon within his horizon, one that somehow diminished his giddiness and calmed his fears. The man slid his finger along the marble top and cleaned up the remains of the coke. He turned on the tap and began to wash his hands. 'Aren't you having any?' Rimini asked him. 'No,' the man said, turning his head to examine himself in the mirror: 'It doesn't agree with me.' Nervous, Rimini glanced at him out of the corner of his eye. No, there was no way of identifying with him: if Rimini and the girl were flat planes, the man was three-dimensional, or vice versa. Sergio had introduced them briefly as he went by, not giving it much importance or at least pretending not to. 'A friend of . . .' he said. Rimini promptly forgot his name and the friend's, but bumped into him a couple of times throughout the night, and could not help eyeing him suspiciously. He was struck by the distance that seemed to separate him from everyone else: the cool, sober detachment with which he moved around the party, always on his own, a glass of mineral water in his hand, and then a few minutes later, he was talking animatedly and was the centre of attraction of those same guests who had previously appeared to ignore him. He was not on the same plane as the rest of them, but in a more controlled, more efficient one, slightly higher than theirs, a dimension which Rimini, standing twenty centimetres from him in the bathroom, somehow saw as a huge gym with loud music pounding out, and filled with people like him dressed in black and sweating all the time as they frantically flexed their muscles in their work-out regimes. 'You two go out first,' he heard him telling them. Rimini felt his voice like a heavy but friendly hand on his shoulder.

They went out – the girl first, lipstick still in her hand, and then

Rimini. He took a couple of steps forward and, like someone coming to the surface after plunging to the bottom of a freezing but invigorating pool, felt a strong urge to embrace the fifty or sixty people dancing in the darkened room. Tall, abandoned, Vera was on the point of giving up her search when she turned and saw him coming out of the bathroom preceded by the girl, who was blindly redoing her lips. It all happened too quickly. Rimini did not recognise her, or was slow to do so, bit by bit, as the rhythmic strobe light picked out her fleeing figure. The first thing he saw was a pair of eyes staring at him. He thought then it might be her, but when he looked again, she had disappeared. He spotted the outline of a body heading for the door, but by the time he had thought he recognised her hair, her hairband, the slightly athletic way she pushed through the crowd of people, something got in the way of the image – an idiot shaking his hips in front of him – and he lost sight of her again. He could see everything clearly, but could only *read* what he saw after a second's delay, as in those films where the sound reaches the ear slightly after the image, so that when he was sure it was her, she was no longer there to confirm it. He saw the flash of a white handbag close to the door, saw the door open, and then almost at once a hand shutting it with a double twist of a key. He was only able to verify what he had seen ten or fifteen minutes later, when, after looking everywhere for her, he burst into the room where the coats were being kept and Sergio, head peering out from among the jackets, told him he thought he had seen her leave.

The next day, after several fruitless phone calls, Rimini finally caught up with her. 'Be quick, please, I was just going out', she said, in a flurry of keys. She was full of exaggerated, self-absorbed anger, the kind that needs to feed off itself in order not to collapse. Rimini asked why she had left in the way she had. 'Why? What way?' she said. Jealousy had sharpened her hearing, and she used it above all to stress how cruel the other person was being, to emphasise the causes of her suffering in the words she had just been forced to hear. 'Yes,' he insisted, 'why did you leave like that?' but before he could go on, he had the impression that an enemy army was charging down the phone line. He heard a stinging condemnation of redheads, another, so obscene that he blushed, about how cosmetic firms had not yet been able to make lipstick that was proof against ejaculations, and then the cold, almost

70

bored description of the obvious plot Rimini had hatched with Sergio to make her look ridiculous. 'But I didn't even know her!' Rimini protested. '*You didn't even know her!* That's worse still,' shouted Vera, 'far worse!' and slammed down the phone. Rimini called her again once, three times, ten times. Each time he let the phone ring a little longer, as if the number of rings carried with it some loving code. He was certain that Vera was still there, next to the phone, and the satisfaction he could sense she felt – her enjoyment of having him ring in vain, or of seeing him, thanks to that kind of clairvoyance that disdain gives us, uselessly dialling the same number again and again – multiplied in an incalculable way the satisfaction that he was experiencing, all alone, defenceless, already hopelessly caught in the web of love.

Vera never answered. It was evening before he managed to get in touch with her, following his first trip out to buy drugs. He had the twist of paper in one hand, the phone in the other. He was trembling. Never before had he realised so clearly how far enthusiasm is born of terror, pure, vulgar terror, the sort that makes people tremble, makes their hands sweat and their mouths dry. He put the receiver between cheek and shoulder, just as he had seen Vera do in her shop, and while he dialled the number he unfolded the sheet of paper with his other hand. Vera answered at once. She seemed depressed, sedated, or perhaps both things. In his imagination, Rimini saw her sprawled on an unmade bed, the blinds drawn and the TV on with no sound, surrounded by plates smeared with uneaten food and filthy ashtrays. They had a long conversation. Vera translated her noontide allegation into the civilised language of inevitability. But all that had happened was that time had passed; her ideas had not changed. Described as a 'bathroom sex maniac', Rimini discovered in himself a promiscuity he had never even suspected; but he also discovered, smiling as if faced with a miracle, that there was no need for the raw material of love to be a shared, unconditional and unbroken conviction; in fact, it could be just the opposite: a radical disbelief, mistrust, suspicion. He laughed and denied everything. Vera accepted his version only so that she could move on to something else, but beneath her docility Rimini (who like everyone who finds themselves the object of jealousy was also developing a new sense of hearing, tuning it in to the almost imperceptible frequencies that jealous people use to transmit their deliberations) could still make out the undertones of suspicion. 'Wait a minute,' he had to say at one point. As though doubled up in pain, he stopped speaking. But it was not pain, it was something more obscure: it was as though he had been skinned alive, and contact between him and everything outside him – first and foremost, Vera's voice – was immediate and without any barriers, like the collision of two raw entities. He stood there silently for a few moments, eyes closed. Then he put his hand over the mouthpiece, bent down over Sofia's young, tanned face, and snorted the long line of coke he had made. 'You aren't with someone, are you?' Vera asked him when she heard him on the phone again. Rimini had no difficulty reassuring her. Emboldened by the drug, whose effects seemed much more noticeable than the night before (perhaps because this was the first time he had actually bought some), he spoke a lot; a lot and with a rare precision: he picked up on every point as if he were trying to use his words to occupy all of the tiny cracks that Vera's doubts opened in her mind. He was not exactly aware of what he was saying, but something inside him that was not his will power, nor his common sense, but more perhaps a mixture of loving devotion, cynicism and self-control – exactly the kind of disparate elements that cocaine is perfect for bringing together, so much so that once they have amalgamated no one can imagine them apart – something told him where to tread, where to push and where to yield, when to take the lead, what to say openly and what to hide. As he spoke, Rimini was astonished to confirm through Vera's silence that his words were working in an extraordinary way. Like a lifeguard returning a foolhardy swimmer to the beach, saving him from drowning but also neutralising the blows, the thrashing feet, all the resistance he puts up unconsciously or out of a sense of shame, Rimini brought her back to land from the whirlpool of hatred where she was struggling, or rather brought her to that intermediate stretch that is no longer the open sea but is not dry land either, the territory where the spent fury of jealousy returns to the matrix from which bitterness expelled it: the matrix of helplessness. And then, when after his lengthy monologue he heard her voice again, by now not hostile but hesitant, defenceless, like someone who having learnt of the disaster they have just caused, refuses to accept all the blame but avoids appearing openly in public, and she, in the faintest of voices, first asked him, then begged him and finally *demanded* of him (with

72

that moving quality which demands made from a position of extreme weakness have) that if he should ever desire another woman, if there *were* another woman, he should tell her straight out, because, as she said, what she found intolerable was not the betrayal or the abandonment but the fact of not knowing – then Rimini said yes, he promised and swore that yes, he would tell her, even though he doubted this could ever happen, and felt certain that his life really had begun to change.

A short while later when, scared by how often they were seeing one another, they each independently began to feel that strange eagerness that distinguishes relationships with a future from merely passing fancies, something that seems less a feeling than a physical effect, similar to what lungs must go through when, after being unable to draw breath for some time, they receive a sudden injection of air, Rimini was able to confirm how far the words *spoken*, which for anyone in love, however committed they feel, always retain a certain levity which allows them to be changed, modified, contradicted even, without thereby threatening the love contract as part of which they were uttered in the first place – how far for any jealous person, especially when they refer to any hypothesis of betrayal, the secret heart of the drama, sees these words as gospel, set in stone. They no longer belong to the ethereal dimension of love as much as to that other one, as familiar to the jealous person as it is strange to everyone else, of legal affairs, a kind of 'law of love' in which every promise is an oath, every declaration a commitment.

One day they met by chance near his Las Heras apartment. For a few moments they had no idea what to do. It was two in the afternoon – apart from the day they had met, they had never seen each other in daylight. They looked at each other like two people who work together and are meeting for the first time out of uniform, in their normal clothes. Furthermore, a few hours earlier they had agreed on the phone that Vera would pass by Rimini's place in the early evening, and this only confused things still further. What could they do? Keep to the original arrangement, and say goodbye until later on? Put this chance meeting and their date together? What if they discovered that love was only a nocturnal illusion? But they were both starving, and as they stood there at a loss, his stomach started to rumble, as clearly

73

as in some TV cartoon, and Vera's followed suit, so they both laughed and glanced away in the same direction. They saw, with that kind of crazy and completely disproportionate astonishment that self-obsessed people feel when they suddenly realise they are in the spot it was obvious for them to be in, that they were right next to a take-away food store. They bought food, lots of it, as though they might be shut away for months, taking turns to ask for things, first him and then her, less concerned with the idea that they were going to have to eat it all within ten minutes than in displaying for each other the wide range of their personal tastes. They went up to Rimini's apartment, and while he was spreading the cartons of food out in the kitchen, Vera shouted from the living-room, asking if he minded whether she put some music on. She had been haunted by a song all morning, and wanted to listen to it with him, to see if he liked it. 'Play whatever you like', said Rimini. Busily organising lunch, he sensed that Vera was still talking to him, but her voice began to fade, as though she had moved away from him. He opened the fridge, looking for everything he knew he did not have, then slammed it shut again. 'I thought I had some mustard ...' he complained out loud. 'Or mayonnaise ... or ketchup ... or butter ...' he said, half to himself and half to Vera, as though to entertain her with his hopelessness. He quickly washed two glasses, and hesitated between offering her a plastic knife (booty stolen from some airline or other) or a fork to cut with. 'Don't be put off by the luxury ...' he shouted. All of a sudden his voice sounded too solitary to him. He paused and listened. Nothing: no music, no footsteps, nothing. A spasm of terror ran through him. He recapitulated as quickly as he could: he had gone out in the middle of his work, thinking he would be back almost at once, and without anyone else; he had just started taking his daily dose of drugs; he hadn't taken any precautions – he left the tray in the living-room and tiptoed over to his study. Vera was standing stock still by his desk. Rimini walked slowly over to her. She was very pale, apart from one red patch that was invading her cheek, and another on her chin. She stared at him steadily; she was clutching her bag so tightly that the strap had made red furrows in her hand. 'Who is this?' she asked at last, with a voice from beyond the grave. Rimini saw the photograph acting as a page-marker in the dictionary; the first thing that caught his attention were the traces of cocaine scattered on it like

74

vestigial clouds, and it was only a few moments later that his gaze lit upon the radiant close-up of Sofia, a lock of hair tumbling over her left eye, the blue expanse of sky, the tip of the red flag in one corner, the birthmark on her right shoulder . . .

He had to act quickly. Rimini weighed up the pros and cons, and decided that Sofia had to go underground – precisely the option that he had discarded in his mental debate about it. Why? Why – if he was sure that everything was over, and Sofia was no longer any kind of threat? And yet, as soon as he had taken the decision, Rimini felt an immediate satisfaction, as if despite being irrational, or perhaps because of it, what he had decided fitted perfectly into the framework of uncertainty that had been besieging him in recent days. Until now he had simply been postponing the decision, in the hope that this dissuasive policy would dampen any illusions Sofia might still have. Now suddenly it had all changed. Now he would remove Sofia from his life. Vera would be his Cause – Vera, whose fits of jealousy, however disturbing they might be, at least confirmed one of the few principles that Rimini acknowledged in his romantic life: namely, that a true love does not die a natural death, but one bathed in blood, battered to death by another love, not necessarily a true one (because in this sense the laws of love, blind to any claims to nobility, show no mercy), but at least opportune, and above all driven by that wild kind of cruelty that every youthful emotion reveals.

Time, cocaine, the hours spent poring over translations, and Vera's visits did the rest. Uprooting Sofia became a daily process. She would call, and Rimini would leave her talking into his answering-machine, shouting questions and reproaches for an impossible posterity. Soon, when he realised she would not give up, he turned the volume down to zero. He went through the day's messages at two or three in the morning, while Vera was sprawled fast asleep in his bed and he, kept awake by the drugs, had started translating again. Whenever he caught her voice, he fast-forwarded to the next message. He almost did not have to hear her to know who it was: it was enough for him to recognise the tense, desperate silence – Rimini could hear her catching her breath – during which Sofia, upset at having to talk to the machine for the umpteenth time, mentally went over the message she had prepared, carefully balancing the serious and less serious, and decided to replace it with the needy laments she eventually always left on the tape. The photos, the photos. She always ended up returning to the photos. She grew angry, and her direct, instinctive anger spoke of immediate pain. She also tried leaving calm, mature messages; she said she perfectly understood Rimini's disloyalty – because, if she wanted to, she could behave exactly like him – and was as indulgent with him as a mother who has surprised her adolescent children *in flagrante*. She too, if she wanted to, could pretend she was not involved in any way: it was enough for her to know that someone other than her was taking care of everything. But understanding is a quality which demands a response. If there is no reply at all, it withers and dies, and in the same earth where tolerance previously flourished, the bitter, arid fruits of war now took its place. 'Hi there. It's me again. Please could you give me a call. We've got things to sort out. Today I'll be at home between seven and nine or nine-thirty. No, between seven and nine. You've got two hours.' Concise, telegraphic, emotion degree zero – with only the slightest tinge of annoyance, the indignation which a stupid misunderstanding produces. But 'things to sort out' was too general, too vague: nobody would respond to 'things'. The photos on the other hand did require a proper meeting: they were a concrete object, capital, shared goods which could be divided and change hands. Rimini might not turn up – which is what in fact happened – but each time he missed the appointment he was demonstrating the selfish and arbitrary nature of his decision. His failure to reply was no longer him exercising a right, but an inexcusable slight. Rimini was well aware that he was failing her, but what could he do? Nobody breaks off an operation halfway. He had to go on, even if it meant being spattered with blood, the old, well-known blood, and whatever he was cutting out would be there too somewhere, a constant reminder of his monstrous crime. Besides, there was Vera. If just one photo of Sofia had brought her to the verge of catatonia, what on earth would the other thousand still to be gone through do to her? And how could he possibly get through the long evening of torn intimacy between him and Sofia when they did the sharing out? A single photo marked the absolute difference, the threshold between happiness and hell.

That afternoon – the one of their chance meeting, the one of the photo – Rimini tried to calm Vera's tears by offering a shortened version of his past with Sofia, a dry synopsis stripped of all flesh and bone, soul, and emotion. But he only succeeded when he made a promise: he would get rid of the photo. Vera did not stop crying, but she raised her eyes and looked at him for the first time in a long while. Rimini repeated his promise syllable by syllable, as if he were speaking to a foreigner. Vera sniffed, shook her head, pressed her handkerchief – the same one she had used since she was six years old – against her reddened nose. 'I- do- n't be-li-eve you,' she said, still sobbing. 'I swear I will,' he said, unsticking a long wet strand of hair from her cheek. Vera choked back a final sob. 'You'd do that?' 'Of course,' he said. He was overcome with a sort of ecstasy; he felt as if he were about to faint. 'Right now?' she said.

The photo was still there, but instead of one life, it now had two: a useful daytime one on his desk, in amongst books and dictionaries, a life that was renewed whenever he poured the tiny grains of white powder on to its surface; and a sterile, suffocating night-time one that began on the dot of seven in the evening when Vera pressed the intercom buzzer and Rimini, even before letting her in, quickly hid it between the pages of a particularly unreadable book, and then carefully put the book in the remotest corner of his library. And yet Rimini had freed himself from the photograph. The proof is that on that afternoon, while clothes were thrown on to the bed and they collapsed and made love on the floor, aroused by the way their clothes seemed to be resisting them, as if the zips, shirts and blouses, the elastic on her panties, the fastening on her bra, their trousers, all these obstacles had recreated in them a sort of clumsy, virginal ferocity, the portrait of Sofia was languishing in the kitchen waste-bin. It was there that Rimini found it half an hour later, still all of a quiver after saying goodbye to Vera, when he went into the kitchen to get a drink. As he opened the fridge door he knocked the bin over and in among the jumble of fruit peelings, lettuce leaves and bits of paper, he caught sight of the shiny, hard tip of something. It was only a little while later that it dawned on him this was the portrait. What first struck him in fact was the shocking contrast between the glass and the scraps of food, the metal frame and the rubbish, the colour tones of the face and the organic matter decomposing around it. There was something monstrous, something nightmarish about it. Controlling his distaste, Rimini quickly rescued the photo, as if a few seconds' delay might mean it did not survive. No, he had not saved it out of a sense of affection or even loyalty; it was more a question of correcting this casual aberration. When later Rimini realised it was Sofia's portrait and decided to keep it, thus doubly betraying the newly re-established balance in his relationship with Vera (on the one hand because by keeping the photo he was running the risk of hurting her, on the other and more importantly because he was secretly violating the promise he had just made her) it was superstition that made him do so. Rimini thought: 'Neither Sofia nor the existence of my past with Sofia depends on this photo.' He thought: 'The existence of my relationship with Vera depends on this photo.' He thought: 'There's something deeper still, which has nothing to do with my past with Sofia or my relationship with Vera that depends on this photo.' He was unable to define exactly what that might be. But as if to make up for insulting it, he carefully wiped the portrait clean, and five minutes later, sitting at his desk and with everything ready to start work once more, his nose zoomed up and down the glass again, snorting another long line of coke.

CHAPTER 13

After that his life was one long high. He ate a late breakfast, then at two in the afternoon sat down to work naked in a state of unbelievable excitement. The books, the typewriter keys, the bits of paper he had written different suggestions down on the previous evening as he translated, the desk itself with its dark wood and rough patches – it all seemed to him somehow incandescent, voluptuous, as if everything were made of flesh and shot through with millions of nerves. Sitting down was in itself a deliciously masochistic ritual: his buttocks lined by the wooden slats of the seat, the vertical bars pressing painfully into his kidneys ... Rimini felt as though he were at the epicentre of a sexual storm. He would open the top drawer of the desk, rescue the wrap of cocaine paper from his card wallet where he kept it hidden, and free Sofia's portrait from its jail on the bookshelves. He could feel the first tingling sensation when he unfolded the foil, poured a little of the drug on one corner of the photograph, and nudged it until it spread across the glass surface. Then, as he was making the first lines, the tingling became a pressure and the pressure gradually turned into a powerful erection. The tip of his prick touched the bottom part of the desk's central drawer. As he snorted the first line – always the longest of all – the coke acted as a sort of brutal piston that cleared his head of everything that had been in it since the last time he had taken the drug the previous evening. This selective abolition of the past was one of the first things that struck him about cocaine. Whereas marijuana, due to the digressive nature of its influence, always encourages a sense of distraction, a tendency for the mind to stray, cocaine was self-referential: it literally obliterated anything other than itself. Even more than the elegant silver folds of the paper, or the powder, in the case of cocaine the drug was the action of snorting. More than once, during this almost completely reclusive phase that lasted six months, Rimini would have given anything for this pleasure – not to get his hands on the purest,

79

most expensive cocaine, but to enjoy the longest snort, one so long he could snort the whole world. That was why the first line of the day was so crucial: he edited that particular point in time with a similar point from the past, the sentence Rimini had before him now, intact, protected by the skin of its original language, with the last sentence he had translated the previous evening, the one which, as soon as he heard the entry-phone buzzer, had marked the end of his day's work. Then, as he got into the translation again, and his mother tongue began to spot and recognise the savours of the other language, the starting point for a search that soon turned into a hunt which Rimini threw himself into blindly day after day, driven on by some unknown force, and from which he emerged at the end of each day's work lost, exhausted, with only enough strength left to promise himself what he always promised and never carried out, that he would never again accept that particularly cruel form of enslavement that is the translator's lot – the erection subsided, the prickly sensation around his anus and his balls died away, and a lazy indolence that at first was extremely agreeable replaced the earlier sexual tension covering the entire area with a gentle, freezing dew. He translated and snorted, translated and snorted. He only changed position when he went to pee, something he always did impatiently, shaking his prick time and again and contracting his sphincter to speed things up. Often he even interrupted his peeing before he had finished, which led to a trail of drops on the wooden floor, a sure sign he had returned to work too speedily, or a sign of his trips to the kitchen, where he went to replenish the bottles of mineral water he drank one after another straight from the bottle (the presence of a glass would have driven him mad) – gulping down as much as a quarter of the contents in one go – all of which was accomplished in a state bordering on complete exasperation. Sometimes he would stand up and then collapse back into his chair, unable to stay on his feet. His legs went to sleep and Rimini only realised this when he tried to use them. So did his buttocks and his genitals, so that whenever he flopped back into his chair, inert but already irritated at the length of time it would take for his limbs to react and for him to re-establish control over them – a complete waste of time, or so it seemed to him, which in his current state was the worst thing imaginable, the worst beyond all question – at those moments he thought he could understand, if only for a second,

what those invalids must feel (or rather, not feel) – the invalids which
as a child leaving school he had seen through the wire netting patrolling
the basketball court of the Institute for the Handicapped in their wheel-
chairs – not pain, or atrophy, or even astonishment – simply nothing
at all. But this falling asleep of his flesh, which was the result of his
immobility and the way he became totally wrapped up in himself,
sooner or later started to subside, so that after a few minutes – which
he tried to shorten by pinching himself, sticking the tip of ball-point
pens into his arms or, in the most extreme cases, slapping himself with
a long plastic ruler (probably the only souvenir he still kept of his
secondary school days) Rimini regained possession of his body. There
was also another kind of somnolence, more worrisome although less
dramatic, which lasted longer and which, just as stealthily as the other
one, because that other one often eclipsed it and Rimini was not even
aware of it because he was so caught up in his translation, nevertheless affected him on a much deeper level, apparently acting on some
central organic plane. In fact this was not so much somnolence as a
kind of torpor, that strange halfway house that a limb inhabits when
it has been given a mild anaesthetic: it has not disappeared from view,
it is still aware of external stimuli, but who could be sure that faced
with a need to act, to move, to respond, it would be able to do so satis-
factorily? These effects were nothing new; Rimini had already experienced them on the very first occasions when, after snorting a line
(painstakingly copying the operation he had seen a former boss perform
many years earlier, a man who worked as a copywriter in order to earn
a living, but really a writer and editor of orphaned writers, as he liked
to describe himself, someone who above all Rimini thought of as the
first – not only the first to do cocaine with him present, but also the
first to wear deck shoes and to write with an old-fashioned Mont Blanc
fountain pen – three habits which given the date [nineteen seventy-
seven or perhaps eight, at any rate the early years of the military dicta-
torship] made him a real pioneer) Rimini would scoop up the remains
of the drug on his fingertip and rub it on to his gums. In the space of
a few seconds, his mouth would go numb, to such an extent that if,
thanks to some mishap or other, any of it came into contact with his
lips, Rimini found himself unable to drink from the bottle without
spilling the water all over himself, and so had to make do (like some

kind of person on their sick-bed) with taking tiny sips of it from a teaspoon. He could have accepted these unfortunate consequences if they had been the result of a painful visit to the dentist's, but not from a freely taken decision to seek stimulation, and so it was not long before he gave up the practice. Yet thanks to this experience Rimini had been able to get a fairly accurate idea of the purely chemical effects the drug had on his body, as well as of their paradoxical nature: on the one hand they led to hyper-activity, with boundless reserves of energy, superlative powers of concentration, and the wish to exhaust all the possibilities of the present moment; on the other anaesthesia, absence, disaffection, lack of feeling. And since he was aware of this kind of effect – which because it came directly from his gums was extremely clear in its origin – he was not surprised when he discovered it happening in another part of his body, not so directly involved in its application. He translated and snorted, translated and snorted. His flesh, blood and bones seemed to belong to an ancient dimension he had somehow surpassed, a dimension in which complexity was still valued and diversity was the praiseworthy state of affairs. Thanks to the drug, everything had become smooth, homogeneous, uniform: all he had to do was abandon himself to the fury that devoured sentences, pages, hours. And yet the body returned – or rather, the worst aspect of the body returned: the evidence that it had disappeared. Everything was fine so long as Rimini went on blazing away, as long as the trans- lation continued smoothly, like a sports car hurtling down a deserted highway in the night. But every so often, something forced him to brake, some irregularity, some accident or other that he had missed during his first reading – that broad but careful overview he under- took prior to the moment of real translation – and, forced to resolve the problem, not so much in order to clear up the difficulty, still less to make sure it did not figure in the other language, but simply out of a need to get moving again, to press forward as quickly as possible, then, due to the very logic of the accident, which disturbs continuity and therefore works to insert time in time, Rimini all at once remem- bered that there was something known as a body, something belonging to him, but abandoned, something which the frenzy with which he translated had alienated him from for hours. So, while he consulted dictionaries, style manuals, compendiums of difficulties, and previous

versions, while he changed, inverted or tried a thousand different ways
to accommodate the sentence resisting his efforts, with the same overwhelming energy he had employed a minute earlier to devour the
following sentence, but forced now to stop, motionless, to perform in
the emptiness of the same spot, Rimini, confused, as though coming
round from a moment's collapse, gradually regained an awareness of
his feet, his ankles, his knees. And no sooner had he recovered them
than he realised, in a flash of horror, that they were useless to him,
empty. Like someone who touches a pocket that a speedy hand has
just picked, Rimini felt for his prick to make sure it was still there
between his legs, and wondered if this was how a cock should feel, so
tiny and soft. He stroked it, pulled gently at the foreskin, lifted it and
let it drop on to the wood of the chair. Yes, he could feel everything,
but far off, superficially, the way you sense a foreign language you know
nothing about: yes, you can clearly make out the outline of the sound,
but have no clues about how it is organised – just as once, lying face
down on a black imitation leather couch under the effects of a local
anaesthetic, he had felt the tip and the blade of different surgical instruments poking at a cyst that had grown on the back of his neck. Then
he suddenly remembered Vera was coming to see him that evening.
He glanced at the time. It was never late, but it was not early either.
There were still three or four hours until she came – it had been two
or three since he started translating and snorting. He was in the middle,
and wondered if the drug had emptied out his prick. At four in the
afternoon he started to masturbate – by half-past four at the latest. He
went to the bathroom and, standing in front of the toilet bowl (a position he took up because it was simpler, because he would not have to
bother about wiping up the semen afterwards, and also because of the
similarities he recognised between semen and other human excres-
cences) he leaned against the wall tugging at his cock, that dead fish
he would have loved to be able to call a cock, until after a while he
gave up in disgust and went back to his study. He looked again at the
clock and searched on his shelves for a pocket edition of *Les Onze Mille
Verges*, one of the few souvenirs he had kept of his time at the advertising agency where, in addition to working on campaigns which never
saw the light of day, writing screenplays which were never filmed, and
creating, at his boss's bidding, imaginary products for imaginary needs,

he had started to translate some of the classics of literary pornography, including *Les Onze Mille Verges*, for a collection which the deck shoes' pioneer was hoping to sell on news-stands in three-volume packs. Rimini returned to the bathroom. He flicked through the book, which by now he knew by heart, trying to find as quickly as he could passages whose sexual density was not completely neutralised by the overall humorous tone of the novel, and started jerking off again when he had found a page, which he raised his eyes from only once he had managed to ejaculate a long while later, sometimes ten or even fifteen minutes. Very soon, the sentence which starts the orgy sequence that the Serbian vice-consul enjoys in the diplomatic residence, in which the protagonist becomes involved without being invited: *Reaching the front door of the Serbian vice-consulate, Mony relieved himself at length against the wall, then rang the bell*, became the safe-conduct offering him access to an irresistible scene and guaranteeing, after a reasonable length of time, the full restoration of his prick and his sexual desire. After which, he wiped the lid of the toilet with three or four bits of toilet paper, making sure he did not miss the slightest splash, then, relieved, went back to sit at his desk, touching his already relaxing prick once more to make sure it was still there. Rimini would concentrate on the book again, locate the knotty problem that had forced him to stop (indicated in the text thanks to the same plastic ruler he used to wake up his legs when they went to sleep on him), solve it with miraculous ease – as though while he was spilling his sperm on to the white porcelain, someone had taken advantage of his absence to completely simplify it, and then, as a reward or perhaps to celebrate the new part of the day that the ejaculation had ushered in, he would snort two long lines of coke, the first in his right nostril, the second in the left; after which he flung himself back on his typewriter. He translated without stopping, almost without moving, for an hour and a half, pausing only to wipe the remains of the drug on his nostrils, without interrupting his work. He could have spent years, centuries even like this. To some extent, when he thought about it, the cocaine was irrelevant. The drug, the real drug, was translation: that was the real addiction, desire, the promise. Perhaps everything that Rimini knew about drugs – neither a little nor a lot, but completely disproportionate to his beginner's experience – he had learnt without realising it through translation.

Perhaps translating had been his schooling in drugs. Because on sunny spring afternoons in adolescence, long before he had taken cocaine for the first time, when his friends rushed to the local squares wearing their favourite football teams' shirts, Rimini would close the shutters in his bedroom, switch the radio on to the station transmitting that afternoon's most important game, and then in the darkness, with the only light coming from his desk lamp and dressed in his pyjamas, he would literally devour books with his translator's hunger, finishing them off but at the same time coming under their spell, as if something hidden in the folds of their lines forced him to bear witness, to tear them out of one language and put them into another, so that even then he had discovered that translation is not something freely entered into, chosen calmly and collectedly, but a compulsion, the fatal response to an order, a command, an entreaty buried deep in the heart of a book written in another language. The simple fact that something was written in another language, one that he knew but which was not his mother tongue, was sufficient to awaken in him the idea – a completely reflex one – that this book, article, short story or poem was somehow in debt, a debt so huge it was incalculable and therefore impossible to repay but which he, Rimini, the translator, had to take responsibility for by translating. So he translated to pay off the debt, to free the debtor from the chains of its debt, to emancipate it, which is why the task of translating implied physical effort, sacrifice, submission, the impossibility of renunciation, just like forced labour. People, especially his parents' friends, asked him if it was hard to translate. At a loss, Rimini said it wasn't, but secretly wondered what importance it had whether it was hard or not. They asked him how he managed to translate, but Rimini said that no, no, translating was not something that he managed to do but something he could not manage without. Even then, at thirteen or fourteen, still a novice, with only a little though surprisingly intense experience behind him, he had confronted the evidence that sooner or later every translator must come to face: that one is translating the whole time, twenty-four hours a day, non-stop, and that all the rest, everything that is commonly known as life, is nothing more than the modest sum of truces and holidays that only a translator with an iron will can succeed in rescuing from the torture instrument that is translation. In one weekend, from when he started at ten or eleven at night on the Friday, to early on Monday morning, two or three hours before he had to get dressed, befuddled by lack of sleep, and put away his books, dictionaries and notebooks and destroyed all traces of the fever that had gripped him before he set off for school, he could translate an entire book, making not just a provisional version in which he had skipped over the difficulties and left them for subsequent revision, but a definitive text, with the footnotes, corrections and adjustments required for it to be published. He practically never even lifted his head from the book. Even then, when cocaine still meant nothing to him, the slightest interruption – a phone call, the entry-phone, even the need to eat or go to the toilet, or any human presence, that of his mother or her husband (which did not happen that often because, at his insistence, they spent most of their weekends at a rented country cottage) – the slightest intrusion of the outside world was enough to drive him wild. Whenever the phone rang he would yelp with annoyance from the bedroom. When the entry-phone went, he would kick the furniture and throw things on to the kitchen floor. So it was that twenty years later cocaine had not added a thing, but merely formalised, put in writing as they say, the abysmal nature of what it means to translate; above all, its chief addictive ingredient: the countdown element. The book had a beginning and an end, just as the weekends he spent shut up in his adolescence had, just like counting down from ten to one: every translated sentence, every hour spent translating sentences, inexorably shortened the distance between him and the last full stop. Ten, nine, eight, seven, six . . . he *had* to finish. But an hour and a half later, when following the initial jolt the effects of his last snort had gradually worn off and left him in a state of general apathy that was made worse by the tiredness brought on by hours of uninterrupted toil, Rimini again began to feel afraid. Vera would be coming in two hours, and he felt nothing but a great gap between his legs, in the place where a short while before his two hands, reflected in the old yellow tiles of the bathroom, had taken turns and finally produced a soft groan of pleasure. To the hard-on the drug had given him, he now had to add the one he had given himself, and its satisfaction. What happened if Vera came early? He imagined her in the bedroom, waiting for him, and felt for his prick to establish or make more explicit the connection between this image and the dim background where his desire lay sleeping. He searched and searched for it, and it was only ten seconds later that he realised he was already holding it in his hand. It did not even weigh anything. His mouth felt very dry, and he was trembling as though he had a fever. He looked for his copy of *Les Onze Mille Verges*, went back to the bathroom and for a few moments, rather than masturbating he was simply rubbing himself, kneading his genitals, as if before he could give himself pleasure he had to recognise the organs that had been given to him. But *Vibescu approached her slowly and, slipping his beautiful cock between Mira's huge buttocks, he pushed it in to her open, moist cunt*, and Rimini had the impression that a distant shudder, fleeting as the blink of an eye, was timidly stirring the shapeless clay he was kneading. By this stage it took him a quarter of an hour to convert this slow awakening into a reasonable erection, and a further ten or fifteen minutes to come, which this time, unlike the first, he was so anxious finally to achieve that he took no precautions whatsoever, abandoning himself to wherever he might happen to spurt, indiscriminately staining the granite floor, the sides and top of the toilet, or even one of the unwary wall tiles. What did Rimini care if he had to kneel down and clean the freezing floor, where there was always the danger that some tiny drop had fallen, or to follow every splash and wipe it up so that he could be sure Vera would not come across any of them, if he had managed to prove he was not one of the living dead, that there were still blood and nerves in his body, in his (properly stimulated) sex – and Rimini was confident that not even the wildest adventures of the protagonist of *Les Onze Mille Verges* could compare to the attraction Vera held for him, so that he was capable of functioning in a perfectly normal way. That called for a celebration, so Rimini polished off the lines he had already made on the portrait, and his fear subsided. But then he had to make new ones, as quickly as possible, not so much in order to snort more there and then, but to know they were there if he needed them, in their neat and tidy lines, and also to avoid the image of the empty portrait, by far the worst thing Rimini could imagine on this afternoon devoted to translating, but after unwrapping the foil and shaking the paper in the air, he realised that the tiny heap of powder he could see, which by chance was whitening the pupil of Sofia's right eye, was all the drug he had left. He was never able to tell whether it was a little

or a lot. Cocaine left him only two alternatives: either he had it all –
and this, whether he had bought one gram or ten, thirty dollars or
three hundred, was the inevitable feeling he had when he left the place
where he bought it, an inner apartment on the corner of Rivadavia
and Bulnes, always lit by the white, nocturnal light from two neon
tubes, and furnished with those chairs and tables made of very rough
yellow wood that usually come included in the price of the rent – or
he had nothing, which was the terrible revelation that shook him when,
normally somewhere between six and six-thirty in the afternoon, he
realised, with a rather inexplicable jolt, as though the dose he had got
out of the desk drawer at noon had not been diminishing bit by bit,
sniffed up his own nostrils, but had suddenly disappeared as if by
magic. The amount of the drug he had only seemed to him relevant,
something which in fact changed his mood, and even his organic state,
when he saw it as something that was threatened and when he subsequently realised just how far, with what absolute conviction he, the
person who needed the drug, had believed that his stock of cocaine
would never run out. The amount was always a retrospective problem,
existing only in that strange mixture of hindsight and anticipation that
took hold of Rimini when, before finishing his dose, he was already
considering it from the viewpoint of someone who has already run
out. What was he to do? Buy more? Not a chance. Vera was arriving
in an hour at the latest, and Rimini never snorted with her there. And
he could not bear the idea of having a gram in his desk and being
unable to use it. What could he do? One possibility was to divide what
he had left into a lot of small lines and snort them bit by bit, at more
or less regular intervals, in order to fill the length of time and work
before Vera arrived. The other was to make two opulent lines and snort
them once and for all, right now, in one grandiose moment that would
close his day. But as he could never decide on a single course of action,
Rimini alternated between the two. Whenever he divided the drug up,
he would sniff the first line and even though this left him dissatisfied,
because his urge to inhale was always inversely proportional to the
amount of drug still left on the portrait, he would start working again,
and the task of having to translate, which was a drug in itself, seemed
at first providentially to spread the effect of the cocaine. But even so,
the lines of coke were so meagre, and he was so anxious, that he began

to snort them more and more quickly, so that by the end of half an hour he had translated only some thirty lines, at most a page, and almost always with all kind of mistakes, confusions and provisional solutions, which meant he had to revise them and sometimes completely re-do them the next day, when everything began all over again – but by this time he had completely depleted the hexagram of white powder he had constructed on the glass frame of the photograph. Then, like someone possessed, he would stand under the shower. First he would remove all remaining traces of the drug from his nostrils, cleaning them with soap and water in order to avoid Vera sticking her tongue in there (as she had already done) and finding the sharp taste she had taken for novocaine. Then he stood for a long while soaping his body up and down, massaging his muscles, revitalising the parts most affected by the drug's anaesthetic action, those which he guessed he would most be in need of when Vera arrived: first of all his hands, which felt as though they were being pricked from inside by millions of tiny needles; then the whole area around his mouth and nose, where it felt as though his skin had completely dried out and the muscles were so taut it seemed as though they had snapped; and finally his thick, heavy tongue and his prick, that limp sausage, which showed not the slightest sign of life and which he could close his fingers round. He began to pull on it absent-mindedly, as though this stimulus, combined with the massage from the shower, would be enough to bring it back to life, but soon he was concentrating furiously on it, lubricating it with the soap lather and beating it about until after twenty minutes' hard work, and with an acute burning sensation (doubtless caused by the soap coming into contact with the irritated skin of his glans, which by now was almost blood-red in colour) he produced two or three drops of abnormally thick semen that looked almost grey compared to the white of the lather, which lay there for a few moments stuck to the skin between thumb and first finger, only to be washed away by the flow of water. Whether he snorted the drug in tiny portions or in one single, lengthy, seemingly interminable go, by the end of which he sat quite still, in a state of highest tension, with the veins on his neck standing out, and after which he found it impossible to go back to translating because he knew he had no more cocaine, either way the shower was an absolute necessity – the shower and also, of course, the final masturbation under the shower, carried out almost as Vera was due to arrive and therefore at the height of his anxiety. Despite their pathetic lack of life, these few drops of sperm, but above all his erection, slow but hard and ardent, filled him with a strange vitality, the kind of integral enthusiasm and satisfaction sometimes felt after some exhausting physical activity, and he would leave the bathroom with a towel knotted round his waist and lie on the floor of the living-room right next to his loudspeakers and allow himself to be swept up in (or because the music was so loud, literally to be crushed by) the musical freaks that were the top five best-selling records played by the cheesiest station on the dial. The tunes seemed to grip his heart directly, without passing through his hearing; he had heard them so often that he knew the words by heart and so started to sing them softly, following the rhythm and the sound of the singers' voices, and then more loudly, as if he were fighting against what he could hear, and finally at the top of his lungs, shouting and screaming and kicking the parquet to signal when he should come in, in such a wild, uncontrolled state that more than once his downstairs neighbour had come up and hammered on his door to complain, until the sun went down and a purple stain shone in the oblong patch of sky he could see through his window, and the entry-phone started to buzz and, flat on his back on the floor, Rimini said to himself with great relief: It's her, it's Vera.

CHAPTER 14

One night, Rimini finished playing back the messages on his machine, and realised something was missing. No sighing, no suspicious silence, no disgusted hanging up of the phone, no insulting recording. (In the last one, with a radio station blaring out tango in the background, a melodramatic voice had predicted all kinds of exotic ailments for him.) He thought about it; there had been no surprises on his answering-machine for a week now. It seemed to him as though this lack contam-inated the night air, and so, sitting there naked next to his desk, he listened intently. He could hear Vera's childlike snoring from the bedroom, interrupted every so often by an intake of breath that sounded like a hiccup. From the living-room came the steady sound of the stereo. They had both been too lazy to do anything about it, and the result had been a sad stalemate: neither of them was willing to get up and go and switch it off. Rimini was the apex where all the noises of the apartment coincided.

He felt relieved – with the telephone 'clean' now perhaps he could play back all the day's messages in front of Vera – but above all he experienced a kind of triumphant, strangely benevolent euphoria, the kind of pride that must fill doctors when the remedy they have prescribed, scandalising their patients, and which to begin with, far from alleviating the illness only made its symptoms alarmingly worse, begins to show itself to be as effective as only they had faith it would. Perhaps Sofia had changed her mind. Rimini would allow some time to pass, enough for the new situation to settle down, and then he would probably call her. By then, he calculated, sharing out the photographs would be nothing more than a routine chore.

A few days later, a Friday, it was his father's birthday. Rimini decided to surprise him by stopping by his office and taking him out to lunch. He walked along Calle Florida looking for a present. Compared to the way it shone in his memory, the street's bargain stores, leather jacket shops, tourist bookshops, its beggars, fast-food outlets and salesmen who, tired of seeing their premises empty, came out into the street to buttonhole customers, offering handbags and mink stoles in the same surreptitious whisper as four or five blocks further on, where Florida suddenly changed status, the touts were trying unsuccessfully to persuade people to come for a sauna or a non-stop striptease, seemed to him merely vulgar. He reached Calle Viamonte and decided to turn back. The smell of frying food was growing stronger; close by him, distorted by a megaphone, a woman was threatening the passers-by with a particularly cruel, but avoidable, punishment from God. Rimini was already beginning to think again about buying a present when in a shop window he saw a thick cardigan with a zip and leather patches on the elbows. He went in and bought it. No sooner had he re-emerged, with the cardigan in a paper bag, than he was beset by all kinds of doubts. The colour – a dark bordeaux that was almost purple – was not exactly suited to his father, who apart from black, grey, white and beige (his only concession to colour) regarded everything else as garish, extravagant or too feminine. The inclusion of a zip would also confuse him, and the patches – the word 'elbow-pad' suddenly appeared in Rimini's mind, then vanished again almost at once, leaving a small eddy in the air. But by the time he had reached the building where his father worked, Rimini had added up all the objections that had troubled him for the last three blocks and decided to turn them into the positive reasons why he had decided to buy the present.

The door buzzed. Rimini struggled to push it open and headed for his father's office, the last of a series of identical partitioned spaces. He went straight in without knocking: the first thing he saw was a large bordeaux blob moving in front of him. He froze in the doorway, his hand still on the doorknob. For a moment he thought he was hallucinating: two metres away from him he saw the cardigan that was lying at the bottom of his bag. But it was his father, who was struggling with the zip of a thick woollen bordeaux cardigan, with elbow patches, the twin brother of the one Rimini has just bought. His father managed to do up the zip, and with the air of bemused satisfaction of someone who has overcome a difficulty without quite knowing how, smiled at him, spread his arms wide and said: 'What do you think?' It looked perfect on him. This was exactly how Rimini had imagined *his* present on his father's body, always supposing he had got him to try it on. But he twisted his lips and said: 'Mmm . . . I'm not sure about the colour. And since when did you go for cardigans with zips?' 'I don't go for them,' his father said, pulling the cardigan down. 'Someone just gave me this as a present. But it's not bad, is it? If only there was a mirror . . .' He walked past Rimini into the corridor. Rimini caught a glimpse of the label hanging from the cardigan collar: the same shop. He followed his father out, furious. He was looking at himself in a vertical mirror that was so narrow he could only see one arm at a time. 'Happy birthday,' said Rimini, instinctively hiding the bag with his present behind his back. 'Not bad at all,' his father said again, pleased with it; then, looking at the patches, added: 'Even the elbow-pads.' 'The what?' Alarmed, two or three heads turned towards Rimini: he realised he had shouted the words. 'These,' his father said, pointing to the suede patches, 'are called elbow-pads.' Rimini wanted to smile, but his mouth twisted more ambiguously. 'It's true. Sofia told me,' his father said, then went on quickly: 'She gave it me,' in the negligent whisper he used for things he did not want to keep quiet about, but which he did not want to cause trouble either. Rimini looked him in the eye: 'You've seen Sofia?' 'She's just gone. If you'd been five minutes earlier you'd have run into her.' He shut the office door, pretending not to notice the bag Rimini was hiding behind his legs. 'I owe you the present,' Rimini said, 'but I'll take you to lunch.' 'Great. What's the weather like outside?' 'Chilly.' 'I'll wear the cardigan then.' 'You'll be hot.' 'I'll take it off if I am.' They were on their way out. 'It doesn't upset you, does it?' 'What?' 'Me going out wearing the cardigan.' 'What are you talking about?' 'I don't know. Different people have different reactions.' They went past the receptionist. 'I'll be back at three,' Rimini's father said. While they waited for the lift, he stroked the cardigan as though to smooth it down. 'She looked good. Better than the last time I saw her, anyway. She sends you a kiss.'

Seated at a back table in an Italian restaurant and threatened as ever by an enormous poster where the coloured lights of Brooklyn Bridge flashed on and off above their heads, they were surprised there were so few customers. They said as much to the waiter, who had been serving them for years. Yes, he admitted, the number of customers had fallen off, but that was perfectly normal given the incident that had

93

happened the week before. 'Incident?' queried Rimini's father. A tourist couple sat at a nearby table. The waiter leaned over and said in a confidential whisper: 'Some robbers came in. Three of them: two fat guys and a woman. By sheer chance, there was a cop in the toilets. When he came out, he drew his gun on them. The woman fired first. *Madonna santa*. A real shoot-out. I threw the *rigatoni* for table sixteen away and dived to the floor. Right here. You should have seen it! Result: one customer dead, another wounded. The cop had a scratch, one of the gang was shot, the other two got away. *Due spaghetti carbonara*, as usual?'

As if to celebrate their renewed intimacy, as soon as the waiter had left them Rimini's father tapped him on the hand and said: 'Go on then, tell me what you've been up to.' This was the peremptory, one-sided formula that was typical of their encounters ever since Rimini and Sofia had separated. For years it had been the other way round: from the lofty summit of his rock-like emotional stability, Rimini had lent his ears and his infinite capacity for understanding to his father, a professional divorcee who had a string of girlfriends, changed homes like shirts, fell in and out of love, was constantly negotiating with solicitors, got married via Paraguay or Mexico, and went on surprise honeymoons. He was also a regular at private gambling dens where he played (he called it 'investing in') poker and fleeced or was fleeced by the same managers and commissioners who during the day said hello to him without any sign of recognition in the business centre of Buenos Aires, or sated his passion making quick trips to the Casino. Now that Rimini was 'single' again – in other words, without Sofia, the only thing his father seemed to take into account when deciding his civil status – it was he who was the possible source of tales of adventure. But in this invitation to talk that his father raised each time they met, Rimini thought he could discern, as well as a sense of anticipation, a kind of condescension that annoyed him, as if his father thought that he was the one who was responsible for the change in Rimini, or that he had decided to allow him the privilege of leading a more or less adventurous life rather than this emerging from the internal logic of Rimini's life. Despite this, Rimini acquiesced and made his report. There were topics that were guaranteed success: how he was looking after himself, his new-found freedom, the lack of limits in his daily life. And of course, his relationship with Vera, whom his father said without any great conviction that he must meet, as if he suspected Rimini might have invented her out of shyness or anxiety, which he did not want to confirm in order not to upset him.

This afternoon, Rimini had the impression his father was not listening. He nodded and gazed at him with his moist, ageing eyes; every so often he slapped the table-top, scandalised or amazed. But beyond these meaningless signs of attention, there was nothing. They stirred their cups of coffee together. Rimini had already talked of Vera, of the mounds of work he had to get through, and even of his experience with cocaine (although he had thought it wise to underplay the amounts and frequency with which he took it), but when he looked across the table at his father he saw he had closed his eyes and was nodding off. He looked old, cut off and at the same time protected by his world of slow digestion, sudden chills, and unintended naps. The cardigan stood out like a rich tourist in a poor country. Rimini touched his hand gently, and asked him about Sofia. His father reacted at once, as if this were the only question that could wake him up, but tried to avoid a proper answer with a couple of banal sentences. 'Papa,' Rimini interrupted him, forcing him into an awkward smile. 'It's just that I don't want to . . .' his father began apologetically. 'You don't want to what?' said Rimini. 'You've had the cardigan on the whole of lunchtime, and now suddenly you're bashful?'

No, she had not looked well. Not at all. Lines round her eyes, his father said. As if she wasn't getting enough sleep. She switched from moments of inexplicable enthusiasm to others when she sat silent and did not move. She looked rough, as though she hadn't been home in days. Her hand trembled holding her coffee cup. Her voice quavered as if she had just been crying or was about to start. Rimini's father could not be sure, but it seemed to him that at times she was going cross-eyed. 'Did you talk about me?' asked Rimini. 'A bit, in passing,' his father said. 'What did she say?' Rimini pressed him. 'Nothing.' 'Papa . . .' 'What all women say when you leave them: that you're avoiding her. That you vanished.' They fell silent. Rimini could feel the weight of his father's gaze. 'I'm living my life. I have a right to after twelve years, don't I?' 'I don't know,' his father said. 'To have to cope with that, after all this time. It must be hard.' 'Those are her words, aren't they?'

said Rimini, growing angry. He stared at the cardigan, with its anachronically thick wool, the way the edges of the leather patches had been artificially rubbed . . . He felt like asking his father to take it off. 'Why can't you give a little?' his father said. Rimini raised his hand to ask for the bill. 'I know what she's like. I'm not saying you should see her. Just give her a call occasionally. Until everything settles down. You'll see, it's just a phase. It'll pass. Then everything will be back to normal.'

Rimini wanted to get out of there. He wanted to go back to Las Heras, where a full wrap of cocaine was waiting for him, as were thirty pages of translation and the wardrobe where he could finally get rid of the twin cardigan. He said goodbye to his father in the street, outside the entrance to his office building. He was in the habit of standing there and watching him disappear inside. Still pulling down the new cardigan, his father reached the lifts. Then he put his hand in his pocket, and turned round and came back towards him. At first Rimini thought he was going to give him money, as he always used to do every Friday fifteen years earlier when they were saying goodbye. But what he pulled out of his pocket was a small black-and-white photo. 'She gave me this for you,' he said – but a shocked Rimini was already studying the photo before he took it, and had gone ten, twenty, thirty years back in time to become once more this creature in uniform, short trousers and ankle boots thrusting his rapturous young face in through the bars of a cage at the zoo.

He returned to Las Heras in a state of great agitation. The taxi-ride was a nightmare. From the waist down he felt hyper-sensitive: as his underpants rubbed against his thighs he gave a groan that was halfway between pain and arousal. For a few seconds, everything was in turmoil: he went into his apartment, double-locked the door, switched the radio on full blast as if trying to drown out a whole host of hidden microphones, and got into bed fully dressed. It was only with the sheets pulled up to his chin that he dared look at the photo again. He turned it over and read what was written on the back: *I don't want to talk to the guilty person who confuses living with running away, hiding, 'protecting himself' from what he loves (and what loves him). I want to talk (because I know him, because he moves me, because he was there before all the rest) to that innocent little seven-year-old (you were seven, weren't you?) who lit up each afternoon with his curiosity and got his shoes covered in*

dust. If that person is still alive, if he is out there somewhere (and I think
he is) he should knock three times on this photo, and I'll open the door.

Rimini studied the back of the photo closely and confirmed his
worst fears: it was written in pencil. A classic Sofia move: one of her
chosen ways to appear, intervene, and make her mark in the world,
leaving a respectful, almost invisible notch that at the same time was
decisive, because, demanding as she was, it was enough for one person
to be able to detect it – just once – for its meaning (like those tiny,
dried-out animals which thanks to the way they absorb water swell to
fill enormous fish-tanks) to take on astounding proportions. By writing
in pencil, and soft pencil at that, making it easy to rub out, Sofia was
giving him a choice of options: to read the message and do nothing,
read it and rub it out, rub it out without reading it: all of which left
the photo itself unscathed. Yet again, Rimini felt he had been trapped.
Sofia could call him on the phone, send him letters or bamboozle his
father with her pathetic tricks – his father, who after three divorces
still emerged from each successive amorous disaster feeling certain it
was he who was the real one to blame – that was not the problem. The
problem lay with Rimini: his way of smelling, of intuiting, his sensitivity to the subtle way that Sofia could tiptoe into the furthest reaches
of his life. What was the point hiding, turning down the volume on
his answering-machine, ignoring the recorded threats, if Sofia needed
no confirmation to know that her message, and not just the words and
what they meant, but also, and above all, the fact that they had been
written in the knowledge that one of the fates they might encounter
would be to vanish without trace, and instead of doing everything
possible to avoid this happening – on the contrary doing everything to
allow it to happen – her message had been received, had hit home, had
been interpreted in exactly the way that she, without saying so, had
wished? What Rimini would not have given for a tiny dose of indifference. Shivering in bed, he felt weak, vulnerable, but above all
disheartened, like a convalescent patient who, after several weeks of
steady progress is almost free of the symptoms, has reached a point
when – were it not for the hospital gown he was wearing – he might
be mistaken by other patients, the nurses, and even the doctors, for a
healthy visitor, suddenly suffers a relapse, returning to the state of
collapse he thought he had left behind for ever, and in so doing

discovers, less with a sense of horror than of anguish, that what he thought of as health was something so delicate, so fragile and fleeting that, like the first skin growing back over a wound, the slightest pressure is enough to puncture it.

Rimini did not give in. In a typical act of vengeance from someone who refuses to act, he comforted himself with the thought that if Sofia had not chosen this indirect, blatantly sentimental way of interfering in his life again, he would probably have called her or replied in some way to one or other of her signals. He even lied to himself; he invented urges (for example, to ring her up, or to return one of her letters) that he had never felt. He constantly submitted everything to a maniacal rewriting. It was not that Sofia had re-opened a wound that was still raw, whatever he thought, in spite of the 'healed' life he was leading; no, Sofia had unforgivably missed an opportunity, and Rimini, bolstered by the verdict of this questionable retroactive justice, could now do what until that moment, out of either love or fear, he had avoided doing: namely, forget her completely.

He put the photo on one of his bookshelves, leaning against the spines. More than once that afternoon, during the six hours he spent translating, snorting cocaine, and, on three occasions, masturbating in the bathroom so frenetically that by the end of the third time, the one which cost him the most effort and desperation, a thin trickle of blood, produced by the wearing away of the skin of his glans, stained the miserable little trickle of semen he had managed to force out of himself bright red, Rimini found himself looking up and staring at it with a strange unease. Every time he glanced at it, something seemed to hide itself – something which, invisible but lying in wait for him, meant that the photo was not entirely his. As he was putting away *Les Onze Mille Verges* on his way back from the bathroom, an alarming idea struck him: what if the photo was possessed? Perhaps Sofia was not giving him something back: perhaps the photo was simply the means, the only one Rimini had not blocked or blotted out, by which Sofia was trying to insinuate herself into his new life, to get in and establish herself there without having to move – as though the photo was her remote-control device, her phantom.

Vera arrived as night was falling and he, thanks to the cocaine boost that turns an addict into a king and all the rest of the world provinces that could become part of his kingdom, suggested the idea to her. 'Possessed photos?' Vera smiled and pointed at him with a knowing finger: she had discovered how he spent his famous 'working' afternoons. Rimini hesitated and stayed as still as possible, as though on the edge of a cliff. 'Watching horror movies!' she crowed, moving closer to him, forcing him down into an armchair and pinioning him with a knee on the chest. Vera – an Amazon with skinny arms and chewed fingernails, a prey to blushes, anger, beauty. Rimini felt enormously privileged. Five minutes earlier, before Vera had arrived, the world had seemed an inhospitable place, aged by rancour and intrigue, full of useless concealed compartments. Now, as he pretended to struggle and flailed his head from side to side, like a young maiden about to be raped, trapped by the force of this body that was completely unafraid of him, Rimini felt he had been given a miraculous reprieve. 'I'm pissing myself,' said Vera, and hopped off him as easily as she had jumped on, then disappeared in search of the bathroom. Rimini lay sprawled in the armchair. As a drug-user, this was the vaguest time of day for him: he was not going to have any more until the next day, and the last lines he had sniffed, divided into tiny amounts out of necessity, were fading fast, and yet his heart, his perceptions and above all his sense of time were still affected by the cocaine, so that his relation to the world around him changed from minute to minute. Vera's disappearance, for instance, had been almost supernatural, something as sudden as a lightning flash but at the same time as long drawn-out as watching the clouds drift by, but concentrated into the tiniest of spaces – something which at first he had only been able to contemplate helplessly, as if it were taking place in another dimension, so that it was only some time later, when he realised that the yellow shadow of her dress was taking too long to reappear, that he reacted, sat up in the chair and then rushed nervously out to the bathroom, trying to imagine what could have kept her. Just before he reached the bathroom door, one if his bare feet landed on something that almost made him slip. It was more than 'something': it was a piece of his face, the face that had been his aged seven, but it was no longer in a state to light anything up. He bent down and recognised torn bars in another fragment, then part of an elbow or a knee, a piece of sky, an ear lobe sticking out from some blond curls, bits and pieces of a sentence ('... *noon with his / ill alive*

/ *ock three times*') which all but made him cry out in pain. The sound of the lift startled him. It was coming up. Vera was no longer in the bathroom: she was standing out in the stairwell, crying, with her face pressed against the wire cage of the lift. 'Why?' asked Rimini. He tried to take hold of her arm, but she jerked it away. Rimini touched her again, as if he was trying to make sure she was there and was real. 'Get your hand off me,' she said, 'you're a piece of shit, a real bastard.' 'It was me,' Rimini tried to tell her, 'me when I was seven, at the zoo. My father took the picture on his Kodak Instamatic.' Vera turned and stared at him with horror, as though she was seeing a monster. 'You can't be that cynical,' she said. 'We used to go every Saturday afternoon. I used to take a Canson sketchbook . . .' She threw herself at him, like a machine that starts up all its mechanisms at once: she started to hit him in his face, to scratch him, to pull his hair, all the while pushing him backwards. The door of the apartment opposite opened: two husky puppies began to bark at them, pulling on their yellow leads and forcing a man with a shell-suit and clumps of reddish hair brushed forward over his head out on to the landing. When he saw Rimini in his dressing-gown, he averted his eyes. Rimini saw Vera's face right next to his own: it was huge, contorted with rage, monstrous. He hit her: a quick, soft slap. Vera was paralysed. Even the huskies fell silent. The lift had just arrived at their floor, and flooded them with a rectangle of light. 'And a box of thirty-six coloured Stabilo pencils that my grandmother gave me . . .' Rimini said, slapping her again. Vera stepped back and collided with the lift door, scaring off the dog trying to sniff at her shoes. 'We used to buy those animal-shaped biscuits. I would put them on the paper and draw round their shapes with the black pencil . . .' Rimini's third blow missed its target: Vera had turned towards the lift, so his hand bounced forlornly off the side of her bag and got caught in between the metal bars just as she was flinging it open. Rimini howled as loudly as if his hand had been slashed by a pair of scissors. Vera leapt into the lift, followed by the excited, yapping dogs and the man in the tracksuit, who cast Rimini a look of utter contempt as he went by. It was only then, as his neighbour and Vera coordinated their efforts – him slamming the outer door shut, her shutting the inner one and pressing the ground floor button, that Rimini could extract his throbbing hand.

Three or four days later, standing only a metre from where all this had happened, Rimini held a post office form in his bandaged hand and with the other, his left, scrawled a comic signature in the box by his name. In return for this display of invalidity and ingeniousness, an asthmatic postman handed over a padded envelope. This time, the photo had serrated edges: Rimini was travelling slowly, so slowly it was almost imperceptible, across the Rosedal lake, his head on his father's chest as the older man pedalled the pedalo. This time there was no message. Nor was there a few days later, when another postman gave him another package with another photo, although this time Rimini found it more difficult to recognise himself. Here he was six, proudly showing off the haircut he had given himself with no other help than a pair of scissors stolen from a sewing basket at siesta-time, which by some miracle had not cost him an ear. If he was alone in the photo, standing apart from the other boys, hands in his pockets, staring intently at the shape and size of every twig his feet were crushing, it was not so much because of the reprisals taken against him which, apart from insisting he pick up the remains of his hair from the floor and throw them in the dustbin, had never been anything more definite, but out of conviction, loyalty to the image of anguished precociousness he had ushered in with those half a dozen wild slashes.

It was obvious that Sofia had changed her mind, or at least her strategy: she was replacing her siege with a regular, benevolent presence which at the same time solved the problem of how to share out their photos. On his side, Rimini was recovering the inheritance of both his childhood and his photos. He had not given in, but he did not have any illusions either. Even though he was benefitting from Vera's tolerant attitude towards his outburst, he knew he could never share anything relating to his past, a word Vera could never pronounce without swallowing hard, which she used to refer not to Rimini's earlier life in general, but to his life without her, which included not only the adult Rimini, who was active both sexually and emotionally, but also, however harmless they might have been, Rimini the newborn, Rimini at his mother's breast, Rimini with teeth missing, Rimini scared of the dark, Rimini the tireless drawer of animals, the occasional dyslexic, the fan of *Those Incredible Men in Their Flying Machines*, *Chitty Chitty Bang Bang* and *Blood for a Silver Dollar*, all of which only went to prove that she had not always been indispensable to him. The result was that he received the two photos and, almost without thinking, as though the incident by the lift had divided his life into two parallel but mutually exclusive periods, put them away in a box bought specially for this purpose, which he calmly, as if it were the most natural thing to do, stored in the top drawer of his bedroom wardrobe. Slamming the front door behind him, Rimini felt a shiver of excitement as he wondered: What will the next one be like? How old will I be? What game will I be playing?

But there were no more photos. One morning, Rimini was lying in the bath while Vera, wrapped in his dressing-gown, was reading him tit-bits from the newspaper while she nibbled on a piece of toast. This was a habit they both enjoyed: Rimini liked having the newspaper delivered each morning, but could not be bothered to read it, whereas Vera, who was not the slightest bit curious about any but the most outrageous pieces of news, loved to read out loud. She did this with extraordinary dedication and enthusiasm, perfecting her diction like a language teacher and making sure she pronounced all the syllables. Rimini was trying to catch the soap, a sort of huge creamy brick he had spent a lot of money on at the recommendation of a pharmacist friend, when he thought he heard the word 'Riltse'. The soap escaped him completely, bounced twice off the tiles, hit the shower curtain, and ended up vertical on the floor. Vera passed it back to him as she read: 'this Thursday, at the end of an international tournée that began nine months ago in the Palazzo Pitti in Florence, continued in the Centre Beaubourg in Paris, then in the Sperone Gallery in New York, sees the opening in the Museo de Bellas Artes of the exhibition *The Minor Hand*, which brings together drawings, studies, sketches, and other "private" works by this extraordinary British artist . . .'

In the same way as some recurring dreams, which not only torment the person who has them while they are asleep, but pursue them even when they are awake, Riltse's reappearance cast a pallor of gloom over Rimini's entire day. He did not think directly about him, but in some part of his brain he could always feel the discreet but ceaseless pressure of a foreign body, like a distant reminder of pain. He threw himself into his work. He was translating, or rather rewriting, an anthology of unreadable texts about perversion, and looked forward to the description of each clinical history with the same anticipation that summer readers have for the sex scenes in a serial set on some Asian beach. He took more drugs than ever. In one go a few moments after Vera had left, he consumed the quarter part of the previous day's wrap of cocaine he still had because she had surprised him by arriving early that evening. He did not even bother to change nostrils. The combination of desire and lack of feeling that this brought on was so overwhelming that he found he had to masturbate four times in the next three hours. Given the impotent state he had been left in the previous three times, in order to successfully complete the last operation he had to wrap his prick in one of the pairs of Vera's knickers that for some time now she had regularly begun to forget in his apartment.

Out of all the consequences of the separation, at least those of which he was conscious, the only one which truly continued to surprise him was the fact that those tokens of the love which had been left behind, tokens of 'the other life' as he often liked to call it, could have survived the catastrophe, and be still alive more or less intact and still imbued with their old meaning in the midst of his new life. How was it possible for everything to change apart from that? What kind of creatures could possess the necessary strength and obstinacy to cross the real change of geological era that the death of a twelve-year love affair signified? Sometimes while he was walking along the street, he found that he raised his eyes and discovered, or literally bumped into, an advert with the name of a bar, a poster for a make of clothing, a metro station entrance, the cover of a book on a market stall, a magazine displayed at a news-stand, a breed of dog, a beach being promoted in a travel agency, and felt that it only took one of these banal signs for a huge block of his past to loom up unexpectedly out of the night, making his soul creak and groan as though it were about to split it in two. So, in the throes of this physical tempest, the result of the collision of two epochs rather than two different emotional experiences, Rimini began to think that if there had been an operation which could guarantee the removal of each and every one of those tokens and return him to his original state of blindness, he would have accepted it without a murmur. Or he dreamt sadly of a world in which the personal, voluntary use of amnesia was fostered, a life in which anyone could learn a few simple tricks that would remove all the meanings that the passage of time had rendered unnecessary, in the same way that with each New Year people leave out unwanted phone numbers from their diaries.

At six, six-thirty, with throbbing head and a mouth as dry as dust, Rimini got up from his desk and went to the kitchen for refreshment. He felt wrecked. The slightest movement produced a string of loud, bad-tempered groans. For the first time, the idea of taking drugs seemed to him a cheap, unsatisfactory child's game. Even though alcohol had never tempted him, he was relieved to find a bottle of whisky at the back of his cupboard. He did not even remember buying it. He poured out two fingers and drank it straight off. He shuddered: a fiery trail coursed through his veins. He was just pouring himself a second glass when the sound of the lift starting up gave him a jolt. He became anxious. He poured a little more whisky into his glass but then suddenly slightly raised the neck of the bottle so that the liquid formed a wavy line inside the bottle and then steadied. The lift was on its way up. He got another shock when the cold edge of the marble kitchen table rubbed against his prick, which was peeping out of the folds of his dressing-gown. He felt as though he was waking from an infinitesimal dream. But when he tried to focus his mind on something else, a premonition brought him up short: the not entirely absurd idea that something important might depend on him being or not being there, on guard in the kitchen. The lift was ascending with a steady hum that was less a noise than a deep internal vibration. As it passed each floor there was a kind of metal click, as if it were crossing a barrier. Rimini started to count the floors in his mind. He heart was beating faster and faster. 'Second . . . third . . . fourth . . .' He stopped counting when he thought he heard, above the whirring of the lift, the sound of a woman's voice humming a tune. There was another jolt, this time quite close by, then the vibration ceased. For a few seconds, all the other noises in the building surfaced, then were swallowed by silence. Rimini did not budge: he was suspicious of everything. Was it on his floor? Lower down? Why couldn't he hear anything? He felt *seen*: a sense of shame forced him to do up his dressing-gown. It was then he heard the lift doors opening. He felt like running and peering through the spy-hole, but thought he might not get there in time: the most important thing now was not to give himself away. He raised his eyes – the only noiseless gesture he could think of – as if to distract his own attention, and looked out through the dirty pane at the kitchen window of the apartment opposite, a floor higher than his. He saw a clean-shaven face wearing glasses staring at him. Outside his front door, he could hear someone's feet shuffling round in a circle like a sick person, as if they were testing all the doors before deciding which one to ring at. A few seconds later his bell rang: a short sharp ring that sounded not in the air outside but right in the centre of his brain. He drew in his stomach and held his breath. The second ring was louder but further off, and was accompanied by the sound of a key turning in the lock of a neighbouring door. Rimini recognised the huskies' clawing on the floor tiles, their gruff barking, the whisper of their owner trying to calm them down. After that, a steady but rather weary hand knocked three times on his door. 'Keep on trying, he's in there,' he heard his neighbour say, as the dogs pushed against the lift doors. He also heard someone thanking the man, and then five light taps, not so steady this time, on his door. The lift was on its way down, bearing away the traitor and his bloodhounds. Rimini's legs were aching; cramp was beginning to affect the arch of one of his feet; his back was bathed in sweat. He had to look hard at the bottle of whisky he was holding to remember he had a hand. He would answer, he thought. He would open the door, and that would be that. He took a few hesitant steps – they felt like the first he had taken in years – and left the kitchen. He reached for the doorknob with one hand, and was on the point of opening it when the floor creaked beneath him. He stood stock still, and had the impression that whoever was on the far side of the door was doing the same. But after a few seconds he heard the rustle of clothing, the sign that someone was bending down, and when he glanced at his feet he saw the tip of a lavender-coloured envelope being pushed under the door.

CHAPTER 15

Yes, I hate you. Yes, I forgive you.

Love is a rushing torrent.

Because I know you won't be capable of going to the Riltse exhibition on your own (I can already hear you: too many 'memories' – the inverted commas are yours), I'll be at the entrance to the museum at seven on Thursday.

I'm the small girl with lines round her eyes who'll be wearing a yellow mac (if it's raining) or who will have just got off her green bike out of breath (if it's good weather).

You can't mistake me.

I hate to have to tell you, but this is your last chance.

CHAPTER 16

It rained for twenty hours, from dawn until well into the night, without stopping. It rained so hard and with such a steady, intense violence that a continuous roar, like an endless squadron of planes, filled the air the whole day. The lower areas of the city were completely flooded; real rivers rushed along the path of the streets and swept cars along for several blocks before crashing them against a monument or directly sweeping them into the reception areas of the more elegant buildings in the low-lying neighbourhoods. Rimini had witnessed the start of the deluge. Unable to sleep, he was reading in the living-room with the music turned down low so as not to wake Vera, when he saw that two or three CD covers piled on the table had begun to vibrate and rub against each other, until the one nearest to the table edge fell off on to the floor. It was only then that he heard the distant, subterranean roar approaching. He stared out of the window, and in no more than two minutes he saw the sky turn from the deep, uniform black of night to a reddish grey and then, in a matter of half a minute, to a yellow the colour of sick, unhealthy skin, marbled by fleeting electrical discharges. He opened the window and a burning-hot gust of wind enveloped his face. He saw people going out on to their balconies, dazed men closing their shutters, women doing up their dressing-gowns or calming babies in their arms, and these few moments of anonymous complicity, strangely suspended in the middle of the night, reminded him of the sense of companionship which as a boy he liked to iden-tify with in disaster movies. It was only then, when Rimini understood that what he had thought was an underground tremor was in fact the reverberation of a roaring sky, that he realised just how huge the storm was. There was a tremendous thunderclap – one of those which seem certain to shatter the whole world, and he felt the first drops of rain on his face. Within a few minutes, this spasmodic, uncertain pattering had become a fierce curtain of rain that made it impossible to see more than two metres. Rimini went to bed with the image of a yellow patch imprinted on his mind – not the yellow raincoat Sofia had promised to wear, but the rubber slickers motorcyclists wear when they have to make deliveries on rainy days.

By the time he woke up, late, the sheets of water were so thick and were falling so steadily that they seemed almost not to be moving. Vera had left. Rimini dragged himself to the bathroom, crushing the backs of his slippers as he did so. He came to a halt in front of the wash-basin, and when he looked up he almost jumped out of his skin: instead of his face, on the glass door of the medicine chest was a goodbye message stuck on with a piece of tape. He recognised Vera's school-mistress handwriting, full of curlicues, and tore it off without reading it. He detested surprises when he was getting up, because only the most monotonous of routines could guarantee him safe passage to the state of being awake. There was also the unpleasant and unacceptable fact that Vera's messages, young, romantic and healthy as they might be, were nevertheless distant relations that fell into the orbit of the chain of messages that Sofia sent. They even seemed to share her maxim – *write down everything that love makes it impossible to say* – so that Rimini, who on principle was against any comparisons, could not help but see them as imitations doomed to failure. The result was that he left the bathroom and started to take cocaine much earlier than usual, before he had his breakfast, even before he had brushed his teeth, a completely mechanical operation which he somehow saw as the real frontier between night and day. Before two that afternoon, the time he was thinking as usual that he should sit down and start translating, he had already finished the stash that should have lasted him all day. He called his dealer, told him he would be there in fifteen minutes, and hung up before anyone could reply. He left his apartment block beside himself, in a state of great impatience, and it was only then, when he saw the water round his ankles, that he remembered the storm which had been raging in the city for almost eight hours. The only vehicles on the street were lorries, and they were travelling so slowly that Rimini, walking alongside them, was able to get well ahead in a single block. At a quarter to four, completely soaked and chilled to the bone, he arrived at the apartment in Bulnes and Rivadavia. A huge chunk of masonry, doubtless loosened by the continuous downpour, fell beside him in the long internal passageway leading to the rear block of the building, only missing him by a miracle.

The door opened. The lights shining in every room, the gas stove giving off its gentle, perfumed heat, the dealer's smiling face and the two presences Rimini noticed in the apartment – two people who interrupted what they were saying for a moment to look at him and then, smiling in the same way as the dealer, returned to their conversation – all this made him feel at home. It was as though this scene – made up of elements that Rimini would normally have objected to: first and foremost, the gas stove with no outlet to the outside, and connected to the gas supply through a rubber tube; after that, the older of the two men talking animatedly around the table, a relatively famous singer, with straight, layered hair, whose name Rimini could not recall but whose face he had seen several times on a Saturday night TV show, always performing the same repertoire of romantic ballads, and rewarding with a flashing smile all his female fans crammed into the front rows of the studio audience, and where more than once Rimini had seen him declare his visceral disgust for the scourge of drugs, boasting of the charity concerts he gave to help those institutions which like him were dedicated to stamping out this curse – it was as though for the pallid witness that the deluge outside had made of Rimini, this scene somehow encapsulated all that remained of a lost civilisation. He was given a dry towel, a cup of coffee, and was asked to join in the conversation, the 'fireside chat' as the singer called it, which they regularly stimulated by bending over together and snorting the lines of coke on a transparent plastic tray – it was on the house, the dealer said. No sooner had Rimini sat down than the singer, without looking at him or pausing in the story he had launched into – a detailed report on the sexual proclivities of a colleague he often went on tour with – pushed the tray in his direction. 'Two lines,' thought Rimini, 'two lines and I'll go'. He could not hide his distaste for the singer, made worse still by the wicked pleasure he was getting from revealing his colleague's obscene details, and by the skin of his face which, seen close up by the light of a lamp hanging over the table as though this was a gambling-den, looked shiny and leathery like a lizard's and was full of tiny pockmarks, but he did not want to seem impolite either, so he snorted the first two lines and waited. Rimini decided he would let a few minutes pass, buy his cocaine, and then say goodbye. But the minutes slipped by, and his dislike of the singer changed to curiosity, which in turn became an interest and eventually a kind of trust, which immediately sealed the sort of intimacy that friendships usually take years to achieve. They were soon treating each other like childhood friends. The singer dug up distant stories from his professional past and Rimini, who had never heard them before, always came out with the right response, giving rise to a thousand enthusiastic developments. They agreed about everything; they, as the saying goes, took the words out of each other's mouth, and celebrated each point of agreement as the sign of something deeper still that they might pursue later on. Suddenly, Rimini seemed to know all the songs the other man mentioned, usually to boast about the platinum discs he had been awarded, all the festivals where he had won prizes or the female admirers with whom, thanks to the spell his music cast on them, he could fornicate in his dressing-room, the camper van that took him to his gigs, or the hotel suites where he stayed on his tours. By now they were laughing their heads off. The singer's whole body shook; Rimini slapped the table with his hand, stamped the floor with his foot. It was as though they had a fever. At half-past five, when Rimini tried to stand up, he felt he had to struggle out of a wrapping of cotton-wool covering him from head to foot. Was it his body, or the fumes from the stove? 'I'm going to take a piss,' he said out loud. He had to pass behind the singer, who was smoothing his hair at the back of his ears with two fingers, and when he looked down he saw the scars which ran like ants' trails along the edges of his scalp. In the bathroom, Rimini took some time to find his prick, which had shrivelled to almost nothing, and stared at the incredible array of clean towels, and the collection of fixatives, gels, dyes, and hairsprays that filled the two shelves beneath the mirror. He left hurriedly, as if trying to make up for lost time; he was in such a rush that he did not open the door properly, and hit his head against the edge. Neither the dealer nor the singer saw him; they were in the kitchen, whispering together. Rimini walked past them, muttering a confused farewell. The pusher stopped him as he reached the front door. 'Are you going to leave empty-handed?' he heard him say behind his back. Rimini laughed at his own stupidity. He would buy two grams. The dealer sat at the table, picked up a red strong-box the size of a holdall from the floor, opened it and took out two wraps of purple-coloured foil. Rimini realised he did not have enough money. 'Take one then,' the dealer suggested, keeping the other wrap. 'Don't be such a tightwad,' the singer said, taking out a bundle of notes from the pocket of the raincoat he was putting on. 'Are you going to argue over a gram?' Rimini did not react. The dealer dropped the second wrap into his hand. 'It's on me: you don't owe me a thing,' said the singer, closing Rimini's fingers round the bit of paper. Then he asked: 'Want a lift?'

It was still raining. The sky was a black dome, the deserted streets were glistening. They travelled for a few minutes in silence; the only noise was the hum of the Japanese car's engine. 'Want some music?' said the singer, plunging two fingers into an ashtray full of butts. 'No,' said Rimini, watching him rescue half a joint. The smell of marijuana soon joined that of the car air-freshener. Rimini felt slightly car-sick. Drawing the smoke into his lungs, the singer offered him the cigarette. Rimini shook his head; he was watching the medallion of the Virgin Mary swaying from the rear-view mirror. They went down Calle Billinghurst, sluicing the pavements with water as they went, then turned into Las Heras. As they got closer to Rimini's apartment, the singer, who had slowed the car down almost to walking pace and was staring, intently but without any show of emotion apart from a mocking curiosity, at the darkness on both sides of the car, began to talk about the flood – the tidal wave, he called it – which had literally erased from the map the town of Fortín Tiburcio, in Buenos Aires province, where he was born. The singer said that when he was twelve he had seen this arsehole of the world, as he described it, where he had been bored out of his mind, overwhelmed by three days of continuous rain and transformed into a stinking lake where dead cows and sheep, mattresses, trees uprooted by the wind, even dead bodies, floated round and round in circles, pulled by some imaginary drain, spreading their stench for twenty kilometres in every direction. If it had been up to him, the singer, Fortín Tiburcio could have stayed beneath the waters for ever. Compared to that pigsty, where between five and seven o'clock every single afternoon of the year without fail, a foul cloud that was a mixture of dung, decomposing animals, stagnant water and hen-sheds descended over the dump and hung there like a curse, Junín, where he had been evacuated to with all the others, had seemed to him the height of civilisation and prosperity. Like the others, however, as soon as the floodwaters had receded, the singer had returned to Tiburcio, and had returned, against his will of course, to help rebuild it. But two days later, his mind poisoned by all the songs the heads of the neighbourhood reconstruction teams (his father among them) kept singing to raise everyone's spirits, the singer fled the place, never to go back.

They reached Rimini's apartment block. Like the rest of the street, it was in darkness. The singer leaned over Rimini as if to stare up out of the car window. 'What floor do you live on?' he asked. 'The sixth,' said Rimini. 'Poor guy,' said the singer. 'Don't you want to spend the night at my place? I've got a generator.' The two of them were very close. The singer was looking up at him, strangely submissive. Rimini could see tiny flecks of dandruff shining every now and again on the shoulders of his coat. 'No, thanks,' said Rimini. 'So many no's, sweetheart; do you never say yes?' Rimini tried to move a hand to open the door, but was trapped by a heavy weight. 'Mmm, my mouth is so dry,' the singer murmured, and leaned still further forward. His voice seemed to be coming from somewhere between Rimini's legs, pleading with him: 'Just say yes, Doctor No. Say yes,' came the whisper. 'Yes,' said Rimini. He felt the zip on his trousers being pulled, and some kind of trembling, moist female animal slipped inside his underpants. 'What's wrong? Don't you want to come out to play?' the singer said in a childish voice. 'Let's see.' He opened the glove compartment. A stream of light flooded the car interior. Rimini looked down and saw his tiny, frightened prick in the singer's hand. He could not help noticing his shiny, impeccably manicured fingernails. The singer pushed the cassettes in the compartment out of the way and found the wrap of cocaine hidden at the back. He opened it quickly with one hand and poured the small amount remaining on to Rimini's glans. 'This'll bring him back to life, you'll see.' He licked the tip for a while, rubbed it against his gums, and finally plunged the whole prick into his mouth. Rimini sat quite still, bolt upright in his seat, staring out at the tunnel of the avenue swept from time to time by the headlights of an ambulance, or reading the titles of the cassettes – all of them recorded by the singer – which were still in the glove compartment: 'Only You' 'Something to Tell You', 'Goodbye to Love', 'A Cure for Melancholy'. He did not feel anything directly: his entire body was floating in a kind of giant fish-tank. He floated and spun slowly round, floating and spinning, just like the dead animals in the Fortín Tiburcio flood had done, first of all slowly, lazily, and then more and more rapidly as the force of the depths took hold. But Rimini only took a few turns, because the singer suddenly straightened up and, flinging the cassettes back into the compartment, said to him: 'Is that what I poured out my heart to you for?' Rimini looked at him shamefaced. 'You're no use to me: I don't want to have to drag it from you. Get out.' Rimini could see his furious cheeks, the bright red of his lips that looked like paint had run, the waxwork shine of his skin, the waves of straight hair gradually settling back on his head. He smiled a stupid smile. The singer leaned across him, opened the car door scornfully, then started to kick him as though trying to push him out into the street. Quivering with emotion, he shouted: 'Get out, you jerk. Piece of shit. Prickless homo. Lowlife cunt. Get out before I rape you, or cut it off, or smash your face and arse in.'

Until half-past eleven that night, when the light came back on and his apartment, the building, the block, and the entire city seemed to come back to life, Rimini lay sprawled on the living-room sofa with his eyes wide open, waiting for his beating heart to calm down. The phone rang a couple of times. He did not answer. Vera did not show up, and Rimini, who guessed it was probably her who had called, did nothing to check the message. By midnight, when he left the sofa to go to bed, without even bothering to switch the lights of the apartment off, it had finally stopped raining. Gaps had started appearing in the rusty red of the sky, and the people in neighbouring apartments were going back out on to their balconies, this time to share their sense of privilege at having been spared. Rimini watched some television. All the midnight news was given over to the meteorological disaster that had paralysed Buenos Aires. Rimini saw evacuees wrapped in blankets in hospital wards, suburban houses practically covered in water, cars squashed by trees, schools that were closed or had been turned into refuges, helicopters, a family rescued from the rushing waters. In the midst of this series of emergencies, he thought he recognised the incongruous faded pink of the walls of the Museo de Bellas Artes, and sat up in bed. Trying hard to balance on the staircase of the museum, an unsteady camera spotted with raindrops followed the attendants who, wrapped in dark-coloured capes, were shutting the glass front doors as quickly as they could. Rimini watched them struggling with the wind and the locks until the camera shifted, scanned across a huge red and black poster (Riltse's favourite colours) and then paused for a second on the museum entrance. A woman in a yellow cape, who was soaked through despite the umbrella she was holding, was looking hopefully all around her, a twisted grin on her face.

CHAPTER 17

Was he being followed? One afternoon he had just handed in a translation to a publisher in Congreso when he recognised the same grim, smooth-cheeked face that had attracted his attention that morning as he got on the metro at Carranza. Two days later, in the midst of a sudden downpour that was too short-lived to ruin the clear morning blue completely, he found himself fighting for a taxi door-handle with a woman who looked a lot like the one who had accosted him the previous afternoon, weighed down with surprisingly light packages, who had said she was totally confused because she had spent hours looking for Calle Paunero, although she was standing beneath the street sign at that very moment.

Unable to continue postponing a long-standing family invitation, Vera had gone off for four days to the Iguazú waterfalls, upset because Rimini had refused to go with her. How could he have been so stupid? It was not so much her being there that he missed, but the protection her jealousy gave him, the unconditional manner with which it kept at bay the brutal attempts the world made to seduce him or attack him when he was on his own. It was enough for Vera to leave for everything suddenly to become slippery, threatening. As if by common accord, a couple of friends he had shared with Sofia, and who had survived their break-up more or less intact, started having problems seeing him, or even talking to him on the phone or answering his messages. When he finally managed to confront them, the explanations they gave seemed even more suspect than their silence and distance. One particularly chilly midday, his father left him standing in the doorway of a Scandinavian restaurant in Calle Paraguay. When Rimini called his office forty minutes later, his father himself answered the phone; he sounded as enthusiastic as he always did when the two of them spoke after several weeks of not hearing from each other. He flatly denied having agreed to the lunch date he had not kept, but since he did not want an argument, he dropped everything and appeared at the restaurant two minutes before Rimini, who was walking back from the public phone opposite. They sat at a table against the wall, and when his father got up to study the buffet of hot dishes, certain he would discover the one that would convince his son they had come to the right place, Rimini found himself staring at the side view of a prematurely bald young man, who was eating alone, alternating a spoonful of soup with a paragraph of the book he kept open with his other hand. Something about him – his small stature, elusive as a fugitive, or the sense of distance he conjured up within the dimensions of his table – seemed familiar to Rimini, familiar and disagreeable. He thought of a furtive neighbour of his in Las Heras, or an assistant at the typewriter shop where he usually bought ribbons. No, not them. In order to identify him, Rimini looked closely again, running the risk of being found out, but at that moment the man tried to stifle a coughing fit, puffing out his cheeks and swaying forward as if someone had just patted him on the back. Then, after two or three brief spasms, as though he were having an attack of hiccups, with the soup spoon wavering level with his nose, he began to cough uncontrollably, spraying the whole table with drops of tomato soup. He lowered his head, looked quickly all round and was busy trying to hide behind his napkin, still coughing, when his wandering eyes encountered Rimini, moved on, and ended up staring into space. Even though he was no longer looking at him, Rimini still watched him; he sensed the other man had changed his mind, was surreptitiously turning his head back in his direction. At that moment his father, who was coming back empty-handed, got in the way and destroyed the whole manoeuvre. Ten minutes later, Rimini surmised that the stranger was shutting his book, asking for the bill, paying and standing up to leave. He wanted to have one last good look at him, but just then thirty-five Japanese all got up together from their table, which zigzagged across the centre of the restaurant like an inspired Scrabble word, and the stranger slipped in among them and vanished.

Rimini saw him again at a party he had decided to go to in the hope of seeing his dealer, whom he had been phoning for a day and a half without result. He was not there: someone told Rimini he had dropped in, then had left, and would possibly be back. Rimini decided to wait for him. He got drunk very quickly, drinking from glasses he kept leaving in different parts of the room, so that when he felt like a drink there was always one that might have been his to hand, and he downed it without a second thought. He had just spat out a mixture of punch and cigarette ash when he saw him: he was in the middle of the dance-floor, gyrating under the flashing light. Something about his body – perhaps the curve of his weak back, which the dancing converted into a gentle hump – caught Rimini's attention. And while the music, the people dancing, the bottles, and the bodies sprawled on the sofas gradually but inexorably diminished in size, victims of the way his drunken states made the present smaller and more distant, the stranger's true identity emerged from the dark corner where it lay sleeping.

He was the man in charge of the desserts at the end-of-year celebrations Frida Breitenbach held for her disciples and patients. It was like being present at the restoration of some ancient, submerged world: the clothes-rail full of coats, rugs on top of each other, the small living-room crammed with people standing still and talking quietly so they would take up less room – and there was Frida, short but massive, sitting on her individual throne, the only point in the room that was reached because of a decision rather than a lack of space; there too were the disciples squeezed on to the couch, and opposite them, piled on to the big sofa, or scattered through the rest of the apartment, the paraplegics, the hyperactives, the Parkinson's sufferers, the scoliosis-sufferers, the insomniacs, the lame, the obese, the pianists, the female dancers: the vast, picturesque court of Breitenbach's patients. In his mind's eye, Rimini saw the table covered with puddings and tarts, the arsenal of pretzels and cereal breads, the pitchers of bilberry juice, and once again felt the stifling heat that once a year, almost twelve in a row, left him drowsy and apathetic. Then he saw the scene missing from the jigsaw: Sofia was holding out a plate, and the stranger was serving her the piece of tart that Frida had just demanded in her imperious way, banging the floor with her stick. And Sofia, talking in that strange schoolmistress way typical of voices remembered, was saying: 'Thank you, Javier.' To associate the stranger with Sofia was disturbing, but Rimini was drunk, and the surroundings he saw Javier in now were so different from those he was used to seeing him in, so different, above all, from the surroundings he imagined Sofia in now that they had separated, that he quickly calmed down.

There was a sudden musical crisis. Two people were arguing about what to play next, while the dancers on the dance-floor protested. As though driven by a reflex of cooperation, Rimini threw himself on the hi-fi system. He bumped into a hard, bony object lined with leather, which turned to argue with him but, when he saw who it was, smiled instead. 'Javier,' said Rimini, and realised he had only said the name to enjoy hearing it said here and now, in the present. They stood for a moment smiling, nodding and slapping each other's back, less pleased at having recognised one another than for spotting all the changes that had taken place in the other since they had last met. They started looking at records together, calling out titles, laughing at them and rejecting them, until at some point one of the two men mentioned the past, and they started talking, until someone from the party – someone still interested in the party – came and shoved them aside to put some music on.

No, Javier told him, with that second degree of embarrassment people assume when they recall an embarrassing incident, he was no longer in charge of the dessert table at Frida's gatherings. He was not even one of her disciples now. He was in crisis. All of a sudden he had looked around him and seen just how far his life – and not simply because of his disc problem, which had been dismissed by the specialists he had gone to see, but all of it, from the brand of toothpaste he used to the excuses he had given himself for ending his latest relationship, from the books that should be read or not, to the countries one ought to visit, the means of transport he used, his preferred sexual practices, even the relationship he had with his parents – how far everything in his life was controlled by Frida. Horrified, he had decided to step back and take some time to think. But this period of truce, that he had considered as only temporary, simply to get his ideas straight, and not a break with Frida – which had not prevented her, who could probably see what was concealed behind his decision, from being against it right from the start – had rapidly been replaced by an ill-defined but much more radical kind of need. After two difficult months, in which the exercises and time devoted to his back problems were dramatically reduced, displaced by an endless debate about a decision which

Frida said was born of fear rather than strength, Javier had been left with no other choice (disturbed by this insistence from someone who he, like all the disciples, Sofia included – and when he said the name Sofia he lowered his voice, as if afraid of summoning up a ghost or in order to make it clear to Rimini that Sofia could well be another topic of conversation between them – had always considered his only guru) than to leave abruptly, slamming the door behind him. This was the only way he could protect himself, even if he did owe her two months' sessions, which he had never paid. And in large part, he owed the freedom he felt that night to him. 'To me?' Rimini queried. To him and Sofia, or rather to their separation, which had not coincided with his personal crisis but had set it in motion by showing that even the most solidly built, well-designed constructions could come tumbling down, and, contrary to everything he had believed until that moment, there was life beyond this collapse. Rimini blushed. He was embarrassed that anything could be learnt from an event that had happened in his personal life. 'No, seriously,' Javier insisted, slapping him on the shoulder as a sign of gratitude: 'When you two separated it was like the fall of the Berlin Wall for me!' Rimini laughed. Then he thought about it and realised that it was true: while he was packing his bags in Belgrano, Buenos Aires, in Berlin a mob of wildly excited Germans had started taking pickaxes to the most significant piece of masonry of the twentieth century. He stole a glance at Javier's hunched back and felt strangely uneasy. He imagined friends, acquaintances, even people he did not know at all, hearing of the split between Sofia and him and turning it into an example, a lesson about life, and following what they had learnt with the most disastrous results – in Javier's case, in agony for years because of his slipped disc, upping and deserting Breitenbach and her treatment, the only one which after years of searching and trying, and finally resigning himself to having to go under the knife, had brought him some relief. Javier reassured him: yes, his back still crucified him, but it was no worse, and he found it tempting to think that Frida's teachings were responsible in large measure for the pain – for causing it, not relieving it. He wasn't sorry about anything. At first he had felt lost, struggling on his own with his suffering, which either in his imagination or in physical reality seemed to have grown much worse overnight. He was a pariah, someone who had exiled himself from the community that had offered him asylum and who therefore had not the slightest chance of going back to it if he repented, condemned to wander with his curse upon his back through a world which had long since given up counting him as one of its members. He had become aware of the secret society aspect of the Breitenbach clan when he told them of his decision to quit, and Frida and her followers, just like an immune system reacting to the presence of a virus and gathering its entire strength to repel the invader, had closed ranks to make him the target for complete condemnation. He had renounced Frida, and with her, unknowingly, all the relationships he had managed to establish over the course of ten years, including Sofia, said Javier, lowering his voice again as he said her name. They did not respond to his phone calls, avoided him, returned the records or books he had lent them, pretended not to have seen him if they ran into him in some public place or other, and behind closed doors, in the intimacy of the living-room on Calle Vidt, on the rare occasion that he and his case were referred to, they did not mention him by name, but called him 'that traitor' – an expression coined by Frida herself. Him, a traitor! When as a young man, after being abducted by the security forces, he had resisted two months of interrogation and torture without ever opening his mouth, without divulging a single one of the names his torturers were demanding – names which because he knew he was about to face punishment (announced by the crash of metal bars being opened, and footsteps coming his way) inevitably leapt to the tip of his tongue. Him, a traitor! That was ridiculous in the mouths of that handful of physical but above all mental invalids who, in the throes of self-delusion, completely identified with the roles Frida had assigned them as guardians of deep emotional balance, took the ravings of an ageing despot for sacred existential truths, saw her wildest ravings as truly therapeutic revelations and, worst of all, presented and defended this scandalous deception as though it were heaven knows what contemporary form of knowledge. Javier paused to get his breath back. His face had gone a bright purple; the veins were standing out at his temples. 'Don't worry, it's all over,' Rimini said, trying to calm him down. 'It's all done with.' He offered to go and get drinks, but Javier did not reply. He did not even look in his direction: his eyes were fixed on some distant point in space, and images of the party were reflected in his pupils as if in a dead mirror. Apparently what had most upset Javier was the *esprit de corps* with which they had all rejected him. If only the Stalinist purges had enjoyed such unanimity! Or Jim Jones. Or David Koresh, said Rimini, hoping that the naturally comic effect of making a list like this would somehow rescue their conversation from the bitter abyss it had fallen into. That's right, said Javier, suddenly alive again: compared to Calle Vidt, Waco must have been like May '68! His guffaws cracked like peals of thunder above the music. Some heads turned their way and Rimini saw his chance. He pointed vaguely towards an adjoining room, muttered 'drinks' and promised to be right back. But a hand grabbed his forearm and held him there. 'You escaped,' Javier said. 'You got out in time.' 'Well,' said Rimini, 'I only went with Sofia. I was never really involved.' 'You know what I mean,' Javier interrupted him. To Rimini, this sounded like a threat. 'You look great,' said Javier. Rimini agreed halfheartedly. And yet, as he started to dwell on the reasons for his contentment, not so much because he really believed in them as to satisfy the vague sense of anticipation he had detected in Javier, he was filled with an odd enthusiasm. He spoke about how young Vera was, how his desire had returned, about her jealousy and the neighbour's huskies, about Vera's ankles and living alone, about Vera's trip to Iguazú and how it had become unbearable, about the vertigo of translating, the sublime sense of renewed life Vera had injected into his existence. After he had finished, when he shifted his weight from one leg to the other and was about to set off finally in search of more drinks, Javier grasped his arm again, stared straight at him and said in a quavering whisper: 'All of them, you realise? All of them. Even Sofia, Rimini. Sofia. You know the relationship I had with Sofia. My God, how could she? How could she do something like that to me?' His voice, incapable of transmitting the degree of suffering he was struggling with, seemed to change its nature and become a massive, soft rumble which covered, or sprang from, a hundred parts of his body simultaneously. 'Well,' said Rimini, 'It's not that important. It's the past. The important thing is you're out of it now, isn't it?' Slowly, as if the mere fact of raising his eyes demanded an incredible effort, Javier looked at him. Rimini could see that the rumbling had risen to Javier's face and was spreading under his skin at lightning speed. He realised that if Javier was still clinging to his arm, it was not so much to prevent him leaving as because he was the only thing in the world that could save him from a complete collapse. Rimini started to prise off the stiff, clawing fingers one by one: as he lifted them, they left tiny craters in his sleeve. 'Out of it?' said Javier in a faint voice. 'Who wants to be out of it? I can't breathe. I've got blotches all over me. I'm pissing blood. My hair's falling out. I don't sleep for days. It's my life, Rimini. I want to be inside. It's the only place for me.' He started to cry. The colour had drained from his face; he was crying with his eyes wide open, sobbing like an animal. 'Help me, Rimini. Please help me.' 'What can I do?' he said, levering up Javier's ring finger. 'Talk to Sofia. Do it for me. Tell her I want to get back into the group.' 'But. . .we're separated.' 'That doesn't matter.' 'I haven't seen her in ages.' 'That doesn't matter. She'll listen to you.' Rimini had got his little finger off. 'I don't think she'd want to. I don't answer her calls. I stand her up.' Javier did not stop crying: he left his sobbing behind like someone leaving a room, simply opening a door. His despair vanished, swallowed up in that invisible dimension where the alchemy of the emotions is concocted. What replaced it was pure hostility. 'Sofia adores you, Rimini,' he said, shaking him violently. 'She'd do whatever you ask.' Rimini stared at him incredulously, as if the very same reason he used to avoid all contact with Sofia sounded insulting on someone else's mouth. At any rate, there was something obscene in the way this almost complete stranger who had no compunction about humiliating himself in front of him, could at the same time pride himself on having access to the most hidden nooks and crannies of his emotional life. 'Let me be,' Rimini said quickly, turning to go. Javier followed him. On several occasions, held up by a crowd of people, Rimini could feel his trembling but insistent fingers pinching his sleeve, his shoulder, his hand. He shook them off like insects. Luckily the music and the conversations were so loud he could not hear Javier's shouts. At a certain point, as he was crossing the large room where people were dancing in black light, Rimini looked round to see how far he was behind him. He found himself confronted with the grotesque image of a wide-open mouth, like in a comic, with two rows of shiny, fluorescent teeth. Near the exit he groped blindly in the darkness and discovered the room where the coats were kept. When he tried to open the door, Javier pushed in front of him. 'What's it to you?' he panted. 'You're strong.

You're saved. You've got nothing to lose.' 'You don't understand,' Rimini replied. 'I don't want to ask her for anything.' Javier stiffened, as though someone had punched him in the stomach. Then, as a blind rage slowly accumulated within him, he stared at Rimini and shouted; 'Why?' – not exactly at Rimini, from whom he knew he could not expect anything more, but at something or someone more in general, less well-defined, a sort of cosmic being he could blame for all his suffering. 'I don't want to owe Sofia anything,' said Rimini. 'Now will you let me through? I want to go.' Javier seemed to regain control, and moved back a step, just enough so that Rimini could get into the room, but would still have to push him out of the way. The room was lit by a weak night-light, so that all the coats thrown on the bed had made a huge haystack it was impossible to find anything in. Sensing Javier's eyes burning his back, Rimini plunged his hands into the pile and tried to feel for his jacket. He touched leather, rough wool, something metallic, then a loose weave his fingers got stuck in, until finally something warm and soft, motionless but definitely alive, made him pull his hands out in disgust. He took a few steps back. Javier was standing next to him, a mocking smile on his face. 'I knew you were naïve,' he said, 'but I didn't realise just how far. You think it's enough not to ask her for anything? Poor guy. Poor fool. You must be an idiot not to see it.' Rimini straightened up slowly and turned to look at him. He was afraid, afraid of discovering how close this cowardly hunchback might be to a truth he himself was completely unaware of. 'See what?' he asked. 'You're in it up to your neck, Rimini. How long were you together: eight? Ten years?' 'Twelve,' said Rimini. 'It doesn't matter. Sofia is the Great Creditor. And you Rimini – listen to me – you aren't even the one in debt. You're the hostage. You're the guarantee that someone, some day, will pay her what she's asking for.' Rimini was staring at him slack-jawed, as if such cruelty had left him witless. Javier burst out laughing. 'When I look at you, my head fills with all kinds of old-fashioned words: gull, booby, dummy, poltroon! And to think that when I saw you at those end-of-year parties, I was jealous of you!' He was laughing so hard he choked and had to stop talking. Rimini seized the opportunity to punch him – at first wildly and without aiming his blows, as if he were blindly flailing in all directions not so much to hurt as to ward off an invisible enemy – but then when he saw Javier curled up in a ball on the floor, covering his face with his hands and groaning, he really wanted to do him harm. He studied him closely to discover his weak points, and started to kick him in the chest, stomach, ribs, everywhere that his arms had left exposed as they protected his face. When a reflex movement led him to lower them to save himself, Rimini kicked him in the head, and when he saw he was helpless on the floor, he kicked him again and again, as methodically as some sort of kicking machine, until Javier stopped moving. It was at this moment that Rimini saw the pile of coats tremble, slide and fall off the bed, taking the lower ones with them. A four- or five-year-old boy with a birthmark on his neck stood up in the bed, stiff as a soldier on his bandy legs, and stared at him sleepily and crossly, like a despot who wonders what trivial nonsense from the world of mortals could possibly have dared to rouse him from the perfect sphere of sleep.

CHAPTER 18

But Vera came back, and when Rimini caught sight of her in the airport, zigzagging between her fellow passengers to pick up her suitcases, and saw how her beauty and grace, unaware of him admiring them from a distance, blossomed for being carefree, the incident at the party suddenly seemed as insubstantial as a dream. Everything seemed ambiguous, like those images we glimpse on TV screens a moment before we go to sleep, which remain suspended and unresolved ever afterwards. Vera's parents emerged first. She was smoking one of those thin cigarettes in coloured paper that she had brought in from abroad; he was behind her, huge and lumbering, with a face that said he needed a holiday from holidays. They came to a halt in the reception area, looking all round for Rimini, until her mother recognised him and came over, wreathed in smiles. Rimini avoided her powdered cheek, avoided the hand with which the father tried to intercept him, left them behind and also avoided a policewoman before flinging himself on Vera, who was struggling with her suitcase – one of the wheels had got stuck – and kissed and hugged the breath out of her until the other passengers, forced to queue behind them, shouted at them to clear the exit. Vera lifted her head from his embrace, looked up at his face for the first time, slightly taken aback, pursed her lips and said yes, she had really enjoyed herself, everything had been perfect apart from a few problems she would never have had if he, Rimini, had agreed to go with her. Still clasping her tight, Rimini begged for forgiveness. He declared himself guilty on every count, called for the worst penalty, and then bit by bit, amazed as he was at recovering all these lost treasures – the V-shape of her hair on her forehead, the pink patches round her lips, her lips themselves, which looked as red as if someone had just been furiously kissing them – he started to listen to the long list of torments that had beset the adventurer. Most of them were irrelevant, and probably imaginary: turbulence on the outward flight, a meeting with a poisonous reptile in mid-jungle. Rimini chose two: an allergic reaction – too much exotic fruit – which had left her a delicious rash by the sides of her nostrils; and the 'terrible wound' that a particularly aggressive kind of cactus has caused to her calf while she was walking, with spinning head, across a bridge suspended high above the water, a wound that any sensible doctor – not the idiot at the hotel, who seemed less interested in the injury than in his patient's legs – would have closed with a few stitches, a wound that left her struggling in a feverish cloud all night long – the cactus was poisonous, although 'by some miracle' not lethal – a wound which Vera refused to show him in the taxi, even though the safari bermudas she was wearing were well suited to an examination, and Rimini's clinical curiosity was at its height, until they reached Las Heras, rushed in with cases and bags and, without even shutting the front door, collapsed into the bed which Rimini, three hours earlier when he had left for the airport, had decided against making, and following a brief struggle with her trouser-leg, he was able to get a close look at, feel sorry for, brush her 'terrible wound' with his lips – it was a pale scratch no longer than a fingernail, and almost invisible, which any casual observer – though not Rimini, of course – might have taken for an accident with a red biro.

Rimini gave her asylum immediately, without thinking twice. One after another, he accepted all the demands that Vera made with the heedlessness of a young child, sitting bolt upright in the bed while he went to switch the TV on, put a kettle on the stove, shut the shutters, disconnected the phone, went to buy pastries or cigarettes, massaged the soles of her feet, went out again, this time to the chemist, to buy a cream for the rash beside her nose, gave her another pillow, took away blankets, opened the window a bit, then shut it again, let her go to sleep on her own, came running when she called, took his clothes off, slipped under the sheets, warmed her up, entwined his body with hers, her hands between his legs, his hands under her armpits and then, without the slightest effort, without even moving, as if their desire was so intense they no longer needed any physical organs to demonstrate it, they crossed a threshold and dissolved in millions of tiny spasms, then fell asleep without parting.

The asylum lasted eight days: exactly twice as long as her cold and the number of days that Rimini – unforgivably – had left her exposed to the perils of the sub-tropics. After two passionate days that Rimini devoted to winning back her favour, he gave up his translations without the slightest remorse: his desk was left untouched, as though it was frozen in time, with the dictionaries and the books still open, papers everywhere, a half-written page still in the typewriter. Every time he went past, Rimini glanced at it distantly, in the same way as he would have looked at the scene reconstructed in a museum. He spent most of the day out in the street, running the errands and fulfilling the instructions Vera gave him each morning from her headquarters in bed, the sheet sprinkled with grains of sugar and breadcrumbs from breakfast drawn up under her chin. Vera was the unmoving engine, Rimini the repercussion. Or rather, Vera was the source of all light, an absolute, capricious centre which imposed its most primitive weaknesses – freshly squeezed orange juice in the morning, an incredible appetite, white socks, mashed potato, ankle chains, Patrick Suskind, lots of sugar in everything, chewed nails, men's shoes with no socks – with a sovereign shamelessness, and Rimini, who was the planet in closest orbit and therefore the most dazzled, was a kind of loyal, tireless emissary whose main function was to carry and spread her light to all corners of the galaxy. One afternoon, standing in a metro carriage on his way back from paying three instalments she owed at the Alliance Française, he once again savoured the pride he had felt when the assistant took his money – the pride of representing Vera to the unknown representatives of her world – and when he glanced at his reflection in the carriage door window, he saw he had an idiotic, completely besotted smile on his face he had never dreamt he was capable of. The metro stopped at Tribunales; people got on. A ginger-haired, scatter-brained boy in school uniform brushed his cheek with the corner of the drawing portfolio he was carrying, and Rimini had a fleeting but intense urge (so intense that he had to turn his back on his aggressor to avoid acting on it) to smash his red head against the door.

It was logical: he had not been taking drugs for four days – four days in which cocaine had been literally wiped out of his life. But this detox, carried out almost imperceptibly, as only happens in cures brought about by love, was not the only sign produced by his period of devotion. On more than one occasion, returning from one of the 'missions' – as he called them in his own private language – Vera sent him on, he had come into his Las Heras apartment and felt a sense of unease, the strange sensation of someone who leaves somewhere and on his return finds it mysteriously changed. It took him days to realise how, in what way. He saw that they were small changes, which a less alert eye could have put down to a moment's distraction or a sudden breeze. But with hindsight, the clues multiplied: his diary was not where he had left it; drawers he kept locked were slightly open; there were no messages on his answering-machine; some books, apparently rebelling against the alphabetical order he classified them in, suddenly switched places on his shelves – especially the large, inviting books that were ideal for hiding secrets, bookmarks, bar napkins, bits of paper, letters, postcards, photos, phone numbers . . .

Vera was using his absence to spy on him. He felt stupid. Why had he not imagined how the fact of him not going with her to Iguazú would increase her jealousy? He thought about her. He saw her sitting up in bed, shooing him on his way with an impatience which he attributed to love, to the unsatisfactory feeling love always has about good-byes, and then, once she was sure he was out of the apartment, he saw her launching herself on his diary, searching through it desperately to try to dig up a name, a meeting, a vital clue. He saw her as fragile, disconsolate, consumed by the sterility of her passion, and discovering this touched him, made him feel even more powerful. One night he suggested she came and lived with him. Vera's face lit up, but she immediately restrained herself; she stared him in the eye with a long, questioning look, as if giving *him* the chance to think it over. Rimini did not back down, and Vera asked him a thousand times if he was sure, if it was true, if that was what he wanted, if he had thought it through properly, if he was suggesting it because that was what he wanted, or because . . . he said yes, yes, yes, and then she, in a clear firm voice, as though she were reading a legal document, started to list all the defects he was agreeing to live with, separating the ones that could be cured from the other ones, the frivolous from the essential. Hugging her gratefully, Rimini accepted them all; he even added a few she had left out, and as he kissed her on the neck told her he did not think defects could be cured. She laughed. He pushed her away a little to watch her laughing, and saw how a rapid cloud of fear flitted across her face, and her laugh became a grimace of terror. She burst into tears, begged him not to let her go. 'I can't help it,' she said. 'When everything is fine, I always think a tragedy is just around the corner.'

They ate in the Chinese restaurant on Calle Paunero. It was a big, over-lit place, with a clutch of ferns drooping over the empty tables, and another clutch of waiters staring gloomily out into the street. They did not exactly eat. After struggling with the garbled language of the menu, it was obvious that the dishes they were served were not those they thought they had ordered, and it was more than enough just to take a look round the restaurant where – apart from a man sitting with his back to them, which made it impossible to decide whether he was a customer or one of the staff, there was, and had not been for hours or even days, no one but them – to realise just how inedible the food was. As a result, they stabbed vaguely at things with tentacles swimming in a shiny sauce, and decided to drink instead, to enjoy to the full the immunity apparently protecting them from all this horror: the threatening dishes, the waiters' hostility, the décor – dragons, portraits of boxers, paper screens with photos of TV stars cut out of magazines and stuck on them – and even the reaction of the other diner who more than once, irritated by their raucous laughter, had turned round and fulminated at them with a look from his bloodshot eyes. By the time they left, they were drunk. Vera took three steps and staggered; Rimini had to hold her tight to stop her falling. They stood for a while leaning against the trunk of a tree, until Vera successfully answered the simplest of the questions Rimini was testing her lucidity with, and they set off again towards Las Heras.

They turned into Calle Cabello, blinded by the light of the quartz searchlight illuminating the whole block. Vera, who could not conceive of advancing from one point to another without debating all the different options, objected to the one they were taking, and wanted to turn round. 'Down Calle Canning, down Canning,' she stuttered. 'We're going towards Canning,' said Rimini, taking her by the shoulders and turning her in the right direction. 'I'm very dizzy,' Vera said: 'I think I'll stay here.' 'It's only two blocks,' said Rimini. 'Here, it's perfect here,' she said, pointing to a dark entrance. 'No, no,' he said, 'lean on me, I'll take you.' They took a few steps, then Vera stopped again. Her eyes were wide-open, as though she had just remembered something important. 'I think I'm going to be sick,' she said. 'Take a deep breath,' said

Rimini. Vera took a quick, deep breath, closed her eyes and looked about to fall again. Rimini held her tight. 'Open your eyes,' he said; her eyelashes swept the air disdainfully, then Vera's huge green eyes stared wonderingly at the huge patch of light. Something stirred in Rimini's memory – one of those lateral, mechanical recollections that all of a sudden come to life, stir among the ruins, give off a spark. 'Repeat after me,' he said: 'I relax the tongue beneath the tongue.' 'What?' 'It's to help you relax. Repeat: I relax the tongue beneath the tongue.' 'What d'you mean, "the tongue *beneath* the tongue". What does that mean?' That was the question Rimini had always wanted to ask Frida Breitenbach – always, from the morning when he heard this kind of mantra for the first time, from Sofia, in the school playground, a few seconds after she had accepted his invitation to go out together and Rimini had such palpitations he thought he was going to faint, to the last, early in the morning when Rimini, who had just confirmed he was going to rent the Las Heras apartment, was struggling to try to get some sleep in bed a few centimetres from the woman he had decided to distance himself from for ever. 'Shh, be quiet and say, "I relax the tongue beneath the tongue"', he insisted. 'Look, I mean it,' she said, pushing at his chest as if holding him back on the edge of a precipice. 'I'm going to be sick now.' They stood as still as statues, bathed in the harsh white light. At a certain point, something must have passed in front of the searchlight, because there was a sort of eclipse and Rimini and Vera felt a soothing balm of darkness refreshing their eyes. It was only a moment – they were immediately doused in light again – but it was enough to ward off the nausea. Vera set off again. 'My God, what a clown,' she said, 'we're going to live together and I start by vomiting on your shoes in the street.' Rimini laughed and looked in front of them. He saw something detaching itself from the light and coming towards them – a human shape. 'I don't think I've ever been sick in front of a man,' said Vera, screwing up her eyes. 'It would have been an honour,' said Rimini. He shielded his eyes against the light to see more clearly: it was the outline of a woman. Too late: he recognised the aureola of hair shining round her head like a crown of fire, the slightly bowed legs: Sofia. 'I don't want to. If I'm sick I'll feel so ashamed I'll have to leave you,' Vera said. Rimini broke out into a cold sweat. He thought of crossing the street, but was so terrified at the idea of the slightest movement that he preferred to stay still and wait. 'Are you cold, my love?' he heard Vera say. He realised that, in his terror, he was not so much hugging her as throttling her. He had a brief hope that the silhouette was not coming towards them, but going away – and he encouraged it, urging it on its way with a determination he had never had before, which crumbled as soon as he realised that the throbbing inside his head was not his pulse but a fateful countdown. 'My love, my love': now it was Vera who was clinging to him, pushing him against a metal fence. 'Do you like it when I call you "my love"?' He was done for. He started reciting a mental plea: he repeated it over and over to himself, in the monotonous, superstitious tone he remembered Sofia and Frida and all her disciples adopting to chant the formula, and as Sofia came closer the interior volume of his pleas grew until it was deafening, more pitiful than any sobs, his hands intertwined, bending a knee – please, spare my life, please, please, do this for me: spare my life now, now, now – three, two, one – *Now*. It was only then that he caught a good glimpse of her, as Sofia's slight body, wrapped in some kind of poncho, got sufficiently close to move out of the light. 'Have you ever been called "my love" before, my love?' Vera repeated, throwing her head back as, with eyes shut, she ran her clumsy fingers over his face. Sofia was next to them, only half a metre away, but she did not look at Rimini. Instead she examined Vera from head to foot, as though appraising her, then smiled and passed straight by him without even slowing down, simply brushing his arm with her gloved hand, as if they were two spies exchanging a secret signal under the enemy's nose – and it all happened so quickly and so harmlessly that Rimini had to turn and look over his shoulder to be sure he had not dreamt the whole thing.

CHAPTER 19

He owed her his life. And like every good debtor there was only one thing he was afraid of: that she would come back to demand payment. Rimini knew there was no way he could repay her, but this inability, which might have reassured him, instead set him on the path towards a strange scaffold. He could not help thinking about the alternatives Sofia must be considering to allow him to pay: getting together to sort out the photos, for example, speaking on the phone once a week, or meeting, just as friends, to exchange chit-chat for a quarter of an hour and then, at the first awkward silence, to concentrate on digging up the past; but this did not happen: Sofia did not reappear. As the days went by, Rimini's mood changed from one of feeling completely vulnerable to a kind of dignified, acceptable stoicism, in which he no longer saw himself as a lamb, offering his throat to be slit, but as capable of arguing, proposing, negotiating conditions that would make the repayment more convenient. And later, when he felt the threats hanging over his new life lifting, and felt himself more robust again, at least sufficiently to live it spontaneously, without being scared of ruining it all himself through some clumsy mistake, just when he found that he *wanted* to meet Sofia to prove that he could survive her, he realised that this was not going to happen, that Sofia had disappeared again. This took the wind out of his sails, as if he had won a very tough competition and now, owner of the trophy, discovered that his opponents had never shown up.

A week later, as he was emerging from the shower, Rimini put his foot up on the edge of the toilet to dry it and saw that half of one his big toenails was completely yellow. He put his foot on the floor next to the other one, and saw that the nail there was in the same condition. 'Fungus,' his homeopath said. 'It's very common.' He was a vaguely Japanese man, who sometimes used his Argentine wife's name, and whose features could look more oriental or western at unpredictable moments. Rimini trusted him so much that, despite the fact that he had been both his and Sofia's doctor, the separation (which had so deeply affected everything they shared) scarcely even seemed to have touched him. 'Aren't you going to look at my toenails?' Rimini asked. He immediately cursed himself: he knew that the iris of the eyes was the limit of what any homeopath could want to look at. 'There's no need,' said the doctor. 'Unless you want me to.' 'No, no,' said Rimini, almost apologetically. 'What do I have to do?' 'For now, nothing,' said the doctor. 'Nothing?' There was something about the homeopathic administration of time – an unconditional wager on the future – which he could never accept. 'The only thing there is,' said the homeopath, 'are antibiotics. But they are toxic. And besides, they would interfere with the treatment, so we'll leave them for later.' 'What treatment?' 'Aren't you taking any pills?' 'No,' said Rimini, 'I haven't been taking anything for months.' 'Let's start you on some, then,' the doctor said with a burst of enthusiasm, leaning forward across the desk. 'What else?' he wanted to know, his voice challenging now. Rimini delved into the previous few months of his life. 'I don't know. I can't think of anything,' he said, and returned to the attack: 'They won't get worse, will they?' The doctor raised his eyes from the lined index card. 'I beg your pardon?' 'The nails.' The doctor said nothing; he smiled, consulted the card once more and then swiftly raised his eyes as if trying to catch Rimini out. 'Are you sweating more than usual?' he asked. 'I haven't noticed any change.' 'Do you sleep all right?' 'Yes.' 'So you don't have insomnia,' the doctor said. 'I've never had insomnia,' said Rimini. He was starting to feel uncomfortable ease. He felt that the haphazard questioning, so typical of homeo-pathic doctors' wandering attention, this time was only a façade hiding some kind of premeditation. 'Do you still see those tiny silvery insects flying in the air?' 'I suppose so. Sometimes. I don't know, I haven't given it much thought.' The doctor sighed, and placed the card face down on his desk. 'How are you feeling?' he asked. 'Fine,' said Rimini. He decided not to add anything more, but the doctor stared at him so long and so impassively that he had to give in. 'Everything is falling into place again,' he said. 'I understand,' said the doctor. Then, almost casually: 'Any excesses?' Rimini became wary. 'Why do you ask?' He was trying to be sarcastic, but the laugh that came out between the words sounded more like nervousness. 'The last time we met, you were married,' the doctor said. He was not looking at Rimini, and for some reason this gave his voice a special gravity. Rimini felt he was about to hear a dreadful diagnosis. 'People do not always choose the most sensible way to get things back into place,' he said softly, as if reciting an axiom from his private catechism. Then all of a sudden he added: 'Any change in your habits? Drugs? What about your sexual life?' Rimini scoured the room, searching for the door of the secret cupboard where Sofia and in all likelihood Javier, her battered informer, must have rushed to hide a second before he came in. 'Do I look so dissolute?' he asked, recovering some of his poise. But the doctor ignored his sarcasm and said: 'Have you weighed yourself recently?' 'No,' he said. 'Do I look thinner?' 'A bit. Three or four kilos,' the doctor said. He turned the card over and wrote a few hasty words, at the same time pulling the prescription pad towards him with his other hand. 'Aren't you going to weigh me?' asked Rimini. 'No,' replied the doctor, busy now writing the prescription, 'not unless you're particularly interested in being weighed.' Rimini hesitated. The doctor tore off the top sheet from his pad and deposited it under Rimini's nose with a flourish. 'Lycopodium ten . . .' he started saying, but Rimini interrupted him. 'Yes, on second thoughts, I think I would like to be weighed.' The doctor smiled again: 'We're going to have to leave that for another day,' he said, standing up and slipping the prescription between Rimini's fingers. 'Lycopodium ten thousand, in a . . .' he paused, then added quickly: '. . . paper. Before you go to bed. You know how to take it, don't you?' He simultaneously shook Rimini's hand and gently but firmly pushed him towards the door. 'You pour it under your tongue and let it dissolve. Call me in a fortnight.'

Out on the landing, in front of the lift that had just arrived, Rimini felt gripped by a cold despair, as if the machinations of which he had just been the victim had turned him into some sort of pariah, left out on his own in the storm. He went back to the clinic and rang the bell. The doctor opened the door slightly and peered out, frowning. 'I don't think I can carry on coming to see you,' said Rimini. He handed him back the prescription. The doctor would not take it, but opened the door wider and with a paternal gesture invited him to step in. Rimini turned his back on him and headed towards the lift, which someone had called from a lower floor. Rimini pulled the outer door open to stop it. 'I don't think this is the moment to take such an important decision,' the doctor said. Rimini said nothing. He opened the inner lift door. 'You've run yourself ragged,' said the doctor. Rimini got into the lift; the person waiting down below was growing impatient. He started to go down; when he looked up he could see the doctor's brown shoes at the edge of the lift-well. 'You need help, Rimini.'

Night took him by surprise. He felt defenceless, lethargic, irritable. Without thinking, he stopped at the first public phone booth he came across, and dialled Sofia's number. He had no idea what he would say to her – he was acting out of a desperate determination. At the other end of the line he heard a male voice, which sounded slightly hoarse as though he had not spoken to anyone for a long while. It took Rimini a few moments to realise that it was Rodi, Sofia's father. 'Is Sofia there?' he asked hastily, running the words together as though to disguise them. 'Is that you, Rimini?' the father asked, with a note of pleased astonishment. Rimini said nothing. 'Hello?' 'Yes, it's me,' said Rimini. 'This is Rodi, Rimini. It's good to hear you,' he broke off, sighed deeply, then went on: 'It's good to hear you after all this time.' Rodi moved away from the phone and muttered something, as if he were speaking to another person. 'I wanted to talk to Sofia.' 'Yes, of course,' said Rodi, but his voice sounded weak or frightened, and the ensuing silence lasted so long that Rimini became worried. 'Is she there?' asked Rimini. 'Er, no. Not at the moment. She's in the clinic.' Rimini heard a loud noise, as if her father had sneezed into the phone, followed by several long complaining sounds. The moment dragged on. Rimini had to steady himself against the phone. 'In a clinic?' Silence. 'Yes,' her father said, coming back to life: 'she was operated on this morning.' Rimini shuddered: he wanted to go back, wanted the whole day to go back with him so that he could start afresh. 'Oh, I thought you knew,' her father said. 'No, no.' 'Don't you talk to each other, Rimini?' 'No.' 'It's too ridiculous. We love you so much. Sofia loves you so much . . .' The other person butted in, forcing him to move away from the mouthpiece. Rodi was arguing. He blew his nose. 'Why shouldn't I tell him? It's the truth. Why should I keep it to myself?' Then he spoke into the phone again: 'They're telling me here that I shouldn't . . .' he clicked his tongue angrily. 'Is everything all right?' asked Rimini. 'All right, yes, no problems. A bit older, that's all. And a bit sad. What a thing to do, Rimini. Twelve years. And when people find it so hard to stay together. Tell me, is there no possibility that . . .' 'I meant, is Sofia all right?' Rimini cut in. 'Is she OK? What was the operation?' Rodi got involved again in a parallel discussion. '*I'm* going to invite him,' he said, 'then he can do as he likes.' 'Hello!' Rimini shouted into the empty silence. 'Hello, Rodi!' Rodi came back on the line. '*Che*,' he said, sniffing, then added with wild enthusiasm, 'I have a show opening on the 12th in Balderston. The same gallery as always. Oil paintings. Beach scenes on cloudy days. That's what I'm into at the moment. I'd love you to come. Seriously, for me, for all of us it would be a . . .' there was a sharp, brutal click – the last five-cent piece had dropped – and Rodi's voice was cut off.

Rimini did not dare call back. That evening, while Vera was having a shower, Rimini shouted that he was going out to buy something for dinner, and ran to the public phone on the corner. He stood for a while staring at the lights reflected on the wet pavement, the easy glide of cars along the avenue, the regular wink of the traffic lights, and this self-absorbed, logical progression of the world beyond him filled him with a childish distress. He called Victor, but all he found was an answering-machine. 'My God,' he thought, 'Victor's at the clinic. They're all at the clinic.' He decided to leave a message anyway: 'Victor, it's me, Rimini. Please pick up if you're there. It's important; very important. Victor . . .' 'Hi there!' Victor shouted at the other end of the line. He apologised: he was cooking. *Orecchiette* with a leek sauce. Had Rimini eaten? 'What's wrong with Sofia, Victor?' Victor said nothing. 'Don't try to protect me, please. Tell me everything, tell me the truth.' He told him about the conversation he had had with Rodi. He surrounded the word 'clinic' with two ominous pauses, but Victor only burst out in compassionate laughter. 'Poor angel.' Silence, he was tasting something. 'Too much cream. She had a nose job, Rimini. No big deal. I talked to her half an hour ago. "New life, new nose," she told me. She sounded happy. Are you sure you don't want to come and eat? Mademoiselle Vera is invited too, of course.'

Mademoiselle Vera had not been in such demand for ages. Rimini found her wreathed in steam, painting her toenails, a towel wrapped round her head, a cigarette between her lips. He knelt beside her and began gently to kiss her calves, stopping every now and then to blow on the pink patches she had come back with that afternoon after having a wax treatment. Vera took a deep draw on her cigarette, then threw back her head to avoid getting smoke in her eyes. Rimini took the cigarette from her mouth. 'Thanks,' she said, puffed out the smoke, and as she put her legs together to examine her painted nails, added: 'A very polite gentleman has just invited me to a painting exhibition.' She paused, cocked her head slightly, still peering down at her toes, and spotted a hair that had got stuck in the nail polish. 'On the 12th, I think he said. The Badmington or Masterson gallery, or something like that. I wrote it down on the notepad. She tried removing the hair with her little fingernail. 'Ah,' she said, 'he said you weren't to worry. It's nothing: she didn't even have to have a general anaesthetic.' Vera looked up, and let her eyes fall on Rimini as if by accident. She twisted her mouth in a brief, condescending gesture. 'They straightened her nose out a bit, that's all.'

Rimini was dumbfounded. Vera had crossed the minefield without hesitating or pausing, and without being hurt, and was now looking at him safe and sound, untouchable, from the other side, with that look that survivors of a terrible experience have. He immediately suggested they choose an apartment and move in together. When he woke up the next day, Vera had already gone: she had left his breakfast things ready, with his coffee prepared and the newspaper open at the flats to rent section, the pages of the newspaper protected from any breeze through the living-room window by a marker pen. The coffee was slightly burnt; his spoon had a thin layer of dry sugar on it, and the butter, although it was soft now, showed signs of having been viciously attacked; but there were eight apartments (alarmed, Rimini counted several second- and third-floor places with no lifts, all of them advertised with huge exclamation marks) already floating in their fluorescent bubbles.

Two weeks later, a van pulled up in a desolate street in the Abasto district, and following the threat of a mutiny, which Rimini managed to quell with the promise of extra money, two porters with bloodshot eyes hauled up three endless flights of marble staircases the variegated fruits of a double move: the furniture Rimini had in his Las Heras apartment, and the keepsakes Vera insisted on bringing with her from her family home: the doll's house, the pink wardrobe, the shoe container (a huge wooden box covered in stickers that fell apart as the men carried it upstairs), the white fluffy stool, the bathroom mirror studded with little white lights – a souvenir, Vera confessed, of an end-of-year school celebration when she played the role of a great dance diva saying her last farewell to her public. 'So what was the mirror for?' asked Rimini, hoping against hope that thanks to some autobiographical slip this particular accessory would have no significance and could be left where it was. 'It was part of the décor in the dressing-room,' Vera said: 'the whole scene was the ballerina talking to herself in front of the mirror.'

Two, three months went by and Sofia, whose nose Rimini thought he glimpsed in cameo roles in his dreams – once shut in a glass box, next to a red rose, a second time seen in profile, against the light, dripping – Sofia still had not appeared. And Rimini's debt to her began to lose its urgency and started to languish, like lost objects which nobody reclaims tend to do, until it lapsed entirely. One afternoon, while he was waiting to see the dentist, Rimini was flicking through a private medical insurance magazine when he came across a photograph in the society pages: it was Sofia with her father, both of them standing stiffly with plastic mugs in their hands like two guardsmen, one on either side of a big painting that showed a flooded field, or a beach, or the tall waves of a sea in which animals or boats were sinking, which according to the caption (which confused Sofia with a promotional director called Starosta) the painter had entitled *Emotional Landscape*. Nothing about Sofia's nose particularly struck him, although the photograph, taken either by an amateur or one of those birds of prey who dazzle people with their flashes at every opening, was slightly blurred and had too much green in it. A few days later, Rimini returned home, and when he checked the day's messages on the phone pad, was brought up short by one he did not recognise: Sonia. It was such a blatant synonym, the reference so obvious – Sonia, Riltse's younger sister, who was drowned at the age of sixteen in an accident – that it would have been less glaring if she had used her own name. He thought that something as obvious could only have been doubly so for Vera, and started preparing himself to meet the storm. 'A friend of Victor's,' was all she said, showing no signs of being suspicious or of hiding something. 'What did she want?' asked Rimini. 'I don't know. She asked when you had last spoken to Victor.' 'How odd,' he said. 'I'd phone if I were you,' said Vera. 'Did she leave a phone number?' 'Call him, call Victor. She had a strange voice, like she wanted to tell you something important.' 'Why didn't she tell you?' he said, then was immediately horrified at the way everything seemed to be going topsy-turvy. For once Vera trusted him, and here he was undermining her trust with suspicions that could only harm his own position. 'Because it's important, I suppose,' she said, looking at him wide-eyed, as if this was the first time she had seen the scared little kid that until that moment her jealousy had prevented her from seeing. She handed him the phone. Rimini sat down and picked up the receiver, all in fateful slow motion. He realised his hands were sweating. He was done for. Sofia had penetrated his fortress. Not only had she fooled Vera; she had recruited her. Vera was the guarantee that her message would get through, and it was because of her, because of Vera, that Rimini found himself more obliged than ever to come up with a reply. The threat was no longer outside but inside, and it was not a hostile force but was what Rimini loved most in all the world, the only thing that kept him afloat. Done for was putting it mildly. All of a sudden he saw Vera as an instrument of evil, an innocent hit-woman, a terrifyingly efficient one. As he dialled Victor's number, he had the sensation that he was entering a new phase in which the weapons and the rules he was used to were no longer relevant. But Victor was in hospital. 'Tuberculosis,' said the girl who answered, who a second earlier had asked him his name, as if she had a list of the people authorised to hear the medical bulletin. 'Who's that?' asked Rimini. 'Sonia,' said the girl, a cousin of Victor's. She lived in Entre Ríos, had come to spend a fortnight in Buenos Aires – an advanced seminar in something or other, cosmetology, cosmology, climatology – and Victor had asked her to drop by his place to water the plants and pick up any messages on his answering-machine. 'Yes, yes, of course,' Rimini stammered shamefacedly, while a sarcastic chorus trampled on all his suppositions.

He went to visit him at once, anxious to free himself of the guilt. There he was fiddling about with his suspicions, while Victor was laid out in bed, spitting blood. How could he be so contemptuous? He reached the German Hospital, walked in and avoided looking at the reception. Whenever he went into a hospital it was just the same as when he was stopped at a border checkpoint: he felt sure he did not have the proper papers to be allowed in. 'Room 404,' he had been told by Sonia, who existed and was real, much more real than this hospital entrance and the receptionist who looked as though she were about to get to her feet to intercept him. He went straight up to the fourth floor. Beneath the harsh neon light he felt slightly dizzy, as if something at the back of his knees were giving way. He passed the time observing the man next to him in the lift: he was small, ill-shaven, and he drummed his fingers on the floor indicator. Whenever the lift stopped at a floor, he stuck his head out and stared in both directions. When Rimini got out at the fourth floor, the tiles were so shiny that they blinded him. It was like walking on the surface of a mirror. An elderly man was snoring on a long bench, his head thrown back, while at his feet a young boy was tying the lace of one of his shoes to the other.

Rimini went in without knocking. He was struck by how cold it was inside: far colder than he would have expected, and the sharp, almost hyperventilated quality of the air seemed to him too rigorous for a sick person. He tiptoed past the bathroom, from where he could hear the sound of running water. Suddenly embarrassed, he peered cautiously into the room. Before looking at the bed, his eyes alighted on the visitor's settee, where there lay a black cord jacket, a beret and a hand-woven bag, which was still across the shoulder of the jacket, as if the woman wearing them had taken them all off together. Considered separately, none of these three things meant anything to him. But as soon as he stopped looking at them, something brought them together, like drops of mercury, and then they took on an unmistakably familiar look. Rimini glanced towards the bed, and saw a nurse who turned towards him and as she got to her feet, handed him something. 'Here. Warm this up,' she said. Rimini saw Victor flat on his back in the bed, eyes closed, and then, in the nurse's hand close to him, really close, the cylinder of a syringe full of blood. 'Come on,' the nurse repeated, rubbing Victor's vein with a piece of cotton-wool, 'Warm it up for me.' Rimini obeyed, even though he was thinking: 'What's the point, it's blood. It's already warm.' He felt his knees go weak again, and the pit of his stomach froze. His eyes clouded over. The last thing he heard before he fainted was the noise of the bathroom door opening, footsteps that stopped just behind him, and the nurse's open mouth shouting a warning he never got to hear.

A voice and a pair of invisible hands rescued him from a deep basement. Lying on his back on the floor, he saw a shadow with a gleaming, blonde halo moving towards then away from his face. All at once, as if in the central control room where he had been disconnected, they had suddenly switched on his senses again, the sounds of the room came back: above became above once more, and below below. His body began to regain a tenuous three-dimensionality. He recognised the nurse's voice – 'A little tube of blood, who would have thought it?' – as she rubbed something on the floor, near one of his hands, and then bit by bit the head between him and the light emerged from its anonymity: bushy, unkempt eyebrows, dark lines round the eyes, slight swellings at the base of the nose, the luminous halo of hair. He sensed a soft, delicate musical rain falling on him. Sofia was singing. She was singing *to him*. She was hardly moving her lips, which meant that what came out was more like a soft whisper, which was spread not so much by travelling through the air as by their proximity, by physical contagion. 'Poor little boy,' said Sofia, smiling when she realised he had recognised her. Rimini moved his head, and found it was resting on her lap. He tried to sit up. He felt an unpleasant tingling in the palm of one hand, and saw that the nurse was digging some glass splinters out with a pair of pincers. Rimini saw the small pool of blood and looked at the nurse. 'Don't be scared, it isn't yours,' she said. Rimini moved on to his side. Sitting on the edge of the bed with his legs dangling over the side, Victor waved at him. Rimini put one hand on the floor, then his knee, and gradually got on to all fours, sensing Sofia's hands accompanying his movements without actually touching him. 'Slowly, take it easy,' she said. Rimini saw the bed and calculated the distance; he grabbed for the metal frame and missed, slipping on a patch of blood the nurse had not noticed. Victor burst out laughing. 'This guy's a danger to everyone,' the nurse said to Sofia: 'Why don't you take him to the bar on the corner?'

They crossed Avenida Pueyrredón, with Rimini up ahead, leaning over slightly as if to refuse any possible offer of help. He was already pushing open the door to the bar – one of those typical hospital cafés, with doctors grabbing a meal under a cruel white light – when Sofia suggested they went somewhere else. She knew a less sordid place not far away, she said, where at least they had tablecloths. 'We're already here,' Rimini protested. He was less interested in comfort than in easy solutions. They went in, and there was a brief pause while they decided where they should sit. Each of them had a table in mind – Sofia one with four chairs, recently cleaned and by the window; Rimini a table for two, on the way to the toilets, piled high with dirty cups and plates – and they both knew they were different. They looked at each other and shrugged non-committally, raising their hands and pointing into space, until Rimini (who was not really bothered anyway) gave in and went to sit near the window with her. He was starving, as though he had not eaten in days. A tall, weary waiter came over to take their order. He stopped by their table, and stood there silently, staring at something out of the window. Rimini chose a Super Pueyrredón, with gherkins and a fried egg, the last option on a long list of hot sand-wiches. 'Are you sure?' Sofia asked. Rimini stared out at the street. Sofia looked up at the waiter: 'Bring him a mixed toasted sandwich and a plain whisky. I'll have a hot milk with a drop of coffee in it.' As the waiter moved away, Rimini started to try to protest. 'Why . . . ?' he said. 'You'll see, you won't regret it,' Sofia butted in, 'I know what I'm saying.' A harsh, awkward silence descended on them, until Sofia stretched out an intrepid, sudden hand, waited for Rimini to carry out his typical defensive ritual of pushing back in his chair, then lean forward again, and then forced him to open his own hand, the one that he had hurt when he had fainted. 'What an idiot,' he said, while Sofia assessed the damage. He realised he had not asked a thing about how Victor was, and felt doubly ashamed. Sofia gave him a detailed report. So they talked for a while about Victor, but not for long, although they were surprisingly vehement about his situation, as though his case was neutral territory where they could show themselves more or less openly without feeling pressured or having to search for disturbing hidden meanings. The waiter brought their order. Rimini reached hungrily for his toasted sandwich. 'Have a drink first,' said Sofia, pushing the whisky towards him. Rimini hesitated. 'It'll help your blood pressure.' Rimini lifted the sandwich and brushed it against his mouth, so that when he put it down again a few crumbs were left stuck to his lips. He took a quick sip of whisky, as if he were getting a tiresome chore over with, and at almost the same time pushed a piece of toast into his mouth. As she watched him eat, her eyes started to sparkle. 'You're really handsome, aren't you?' she said, with a sad smile. 'I shouldn't be saying that: you've got someone who tells you it all the time. But I'll say it all the same: you're really handsome. That's the way it goes,' she sighed: 'We're separated, you've got a beautiful young girlfriend, you can't bear the sight of blood, we've got a friend who is ill, and you still have no idea where to sit in bars or what to order. And you're good-looking. A handsome rebel.' She put a hand on top of his. 'There's no reason for you to rebel, you know. I'm not going to do anything to you.' Rimini laughed, but felt awkward, unhappy with the role he had been given. Despite her purple nose, her nervous squint, her freshly combed hair, Sofia was performing with unshakeable authority, as if she knew it all by heart, whereas he took refuge in silence to hide his inadequacy. He stole a quick glance at her face, trying to avoid her reading anything significant in his gaze. The sparks in her eyes were as fixed as though they had been implanted in her pupils, but they gave him a clue as to the reason for their unequal roles. Sofia had a cause; he was a mere deserter. To her, the meeting in the hospital, the way Rimini had cut his hand, the bar, the inattentive waiter, the crumbs on his lips – it was all part of a plan. For him, everything was a string of unfortunate, possibly malevolent coincidences, as lacking in meaning as any chance occurrence, like a stray bullet that wounds a victorious soldier just as he is leaving the battlefield.

Rimini laughed again. 'Me, rebel?' he said. 'I don't rebel. Why do you say that?' 'You work so hard at it. You force yourself the whole time,' she replied, almost affectionately. 'Look, you force yourself not to call me, not to come and get your share of the photos, not to answer my messages, to leave me stranded at the Riltse exhibition. You never relax, Rimini. You have your hair cut short, because you know I don't like it like that. You sniff cocaine. You wear hoodies (by the way, they've invited the Witch to give a seminar at the university you've got on your chest). You go out with very young girls. (Javier told me she's terribly jealous, is that right?) You abandon the homeopath who cured your psoriasis . . .' Rimini wanted to look at her, but couldn't. He chased the crumbs around his plate, building them into tiny anthills. He shrugged. 'You're like a political militant. Isn't it too much? That's enough, don't fight it all the time,' said Sofia. 'Relax. You don't have to be changing your life *all* the time. Do whatever you want. And don't worry: nobody's going to force you to go back.' Rimini raised his head and fixed his eyes on the upper part of her cheeks, where the bruises from her operation had turned a pale yellow, like old paper. 'What?' she said, taken by surprise. She lifted a hand to her face. 'What's wrong? What a bastard, you didn't say a word. What do you think of it? It's all still . . . You can't see it properly . . . Once the swelling goes down . . . Yes, I had an operation. I did it. You moved out, I changed my nose. Do you think it looks all right?' 'Yes, I guess it does.' Rimini took another good look at her, this time without any ulterior motive. He recalled her original face and compared the two noses, trying to discover some difference. 'He's a special surgeon, one of a kind,' said Sofia, as if she had read his mind. Her hands were fluttering around her nostrils. 'He's a sworn enemy of the "snub-nose" industry. He says that there's a face for every nose, and a nose for every face. He says the best plastic surgeons (the real ones, not those butchers who treat faces like cars on an assembly line) work with that relationship. What do you reckon? Can you tell the difference? Because there *are* differences. Look here, look at this bit. You haven't noticed a thing. It'll take time, it's still quite . . . but say something, please. If you didn't know me, if you saw me for the first time today (well, not exactly like this, imagine that my face is OK, with all the swelling gone, without this yellow patch here) would you fall madly in love with me? Rimini half-opened his mouth, more out of amazement than any desire to respond. 'Just a joke, kid. A rhetorical question.' She laughed imperiously, like a queen pardoning a condemned man two seconds before his execution. Then she glanced at him out of the corner of her eye, emboldened by a rush of desire, and said: 'Although in fact, yes. You could reply. Would you fall in love with me all over again? You can lie if you like. But I'll know. You know how I am . . .' Rimini stuck his hand in his pocket, pulled out some notes and left them on the table. 'I have to go,' he said. He would have liked his voice to sound firm and solid – the voice of a very busy person who has generously donated a portion of his very valuable time but now, alerted by a secret alarm, suddenly realises he has to get back to his demanding routine – but instead it sounded tremulous, almost questioning. He had advanced cautiously into the sea, interspersing his strokes with regular glances back at the shore; but now he was out of his depth, and all he could see was the undulating surface of the water, the sea around him, and only far off in the distance, shimmering in the air, the dim outline of the by now unreachable coastline. 'What!' said Sofia. 'Suddenly you're in such a hurry.' Her mouth twisted in a bitter grin. 'Yes,' he said. He signalled to the waiter. 'Come on then: what do you have to do? What is it that's so important?' 'Nothing. Things,' said Rimini. He checked the bill, realised he did not have enough money, and started searching through his pockets. Sofia followed his movements with a compassionate scorn. 'You're like Cinderella. Is that why you left me? To clock in? To work nine to five?' 'Sofia, please . . .' he said, hauling out on to the table a set of keys, and old invoice from the French Institute Library (for Tchou's *Dictionnaire des injures*) on the back of which were scrawled lots of phone numbers, two cinema tickets, and an empty strip of aspirins, with each compartment hanging open like an eyelash: but there was no sign whatsoever of the money he needed, not a cent. The waiter came over. Rimini looked imploringly at him and plunged his hands into his pockets again: 'I'm sure somewhere I had . . .' 'I'll pay,' said Sofia. Then, still looking at Rimini but talking to the waiter, she said: 'But not yet. Bring me another milky coffee.' Rimini watched as the waiter's white back moved away from them, carrying with it his only hope of survival. 'Just another five minutes, that's all,' Sofia said. 'I'm worth another five minutes, aren't I?' 'Don't be silly,' he said, gazing around him as if in search of the emergency exit. All at once something in the atmosphere caught at him, filling him with a long-distant sense of grief. 'What's wrong?' said Sofia. 'Nothing,' he said. 'Nothing? You look as if you're about to cry, Rimini.' This mixture of smells – freshly ground coffee, air-freshener, perfume. Where had he smelled it before? He rubbed his eyes with his knuckles: when he opened them again, at first everything was black, then he saw a hail of silver needles, and finally Sofia's face. 'That smell. Can you smell it?' 'Yes,' she said. Rimini hesitated. He wanted at all costs to avoid confiding in her, but he calculated that if he offered her something personal, a modest but real part of his personal life, that would perhaps placate her. 'It's as though I've smelled it before,' he said. 'Aha. You've smelled it before,' said Sofia. The tone of her voice was so enigmatic that Rimini had to screw up his eyes to look at her. 'Are you joking?' she said. 'No. Why?' Sofia leaned forward, planting her elbows firmly on the table. 'Rimini: this is the bar we were in when your grand-mother died. We were sitting over there. Your father came over here from the hospital to tell you.' Unconvinced, Rimini looked all around him. He knew he would find nothing, and smiled half-heartedly. 'We hadn't slept all night,' Sofia said. She too began to smile: she was curling up in her memory like someone getting into a newly made bed with clean sheets. 'Well, you had,' she said, her voice trembling slightly, 'at one point you fell asleep on my shoulder. Over there, at that table. Then I put some chairs together for you and you stretched out with your head on my lap. Like a kid who goes out to eat with his parents and fall asleep in the restaurant.' Sofia stopped, looked at him. She was expecting something: she was expecting him to pick up the end of the ball of string she had thrown, and to carry on unrav-elling the scene. 'Nothing. I don't remember a thing,' he said. He looked down, feigning embarrassment, until he heard the waiter placing her coffee cup on the table, and only then did he risk looking back up at her, as if this china witness could guarantee him some kind of immu-nity. What he saw on Sofia's face was not so much incredulity as repu-diation, the kind of painful rejection that characterises those angelic creatures who, overnight and for no obvious reason – and while at the same time losing none of their normality, turn into completely inhuman beings. 'I see,' said Sofia. 'That's what moving on means for you. Everything you rub out is another step forward, isn't it? You wipe the slate clean. You get rid of anything that's no use to you any more. What's the point of so much baggage? It collects dust, takes up space, you're always having to tidy it up. Better just to jettison it. "Set your-self free". That's why you went for that girl, isn't it? She's young . . . She has no past (Vera's her name, isn't it? Vera. I like it). She's ideal. There's nothing behind you any more. Everything is in front of you.' She broke off; her rejection had become disappointment, that kind of melancholy that often accompanies objective verification of the truth. 'You see?' said Rimini. 'You see why it's so hard for me to meet you?'

'Yes, I see,' she said, softening. 'I never met anyone less alive in my life.' She pulled a crumpled bank-note out of her bag and dropped it next to her untouched cup. 'I don't know you,' she said, standing up. 'I feel sorry for you.'

CHAPTER 20

He heard nothing more from Sofia until that night in the restaurant, the night of his birthday, when Victor, whose lungs no longer bore any trace of the bacillus, and even less of healthy tissue, so far had the army of malign cells advanced in their attempt to colonise them, slipped him the note full of reproof for his insistence on celebrating his birthdays without her. This came as a relief for Rimini. As he read it, he could picture her just as she described herself, in her nightdress and slippers in the middle of the street, at that early hour of the morning that invites lunatics to perform their antics in public. Rather than horrify him, the image pleased him; it was cheerful, too picturesque to be true, too true to be cloying. She had stolen it from Fellini, or better still from Giulietta Masina, who for Sofia was, after Frida Breitenbach, the greatest authority on earth about emotional matters.

Then, some time later, he went to pay Victor a visit – Victor, who a relapse had confined to his home, his room, his tartan bedspread, and the company of some monosyllabic, furtive children who seemed always to have just had or to be about to have a shower – and Victor, like someone relieving himself of a weight he has carried for a long time, ordered him to go to the chest of drawers, get the present Sofia had promised him in the letter, and take it with him once and for all. Rimini found it straightaway – a long, thin package wrapped in expensive-looking foil. He weighed it in his hand slightly uneasily, then decided to open it in front of Victor, as if having a third person present would make the situation less compromising.

It was a pen: one of those black, elegant fountain pens that justified the existence of that pompous term 'stylographic' – the sort of pen that doctors used to use for writing on their prescription pads, disturbing the silence of their consulting-rooms at dusk with scratching sounds from another century that made Rimini shiver with joy. 'Well, well,' said Victor, impressed by the satisfied smile spreading across

Rimini's face as he stared at the gift. 'It looks as though this time Madame hit the target.' Rimini scowled at him, as if he were being insolent. In fact, he was frightened: he was only too aware of how Sofia could use that smile if Victor somehow let it slip, or even succumbed to the twisted pleasure of acting as a go-between. 'Sorry,' Victor said. 'Don't worry; it'll go no further than this room. She'll never find out about it. I'll tell her I never gave it you.' Rimini twirled the pen between his fingers. He was in ecstasy, but a simple ecstasy that had nothing to do with love. Stripped of the amorous impulses that should have invigorated them, Rimini discovered just how far moments like these demonstrated something which for Rimini only appeared to exist in a vague, metaphorical dimension: the idea that love, true love, love beyond all posing, had nothing whatsoever to do with effusion or sensibility, or the overwhelming nature of feelings, but everything to do with precision, economy, and that ancient and unjustly derided art known as marksmanship. Love does not enfold, thought Rimini: it wounds. It does not flood, it pierces. How did Sofia still manage to have such a good aim?

He unscrewed the top, brought the pen up to his eyes, and studied the nib, those two little metal feet protruding from the tip like a metal fingernail. What was the word for it: hitting the bullseye of an absent target? He turned the pen over to examine the dark region, hidden and exposed at the same time, through which the ink had to pass before flowing on to the paper, which Rimini remembered as being slightly rounded, like an insect's abdomen, dull when it was dry, but shining bright when there was ink in the reservoir. Then he put the nib gently against the pad of his index finger, so that when the ink came out it would follow the line of his fingerprint. Nothing appeared on his fingertip. He repeated the operation a couple of times, pressing harder and tilting the nib to one side. Still nothing. He studied the nib closely. It was still dry. He sensed that nobody had ever taken the trouble to fill it. Victor passed him the sports supplement from the newspaper, and he shook the pen over a photograph of two black players in green shirts who were intertwining their legs in an unlikely ballet. When nothing happened, he repeated the operation with more force, hitting the edge of his hand against the table. 'Perhaps it's not loaded,' Victor suggested. It was such an obvious possibility, and it was so incredible that Rimini had not even paused to consider it, that he rejected it out of hand. And yet he held the pen closer to the light, and began to unscrew the barrel. The slender golden ring that separated the two halves of the pen was left dangling from the rubber reservoir. A vague suspicion flitted through Rimini's mind. He put the pen down on the newspaper, and bent over the ring, moving it more and more slowly as his suspicion was confirmed. Then he saw the letter. He saw the tiny *R* engraved in the gold metal, and sensed the floor moving beneath his feet. He felt for support; without moving from his bed, Victor pushed a chair towards him. 'What's wrong?' he asked. 'She got them to engrave my initial on it,' said Rimini, passing him the pen. 'She's out of her mind.' 'Where?' 'Take a look at the gold ring.' Victor brought the pen up close to his eyes, then all of a sudden held it at arm's length. 'I need glasses. Urgently. What initial? Are you sure?' 'What am I going to do?' said Rimini. It was not exactly a question, more one of those deep, private sighs of despair that often precede theatre monologues, when the main character, alone in the centre of the stage, reviews out loud all the dramatic events that have happened to him. 'Give it back to her? If I keep it, it means I accept everything. The pen is the least of it. I accept the idea of presents; I accept as natural the possibility that, even being apart, we give each other special gifts, just as if we were together. I accept not only the effort and devotion she put into finding the pen – which incidentally I adore, as she well knows, even though I've slightly distanced myself from that kind of thing these days – but with it all the meaning she put into having my initial engraved on it. I accept everything that there should be between us to make a gift of this sort something perfectly normal, rather than what it really is, a completely misplaced gesture from someone who is deceiving herself, allowing herself to be carried away by some delirious fantasy, or is quite simply crazy.' 'Do me a favour,' said Victor, 'pass me the top.' Rimini handed it to him. It was all very quick, like a background move- ment. 'But if I refuse to accept it,' Rimini went on, 'if I respond to so much with so little, refusing to join in – doesn't that mean I'm making things worse?'

'It's the make of the pen,' said Victor. There was an abrupt silence, as though the air had been split by a crack. Victor handed him back the pen. 'It's the R from Reform, the make of the pen.' Rimini took the top reluctantly. 'Look, it's on the clip too. The same R.' Rimini recognised the capital letter – so pompous, so offended at being given so little space on the clip – and the other five letters in flowing but discreet lower case. He felt something collapsing inside him and smashing against a smooth, crystalline surface far below, like a coin hitting the bottom of a well. Then, like a window being blown open by a gust of wind, Rimini saw the original scene in which that R and that make, Reform, had burst into his life, and got some idea of just how great a mistake he had made that evening, in Vienna train station, when Sofia, desperate to make up for the time and kilos that her bout of flu had cost her, came to a halt on the platform (just as Rimini was trying to load their luggage into their compartment) and insisted he stop everything to look at her, and accept the black velvet box containing the present she had bought for him two days earlier in the pen, pipe and tobacco shop at their hotel. He saw the scene a second time: he saw a younger version of himself, with long, straight hair, pale skin and lips puffy from the cold, opening the box (a luxury miniature coffin) and finding the Reform nestling in the centre of a red bed, held in the middle by a black plastic band, and thinking – thinking and, compulsive collector that he was, saving the thought as he was thinking it – that whatever happened, whether they were together a thousand years, ten, or only a single day, he would never forget that moment for the rest of his life.

But he had forgotten it, and now that he had the same pen in his hands, like one of those objects which in fairy stories go through a whole series of challenges before returning, identical but full of experience, to their original owner, Rimini, staring at it in amazement and fear, understood to what extent the unforgettable nature of things, or that interconnected tangle of facts, people, things, place and time that we call a moment, arises far less from the things themselves, is far less to do with the way that things relate to us, become part of us, affect us, than is the result of a wish to preserve something, a wish that even as it is being formulated, knows it is in danger of failure. We say something will be unforgettable not merely to reinforce (converting it already into part of the past) the intensity with which we are experiencing it here and now, but above all to protect it, to guard it with the jealousy and care we feel are necessary, with the aim of ensuring that some time in the future, when neither the world nor we are the same, this fragment of experience will still be there, waiting for us, demonstrating that there is at least *one* thing capable of resisting everything. But there was nothing that could not be forgotten. There is no immunity against forgetting. Rimini looked again at this little vertical, armless body, dressed in mourning. If he could look at it for two more minutes like that, he would no longer recognise it. How could Sofia have given him the same thing twice? And how could she give him something that was already his? 'I wouldn't take it too seriously,' Victor interrupted, 'She's got a boyfriend.' Rimini stared at him as though dazzled. 'Sofia,' Victor repeated. 'She's got a boyfriend. He's called Cyril or something like that, some name like a pervert out of a seventies' film. The sort of role that was perfect for Pierre Clementi. A percussionist, I think. German. He lives in Hamburg. Which is where Sofia must be at this very moment. She's away on a trip; didn't you know? It seems they met at one of those seminars she gives with that Witch Breitenbach.'

Rimini sighed. It was as if someone had waved a magic wand and emptied a room cluttered with furniture. He filled the Reform with black ink and kept it, nib downwards (a sign that he intended to use it) with the other pens in his collection. But he never used it. He came across it a couple of times when he was choosing another one, but always regarded it indifferently. Then one day when he was determined to sort out his study – which he had set up in the maid's room – he picked up the mug where he kept his pens and gave them a routine inspection. The Reform did what it could: it had a surprising debut – the line it made was so thick and fluid it seemed as if it had been used only ten minutes earlier – but the nib quickly ran out of ink, stumbled, tried to come back to life (the attempt lasted barely enough for Rimini to write half his name) then fought with the paper and fell silent for ever. Rimini tied the failed pens with an elastic band – there were six altogether, all of them funereal relics – and the Reform had to endure being transported squashed between a Pelikan whose top did not screw on properly and a Tintenkuli whose point had been bent after being dropped, so that it was shaped like a question mark – and threw them in the waste-paper basket. He did not feel a thing. It was not a moral act, but a hygienic one. For months now, he had been doing fewer and fewer written translations (books, articles, documents);

they had been replaced by an increasing number of calls for him to do simultaneous translation. Worried by a transition he had not envisaged, Rimini had begun to feel he possessed too many useless things. The most flagrant proof of this was his desk. The quantity of different papers, the welter of fasteners and clips, the wide variety of folders, from the classic ones with hard black covers and big rings inside that snapped shut with a terrifying clunk, to the most up-to-date transparent, lightweight sort, the range of pens, pencils, propelling pencils (the only thing he would use to underline the translations he had to do) and marker pens: all these tokens of an opulence that used to comfort him, tokens he considered essential to enable him to carry out his work, had begun to lose importance and to gather weight, with the result that what he had always seen as welcoming surroundings now looked to him like a baroque landscape, full of unnecessary objects, one it was difficult to move around in without causing a tragic accident: spilling ink on a freshly typed sheet of paper, creasing twenty pages he had to hand in half an hour later with his elbow, dropping a pencil box full of loaded pens on to the floor.

He got rid of it all in an afternoon. Vera found him half-naked and wearing sandals, like a Roman gladiator, going up and down the steep staircase that led to his study, carrying cardboard boxes and big refuse bags that the sharp corners of the folders, the tip of a ruler, or the point of a biro were threatening to tear open at any moment. He was coming and going without stopping, with that frenzied determination of someone afraid that any hesitation might lead them to change their mind about the whole thing. Sensitive like any 'jealopath' person to the slightest need Rimini showed to throw things away, Vera joined in without a word. She helped him carry the bags down the three flights of stairs, and only wavered out in the street, where Rimini, who had gone back up to get the last load, had just left the bag with the pens in it, and she saw the tiny hole that the Reform, from its prison inside, had dug through the polythene skin.

CHAPTER 21

Poussière was arriving the following week. In between, like a preventive balm, they had a long weekend. Anticipating that the linguist's visit would completely take Rimini over, they decided to make the most of these three empty days to get away from it all in the house Vera's parents had in Valeria del Mar. They travelled on the night bus, curled up against each other, rejoicing in the Arctic cold of the bus, and feeling privileged to be eating dried-out *alfajores* and the watery but scalding coffee that a spluttering machine served intermittently (Rimini tenderly kissed the pink blisters that the brew caused on the back of her hand), the rough, too-short blankets that the auxiliary driver had handed out to the passengers a few minutes before the lights were switched off in a ceremony that smacked somehow of prisons. On the point of falling asleep, Rimini, who had the aisle seat, stared at the empty road ahead, heard the hum of the engine, saw two rows in front of them a foot with a shoe that was about to fall off, then smelled the different odours in the coach: musty carpet, wafts of piss, a mixture of tobacco and cheap perfumes, pine air-freshener, and in all this had not merely the impression but the evidence that love truly did wield an extraordinary alchemy, the only force capable of transforming the poverty of this world into sublime luxury. He fell asleep, rocked by Vera's purring against his neck.

A short time later, he was jerked awake by a sudden feeling of danger. He opened his eyes, and was blinded by a dazzling white light. He almost shouted out loud, but the flood of light seemed to become more concentrated and clearer, gradually splitting into the two parallel beams of another bus coming in the opposite direction. Then everything went dark again. On the TV screen suspended from the roof, a fat comedian, dressed in a fake doctor's coat, was trying to give some sort of injection to a redhead who was rushing about a small consulting-room with shaky walls in her bra and panties. Rimini did not know if he was dreaming, but the image aroused him. He turned to clutch Vera, who was sleeping facing away from him, and began to rub himself very gently against her, following the swaying of the bus, until he came. It was an inoffensive ejaculation, which sleep soon drew a veil over. Rimini could only really enjoy it the next day when he remembered what had happened, and throughout the weekend, during the half a dozen times they made love – always in a different part of the house, based on a partly athletic and partly touristic programme of activities of which Vera was inordinately proud.

Strictly speaking, that was all they did, apart from using the terrace to play racket-ball tournaments (they were much more than games) which left Rimini completely exhausted, not so much because of the way she fought over every point, but because of the number of times he had to go up and down the pine cone-covered bank that linked the house to a nearby wood, which was where the balls always seemed to end up. Apart from that, they walked barefoot along earthen paths, stuffed themselves with chocolates in a tea-room straight out of Hansel and Gretel run by a couple of bossy Hungarian women, and in the evening ate barbecues at a restaurant that had walls of clear plastic and bored waiters dressed up as *gauchos* who after eleven at night swapped their trays for whips and *bolas* and converted the restaurant into a passionate theatre of folkloric prowess. It was three days of crazy, unalloyed physical joy, Siamese happiness. So much so that once or twice, astonished at finding himself alone, Rimini insisted almost perversely in trying to find the cracks that his sense of complete well-being probably prevented him from seeing. He wanted to be disappointed. Yet everything he discovered was impeccably clear, like one of those bright-blue skies that last an entire day and seem so invulnerable they could go on for ever. Nothing could harm them. They were protected even from foreboding.

Rimini did not even react when Vera had to sign a credit card bill and casually got out the Reform pen he had thrown away a few days earlier; not only that, but to his astonishment and dismay, got it to work perfectly. 'I felt sorry for it, so I kept it,' she said, smiling so that he would forgive her. 'You're not upset, are you?' No, he wasn't upset. Nothing could upset him. The world was far, far away, and Rimini felt as if he were invisible. He would have given anything to be able to avoid the misfortune, pain, and disenchantment he knew were lurking in some secret compartment of his destiny. He felt he would never be so strong, so capable of facing up to them as now. He wanted to take advantage of the moment. If he did not do so, it was because by nature happiness is against all administrative concerns. Joy means losing, using, throwing away – and weariness.

Rimini had never known his legs to feel as tired as they did when he got on board the bus back. This was not due simply to his walks on the beach, the hard-fought battles on the terrace, nor even the strange, uncomfortable but stimulating gymnastic challenges he had found himself put through when they made love out in the open on a couple of occasions. It was a weariness that came from his happiness being so pure, so smooth, so homogeneous – the weariness not of swimming in, but of floating in, an element that is always the same. As a result, he got on board the bus and was asleep even before it had pulled off – his only lack of courtesy in what until then had been a perfect display of manners. The very next thing he felt was the bus braking sharply, followed by two or three further short and smaller jolts like aftershocks, until the bus came to a complete halt and, with a noisy sigh, seemed to settle on the ground, as if all its tyres had gone flat at the same time.

As the ceiling lights went on, Rimini peered over the back of the seat in front and saw the outline of the driver standing up and stretching. Rimini took in the images more quickly than the sounds. The spare driver was standing in the middle of the aisle, hands up on the luggage racks, but his words only reached Rimini a few seconds later, muffled as though wrapped in cotton-wool, by which time the man was already doing up his jacket and venturing out into the early morning cold. The door was open, but he only heard the lengthy sigh it gave on opening when the shadows of the other passengers were already starting to move in their seats. Everything seemed hostile: the bright lights, the icy draughts that cut through the stale air in the bus, the noises from outside that flashed like sparks across the cosy background of sleep. And yet how pleasing was the sharp, brusque way in which these demands – stopping, switching the lights on, waking up, standing up, getting off the bus – tore the cocoon of rest, how exciting it was to be forced awake in the middle of the night, in a deserted café on a deserted road . . . Rimini watched the first passengers file slowly off the bus, as though dragging the chains of sleep with them; he turned to Vera and gently shook her.

They sat at a table at the back of the café, the furthest from the door but close to the drivers, who were already attacking two huge French bread sandwiches, and to a table where an elderly woman with an old fur coat across her shoulders was busy tearing a pastry into bits for the little girl sitting opposite, who was studying her fingers with the rapt attention of a sleepwalker. They ordered coffee and croissants. Using one of Rimini's arms as a pillow, Vera lay her head on the table. She yawned – it was more like singing than yawning – then launched into an account of a dream that was so full of adventures and misunderstandings it sounded made-up. And whilst a younger, paler version of herself, half her face disfigured by a red birthmark – one of the many demonstrations of imperfection with which in her dreams she tried to minimise her beauty – was coming down a spiral staircase holding the hem of her nightdress in one hand, worried about being in time for one of those appointments dreams torture us with, Rimini, who was stroking her head, lost track of what she was saying and surveyed the whole café with one of those superficial glances that are typical of people who have just woken up and know they will soon be asleep again. He took in the stand selling *alfajores*, the one with books (where a slim, blood-red novel poked its head daringly above the metal frame), the newspaper stand where the previous day's papers lay unwanted; he passed over the irregular shapes of his fellow passengers' heads, and as his gaze was returning along the chequer-board pattern of the floor to their own table, at precisely the moment when in her dream Vera, who had forgotten something essential, was climbing back up the staircase while a phone rang somewhere far off in the castle, Rimini's eyes found an enormous, serious-looking face blocking his view. The size was due to it being so close: the little girl was standing beside him. There was a black sugar moustache on her top lip: she was offering him a bit of her pastry. Rimini accepted with a smile. The girl stood staring at him without moving, almost without blinking, as if she wanted to make sure that Rimini was not going to refuse her gift, and only agreed to return to her own table, dragging a small pillow behind her, once she had seen him put it into his mouth and start chewing it. Seeing that her grandmother was looking elsewhere, she stole another piece from her plate and, not lifting her orthopaedic shoes from the floor as she shuffled back across to Rimini, offered him that as well. 'Thank you,' he said. The little girl was blonde, with a rash on both cheeks, and a general air of being uncared for, as if she had been wearing the same clothes for several days. 'Eat,' she ordered him. Her voice was extraordinarily deep and seemed to come from somewhere else, as if someone in the distance were speaking through her. Rimini started chewing on the bit of pastry. 'It's very good,' he said, exaggerating his jaw movements. As he watched her walk off again, walking like a broken doll and dragging along her pillow-talisman, which swept up everything in its way on the floor, his eyes filled with tears. The girl picked up another piece of her pastry, turned again, agreed with her tautological grandmother without even looking at her: 'Are you giving that gentleman something to eat?' and headed back towards Rimini's table with outstretched arm, and looking him straight in the face. Rimini smiled at her, but began to feel slightly awkward, as if something in the scene was not entirely genuine, had been rehearsed or was being performed for someone, an invisible eye secretly watching them. The girl put the last piece of pastry on his plate, then stood there quite still, looking first at him, then at the plate, then back at him. All of a sudden, like a wilting flower, her mouth crumpled into an inconsolable pout. This was the last piece: she had realised it was the end of their game. Moved by her despair, Rimini was about to play his part when a fork – flashing down like a streak of lightning – stabbed the piece of pastry on the plate five centimetres from his hand, in exactly the spot where the little girl's grubby fingers had ventured a few seconds earlier. It was as though a second, deep and sinister silence had been created within the silent atmosphere of the café. Rimini turned towards Vera and saw her brandishing the fork in a trembling hand. 'What else,' she hissed. 'Why don't you just go right ahead and lick her cunt?' Her face was white as a sheet; her eyes glowed red; Rimini thought he could hear the chomp of her jaws, see the flecks of foam at the corner of her lips. It was all over in a matter of seconds. Suddenly, as if the same energumen that had put the fork in her hand had now given the order to retreat, she stood up, left the table – banging her hip against a corner as she did so – walked across the whole room, slammed the door behind her, and disappeared on board the bus, where she began a silent strike that she kept up for the next forty-eight hours.

CHAPTER 22

It was intolerable. And yet . . . Rimini devoted the two days of distance between them – and the following five, when, newly reconciled, the obligations that Poussière's arrival placed him under began to separate him from Vera – to thinking almost exclusively about that *and yet*. Perhaps that was where the secret of the force of her jealousy was to be found. That absolute flash point, which reduced him to stupefaction and literally flayed her alive: was it not also the greatest proof of love that Vera could offer him? Perhaps due to a professional quirk, made more acute by the marathon he was soon to be caught up in with the arrival of the Belgian linguist, Rimini had a tendency to think of jealousy as an arbitrary but implacable machine which specialised in translating the diaphanous language of love into a nightmarish slang: love flowed freely until it came across some impurity, the impurity created an obstacle, the obstacle created a blockage, the flow of love slowed to a trickle, until all at once positive became negative, and Rimini, who a minute before had been the embodiment of a promising prospective father, became a shameless, savage paedophile.

What could he do? He had tried everything. An emotional conservative deep down, like all monogamists Rimini took literally the platitude Vera used to try to justify her attacks of rage: 'Put yourself in my place!' and had tried to see himself and the rest of the world through the eyes of jealousy. He did not doubt himself; there was nothing that could spoil his belief in this unique love. But the world, that unending murmur which this unique love saved him from, slowly began to make itself felt, to fill with intention and send him messages. Rimini began to feel unprotected, out in the elements, like a weaponless soldier on a battlefield, and so had no option but to turn to the first thing that came to hand: suspiciousness. He listened, mistrusted, learnt to read between the lines. He discovered the voluptuous mechanics of interpreting and deduction. An alleged executioner, he embraced the cause of jealousy more fervently than the proven victim Vera could ever manage. He developed a prodigious imagination. He began to believe he could detect in everything the presence of desire lying in ambush – as if the innocuous froth of everyday life was continuously hatching imperceptible, bubbling passions that were linked by a single common denominator: that of making him, Rimini, their object.

Why were women interested in him all of sudden? The phrase 'married but not castrated' came into his mind. He had heard it ages before in a garden in Temperley, spoken by a study group colleague, a tall, knock-kneed fellow with a beard and abnormally small hands, who, after boasting about the exciting parallel lives he experimented with in the margins of his marriage, asked him somewhat bitterly why he had not brought Sofia to the barbecue. In Rimini's case though, it was quite the opposite. If women were suddenly beginning to notice him, it was precisely because Rimini was a lost cause for them. By forcing his withdrawal from the love market, Vera had added to his prestige, had increased his value, made him a collector's item. (This is every jealopath's nightmare: they kidnap the object of their love and remove them from the world, but then in the solitude of their imprisonment, like a demented collector they beautify them with a taxidermist's dedication and patience, so that finally, when the job is done and the love-object is at last the dazzling, perfect doll the jealopath always wanted them to be, that love-object brushes his teeth, ties his shoe-laces, finishes his cup of coffee, gives the jealopath a kiss and then, leaving them aghast, goes out into the world handsome, irresistible, and rejuvenated, as if all the devotion, the maniacal care and everything else that the jealopath trusted would make them their exclusive property was in fact merely the guarantee that soon, very soon, they will lose them.) No sooner did Rimini detect any hint of desire from a woman, any woman, someone he would probably never see again in his life, than he fled, fled like a criminal in the midst of a crowd, or like an explorer who even after he has safely left the jungle continues to slash wildly at the air with a machete. When he got back, as white as a ghost, to Vera, to her trembling arms he was overcome with an immense joy: the joy of being a soldier of love.

A second phase followed: that of transforming all the world's snares into innocent coincidences. Relieved, Rimini stopped being suspicious of everything and fell into the role of a drowsy spectator, watching a firework display without really seeing it. The world was still full of evil intentions, and he was still their preferred target, but he no longer cared. The epic period of siege and resistance was over. He discovered he no longer needed all his obstinacy or his sense of sacrifice to be sure that his love was safe. He was a veteran of wars he had never fought. And so for the first time in his life, floating in this limbo of indifference, in the same way that an invalid dreams of doing what life will no longer permit him to do, Rimini allowed himself the luxury of dreaming (*only* of dreaming) of the delights of a secret adventure, instigated by one of the many insinuations he had previously spent his life avoiding and which he now regarded with scorn: a woman who approached too close to speak to him; another one he surprised staring at him from afar; another who asked him for a light and, when he held out the lighter, rested her hand on his for a little longer than necessary; a trivial conversation which suddenly, like an aeroplane losing height, entered a zone of turbulent intimacy; then there was his zodiac sign, his name, the title of a favourite film or book – all these childish coincidences that appeared out of nowhere and threatened to attach him without warning to the life of the stranger to whom he had just been introduced.

CHAPTER 23

Jeremy Riltse killed himself in London early one morning in 1995. He first shot Gombrich in the bath-tub, with a bullet to the head. Then he pressed the barrel of the revolver just below his left nipple and fired. Although he died on the spot, the bullet only reached his heart after zigzagging, bouncing off a couple of bones, changing direction, losing itself on inexplicable detours. He was seventy-eight years old and had no heirs. Apart from a few small health problems – psoriasis, rheumatoid arthritis, vertigo: the consequences of infections he had got as result of his Sick Art experiments – there was nothing in his medical history that could offer a convincing explanation for his decision. The nomadic years were behind, far behind him, in that remote province cut off not so much by time as by repentance, the vague noises from which are only of interest to biographers or blackmailers. He lived with his dog. He went out only rarely. Now that he finally accepted his fame, he was in that bourgeois phase when artists claim the right not to have to move and, like gurus, simply receive – except that Riltse, who had never bothered to repair his door-bell, did not even do that. Every so often he cooked partridges, his speciality, for a handful of friends. Riltse had their phone numbers; they did not have his. After Pierre-Gilles (alias Albert Alley, alias Bart Bold, alias Chris Caistor . . .) who, following their break-up and the famous self-castration, had continued to pursue him until a court order managed to restrain him, with far from happy results for his mental equilibrium, Riltse had never again known what he himself termed 'the horror of love'. A few protégés, usually young and poor – whom he recruited at the gates of army barracks, on building sites or in the personal section of the newspapers, and then used as models for his paintings, where they appeared disfigured in ridiculous bestial guises – brightened up his life with quick erotic services (Riltse hated things to last too long) and with robberies he himself planned in a state of immense excitement, devising ways to make sure the latest rent-boy got a good view of the bundle of notes, the piece of jewellery, the silver cigarette-case or bottle of Pomérol that he was dying to sacrifice. These sporadic moments of satisfaction never caused him any problems: on the contrary, they are perhaps the source of the most important works of his later years; the most important, though not necessarily the best. Because if there is something for which contemporary art has to thank Zookitsch (as the last part of his career is known), it is not masterpieces – for contemporary art, the maestro was already dead and buried after Sick Art – but the annihilation of taste as one of the variables of artistic perception.

At his biological death which, following the initial commotion, came to be assimilated into the Riltse legend with a curious ease, as though any other way of dying would have been highly incongruous, there were no irregular transfers from his bank accounts or his estate, and nothing in the spot where he was found (the old, three-storey house in Notting Hill, built in brick and with a walled rear garden, the same garden where he found himself trapped one New Year's Eve – a sudden gust of wind had slammed the house door shut, and there was no handle on the outside – he was wearing only a t-shirt and the mustard-coloured short-sleeved cardigan he could not bear to be parted from – he had twelve exactly the same – and grew colder and colder while in neighbouring houses people were slicing turkey or opening bottles of fizz, until he managed to use a climbing shrub as a ladder, scaled the high wall and escaped), nothing led the police to suspect that the suicide might have been anything other than his own personal decision. There were no fingerprints, apart from those of the Indian maid, but she left them after she had found the body; none of the windows were broken, and no door had been forced. There were no threatening messages on any answering-machine – Riltse had sworn he would never allow that kind of thing into his house – no second cups of coffee still steaming, or half-smoked cigarettes apart from those Riltse himself smoked; no signs of violence hastily concealed, no clues that might suggest a dark motive, a threatening presence, any outside criminal intervention.

At the bottom of the kitchen waste-bin, between a frozen pizza box and an old volume of the London telephone directory, they found a large pile of letters, all still with their envelopes, wrapped in a rubbish bag. The letters were grouped in individual bundles, each with a label on it. There was no obvious system to the categories: 'Hotels' said one label; 'Prepositions', said another; 'Blacks' was written on a third; a fourth stated: 'Organs'. One of the bundles – the first to be put up for sale, and the only one not to find a buyer – said 'Argentina'. The three letters in it were signed by the director of the Museo de Bellas Artes de Buenos Aires, and two of them had been written on the museum's headed notepaper. The first, sent soon after Riltse had begun legal proceedings against the Argentine state, the museum, and the director himself for damage that a host of leaks had caused to his work during the first three days of his exhibition in Buenos Aires, was full of apologies, excuses – out of the forty lines of writing, twenty were devoted to a weather forecast that predicted the storm on that day, but put it in the far north-west of the country – and promised all kinds of compensation (although the English the letter was written in made them sound like threats) if the artist reversed his decision. The second arrived a week later, after the museum director had personally tried to convince Riltse of the benefits of accepting the offer made in the first one. Riltse apparently never agreed to meet him. All he did was study him out of a second-floor window while the Argentine director stood guard on the railings outside. 'You should see him,' the painter told a friend he was speaking to on the phone: 'He's been there two days. I think he even camped out there all night. He doesn't even want me to withdraw charges now, all he wants is to meet me! I think it's the same fathead who Rolandine mentions in passing in the diary of his pathetic nocturnal wanderings!' In the letter, written this time in Spanish, the museum director had adopted a different strategy: he offered personally ('the lamb of Art', he called himself) to pay for the damage caused. He had a mansion in Punta del Este, the best collection of Tehuelche rugs in the world, and a seventeen-year-old daughter who was a model in the Ford agency. The third letter arrived two months later, by which time the director was on sick leave in Ascochinga, Córdoba province, leave granted him by a board of psychiatrists following a confused episode when he barricaded himself in his office and resisted all attempts to dislodge him. As jerky as an electrocardiogram, it was handwritten on the stained backs ('*mate* tea' according to one of Riltse's protégés, who had rudimentary Spanish thanks to spending two seasons as the star ice-skater in *Holiday On Ice* in Buenos Aires) of the museum's newsletters. Riltse hesitated: should he throw it out or donate it? The chief archivist in the London Hospital for Nervous Diseases would appreciate it. It was not even a proper letter. In a dozen disgusting pages, after announcing an 'essay on Riltse's World', that 'ashen monster' had flung together without the slightest logic all kinds of insults and obscenities, the typical ravings that those who are 'speaking in tongues' find it obligatory to write, with a string of judgements about his work, all of them less enthusiastic than Riltse might have expected, and all copied from an old Tate Gallery catalogue for a Lucian Freud exhibition.

In addition to interrupting an early morning session of ablutions – Riltse's face was only half-shaved when they discovered him, and his toothbrush was dry – the fatal bullet left the painting he was working on unfinished. This was *Icy Silence*, a calm, monumental work (six metres by three) in which, to judge by the pencil sketches found later, the painter was intending to portray a picturesque canine gang-bang in which the lead role was taken by Gombrich, his faithful Weimaraner puppy.

CHAPTER 24

Rimini studied the card, the horizontal rose, the small white plaque. 'Riltse,' he read. Read it and thought it, with that slight delay that thought takes when it is also trying to remember. Then he said the word out loud a couple of times, as though to prove to himself he still knew how to pronounce it. But when the body remembers, it is not like memory: its desire to forget is a hundred times stronger. Rimini – or rather his tongue, annoyed at this childish challenge that Rimini was setting him – gathered speed, launched itself across the 'I', stumbled on the three consonants in the middle, went back, tried again, failed, charged wildly at them, and was repulsed. This stumble brought a smile to his face. As he looked for somewhere to hide the card, Rimini wondered if there was anything else from the past that his body, not him, would refuse to accept. *Riltse.* He spelled it out silently, with all the astonishment and tenderness of an adult peering at the fragile marvels that enchanted his youth. He felt overtaken by a strange sense of cruelty. If he could have laid his hands on his adolescence, he would have smashed it to smithereens. He surveyed everything with the detached calm of a surgeon looking at the vital organ he has to remove; and yet at the same time, he could not help laughing. It was so obvious to him now that the mystery of Riltse did not lie in his paintings – he tried to remember some of them, but the only image he could summon was of the horizontal rose and the commemorative plaque – but in the foreign sound of those three consonants together. *Riltse.* His diction was improving.

But Riltse was dead, and Rimini sensed something in his mouth, something bitter like a split lemon pip; he thought he was going to retch. Wasn't he already dead? He let his eyes drift and once again saw the yellowish stain that Sofia's hair had left on the photo. He thought of vaguely supernatural things: apparitions, the holy shroud, cataleptics, a woman on an island walking barefoot at night under a full moon, following the sound of distant drums. Could you come back dead from the dead? He heard footsteps on the stairs, the sound of Vera singing and her steps dancing to the rhythm, so he slipped Sofia's card in between the pages of the Petit Robert on the coffee table in the living-room, next to the original of Poussière's opening lecture. His heart in his mouth, he closed the dictionary just as Vera's key was scraping in the lock. Nothing to be worried about, he thought. If the card had just arrived and was with him, Sofia, who had sent it, must be far away.

PART TWO

CHAPTER 1

In the interpreters' booth, while Rimini was mopping his face with the handkerchief Carmen had just put in his hand, he heard Poussière spit the final words of a long sentence full of incidental clauses and invisible italics and, pressing the headphones against his ears, muttered to himself the simultaneous translator's mantra: 'Please let him repeat the sentence. Please let him repeat the sentence.' But Poussière was completely self-absorbed and did not repeat a word, so Rimini translated from memory, badly, and waited for the next sentence, head down and eyes shut, as though he were gathering himself to face a catastrophe. Then Poussière suddenly fell silent: not only did he stop speaking, but he seemed to impose silence on all the sounds in the theatre and the world outside. It may only have been an interruption, one of those pauses that Rimini was usually grateful for, like a welcome truce, and used to catch his breath or look ahead. The stage was down below him; he needed only to glance through the cabin window to see it, and yet he did not have the nerve. He was frightened. Saying nothing was the most threatening sort of silence; especially when it cut short the kind of vertiginous monologue that Poussière had been engaged in for more than forty minutes now, each sentence snapping at the heels of the previous one. No, Rimini told himself, this was not a respite, it was an accident. Someone was falling into that well. He steeled himself, looked up, and saw Poussière sitting there, motionless, leaning forward slightly over his sheets of paper. Rimini looked beyond him, his eyes coming to a halt on the water-jug next to the microphone. This was the fourth time Poussière had given a public lecture during the week, but the first when he had reached the mid-way point in his talk without touching it.

It was a glass jug, with a thin, curved neck like a swan's. Poussière took it everywhere with him. It was the first thing he searched for in his suitcase when he had got to his hotel room an hour after landing in Buenos Aires. In order to stay awake, Rimini tried to keep a banal conversation going: details of the flight, the polyglot attempts to show off by the immigration official when he read 'Linguist' on the entry card, the advert for female underwear that Poussière tried to keep looking at even though it gave him a crick in the neck, the secrets of the Rio de la Plata climate – but Poussière simply turned his back on him, opened his case and plunged his hands down past several layers of shirts and pullovers (he was as suspicious of South American summers as he was of any hint of local colour) until, reaching the bottom, he started casting about desperately, disrupting the careful arrangement in which his luggage had crossed the ocean. When he pulled out his hands a few seconds later, they were triumphantly holding a pre-packed parcel. 'I wrap it myself. I don't trust those people at airports,' said Poussière, starting to open the package, ripping off the tape and tearing the outside layer of brown paper. When he reached the second layer, of tissue paper this time, he became calmer, his gestures more delicate. He slowly unwrapped the jug, removing every piece of paper with his fingertips and laying it carefully beside him on the bed before moving on to the next one. As he laid out each sheet he breathed in cautiously, as though he were disposing of a bomb. Rimini felt a sudden flush, and caught sight of his red face in the mirror. The scene was too intimate for his prying eyes; he should leave him on his own. If he did not do so, but stood there half a metre from the bed trying hard not to look as Poussière finished unwrapping his treasure, it was partly out of curiosity, but partly also out of politeness: after all, of the four members of the welcome committee (that traitor Carmen among them) Rimini was the only one who had kept his word and turned up at the airport. Poussière removed the last sheets of tissue. The paper stuck to the glass for one final moment, as though sad to be saying goodbye. Poussière smiled as he admired this effect of statics; Rimini stared with almost open-mouthed disappointment at the jug. 'It's a professional failing,' the linguist shouted from the bathroom as he turned on the tap to rinse it out: 'when I speak in public, my throat goes dry.'

The silence was so intense it changed the quality of the air all around. Carmen was trying not to breathe. Slowly, Rimini looked again at the lecturer. It was him, it was still Poussière, but there was something artificial about the way he sat there rigidly, something about the tension of his body that was lasting too long. His buttocks dangled over the side of his chair, as if he had been petrified by a sudden lava flow just as he was about to leap into the front rows of the audience. The only things that still connected him to the world were his hand, still clutching the base of the microphone, and his eyes, which were staring wildly at something in the middle of the lecture hall. 'A heart attack,' thought Rimini. 'He's going to keel over in the middle of his talk.' He turned to Carmen and was horrified to see the same glassy stare he had just noticed in the lecturer, as if they had both been frozen at the same moment by a magic spell. Rimini hesitated with his hand in mid-air, only centimetres from Carmen's bare shoulder (a shoulder tanned by the sun, with a slender white line dividing it into two coppery halves); he felt suddenly lost, as if this detail had caught him in a moment of weakness; he tried to take his hand back and searched in the darkness for an imaginary handrail – but he slipped or stumbled on something, and all at once found himself on a breakneck journey to the secret centre of Carmen's shoulder. Was that a strap-mark? An old scar polished by time? A Japanese brush-stroke? The track that an army of ants traces on the bark of a tree? He shuddered. And then Poussière, the stricken Poussière, the whole host of colleagues and disciples filling the hall, and the unbearable heat, the university theatre with its worn stage curtains and creaking seats – all of it silently burst into flames, and became focussed on one point, one single brilliant particle rushing away into the distance at the speed of light until it hung there in the dark depths of space, vulnerable but twinkling, like the dot which lasts for a second on a television screen after it has been turned off. Everything had disappeared – everything except for Carmen's shoulder and her nonchalant white mark.

CHAPTER 2

As so often happens when people fall in love, concentrating in a second
a process of erosion that has been going on for days or even years,
Rimini was doubly shaken: everything seemed to him speeded-up and
yet in slow motion at the same time. If falling in love is a chance
collapse, an event brought on by time and space like a traffic accident, the exact moment and place where it occurs depending on coincidence and never the will of its participants, then Rimini felt he
had been unpunctual with Carmen: he had arrived too early, and yet
also too late. He thought over the five days they had spent together,
taking it in turns to interpret for Poussière. Many of the scenes in
which they had found themselves – late night suppers in too brightly
lit restaurants, work sessions in the Hotel Crillon lobby, which
Poussière used to yawn in, or to check out the uniformed female lift
assistants; reading sessions when they pored over his speeches, which
Rimini underlined with a propelling pencil, and Carmen with a yellow
marker pen, and which they both tried to enliven with feeble jokes;
the moments before each lecture when, closeted in a green-room, they
exaggerated their own personal panic attacks – Rimini's sudden fevers,
never confirmed on any thermometer, Carmen's desire to sleep – with
the simple aim of attracting the other's pity or commiseration; their
unkind comments about Poussière, his water-jug, the tartan tie he used
as a belt, the tufts of hair growing out of his ears and nostrils, the turn-
ups of his too-short trousers. . .and the shoulder, Carmen's naked
shoulder bursting into each and every one of them, sometimes in the
foreground, as when they were eating sitting next to each other, at others
in the background or out of focus, but always, in each and every case,
with the reluctance and pride that certain attractive features that habit-
ually go unnoticed display when they finally surface – all these scenes,
removed now from the insipid surroundings where they had been
slumbering, struck Rimini almost as if they had been real blows, just

as a passer-by is struck by a warning sign that he saw but disregarded and remembers at the moment when he is in the street and finds (too late) that the danger is about to engulf him.

Rimini understood: he had been falling in love with Carmen for five days, and the certainty that merely stupidity or terror had prevented him from realising this only served to increase the speed at which the sweet poison spread through his veins. Now, when it was too late to turn back, Rimini discovered that this gentle woman, with prominent bones and a too-small mouth, who looked at everything through screwed-up eyes, as if there was always a wind blowing in her face, this woman who was a foreign-language expert and still lived cooped up with her parents, was exactly the sort of woman who five days earlier he would have sworn he could never fall in love with. It was as if someone else had carefully noted down on his behalf all that he would have felt proud of not noticing during those five days, and injected him with it in imperceptible doses, without him realising it, so that the more indifferent Rimini believed he was, the more in control of the situation, the worse he was affected by the illness, and the less control he had. So, as the measure of the depth of falling in love comes not from the intensity of the process but from how invisible it is, Rimini discovered he was a hopeless case.

Every love has its beginning, a kind of private big-bang, but this by definition is a lost moment which the lovers, however observant they are, are not contemporaneous with. In reality, every lover is the tardy inheritor of an instant of love they never see, fixed as it is for ever in the darkness of its creation. Except that now, with the frantic ability of those who know they are already lost, Rimini was able to look back-wards and search for that original signal, to try to identify it or even to choose it. He could, for example, linger for a moment on an image – Carmen pushing away a lock of hair in order to wipe her mouth with a napkin – and then reject it, only to let himself be captivated by another – Carmen on the theatre stage, in her flat shoes, rocking her childlike heels and just slightly moving the hem of her skirt, as though about to launch into a dance – and then in the end, he jettisoned the whole album and fell to his knees to worship a sound, a single sound – Carmen's voice on the phone, shy but always inconvenient, reciting the paragraph from Poussière's lecture that she was losing sleep over.

But not even that – none of these images from the past could compare with the memory Rimini had of his own face on the evening of the first lecture when, five minutes before the start, with Poussière already on stage and the hall full, he was standing in the interpreters' booth and suddenly had the feeling that Carmen was not going to come. It was a moment of private despair, without witnesses, but it remained engraved on Rimini's mind with extraordinary, hyper-realist intensity. In fact he had been afraid, had sensed an inexplicable fear he could feel growing inside him with a suicidal eagerness, like a huge set of fangs bent on devouring itself. Now, forced to re-read the past few days, Rimini stumbled across pages he had never even noticed, entire sentences to which someone – doubtless the same person who had been injecting him with the love poison – must have been adding diabolical comments in the margins, comments which changed every-thing. Each stab of love had pierced and fatally wounded him, only to vanish immediately, as if erased by instantaneous cauterisation.

CHAPTER 3

An expert in this kind of scar tissue repair, Rimini had an even better reason to practise the skill on this occasion: Vera, and Vera's jealousy. The incident in the roadside café had been so arbitrary and outlandish as to almost beggar belief, but a long while before that he had been warned: the morning that Bonet had called. Vera was having breakfast on the floor, sitting in a patch of sunlight with her legs crossed and reading a newspaper splashed with drops of coffee. At the second ring of the phone she smiled wryly, as if she knew something awful was about to happen, but was pleased that she had been able to anticipate it. (Nothing was so indicative of the threat from Rimini's past as the sound of the phone.) Vera let it ring, in the hope that whoever was interrupting them would think better of it at the last minute, and then eventually got up, went over to the phone rather smugly, and picked it up. Bonet's sex, voice, age and foreign accent all took her by surprise. Carrying two glasses of orange juice back from the kitchen, Rimini saw her turn serious and feared the worst. 'Yes, yes,' she was saying in a monotonous tone, lowering her eyes. 'This is his wife. Vera. He's here. I'll put him on. Just a minute.' She left the handset on the table and collapsed on to the sofa, as if putting so much effort into a false alarm had exhausted her. Rimini set the two glasses down on the newspaper, then picked up the phone, holding his breath. 'Congratulations,' said Bonet. 'I didn't know you were married.' Rimini muttered his thanks and for a brief moment – until he looked round and saw Vera – thought of slightly lessening the state of the relationship his former linguistics professor had congratulated him on. Marcel Poussière was arriving in a fortnight to give a graduate seminar. Could he count on Rimini to do the interpreting? Rimini accepted on the spot, without even asking about dates and fees, as if the mere fact that the person who had phoned was Bonet, an inoffensive seventy-five-year-old ex-philologist, and not some predatory woman appearing from the shadows with the sole

177

intention of shattering his fragile marital equilibrium, were enough to turn him into a pardoned prisoner, someone who had no rights and only one obligation: to be grateful. 'I thought of you and Carmen,' Bonet said. Rimini hesitated. 'Carmen Bosch. I understand you studied together.' 'Carmen, yes, of course,' Rimini said, and had no need to turn to look at Vera to know that a smug smile was spreading across her face. 'A very capable young woman. She's doing a doctorate with me,' Bonet went on. 'I think you'd make a good couple.'

Carmen Bosch. Rimini had forgotten her, just as he had all his other university classmates. He hung up. For a few seconds, standing by the phone, he struggled with the box where he thought he might have kept (secretly hoping to lose them) all those faces and names. He revisited and rejected corridors, tiled walls, stuttering neon lights, toilets daubed with scrawled exam notes, the toothless face of a janitor leaning on a broom like a golf club, the sick feeling in the morning that only subsided with the first cigarette, the impression – a minute before having to take an oral exam – that his head was completely empty, as though a gang of thieves had come in and emptied it while he slept. A few silhouettes glided past and disappeared. He heard voices he did not recognise, but which bewildered him. He could not see any faces; at most two or three blurred photos that a cloud of dust obscured and finally buried. Not a trace of Carmen Bosch.

But Vera was waiting. She was being civilised, but the mention of an unknown woman's name had put her on her guard. Rimini played for time and told her about Bonet, his straggly eyebrows and shirts with missing buttons. In what was for him a highly unusual theatrical gesture, he even imitated his typical way of walking – a completely fake imitation because while he was doing it Rimini was not thinking of Bonet, who walked like any seventy-year-old did, but of a caricature he himself had just invented in a panic, made up out of half a dozen eccentric passers-by he had seen. Then he launched into a detailed description of the work he had been asked to do, as if his only aim was to silence Vera's suspicions. He included dates, times, places – everything he had neglected to question Bonet about on the phone – and even invented a biography for Bonet that was as false as his way of walking. Vera listened to him patiently, nodding from time to time, like someone who detests all these pre-ambles but is too well-educated to object. Eventually, with the furtive, casual manner of a smuggler hiding a diamond among fake jewellery, Rimini let slip the name of Carmen in the middle of some sentence or other. It was little more than a second, the four consonants were hardly even audible, but Vera lifted her head, looked at him, and smiled. Deep in her eyes Rimini caught the gleam, the triumphant flash of lightning that women only display when they have confirmed an act of betrayal, and are able to put an end to the torture they have being going through while awaiting the confirmation. 'Who is she?' she asked. In her voice, Rimini detected that kind of frail, forced innocence that ex-porn queens adopt when they become presenters of TV children's shows. 'Someone from the faculty, I suppose,' he said. '*I suppose*,' Vera echoed him, making it sound like a question. 'Don't you know her?'

Which torture is worse for a suspicious heart: a clear image of the past, or amnesia? Rimini knew Vera was so conditioned by her jealousy to reject any immediate denial of this sort as untrue, that telling her the truth ('No, I don't know her, or at least I have no recollection of her') would sound as suspect as any story invented to hide a secret, and would therefore mean he was convicted of something he had never done. He also knew that if he lied ('Yes, I know her, we took Socio-linguistics together, she was the only one in the whole faculty who had really read the latest Chomsky') this might lessen Vera's mistrust by proving it to have been justified, but at the same time would arouse a desire to know more, and so open the way for an interrogation which, by putting him at risk of contradicting himself (Rimini was not lying in order to hide anything, simply to avoid awakening Vera's jealousy), robbed him, guiltless as he was, of the possibility of lying, due to all the incongruencies that lie in wait for anyone who attempts to improvise – he would inevitably find himself declared guilty. If he told the truth, that would unleash a catastrophe; by lying he might win a reprieve and buy some time, but sooner or later as he tried to keep the lie up he would be bound to become its prisoner, and a simple chain of imprecise answers would be enough for his lukewarm first admission to come to seem, in Vera's feverish imagination, like the confession she had feared and sought from the start.

And yet, emboldened by the success of his portrayal of Bonet, Rimini started rummaging among his university memories again and with the information he gleaned, all from different parts of his files, he managed to construct an emergency curriculum for her. According to this, throughout her university career Carmen had excelled in one thing only: contradicting herself. In the short but colourful few minutes of his evocation of her, Carmen changed surnames three times: Bosch, Boch, Bohm. She entered the faculty the same year as Rimini, or two years later; specialised in linguistics or in ancient and medieval history; grew fat and then thin; was a militant in the Santiago Pampillón Front and a cadre in the Franja Morada movement; rich and poor, cheerful but depressive, a shining light and a pale candidate for a life as a schoolmistress. By the end, Rimini was exhausted – exhausted and perplexed, like someone who digs a hole to escape only to find that the walls of earth are piled so high around him that there is no way he can climb out. Vera said nothing: she never spoke when she was smiling. She bent down for the glasses of orange juice and handed Rimini his. 'Wonderful,' she said eventually, clinking their glasses and spilling some of Rimini's. 'So now *we* have a job.'

For days, that '*we*' cast a tormenting shadow over Rimini. He saw himself with Poussière and Carmen Bosch in the terminal at Ezeiza, pushing his way through knots of down-at-heel cab drivers when something about the furtive appearance of an air hostess snooping around nearby, perhaps wearing too many clothes, reminded him of the agitation that gripped Vera whenever she was worried. He pictured himself in a bar, translating Poussière's ideas for a journalist's tape-recorder, or being bored at a cocktail party at the Belgian Embassy, or sharing endless academic discussions in restaurants, with Bonet at the head of the table and a harassed Poussière surrounded by a swarm of language teachers – and in all these scenes he imagined he could see Vera in the background, trailing them with the shy persistence of admirers who can never screw up the courage to present themselves to their idol, but never give up either. At some point he even saw her hiding behind a column, like a special agent sent by an anti-Poussièrist commando, three or four tables away from where he and Carmen were trying to unravel the linguist's latest contributions to an already moribund discipline. It was Vera herself who reassured him. She stepped aside, avoided asking him any questions, was no burden, made herself almost invisible. A few days before Poussière's arrival, when meetings were piling up and Rimini got home very late, red-eyed and with his clothes reeking of cigarettes, a smiling Vera was awake waiting for him, food in the oven, interested in his day, his stiff neck, and his cough, and in replacing his smelly clothes with a clean dressing-gown, but not the slightest bit concerned about silly university nonsense that had kept him from her all day. Confused but pleased, Rimini could feel his love blossoming anew.

But then Poussière arrived, the seminar started, and Rimini spent hardly any time at home. Now she was asleep when he returned – although she let it be understood that she was only sleeping so as not to oblige him to waste his few crumbs of free time on her – but each time he opened the front door, Rimini was presented with a thousand tokens of her devotion scattered throughout the apartment. She left two or three dim lights on so that he could get around without banging into the corners of any pieces of furniture. The table was laid; a line of fluorescent lights pointed from his empty plate to the dish still steaming in the oven. There was a fresh message of love every night on the bathroom mirror, and next to the phone was a list of the day's messages. Vera jotted them down, almost casually, on separate bits of paper, but before she went to bed wrote them out on the lined notepad, so that its pages soon filled with her tall 't's (like miniature Eiffel Towers) and a critical gloss around the names and surnames. 'The video-club: they need *The German Miracle* urgently. Why do you keep on renting black-and-white movies when you know I can never finish watching them? Ivan – half-past three, something about a dictionary. He's at home until six. I know it was wrong of me, but I told him I'm not deaf. From the administrators: when are we going to pay our rent arrears? I put on a Paraguayan accent and claimed I was the maid.' And when Rimini, by now undressed, tiptoed into the bedroom, carefully avoiding any loose floorboards that might creak, the scene Vera had set for him moved him almost to tears. The night-light was on, the window open; there was a fresh bottle of mineral water on the bedside table. His favourite pillow – the one she usually stole from him during the night – was lying intact, as if protected by a sacred halo, on his side, and his half of the bed gave off the sweet smell of clean sheets. Vera, who had even somehow managed to stop snoring, was curled up asleep on the far side, with her back towards him. Before, Rimini would have seen this as a sign of indifference, but now it seemed to him the height of consideration: Vera was turning her back so that he would not have to worry, to avoid him feeling the remorse that would have stricken him if, on getting into bed, he had somehow clumsily woken her up. This made Rimini so cautious in his movements that he all but gave himself cramp as he sneaked into bed like someone penetrating a sanctuary made of paper. As he watched her sleep, he found it hard to believe that even there, caught in the cave of sleep, whose laws usually permit the least considerate acts, Vera could still transmit the impulse of her loving devotion. It was as though she were dead, or as if, before leaving him for ever, she had scattered the posthumous traces of love by which she wanted to be remembered in every corner.

This went on until the day of the final lecture. At six in the evening, ten minutes before he was due to meet Carmen in a bar close to the university theatre, Rimini was still trying to sort out his belt and the loops on his trousers. He had started to sweat. Wrapped up on the bed in her white flannel dressing-gown, Vera was finishing painting her toenails while a man with crazy, staring eyes was gesticulating on the TV screen with the sound turned down. She gave one last flourish, cleaned off a mistake with the tip of a cotton bud, and removed the other white fluffy balls from between her toes. Rimini groaned: the loops were too narrow, the belt was too broad: he found it impossible to decide which of the two to eliminate. 'What time is it?' he asked in despair. 'Leave the belt; you don't need it,' said Vera without turning round, but screwing up the bottle of nail varnish. Rimini obeyed on the spot. Finally ready, he ran into the living-room to look for the text of the lecture. A disheartening mess of papers lay waiting for him on the coffee table: photocopies, pages of notes, translation suggestions . . . He knelt down on the floor and plunged his hands into them, as if he could recognise the copy of the lecture by the sense of touch. He encountered a sheaf of papers stapled together. 'Programme of activities for Prof. Marcel Poussière in Buenos Aires', he read at the top. He started searching again, pushing the piles out in circles: the shock waves knocked over an empty glass, a full ashtray, a lighter. Vera's voice came softly but surely to his rescue: 'In the green file, on the dining-room table!' Two minutes later, when Rimini popped back into the bedroom to say goodbye, Vera was reading, her eyes screwed up from the smoke of a cigarette, wiggling her toes to get the circulation going again in front of the TV screen, as though trying to speed up their drying by the light of the images. Rimini speared the bed with his knee. Vera smiled at him and ran a hand over his forehead, brushing away an imaginary lock of hair. Rimini closed his eyes. It was not a caress – the tips of her fingers had not even touched him – but he felt an imperceptible, distant ripple, like the change in temperature a shadow brings when it is cast over a body. When he opened his eyes and saw her busy with her tasks as if nothing had happened, he suspected the gesture might never have happened, that it had been a mirage, a premonition or a memory. No, Vera was not getting rid of him: she was freeing him. Yet again, she had sacrificed herself for him. Now all that was left was for her to vanish, like some fairy-tale creature. He felt immensely sad. 'Why don't you come?' he suggested, without much hope. 'Should I?' she said. 'It's the last lecture,' he said: 'I'd love you to be there.' 'Won't I make you nervous?' she asked. 'I don't care,' said Rimini. 'I'll be bored: I won't understand a thing,' she protested. 'Do it for me,' he insisted. Vera got up and switched the TV off. 'I'd have to get dressed,' she sighed. 'Aren't you very late?' 'Carmen's never on time,' he said, moving over to the wardrobe. Vera got there before him; she opened the door, pushed a heap of coats aside and, with a rehearsed yelp of surprise, found exactly what she had been looking for: a hanger with a complete set of clothes on it, just waiting to be put on. 'You'll have to go to the bar on your own, though,' she said as she stripped off. 'I'll see you in the theatre. Do you think I'll be all right in this?'

CHAPTER 4

Everything returned to normal, as if the lights had come back on. Poussière still looked as if he were about to collapse. A couple of seats creaked, someone coughed, two heads came together to whisper in the darkness. An Underground train went by, shaking the whole auditorium. Rimini bent over Carmen, coming within the perfumed orbit of her face. Vanilla or almond, he thought. But he said: 'What's going on?' Carmen did not look at him, but lifted her chin towards the audience. 'There, in row five,' she whispered in his ear, her breath tickling him like a feather. Rimini counted, surveyed the whole row and came to a halt at Vera, who was yawning in the seat next to the aisle. 'Why on earth did she come?' said Carmen, horrified. 'She must be crazy: look how she's dressed.' 'What about it?' asked Rimini. 'Just look – she came to seduce him!' Rimini stared at Vera, who by now was chewing on a rebellious cuticle, and examined her attire in disbelief. 'Vera? Who is she trying to seduce?' Carmen looked at him in astonishment. 'Is she called Vera? Like your partner?' 'She *is* my partner,' Rimini said. Carmen glanced down at the audience and tried hard not to laugh: 'Your partner was Poussière's lover?' 'What are you talking about?' said Rimini. He wanted to hit her – to hit her and kiss her and scrape her cheeks with his lips and disappear with her into some luxurious tropical paradise full of carnivorous plants and giant termites. 'I'm sorry, is that woman in the green and white diamond dress your partner?' Rimini shifted the direction of his gaze and saw sitting next to Vera a fat, dyed-blonde woman who seemed to be bursting out of the top of her harlequin suit. 'No, the one next to her. Does Poussière have a lover in Buenos Aires?' 'He did. Didn't you know? They had a fight two days ago. It was a huge scandal: they nearly threw him out of his hotel,' said Carmen. She glanced at him pityingly: 'You're a real dummy, aren't you? You hadn't realised anything was going on, had you?' 'No,' he said, avoiding her eyes, 'I'm always late for everything.' 'Like all good Tauruses,' she said with a smile, before something – a knowing mix of curiosity and disdain – drew her eyes back to the fifth row. 'Your Vera is beautiful,' she said. The two of them fell silent for a moment, as if they had been beamed up to two different planets. 'Yes,' he said, and then, without looking at her: 'I think I'm in love with you.' Silently, Carmen pushed back her chair. When he had the courage to look at her, Rimini thought he could see the traces that a rapid blush had left on her face. He wanted to say something more, something to correct or minimise or amplify what he had just said, anything so that things did not stay as they were. He was about to speak when Poussière seemed to recover, opened his mouth and broke the silence by groaning directly into the microphone. There was a deafening microphone noise. Poussière leapt backwards, then recovered and threw himself on the microphone as though trying to tame it, but the water-jug got in his way. As he knocked it, there was the vaguely musical sound of glass: the jug wobbled, its rounded belly swaying, then smashed on to the stage floor.

The chaos must have lasted five minutes. Poussière disappeared through one of the stage flats, Carmen rushed out of the booth, someone appeared with a broom and began to sweep up the bits, while the people in the front row examined the damage done to shoes and note-books. The light in the hall blinked, went off, came on again. A buzz of excited consternation ran through the audience. One group sitting in the middle of the row made as if to get up and leave, but sat down again when they saw their neighbours' hostile looks. Rimini peered at the fifth row: elbows on her knees, Vera was trying hard not to laugh, while Poussière's former lover was taking advantage of the confusion to re-do her make-up. Then an assistant came down the aisle to the end of their row, and waved to catch her attention. She stood up, left her make-up bag open on her seat, and clambered over Vera's legs to get out. Rimini watched as they talked to each other for a few seconds: the assistant was smiling too much, she was being too reasonable. With the politeness of someone guiding a lost person, he took her firmly by the elbow and led her to the exit. Halfway there, she tried to go back, but the assistant blocked her path; angrily, she pointed at her distant seat. Vera, who had followed the entire episode, picked up her make-up bag and waved it in the air. The assistant came over to get it, but the woman snatched it from him; they turned on their heels and disappeared, banging the doors as they went.

Poussière poked his head round one side of the stage, cast a fearful look at the audience, then walked out under the stage lights. Carmen followed a few paces behind, protecting him and blocking his exit at the same time. She was carrying a plastic cup and a bottle of water. They sat down together. The linguist covered the microphone and whispered something in her ear. Smiling, Carmen filled the cup with water and practically lifted it to his chin. Poussière downed it in one. Then, as he was crushing the cup in his hand, he looked at the pages of his speech and searched hopelessly for his place. Carmen shot a quick glance at the script, and then pointed benignly at the right page. Poussière cleared his throat. Carmen lifted her head, bewitched Rimini with her pleading eyes, then seemed to be saying yes.

Half an hour later, the lecture ended peacefully. Vera signed to him from afar that she was going outside to smoke a cigarette, a resplendent Poussière, keen (like all survivors) to take on a fresh challenge, was attempting to respond to the audience's questions without an interpreter, and Rimini and Carmen were kissing each other in the darkened green-room, leaning against the wall of an Indian wigwam which did not take long to collapse, as it had a merely decorative function in the Wild West show it had been bought for. They stumbled, fell over, but did not stop hugging each other. A pile of cushions and cowhide rugs broke their fall. When they got up again, giddy from their moment of ecstasy, Carmen's head was crowned with feathers, and Rimini had a necklace of wild-cat claws dangling from his shoulder. They laughed in unison. Carmen was allergic to feathers, and so a fit of sneezing followed her laughter. Rimini grabbed her again. He felt as though he could wrap his arms round her whole body. As he patted her on the back – some strange medical intuition told him that allergies and coughs are closely related – he burst into tears, so confused and happy he felt intoxicated.

Suddenly they heard noises. 'Carmen! Rimini!' the assistant shouted from the stairs. 'Poussière can't understand a thing, and we've taken more than ten questions. We need you back up in the booth!' Carmen tugged at the claw necklace and broke it. Rimini blew on her head: the feathers floated in a clump through the air, until one was separated from the rest and landed on Rimini's wet cheek. 'My little Indian. Little tearful Indian,' said Carmen, trapping the feather in two timid fingers as though it was a butterfly's wing, and then putting it away somewhere. 'What have you done to our life?' On the way up to the booth, she stopped: 'No, it's better we don't come out together: I couldn't bear to be right next to you and not kiss you,' she said. Her hand fluttered a brief farewell, and she disappeared into the toilet. Rimini went on alone. Still trembling, he put on the headphones and stared at the dimly lit hall, the audience sitting quietly, the seat where Vera had once sat, two hundred and fifty million years ago, when something like a world was growing and orbiting around her body. Leaning against the back of the seat in front of him, a student with drooping shoulders was stammering out a question. Sitting sideways on to the audience, Poussière was urging him on, tearing what remained of the plastic cup into regular strips. 'Everything is the same,' thought Rimini in amazement as he translated the student's speech. There was something impassive, brutal even about the contrast between the emotional upheaval he was going through and the way he could still identify what was happening in the world. Everything was the same, but somehow clearer: Rimini could see it all in great detail, like the countryside after a shower of rain. He had the impression that if he had been outside at that moment, in a park or out in the fields, he could have described the veins on every leaf with complete accuracy. At the same time, dazzled by the brightness of everything, it seemed to him that the only thing to have changed was time. He could sense a kind of generalised slowing-down. Poussière's voice (he was busy disentangling the question by now), Rimini's own voice echoing his – didn't they sound far too quiet? And most surprising of all: how could there be this slowing-down without everything getting older? He could understand this in his own case: he was in love. But the phenomenon seemed to arise from the very heart of the world, as if this extraordinary stretching were the ultimate consequence of its determination to go on being exactly the same as ever. Or perhaps everything seemed so long drawn-out simply because Carmen was not there. Perhaps at that very moment Carmen was peering at her face in the toilet mirror and finding it impossible to see her own image, caught in this same slowing-down process . . .

'. . . according to the formula,' he finished translating, 'by which all lack of meaning is obligatorily negated.' Rimini fell silent, but in his earphones he could hear Poussière's voice continuing a few seconds longer. The original arrived later than its interpretation. Rimini was stupefied. Time had never been so dense. 'What now? What else is there room for?' he wondered, as taken aback as someone who has just moved homes and watches in horror as a gang of workmen ruin the clean empty spaces of a room with furniture and crates. Standing by the front row down below him, the assistant surveyed a list, consulted his watch, and called for the next question. Rimini managed to spot something moving in the darkness at the back of the hall: the whitish blur of a sleeve, an arm poking out in a timid but relaxed way from behind a concrete pillar. The assistant walked up to the back rows with the roving microphone, which was passed along the row of seats before it disappeared behind the pillar. There was a silence. Then someone cleared their throat, an imperious finger tapped the microphone, the wide sleeve flapped through the air. 'I'm not a linguist,' the woman said in impeccable French tinged with a hostile reserve, 'and apart from the accident with the water-jug, I'm not sure if I understand anything that has gone on here tonight. I don't know all the specialised terms, so I'm sorry if by chance what I want to ask has already been answered at some point . . .' 'What's your question, please?' the assistant pressed her. Rimini felt a sudden emptiness in his chest, as though his heart had skipped a beat. 'This is an inter-disciplinary meeting, isn't it?' the woman counter-attacked, speaking in Spanish now. 'I'd like to think you accept interventions from other areas, don't you?' An embarrassed titter spread through the auditorium. Rimini isolated and recognised the note of rancour in the voice. He looked down at the column where the sleeve seemed to be talking just to him, in a private language whose remains, buried in some far-off corner of his memory, were starting to come back to life. 'Of course,' the assistant said, 'but it's late and there's still a list of people . . .' 'I haven't got all night either, so with your permission, I'd like to get on,' the woman said. She took a deep breath – amplified by the microphone, the rushing noise echoed round the theatre like the start of a storm in a children's play – changed languages again, and began to say: 'I work with the body . . .' Rimini felt he had been found out, as if the beam from one of those high-security jail searchlights had picked him out against a dark background just as he was trying to sneak across unseen. There was nowhere for him to hide. He looked towards the back of the hall, saw two or three heads turn towards the pillar, saw the pillar, the arm in its sleeve – a 'hindu tunic' – the hand holding the microphone and then, like the last domino in the line to fall, the flash of exuberant blonde hair: 'I don't know if the professor (and his European colleagues, or even linguists in general) are aware of the Breitenbach school, of the school or method (what exactly it is has still to be decided) developed by Frida Breitenbach . . .'

CHAPTER 5

He heard voices clamouring around him and came to. He saw the rough walls, a small light bulb swinging above his head, the row of metal cabinets lined up like soldiers. A very delicate object touched his nose, making him sneeze. A feather. He tried to stand up, a shadow bent down to help him and as he stretched his hands out to the floor he could feel a cold, wet material that was somehow familiar. The plastic of the Indian wigwam! A wave of relief flooded through him, the most intense he had ever felt, but then his legs gave way again and Rimini toppled very slowly backwards, smiling beatifically as he fell at all the faces gathered round him trying to help. A moment before, blinded by the dark well he was emerging from, he had not recognised them: now he did not know who they were either, this time because he was so foolishly happy to discover it had all been a dream. As he was being lifted to his feet again, he analysed what remains of reality had survived the black-out: he had gone with Carmen down to the green-room, they had kissed in the darkness, and had fallen over while they were embracing. It was obvious he must have hit his head against something and lost consciousness. Everything else – a series of minor facts and details, which Sofia's appearance drew out like a magnet – seemed to be floating around aimlessly inside his head and slowly dissipating, like the shadowy images of a nightmare. 'You fainted,' somebody told him. Rimini identified the assistant's voice and smiled. 'I'm fine now,' he said, patting a shoulder that turned out to belong to someone else. He tried to ask about Carmen, but as soon as he opened his mouth somebody poured a sachet of sugar under his tongue. He had no problem climbing the stairs, and even refused the assistant's help, but when he reached the stage he felt such a black, freezing hole in his chest he had to come to a halt. It was as though the act of fainting, by penetrating into the most secret part of him, had robbed him of the breath that supported not his body, or his organism, but his life itself – and not the real, tangible life from which his body and organism were indistinguishable, but all that was left for him to live. What he was lacking now was not strength: it was *time*. And if he felt tired it was not because he had overdone it, but because he had lost something – a second, hour, or year – that he could never recuperate.

He walked slowly across the stage like an old man, watching as some workmen carried away the table, the chairs, the baize tablecloth and microphone – all the sad trappings of the lecture. Everything had finished some time ago. How long had he passed out for? He wanted to ask the assistant, but when he turned round all he saw was his back as he walked off the stage. There was a click, one of the stage lights went out, and in a few seconds the light faded. Caught out by the darkness, Rimini felt for a wall. A few moments later, when he could again make out the outline of objects around him, he climbed down a small set of steps in one corner and headed up the aisle towards the exit. At a certain point he was frightened he might bump into something, so he raised his head. A few steps further on he could make out the shadows of two people talking. In fact, only one of them was talking; the other, taller figure, seemed trapped against the brick wall. At that moment the door to the lecture hall opened, one of the workmen entered, and with him a shaft of light which briefly lit the aisle. As though taking advantage of this short interlude of confusion, the taller figure turned towards Rimini. He saw it was Poussière, a wild-eyed version of Poussière, who let out an 'Ah!' of relief when he recognised him, struggled free from the other person's unwanted attentions, came up to him and smothered him in a whirlwind of over-acted phrases and gestures, embraced him once, twice, three times with comical euphoria, then rushed off as quickly as he could back to the stage. Dumbfounded by this outburst, Rimini stood rooted to the spot, until a sense of compassion led him to look at the silhouette Poussière had just fled from. Sofia. Sofia, who was already by his side, was already laying her hand on his arm, already giving him a kiss and enfolding him in a cloud of exotic perfumes. 'Did you get my postcard?' she asked.

They were in almost complete darkness, but Rimini stared long and hard at her, as if he had to cross an endless distance to reach her. He felt something very strange, something which when he thought about it had always seemed to him the height of the impersonal, similar to a theorem for example, or a law of physics, or one of those processes which take place over such vast periods of time that they go beyond human understanding – he felt he was living in several worlds at the same time. In one he was fainting; in another he was getting a postcard from a former lover; in another he was meeting that former lover, who had sent him the postcard; in another he was happy with a jealous woman; in another still he was falling in love with a woman who was not his type. 'You're looking at me as though I was a ghost,' said Sofia. Rimini smiled. He realised just how weak his smile was, and looked anxiously towards the door. 'Don't worry about Vera,' she said. 'She's gone.' She linked arms with him and guided him towards the exit. 'I saw her outside, in the foyer (no, she didn't recognise me, I'm sure of that) and I heard her say she was leaving. Is it just me, or is she a bit more civilised now?' 'Why do you say that?' Rimini talked like someone who is patting his own body to make sure it is really there. 'Somebody asked her to stay because you were all going out to eat together. Him,' Sofia said, pointing to the assistant who was coming towards them between two rows of seats, and when he saw Rimini, asked if he was feeling better. 'Yes,' said Rimini. 'Is Vera outside?' 'I think she left,' the assistant said. As he passed by Rimini he avoided looking at him but whispered: 'the one who's looking for you is Carmen.' Rimini felt bad not acknowledging this token of complicity, but the man was already climbing the stairs to the stage. Almost at once the fact that something so precocious as what had happened between Carmen and him was already a secret (and one shared with somebody so remote from the event as the assistant), which could possibly have lessened the solitude into which his emotional catastrophe had plunged him, not merely the *coup de foudre* with Carmen, whose taste kept returning to his mouth, but also this supernatural appearance by Sofia, instead only increased his sense of abandonment. He felt someone tugging at his sleeve. 'Why did you faint?' – it was Sofia, dragging him towards the exit. 'Oh,' Rimini protested, 'it was just low blood pressure.' 'It's not the first time, and this time there was no blood involved. Shouldn't you see a neurologist? Or were you just embarrassed by the question I asked?' Rimini stared at the vertical strip of light between the two doors and quickened his pace towards them. 'Anyway, you didn't answer me, Rimini. Did you get my postcard or not?' 'When did you arrive?' he asked, hoping that by changing topics he was taking the initiative. 'This morning. I bought a paper at Ezeiza, saw the lecture was announced, and decided to come. And don't go thinking I do this sort of thing for everyone. I'm dead tired, Rimini. How long is it since we've seen each other? Why do foreigners who come here to give lectures never answer the questions they're asked?'

They shared the two exit doors: Rimini pushed open the one on the left, Sofia the right-hand one. When they emerged into the foyer, Rimini was disappointed: he was hoping to find faces, people, noise, the exaggerated hubbub with which an audience compensates for the forced vow of silence they are obliged to take inside theatres. Instead there were only two or three students idly staring at the poster, an old man in a cap who was limping across to put a chain on the street doors, and a harsh light that seemed to be bleaching everything white. 'Shall we go for a drink?' said Sofia. Rimini looked at her – first at her face, and then all of her – from head to foot: her trousers looked new, but one of the turn-ups was frayed and a big oval patch of oil or grease stained one of the pockets. She was wearing three or four rings on each hand; not jewels, but the usual handicraft ones she always wore. They looked noble and austere, but each of her fingernails was crowned by a half-moon of dirt, and all her cuticles had been chewed raw. This was not a lack of care, or negligence; on the contrary, it showed how much she demanded of herself, even if in a misguided fashion. It took Rimini some time to realise that the perfume he could smell, a dense mixture of chewing-gum and alcohol, was coming from her make-up, and that what was making his head whirl was the difference in size between her eyes: the one on the right was much more closed than the other one, its eyebrow sprinkled with black eye-liner. 'No,' said Rimini, 'I can't. It's the end of the seminar: I have to go and eat with everyone else.' The theatre doors burst open and Carmen appeared in the foyer. She looked worried, and was carrying a bunch of flowers. Close behind her was a tanned older man, wearing a Prince of Wales check suit, who was sneezing repeatedly into a handkerchief. When Carmen saw Rimini she came to an abrupt halt, with her right foot stretched out but still in mid-air, and the left one tensed to push off, showing her ligaments. Rimini felt like one of those minor deities who, consumed with lasciviousness, desire, and the basest passions, catch sight of the beautiful huntress who is driving them wild in the heart of a wood, and because they cannot possess her either because their lowly place in the divine hierarchy will not permit it, or because some higher-ranking god has already chosen her as their prize, choose to turn her into a stone statue. But Carmen's foot eventually landed on the floor, the cellophane on the bouquet crackled, and one final sneeze rang out in the theatre foyer. As they approached, Rimini thought he could see a purple blotch on Carmen's neck just beneath the ear lobe: the signature of a vampire's lips. The fact that he had no idea who had caused it filled him with a blind rage. They met and smiled, the first stage in a pathetic goodbye ritual: they raised hands, only to abandon the gesture halfway; said yes to all the unspoken phrases, made as if to introduce the others when there was no need. In a few seconds they went through a whole array of mental and emotional states they would probably need more than a lifetime to feel. In the end, Carmen took the plunge: 'Are you going?' she said, pointing towards an imaginary restaurant where Poussière and the others must already be raiding the bread baskets. 'What about you?' asked Rimini. 'No,' she said, her mouth twisting in either a sad or tired expression. Her eyes brushed against Sofia, as if she did not want to disappear without having something of her to take with her, an image on which later, when she was on her own and felt calmer, she could unload all the questions piling up in her brain. Her gaze settled back on Rimini and then, shyly, irresistibly, lowering her eyelashes, she said: 'Well, see you then.' And left. The beau with the handkerchief was left at a loss, as if he had only rehearsed the scene this far and now, with no text and no direction, had no clear idea of what role he was meant to be playing. He finally gathered himself, cleared his throat, put the handkerchief away and declaimed 'Good night' like an old-time Argentine movie star. Stifling a laugh, Sofia shouted 'Farewell! Farewell!' as if waving him goodbye from the dockside. Then suddenly, as if she had torn off a mask, everything about her changed in an instant. She rounded on Rimini: 'Is that Carmen?' 'Yes,' said Rimini, 'why?' 'You like her?' 'Sofia . . .' 'Not bad. She's your age. That in itself is progress. Nice ankles. Very delicate. Vaccination on one shoulder. A good choice.' Rimini felt as though the words were being spoken separately and distinctly, like the description of a scientific classification: 'affectionate, sensitive, very feminine.' 'Sofia, that's enough. What's wrong with you?' 'I don't know. I feel as though I'm sleepwalking. It must be the jet lag. But good for you: you're getting a good deal. What you lose in passion you gain in maturity. I suppose you know what you're doing. It won't do you any harm. Vera's had it. You've got what you can from her. Like stocking up on haemoglobin. When it comes down to it, you're like a stockbroker: you take youth from here, you invest it over there . . .'

By now they were in the street. The theatre lights went out one by one. A gust of wind swept over them. All of a sudden, Sofia looked fragile. 'I'm cold. This time yesterday I was . . . Shall we have a coffee?' 'No, Sofia. I told you: I'm going to eat with . . .' 'What's the point?' she butted in, 'if Carmen's not going?' 'What's that got to do with it?' 'Rimini, don't make it such hard work. We really don't have to start from the beginning, do we? That's an advantage. A big advantage. There's a bar on the corner.' Sofia huddled against him to protect herself from the wind, and forced him towards the café. 'I can't, Sofia. I really can't,' he said, moving away from her, 'they're waiting for me.' For a second, neither of them said anything. A fresh gust of wind forced them to screw up their eyes, and swept a sad raft of papers along the avenue. Sofia coughed. She tried to cover up, reaching a hand to her neck, but her dress had no collar, so she left her hand on her chest while with the other she pulled back the locks of hair the wind was blowing into her face. 'Will you at least take me to my car?' 'Where did you leave it?' 'What street's that?' 'Uriburu.' Completely lost, Sofia stared all round her. She got out a set of keys, took a few hesitant steps, then came to a halt by a Renault 12 parked right next to Rimini. She slid the key in the lock, thought hard and then, as she was opening the door, she said: 'Did you at least get my card?' Rimini nodded without a word. Sofia smiled and got into the car.

Rimini walked away before she pulled out. Sofia was in the car, he was on the street: this was a slender advantage, but he would have given anything not to lose it. He started striding purposefully towards Avenida Callao, energised by a general sense of absolution, but the further he got from Sofia, the further he left her behind and approached safety, at the moment when he was starting to enjoy the renewed vigour he felt whenever he survived a meeting with her, everything she had said and done during the ten or fifteen minutes they had been together: her gestures, offers, demands, suggestions – the radiation she had exposed him to, and the traps she had set (which he had somehow managed to avoid), the whole of that influence, which Rimini imagined he had sealed off in some water-tight compartment of his soul, suddenly reared up again to threaten him. With Sofia gone – like the note on a piano which the foot pedal leaves hanging in the air long after the finger has been lifted from the key – what were left were her actions, her effect, the strange resonance that prolonged the life of her words which, unencumbered by the situation in which they were uttered, turned into dire warnings. Yes, Rimini was safe, but like a virus the threat had only changed shape: as though quitting a no longer useful means of transport, it had abandoned Sofia, and had now turned into an infinite number of rapid, tiny particles in the air which pursued him so closely that they buzzed in his ears and were starting to rip him open with their sharp little rows of teeth. Rimini had survived, but he was left defenceless. Sofia's influence was destroying the wrapping between him and the world, making him transparent and porous to such an extent that as he walked on, Rimini no longer felt the wind gusting around him, but felt it inside his body, in his stomach and his lungs, an icy presence that froze his heart. He stopped, teetered on the edge of the pavement. He felt the utter despair of someone who has no secrets. After disembowelling him, Sofia had turned him inside out. It was true: Rimini had fallen in love with Carmen. He still felt shaky in the legs, the warm sequel to the ecstasy they had reached together in the theatre green-room. But what did he have to offer her? Nothing. The chain tying him to the other world of the past – and Vera. Worse than nothing. He glimpsed – as if it were a film preview – the disappointment etched on Carmen's face, her eyelids closing again, this time to condemn rather than bewitch him – he, Rimini, who had just come into her life and who could not dream any more of living without the warmth she had given him. He felt so ashamed of himself that he stepped down into the street with his eyes closed. A dark shape without any lights turned the corner with a screech of tyres and pinned him against the kerb. It all happened so quickly he did not even have time to be afraid. Sofia was already next to him. Shouting at him. At first he could only see her mouth moving – the only living part of the pale mask that was her face. Then little by little he could make out the sounds: '. . . who the fuck do you think you are, you son of a rotten bitch? Twelve years together and you've no time to spare? How can you be such a shit? You think you're going to get away with it? You think you can carry on in life completely freely, as if nothing had happened? You're going to pay, Rimini! You can do whatever you want with me, but you . . . You're the one who is the problem! You, your miserable life inside, your soul! That miserable, terrified stone you have in place of a heart! You're such shit! Say something. You're sick! You're going to rot! You're already rotting! It's all bubbling up inside. All of it! Look at me, you coward, when I'm talking to you! It's me, Sofia! Go on, say something. Right now, because if you wait until you realise what's going on, it'll be too late. I know you'll be back. You'll come crawling back. Begging for my help. And me . . . you know what, Rimini? I'll be dead. And what are you going to do if I'm dead? Who's going to look after you? Who's going to think about you when I'm dead? Who's going to want to . . .' – she kissed him. She leapt on him, grabbed hold of his ears as if she were going to pull them off, then pushed at his mouth with her lips and tongue until she had forced it open. Once she had got past the twin rows of teeth, Rimini felt that a blast of cold, damp air – so harsh it seemed to come from the depths of the earth – was scorching his mouth and throat. Horrified, he let her carry on, hearing the protests of the drivers Sofia's car was blocking in the distance. He would probably never have seen the accident if a few seconds earlier he had not heard, clearly but faintly in among all the car horns and shouting, the voice of a man asking: 'Do you feel all right, miss?' He heard it, and the astonished, worried tone, the lack of interest it showed in the spectacle that Rimini, Sofia and her Renault were offering in the middle of the street, forced Rimini to look to one side, to spot the tall, skinny old man wrapped in a blanket and leaning on a Zimmer frame who had spoken the words, and then after a rapid panning of the peeling façades, to light on Vera standing on the street corner, staring at them with a terrifying lack of expression over the roof of a car on which one of her small white hands was resting. Seeing her there, Rimini finally reacted: he freed himself from Sofia's kiss, and as she immediately began cursing him again, he turned and shouted

Vera's name. But Vera had vanished. Rimini saw the old man come into the picture, shuffling along as fast as he could, wide-eyed and with his mouth half-open, and stood motionless for a second, wondering if he had really seen her, until – more from inertia than anything else, from that kind of half-interest with which we decide not to miss something chance has put before us (even if it is not what we were expecting) – he followed the direction of the old man's gaze, peered down the avenue to the next intersection, and saw Vera sprinting diagonally across the road, turning her back not only on him, the old man, and the vehicles still held up by Sofia's car, but also on the cars hurtling down the avenue at top speed, encouraged by the lack of traffic at that late hour. Vera's trajectory seemed to him so erratic that he could not help but smile, as if what he was seeing was not something real, taking place in the here and now, but an empty hypothesis backed only by the imagination that had just dreamt it up, until he heard another set of tyres screech, smelled the burnt rubber, felt the dull thud, and after a moment's confusion saw Vera flung into the air – flipping over just as he had seen all the bits of paper tossed by the wind only a short while before – and then, as Vera seemed to float through the night, heard the crash of metal and broken glass, so that by the time Rimini looked away it was all over: Vera was lying face upwards on the tarmac, not moving, with a strand of hair dangling down her forehead, beside a truck wheel spinning in the void.

CHAPTER 6

He was losing everything. Losing it bit by bit, in no particular order or logic. One afternoon an entire conjugation in French might disappear, then two or three days later the scheme for accents, a week later the meaning of the word *blotti*, an hour after that the phonetic distinction between a promise of food – *poisson* – and that of death – *poison*. It was like a cancer: it could start anywhere, was no respector of hierarchies, reacted in exactly the same way faced with the simple or the complex, the essential or contingent, the archaic and the new. The damage, at least as far as he could tell, seemed irreversible: the lost areas were gone for ever, and every time that, encouraged by a glimmer of hope or by the whimsical nature of the illness, Rimini took the trouble to return to a problem area to see if anything had changed, all he met with was the same desolate panorama that had frozen his blood the first time he found himself robbed of the possibility. The deterioration was not even choosy about what it affected. It was neither uniform nor homogeneous, and yet for some reason the four languages that Rimini knew well suffered from it equally. Occasionally the loss was more noticeable in one of them, but soon afterwards the others caught up. The only good thing about the illness was also its main curse: it was unpredictable.

The first blows were doubly hard, not only for the kind of shock they produced, and their immediate consequences, but above all because they came completely out of the blue, which only seemed to intensify the scope of the damage. They were brutal, unexpected, unbearably cruel, in the way that a blow we sustain when we are walking along a dark corridor we know well is cruel: we walk along blindly but confidently, in other words doubly blind, so that when we bump into the window and the sharp metal frame hits us on the forehead, what most upsets us is not the physical wound itself, however deep that might go, but the sense of moral outrage the accident causes our faith, which had bet on a specific outcome – a smooth passage, with no hitches – to the complete exclusion of all others. The very first time it happened was in the Teatro Coliseo, in front of six hundred people: after sticking as close as a shadow to the Italian deputy foreign minister for forty minutes, Rimini felt a kind of dry crack (similar to the noise he sometimes heard beneath his ear when he bit into something) and a sudden, impenetrable night like the one formed by huge storm clouds when they sweep across the sky descended between the speaker's voice and him. It stayed for two or three long minutes while Rimini, who had fallen silent, rolled up his eyes, the deputy foreign minister pretended to admire the august sobriety of the theatre, and the audience – the most amazing conglomeration of dark suits Rimini had ever seen – went from respectful bewilderment to polite protest. While it was an unpleasant moment, there was no reason for Rimini to be unduly alarmed: these lapses by interpreters were as common as footballers' sprained ankles.

By dint of repeating this comparison to himself over and over again, he recovered sufficiently from the accident three weeks later to accept the job of interpreting for the first public talk by Derrida in Buenos Aires. Everything was rolling smoothly along. The philosopher, who was pretending to be improvising, was speaking with exaggerated slowness, as if he were talking to an audience of deaf mutes rather than Spanish speakers. Rimini felt light, alert, flexible. He was vaguely excited by the smell of wet leather the theatre gave off, so pleasantly different from the stale smell of the university auditorium where he had yielded to Carmen's charms – and Carmen herself was in the stalls, sending him comforting signals of love and encouragement. It was all going fine: the incident at the Coliseo was completely forgotten until the moment when the philosopher – who had wandered off on a digression about what he called the 'Prague affair', the time he had been arrested and accused of trafficking cocaine by the Czech police, who had picked him up at the airport just as he was boarding a flight back to Paris after giving a clandestine seminar to the students in the Jan Hus Association, the same secret police who then put him through what seemed to him inexplicable photo sessions, not only photographing him in his classic French thinker's garb, but also (the worst humiliation) in the nude, and even in a striped prison uniform – until

Derrida, with a bitter, sarcastic smile, turned over one of the pages he was reading (without betraying the fact that he was doing so, in order to preserve the illusion that is so crucial for people who go to this kind of public event, that everything which happens there is happening at that very moment, before their very eyes), took off his glasses – first one side, then the other – and recalled that throughout the interrogations that the secret police had subjected him to he had often mentioned Kafka (at the time he had been working on a short commentary on the story 'Before the Law') while his captors, thanks to an irony they doubtless had nothing to do with, must have taken advantage of his visit to Kafka's grave to go to his hotel, enter his room, and plant the cocaine in his suitcase – and when he came to the word *valise* Rimini suddenly experienced the same dry crack as at the Coliseo, felt as though a strange force was pushing him away from everything, and the philosopher's voice, which until then had been crystal clear, became completely impenetrable. He could not go on. He struggled long and hard to try to get the philosopher to admit that *valise* was another of the inspired neologisms he specialised in, and when Derrida decided to cut short the interruption and get on with his talk, Rimini was lost in a forest of mysterious sounds. He gave a weak yelp of panic. It was a stroke of luck that Carmen was there to hear him, give him a kiss on the lips when he was led away, and also to replace him. It was bad luck though that she was away working in Rosario the following month at the very moment when, back in Buenos Aires, Rimini, bolstered by his new slogan 'Third time lucky', was at the same time starting and finishing as head of the Alliance Française's interpreting team, thanks to his translation of the introductory paragraph of a speech by a former minister of culture from the Mitterand era into the secret (even to him) language of his own perplexity.

In the space of a few months, Rimini went from being a polyglot star to a clinical case, almost a professional curiosity which his colleagues debated furiously, as if he were a martyr to the cause, in the corridors of publishing houses and the faculty. Contrary to what he himself would have believed, the syndrome, as he liked to call it, was not in the least bit painful, quite the opposite: besides being limited strictly to the area of his linguistic competence, the losses were in fact pleasurable, in the same way that in summer Rimini stayed out in the sun too long, and then derived hours of pleasure from peeling off strips of burnt skin. However, he yielded to Carmen and his father's pressure and went to see a neurologist. The doctor, a portly man who glanced at his watch every minute, as though he had put a time-bomb in a rival's consulting-room, got him to lie down on a couch, smeared his head with gel, stuck a dozen electrodes on him and then, after a cursory, almost irritated glance at the long strip of results, sent him on his way with a few pats on the back, a diagnosis of stress, and a prescription for tranquillisers.

Rimini wanted a second opinion, and decided to change homeopaths at the same time. Victor had told him that Vázquez Holmberg had just opened his list for new patients. This was Rimini's chance: a renowned teacher of doctors, Vázquez, as his followers called him, had trained his previous homeopath, enjoyed a remarkable reputation based on his knowledge and extravagant behaviour in equal amounts, and had so many patients that each new gap, which happened every once in a blue moon, was celebrated as a miracle. Rimini waited four and a half hours in a courtyard covered with a tin roof, dozing off and then waking with a start to realise that the patients sharing the waiting-room with him before he fell asleep had been replaced by others, and that the doctor's secretary, a tall, bustling forty-year-old with traces of lipstick on her teeth and a general air of slovenliness that immediately aroused him, was showing them into the doctor's surgery according to a less conventional, more secret system than one based on the order in which they had arrived. He finally got in, preceded by the secretary's wafted perfume, and almost felt his way through the darkness, trying to conceal the massive erection he was having, until he saw the glow from a lamp and sat down opposite a very ancient-looking gnome with no hair or teeth, who seemed to be visibly shrinking second by second inside his spotless white coat. 'Your heart is pretty healthy,' Vázquez informed him after looking at and getting caught up in the electro-encephalogram. Then he dictated some medicines to his secretary and by way of a farewell, in his strange toothless mumble (which ironically Rimini could understand perfectly), recommended he do sport, lots of sport, and especially rugby.

Rimini ruled out the sporting suggestion, even though Carmen protested that she was dying to see him in shorts and with muddy

knees, but brought home the globules and other homeopathic remedies. Carmen was not happy about this either: she held the glass phials
up to the light, anxiously observed the strange ballet of oils going on
inside, and was on the point of throwing them away. After this, Rimini
more or less retired. He left the public arena, the live audiences, the
histrionic but electrifying vices of instantaneous translation, and went
back to paper, to written translations, which also had their moments
of crisis, but which could be resolved discreetly, in his own time and
in solitude, far from the pressure of an anonymous mass of spectators. He imagined, with a sense of perhaps unjustified nostalgia, that
his state of mind – a mixture of contentment and anguish – must be
somewhat similar to that of sportsmen who decide to retire at the peak
of their achievements, after they have won all the championships, prizes,
and money in the world. Rimini was not rich and although intense,
his career as an interpreter had not brought him any great recognition. But he did have Carmen, that priceless treasure; he had her just
measures of passion, light-heartedness and good humour, her compulsion to belittle everything she loved, that odd, smiling way she had of
making her way in the world leading him by the hand – not as though
she were helping him, but rather creating the impression, and leading
him to believe, that he, Rimini, was the real driving force whereas she
was merely the material manifestation of movement.

Rimini began translating at home, and Carmen went out to work.
Although it was Rimini's crisis which had brought about the change,
they saw it less as a reaction to adversity than the choice of a different
life, one perhaps more in keeping with the fresh needs of their life as
a couple. It was then that the invitation to a translators' congress in
Sao Paulo arrived. From the start, Carmen took it for granted they
would go together. She only realised that Rimini did not feel the same
way when a week before they were due to travel she went to collect
the two tickets – one for her, the other for her companion (a privilege
she herself had won thanks to quiet but determined efforts) and came
home to find Rimini sitting on the floor sifting through the small
number of photos they had taken of each other since their marriage.
The sight of him moved her: he had no shoes on, and his short, white
cotton socks made his feet look like a child's. 'What are you doing?'
she asked. 'I'm choosing the photo of me I want you to take,' he told

her. She had no difficulty convincing him that he was going with her; there was no fight, no negotiations were necessary. To Carmen, their travelling together was not a possibility but a fact, an accomplished fact, and the ticket she waved in Rimini's face was not a means of persuasion but irrefutable evidence. Rimini read his name on the first page, and his eyes filled with tears.

It was not the idea that they would be travelling together for the first time that moved him so much; it was more the solitary determination with which Carmen had conceived and carried out her little project, and the role of lifeless, voluptuous object he had been reduced to. And yet that lack of symmetry, which in some way crystallised his deepest feelings about love, was at the same time the still invisible but already active sign of an insidious mechanism that was just starting up in some distant part of his soul. That word 'companion' started to buzz around his brain like a bothersome fly. For the first time, he really did feel ill. Even before they had started out on it, the journey to Sao Paulo achieved what his linguistic failings, his lapses of memory, his public humiliations, his colleagues' opinions, or even his decision to quit interpreting had not succeeded in doing. The night before their departure, with bags packed, travel clothes chosen, and Carmen asleep beside him, Rimini found that the film *A Star is Born* had just started on one of the cable channels, and sat for more than two hours glued to the screen, on tenterhooks the whole way through. He only collapsed as dawn was breaking.

CHAPTER 7

The journey lasted an hour and a quarter, only fifteen minutes more than they had told him at the hotel, and forty-five less than it would have taken him by car, but still it seemed endless to Rimini. He spent the whole trip standing up, pressed against the carriage door in case he discovered just as the warning signal went that *this* was the station where he was meant to get off. He was sweating, and struggled to read the map he had snatched from the hotel reception, which seemed to have a life of its own and kept unfolding endlessly, and another diagram showing the whole system of Underground stations plastered high on the side of the train. Successive waves of local passengers regarded his plight showing no sympathy, and left the carriage without even glancing at him, their mouths twisted in a grimace of satisfaction.

He had already begun to regret the whole thing when he had left the hotel and tried to go down the wrong part of the Underground entrance: a flood of passengers coming in the opposite direction forced him back into the street. He regretted it still further when the carriage doors closed on him and he found from the Underground map that all the lines – including the one he had just taken, although he was still not quite sure which one that was – followed a more or less straight, comprehensible trajectory until they reached a certain point, a myste-rious subterranean maelstrom, after which they ran amok and shot off in a delta of smaller tributaries, curved back on themselves, traced improbable arabesques. He regretted it even more at every station he passed through (twenty-nine altogether) each time the train braked and, crushed in a heap of bodies, packages, hair-dos, kit-bags, he tried to peer out and read the name of the station outside, to make sure it coincided with the timid idea he had in mind. And he completely regretted it when, after getting off the train, happy simply to have arrived at his destination, he emerged into the street and a white sky blinded him, while the smell of frying food and stale fish swirled around him and the landscape where he had planned to spend the next few hours of his life slowly came into focus: a deserted avenue, dogs, a service station, abandoned cars, low, squalid houses, car workshops, empty lots piled with scrap. In the background, beyond the shimmering heat of steam and oil vapours, he could make out the two huge sheds where the Sao Paulo city council had decided to move the Book Fair.

What a mistake, thought Rimini. He started walking towards the sheds, roughly judging the distance and multiplying it by the heat of the sun, the humidity, the diesel fumes, the inhospitable poverty of the neighbourhood, the tourist-murdering gangs he could sense were about to pounce on the far side of the long, bare, brick frontage. Nothing about the Book Fair particularly interested him. But what other options did he have? To stay in the hotel, where the maids and the bell boys were already looking askance at him, as if he were a cross between a conman and an invalid? Go with Carmen to her congress? He had done that. The first day he had clambered into the minibus with her, accepted the badge that the smiling group coordinator had eventually been obliged (at Carmen's insistence) to give him – it belonged to someone called Idelber Avelar, a translator from Porto Alegre who had never turned up – went to all the sessions, had lunch with Carmen and her colleagues in the cafeteria, and afterwards, feeling drowsy from a caipirinha he should not have drunk so early in the day, had gone on the guided tour of the conference site with them. He had sat through all the afternoon's events, sometimes accompanied by Carmen, who left her post to offer him furtive caresses, but more often on his own, increasingly so as the afternoon advanced and the public – translators, language teachers, students, a paunchy, dishevelled poet who had enough energy to make Picasso look like a consumptive librarian, and who every so often rose to his feet, glass in hand, to recite irascible verses in a variety of languages – became increasingly sparse. He only gave in towards the very end when, almost entirely alone by now in the front rows, he nodded off into a dreamless sleep, only to be awakened by a loud microphone noise. The next day was a sad repetition of the first. In the minibus, a quick and apparently random pincer movement by three Canadian translators separated him from Carmen and condemned him to the most uncomfortable seat at the back of the bus, at the mercy of the body odours of an editor from the Dominican Republic and a

Spanish literary agent's garlic breath. A strange insect, somewhere between a beetle and a scorpion, took advantage of the sleepy atmosphere of the first session after lunch – 'Towards Cybertranslation' – to bite him invisibly but incredibly painfully in the calf, and everyone, absolutely everyone, began to call him by the name on his badge, a piece of paper so essential he could not even think of throwing it away, because it was the only way to get in, move around, eat and even to use the toilet facilities in the building; 'Idelber this', 'Idelber that', a flagrant abuse that the Brazilian participants employed to address him directly in Portuguese, as if that banal rectangle in its plastic cover were sufficient to give him a new nationality.

Yes, the excursion to the suburbs had been a mistake, but by this time Rimini preferred to face any challenge it threw at him rather than having to turn round whenever he heard a name that was not his, or explain to the waiters in the hotel restaurant that if he was not on the list for lunch it was because he was at the translation congress in the guise of a companion, or being forced to say Carmen's name because in the hotel register she was the one who had booked the room, so that the desk clerks, already reluctant to satisfy any requests, would agree to give him their messages or phone calls. A mistake then that Rimini was prepared to take to its ultimate consequences. For ten or fifteen minutes he walked in a kind of incandescent cloud, until he finally reached a completely deserted concrete esplanade where different countries' flags were flying alongside the official Book Fair banner. In another ten minutes, Rimini had reached one of the sheds, and was searching in vain for a doorway in the vast corrugated-iron wall. He fiddled with a small gate locked with a piece of wire, then stepped back and, hands on hips, surveyed the shed from top to bottom. Just as he was wondering how on earth the main entrance to the Sao Paulo Book Fair could be so inconspicuous, a security guard appeared on an electric cart and with a mixture of Portuguese and gestures, circling round him all the time as though worried that if he came to a stop, his vehicle would never start again, succeeded in giving Rimini a simple if somewhat embarrassing explanation. Yes, he had reached the Book Fair, but he was at the back of it; the main entrance was this far down, but on the other side of the building, a few metres from the Underground exit where he had started.

Rimini went in and savoured the carpet with his feet, as if this red, threadbare tongue could compensate for all that he had suffered. No sooner had he gone through the entrance, refusing the fruit juices that two girls dressed as jungles offered him in plastic cups, than he felt a sudden chill in his stomach that was somewhere between nausea and vertigo. He had to stand still for a few moments, gazing up at the high roof of the building (he discovered he could make out even some of its tiniest details) until his body finally understood that the sunshine and heat had gone, and slowly got used to the abstract air-conditioned atmosphere. He wandered down the aisles, allowing himself to be carried along by the knots of people (not many of them, as it was still early), and stopped a couple of times to hear the announcements that the distorted voices of a man and a woman made over the PA system. He ate a *cachorro quente* and two *milhos*, became a fan of *maracujá* juice, and as he passed by the South Africa stand, wiped his fingers on a glossy foreign affairs magazine. At one point he let himself be carried along by a group of pilgrims and found himself queueing up outside an empty room surrounded by people clutching the latest book by Paulo Coelho. Rimini, who detested Paulo Coelho in the same way as he did all the other ex-addicts, ex-criminals, ex-terrorists, ex-prostitutes, ex-businessmen, ex-wifebeaters, ex-rapists, ex-politicians and ex-artists who produced their literature of rehabilitation (that sub-genre of catechism), stood in line for a while. As he watched the queue grow at an astonishing rate, he felt comforted by a strange sense of well-being, as if despite the outrage to his principles, made worse in this case by the nature of Paulo Coelho himself and the massive, unconditional devotion he aroused in his followers, and above all by the fact that while the line to see, hear and touch the pope of the converted went on growing and growing, sitting at a table in the next-door room, a young, badly shaven writer was checking the text of a speech he would never give, for one simple reason: the lack of an audience – the complete lack of an audience, unless you included his translator, the sound engineer, two female security guards who were yawning in the back row, and the lost couple who came in at the last minute and asked if this was where Paulo Coelho was signing copies of his latest book – as if, despite all this, the contact with this crowd of strangers offered Rimini some kind of warmth and shelter. So Rimini stayed where he was and then, once the queue began to move – anticipating the crush, Coelho must have slipped in by a back door (the same one, probably, that Rimini had struggled unsuccessfully with some time earlier) – and it was his turn to go in, he stepped aside without a word and dropped out of the endless caravan of worshippers.

Later on, crucified by his aching feet and by the vast waves of people crowding the fair, Rimini sought asylum in an ugly waiting-room furnished with chairs and a garden table. He rid himself of the pile of pamphlets, notebooks, flyers and advertising he had picked up in the previous half-hour, incapable by now not only of saying a single thing in Portuguese but even of saying no, or shaking his head, slipping them all surreptitiously under the cushion on the chair next to him, then let himself be hypnotised by a TV showing an old documentary in Portuguese about a famous painter who had no hands. He had not been sitting there more than ten minutes, plunged in this ridiculous stupor, when a deep rumble that was both multiple and strangely uniform, like the sound of a troop of galloping horses, began to grow louder above his head, on the roof of the building. It was raining – one of those sudden raging storms that seem to herald the end of the world, only to fall silent again a few minutes later, as though silenced by some god or other. But the roar had woken Rimini up again, so he ventured out into the ant-heap once more. He saw that all the people who a few minutes earlier had been rushing ceaselessly around, going up and down the main avenues and the smaller aisles, filling and emptying rooms, buying, scrabbling over food and book stalls, strictly in that order, had calmed down and were moving now very slowly or not at all, so that what before the parenthesis that Rimini had used not only to take a rest, but to learn all about the life and work of the handless painter, whose canvasses done using his feet after his maiming showed absolutely no difference, for good or ill, from those he had produced earlier in life painting with his hands, except possibly in terms of their price, had seemed to Rimini like a swirling mass of bodies, colours, and voices, now after the storm had broken (it was still lashing the tin roof with ferocious intensity) appeared to him like a static spectacle in which instead of moving around, the same people formed evenly spaced unmoving clumps as if posing for a gigantic painting under instruction from a gigantic painter.

Rimini took a short-cut he had spotted on his left. He felt his feet dragging in a very pleasant way – he found himself climbing a very gentle ramp – and came to a Brazilian publisher's stand. The lighting was too bright, and the three girls on the stall all smiled at him at once. Rimini did not want to offend them by leaving straightaway, so he decided to walk round the stand, on condition that none of them tried to speak to him. He quickly surveyed the tables: the satin sheen of the book covers reflected the light harshly. Rimini, who by now had given up all hope with Portuguese, dedicated himself to looking at the close-up shots of people on the covers: healthy-looking, shiny faces smiling at the reader with indestructible confidence out of deep black back-grounds. It was as though all of them – men and women, old and young, white people, black and Asian, fat or thin (this deliberate diversity, which seemed to exhaust every category of face, must have been one of the attractions of the series) – had put themselves in the hands of the same team of dermatologists, hairdressers, make-up artists and dentists for the same beauty treatment. And yet, as they all paraded before his eyes, identical apart from slight variations, like the different incarnations (the successful businessman, the missionary nun, the chess prodigy, the movie starlet, the reformed criminal, the footballer, the pale Buddhist saint) of an original prototype, Rimini began to notice that something strange and more or less persistent undermined the apparent impassive surface of all these faces – a minor detail, apparently sliding in unnoticed, which disconcerted the observer for the fraction of a second before vanishing again. There was a wart growing under the chess prodigy's ear lobe; a black or missing tooth spoiled the businessman's smile; and there was a bright red fleck in the nun's right eye ... It was as though each of these blemishes succeeded in restoring – beyond the idea of complete harmony the photographs were trying to impose on the viewer – some connection between the glowing, healthy faces they were showing and their past, an earlier state ruled by dark forces and shapes, as if the vitality the photographer had immortalised for the book covers at the same time offered a glimpse of the jumbled mess of pain, blood and infamy from which it had been snatched. But just as Rimini was beginning to see the abused child behind the magician of gambits, the alcoholic behind the missionary nun, the hopeless coke addict behind the multimillionaire – he thought it over, and stopped. He looked once more at the covers, that exhaustive portfolio of life stories, and realised that there was as much regularity and calculation behind these blemishes as there was in the signs of boundless vitality the photographs showed, and that everything which he had naïvely thought he could use against that repulsive happiness fabricated by the professional make-up artists was in fact the work, and doubtless a masterpiece, of those same professionals, who were as expert at creating monstrosity as beauty. He smiled, and admitted defeat. He was about to move on when one face, the furthest on the table, caught his attention. It was the portrait of a blond young man with dreamy eyes that were so light-coloured they looked almost transparent; whose cheeks were as smooth as a baby's, with traces of blushing pink that the make-up had not succeeded or perhaps wanted to hide. Like all the others, he was smiling, but there was something pallid about his smile, as if it came from the distant past, and this made it a little vague, made it unsteady, somehow shaky, as if it were about to fade away completely. The effect it created was so strange that Rimini stood for a while looking down almost vertically at the book cover, waiting for the phenomenon to happen.

Rain was still hammering on the roof of the pavilion. Perhaps he recognised the face. He knew or thought he knew all the others – they were public figures, many of them celebrities, so that there was no great difference between knowing them or thinking he did. But Rimini could have sworn that this last face, which although the book belonged to the same collection, he had placed in a different dimension of time and space, was the only one he really did *not* know. Perhaps this explained why it had attracted his attention and why it was that now, instead of moving on, he picked the book up from the table, where the reflection from the stand lights meant he could not examine the author's face properly, and peered at it. He looked more closely at the smooth, rosy skin – like an embalmed child's – and then, fascinated by some internal contradiction in the face (in the same way that sometimes when he was reading, a sentence, turn of phrase or unexpected construction in the text took him by surprise and he felt he had to break off from reading to study the photograph of the author on the inside cover, as though the face held the secret to the mysteries of the language) he studied the name written above the photo: Caique de

Souza Dantas. He muttered the name under his breath to himself, but this only increased the enigma, so Rimini turned the book over and, beneath a miniature version of the photo on the front cover, found two or three lines in an accessible Portuguese which outlined the life of Caique de Souza Dantas, born in 1957 in Rio de Janeiro, actor, TV soap star, died of AIDS before his thirty-eighth birthday.

All at once he had to lean on something. One of his hands knocked over a pile of books, and he heard how, in the distance, their spines crashed against the floor. As one of the assistants bent down to pick them up, Rimini could sense an image emerging from the mists of his memory, becoming sharper the closer it got. Without having to look at the photo again, he could see the dead man's face; he saw a caterpillar of ash about to fall from the tip of a cigarette smoking between two gaunt fingers; he saw the branch of a tree, a foot with a sandal also about to fall off, a shirt with rolled-up sleeves, Sofia's rapt profile, half a wrought-iron chair, sun flickering on foliage, a stretch of pebbled ground, the brim of a light-coloured hat, the crossed tips of a pair of boots – his – and finally, like someone very slowly opening a valve, he heard the noises of the scene: the murmur of trees and water, birds, background voices from a group of tourists getting off a bus – and Caique's voice speaking Spanish, the sibilant Spanish he had learnt in Buenos Aires. And Sofia's laugh: a soft, irrepressible, frank laugh – the laugh of happiness. A chair creaked, and Sofia, doubled up with laughter, let her hand fall on Caique's bare forearm. The same laugh which for Rimini, who had produced it twice or at most three times in the twelve years they were together, was the one true proof (truer even than any emotional or sexual demonstration) of amorous possession.

Someone was talking to him. Rimini looked up and saw the worried face of one of the girls on the stand. She was close by, yet somehow blurred, as though she was behind a wet pane of glass. Rimini realised he was crying. 'I'm fine, I'm fine,' he said. The girl stepped back to let him past and smiled at him, and when Rimini, still grieving, stumbled by her, she held out a timid hand to reclaim the book. He thought she was trying to help him again, swerved to one side to avoid her and strode on until he was lost in the crowd.

As he left the Fair he bought a pair of cheap plastic sunglasses and, camouflaged as a fly, spent the whole of the return journey in tears.

He only discovered he was still carrying the book when he turned to read the name of a station and saw the man in the seat next to him leaning over and trying to read what he thought was the edge of his hand. Then, like someone plucking up the courage to touch a magic object that has suddenly appeared out of nowhere, he opened the book and started leafing slowly through it, amazed at finding writing in it, and then all at once impatiently opening it at the centrefold photographs. He devoted an equal amount of time to each one, as though fulfilling some sacred, austere funeral rite. 'Rio, 1959: Caique – the precocious actor – with burnt cork moustache. Sao Paulo, 1967: Caique with the flag. Sao Paulo, 1974: Caique as Puck in a school version of *A Midsummer Night's Dream*. London, 1975: Caique in Carnaby Street. Paris, 1975: Caique and Pascal. Friendship. Rio, 1977: Caique (second on the left, between Carmen Miranda and Marilyn Monroe) on his nineteenth birthday). Buenos Aires, 1980: Night on the town.' Rimini could see everything extremely clearly, as if the tears had polished his eyes. A smiling Caique, a red-eyed Satan thanks to the flash, is raising his glass to the camera. He is sitting barefoot in the lotus position on a dark carpet, a pile of records between his legs. Behind him, on a big leopard-skin sofa, sit two women in profile, talking and smoking, with glasses and cigarettes in one hand, while a younger boy and girl, alerted by the flash, turn towards the camera with baleful looks: the girl is so blonde her head looks as though it is aflame; the boy . . .

Rimini howled with pain, shut the book, buried his head in his hands. He felt overwhelmed, and the discrepancy between cause and effect only served to make him feel even more miserable. After all, Caique had never meant that much to him. It was the photo rather than the memory which proved that one night they had been less than half a metre from each other. His memory preferred to recall the scant furniture in the apartment, the fluffy carpet (the only reason to explain the epidemic of bare feet), the repulsive obesity of the woman owner. Then there was their meeting in the Floresta of Rio de Janeiro, clear and calm thanks to the cool breeze, the tree foliage and the determined enthusiasm which Sofia and he brought to their trip, despite all the discomfort, misunderstandings, and boredom – because not only had they shared very little, almost nothing, with Caique in Buenos Aires, but what little they had shared tended inexorably to become lost with the change of scenery and roles. Even so . . . his head filled with wild suspicions. Perhaps Sofia had been in love with Caique. Perhaps Caique had been in love with Sofia. Perhaps they had had a clandestine romance in Buenos Aires, and what Rimini was describing as calm and clear was not so much thanks to the charm of the ecosystem in the Floresta but to the nostalgic, knowing ease that Sofia and Caique seemed to share, so close to the feeling ex-lovers have when they meet in public and, in the presence of a third person who knows nothing of their relationship, decide to keep their past a secret. Every hypothesis seemed plausible but irrelevant. Digging up those virtual pasts where now all three of them – Caique, Sofia, he himself – were playing different roles to the ones the real past had assigned them, might perhaps have been of some use if Caique had been the reason for his sadness or at very least that strange whim of fate which had decided that Caique should reappear in Rimini's life only for Rimini to discover that he was dead. For Rimini there was something even more tragic than looking at the face of a dead young man, something that made him even more inconsolable because of making him feel even more alone: the evidence that *he had not died with him*, with *them* – with Caique, whose made-up face filled the cover of the book, but also not with that Rimini and that Sofia, who were displayed like mummies in the photo of that London interior. It was then that Rimini understood why he had always refused to share out the photos with Sofia, why two days after the accident he had burnt the ones of him and Vera, why he had forbidden any photographs on the afternoon of the civil marriage ceremony with Carmen, and why stories about vampires had never frightened him but instead had inspired a sense of intimate, very familiar sadness. No, when he looked at a photo he did not say: What I am looking at happened; he said: What I am looking at happened, has died, and I have survived.

He returned to the hotel with a single thought in mind: to write a letter to Sofia. As he left the Underground, the sky was disintegrating into clouds and purple stripes. It was night by the time he arrived: Carmen was not back. At reception, a new, young and friendly clerk handed him the room key on a small tray between two messages. Rimini asked for three beers and a bottle of tequila to be sent up. The clerk apologised: only the people on the hotel guest list could ask for room service: but before he had even finished, Rimini was already shooting out of the hotel to the self-service store opposite. Something about the way he clutched the supplies to him – the bottle of tequila under his right arm, one of vodka (a last-minute addition) under the left, and the beers (six instead of three) hanging from his mouth by the plastic strip holding them together – must have worried the owner, who glanced at him furtively while taking his money. Less out of greed than a desire to get back at him, Rimini added some chewing-gum, a chocolate coconut bar, and two bags of crisps. He returned to the hotel, crossed the lobby waving the bottles defiantly, and got into the lift. He read the messages by its flickering light: one was from Carmen, telling him that the evening session was still going on, and promising to call him as soon as it had finished; the other was from Idelber Avelar, who was in Room 610.

For the next few hours, Rimini did three things, always in the same order: he drank, he wrote, he threw what he had written away. He drank: first of all, two beers, then half of the tequila straight from the bottle, then another beer – the aluminium strip that remained when he pulled the can open cut his top lip – and finally, using the glass from the bathroom, which gave the vodka a gentle hint of mint, almost the whole of the Stolichnaya. He wrote: a sort of belated, confused summary of his relationship with Sofia that at its most inspired was quite dishonest, since the reason behind it was not to shine light on the past but to exorcise (thereby finally giving her what she was supposedly demanding from him) any possible ghostly reapparitions of the kind he had just suffered, disguised as a souvenir from Rio; an invitation to re-create that afternoon in the Floresta that began in a mature, balanced tone but rapidly changed to one of suspicion – 'I don't know how long you and Caique took to come back with the pineapple juices, but I remember it was too long . . .' and ended with a threatening list of questions, numbered from 1 to 25; followed by an equally fraudulent *mea culpa* in which Rimini, desperate to rid himself of Sofia rather than to reconcile her to his points of view, for the first time bared his soul to her, accepting the responsibility for everything and drowning in the mire of his own shortcomings, which had not only separated him from her but also, as he was beginning to suspect, from 'the possibility of love in general'. Then he threw away: he tore the sheets off, let them drop on to the carpet, rolled them into balls and flung them against the half-open window, tore the sheets into bits and dropped the pieces into the toilet bowl, where he bathed them in sarcastic jets of piss, burnt whole pages of them in the bath-tub. As he was doing this, he caught sight of his dishevelled image in the bathroom cabinet mirror: he was naked, bathed in sweat, his face bright red from the drink and smudged with ink.

He could have carried on like this for hours. Failure only spurred him on, multiplying his ambitions in a diabolical fashion. He wanted to drive Sofia away, to excuse himself, to disappear for ever so that this handful of lined sheets would be the very last thing left of him; he wanted to purify himself and at the same time to annihilate, to annihilate something living, anything. He wanted to write a letter commensurate with his body – like a resistant, durable skin that would protect him always against everything. But the phone rang and Rimini, who had heard it ring and ring earlier as if in a dream, crawled across the bed like an infantryman and answered it. It was Idelber Avelar. He introduced himself formally, repeating the three lines of biography that were in the congress programme, and then started on a long, confused explanation that Rimini cut short before it could take the form of a coherent complaint, with an avalanche of indescribable obscenities. Avelar hung up, and Rimini was left for a moment with the sound of his own breathing. Then he ran to the bathroom to throw up. All he managed to produce were a few dry retches, but these proved sufficiently strong to lift the mist before his eyes slightly. He went back to the phone, started to get dressed, and played back the messages that the flashing red light was promising. There were three of them, all from Carmen, and all of them accompanied by a swarm of voices, laughter, the clinking of glasses, music. The first told him the address of the restaurant where they were celebrating the close of the congress; the second was in tiny childish yelps, asking him where he was; in the third her voice was either worried or weary, repeating the address like someone crying for help. Rimini searched for something to write with, struggled with the sleeve he was trying to put on, lost time, and just as he was writing down the number of the street where the restaurant was, the message ran out. He tried to listen to it again, pressed two wrong buttons, and found himself talking to the laundry service (what were they doing open at this time of night?) and with the extension for valet parking. Finally, after attempting in vain to get through to reception, the red light stopped flashing and went out once and for all, to be replaced by the voice of Idelber Avelar, the voice of a reasonable person who has decided to pretend that what happened never in fact took place, who never heard what he thought he heard, and wants to begin again from the beginning. Could he have his badge please?

Rimini cried, cried, cried, until his eyes stung so much he had no alternative but to go to sleep. He dreamt of ceiling fans turning exasperatingly slowly, with ashes in water, with bells, with the distant rumble of a moving lift, with a door creaking open, fingers caressing his hip, his thighs, his feet – at that point he half opened his eyes and managed to say – although he was not sure if he said it in his dream or in the hotel bedroom – 'the light, the light', and a woman who looked remarkably like Carmen took pity on him, said 'yes, my love, yes, straightaway', then moved away from the bed (with his trousers in her hand) and switched off the light. She came back, speared her knee on the bed again, and started to unbutton his shirt. Rimini could feel her fingers brushing against his chest and shuddered, then heard Carmen laugh and say: 'Mmm, what an enthusiastic welcome', and when she sat on him and began to move, he screwed up his eyes and plunged into a bottomless black pit. Everything he had been dreaming about before Carmen arrived came back to him, projected on this black background: the same images, but spinning backwards – first her fingers, then the sound of the door, then the lift going down, and so on and on until it was Rimini himself and not the blades of the fan spinning around in the bed. After that it seemed to him that the light had gone off for good, and he passed out, only coming round for an instant when Carmen returned from the bathroom, gave him a gentle push to make room for herself, slipped in between the sheets and, curling up against him, brought her lips to his ear and whispered that she might be completely crazy and that he should not ask why, but that she thought she had just become pregnant.

CHAPTER 8

He went into the bathroom and saw her standing there, back towards him, with her legs apart and holding the hem of her nightdress high up on her thighs. He went over to her slowly so as not to alarm her, and when he came level with her saw she had her head down between her shoulders and was staring fixedly at something on the floor – something she did not yet know whether to admire or to be afraid of. Rimini touched her arm. Carmen did not move; she had not even realised he had come in. Following the direction of her gaze, Rimini came up against two small pools gleaming on the black tile in between her feet. As his eyes travelled up from the insteps of her feet, her ankles, her swollen knees, he saw that two thin trickles of water were running down from the inside of her thighs.

Too late again – or too early. Things never happened following the logical course of events, but in a sort of treacherous backwater added accidentally to time, a place where things, like those faces which look old although the person is still youthful, seemed to stagnate in a state of unbearable indecision. It was just after midnight. Carmen's belly – despite its size, which brought on paternal instincts in the obstetrician and groans of perverse pleasure in Rimini – was only at thirty-two weeks. They had not prepared anything: no bag, no clothes, no money, not even the proper reaction designed to lessen their terror when this moment arrived – nothing of what they had been promised they would learn to do and have ready when they had gone to their one and only antenatal class along with another half-dozen couples. But no preparation would have been of any use: even though the waters breaking and a premature birth were not that unexpected, they both seemed to have prepared for it on their own, in a sort of individual world of speculation, separate from the other person's, and never in the same orbit where they might have coincided: so that now that Carmen was staring like an idiot at her streaming vagina, while Rimini was covering her with the first thing that came to hand – an old green coat with a thread-bare collar, one pocket hanging loose like a tongue, the other stuffed with mothballs – and trying to get her to put on a pair of sandals, what most affected them was not so much how unprepared they were, nor how dramatic the situation was, but also, and above all, the crash with which their two worlds had collided and merged into a shared horizon of fear.

They took a taxi and travelled in silence. Her legs spread wide, Carmen took up almost all the seat. Rimini was squashed up against the taxi door, his mind alternating between a blind, shapeless panic and a much more focussed concern about the possible effects of the amniotic fluid on the leatherette upholstery. They held each other's hand, took turns to stroke one another, sought refuge in each other. They were together in a way they perhaps had never been before, because, as well as love, what brought them close at that moment was the same sense of disbelief and horror that brings two strangers together in mid-flight when they both look out of the window at the same time and discover that one of the plane's wings is on fire. 'Music bother you?' the driver asked, raising a threatening hand towards his radio. They looked at each other and said nothing, but a few minutes later, when the taxi was going through the third red light, Carmen said something very softly, and Rimini leaned towards her and asked: 'What?' 'It's Virus, isn't it?' she said. Rimini looked at her as if she was delirious. 'The group playing,' she said. 'Ah,' he replied, and listened more closely: yes, it was Virus. They listened together in silence, concentrating hard, as though expecting to hear, hidden in some words or in a chord, a message meant only for them. Carmen started humming the tune. Then she felt her vagina, and when she had lifted her hand to her nose, said: 'It's water,' in a disappointed way, holding her fingers out to Rimini. He did not take her up on the invitation, but merely nodded, kissed her hand, and kept it pressed against his lips for the whole of the rest of the journey as though it were a talisman. 'Shall we take Gascón or Potosí?' the taxi-driver asked a few blocks before they got there. Rimini hesitated, confused by the superior tone he had detected in the question. He turned towards Carmen, who was staring out of the window, her mouth half-open. She looked far, far away, as if she had gone on a solitary journey without telling him. 'What's the difference?' asked

Rimini. The driver smiled in the rear-view mirror. 'You need Potosí, sweetheart: Maternity is in Potosí.'

After he had installed her in an old wheelchair, the paramedic walked off, his rubber soles squeaking on the floor. He was replaced by a young woman doctor who asked them to follow her down a corridor. Rimini started to push the chair. To him, who saw this moment as a threshold, and the hectic sequence of events to follow as only ending with the birth, it was all over far too quickly. It was only a metre or so from the lobby, where they had sat in ragged chairs for a few minutes (Rimini ready to do battle, indignant even at the passing of time, as if Carmen were bleeding to death in front of everyone in a hospital, and nobody was doing anything to help her; Carmen sitting in silence, slack-jawed, sinking deeper and deeper into the stupor she was only roused from the next morning when after a silent, sleepless night, the obstetrician – disguising his concern as indifference, haste, or boredom, as if Carmen's case, despite all the risks, were not complicated enough to offer anything original – told them that whether Carmen liked it or not, the birth would not be put off any longer than that night) to the duty consulting-room where there was barely enough space for a couch, a coat-stand and a tall stool like something out of a 1970s whisky bar. The wheelchair made the transfer difficult: its front wheels needed oil and were buckled: every so often they splayed out perpendicular to the direction Rimini was pushing it in, so that he had to stop, shake the chair carefully in order not to disturb Carmen too much, and then do the same thing all over again a few metres further on. The woman doctor went into the consulting-room and called them in. She hung a stethoscope round her neck and told Carmen to get up on the couch, and Rimini to wait outside. Rimini wavered: he did not want to let Carmen out of his sight. He helped her from the chair, held on tight as he walked her over to the couch, then forced her to sit down with exasperating slowness, as if her body were made of glass. As she slid backwards, her elbows jutting into the black oilskin, he lifted her feet with both hands, like a magician preparing his assistant for a levitation trick. After settling her on to the couch, Rimini turned and bumped into the doctor, who was looking at him with a sort of tender insistence. 'Outside, please,' she said again. Rimini felt a flush of useless heroism, the same compulsion to sacrifice himself that he used to feel as a boy when something was prohibited and he realised that nothing he could do would change a thing, and so redoubled his efforts. He looked despairingly at Carmen to try to spot some obvious heartfelt emotion that could justify his posturing. 'Go on, go on,' she said resignedly.

The consultation lasted less than ten minutes. Rimini stayed on guard the whole time outside the door. Every so often, after confirming no one was in the corridor, he pressed his ear against the door to try to hear something. He never recognised anything apart from his own beating heart. He saw a paramedic go by pulling two empty trolleys, a nun in glasses, two doctors with masks round their necks and feet covered in sterilised plastic bags, a nurse pushing a wheelchair in which sat an old man wrapped in a tartan blanket. As he passed by Rimini, the man turned his head slightly, lifted a dying hand from between the folds of the blanket and waved it in the air, as if in greeting or calling for help. At that moment the consulting-room door opened and Rimini, who had been leaning on it for a moment, almost fell on top of the doctor. 'We're going to keep her in,' he heard her say. She gave him a sheaf of papers. 'You go down to the first basement and get the paper-work over with.' As simple as that? Was that all? Rimini wanted to protest – a childish reaction, but one that could be effective: it was enough for him to start protesting to feel that the situation was no longer out of control, but was heading in some direction at least – but the doctor, who was already skipping away down the corridor (she was wearing trainers, and no sooner had Rimini spotted the faded orange marks on the sides of the rubber soles than he felt an extraordinary urge to play tennis on a hard clay court), left him standing there waving his arms on his own.

He went into the consulting-room; Carmen was lying back in the same position he had left her in. She had been covered in a grey blanket, and her pale arms stood out from the wool as if they were prosthetic, like fragile exhibits in an anatomical exhibition. She was smiling placidly, the smile of someone who has been drugged and is no longer suffering because she has lost all feeling. She seemed perfectly comfortable, as if the black oilskin of the couch, the flimsy partitions or the neon light tube buzzing on the ceiling were not casual accessories but pleasant details of surroundings in which she was going to spend a long time.

And there he was, disturbing this strangely peaceful scene with his vehemence . . . He wanted to backtrack, but it was too late – he bumped into the stool, leaned over Carmen, took her hand. He was taken by surprise at how cold it was, and the bluish tinge the veins gave to her white, almost transparent skin. He whispered firmly into her ear, as if she was very close but very far away at the same time, and swore he would never leave her side, that he would not go and do any of the paperwork, that he would stay with her until the obstetrician arrived, that he would not allow them to . . . 'Go on,' said Carmen, freeing her hand and using it to pat him gently on the shoulder, as though consoling him. 'Seriously. I'm fine here. Don't worry. Go and look round, then you can tell me what the hospital's like, OK?' Rimini straightened up, bewildered by the ease with which Carmen's simple stoicism was enough to undermine all his attempts to fuss over her. He turned to look at her one last time, and as he caught in her face the last dying echoes of the pity he had aroused in her (his fears, his helplessness, his touching incapacity) a whole string of worrying eventualities sprang up in his imagination. He left and Carmen was transferred, but nobody could tell him exactly where she had been taken, to which ward or room. He left, and Carmen had to have an emergency operation for an illness they had only just discovered. He left, and Carmen was abducted, gave birth in captivity, and her kidnappers took the baby and sold it. He left, and Carmen gave birth without him, but the child was dead, or deformed, or was somebody else's. He left, and Carmen died in the delivery-room, far from him, without even realising she was dying or that he was not by her side . . . Rimini opened the door and waved his hand slowly and melodramatically, perfectly aware that he was prolonging the gesture so that Carmen would have it engraved on her memory as the last thing she had seen him do, something she would spend the rest of her life cherishing, or forgetting – until she raised her own hand, a slight, pallid hand that seemed to be slapping the air, and drove him out.

Near the hospital entrance, a porter was successfully struggling with a sticky caramel wrapper. When Rimini asked him how to get to the admissions desk, he gave him long, confused directions of which he retained only the first part: how to get from the maternity building they were in to another one, the original hospital, built in 1907 according to the porter, where all the administrative offices were to be found. It took Rimini fifteen minutes to get there. The hospital was immense, but its dimensions were multiplied due to a diabolical system of signs which in the main consisted of handwritten posters and arrows, figures painted with marker pens obviously running out of ink, sheets from computer print-outs stuck to the wall with Blu-tack, some spatial (left for right and vice versa) and numerical (ground floor for first, first floor for second, and so on) liberties, as well as a whole chain of human informers dotted all along the route – easily recognisable thanks to their uniforms: white undershirts, unbuttoned overalls, flip-flops, some kind of cleaning implement in their hands, and a kind of shared dialect made up entirely of grunts and onomatopoeias – who accosted any visitor, smiled in a friendly way to reassure them and then, as if coming under the influence of some dreadful potion, began to dampen their spirits with dire warnings ('You have to go back to the door where you came in . . .'), made them giddy with contradictory advice, and whenever the other person tried to point out an inconsistency, grumbled and walked away, cursing at the world's ingratitude, to busy themselves with the imaginary task they had been forced to abandon. In addition, the hospital was like a theatre in ancient times, split into two tiers: the upper one represented day, and the floors shone, there were windows on to the street, the doctors spoke quietly and the nurses walked by, stiff and proud; the lower one was night, with peeling walls and a smell of food – here the values of the upper floor were turned upside down, and a vast dark basement was peopled by hopeless slaves, the lowest rank of nurses, maids, porters, kitchen assistants, janitors, security and cleaning staff, as well as an entire fauna of society's outcasts: chronic or poverty-stricken patients, sellers of lottery tickets and cheap jewellery, the homeless, street kids, beggars who had either managed to avoid the hospital authorities or had somehow gained their consent to squat in this cellar where in summer or winter the temperature was always infernally hot. Apart from the two shortcuts he took – two very instructive failures (the first led him straight to the morgue; the second to the depths of the underworld and something an old sign said was the 'machine-room') – Rimini did not get lost. He went down corridors, crossed entire wards, climbed up and down stairs, took lifts, went through reception areas and transitional areas, astonished at his own determination to find his way around this unknown world. He stopped only once, for a few seconds, when he recognised the woman doctor who had taken Carmen in, even though she had swapped her white coat, now hanging from her arm, for a dark outfit. In a fit of unusual daring, which he regretted almost immediately, he went over and asked her how Carmen and the baby were *really* doing. In response, partly because she was annoyed at being bothered with work matters after she had finished for the day, and partly due to Rimini's confidential tone, as if he took it for granted that her diagnosis had been one long lie from start to finish, she reeled off an avalanche of technical terms of which Rimini understood not a thing, although some of the suggestive terms – drip, contractions, nil dilation, caesarean – stuck in his mind when he continued on his way to the admissions desk.

It was the time when they were changing shifts. As he advanced through the depths of the hospital, Rimini thought he could make out the signs of a subtle movement that was hard to pin down but which was definitely bringing about a profound change in the appearance of his surroundings. It was as if he could see the tides moving back and forth at the very moment they were doing so. Faces lined with tiredness gave way to freshly shaven, bright ones. Forms, lists, medical records changed hands. Superfluous lights were switched off, leaving whole areas in darkness, and footsteps, which previously had merged into the general hubbub, now rang out clearly, amplified by the emptiness. Doors were locked, people said goodbye, the loudspeakers announced the end of visiting time. Rimini was scared of arriving too late, and hurried even more. He knew he was close by now, but could not avoid asking a woman who was tidying a pile of papers. 'Down those stairs,' she said. When he got there, a woman with an enormous mole on her lip was covering the gap at the bottom of the window with an oblong piece of cardboard. Rimini waved his forms in front of the glass. The woman did not even look at him. She merely nodded once in the direction of something to Rimini's right, then turned her back on him. Rimini spun round and saw two women queueing a couple of metres away. The one behind was writing something on one of her thighs, which she had raised in the air. Rimini barely looked at her, simply registering her stooped heron silhouette, but as he drew close something happened; the ballpoint

224

she was using to fill in the form ran out of ink, or the sheet of paper got torn, or she wrote her civil status in the box for her telephone number, whatever it was, the woman was visibly irritated and she stumbled. The piles of photocopies she had been resting the form on started to slide out one by one and floated to the floor like leaves. Rimini bent down to pick them up. Each of them contained an out-of-proportion drawing of a different part of the body that was slightly askew, as if it had been done by a child. There was a face, a thorax, two feet seen from below, as if they were on a glass floor, and there were lines stuck like needles into different vital points. As he straightened up, photocopies in hand, Rimini found himself staring into Sofia's face. She was gazing back at him, wide-eyed. 'I don't believe it,' she said, a smile spreading across her features as she looked at him more closely, taking in the whole of his body, like an x-ray machine, with her gaze. 'You're fat,' said Sofia, and repeated: 'Fat,' as though finally accepting some astonishing truth. Her astonishment was genuine. Rimini felt that however banal her comment might be, it tore him out of the present, in the same way that as a child he imagined it happening to Douglas and Tony, the heroes of *The Time Tunnel*, when from central control they succeeded in getting them to change epochs – and deposited him in this new, bare and slightly hostile environment where he and Sofia met again like the only two survivors from an extinct planet. Rimini was hurt. 'I stopped smoking,' he said, handing her back the photocopies. 'It's incredible,' Sofia repeated, unable to take her eyes from him. 'Why? It's like a light switch – I can put it on or take it off when I like.' 'No, I don't mean that. Only two minutes ago I was talking about you with Frida. I'm getting her admitted to hospital. She keeps fainting. She fell twice in the Underground. I went to her place today because I had a class, but nobody answered. I rang and rang: nothing. Luckily I had a key. (When she goes away on trips it's me who waters her plants and feeds her cats. You remember.) I found her on the floor in the bathroom, naked (just imagine!) with the shower running for heaven knows how long. She could have cracked her head open. The fact is, that's what she may have done. She's got a cut here, and it's all black around her eye. They were taking some x-rays. Yes, sorry.' She took a step forward, smiled at the face waiting for her on the other side of the window, and slipped a credential and some sheets of paper through the slot. The clerk kept the top sheet and passed back the three bits of anatomical art he would not be needing: a male reproductive system, an abdomen, a lumbar region. 'I called Nolting. Do you remember Nolting? Because of course she didn't have any kind of doctor. Frida hates doctors. What? Oh yes, I'm sorry. 13-82 . . . No, 13-80, no: 8 . . . What is this? I can't even remember my identity card number. 13-80 . . .' she turned to Rimini, horrified. '13-82-322,' he said, going up to the window. The clerk looked at him. 'Are you two together?' he asked, waving the blunt pencil in his hand at them in turn. 'Yes,' Sofia said. Rimini felt warm pressure on his forearm and entered a cloud of perfume. 'That's great: with you beside me, I could just let myself forget everything. Rimini cast a surreptitious glance at her out of the corner of his eye. Her hair was cut shorter, she was not wearing much make-up and looked fresh and enthusiastic, like someone who has just finished some sporting activity. A reddish scab was prominent on one of her ear lobes, escaping the ear-ring that had been put there to hide it. 'Just now, five minutes ago,' Sofia went on. 'I don't know what I was saying, something about the room (oh, yes, it was about the instructions for raising the bed – they're in English, have you seen?) and Frida mentioned your name. Off her own bat – I hadn't said a word.' The clerk stamped her forms, kept the original in a folder, pushed the copy back under the window, and then got up from his seat. 'Wait a minute,' Rimini shouted, flinging himself at the window. The clerk said, turning back to them: 'Weren't you two together?' 'No, no,' said Rimini, pushing his documents through the gap under the window. 'I've . . . got my wife up there, in Maternity. Her waters have broken'. Rimini shot Sofia a quick glance and had a proper, clear view of the way her mouth was starting to twist in disbelief. He could feel a huge lump in his throat, and barely managed to get out the words: 'I'm going to have a child.' The phrase sprouted, flew through the air, penetrated Sofia and mingled with her blood, and it was only when it surfaced again as she started to shiver, turn pale, go cross-eyed as she had always used to, that he realised it was the first time he had said it. 'I'm going to have a child,' he thought. Sofia stepped back. Perhaps she was preparing to run away; perhaps she needed to distance herself to comprehend fully what she had just heard. 'I can't believe it,' she said. 'Nor can I,' he replied. Sofia gave a weak smile, rushed up to him, and started beating against his chest with her open hand. 'Without me. You're going to have a child without me,' she said, hitting him two or three times without any force, merely for emphasis, as if she were trying to find the physical, material proof of the emotional sterility she had always accused him of. Then she crumpled, lifted her eyes and looked up at him. 'Son of a bitch,' she said, 'so you were capable of it.' She hugged him.

Arm-in-arm, they walked away from the window. Sofia was crying; Rimini felt overwhelmed by a powerful sense of vitality. He felt like running as fast as he could along the hospital's subterranean corridor, like a demented athlete; he imagined all the steps he had climbed and descended and saw his feet literally swallowing them up two, four, six at a time. Sofia was still crying, drying her tears on his shirt sleeve. 'Son of a bitch. Son of a bitch. Just as well I'm fine now,' she said. 'If you'd told me three months ago, I'd be dead. Now I'm happy. You're a son of a bitch, but I'm happy for you. It gives me . . . hope. Everything is so unbelievable. I arrived two days ago from Europe, I'm off again next week, today this happens to Frida, and now I've met you . . . isn't it all unbelievable? And I'm in love.'

His name was Konrad. He was German, from Munich. Sofia showed Rimini a photo while she was pushing him into a lift he could not remember having taken: a yellow wall with bookcases, books, masks, and in the foreground, almost singed by the flash, the outline of a figure raising a hand to the camera either in greeting or in protest. It seemed to Rimini he had red hair and that he was in his underpants or had a towel round his waist. He preferred not to ask. By the time the lift doors opened again (after going up and down a couple of floors for no apparent reason) Konrad, who had become an orphan (an avalanche in a ski resort), was going to live with Liselotte, a deaf spinster aunt, in her luxurious but run-down mansion in the suburbs, seven of whose thirteen rooms she used to house students from all over the world. Sofia had briefly become part of the commune. She had ended up at Liselotte's mansion – by now, Liselotte (Sofia was steering Rimini across a deserted hall, and casually greeting a very elegant nurse with a coif and glasses) was not only deaf and a spinster but wore bootees without socks, all the rage with lesbians in the Black Forest – when after a particularly difficult moment during her trip before last with Frida she had quit the hotel room they were sharing due to a dreadful argument about the possibilities of rehabilitating (unlike Frida, she thought there was a good chance of it) one of the children on their summer school, half of whose body was paralysed by an unusual sort of conversion hysteria. It was not the first time, and would not be the last. Rimini knew what Frida was like, and knew that nobody who had a relationship like the one Sofia had had with her for almost twenty years now – more than enough time for two women of such different ages to have experienced practically all possible forms of emotional exchange – could imagine they were safe from this kind of clash. In fact, these tensions were not so much accidental as the driving force of the relation, its sustenance, its possibility of moving forward. Sofia spent only a week in the Pension Liselotte, as Konrad had called it when they had become friends after only two days. It had been love at first sight, Sofia said, tugging at Rimini's sleeve. It had only taken two days in that fin-de-siècle mansion, establishing with Konrad the kind of contact that exists between host and guest – morning encounters in the kitchen, at breakfast, poring over maps of the city together, asking for fresh towels, the exchange of linguistic curiosities in their respective languages – for Sofia to realise just how far Konrad, who was quite a lot younger than her and kept the books for the Pension Liselotte, was dominated by his aunt, and lived in an atmosphere of fear that was imperceptible or irrelevant to anyone but Sofia who, as Rimini was well aware, had a special nose for everything that went on under the surface, and how far the house, where at that moment (it was not a very successful season) twelve students from the four corners of the globe were living – students from Singapore to Quito, Vancouver to Athens – with its well looked-after plants, its traditional food, its CDs of Bavarian music played on small loudspeakers installed in every room, its impeccably white lace mats, made by Liselotte herself, was in fact a complete madhouse. The domineering lesbian aunt, the fragile orphan nephew, the house pretending to be a refuge, opening its arms wide only to clamp them round its victims like a trap; Sofia could see the blackmailing logic of the situation, while at the same time she was falling in love with Konrad's shyness, the traces of his adolescent acne, his old man's slippers, his hairless chest, the rough, forced, moving way he had

228

of pronouncing (or rather, of hammering out) words like 'Argentina', 'emotion', 'profundity' and 'beloved'. Yes, Sofia was happy. Did she need to tell him everything she had found in Konrad that reminded her of Rimini, the *first* Rimini? No, there was no need, said Rimini – desperately wanting to ask where they were, and if this corridor with numbered doors on each side actually led to Maternity, if the bodies he caught glimpses of in the beds were women about to give birth ... In the week she had been there though, Sofia had managed to turn the madhouse on its head. It all began with an innocent request to have the heating turned down. The request – which in any other of the hundred or hundred and twenty family houses in Munich which rented rooms to foreign students would have been unnecessary, given the fact that it was high summer and a 32° average temperature, which meant that even ten per cent of the constant heat given off by the Pension Liselotte radiators was stifling – was the spark that set everything alight. Even though it had been Sofia's idea, the person who relayed it to the higher regions was not her, but Konrad. She was well aware of the potentially explosive situation when she chose him as go-between – partly, as she admitted, because Liselotte intimidated her, but mostly for therapeutic reasons – in an attempt to free him from the despotic pact into which his aunt had forced him. 'He had never asked her for anything, you see?' said Sofia. 'It was crazy: the aunt was all he had in the world, and he had never asked her for a thing. And if he went on not asking for anything, he was going to have to accept whatever she felt like giving him. And what was that? Nothing. Absolutely nothing. Or rather: she gave him red hot radiators in the hottest summer for the last fifty years.'

That had been the start of a real revolution. At first, Liselotte had denied that the heating was especially high; she had not touched the controls on the boiler that constantly pumped out heat in the basement for more than twenty years. Then, when Konrad suggested (only suggested, because after all, however crazy and despotic she might be, she was his aunt and he loved her, and would not have wanted to offend her unless it was a really life-or-death situation) that it was summer outside, and also that over the past twenty years the temperature in general might well have got warmer, Liselotte, apparently beside herself, in a violent rage such as Konrad had never seen in her before, not even when one of the neighbour's sons, a skinhead who according to her went out on Saturday nights with his gang of layabouts to molest the Turkish maids in the neighbourhood, dealt a fatal taekwondo blow to Kim, the fox terrier cross who had been her faithful companion for ten years, almost kicked him out of the kitchen, pausing only to shower him with insults and accuse him of screwing around behind her back – in her own house where (doubtless egged on by that woman) he had dared to criticise the level of the heating – screwing around with a South American whose sole purpose was obviously to destroy the only family tie he had left following the tragedy, and in doing so bring about her ruin. 'Screwing around, would you believe it? We hadn't done a thing up till then, nothing! Not even a kiss, Rimini! Oh well yes, there was some kissing, not in her house but once in the cinema, when we saw *West Side Story* ... She's sick, a complete psychotic!'

They had to come to a halt. Someone was being transferred: a woman so thin that two of her would have fitted into the nightgown she was wearing. The porter could not get the bed round the corner without hitting the corridor walls time and again. Rimini felt a wave of anguish. 'I have to get back,' he said, or let slip, as he turned and peered at the far end of the corridor, where a yellowish light – his last hope – appeared to be slowly going out. 'Give me a hand,' said the porter, who had stopped pushing the bed in order to straighten the bag of saline solution that was threatening to fall off its hook. The woman groaned; as soon as she did so, a string of other groans rose in reply from the corridor rooms. 'Rimini!' Sofia scolded him. Rimini started pushing the bed, going over in his mind ways he could escape: 'I don't have ... I ought to be ... My wife ... Maternity.' 'That's the other building. The new one,' the porter replied at once, as if he had been trained to react automatically at the mere mention of any word in the hospital's lexicon. Rimini pushed as hard as he could, screwing up his eyes. His hands were sweaty: he let go of the aluminium rail and put them directly on to the plastic covering on the bed. As he did so, his fingers touched something rough, hard, completely dead. He opened his eyes: it was one of the woman's feet which all the jolting of the bed had exposed when the sheet slid off, a foot like a stone wrapped in a dry, wrinkled skin ... Rimini felt dizzy, but instead of looking away found himself staring intently at the claw-like toes all bent towards the big one, like a herd fleeing a predator and seeking refuge against the big yellow nail ... Rimini lifted his head and felt fresh hope. They had reached a big hall lined with three lifts. While the porter manoeuvred the bed and the woman barely raised her head, looked all round her and asked if this was the operating theatre, Rimini sensed a powerful hand pulling at his clothes, taking him away from them. A door opened behind him, a rush of hot air engulfed him. When he tried to work out what was going on, he found himself running down a flight of steps, pursued by Sofia. 'Are you sure that ... ?' he started to ask. She shouted 'Shortcut!' or something that contained the word 'shortcut', and when they reached a platform jumped up five or six steps at a time, getting ahead of him without even touching him. She opened another door – the cold air hit him in the face and chest again, and pushed him into a hall identical to the one they had just left. 'It's this way,' said Sofia. And then, as Rimini struggled to follow her, she added: 'She threw him out.' 'What?' said Rimini. 'She threw him out in the street. Didn't I tell you she was a psychotic? We went to a hotel. Poor thing: I knew Munich better than he did. He was like a fledgling fallen out of its nest. My Kaspar Hauser, you would call him. And you can laugh: Konrad was a virgin. Do you know anyone who's still a virgin at twenty-five? One hundred and twenty-three, one hundred and twenty-five, one hundred and twenty-seven: this is it. I fell in love, Rimini. Head over heels in love. I couldn't lie to you. One hundred and thirty-one: now I can't remember if it was odd or even. And do you know what was most fantastic of all? We couldn't speak a word together. I can hardly understand German, he doesn't know a word of Spanish. It's like being naked the whole time. It's love, Rimini. You know what I'm talking about. Pure love.' Sofia stopped outside the half-open door to a room. She raised a nostalgic hand and brushed his cheek with the back of her fingers: 'Like ours once, perhaps ... no?' She kissed him quickly on the lips, the way one kisses someone asleep in order not to wake them. Then, as she carefully pushed open the door, she added: 'He's still a virgin. We couldn't do it. Besides: we've got time, haven't we? He's taking singing lessons now. When I met him I said: "you must be a good singer." "No," he told me. So I said: "that can't be right. You've got to sing."' 'Sofia?' a voice called from inside the room. 'Come on, you go in first,' Sofia whispered, dragging him inside: 'she'll be so pleased to see you.'

He recalled her as *more*: paler, bigger, more threatening. But that was how most things seemed to him in memory, not just Frida Breitenbach. And even though she was on her back in bed – not lying flat since, aware of the image of weakness this position would have created, she had taken the trouble to convince first Sofia and then the nurse to raise the back of the bed slightly so that when she talked she would not always have to be looking up, like someone about to die; her entire body, shrunken by age, and her bruised and wounded face, but above all her still bright, lively eyes that seemed encrusted in the folds of flesh, and the flaccid jowls her face dissolved into around her jaws and neck, and even, half-sitting up as she was, into the upper part of her chest – everything about Frida still gave off the arrogance, the malign perspicacity, the remote sensitivity that managed to be both vibrant and contemplative, which for twelve years had kept Rimini in a state of constant alert, oscillating between fascination, horror, and wariness. Battered as she was, at the mercy of doctors, nurses and diagnostic machines – three things she had never believed in and which in her own way she had combated all her life – she was still the same female Buddha who, through all those years, had been the immobile centre of a virtually infinite galaxy of sufferers in the gatherings at her Calle Vidt apartment.

Rimini saw her before she spotted him. She was too busy casting one of her famous withering looks at Sofia, who was approaching her bed, a look full of reproach and scorn, one of those fateful bolts of lightning that often reduced her disciples – and sometimes, if through some unforgivable weakness they had betrayed the principles of her discipline, her patients as well – to a state of slavery that could last for months. 'Might I know what . . . ?' she said, speaking to Sofia, and as her voice came rumbling out, Rimini could see her whole face vibrating and starting to shake. She would doubtless have fired off a barrage of insults if Rimini had not bumped his knee against the bed and attracted her attention in mid-sentence. For the fraction of a second, Rimini found himself the object of her fury. It was only an instant – less than that even: the gap between two instants. This was because as soon as she saw who it was, the scornful twist to her mouth changed into a bright, beatific smile, and Frida opened her arms wide to receive him. 'Darling,' she said emotionally, hugging him to her, while Rimini clung on to the edges of the mattress, his fingers digging into the seams of the cotton sheets. 'My darling,' she repeated, letting go of him in order to get a better look. He smelled the same stale, wet perfume he had noticed on Sofia when she had kissed him in the middle of the street two years earlier. 'Just because you split up with this harpy here didn't give you the right to abandon me.' And then immediately, as if regaining control and suddenly remembering how she must look, she said coquettishly: 'Get away, don't look at me,' and hid the bruised side of her face in her pillow, even though due to the dim light in the room, Rimini had not even noticed it. 'I must look like a monster.' 'Does it hurt?' Sofia asked. 'No,' said Frida, 'I don't feel a thing. No pain or anything. Do you think this is how death starts? Come here,' she said, holding out a hand to Rimini and drawing him back towards her. 'Where have you been all this time, if I may ask?' Rimini sat on the edge of the bed. Sofia replied for him: 'He's going to have a child.' 'Don't talk nonsense,' said Frida, tapping Rimini lightly on his right cheek. He felt strangely uneasy: it was as if Frida had forged them into a single being, in which Frida was the voice and Rimini the body. 'A child? Who with? You're not really going to have a child, are you? You're so young, so intelligent, so handsome. And you're going to ruin all that with a child?' She shook him vigorously; in her eyes Rimini thought he could see a fierce, evil glow, so he pulled away. Frida collapsed on to the bed: her breathing was suddenly laboured. 'Call the nurse,' she said. Sofia went over to the bed. 'Let's ring the bell.' 'No, go and call her, don't be so mean,' Frida shouted. She seemed to be choking, and started to cough. As soon as Sofia was out of the room, Frida raised her head and fixed her eyes on Rimini. 'You two were so beautiful. How old were you? Seventeen? Eighteen? I remember the first time Sofia brought you to Vidt I thought: "They're so beautiful they ought to be disfigured." What an idiot: why didn't I do it? If I had, you'd still be together today. Drawing the right amount of blood at the right moment: that's the secret of immortality. I took pity on you. I was always too sensitive to beauty: that's my karma. And then what did you pair of criminals do? You decided to be . . . normal. Normal! You decided to split the cell, to get some fresh air, to fall in love with other people . . . Hopeless. You didn't have the right.

You were part of our world heritage. If society were just – no, not just, intelligent – young people would all be slaves, slaves of the old, and would have to live governed by their points of view, their whims, their violence even, until the first sign of corruption started to appear. Only then would they be set free. "Free". If anyone who has started to rot can be free, that is. How old are you now? Thirty? Thirty-two? It's late. Very late,' she moaned, starting to beat her breast with both hands. 'What have you done with your life, you wretch? You've lost everything! You two have wasted everything! So now you're going to have a child and you think that will make you young again, do you? That you can live again. Poor fool. Is that why you gave up? For a child? Listen to me: there's no such thing as children. There are no children. There are foetuses – and you still have time to change your mind – and then there are parasites, and it's too late. Do you want to know where the next few years of your life are written? In your wife's tits. In the nipples of your wife's tits. Flesh does not lie. That flesh is your horoscope. Keep in mind what I'm telling you. Everything dries up, Rimini. Have you seen what happens to plums when they're left out in the sun? Their flesh turns to mush. Their skin splits and breaks. There's nothing left to suck, Rimini. What about life, you think. Life got stolen by the kid, you stupid idiot. My God, how could you two . . . You're still handsome. You could still pass for being young. But you don't fool me. I knew you when you were really young. I enjoyed your youth, Rimini. Often at New Year, after the reunions were over and everyone had gone, I would lie back exhausted on the living-room sofa, take my shoes off, and remember you two: you coming in, always so well dressed, something old-fashioned about you, always blushing, half-hidden behind Sofia; and Sofia herself, who agreed to hide you without a murmur, without asking for anything in return, with that little moustache of hers bleached with peroxide, her smooth skin – the most beautiful I've ever seen – and then, while I was remembering you, I would masturbate, lying on the sofa with my skirt pulled up, surrounded by all the plates with bits of food on them, the ashtrays overflowing with butts, dirty glasses, napkins smeared with chocolate, coffee, or lipstick – the sad remains of an orgy that had never taken place, an orgy where you two angels had been my idols, my executioners, my nectar.'

CHAPTER 9

But that night there was a child, a small, slippery, shiny animal, purple as a plum, who poked his head out between his mother's legs, slid down with an underwater ease, and plopped into the hands of the midwife. Then, while Carmen, raving from the anaesthetics, wanted them to tell her once and for all if the baby was alive or not, he was passed from hand to hand like a magic, very fragile, or very dangerous object, until he was in the arms of the short, slightly tipsy fellow who was to look after him throughout the thirty-five days he spent in the hospital's intensive care unit, sleeping in an acrylic dome with infrared, vaguely Martian radiation from a lamp twice the size of his head. He did not cry, but Rimini was too stunned to ask why. He accepted the idea of him disappearing with the obstetrician as though this move (despite the fact that there were none of the clichés that Rimini had always associated with after-birth moments) formed part of a protocol he was unaware of – doubtless the main topic of one of the classes for future parents that the surprise arrival of the baby had cut short – that was as hermetic and effective as all imperial protocols. Ten minutes later, when he saw the baby reappear, by now confined to his tiny transparent cell, Rimini could feel his legs buckling. He grasped at something to lean on, and squeezed it as hard as he could so as not to fall. 'Ow!' the anaesthetist howled. 'That's my shoulder!' Rimini withdrew his hand and surveyed the little king. He was lying face down on his left side; his eyes were extraordinarily open and brilliant. Rimini could feel himself being drawn into their dark depths: he could have sworn the baby was looking at them, and the profundity and patience he thought he could see in that somehow both inexplicable and threatening gaze left him feeling strangely intimidated, as though what he had just witnessed was not an everyday rite that the human race carried out every second, all over the world, but something sacred, an esoteric ceremony which committed those present to swear some mysterious vow of loyalty or silence. The three of them stayed as they were, staring at each other without moving for a long while. Even the medical staff lowered their voices. Then the obstetrician said: 'The fencer's reflex.' Rimini stared at him blankly, but the doctor pointed out the way the baby was lying, with his right arm stretched out next to his head, and the left one down against his side, his right leg straight, the left bent at a ninety-degree angle. A perfect swordsman. 'It's true,' murmured Carmen, and raised her face to Rimini to get his approval. Rimini did not look at her: he had just discovered this was the position he had slept in all his life.

That night was unusually hot. The sky suddenly turned red and threatened a storm which never arrived. Soon afterwards a gentle breeze sprang up, the reddish layer of clouds was blown away, and the stars came out. It was as if the world had renewed itself completely without the slightest fuss, imperceptibly, with astonishingly good manners. Luckily, the hospital was as lax about visitors as it was about its signs, so that the small crowd of relatives Rimini notified from the public telephone on the ground floor was soon able to fill Carmen's room noisily without much problem. As expected, Rimini's father got the nurses firmly in his sights, especially their uniforms and two-tone shoes, and demonstrated all the generosity, enthusiasm and carefree negligence his son knew so well, reinforced on this occasion by the drama of the premature birth and the one kilo six hundred and seventy grams birth weight. The jeroboam of champagne was warm and had lost its sparkle, the bitter bar of German chocolate was huge, but had arrived at the hospital completely melted, and the two dozen lilies beneath which he almost buried Carmen and which filled the air of the room with a sickly perfume, looked faded and withered, as though they had had to cross a wide desert to get there. (Yet Rimini gave a huge sigh of relief when his father took him to one side surreptitiously, like a neighbourhood mafia boss or conman, led him into the bathroom, then stood against the door as though to stop him escaping while at the same time concealing what he himself was doing – a purely theatrical display of caution, because nobody could see them – and handed him an envelope with the money to pay the anaesthetist, the midwife and the obstetrician.) Then Carmen's parents arrived. They cried a bit, dusted off a few stories from Carmen's childhood, and when they were starting to think of settling in for a while, and her father was already suggesting they make a quick raid on a neighbouring room to get some more chairs, Rimini's father's enthusiasm – he was always quick to respond to the sporting aspects of emotion – suddenly went into overdrive. He became euphoric, a childish, impudent euphoria bordering on the indecent, full of jokes, hints, and sarcastic comments that inhibited the other two so much they felt obliged to leave. Shortly afterwards, two of Carmen's friends burst in, weighed down with the sandwiches and drinks Rimini had asked them to bring half an hour earlier. They ate, drank, and laughed outrageously. They said very little about the baby, and nothing about the birth. The little that they did say – especially Carmen, who was riding a wave of hyperactivity, seemed to turn the delivery into a kind of superhuman deed. Carmen had survived – nothing else was important. Occasionally, less to scold them than to blend in, because her appearances coincided with the moments when their high spirits had yielded to exhaustion, a nurse appeared to remind them of certain hospital rules, smooth the bedcover that the visitors had crumpled, and then left, taking with her the wrapping paper from the flowers, the empty bottles and the overflowing ashtrays. They decided to forget the baby, to wipe him from their minds in order to live the illusion of what would probably be their last night on their own together. It was only by ignoring the new monarch for a while that they could gather the strength for the long life as his subjects stretching before them. When the visitors left, and the room was empty and they could hear their own voices echoing forlornly around the four walls, Carmen slumped on to the bed and Rimini, without getting undressed, stretched out beside her but upside down, with his head at the bottom of the bed and his feet at the top. They lay like this for a while in silence, enjoying the supreme delights of exhaustion, while the first dawn breeze gently stirred the window curtain and brought the friendly sounds of a conversation between two doctors, a radio, the creak of wardrobe doors opening and closing. They forgot about the baby and then at a certain moment, without a word, they both began to cry, in a kind of euphoric despair, while they shared out loud (with that slightly artificial eagerness with which we choose someone and construct his first memories for him) the image of the swordsman prince studying them and welcoming them from atop his throne.

It was late, and day had almost dawned when Rimini half-opened one eye and saw Victor's pale face poking round the door. Carmen was fast asleep. Rimini thought he must be dreaming, and stretched out again against her legs, until he felt a hand shaking his shoulder. 'Victor,' he said. 'What time is it?' 'I don't know,' said Victor. They hugged each other. Victor smelled of cigarettes, of stale rooms, of that sordid combination of smells that funerals leave on clothes. 'Let's go out,' said Rimini, struggling to get up without waking Carmen. Out in the dark corridor, still befuddled by sleep, Rimini thought he could detect a strange tension in Victor's face, like someone trying without much success to hide something. He took a good look at him. His eyes were red, and his cheek looked as though it had been smudged by ink. 'How was it?' Victor asked him, rubbing his chest with the palm of a hand. Knocked off balance by the gesture, Rimini swayed backwards, bounced off the wall, and came back to his original position. 'Good,' he said. He thought about it: 'Good?' 'Good,' he repeated. His voice sounded hollow. 'It must be really late. Or really early. I don't understand how they let you in,' he said. 'Have you got him in there with you?' asked Victor. Rimini shook his head. 'Incubator,' he said. Victor heard the word 'incubator' but seemed confused rather than worried by it. 'He can't breathe on his own yet,' Rimini explained. 'There's something in his lungs, some sort of membrane, that hasn't formed properly . . .' They stood there silently for a moment. Then, with an almost theatrical lunge, Victor hugged him again. Revolted by the smell of his clothes, Rimini felt sick and pushed him away roughly. 'What's wrong, Victor?' Victor hesitated. Rimini realised he was weighing something up. 'Victor,' he repeated, trying to pin him down. 'Sofia rang me,' said Victor. 'Frida died. She had a heart attack when they were taking her for x-rays. A massive heart attack. Her heart was torn apart – it's dreadful. Sofia was on her own; she called me. I had to come. Afterwards, Frida's sister arrived, a few students and patients of hers. Then when the two of us were in a bar having a coffee, Sofia slapped her forehead and said: "Rimini!" She told me everything. She thought the baby must have been born by now. She wanted to come and see you, Rimini. With Frida's death certificate in her hand. I told her she must be crazy. "You're right," she said. "Let's both of us go." I gave her two drops of Rivotril, put her in a taxi, and took another cab so she would think I was leaving too.

Three blocks further on I told the driver to turn round and bring me back here. They already knew me, so they let me in. Have you chosen a name?'

No, they hadn't chosen one yet. And if, ten months later, sitting in the sun on a café terrace, Rimini could allow himself to prevent – with a shout of Lucio, no! – that same baby (a magnificent, amnesiac and particularly stubborn version of the swordsman prince who with the excuse of combating severe jaundice had spent the first month of his life getting a tan in his mobile solarium) from shoving one of his typical concoctions into his mouth, a dish composed of a cigarette butt he had picked up off the ground, a torn packet of sugar – part of which was already spilt down the front of his romper – a tasteless dummy and the already well-salivated bill for the coffee that Rimini had been trying to drink for the past ten minutes – it was not strictly due to the fact that at a certain moment they had decided to choose that name, nor even because he, the chief supporter of calling him Lucio, had succeeded in getting Carmen to accept it, defeating rival candidates such as Antonio or Vicente, but chiefly because the days were going by, and the label with the blue border hanging from the incubator still said simply 'Rimini', and Rimini, who had grown used to whiling away the time that Carmen spent shut up on her own extracting her milk in a tiny room in the intensive care unit by chatting to the nurses, the obstetrician, and the parents of the other babies dozing in nearby acrylic bubbles – some of whom, whose birth weight was less than five hundred grams, were hardly any bigger than the fluffy teddy bears their parents tried to keep them amused with during their stay in the incubators – found himself casually using the name Lucio, dropping it into phrases here and there, as if taking for granted with all of them – the ones who spent most of the time with the baby – that the baby had always had that name. In this way, when after three weeks in the incubator Rimini and Carmen already felt they were part of a new community and the rituals of their visits to the intensive care unit – ringing the bell each morning to gain entry, waiting, washing their hands with disinfectant, putting on the gown and mask, covering their shoes in those white cotton bags – had become a routine like any other, Rimini had no need to return to the charge and praise the virtues of the name he preferred, because all the other members of the community, perfect strangers whose faces and voices had nevertheless become more familiar, trustworthy and friendly than those of their own relatives or friends, called the baby Lucio as naturally as though there could not possibly be any other name for him in the world.

Despite all Rimini's fears, which the premature birth had only served to intensify, being a father turned out to be one of those secret abilities which, whilst nothing in the world around us makes them necessary, often go unnoticed by us, but once they are summoned – or as he liked to think, invented – thanks to the pressure of a new outside stimulus, become obvious and are displayed with miraculous efficiency, demonstrating not only their authenticity but a whole range of skills we never knew we had. To be a father, thought Rimini, was something just as arbitrary, just as similar as being taken over by someone else's will, as was speaking in tongues – a significant comparison from someone who, at the same time as he could amaze his father by changing nappies with one hand, could just as naturally and easily give up the languages which until a short time before had been his vocation, his main area of interest, and his chief means of survival. Rimini shed his languages like someone shedding skin: sometimes more, sometimes less, but a little every day. The soreness soon wore off. The scar healed, the raw part was sealed by a layer of dead tissue. This painless process was also irreversible. If the seven months of Carmen's pregnancy had managed to conceal the presence of the illness (which Rimini, after the Sao Paulo affair, had started to call 'my precocious linguistic Alzheimer's') by relegating it discreetly into the background, everything that happened thereafter – Lucio's birth, of course, but above all the way their lives became absorbed in a general process of hospitalisation, the rules of which they had to learn from scratch, and which at first they suffered from like prisoners having to learn the rules of the jail they have just been locked up in, but which in no time at all they came to feel grateful for, because everything that novice parents normally have to learn by experience, responding to the emergencies with which the newly born test out the equilibrium of the family, getting it right by sheer chance, making catastrophic blunders, or learning from the experience of those who had once been parents (starting with their own parents, in this case the grandparents, who, as is only logical, had completely forgotten everything about this initial phase of having a first child –

if they had in fact ever known anything), Rimini and Carmen could learn from the army of professionals they practically lived with during the month Lucio was interned – all but totally wiped it out, as if it had been nothing more than a bad dream.

That was until one stupid afternoon, one of those afternoons which, with hindsight, we could perfectly well pick up between our finger and thumb, lift out of our lives and deposit in some waste basket, when they decided to go to the cinema. They had just had lunch out. As well as being stupid, the afternoon was cold and hostile. Lucio had finally fallen asleep on Rimini's chest. They wandered about the city centre in a lost fashion, as if they were out of training, taking decisions they immediately changed their minds about, until they finally ran into the amusement arcades, the bargain clothes shops, the smell of fried food, the girls in uniform doing promotions, the maimed beggars of Calle Lavalle. After a year and a half's abstinence, moved almost to tears, the only thing they saw were the cinema foyers. They could have fallen victim to the rashness, lack of discernment or gluttony that can assail usually demanding people when they emerge from a long period of enforced chastity. Rimini, however, categorically refused to see any action film. He was worried that the four-month-old Lucio would wake from some voluptuous dream to find the world, reduced to the size of a dark, damp box, welcoming him with a burst of machine-gun fire or an exploding service station. Instead, they fell for the fraudulent promises in the foyer ('the most daring example of new French cinema', a handwritten sign said) and found themselves guided by the usher's torch into a decrepit auditorium. The old wooden planks of the floor creaked beneath their feet, and so did the seats as they settled in, immediately falling into an extraordinary state of enchantment, like country bumpkins in the big city. When they plucked up the courage to raise their eyes and saw the enormous image of a maid wearing a short white polka-dot apron, feather duster under her arm, searching through the only sinful drawer in the chest in her employer's bedroom (the film had already started) they felt for each other's hand in the darkness across the split seat rest – Carmen stifled a cry of pain – then intertwined them passionately, at almost the very same instant that in the distance above them on the screen (which every so often gave out strange sounds of protest), the employer's wife, who had just slipped

241

unnoticed into the bedroom, closed her fingers round the maid's in the drawer, against a silky background of female lingerie. But then all at once the image filled with hairs, or tapeworms, or scratches, and bubbles appeared and spread, while the actor's gestures became stiff and jerky, as if somebody had stolen the moments of transition linking each gesture with the one that followed, and just as the action was reaching its climax – after snatching the crucifix from her neck, the maid was pushing her mistress towards the bed; the other woman had opened her legs, and her mouth was twisted in an evil smile as she lifted the hem of her skirt with one hand, and avidly clasped the floral bedspread with the other – the projection seemed to stutter and come to a halt, a black square fleetingly interrupted the story, then there were more scratches, more tapeworms, more hairs, banging noises as if someone had spat close to a microphone; and by the time that some more or less recognisable shapes had hurriedly returned to the screen, as though in response to an emergency call, the action had moved on: a kettle was boiling, a lifesaver in swimming trunks was patrolling a beach, two men were proposing a toast in a restaurant filled with plastic flowers, the sun was coming up or going down, a traffic light changed from green to yellow, someone was taking a grey suit from a hanger. Rimini, who in any other circumstances (and with much less of an excuse) would have leapt out to the box office and demanded his money back, simply settled down in his seat, enjoyed the feeling of Lucio's weight dissolving into the warmth of his own body, savoured the heat, the enclosed atmosphere and the dank smell of the cinema as though they were rare privileges, and surrendered to the erratic performance of the film projector, whose inconsistencies seemed to him as bewitching as the imperfections of primitive art.

He had not even realised that the film was in French. He only became aware of it when the image slipped and the two lines of subtitles disappeared from the bottom of the screen. He realised that everything he had understood up to that point had been thanks to the subtitles. Without them, left only with the voices that were still speaking French, Rimini discovered the language meant absolutely nothing to him. 'Framing!' someone shouted from two rows in front of them. Rimini looked at Carmen. Her tranquil face left him in despair. 'How . . . ?' The answer was obvious: Carmen could understand without having to read. He was the orphaned one; he and only he was losing everything. He got up, pushed past knees, an open case, an umbrella, ran up the aisle towards the two thin streaks of light shining through the middle of the doors, rushed out – the ice-cream seller turned his eyes on him in slow motion with a look of bovine stupor – and ten seconds later, clinging to his still sleeping son, he was howling in one of the cubicles of the men's toilets, staring as though through rainy windscreen wipers at the furtive caveman's drawings daubed on the door: a side-on view of a fat prick, from whose tip, pointing directly at Rimini, spurted some drops of sperm that joined up to form a telephone number.

It was a split-second crisis, one of those that erupt and then subside in a moment. Either because he was upset or wanted to get in on the act, Lucio began to cry as well. This made Rimini stop, possibly out of a sense of shame or because, in accordance with some mysterious rule that nobody had imposed on him but which he obeyed as if it were sacred, since to him it formed part of the long list of vague but peremptory instructions and prohibitions that sprang into his mind whenever he thought about being a father, there was no longer any room in the world for a father to cry at the same time as his son. He felt nostalgic – nostalgic and afraid. What else? He wondered? What other things would he never do again in front of his son. What kind of clandestine existence had he been condemned to? That was the end of his crisis. By the time they left the toilet, Lucio was smiling. The film was over, and Carmen was pacing about the foyer with a worried look on her face (she had only realised she had been left on her own when the lights in the cinema came up again) while two or three evening masturbators jostled round her like crows. Rimini saw how his son's smiling pink gums almost immediately lit up his mother's face and felt as though for the first time, in his own flesh as they say, he had understood the meaning of 'flesh of my flesh' which before, despite its attractive sound, he had always been wary of because of its religious overtones. But what he now thought he understood was not the usual meaning of the phrase – the obvious shared carnality linking a child with its biological parents – but something more secret, more involved, or at least more unexpected: that the mere fact of conceiving a child together condemned the pair of them, Rimini and Carmen, to share a single flesh, with the result that from that moment on – Rimini felt suddenly giddy, but in a not unpleasant way – everything that Lucio did which affected Carmen would also affect Rimini, and everything that affected Rimini would affect Carmen equally and at the same time.

A whole new world opened up before him, obliging him to learn and submit himself to an infinity of unknown laws. How distant words, languages, the hours spent deep in dictionaries seemed to him now. It was as if all that belonged not so much to another time as to another life ... Rimini decided to surrender. He continued stripping off the old skin, but it no longer mattered, and the last strips of language he left in his wake vanished silently, almost without him realising it, as imperceptible as the millions of cells the body sheds each night on the sheets – cadaverous but trivial flesh, in part because the body the cells are leaving behind for ever never knew they existed, and partly because the fact that on waking the body went on living normally without them proved they were completely superfluous. Flesh of my flesh.

Even though he was reduced to nothing, Rimini felt detached, superior, invulnerable. Four months after Lucio's birth, when Victor, who had just got out of hospital after undergoing the series of tests that kept him in suspense at least twice a year, incapable of doing anything – working, having a social life, or even eating – apart from having sex, something which paradoxically at these times reached levels of frequency, variety and intensity unheard of for him, paid them a visit and, taking advantage of Carmen being distracted for a moment, without a word dropped a small, elegantly wrapped package in Rimini's lap, as if it were burning his fingers. Rimini immediately recognised 'the hand of Sofia', as he had called Sofia's handwriting when she had first started bombarding him with letters, notes, and messages, and had later come to apply to the unmistakable way in which Sofia inserted herself in his life from a distance. This time, to his amazement and delight, he did not feel the slightest unease. He of course recognised the hand of Sofia in Victor's careful discretion, but also, expert as he now was in that business sector that figures in phone books under the title 'baby goods and services', he recognised the wrapping paper used for the present, the kind of paper used only by the most expensive shop in the city, obviously the one place where Sofia would have deigned to purchase something for Rimini's son. This time Rimini did not start to tremble, he did not have palpitations, or feel that his mouth had gone dry. Carmen reappeared in the room and caught him with the package in his hands. While Victor tried to cover up with a close examination of an elephant with bells, Rimini looked at her with no sign of fear. He felt as though he could face anything. Carmen glanced down at the package. 'Did Sofia send it?' she said. 'Yes,' said Rimini. 'Open it, what are you waiting for?' 'That's right, open it,' said Victor, relieved to have been let off. 'And please, make sure you call and thank her,' Carmen added. Rimini tore off the paper and opened the box inside: it was a pair of tiny blue canvas shoes. Very elegant. Carmen brought Lucio over in his push-chair and tried them on – the boy stared at his feet in astonishment, as though the shoes had grown on him while he had been asleep. Rimini cautiously pressed the rubber tip; they seemed enormous to him. 'Perfect,' said Carmen: 'that way they'll last'. Then she turned to Rimini, and threatened: 'If you don't call her, I will. I don't want us to look bad, OK?'

Perfect. Strapped in his push-chair, Lucio protested. As though being given an electric shock, his whole body arched and beat against the padded back of the chair, while his tiny blue feet kicked the air. Before he could launch into the deep, prolonged whine he usually adopted to claim his rights, Rimini made the packet of sugar, the cigarette butt and the bill disappear, then stuck the dummy back in his mouth. He glanced inside the bar and at his watch: Sofia was twelve minutes late. He had two overwhelming impulses: to smoke, and to take Lucio's shoes and hide them in his pocket. With that remarkable deference women show only towards one another, no matter what sense of rivalry or mistrust keeps them apart, Carmen had insisted on using the meeting to have the baby wear them for the first time. She rejected all the options Rimini offered her without even bothering to consider them, nodding vaguely while her fingers, disdainful and indifferent, went on doing up the laces of the blue shoes. Rimini realised this stubbornness was basically a subtle form of retribution, or in other words – in some peculiar way that female etiquette must cover in one of its provisions – a civilised way to settle the debt which being given a present had put them in. But it was hot, and if Sofia did not appear – fifteen minutes now – the gesture would lose any meaning. A couple of tables away, the waiter was offering a foreign couple cigarettes. Rimini could see the ochre strip of the filters, the spirals of smoke drifting up through the air, the elegant ease, at once so commonplace and yet so exceptional, that a cigarette lends the fingers holding it. He felt an incurable nostalgia.

He fought it. He cast about for something to take his mind off his craving, and thought of Sofia, and how disappointed he would be if she did not turn up. In the end it had been Rimini who had called her, not so much due to Carmen's threat as out of a sense of personal, much more urgent, necessity: he wanted to put his own invulnerability to the test; to test it not mentally, for himself, as he had already done a thousand and one times, but with Sofia, in the presence of the only person it was worth demonstrating it to, because she was the only one who could shatter it completely. 'She's not going to come,' he thought. He hated this bar. He hated its pretentiousness, its fake wood panelling, the way in which the waiters pardoned the existence of people like him who were not regular clients. Sofia had suggested it, and Rimini had agreed without any fuss, with that same disregard with which he had agreed to call her to thank her for her present, and that same calm, calculated indifference with which he had said that yes, he would take Lucio, so that she could finally get to meet him. If Rimini had made so many concessions, it was because he had everything, and because he felt that he grew stronger with every concession. But when Sofia did not arrive, all his strength, his immunity, his fatherly prestige – everything that, by separating him from Sofia, he thought had freed him from the need to escape her – all that became empty and ridiculous, like the muscles, the tension and even the new clothes a gymnast sports, only to be told that the competition they have spent months preparing for has been postponed. Rimini felt a wave of anger and looked round him, desperate for revenge. He looked again at his watch: twenty-two minutes. A Brazilian woman laughed a loud smoker's laugh and waved her gold bracelets: they tinkled like cowbells; a yellow convertible raced past, with a broken exhaust; close by – too close – two men in blue shirts, ties and braces were shouting stock exchange instructions on their portable phones. Rimini raised the coffee cup to his lips, knowing it would be lukewarm. He did not even manage to taste it; with a delighted sweep of his hand, Lucio intercepted the cup halfway and spilt it all down his father's shirt and trousers. Rimini did not move, his gaze switching from watching the wet patches growing on his clothes to Lucio's ecstatic smile as he pointed at them with radiant astonishment. 'That's it,' thought Rimini, as if he had finally crossed a line, 'I'm going to smoke again.' He saw the waiter who had offered cigarettes to the tourist couple, and signalled to him. His eyes were too wide apart, like a shark's, and he had a wart on one cheek. 'The bill?' the waiter asked, surreptitiously eyeing the damage to Rimini's clothes. 'No,' said Rimini. 'I wanted a cigarette.' The waiter took a packet out of his waistcoat pocket, shook it slightly until the tip of a cigarette appeared, then stopped when it was halfway out. Rimini reached for the cigarette, then thought it over again. He looked down at his watch – twenty-five minutes – and said: 'Yes, that's fine, bring me the bill.'

He lit the cigarette and blew the smoke out almost at once, as if he was keeping the moment for inhaling it back, for the moment when after a year and a half's abstinence his palate and tongue had got used to the burning tickle. He took two more short puffs; he pushed his mouth out into an O, then blew a long train of smoke rings which Lucio watched pass before his eyes first with amazement, as if he was discovering a new kind of cartoon, and then with sudden hostility, disappointed at the indifferent way these small round creatures treated him, so that in the end he started to bat them away with his hand. Rimini laughed. He took another drag on the cigarette and let out another string of smoke rings, this time aiming directly at the baby's face. Lucio halted the first wave with his open palm, which shattered the rings; the second lot bounced off the padded back of his chair, but the next two hit him right in the face. He screwed up his eyes. He was getting desperate: the smoke rings were coming too thick and fast for him to be able to intercept them. In five seconds he's going to explode, thought Rimini. He took another puff, promising himself this would be the last, and that after this he would finally inhale. But just as he was drawing in his cheeks to make the last burst of rings, a rapid, determined hand flashed across his line of sight and snatched the cigarette out of his hand. 'What a crime,' Sofia said, sitting down between him and the baby, and crushing the cigarette beneath her foot. Rimini watched her do it; he was surprised that Sofia's boot was not done up with laces but with a bit of dirty string that was starting to fray. 'It's criminal, weak and stupid, Rimini. After a year and a half when you haven't touched a cigarette!' Sofia attacked him. Her old squint was back. She turned to Lucio and said: 'So this is your little treasure, is it? Aren't you going to introduce me?' 'It's twenty-five past three, Sofia,' said Rimini. 'Yes,' she said: 'I had problems choosing what to wear. I still get dressed up to see you.' Then, considering the adult part of the conversation closed, she turned back to Lucio. 'Hello there, Lucio. You know who I am, don't you? I suppose your father's told you about me,' she said. The little boy contented himself with studying her with a vague curiosity. 'I'm Sofia. So-fi-a,' she went on, pushing an ink-stained finger in between his tiny ones, and forcing him to grip it. 'I'm the woman who taught your daddy all he knows.' She swivelled back to Rimini. 'Shhh! It's a joke, idiot. An idiotic joke. Don't over-protect him: he knows exactly what jokes are.' Then she turned her attention back to Lucio, whose eyes were alternating between her face and hands, and that enormous finger-log of wood that his tiny drowning fingers were clinging to. Sofia stretched out her other hand towards his head. Her hand began to tremble, ran parallel to his downy blond fuzz without daring to touch it, and then followed the outline of his cheek without making contact either. 'You're pretty,' she said. Lucio celebrated getting his hand back by sticking a finger up his nose. 'Pretty, and so white. And shy. Just like your father. I can't believe they called you Lucio. That must have been her idea, mustn't it? A sad idea your mother had? Go on, tell me the truth. You shouldn't lie to Sofia you know. If you don't believe me, ask your father.'

The waiter came over; Sofia drove him away without a word, wafting a scornful hand in his direction. 'Don't you want anything to drink?' asked Rimini. 'Not on your life,' she said. 'This place is a rip-off.' She picked her bag up off the ground and tried to open it, but the clasp would not give. 'Why did you suggest we meet here then?' Rimini asked. '"You suggest we meet",' she mocked him. She looked at him loftily. 'Who called who, Rimini?' She struggled, finally managed to open her bag, and took out a bottle of pills. 'I did,' he admitted, 'but it was you who chose this place.' 'It was the only one I could think of. Is that a crime?' There was a moment's silence. 'I was nervous. Besides, if you made a suggestion yourself sometimes, you wouldn't be so keen to crit- icise.' Sofia opened the bottle, poured four or five pills on to the lid – this operation must have emitted some secret signal that was only perceptible to a child's eyes, because Lucio immediately stopped what he had been doing: trying to stick his finger in the eye of his right shoe, which already had the lace in it, and sat bolt upright in his push-chair in order to study what she was doing all the more closely – counted them, and tipped them under her tongue. 'Are you still taking the sulphur?' Rimini said. Yet again he was amazed at the intensity of concentration Sofia could devote to something – dissolving the pills in her saliva – which was purely chemical and did not depend on her in the slightest. 'Mmm, mmm,' she said, shaking her head. For further explanation, she leaned towards him and showed him her forehead. All Rimini could see was a thick layer of make-up with lines of parallel wrinkles showing through. 'What?' he said. 'Hm,' she said, and lightly scratched the area with a nail – Rimini noticed she had started chewing them again – and as she did so, part of the pink covering came away, to reveal a chain of white spots, ranged in order from large to small, like a disciplined range of tiny mountains. 'And you missed the mouth sores, millions of them. My whole mouth was one big white wound,' said Sofia. She decided she had shown him enough, and sat up in her chair. 'But that's it. Absolutely everything has come out. Now some-thing must go in.'

Rimini shuddered briefly. Hearing that 'something' rang an old, tired but still functioning bell somewhere in his heart, alarmed at the distance between the innocuous word and the raging hunger that lay in wait behind it. Something nearby creaked. He wanted to believe that it was the wicker seat of his chair. It was getting late. Rimini avoided Sofia's ominous shadow and turned his eyes on Lucio. He had often imag-ined him in danger, at the mercy of some illness, an evil electrical socket or rabid dog, but in all these macabre scenes Rimini always burst in near the end, just before tragedy struck, like the comic super-heroes who had ruled his emotional life as a child. Now for the first time he thought of his son as someone – the only one – capable of saving him. He realised that the idea scared him. Lucio, who took his father's expressions as variants of the same over-arching, clumsy but inoffensive tenderness, puffed out his cheeks and sprayed him with saliva. Sofia suggested they went for a walk, and stood up at once, as though any delay were intolerable. Rimini was still seated, feeling for his wallet to pay. When he turned towards her he could see, almost in spite of himself, that the lining of her skirt was hanging down, and that she had two big holes in her stockings.

Two blocks later, Sofia was scraping the side of her body against the wall as she walked. She had started to cry. It was a very peculiar way of crying, which Rimini had never seen before, neither in her, through all the long years they had spent together, nor in anyone else: her face had been completely dry and then all of a sudden there was an instantaneous haemorrhage and it was soaked with tears. She was crying and laughing uncontrollably. 'Don't pay any attention to me,' she said, hiding her mouth behind what looked like a doll's handkerchief, as if she had teeth missing. 'I'm far too emotional. When I see you with that push-chair ... You had a child with another woman; you're a traitor. A traitorous son of a bitch. But now at least I know that when I imagined what you'd be like as a father I wasn't wrong. You make a good father.' They reached a street corner. Rimini stopped the push-chair at the kerb, with the front wheels dangling in the air, then edged the back down on to the street. Sofia applauded his expertise as she launched herself across the road. Out of the corner of his eye, Rimini saw the bonnet of a black-and-yellow speeding vehicle coming up Ayacucho, but did nothing more than open his mouth. A woman who was level with Sofia held her back gently, without knocking her off balance. The taxi passed by less than half a metre from them, sounding his horn in a long protest. Sofia did not even notice. They crossed the street. Sofia's guardian angel strode ahead of them, turned round silently, and shot Rimini a quick but withering look. Feeling threatened, Rimini glanced down at his watch. How much longer did he have – fifteen minutes? Half an hour? – of this torture? But when he turned towards Sofia and saw her playing round the push-chair, coming closer then moving away, disappearing from Lucio's sight and suddenly reappearing, tickling one of his feet, his stomach, his cheek, he was ashamed of being scared. Now Sofia was sticking her finger in Lucio's belly-button and making him giggle. 'Perhaps, after all . . .' he said to himself, buoyed by a sudden wave of optimism. He thought about his own inflexibility, about how hard it was for him to admit that accidents related to things were part of those things, that the logic of things was a lack of continuity, a coming and going, the rhythmic alternation of more or less arbitrary accidental moments and more or less predictable moments of stability. Perhaps after all, beyond what he thought of as 'torture' there was always something else that was not torture, as he tended to think, stuck as he was in the belief that the internal movement of things followed only two parameters: less or more, but for example could contain stretches of calm happiness, bucolic scenes, epiphanies of a scandalously bourgeois harmony of the sort he could see now. His spirits rose. 'Should we have an ice-cream?' he said forcefully, with the theatrical, slightly out-of-place emphasis he always used to compensate for his lack of initiative. Sofia was shaking a set of keys between Lucio's despairing fingers. 'We could sit here on the pavement . . .' he went on. Sofia frowned and looked at her watch. 'Are you busy?' he asked. 'A bit . . .' she said, confused. Lucio triumphantly pulled on the key he had managed to grab. Then her face brightened as she thought of something. 'Unless you give me a lift,' she said. 'Where are you going afterwards?' 'Home,' he said. 'By taxi?' 'I suppose so,' he said, slightly taken aback. 'Then I will have an ice-cream,' she said, smiling and tugging at the keys, so that Lucio was left with his hands extended towards her, like someone imploring or venerating an absent god.

The ice-cream parlour was deserted. Rimini insisted he paid. Sofia hesitated over what kind and size she wanted, while the cashier, an understanding man with a middling musical instinct, drummed on the keys of his till. Sofia finally decided on two scoops, but a few seconds later, faced with the board showing all the flavours, she not only began to hesitate once more, but changed her mind, so that Rimini ended up giving her his larger cornet. They were the only customers, so they were served at the same time. But as Rimini scooped the top off his ball of lemon with the edge of his plastic spoon, Sofia was still empty-handed, caught up in her fourth or fifth dilemma – Russian cream or *zabaglione* – and the assistant was surveying her with professional patience, both hands resting on the aluminium counter where the drums of different flavours, which Sofia had made him open one by one, displayed a whole palette of edible watercolours. 'Oh, I don't know,' she groaned, turning to see what Rimini was having. 'What did you ask for?' 'Lemon,' he said. 'Just lemon?' she said, licking one side of the ball that Rimini had been saving for later. 'Yes.' 'You always were really boring when it came to ices,' she said. She turned back to the assistant and said: 'Lemon. Just lemon, please.' They sat outside in the sunshine. As usual, Rimini finished his ice-cream first. It was not that he was greedy; in fact, nobody who had ever eaten with him realised during the meal just how quickly he polished everything off. It was more of a retrospective discovery: at a certain point they saw him lick his lips, leave his napkin on the table or line up his knife and fork on his plate, and they realised that, as well as talking, Rimini had been eating, and that for every mouthful they swallowed, he must have eaten at least three. Rimini stood up to throw away the paper napkins he had used to clean Lucio's mouth – in his son's linguistic world, apparently, the terms swallow and spit belonged to a new category of synonyms. Unable to avoid an ingrained sentimental habit, he calculated where Sofia would be up to, and when he cast her a fleeting but accurate glance, he found her ice-cream was still untouched: it was exactly as they had served it to her, but because the sun had slowly melted it, the ice had become a Lilliput version of the original. Trails of liquid lemon shone on Sofia's hand and were stuck to the cuff of her blouse, the sleeve of her coat, and her skirt, but all this seemed to be happening far, far away from her. She sat there without moving, stiff as an invalid; the hand holding the ice-cream looked as if it were made of stone. 'Aren't you having any?' asked Rimini, thinking that by attracting her attention in this trivial way he might bring her out of her trance gently, as one is supposed to do with sleepwalkers. Sofia blinked, shook her head slightly, and then looked down in horror at the mound of lemon ice turning to liquid in her hand, as if seeing it for the first time. She lifted it to her mouth with a mechanical gesture, the reflex of a habit that once, in another life, she had known how to do properly. But she failed, the ice-cream hit her on the side of her mouth, and a lump hung there for a second until it began to run down towards her chin. Rimini stretched out a hand and stopped the trickle of lemon with his finger. Sofia's face lit up in an instant smile – the smile of a sleeping beauty awakened by desire or resentment – and she caught his hand just as he was trying to withdraw it. 'I was thinking . . .' she said, but as she had not spoken for some time, her voice came out as an unintelligible hoarse croak, forcing her to stop and clear her throat. 'Do you remember when Lucio was born?' she asked. 'In the early morning,' said Rimini. 'Yes, but when exactly? At what time?' she insisted. 'At two-twenty in the morning.' 'I knew it,' she said triumphantly. 'What?' said Rimini. 'That was exactly when Frida died.'

Then the season of sobs began again, and the tiny embroidered handkerchief reappeared, streaked with the tears and snot she had wiped off during the previous crisis, and from tears she moved on to hiccoughs, and from hiccoughs to choking and coughing, until all of a sudden Rimini found himself patting Sofia's bent back, first with one hand then with both of them, less to console her than to try to hold in check the storm he could see heading his way: he could feel a host of threatening clouds covering the evening sky – clouds of his own making, because although the sun was not so strong now, it was still shining and the sky was still clear. In a strange fit of euphoria, Lucio was celebrating this apotheosis of tears by banging his hands on the padded bar of his push-chair. In order to comfort her, Rimini tried to make her see reason. With a surgeon's cool attention to detail, he reduced the coincidence to a handful of banal, completely unimportant elements. He was hoping this might help neutralise all the drama, but his arguments collapsed one after another against the curtain of tears veiling Sofia's eyes. Then he remembered a phrase: 'Don't try to convince me I'm not suffering.' Classic Sofia: one of those shards love spits out and leaves in an organ to which only it has access, so that not only do these splinters survive everything, even the death of love, but become so essential to the organism they are incrusted in that they cannot be removed without putting the life of their bearer at risk. Rimini changed tactics and decided to distract her attention. Some states of mind are so incandescent that going anywhere near them is simply to help renew the ardour of their flames, to feed their combustion and risk putting yourself in danger; all that is possible is to look away, to concentrate on something else, to realise that there are still things in the world not consumed by the flames, until time, the only truly invulnerable force (capable of changing things without itself being changed) does its work and what were once roaring flames or coals are finally reduced to nothing more than the faint echo of heat, to inoffensive ashes.

Rimini managed to persuade her to give up the ice-cream, that repulsive sticky mess the ice-cream had become, and almost made her laugh when he went to throw it away: when he shook his hand the lifeless blob stuck to his fingers as if making fun of him. Sofia relaxed, and Rimini took advantage to say he was cold and force her to get up from the bench and carry on walking, using the excuse that he wanted to show her some architectural discovery he had made in the neighbourhood. Sofia did not say yes, but did not resist either. Her face dried once again with terrifying speed. She put a hand on the push-chair handle and asked: 'Can I push him for a while?' Rimini heard her and felt she was coming back to life. 'Yes, of course,' he said. After a moment's silence: 'I have to practise,' she said. She stared at him openly, seeking to confirm the effect of her words in his face. Rimini smiled and looked away, but a few moments later began to observe her surreptitiously, without her noticing. It was like a miracle: she was her old self again, walking along erect, head held high, challenging and elegant. 'It's easy,' she said. 'How do I look?' Rimini smiled again, but said nothing. Lucio though turned round, and stood up in the push-chair, still strapped in by the harness he liked to chew on with the edge of his gums, approving of his new driver with a broad smile. Sofia brought her nose down close to his. 'Well, baby? How do I look? Good, don't I?' she said, offering him a nose-fencing match. But Lucio had serious problems reciprocating: giving him something back always made him lose interest. So he ignored the offer of a game and slumped down on to his crumb-covered throne. Rimini felt responsible for Sofia's resurrection, so decided to go a step further. 'How's everything going with your German?' he asked. 'My German,' she said, laughing. 'What was his name? Kurt? Karl?' 'Rimini.' 'What?' 'He's the first man I've been with since we split up, and you can't even remember his name.' 'Is that bad?' 'No, not bad,' said Sofia: 'I don't believe you.' Silence. They passed another push-chair, and Lucio and his colleague, a fat baby who was enjoying chewing the frayed ear of a bear in braces, followed each other with their eyes as they moved apart, as if trying to decide whether the friendship they were passing up was worth it or not. 'Kantor?' Rimini suggested. 'Konrad,' said Sofia. 'Well, I knew it started with "k",' he said in his own defence. 'He's still German, but I'm afraid he's not mine any more. If he ever was, of course.' Rimini cursed himself – he had opened the wrong door. But the thoughtful maturity obvious from the way Sofia was talking about it reassured him, so he took another step forward. 'Did you separate?' 'Not exactly. Nobody "separates", Rimini.

People abandon each other. That's the truth, the whole truth. Love may be reciprocal, but the end of love never is. Siamese twins separate. But not really, because they can't do it for themselves. Someone else, a third person, has to separate them: a surgeon, who slices through the middle of the organ or limb or membrane joining them with his surgeon's knife. Blood is spilt and more often than not he kills one of them at least, and condemns the other, the survivor, to a kind of eternal mourning, because the part of the body that united him with the other twin is still sensitive and hurts, it goes on and on hurting, and at the same time it's a constant reminder that he is not nor ever will be complete, that he will never again have what they took from him.'

They walked on in silence. Sofia sighed: she had spoken very quickly, almost without drawing breath, like someone who has to get up a steep slope and decides to do it in one last rush rather than trying to save their energy. Rimini did not dare look at her, ashamed yet again at how frivolous her emotional intensity made him seem. 'I don't know why I'm surprised,' Sofia said, calmer now, as though it had rained on the flames of her hurt. 'After all, he only did the same as you: he learnt what he had to learn, and then left, a real man. A charming, sensitive, curious, passionate man who I guess some filthy German girl will be taking advantage of, a girl with clumps of hair under her armpits and wearing sandals with socks. But I'm not complaining. That's how things are. That's my mission in the world: to invent, discover people, to bring out their beauty . . . for others to enjoy. That's what I do with my patients. They come to me as invalids, paralysed, given up on by all the doctors: and they leave happy, walking on their own two feet. Their own families have difficulty recognising them. It's the same with men. Those men who women find, seduce, and then shut in their little three-room apartments and turn into fathers of families, those men who over time discover that the women they have spent their lives with are complete strangers who never knew anything about them, never, nothing, starting with the most basic facts – who they were, the men, who they *really* were, what made them happy, what made them ill, what made them go crazy with joy, what they were trying to escape from, what paradises they dreamt of – and then those men die, and the doctor says "heart attack" or "aneurism" but in fact they die of heartbreak . . . But those men, those men like you Rimini . . . I can see them. I see them, and just by seeing them I can split them in two, like those people in the Philippines who operate on people without touching them, and I can see their hearts from a distance, like now, and I can read everything in them, you understand? Each and every one of the wounds and scars they have, the big ones that cannot be cured, even the ones that are scarcely visible. I can also see all that a heart is capable of, everything that not even the owner – him less than anyone in fact – suspects it is capable of, and I tell them what I see, or no, I show them what I've found (because the poor little things run off if you tell them things like that) and then pow! They fall in love with me, head over heels in love, and I fall for them too; then when they start to realise that what I've shown them is there, right in front of them, or inside them, they think they've understood what they are really in love with – not with me, of course, but my power, my Filipino eye, my ability to cure them. So once they are cured and magnificent they leave: much more beautiful than when I found them, young again, in a perfect state to find happiness. Without me, of course.'

They stopped to let a dark, interminable car out of a parking lot. The driver was winding up his window as the car swept its way through the plastic strip curtain. Rimini was enveloped in a sickly-sweet wave of what seemed like cheap soap coming from inside the vehicle. 'That's how it is,' said Sofia. 'And perhaps it's no bad thing. I don't know if I would have wanted to be with Konrad for ever. Not even with you. I get tired too. It's hard work dealing with people with problems. But dealing with men takes a superhuman effort. It's like stripping down a very old door. You have to soften one layer of paint, then another, then another and another, as gently as you can, because if you're too brusque you could ruin everything, and above all because if there's something men are proud of it's exactly that, what they call "experience", those layers upon layers of old, dried-out, rotten paint covered in fungus and damp, all of which you have to remove as patiently as possible so that finally, after years of work, they are naked as the day they were born. And then, just when everything could start again from scratch, when I could get some rest at last, that's when the hardest, the really titanic effort begins. Because when they're naked, men are weak, innocent, helpless, clumsy. They're like animals with the skin missing: anything could kill them. So they have to be held very carefully so they don't get hurt – their bodies are so fragile and they're very easily scared, so you have to reassure them, help them stand up, show them that yes, they can do it, they can walk and . . .' Sofia fell silent. She raised her chin an inch or two, distracted or very focussed, as if trying to recognise something in the air, or as if some secret music had got inside her head. Rimini looked at her, and saw the reflection of a green neon sign flashing in her tear-stained face. He realised night was falling. He was shivering with cold. He saw Lucio's bare legs and was frightened he might get ill. He was about to say something, but Sofia reached out a hand and started stroking him with her knuckles. She said: 'Wouldn't you like to fuck me?', her voice almost inhumanly soft. Rimini laughed. 'Fuck. Here, now. Look – there's a hotel, see?' said Sofia. 'Go on. A fuck. A quick fuck. We go upstairs, we fuck, and *ciao*. We say goodbye. Don't worry, it doesn't mean anything. I'm so hot. I haven't had a prick inside me for so long. I'm so hot my ovaries ache. Feel,' she took his hand and laid it on her crotch. 'Go on, feel. Can you feel it beating? Just a quick fuck. You stick it in, come inside me, and that's that. I'm begging you. For all you hold dear.' Rimini felt giddy – it was neither desire nor rejection, just a kind of immobile movement produced by two opposing forces – growing and diminishing, going forward or back, climbing or descending: exactly the same odd feeling as when in his childhood something would wake him up in the middle of the night and he would find himself seated in an immense, oceanic bed, designed by an expressionist carpenter from the wrong fleet – forces working on him simultaneously, while through his fingers, which Sofia kept softly pressed against her body, he could feel her trembling. Suddenly he was overcome by a devastating idea – so stark and drastic it hardly seemed to have come from inside him but to have been shot at him from some distant heaven by a monstrous intelligence: *sleep with this corpse so I can be free of her for ever.* By the time he could react he found himself in a cramped lift, stiflingly hot, with Lucio in his arms and the push-chair only half-folded beside them. When his eyes got used to the darkness, to the sinful red light shining from the ceiling, in the mirror Rimini saw Sofia's face staring down at the carpet, and Lucio's smiling white features, floating like a pearl in a nightmarish swamp. The lift came to a halt. Sofia opened the door and went out into the corridor to look for the number corresponding to the one on the key in her hand. Rimini leaned out of the lift sufficiently far for Lucio to greet the sight of Sofia in new surroundings with an explosion of spluttering. Rimini tried to get out completely, but one of the push-chair wheels got stuck in the door, so he had to turn back. Seeing Sofia disappear again, Lucio became upset and started to protest violently, hitting Rimini on the head and eyes with his open hands. This blinded Rimini as he struggled with the lift door, the rebellious wheel, and the unfathomable workings of the push-chair which, shaken repeatedly by his violent efforts, suddenly opened up with elegant ease, jamming the whole doorway with its articulated skeleton.

Someone down below was calling the lift. Rimini stuck his head out again, trying to free his ankle from the iron and plastic trap that had snapped around it. He saw Sofia coming back round the corner, and waved desperately to her for help. When she saw what the problem was, she collapsed into a long, scornful burst of laughter, which echoed along the corridor for several seconds. They struggled together – he was sweating, convinced that if this went on much longer he would go completely mad, she was beside herself, intoxicated by her own laughing until, fighting with one particularly reluctant strut of the push-chair, she caught her finger in it, yelped with pain, and took it out on the push-chair by furiously kicking at one of its wheels. Lucio's eyes filled with terror. A maid carrying a huge pile of white towels appeared in the corridor and walked slowly by them, staring in utter amazement. Down below, impatient knuckles beat at the metal door of the lift. Rimini grabbed Sofia by the arm and forced her to get in. He pressed the ground floor button with his elbow. There was so little room the three of them travelled down almost hugging one another. Sofia was still laughing, and blew inside his collar, his right cheek, on to his mouth. 'That's enough Sofia, please,' he begged her. He had never felt so humiliated by someone else's laughter. He asked her to stop once more, and when she didn't, he slapped her, one of those flat, compassionate blows used to snap someone out of an attack of nerves or to bring round a drunk. Sofia's jaw dropped, less from pain than from surprise, and when they reached the ground and the door opened, like a swimmer breathing again after having spent too long underwater, she blew out one last mouthful of laughter all over a couple who were waiting for the lift amidst a jungle of brightly illuminated green ferns.

They piled out into the street like the villains from a slapstick comedy. Rimini appeared first; he was carrying Lucio bodily under one arm, and tugging at one wheel of the push-chair, dragging the handles along the ground like a corpse. He stepped into the road to call a taxi. Sofia was propped up against the hotel wall, still giggling, her body bent forward as if she were being sick. Then all at once she quietened down. Keeping one eye on the street, out of the corner of the other one Rimini glimpsed how she pressed her back against the wall, kneeled down, opened her legs and abandoned herself, still smiling, to a long, warm pee, which trickled through her knickers and then down the narrow cracks between the pavement tiles into the street. An old Peugeot 504 braked alongside him and waited, throbbing and enveloping him in a cloud of petrol fumes. On another occasion, he might have refused to get in, but now he was in no position to choose. He opened the door, tamed a last attempt at revolt by the push-chair and, after forcing it between the back seat and the driver's seat, flung himself into the taxi as though fleeing a nuclear explosion, still clutching Lucio to him. The taxi door was open; Rimini had sat in the other corner of the seat and was too far away to be able to close it, so had to wait for the driver to reach over and do it. While this was going on, he turned his head to look at Sofia, thinking this would be the very last time – promising himself it would be. He saw her slowly getting to her feet, as if this scene were the exact reverse of the last memory he had of her, and once she was upright, take a dazed step towards the street, towards him, probably towards Lucio, who was pointing a cheerful finger at her and looking at his father, as if waiting for his verdict. Sofia was smiling sweetly, the sweetness of the weary or the dying, whose muscles contract in an expression they will no longer ever change, because it would take too much effort for them to adopt a different one. She came towards the car, and as the driver was feeling for the door handle to shut it, Rimini saw her trip, stumble, and look at him, straight in the eye, while the whole dignity of her bearing, which a moment before had seemed so solid and complete, creaked and fell apart. To have someone look at him at the very moment they are falling apart: Rimini could not face that. It was not in hysteria, or coquettishness, or scorn, or the maternal instinct that Rimini located the real truth that women embodied for him, but in this crucial, almost tragi-comically precise moment – a stumble, a misguided movement, the make-up slipping – the moment when all the power of enchantment was dynamited by the ridiculousness of the situation, and was left in ashes. Or perhaps in fact these falls did not so much convey the truth about women as the truth about the effect they had on him, that rare differential which with the speed of a gag made him go from one kind of enslavement to another: from the devotion that goddesses inspire to the abject pity they arouse when they are seen sprawling on the floor, their skirt pulled up and their legs wide open, with bloody knees and the fresh leather of their shoes scuffed and stained. Rimini saw her stumble, Sofia saw him see her, and something in her eyes that was not hostility (she was too busy trying to recover from her mistake to indulge in such a demanding emotion) but something more debased, a mixture of nakedness and pain, wound and shame, again left in him the burning brand that every single woman he had happened to see falling like this had imprinted in him: the impression of witnessing something he should not have seen.

'Wait,' Rimini shouted, and stopped the driver's hand before he could shut the door. Halfway between the hotel and the street – Rimini read the name of the hotel handwritten on the fake marble plaque by the entrance: 'L'Interdit' – Sofia had bent one leg in front of the other and was busy examining something on the heel of her right shoe. 'Get in,' Rimini shouted again, pushing the taxi door open. Sofia continued with her inspection for a few moments – not that there was much point, as there was nothing wrong with the heel, and the only reason for her inspection had been to put the blame for her stumble on to the shoe. Finally she got in, muttering vague reprisals against the shoe-shop or the make, and when she heard Rimini give the address: 'Bulnes and Beruti, please,' she corrected him: 'No, Honduras 3100.' 'Oh,' said Rimini. He was surprised, but wasn't going to abandon his caution. 'When I called you, wasn't that at Bulnes?' he said. 'They take messages for me, but I haven't lived there for months. They threw me out while I was in Germany. The owner sold the place and had to hand it over immediately. He knew I was going to be abroad for several months more, so he took all my stuff out and put it in a storage warehouse in Barracas. A fortnight later the warehouse flooded in a storm. I must be the first person to be thrown out in both hemispheres at once: while

Konrad and that witch of an aunt of his were denouncing me to the German Migration Office (my tourist visa had run out a month earlier) all my furniture was floating around and rotting in a flooded basement for the princely sum of two hundred and fifty pesos a month, which the owner of the Bulnes apartment wanted to make me pay as well.' She paused, apparently checking the stations of her calvary in the car-door window. 'It was better that way,' she said after a while. 'It helped me get rid of a lot of things. Rubbish, stuff, all the crap you drag around with you. That's the good thing about disasters: they force you to completely re-jig your priorities. And I found the Calle Honduras apartment, which has a thousand times better view.' She turned to Rimini. 'Wouldn't you like to come up?' she asked. Rimini looked at her, but said nothing. 'No, it's true, it's late,' she said, as though thinking aloud.

They travelled on a few blocks in silence. When they pulled up at a light, Rimini could not take his eyes off a news-stand. If he did not smoke he would have a heart attack, he thought. Before, when he smoked, however intense the desire for a cigarette was, it always had the slow, languid feel of a luxury. Now, following a year and a half's abstinence, it was as demanding as thirst, hunger, or fear. Sofia wriggled in her seat, as if settling back, and gently stroked Lucio's head. He was staring silently out of the window, three-quarters asleep. 'Oh', she suddenly said. 'Guess who I saw in Germany? Pierre-Gilles.' Rimini thought she must be joking, and looked at her. Sofia turned away, looking for something outside, in the street. When she could not find it, she turned back to him, her eyes skimming over his features as though she did not consider him worth spending much time on. 'You saw him?' asked Rimini. Sofia nodded. 'On TV one evening.' 'I thought he was dead.' 'I don't know,' she said. 'He could have been. How can you tell? Everything on TV looks dead. Anyway, he seemed fine. Better than you or me. They were giving him a prize.' 'What for?' 'No idea. The programme was in German, so I didn't understand much. I think he's a film producer.' 'A film producer,' muttered Rimini. Taken aback, he tried to match the silhouette of the psychotic who had tried to destroy *Spectre's Portrait* with the prosperous stranger Sofia had just planted in his imagination. 'That's how it goes,' said Sofia, 'one dies, the other grows younger. Grows younger and takes up the space left by the dead person. Breathes and eats and looks and enjoys himself for the two of them. A double portion of everything. Survivors, usurpers. What's the difference? What is love if not a kind of natural selection?' Sofia leaned forward and waved her hands in front of the taxi-driver's face, telling him of some shortcuts he could take. She realised she could see herself in the rear-view mirror, and touched the lower edge of her eyelids, which were still puffy. 'I was in the house, you know, in the kitchen (the dyke aunt had gone off to one of her weekly neighbour-hood association meetings. For months she'd been trying to get them to accept the idea of naming an alleyway after her dog, Kimstrasse or something), the TV was on in the dining-room (people talking in German and every so often, a round of applause) and then all of a sudden I heard some verses . . . You're not going to believe it. I thought I was hallucinating, Rimini.' She looked up at the roof of the taxi, and bit her lip. '*Voici de quoi est fait le chant de l'amour*,' she recited. 'No: *Le chant symphonique de l'amour/Il y a le chant d'amour de jadis/Le bruit des baisers éperdus des amants illustres* . . . Do you remember?' Not waiting for his answer, she went on: '*Les cris d'amour des violées, des mortelles violées par les dieux/Il y a aussi les cris d'amour des félins dans les* blah blah blah . . . I ran into the dining-room, and there he was. It was him, Pierre-Gilles, holding a little statue, a kind of cylinder ending in a point, like a huge golden prick (it wasn't a very good picture, the aunt was such a skinflint she reckoned cable TV was the devil's work), Pierre-Gilles reciting *Les vagues de la mer où naît la vie et la beauté* . . . Isn't that incredible?' Rimini looked at her, smiled faintly, then looked away. Sofia kept on looking at him, expectantly. 'You remember, don't you?' she said. 'Yes, yes,' said Rimini, as if in protest, 'but . . .' 'But you don't understand a thing.' Rimini sighed. 'You don't understand what you're hearing,' said Sofia. 'It's just noises. Chinese. So it's true then.' She felt silent, opening her eyes and staring at him with a mixture of alarm, curiosity and excitement, as though the marvel she had just witnessed would have fooled anyone but her, because she was the only one who knew the secret behind it. 'That thing about "Linguistic Alzheimer's" is true.' How did she know about that? Rimini swallowed, and tried to look unimpressed. 'Well, calling it Alzheimer's is a bit harsh, isn't it?' 'That's what you call it, I hear,' said Sofia. Rimini wanted to go on pretending, but found in impossible. 'How do you know?' he said angrily. 'Are you spying on me? Do you pay to receive information? Have you bugged my phone?' There was a silence. Lucio decided to stir: he arched his body, stretched his arms out as far as he could and, leaning his head on Rimini's chest, fixed him with set, wide-open eyes. Predictably, Rimini regretted what he had just said. Any show of passion was dangerous: all the progress he had made so far might come to nothing. 'What are you thinking of doing?' said Sofia. 'I mean, apart from getting angry with me. Because you're in trouble, aren't you? Do you have any work?' 'Not much,' he lied. 'I was tired of translating anyway. Carmen's doing well, so I decided to take a year off.' Rimini waited. He saw his alibi floating in the air, and hoped it could survive. Sofia let a few seconds go by, then eventually said: 'You must be happy. Your dream's come true.' 'My dream?' 'To be a gigolo. That was one of your fantasies, wasn't it?' Rimini could not prevent himself smiling. 'Clown,' she said, punching his arm. 'Do you take me for an idiot? You're the one with Alzheimer's, not me. I remember everything.' 'I know,' he said, 'and I never understood how you manage not to get exhausted.' 'Who says? Sometimes I'm at the end of my tether. For example, when I realise I'm the only one. When all around me, everyone allows themselves to forget, because they know I'm there. I reassure them: they know if I'm there, nothing will be lost. I'm a sort of biological archive. By the way, do you know what the only thing was that wasn't ruined in the flood?' 'I've no idea,' said Rimini, running his first finger down the bridge of Lucio's nose, then off into space, until it finally landed safe and sound in the soft gap between his lips. 'Guess,' she said. 'I don't know: I don't even know what exactly you had ...' 'Guess, Rimini!' she cut in. 'You don't have to know to make a guess. Guessing is the opposite of knowing.' 'I don't know: your clothes?' he suggested timidly. 'Clothes,' she said thoughtfully, as if assessing this answer at an exam board. 'Let's say it was my clothes,' she said resignedly. 'Let's say that my armchairs, books, lamps, paintings, curtains, sheets, were all ruined, and the only thing that was saved were my clothes. If that was the case, darling, can you tell me why on earth I would want to mention it to you? What would you say? "What a shame?" "Fancy that?"' 'So it wasn't your clothes.' 'No. The photos, Rimini. That collection of portraits of dead people you've sentenced me to live with since we separated. I counted them: there are one thousand, five hundred and sixty-four of them. Sofia and Rimini on the esplanade at Mar del Plata. Sofia and Rimini at the Merano *pensione*, just out of bed and having breakfast. Sofia and Rimini eating in La Carcova. Sofia and Rimini next to the *Mona Lisa*. It was the first thing I saw when I went to the storage place: this huge box floating in the water, and inside it the photos were intact, like shipwrecked sailors on a raft.' She opened her mouth wide as if she could not get enough air, and started crying again. 'It's enough,' she said. 'That's enough, Rimini. Please let me be. Give me my life back.'

She was staring straight ahead as she cried, sitting upright with the terrifying dignity of a condemned woman refusing all pity. Rimini realised she was not looking for consolation, or warmth, or under-standing, not even for the crazy satisfaction which ten minutes earlier had made her go halves on a hotel room they had never even used. He saw no cunning, calculation, or effort to seduce in her attitude. For the first time, he felt he was coming face to face with a pure, raw desire. She wanted her life back. That was all. And this naked wish was unbear-able. He felt ill. He thought he was going to be sick. So he dodged round Lucio's head, leaned into the front of the car, and asked the driver if he had a cigarette. Sofia butted in. 'No,' she said, 'don't even think it. Don't pay him any attention. He's not allowed to smoke.' 'I don't have any anyway,' the driver said with a smile, 'I gave up years ago.' Rimini was choking. He rolled down the window and tilted his face towards it, so that the cool evening air blew straight at him. The first rush of air immediately dried the sweat that had been soaking his forehead a couple of minutes earlier. Lucio went rigid, drummed his blue shoes against the back of the seat in front, and let out a long, shrill shriek. He howled without opening his mouth, as if he were biting back his pain, and whirled his arms around like the sails of a demented windmill. Rimini picked him up under his arms, turned him round, and saw that he was rubbing his eye with a closed fist. He asked the driver to switch the light on. 'He must have got something in it,' said Sofia. Rimini examined it in the light: Lucio was pallid, and had dark circles under his eyes. 'He's exhausted,' said Rimini. 'Why not try the dummy?' 'That's what I'm looking for,' he said, annoyed that she had thought of it before he had. He searched for it desperately, while Lucio's fingernails dug ten fiery grooves into his cheeks. 'Stop it, Lucio.

Don't,' he protested. The stinging sensation filled his eyes with tears. He stuck his hand into the push-chair, and pulled it out covered in ice-cream and old crumbs. He felt in his pockets. He was struggling to get off all the bits of fluff that had stuck to the traces of sticky ice, when Sofia pulled at the frayed blue ribbon round Lucio's neck and the dummy reappeared, nestling between the rabbit and squirrel involved in some complicated negotiation on the front of his t-shirt. Rimini stared at it suspiciously, convinced all this had been set up by Sofia, and lifted Lucio to him so that he could put it in his mouth. 'Wait,' said Sofia. She took the dummy between her fingers, popped it in her mouth – amazed at the sight, Lucio immediately stopped wailing – and started to suck slowly on it. A few seconds later, she took it out all shiny and new, and offered it to Lucio. 'Can I?' she asked. Lucio turned expectantly towards his father. Rimini nodded. Feeling ashamed of himself, he looked out of the window and saw a newspaper kiosk shining brightly on the far side of the street. 'Stop!' he said. The taxi-driver looked at him in the rear-view mirror. 'Stop here!' he shouted. He picked Lucio up again, and handed him to Sofia. 'Here, hold him for me.' Lucio settled on Sofia's lap without a sound, staring at her as if she were some kind of goddess. 'Hello Lucio,' she said. Lucio took the dummy out of his mouth and offered it to her. Sofia shook her head and gave Rimini a wry smile. 'Well?' she asked, posing with Lucio as if for a photo. 'How do I look?' But Rimini had already left the taxi and was sprinting across the street, skilfully dodging in between all the car bonnets. He reached the news-stand, put a hand in his pocket to look for money, and for a split second all he could think of were brands of cigarettes: the brand his mother used to smoke in the days when he, as a thirteen-year-old, waited with the packet and the lighter for her to finish her meal so that he could light her cigarette the moment she decided she wanted one; the imported brand his father smoked, with its posters advertising beaches, yachts, fjords and a thousand other exotic rewards; the brand of black tobacco cigarettes that had been Rimini's initiation into smoking, seduced partly by that fact that they were of French origin, and partly to show how virile his lungs were; the brand of light tobacco he had adopted soon afterwards, firstly to 'take a break' as the saying went, from the devastating effects of the dark tobacco, and then, less rationally, to imitate Polanski in *The Tenant*, one of the few films (besides *Rocco and his Brothers*) that Rimini had seen more than half a dozen times with Sofia, who asked for this particular brand every time he went into the bar opposite his house in Paris, capital of the black tobacco empire. He saw all these brands – his whole life flashed by in brands of cigarettes – and with a strangely uneasy feeling, he began to wonder what he was going to smoke now, after a year and a half's abstinence. It was as though the choice of a brand would decide his fate. He realised he did not even know how much a packet of cigarettes cost these days. He asked for a pack of Marlboro and a box of matches, and the mere fact of pronouncing this age-old formula once again was enough to fill his lungs with smoke. The man at the news-stand – a huge fat guy with smooth cheeks, who from the top of his stool seemed to dominate all the counters as if they were extensions of his body – spread his arms wide. 'No cigarettes,' he said. 'The distributors are on strike so I can't get any.' Rimini smiled. He stood there silently, waiting for the man to wink at him knowingly and then scrabble in the plastic containers for a packet, but when he looked up, he saw they really were all empty. So while the man pushed his mobile stool along to the snack bar that was a continuation of the news-stand, and plunged a metal skewer into a pan of boiling water, Rimini, as listless as if he had been drained of all emotion, turned back to the street, noted the soft drizzle falling on the road surface, and looked blindly for the taxi. There it was, with the engine running and headlights flashing. Lucio's two tiny hands hung like stickers from the back window. Rimini stepped down into the street and stumbled. He opened his arms to get his balance, and as he did so, thought of Lucio, who must be watching him from the taxi. He decided to make a joke of it, and convert himself into a human aeroplane flying across to him, but as he was travelling through the damp air, his arms spread wide like wings, and humming softly like an aeroplane engine, he glanced towards the cab once more, and saw it slowly pull away, turn the first corner, and disappear out of sight.

CHAPTER 10

Well, I had to keep something of yours. Something more, something better than those poor drops of warm milk you left inside me in the hotel. How sad all this is, Rimini. It was so easy. I was so hot for you. I deserved better. But not even that, Rimini. (That same night, as Lucio was messing up my sheets with his apple compote, I had a revelation: hadn't we already been once to the same hotel? I remembered because of the name, because the time I think we went [try to remember, Alzheimer, even if it's for the last time: it was a long time ago, we were different people then, and I even seem to recall you couldn't get a hard-on] I remember I thought that L'Interdit [I saw the name on a box of matches] was also the name of the shop where your mother bought clothes – the clothes I was jealous of when we first started going out together, do you remember? And which later on she gave me, and which I think I must still have somewhere or other.) Lucio on the other hand is new and adorable. I wanted you to know that. (You too Carmen: it's great knowing I don't have to hide anything from you.) He's a delight. There's no doubt he takes after his mother: all he has of yours are the eyes. He doesn't have your fear, your 'prudence', or your pathetic emotional stinginess. You don't deserve him, Rimini. But I suppose you'll make it your job to ruin him. I think he and I got on fine. I hope he has a happy memory of his Aunt Sofia. He liked 'The Simpsons', the sound of my keys, the miniature hour-glass I use as a key-ring, the green light on my alarm-clock, and the imitation Calder mobile over my bed which always looks down on me while I'm masturbating thinking of you (I brought a Van Dam dildo back from Germany, a huge black double-headed one that bends into a U-shape so I can stick it in my cunt and arse at the same time), thinking of the day when you will finally accept the fact that you love me and that love is a continuous current. Lucio's had a bath, smells nice, and has eaten, so he's all ready for bed. The clothes he was wearing are in the bag. OK, so the t-shirt I bought him is a bit big. It didn't say the size, it was late, the shops were shutting. Sorry. Nobody's perfect.

PART THREE

CHAPTER 1

He arrived ten minutes late, after getting first the wrong building and then the wrong block, and spending half of the time trying to convince the lift-attendant that even though he was unshaven and had dishevelled hair, a coffee-stained shirt and a shoe missing a lace, he was telling the truth and did have an appointment with the Estebecorena practice. He rang a bell and waited a few seconds, looking at his own shadow in the frosted glass, until an impatient voice asked his name on the intercom. A confused cicada sound followed. Rimini pushed once, twice, three times with increasing force at the door, but to no avail. He finally noticed the little sign saying 'Pull' just as the voice (obviously used to dealing with idiots) suggested he try pulling it towards him. A tall, icy secretary led him along a carpeted corridor – Rimini, who was allergic to the smell of carpet glue, sneezed all the way – and left him in a large, well-lit waiting-room, which had four armchairs and a low table in it. On the table were scattered sports magazines and auction catalogues; a man in his forties with greying hair was leafing through the 1992 Lasalle College Yearbook.

'Coffee, tea, mineral water?' the secretary asked. Rimini raised his head to answer, but saw the offer was not meant for him. 'No, thank you,' the grey-haired man said. 'Are you sure?' she insisted, picking up a dirty cup from the table. 'No, thank you. It's very kind of you.' 'The doctor will see you at once,' the woman added before she left, avoiding imaginary pieces of furniture with her hips. Rimini tried to relax by crossing his legs. Then he realised that the leg he was waving so unconcernedly in the air had the shoe with no laces. He quickly hid it under the table, banging his shin on the edge in the process. Soon after that, the secretary came for the grey-haired man, leaving Rimini feeling even more intimidated, as if the sombre, elegant luxury of the office was taking advantage of them being alone to attack him. Everything was silent and deserted. The carpets softened the noise of footsteps, the wooden panels on the walls deadened the sound of telephones and voices. Rimini heard a ship's siren outside, and it was as though this was the last signal before the world faded away for ever. A door opened, the self-assured boom of a man wishing a whole family well could be heard, and then Rimini saw the forty-year-old's head pass along outside the waiting-room. Now it was his turn. He stood up, and in his mind went over everything he had decided he would say. A few scraps of a line of reasoning drifted through his memory like frightened clouds. 'It's absolutely false that . . .' 'I was as much a victim as she was . . .' 'An unbalanced personality . . .' 'An incurable mythomaniac . . .' Even to him it all sound weak and forced. The slightest scrutiny of any of the excuses could lead to a whole swarm of objections leaping on him and stripping him to the bones in a few seconds flat. He sat down again.

He was tired, his body ached, his hands and feet tingled unpleasantly, and there was a continuous buzzing just behind his ears, as though a pair of insects were following his every move. He had not slept well for days. The sofa-bed his father had lent him was ancient, the mattress was lumpy, and the metal struts underneath jabbed in his back all night, leaving his skin covered in bluish patches. To top it all, his father woke up at first light every morning. He had suffered from mild angina, one of those scares that doctors, employing a narrow but effective range of gloomy predictions, turn into crucial life-or-death moments. His father's body had come out of the ordeal intact, but not his morale. Repenting of the excesses and carelessness he had always abused his health with, he had allowed himself to submit to that modern form of penitence known as rigorous physical conditioning. This began every day in his own living-room, right next to the sofa-bed where Rimini, after struggling with the nightmare of insomnia, was finally entertaining the possibility of getting to sleep, and continued in the Rosedal at Palermo Park, where, whatever the temperature, he ran next-to-naked and drenched his body with bottles of mineral water, closely followed by his personal trainer, a former colleague who had replaced the world of tourism with that of anabolic steroids, and had gained a certain amount of fame by showing off his pecs on a couple of cable TV programmes.

Rimini yawned and smelled his own breath: if he had been someone else, he would have turned his head away. He decided he would sit well away from the lawyer: the distance would disguise his neediness. Paradoxically, this idea calmed his nerves. It was as if he had discovered the key, as when an actor who is struggling to come to terms with his character suddenly discovers a small detail, a way of walking, holding a glass or a cigarette, or of blowing his nose, and all at once everything that had until then resisted him – psychology, motives, personal history, values – becomes clear to him, illuminated by that tiny discovery, so that it is all completely transparent. Rimini picked up a golf magazine, exchanged it for one on polo, and just as he had opened it at the centrefold, where six horses and their riders were crowding round the Intercountries 1999 cup, the secretary appeared in the doorway. She looked at him without a word for a few moments, as if Rimini were the only thing standing between her and more or less complete happiness.

He was shown into a large meeting-room, with an oval table in the middle and a single painting on the wall: in the foreground, a pack of hounds, an impossibly young rider blowing a horn, two Amazons in breeches and helmets pursuing their prey, clouds in the sky, woods, and in the distance a castle reduced to almost nothing, but still remarkably detailed. This hunting scene caught his attention. Rimini searched for some sign of the fox, the tip of his tail or anything else, and when he could see nothing, realised that if the fox were absent, this was because everything in the painting was headed straight at him, and if the scene were to transcend its modest pictorial existence and burst into the real world among the four walls of the office, the hounds, the horses and the huntswomen would land on top of him, crushing him under their feet and hooves, and giving him the *coup de grâce* with their little toy shot-guns. He, Rimini, was the fox. Sitting at the head of the table against the light, with the river behind him, Estebecorena, the man with the booming voice, was conducting a delicate phone negotiation with someone called Fico. Rimini noticed that the secretary had not closed the door. He was about to correct her omission when Estebecorena raised a hand and, still talking on the phone, brought him to a halt. Rimini did not move. He saw the other man turn in his seat, lean over slightly (his voice grew lower as he adopted a more confidential tone, then guffawed) and search for something in a drawer. Rimini pulled a seat out from the table. Following the plan he had sketched out; he was about to sit down at the opposite end to the lawyer, but Estebecorena, who was now facing him again, stopped him in his tracks again with a gesture. He tossed some A4-size papers across the table. They slid along cleanly and came to a stop a centimetre from Rimini's left hand. Estebecorena covered the mouthpiece of the phone with one hand. 'Let's not waste time,' he said, leaning back and pointing to the papers. 'It's just a case of reading and signing – there's no need for you to sit down.' He went back to his conversation. Estebecorena was in favour of Wilson balls; Fico apparently preferred Slazenger. The matter would be settled that weekend on a nine-hole golf course at Pilar. Still standing, Rimini skimmed through the first page, as though taking it for granted he would not understand a thing, but reasoning: 'I'm going to sign, and if I'm going to sign I have to read it, so that if there's something I don't agree with, I can protest . . .' He began to concentrate, and by the tenth line, when he had finished reading about the parties in dispute – he read Carmen's name and then, on the line below, right underneath Carmen's, his own (he realised that this was the closest he would ever be from now on) – his eyes began to mist over and the sentences started to vanish from the paper, as though they were not printed with ink but with smoke. Rimini tried to hide his emotions, and pressed his two hands on the table, on either side of the sheets of paper. He stood helplessly for a few moments bent over the four or five sheets that summarised the fate he could expect, while Estebecorena's voice, like a distant, meaningless, but not unpleasant rumble, undermined his last remaining attempts to concentrate. 'Oh, so you're going to *read* it,' Rimini heard the lawyer say. It was not a question, more an incredulous assertion. Rimini looked at him; all he could see was the point of his skull standing out against the horizon. 'Can you wait a moment?' Estebecorena told the phone, then covered the mouthpiece again and said to Rimini: 'I can save you the trouble. By signing that document, you legally undertake to: One . . .' Rimini saw against the skyline how the lawyer raised his thumb to emphasise his point: 'not come within less than fifty metres of my client; two, not come within fifty metres of my client's son; three, give up all rights to each and every one of the goods and chattels which until now you owned in common with my client; and four, provide my client with a monthly alimony equivalent to the value of three family shopping baskets, without prejudice of this sum increasing if my client's son's mental health should suffer as a result of being deprived of his liberty, meaning that he needs special care or treatment, the entire cost of which is to be borne by you for however long such care is required. That's all. If you sign. And I frankly advise you to sign.' He went back to the phone: 'Sorry, where were we? Oh yes, the tassels. I can't believe you still wear them. This is almost the year 2000, Fico. They went out with Arnold Palmer.'

Client? Son of client? Rimini had seen them cry, had bathed them and smelled them, he had watched them sleep in the darkness . . . He had kissed their lips, their ear lobes, their groins . . . While he tried to find reasons to object to the terms of the agreement, starting with that term itself, 'agreement', he searched for something to write with. He found a top full of ink – but no sign of the pen that had leaked into it; the mustard-stained bill for the two hot dogs he had eaten for lunch half an hour earlier; the plastic credential that the man on the desk downstairs had given him in exchange for his identity card when he entered the building. A modest booty, but he laid it out on the table with a ceremonious and weary sweep of his hand as though these baubles, one of which was not even his, were merely the first samples of a vast collection hidden deep in his pockets. Worried about the amount of damage the rest of the hoard might cause to his impeccable table, his impeccable documents and, if they were to roll off the table (as the pen top had just done) to his impeccable carpet, Estebecorena plunged a hand into the inside pocket of his jacket, and pulled out one of those plum-coloured ballpoint pens (a real one, not the cheap Taiwanese imitations that Rimini had been admiring as if they were diamonds on the Calle Florida stalls). He pressed the button on the top so that it was ready for use, then slid it towards Rimini without even deigning to look in his direction, demonstrating the same skill and precision as he had shown with the papers. And Rimini signed with a trembling hand. He signed the first page and then, following the instructions of Estebecorena's index finger waving at the far end of the table, he signed the second, and the third, and then the fourth. When he had finished, and the desolate gravity with which he had added his signature to the first had turned into a routine gesture, Estebecorena's hand – the only thing he seemed willing to allow to participate in all this – ordered him to come closer. Rimini walked towards him – the hand reminded him about the papers, Rimini went back to fetch them – and after arrogantly dismissing the scrawl Rimini had imprinted at the foot of each of them, Estebecorena, who by now was extolling the virtues of his personal caddy on the phone – he had brought him specially from the Mar del Plata Golf Club – stretched out a limp hand which Rimini shook without thinking, as if he were drugged. Then the hand waved him out of its presence. Rimini turned away, but halfway to the door, he stopped and turned back again. He looked at the lawyer, who raised his head in surprise. 'The letter,' said Rimini, pointing to the folder Estebecorena had taken the papers of the agreement from. Estebecorena covered up the phone yet again. 'I beg your pardon?' he said. 'Sofia's letter. I'd like to read it.' 'I don't see why.' 'I want to read it. It's addressed to me, so technically it's mine.' 'Technically, that letter is legal evidence. And if we were to decide to start legal proceedings against you – something which my client, for the moment at least and against my advice, has decided against – I don't think it would help improve your situation very much.' Rimini did not budge. 'I don't care. It's still mine. I have the right to read it.' Estebecorena gave a disdainful sigh. He had bulging eyes that were so blue they looked almost transparent; the skin on his cheeks was red as though he had just shaved, and he had the most prominent Adam's apple Rimini had ever seen. 'Excuse me a minute,' he said into the phone, opened the file, and took out a sheet of lined paper torn from a notebook. 'Very kind,' said Rimini. 'Leave it on the table when you've finished with it,' Estebecorena said, swivelling his chair so that he was facing the windows, with his back to Rimini. 'And when you go, please shut the door.'

Although this was the first time he had read the letter, he was perfectly familiar with its contents. And yet it was only now, looking at it, that Rimini was able to imagine what Carmen must have felt when she got it. Late on the night of the abduction, whilst Rimini, terrified by his sense of guilt, was busy trying to increase the difficulties in his way, in the hope that an accident, a street brawl, or any other incident could provide him with an alibi, Carmen (who by this time had spent hours phoning hospitals and police stations) answered the entry-phone and heard her son's voice burbling above the sound of traffic. She thought she must be hallucinating. She ran downstairs in her dressing-gown and slippers, her face puffy from all the crying. When she reached the lobby she saw Lucio through the glass front door. He was sitting in his push-chair, staring at the entrance to his own home with sleepy eyes. He looked as though he had just been given a bath: his hair was wet and combed to one side as if he were on his way to communion, and his clothes, apart from the blue shoes, still had the labels with their prices from the supermarket where they had been bought. It was some time later, after she had dried his hair with the electric hair-dryer – as if, not completely content with having burnt all the new clothes, she also wanted to remove all traces of dampness, cold, and perfume from his body, to get rid of the slightest trace that contact with Sofia might have left on him – that she discovered the lock of hair missing behind his right ear. The letter was pinned to the bib of his romper with a paper-clip. When Rimini appeared three hours later still, completely drunk, dragged in by the pizza delivery man he had tried to pick a fight with, Carmen had already taken advice from Estebecorena and had locked the letter away. She did not say a word. She let Rimini collapse on the floor, and heard him being sick as she gave the pizza man some spare change. Rimini crawled over to her, stammering out a stream of excuses. He saw Carmen looking at him expressionlessly, and tried to pronounce his son's name. He got as far as Luz, Luis, Laz – when a clockwork bee with a bent wing came speeding across the living-room carpet and banged into his body. Behind the bee came Lucio, crawling on all fours and shrieking like a karate expert, either to catch it or drive it away. Then, as Carmen poured the contents of Sofia's letter all over him, like some fateful lava, Rimini could feel his arms giving way, and lay his cheek against the carpet. He started to cry and cry, and while in his ears he could hear the crazy duet of his sobs and the enraged bee, a huge weight fell across his back, and he passed out.

A month after that night, Rimini was finally reading the letter for the first and last time. He took it in instantly, all of it, with a ghastly completeness. As he later realised, he was remembering it in order to treasure it. After all, that letter, which had buried him, was his only link to the world from which he had just been exiled. Over the following months, each time the need to know something about Lucio became unbearable, he kept going back to it, to that kind of imaginary shop-window where he had it on display. He was aware that the Lucio Sofia was describing in those lines probably no longer existed, and that his tastes – the last ones Rimini had seen close at hand – had probably been replaced by new ones, which Rimini could imagine but not share. This anachronism was the secret of the letter's attraction. For him, Lucio had been frozen in time, embalmed by Sofia's prose, and Rimini could use the letter to violate the terms of his agreement with Carmen without suffering the consequences. By reading it in his mind, he could visit his son and admire the eternal, intact mummified beauty he had acquired. He could even secretly enjoy the image of Carmen, the sweet, brave Carmen that Sofia's knowing eye had been able to discern in Lucio's features. The letter – or rather the mental facsimile of the letter, a photographic likeness (because whenever Rimini tried to copy it out, after he had written two or three lines he would furiously tear it up because it might reproduce the words but could not capture the hesi-tations, the crossed-out phrases, the defects of the paper, everything that made it unique) – was his refuge, his altar, his funeral chapel.

CHAPTER 2

One night he recited the letter in his dreams, from start to finish, while he was trying to ward off some phantoms clawing at him from mid-air. (This was the first in a series of polyglot dreams: Rimini was dreaming of the letter and, after saying out loud the original words in Spanish, he saw it translated into English, French, and Italian, projected on to the dome of his dream one by one. The translations were faithful to the original while at the same time wildly poetic, but they were always perfect. So then, invaded by a whirlwind of happiness – these nocturnal appearances took him back to what he had once been – Rimini, like a crazed stoker, fed the dream in order to perpetuate it, clinging to all its components and driving away any threat of inter-ference, any new detail that might upset its balance, confident that if he could only make it last long enough, the dream would restore all the faculties he had been robbed of that day . . .) Watching TV by his side in the darkened living-room, his father understood that Rimini was speaking the words with the precision of someone fast asleep, and watched him shouting and tossing and turning without intervening. The next morning over breakfast, shortly after Rimini (anxious to enjoy the fruits of his accelerated nocturnal apprenticeship) had discovered that his memory was as parched and scant as ever, his father gave him an ultimatum: he had to start living again. However hard that might be, there was nothing else for it. His father, alerted by his bout of angina and his change of lifestyle, had decided to revive an old wish of his: fed up with the frantic pace of Buenos Aires, he was going to sell what few possessions he had (among them the small two-roomed flat they had been sharing for the past three months) and go and live in Uruguay. Rimini felt as though the world was collapsing around him. He asked his father to take him too. His father said no. He said it would do no good. Rimini dropped the spoon into his bowl of cereal – splashing the t-shirt his father had lent him to sleep in with drops of milk – and began to chew the tip of the napkin he was twisting in his hands. 'Please,' he begged him, 'Take me with you.' 'No. I want to help you,' said his father, 'but I don't want to be an accomplice in your downfall.' 'Please! I can work. I could pay your bills. Clean the house, cook, wash clothes. I could be your chauffeur. Please take me with you.' 'That's enough,' his father cut in. 'Can't you see you make me feel ashamed?'

No, of course he had not seen that. There were days when the horizon of what he saw and understood was reduced to a complete minimum. He was unable to tell whether the light was on or off, if he was dressed or naked, if anyone was with him or if he was on his own. He was blithely unaware of himself; he had reached one of those states of suspension of consciousness that Buddhist priests achieve after decades of harsh discipline, and for which devotees from the West who visit those monks each year in their temples are willing to pay a fortune. Rimini no longer went out. The outside world – even in its replicated form on TV, the radio, newspapers or the telephone – had slowly ceased to exist for him. It had become a vague, uncertain memory, like something implanted. For example, on a particularly acute day, for Rimini the 'outside world' consisted of the array of objects external to his body that he came into contact with in his recluse's life: the uniform he wore to sleep and live in, for a start – his father's t-shirt, the striped pyjama bottom and a pair of old woollen socks out of which his big toenails poked mockingly, beyond his control – then one or two light switches, which he very occasionally accepted the need for to get from one room to another; water, which he could tolerate only to drink, not to wash himself with; a basic minimum of foodstuffs: sausages, instant mashed potato, fried eggs, dozens of boxes of mint chocolate biscuits, whose wrappings he left all over the apartment, allowing his father to trace his movements while he had been out; the sofa-bed where he spent most of the day; the sheets and blankets he wrapped himself in; the pillow he clung to . . . Even the letter, which in its own way appeared to prove that there was life somewhere out there, a life in which a world and beings lost to him were floating; even that sheet of paper from a school notebook, which was now no more than a stark mental image, seemed to Rimini to be something more internal than his own thoughts, the taste of his saliva, or the rumblings of hunger in his stomach. It was not that he had such a vast interior world, or that this interior world had grown. Rimini *was* pure interior world, what was less certain was whether this world was his.

To his father there was only one solution: to inject him with the outside world. A good dose of it, although (and this was vital) it was to be administered with great caution. Given Rimini's complete self-absorption, any slip-up could prove fatal, like exposing an albino to the summer noonday sun. That was why, in theory at least, the Uruguay plan was ideal. He would put the Buenos Aires apartment up for sale; Rimini could continue to live there, and be responsible for showing people around, while his father looked for something to buy in Montevideo. He would have to synchronise two transactions in two different market-places, each of which was bound to have its own rules and dynamics. This would mean that the operation would take some time, two months at least – which ought to be enough, his father calculated, for the valve to open bit by bit so that Rimini, by having to establish contact with possible buyers (ideal emissaries from the outside world, because while they called for a certain amount of attention, they made no real demands) could receive small, homeopathic doses of a life-giving radiation which might otherwise prove too much for him. He was not going to leave him in the street, but nor was he willing out of a sense of pity to let him consolidate his indifference to the world. Within two months, his father thought, Rimini would be himself again, robust enough to get himself a job and even (with a little help from him – although this meant him cutting back on his dreams in Montevideo, for he was planning to give him part of what he earned from the sale of the apartment) his own place.

On the big day, Rimini woke up early, had a bath, brushed his teeth, got dressed, made the bed, prepared breakfast, woke his father, helped him finish packing his suitcase, and went with him to the port. His father was delighted: the remedy had not even been applied yet, and it was already having an effect. Once on board the ferry, he looked out of the window and saw Rimini, not level with the boat but a little further back, leaning against one of the fake portholes on the landing-stage. His smile was oddly radiant, and he had one hand raised level with his face as though taking an oath. He seemed completely indifferent to the travellers milling around him. His father waved. Rimini did not respond. Was he looking in his direction, or . . . ? His father got up and went out into the saloon aisle. Perhaps if he sat a few rows further back he would be opposite Rimini and could wave and make sure he had seen him. He set off, but at that very moment a flood of passengers emerged from the car-deck and swept over him. This tidal wave ended up pushing him back to his original seat, as the ferry began to pull away from the pier. He turned his head to look: Rimini was at the same spot, in the same position, but now the raised hand was waving mechanically back and forth.

It was eleven o'clock in the morning. The boat grew smaller and smaller in the distance, the landing-stage emptied of people, and Rimini sat down again at the bar table where he had been drinking coffee with his father shortly before his departure. He crossed his legs, pushed his forefinger against the handle of his own coffee cup and started spinning it round, chuckling to himself each time the Italian logo came into view. At half-past nine that night, after taking a long while to make up his mind, a waiter came over, tapped him gently on the shoulder as if afraid of waking him, and the dizzy cup came to a halt, although Rimini's finger was still against the handle. They were about to close, the waiter explained. Rimini drew his finger back as if the cup was burning hot; he uncrossed his legs, stood up, plunged his hands into his overcoat pockets, and left.

He walked home. This was not the first time he had gone forty blocks on foot, but he had never done it in such a state of receptivity. His route was a perfect mix of decision and chance: the general direction was established from the outset, but each point along it offered the possibility of a detour, an escape, a fortuitous adventure. Anything could distract him. He knew his destination and how to get there (he even knew the shortcuts), but everywhere he passed through was a temptation to which he inevitably yielded. He followed the avenue alongside the port, well-lit but deserted at that time of night. At a service station he stopped to observe how an attendant, struggling with the weight of his baseball cap, was filling the tank of a dark van that looked as if it were armour-plated. The whole vehicle seemed to shake to the beat of music blasting from inside. Then, standing beside one of the pumps, he peered inside the all-night café and saw a man and a woman, their heads leaning against the window-pane, drinking coffee and reading out loud to each other what they had previously read in silence in their magazines. He watched them for a while, buffeted by the wind whipping round the service station, until a moped that had just been filled with diesel startled him with its horn and forced him to get out of its way. Rimini decided to follow it, and set off along the avenue again. He spent an hour in Retiro coach station. He went into all the shops that were still open, stopped at all the news-stands, and sat hunched in three different bars without ordering anything. On each occasion he let himself be drawn into the soundless images he could see on their TV screens: a series of brutal tornados, a game show, a cruise through a Greek archipelago. He spent another hour inspecting the cheap stalls that festooned the outside of the railway station. He never said a word. The stall owners called out prices, pulled things from secret cabinets to show him, started up all kinds of household electrical goods and demonstrated them under his nose – even, in one case, using his overcoat sleeve as testing-pad; all Rimini did in response was smile and move on to the next stall, where he would once again be assailed by portable radios, electric toothbrushes, ballpoint pens, umbrellas. A drunken fight with broken bottles, staggering figures, and a poor dog unable to choose between the two sides, kept him entertained for another twenty minutes. Then, as he moved away from the port area, the amusements ran out. For a few minutes he found himself in the shock wave from an elegant party that had no music but boasted a soundtrack full of voices, clinking glasses and laughter, and from the street admired the bare shoulders of a woman picked out in the light from a first-floor window. When he saw two very young girls pressing all the buttons on an entry pad, he walked away backwards without taking his eyes off them. At a cash machine a sweaty, bald man was frowning as he read the receipt the slit had just spat at him. An ambulance went by, a group of men came out of a restaurant, blown about by the wind, an inflatable dummy bounced to and fro next to a garage. It was two in the morning by the time he reached the apartment. He went in without switching any lights on. Although his father had given him permission to use the bedroom, the bed, the sheets, and everything else, so that at least for the length of time it took to sell, Rimini would feel he owned the place, he pushed off his shoes with his feet, stretched out fully dressed on the sofa-bed, and fell asleep.

As was to happen with a certain regularity over the next few weeks, he was woken in mid-morning by the sound of the intercom. He attended it still asleep, his head full of sand, opening the door out of sheer laziness, in order not to have to argue. He fumbled blindly for the button, and as he did so knocked over a bottle of mineral water. It smashed on the floor. Rimini plunged back into the swamp of his bedclothes. He had the rapidest of dreams, full of silent but glittering images, and just as he was entering a more stable phase, in which these meaningless picture postcards seemed to be settling into some kind of story, the doorbell rang inside his head, and he was forced to get up again and open the door. An elderly man, one side of his face covered in a birth-mark, looked at him in a puzzled way. He stared down at the bit of paper in his hand as if to confirm something, cast a sideways glance at the traces of blood that Rimini's feet had just left on the door-mat, stepped back, and started searching round the landing as if he had got the wrong door, or was looking for an emergency exit. Rimini showed him in. The man – the first in a long line of unsuspecting victims whom Rimini tortured with the sight of his decadence – came in and timidly advanced into the darkened living-room, while Rimini ran yawning to seek the refuge of his foul-smelling nest. It was from there, with eyes closed and sheets up round his chin, that he reeled off the apartment's attractions.

Drawn blinds, the fuggy, almost solid atmosphere of stale air, dirty clothes all over the floor, Rimini's voice ringing through the rooms like the fog warning from a dying lighthouse, as it guided wary men and women through the darkness, where they knocked into furniture and doors and tried to escape, only to knock themselves again: the same ritual went on for two months. The only thing that changed was the scale of the disaster: the patches of damp on the walls, a dripping tap, a rotting window-sill, the gas leak in the kitchen. Some of the visitors fled as soon as Rimini opened the door. Once, a woman arrived: he did not so much as look at her, or say a word, or make the slightest move to invite her in, merely opened the door then turned to shuffle off back to his sofa-bed and sit in front of the TV (which had been on all night, tuned into a special report on sorghum or alfalfa on the farming channel) to polish off the remains of an old pizza he tore apart with his fingers. A sudden draught made him glance back at the open door, and he realised the woman had vanished. On another occasion he attended a young couple – just married, he thought he heard them say, or perhaps only engaged. When they saw he was also young, or simply more approachable than the estate agency people they had been dealing with, they told him all about their three-year love affair, the trips they had been on, summarised their affinities and arguments, and after keeping him standing at the front door (which was very unusual) the girl suddenly paused in mid-sentence – something about flowers, or hours, or floors, and burst out laughing. Mollified by all their romantic passion, Rimini made to usher them in, but then realised they were no longer there, that the lift door was already closing, taking with it not only the girl's laughter but the boy's too: it was only when he was on his way back to the sofa that he realised his prick was hanging out of his pyjama front.

Most people entered, wrinkled up their noses and went round the apartment following the instructions called out by Rimini's static voice. Although inevitably they were disappointed by what little they could see in the darkness, they persisted out of a strange kind of morbid expectancy, because while the ruinous state of the rooms, the floors, the painting on ceiling and walls dashed their aesthetic hopes, it served at the same time to kindle their sense of an opportunity, giving them an excuse for asking him to drop the price. But to Rimini, the price was absolutely untouchable. In the vegetable state to which he had been reduced, to sell or not to sell, to have the apartment make a good or a bad impression, for the potential clients to be more or less enthusiastic – all this left him cold. And that indifference made him an unassailable vendor. He was so detached from the apartment that he was inoculated against all the arguments – architectural, financial, emotional – usually trotted out to undermine the traditional seller's will. 'Sixty-five thousand', said Rimini, and his voice, dull and monotonous when it was describing the view out of the back, or the closed-in patio, acquired new life all of a sudden. 'Sixty-five thousand. Not a peso more, not a peso less.'

Apart from a couple of acts of spontaneous charity, both female – one woman who offered to raise the blinds; another who, alarmed at his retching noises, wanted to go out and buy him some cough medicine – Rimini did not receive a single offer in the entire two months.

When his father called him each week from Montevideo, where he had rented an apartment overlooking the river in Pocitos, he told him everything was going fine, that he was showing the apartment on average to four people a week, and that it was only a matter of time before it was sold. 'Aha. Any offers?' 'Several.' And when his father, encouraged by the report he had just heard, pressured him for details, Rimini baffled him with the esoteric but effective language – price rises, price falls, the incongruities of the market – of an experienced real estate agent. 'Why make a bad sale?' he said into the phone, desperately scratching his head and showering his shoulders with a cloud of dandruff. 'No, of course not,' said his father, slightly ashamed of himself, as if compared to Rimini's commercial astuteness, his wish to sell was a sign of rampant greed; he was also moved by the zeal with which his son defended the value of his property. Then, considering that his confidence in Rimini gave him permission to do so, he confessed he was missing his things, and timidly asked whether he could have his furniture. 'Some bits of it at least,' he corrected himself, heartbroken at the thought of his son living alone in an empty apartment. He would see to everything; all Rimini would have to do was let the removal firm in.

Rimini had given in to the passage of time. He lived at a kind of degree zero, as if anything that was not part of his introspection was intolerably trivial to him. He was no longer hungry or thirsty; he did not miss the street, or work, or reading books, or going to the cinema – early one morning he had caught a glimpse of Annie Girardot's silhouette and naked shoulder on the TV, and had stayed staring at them for several moments, just long enough to scorn them as the remnants of an old, despicable way of life. He even began to confuse Lucio's and Carmen's faces with those of anonymous children and women he caught sight of in sweets adverts in the pages of the newspapers he sometimes used as napkins. But he could describe the speed his nails, hair or beard grew at, and the intensity of the smell his body was starting to give off. Rimini was the passage of time – life stripped bare. A masterpiece of inertia, directionless and aimless: self-contained life, life in free fall.

286

CHAPTER 3

One morning Rimini forced his eyes open and found himself staring at the sculptured pectorals of his father's personal trainer shaking him awake. He thought he must be dreaming, so he took a good look. He saw the white t-shirt: a stylised black gazelle leaping over his left nipple, the even tan of the forearms, the copper bracelet (with its enigmatic green secretions) on one wrist, the running shoes without socks. He allowed himself to be intoxicated by the wave of health that enveloped him – a cunningly dosed combination of mouthwash and aftershave – and gave a sigh of relief, as if this sporting angel were not only his personal messiah, the man who would rescue him from the bottomless pit of the sofa-bed, but an antidote that could retrospectively free him from his most recent suffering. Covering his nose and mouth with his hand, the trainer threw open the living-room window, succeeded in making the blinds let in a few shafts of light, and surveyed the devastated apartment with cool aplomb. He was a simple, determined man. He had heard what was going on from the porter, who a few days earlier had witnessed the satisfaction with which two gas company employees turned off the gas supply to the apartment – the same satisfaction shown by the electricity men a week earlier – and thanks to a couple of phone calls from Rimini's father in Montevideo, enthusing about how well the sale of the apartment was going. To the trainer, Rimini was not much more than the son of a client. But Rimini's father, taking advantage of the confessional intervals between, for example, a session of abdominals and another of stretching exercises, had described in some detail Lucio's abduction and the series of disasters this had led to, and this story, so imbued with the father's pain (because, as so often happens, he saw in his son's debacle the proof of his own failure as a father), had moved him in an extraordinary way. He put a few things together, suspected something fishy, and postponed an entire week of training sessions just so that he could be free to take the matter in hand. He had no children, and lived alone. Taking care of his body obliged him to cultivate a very special way of life which implied a whole series of habits and precautions that could not easily be shared. Only someone like him – a female personal trainer, for example – would have seen them as something more than whims. But female personal trainers were not his type. He was used to dealing with *fallen* people. Self-neglect, physical decay, disability, lack of will-power (and all the related psychological effects) were common currency to him. These were the problems that – after several decades in a comfortable position in the tourist industry – he had taken the mature decision to dedicate his life to. Rimini was in a bad way, but not that much worse than the situations he had to rescue many of his clients from. Rimini was shaking like a leaf. The trainer wondered whether he should give him a bath. He remembered there was no gas and therefore no hot water either, but went into the bathroom all the same, judging that the shock of cold water might be even more effective. He turned on one tap, then another, and another, until they were all running. He sat on the side of the bidet and waited. A sort of musical cannon of dry flatulent sounds followed, some of them accompanied by wisps of smoke; then a *seguidilla* of anaemic reddish drops dripped from the bath-tap on to the mouldy rubber mat. He went back to the living-room, wrapped Rimini up in the blanket, lifted him in one easy movement, and carried him far, far away from the disaster area.

The trainer lived in Núñez, on the twenty-second floor of a tower block which in the evening, on windy days, seemed to sway slightly, as if pulled by the speed of the aeroplanes crossing the sky close to it. Rimini spent the first phase of his rehabilitation (the one that, according to his trainer, took the most effort, but was not necessarily the hardest, because for someone at the bottom of a well everything is progress, whereas for anyone who was more or less back to normal, any further progress was a titanic achievement) in what the trainer called the temple: a spacious rectangular room overlooking the river, furnished only with a tatami, a rubber mat the thickness of a carpet, a set of parallel bars, an aerobic belt and two weights machines, all of them duplicated by a ceiling-to-floor mirror on one of the main walls. It was the ideal place, and Rimini was the perfect patient. The trainer designed a special routine for him that made increasing demands, including not

288

only a complete physical exercise programme, but also a diet, with carefully calculated vitamin supplements, and hydrotherapy and massage sessions. Rimini surrendered to all of this mindlessly, as if it were some kind of practical religion that channelled his life in one direction, as all religions do, and so saved him from the exhausting task of having to take decisions while at the same time, unlike other religions, not demanding any kind of intellectual or philosophical communion. Rimini scrupulously followed the instructions, and the time that the trainer was away from the apartment working, which any other patient might have taken advantage of to escape from its strictures or at least relax them, even if only by diluting them through watching TV, talking on the phone, or reading, only served for Rimini to feel more responsible and more fiercely committed – partly because of the combination of will-power and inertia that physical training produces, and partly because the apartment (except for the view of the river, which was almost invisible anyway for most of the day, either because the sun and the bare horizon reduced it to a white haze drained of all definition and colour which blinded him, or because it was obscured by a vast veil of mist) offered few distractions: the trainer had no sound system or radio (he was rather deaf), only read specialist publications such as *Muscle Today, True Fitness* or *Everybody*, which he had translated by a bilingual colleague and kept carefully locked in a drawer – and although he did have a television (he liked to watch a little at night to help him get to sleep, or turned to the home sales channels to keep up with the latest in portable muscle toners, electronic stretching machines, manual lipo-reduction gadgets, silhouette shapers and all the other gimmicks of what he called, half-amused and half-furious, 'the great body fraud industry') he had blocked access to it by means of a secret code, so that there was no risk of Rimini wasting the slightest amount of energy on it. The trainer saw Rimini's collapse as a typical case of energy entropy: first there was disorder, and then the chaotic, enormous leaking away of life spirit. Those leaks had to be plugged; then resources concentrated; once they were concentrated and the organic machine had regained what in some sense was its own combustible, its own energy source, then it was time to go from inside to out, to open up and project the restored self on to the world, and wait for the feedback. Even though he knew nothing about it, Rimini soon became a perfect example of this principle, and showed an astonishing improvement. He had nothing to think about. His mind, his imagination, even his memory – it was all as white and blank as the walls of the temple where, apart from the mirror and a photo of Charles Atlas in the trainer's bedroom (a blow-up of the photo usually seen in old comic books alongside the coupons to enrol for the Atlas correspondence course), the trainer, iconoclast by nature, refused to hang any images, convinced that they wasted energy by taking the mind away from the only truly worthwhile thing: the image of one's own body. It was like being in a prison or a Buddhist temple. Everything was discipline, rhythm, repetition. It took Rimini at least a week to be able to poke his head up out of the ruins. It was as though some invertebrate creature – an amoeba or a jellyfish, for example – had suddenly grown a backbone, a structure, a whole skeleton, and the wobbly, soft object had stood erect, taken on a definite shape, and begun to move in a coordinated manner for the first time in many months.

One morning, ten days after Rimini had been interned, the trainer woke him abnormally late (at eight rather than half-past six) with an abnormally generous breakfast: orange juice instead of water, tea instead of water, a piece of toasted rye bread instead of water. A new phase had begun. The trainer, using – not without the occasional confusion – the forefinger of one hand and the five fingers of the other to count with, listed the most important points of the immediate future, while Rimini sat staring in wonder at the three morning luxuries he had been rewarded with. Point number one: he would start going out. The temple had fulfilled its main function – to cut him off from the outside world, to give him shelter and allow him to gather his strength. If they confined him any longer, especially considering the progress he had made, they would be running the risk of building up the toxic reserves that lie in wait in all artificial ecosystems, however favourable they might be. The concentration stage was coming to an end; it was time to release that concentrated effort, and if the conditions were right (but only under the strictest control) to let it interact with the outside: it was time to renew relations with the world. Second: going out did not mean they were suspending the treatment, merely modifying it. From rehabilitation, which could now be considered complete, Rimini was to move on to the bio-social stage of starting to train, by joining one of the groups that jogged every morning, under the trainer's instruction, in the Palermo woods. Thirdly: Rimini would have nothing further to do with his father's apartment, the cleaning and sale of which the trainer had left in the hands of the porter, in exchange for a substantial tip and the promise of a commission. Fourthly, and most importantly: the trainer promised to keep point three (and also, of course, the pitiful descent into hell which had made it necessary) undisclosed to Rimini's father, who thought the transaction was going ahead according to the terms agreed before his departure for Montevideo, while in return Rimini promised to do everything he could to bring this new phase of his treatment to a successful conclusion. 'And point five . . .' the trainer said, nibbling at the corner of a burnt piece of toast. A shower of coal-black crumbs spoiled the impeccable white of his t-shirt. He thought it over: point five could wait. And a surprise: he had bought Rimini some clothes. He cleared away the plates and cups and plonked a big bag with a sports shop logo on it on to the middle of the table.

Rimini pulled out what was to be his uniform for many weeks: tennis shoes and socks, a pair of grey cotton trousers, a t-shirt with collar and buttons (which the trainer called a sweater) and a troubling garment made up of three interwoven elastic strips and a kind of triangular loincloth. At first Rimini associated it with some extravagant medieval accessory, halfway between a piece of armour and a chastity belt. Then he had a sudden flash of inspiration: thanks partly to his memory, which was slowly recovering, and also to the word 'jockstrap' which the trainer had ceremoniously pronounced as he showed it him, he eventually recognised it as the caveman's garment he had so often seen his father put on in the club changing-room. This was the uniform in which one morning without warning, and without the trainer considering any special presentation necessary, Rimini joined the five members of the Blue group (Tuesdays and Thursdays) and continued to follow his recovery plan to the letter. The clothes and the group were as perfect as the temple, with its bare walls and lack of temptation, had been before them. The others could not have been more ordinary: there was nothing strange, nothing remarkable about them. They complied so well with the stereotype that they blended completely into their surroundings and went completely unnoticed. Although there were five of them, of differing sexes and physical condition, and though their ages varied between thirty and sixty-five, all the possibilities that this handful of variables might create were nullified by the common goal they shared. There was no time for socialising: any expression or exchange of a personal nature was out of place. They did only what they said (while they said it), only talked about what they did (after they had done it). They went from instruction ('Hands on your hips and ... one!') to commentary ('My gluteus is a bit sore') and vice versa: those were the only two registers they seemed authorised to adopt. Reduced to the present, and to that especially reduced form of the present depicted by the vagaries and limitations of the body, they were fundamentalists of the here and now, people for whom past and future were nothing more than harmful fictions, invented with the sole aim of destroying their self-obsession with the poison of a sense of history. Everything was now, this instant, here. A myopic, immediate world, the laws of which permitted only one postponement: that between a badly performed exercise and its corrected version. There was no struggle with origins, or effects, or projections into the future. Nothing was left over: everything was in its place. In the worst scenario, they had to improve, but the parody of a future that this demand created did not so much change as ratify their world's homogeneity. And Rimini stubbornly improved. Between classes, of course, but also in each class itself. He improved every hour and every second, as though afraid of disintegrating if he did not move forward. As he regained control, strength, and suppleness, the same force reviving his muscles cleared the jungle of brambles, ivy, weeds and poisonous plants that had been growing for months, perhaps years, inside his head. Perhaps because of the kind of abyss that Rimini was emerging from, he quickly achieved the sort of perfection (at least to the extent it could reasonably be achieved), which for the other members of the group seemed to be a long-term objective, something vital but distant. He was not surprised; he was too busy carrying out his routines to be able to enjoy the distance necessary for that. His awareness – that tiny minimum of awareness that the training had spared from its general clear-out – judged things on a daily basis, in the strict terms of the everyday accounting exercise that all physical activity entails – number of minutes, breaths, bends, number of times round the lake – which meant he lacked an overall, panoramic vision of the progress he was making. At the same time and in the same way that he was achieving perfection, Rimini was becoming innocent. Only the trainer, who was both part of and outside the commitment his disciple had with the goal of physical well-being – only he, who was capable of comparing the two Riminis, the drowning man he had found on a moth-eaten sofa-bed and the tireless athlete who was now dazzling him in the sunlight, could see the state of perfection Rimini had reached, and understand that the time had come to move on to the next stage.

One morning, while the group, lying on their backs on the grass, was trying to complete the last set of abdominal exercises, Rimini (who had finished them some time earlier) lay stretched out for a few moments watching the tops of two trees swaying together, and then stood up and walked off down the red clay path that bordered the park. The trainer, busy holding down some of the group's ankles against the ground, watched him go. He saw him lean against a tree trunk, flex his leg, then get hold of first one instep and then the other. He saw him walking along, shaking his arms and legs like a rag-doll, whirling his arms round like the blades of a fan. Then suddenly, he saw Rimini come to a halt. His back was to the trainer: he seemed to be studying something on the sole of one of his shoes. The trainer shouted a command to the others, and went over to Rimini, who by this time was examining his other shoe. Rimini slid his finger along the rubber edge, from heel to toe as if he were sharpening a knife. Then he raised his finger in front of his eyes, so close he had to squint to see what was on it. When he saw what it was – his finger was covered in a thin layer of red clay – a beatific smile spread across his face.

He had not been on a tennis court for a very long time – ten, perhaps twelve years. And the last time, the memory of which came back to him in fits and starts (trees, eucalyptus, part of a wire fence, splashing in water, a towel thrown on to the grass, the sun reflected on the water, on the film of oil floating on the water) it had not been red clay: Rimini was running barefoot across a cracked cement surface, avoiding the clumps of weeds growing out of the ancient joins in the asphalt as he chased the ball that his opponent, a faceless girl in a swimsuit, had hit towards him with her backhand, and drew his arm back with unexpected violence – the result of a long, drunken lunch or perhaps in response to the mixed emotions he felt about the way his opponent laughed at every one of his movements – in order to deliver the most crushing blow his tennis racquet would allow (it was a woman or child's wooden Sirnueva, found among a pile of parasols in the gardening shed, with a bare, rough handle and loose, frayed strings).

A strictly orthodox reaction to this irruption of the past, with its colourful details and heightened emotional temperature, might have viewed it as risking a relapse, with all that would entail: back to square one, strict limits, tightened control. But the trainer was not so stupid: he had accounted for the possibility of stray memories in his original plan. And so the tennis epiphany Rimini had experienced became not so much part of his past as of his future, the future the trainer had carefully prepared for him. 'You should have seen him play tennis, he was really promising,' Rimini's father had once told him, possibly to make up for the grim portrait he was giving of his son. And despite the fact that this made the picture even gloomier, because the promise he mentioned seemed irremediably lost, the trainer had taken mental note of it, moved by the way that this simple sporting reference made Rimini seem that much more human, and filed it away in the chest where he kept the weapons he could use in the future. Now was the moment to fish it out. 'Point number five . . .' he said. This was the third and most complicated phase, according to the trainer, because it required a certain amount of independence on the part of the patient. Control over him would be relaxed, which meant that the dangers grew in direct proportion.

Point five was work. The trainer spoke very quickly – the longer the explanation, the less the sense of authority: he did not want Rimini to feel too important just as he was about to embark on this new phase. He had a colleague . . . a coach . . . Argentinian Tennis Club . . . select clientele . . . twisted his knee . . . torn ligaments . . . at least six months out . . . other coaches in the Club could . . . but someone specially recommended by him . . . someone young . . . the Club would be bound to accept . . . he could start on Tuesday. How absurd, thought Rimini. His first reaction was to laugh out loud. But he controlled himself, and a split second later the idea seemed completely reasonable and clear to him . . . in order to change, other people ventured into the most perilous situations: they travelled thousands of kilometres, got lost in unhealthy countries, faked documents, injected plastic in their faces, underwent all kinds of sexual mutilations and implants, suffered from multiple-personality syndrome. All he needed was a change of clothes – less 'sporty' and more 'tennisy' than the ones he had, a double T (titanium and Teflon) racquet, a collection of somewhat old-fashioned Australian videos – the assistant who sold him them read the names Laver, Newcombe and Rosewall on the back and sniggered, but Rimini felt he had in his hands something even more precious and remote than a glorious tennis era – his own childhood, a supply of useless resin (the coating on the handle of his new racquet made it completely superfluous) and two boxes of charcoal tablets. This proved the most controversial aspect of his new identity. The trainer did not want to buy them; he was certain they would bring on the disaster they were meant to stave off. Rimini, who had kept them in his pocket throughout four years of inter-club tournaments, only managed to get him to give way by promising he would only use them during the first week of classes, and then only in emergencies.

He did not need them, in the first week or ever again. It was true, Rimini did have promise, and none of those privileged to witness his *rentrée* that Tuesday would have said it was more than ten years since he had been on a court – except, perhaps, for the insistent way that before he went on, he used the side of his racquet to tap his shoes and remove any wet clay that could only have been stuck in the grooves after he had played. In addition, as sometimes happens with skills that resurface after a long period dormant, Rimini's talent was not only still there, but it was refined, as if the period of hibernation had not merely preserved it, but had freed it from all the nervousness, fear, hesitations, scruples and silliness, all the jumble of vices which had always spoiled his game, and from which very quickly, after the first few tournaments, it had been almost impossible to separate him. It was true that now he was not competing – he was coaching. But his old faults as a nerve-racked player had always found a way to perpetuate themselves without the presence of umpires, official records, a public, an opponent – all reasons for stimulating or even explaining them without ever being their real cause. Rimini would scream at the slightest error: a volley that was too long, a clever shot by his opponent that he saw coming but could do nothing about, a ball that was gifted him but which he hit too eagerly into the net. If he served a double fault he would fling his racquet to the ground, catching it immediately it bounced back if it were not a decisive point, and leaving it there for several seconds to do penance if it meant he had lost a game, while he stood bent over, hands on knees, trying to decipher not so much why he had made the mistake as the reason for the cosmic injustice he was the victim of. He was always strictly fair: he never argued with the umpires or tried to steal a point. It was enough for his opponent to raise a doubt over whether a ball was in or out for him to offer to repeat the point, or to give it to his adversary. But his behaviour on court was dreadful. Between games, when he was losing and it was the other person's serve, Rimini would get the loose balls and hit them to the farthest corners of the court so that his opponent would have to go right out of his way to fetch them. If he missed a simple shot he would point up at the sky and smash the offending ball as hard as he could into the next-door court, then immediately run to recover it, ashamed of himself. He flailed at nets, line tapes, and wire netting with his racquet; kicked balls anywhere, without looking, balls that inevitably ended up in gutters or bounced out through secret holes into the street, or towards the puddles of stagnant water he later had to rescue them from, sickened by the smell. He had a small stock of words of abuse for himself – rude but not illegal: 'dolt!' 'idiot!' 'dummy!' 'useless!' even the extravagant 'no-hoper' – that were always so picturesque that he could repeat them several times without being penalised by the judges, and as time went by, without really intending to (because what drove him to this anti-social anger was not so much a desire to upset – as is common with those subversive tennis players for whom talent and insults are simply the two sides of the same nervous energy, as a complete lack of will, which as soon as he set foot on a court was destroyed by the vast array of variables he had to face in the game), he had managed to refine into an ingenious technique (which the usual parasites were quick to copy), a technique that allowed him to ridicule his opponents with impunity, by cursing himself out loud while declaring (also out loud) his reasons for doing so, and reducing them to one basic reason: the fact that he had wasted the weak, stupid, pathetic, total beginner's shot that his rival had offered him. And while he was acquiring the worst of reputations, that of a player with an unstable temperament –

a reputation that soon went before him wherever he played, and allowed all his opponents to incorporate it into their identikit portrait of him, along with all his technical deficiencies, so that they could take advantage of it – while this was happening, Rimini suffered. Playing tennis was an ordeal, a passion that left him beside himself, a prey to emotions he had not even known he had. His father who occasionally, emboldened by those rare moments of grace when Rimini seemed to be inventing tennis with every stroke, had raised the idea of him turning professional, tried every means possible to cure him of this weakness, by far the most damaging for any sporting career. He talked to him; invited him to look for traumas, causes. When they played together, he imitated him, in the belief that if he saw his reflection in a mirror, the shame would cure him. He insisted, threatened him, even interrupted an inter-club final in Deportes Racionales by bawling at him in front of three hundred and fifty spectators, among them a girlfriend of Rimini's with ominously hairy armpits who could not stand the tension and preferred running away to seeing him lose. His father even managed to arrange with the club trainer for Rimini to be dropped temporarily from the team as punishment. None of these strategies worked. 'He had promise,' was the only proper conclusion. Rimini suffered from the prodigy syndrome. There was no cure, because a player with natural talent has everything from the start: awareness, strength, intelligence, speed, inventiveness, and yet he has all this in the abstract, at its most pure, as though there were nothing more to do apart from rejoice in the gift or admire it, or as if the horizon where the prodigy was called upon to demonstrate his art was an inaccessible, self-contained limbo, a world of harmony and balance far removed from the arbitrary, uneven, brutal world in which one day it is cold, the next hot, or windy, or might rain, where trains roar by in the middle of a second serve, the fencing moves, shoe-laces come undone, you get blisters, where your girlfriend starts talking to a stranger in the stand, plastic cups get blown across the court, a flag flutters too much, where one ball bounces less than another, your opponents never stop chasing, where sweat gets in your eyes.

Now all this had been relegated to the past. If Rimini – 'Coach Rimini', as he read on the morning of his debut in white letters on green baize on the noticeboard in the entrance to the still-sleeping club

– had kept his talent, it was simply as a kind of antique, a superfluous antique, which his new position did not require in the slightest, and which Rimini added to his teaching role as an extra-curricular bonus. Talent has no future; once youth (of which it is a kind of perverse synonym) has gone, there is nothing for it to reflect. But in Rimini's case, this solitariness, which usually depresses unbalanced natures, only served to confer a special attraction on his talent, such as some genuine but unloved jewels suddenly acquire when thanks to a stroke of luck they leave the jewellery box they were lying bored in and instead sparkle and shine on the still pulsating flesh that has decided to show them off. It was an orphaned, unique luxury, and like all luxuries, possessed an anachronistic elegance. And it was the sign of a passion for wasteful expense that sports players share only with dandies.

Nobody – not even Rimini – was able to spot all these subtleties, but on the day of his debut, as nervous as was to be expected, and further upset because of a broken shoe-lace (a sure sign of bad luck), after four and a half hours of coaching, he had managed to give back to tennis the spirit that fifteen years of anabolic steroids, trademarks, and TV coverage had replaced the spirit of sacrifice with. He had an almost insolent sobriety. He played a natural, effortless game, as though his racquet were not so much a weapon or an artificial extension as the vigilant, subtle musical performer of his arm. He never held the racquet in both hands. Fifteen years on, he still confounded his teachers: instead of 'attacking' the ball he preferred to wait for it, which gave his game a touch of aristocratic disdain, as though he always had something better to do than to be there; he hit the ball slightly lower down than normal, almost spooning it up, like tennis players from before the era of doing things for show. He seemed to walk rather than run, and filled the court not so much with his body as with his intelligence, always anticipating his opponent's shots. His own were usually low across the net, and the strangest thing about them was that there did not seem to be any gaps: they made up a single fluid sequence, like the delicate figures that certain martial arts trace through the air, and seemed to continue even when the ball was on the other side of the net. They only stopped once the point was over. Then there was Rimini's clothing, which in itself was almost a declaration of principle: everything was white cotton, the only exception being the two blue stripes running down the V-front of his short-sleeved sweater; white shorts with pockets; canvas tennis shoes, of course, and a loosely woven sun-hat, light enough not to become too heavy if it got wet.

He went, he played, he won – symbolically at least, because, given the wretched level of his pupils (which meant that the balls only managed to cross the net five or six times – ten at the most), Nancy among them, it was unreasonable to think of playing a real game. His success was more cultural than sporting. Taking his time, as though the anachronistic atmosphere not only affected his clothing but even his body, which now moved with an odd nonchalance, he donned his brand-new coach's uniform in the changing-room. After a moment's hesitation, the man in charge of towels and soaps rewarded him with a radiant smile. He left the changing-room, carrying the metal basket full of yellow balls that his unfortunate predecessor had bequeathed him. He crossed half the club in the hot sunlight, looking for his allotted court. As he walked by, a group of locals – a man wearing a cook's apron, a gardener watering a bed of roses with an empty watering-can, someone struggling with an enormous ladder – all greeted him cheerily, nodding their heads like one of those dogs on the back shelf of a car. The court door creaked, Rimini tapped the soles of his shoes with his racquet for a fourth time – this time not because he was confused, but purely out of superstition – and went in. He had a strangely contented feeling. He knew he was an impostor, but was amazed at the banality and ease of the imposture. He was about to step on to the clay court when his foot met a slight dip in the surface and knocked his whole body off balance. A single ball, the one at the top of the pyramid, rolled out of the basket and landed on the court. It bounced once, twice, three times, threatening to escape, but Rimini stopped it with his racquet, hit it a couple of times with the strings until it bounced up again, then scooped it up and put it back in the same place it had tried to escape from. He saw the groundsman looking at him from the far side of the net, his rake dangling from one hand, the other raised in greeting.

Then it was the turn of his pupils. They introduced themselves gradually over the first week of classes. There were six of them, and apart from two – an irritating boy, Damian, a former private school boy whose parents were trying to make up for what he was missing by filling his mornings with languages and sports that he detested; and Boni, an awkward-looking adolescent with a face starred with acne and yellow nicotine-stained fingernails, whose mother, who was in almost sole charge of him, thought that a bit of physical exercise might help sort out his hormonal excesses – they were all women (which was perfectly natural given the time and days the classes were given). They greeted Rimini without any great fuss: the usual mixture of mistrust and curiosity that replacements always give rise to, especially when they are unannounced. Damian cast a mocking glance at his canvas shoes, which compared to his own monstrous creations (like a pair of mutant reptiles) were as austere as something out of the stone age. Boni the smoker – who, with Rimini's tacit approval, missed every other class – never managed to pronounce his new coach's name properly. But they were not very demanding, were easily distracted, and, as Rimini soon learnt, were happy if he ended the classes early. The women were slightly more hard work. They were all very similar: mature, with time on their hands, well-preserved, kitted out with the very latest in fashion and sporting technology. They always chased hard: first in a dignified, haughty manner, then with blind despair, as if they were flagellating themselves. One thing surprised Rimini: whenever they hit the ball, even if it was with the edge of the racquet, or even if they missed it completely, they all gave high-pitched little grunts like a samurai warrior. For the first week, they put him through the classic comparative tests, judging every one of his recommendations, formulas or principles against those they had been taught by his predecessor. The samurai grunt was one of these, as the injured coach told Rimini one afternoon when, at his trainer's insistence, he went to the clinic to thank him for the chance he had given him. 'That way they let off steam,' the coach said, poking a knitting needle into the orthopaedic framework keeping his injured leg immobile, 'and they feel like they're super-professionals.' The comparisons his pupils made were not value judgements, but were strictly neutral, as though they were less concerned about losing a familiar face than the supreme, objective good of tennis. They managed to find a virtue and a failing in everything. Rimini's youth, for example: he was fifteen years younger than his predecessor, which was a plus; but that meant fifteen years' less experience, which made them suspicious. They were relieved by his easy, simple style of tennis, because it freed them from the weight of demands of technique, but at the same time they were scared by it, because without all the showy paraphernalia, they felt lost. However, once this first phase of mutual examination and measurement was over, everything calmed down, and the shocks (together with their expectations) gradually gave way to the boring efficiency of sporting routine, which in the end resolved all their doubts.

Then, as in those beauty contests where all the candidates stand in line awaiting the final verdict, multiplying the same anxiety tenfold, and the judges announce the result – and one of them, just one, steps forwards and bursts into tears while a court of ex-princesses and queens crowds round with sceptres and laurel wreathes, and all the others, from whom the winner had until that moment seemed completely indistinguishable, suddenly become part of one hazy, indeterminate magma they disappear into, never to be seen again – so, in the same arbitrary way, Nancy took a step forward, left behind the flock in which she had been grazing with the rest of the pupils, and swept proudly (gold bracelets atinkle) into the desert of Rimini's life. She wore them when she took her classes, six vermicelli-thin bracelets on each wrist, which Rimini, somewhat naïvely, as he was to learn, took to be the result of weakness or laziness on the part of his predecessor. By the third class, when Nancy sent the sixth ball of the morning to the natural tennis ball cemetery by the train tracks on the far side of the fence, he decided he had to correct the mistake. He jumped over the net – something exceptional from him, because he was not yet sure of his physical relationship to his pupils and so rarely went to their side of the court; if he did do so, he always went round the net, this being the polite, if the longest, way to do things. He skipped over to Nancy as if the proof of agility he had just given had not cost him any effort. She was waiting for him with drooping arms; the racquet dangled from her left hand. She was standing still, rooted to the same spot from where she had delivered her backhand, as if there were some rule that she must not move. As usual her eyes were hidden behind a pair of big hexagonal sunglasses, but Rimini could see her chin had dropped in disappointment. 'Le-et's see,' he said, as if to a child. He stood behind her, and as he moved closer, to show her step by step what she needed to do (like a puppeteer and his puppet) he was enveloped in a cloyingly sweet perfume – a combination of ripe apricots and suntan lotion

– that seemed to be oozing from her every pore. Slightly stunned, he saw at the back of her neck, which he had never been so close to before, a line of droplets of sweat, all the same size, shining like a string of pearls on her tanned skin. Rimini approached even closer, putting his left leg parallel with hers, and touching her left elbow gently but firmly. Nancy responded instantly, as if her elbow were the nerve centre of her whole body: she raised her arm back across her chest, rehearsing the shot, and as she did so the stack of bracelets that had been lying limply on her wrist stirred and came to life. They gave off a faint metallic rustle, and this combined with the perfume to knock Rimini cold. He got an instantaneous erection that was so sudden and intense he almost cried out. Instinctively, he moved away from her. To distract her attention, he remonstrated with her for not removing the bracelets before her lesson, while at the same time he snatched a quick look down at the straining top of his shorts. 'They're gold,' said Nancy, 'I'm crazy about gold.' She took an unnecessary step backwards, catching Rimini, who was now holding her by the shoulders, completely unawares. Her hip brushed against him. That was all. Rimini raised his eyes, saw the tops of the trees whirling against the sky, and stifled a groan in his wristband. His body shuddered in the briefest of flushes, like a streak of lightning that shot through him from head to toe, literally burning him up. His legs buckled. He would have fallen to his knees right there in the dust if Nancy, who, although she was less than twenty centimetres from him but seemed to belong to another dimension, from the ancient, remote world of reality, had not at that very moment drawn the racquet back (the second phase of the shot she was trying to improve) and collided with the unexpected obstacle of his face. A happy accident. The pain brought Rimini to his senses. Embarrassed, Nancy dropped her racquet and stretched out a trembling hand towards his already reddening cheek, as if touching him were a way of apologising. Her hand was shaking in a way, Rimini thought, that he had only seen in old or sick people, or drunks who were completely wrecked by alcohol. And before she could touch him – in fact, to avoid her touching him – Rimini bent down to pick up her racquet, taking advantage of the movement to cast a quick glance at his shorts, where the moment of ecstasy had left its sad reminder. He handed it to her. 'Don't worry,' he said, 'it's nothing. We'll repeat the backhand, but with the ball.' He went back to his side of the net, picking up some stray balls from the court on his way, trapping them between his racquet and the outside of his right foot.

Nancy was shaking like a leaf. Like any leaf aged fifty or more would shake, doped on tons of tranquillizers, slimming pills and dietary supplements, and still smoking an average of forty long cigarettes per day – one, without fail, after every lesson, which she lit with her gold Dunhill lighter as she collapsed on to the bench by the court, racquet still in hand. After which, disdainfully refusing the bottle of mineral water Rimini offered her, and avoiding the changing-room or the showers, she would sit at a table on the club terrace in the deadly midday sun, stretch her sturdy legs out on a nearby chair, and put away two gin and tonics and two more cigarettes in the time it took Rimini (whose every moment she could spot from her observation post) to gather up the balls she herself had scattered all over the court. And at a certain moment, with that mysterious precision that chance confers on the most insignificant actions, everything became synchronised: the basket was almost full, the metal gate on to the court creaked again, pushed open by Boni's reluctant hip, and Rimini, caught in the act of picking up the last ball, looked up at the terrace where Nancy, who had just drained her second glass, was lifting her feet in the air, standing up and heading slightly uncertainly for the club exit, dragging her racquet along the floor like the tail of a dress she was not going to wear again. She shook, and all the accessories she hid behind – the hexagonal glasses, the gold, the make-up, the haircuts that were as varied as her sporting wardrobe, the Japanese car always waiting for her in the club car park – all these tokens of wealth that should have hidden the fact, only served to accentuate her disarray.

She shook with despair because she was empty. Nancy seemed to have suffered from that kind of thorough scraping that surgeons sometimes give to women's infected uteruses. Not her body, whose vitality, despite being very forced, was genuine enough, but her soul, which some monstrous knife (far worse than any surgeon's implement) seemed to have scraped every corner of. She was like a bare pouch, with nothing inside, condemned to a relentless ageing process. And since she had no secrets, nothing she could keep from the surface of the world, the only thing Nancy could do was to multiply: she replaced discretion, reticence and a sense of shame with a logic of greed and possession, compulsive behaviour she could not control, and which often showed itself in an inverted, contradictory way, as when at the start of the month she added an insulting tip to Rimini's fees, and then fifteen minutes later on the club terrace, rewarded lacklustre service from the habitual waiter with an amount that doubled the price of what she had consumed. And although in a strictly technical sense Rimini's sexual discharge had been over in an instant, and its fruits (if there were any) had withered on the vine of his shorts, it was there, on the barren earth of Nancy's greed, that they created a lasting lineage. For Rimini, everything had been born and died at almost the same moment: a suicidal ecstasy like the passage of a shooting star, which only exists as it vanishes. (In the sexual horoscope, Rimini was a dromedary; he got little enjoyment, but was prepared for long periods of drought, the only prospect his desire could envisage.) He had enjoyed the climax, insofar as something lasting a split second can be enjoyed. But what this sexual release did to him, in him, was not to create the hope of it being repeated (something hard to imagine anyway, given the extremely casual nature of the encounter) but rather to bring to an end a long stretch of chastity, or at most to provide sufficient reserves (extremely modest in his case) that would enable him to traverse the desert separating him from the next oasis.

So, whereas Rimini returned relieved to his state of indifference, Nancy reached the kind of boiling point that only goes unnoticed by those suffering from it. It is not certain that on that particular morning on court, with her back to him and given the skill with which Rimini managed to conceal all the evidence, she quite realised what had happened. She had not seen the erection; or the damp consequences it had left on his shorts after passing through the jockstrap. But she had been aware of everything else: the sudden temperature increase, the more rapid breathing, the imminent loss of control that Rimini had succeeded in avoiding, but whose reverberations could still be felt all around. She had noticed this in an indirect but real way, as we register pressure, or movements which take place at the edges of our visual field – movements which may be almost invisible but are often more present than those happening right in front of our eyes. However vague the reasons, the kind of 'atmospheric turbulence' of which Rimini had most definitely been the centre, was enough to set her on fire. She was shaking with desire as well.

There is only one sadder sight than frustrated love: unrequited desire. Love involves both the person who loves and the one who does not, but the person who does not feel the desire is not part of it, and nothing can restore him to the world from which he is excluded. The no of the person who has no desire is absolute, without appeal, and this turns the person who does feel desire into a completely alien being, not just different but heterogeneous: not someone who is in a different 'state' from which they could eventually, after a certain length of time and under different circumstances, 'emerge' or 'leave behind', but someone who is in a different realm. A dog on heat, let's say, is patrolling a square. He spots another dog like him, of the same breed and everything, and without waiting to find out whether it is male or female, if the tiny penis between its legs will discover a hole to unburden itself in, it surprises the other dog by leaping on it from behind, climbs on its back and starts thrusting away blindly. But it so happens that the other animal does not want it. It does not want it, and that's all there is to it. This not wanting is everything: it is as pure and all-consuming as the other's desire. It stands there, tongue lolling out of its mouth, staring at something in the distance until its attention is caught by something else and it shifts its head slightly, and looks at that. All the while, the dog on heat is frantically trying everything, but to no avail. Who has not found themselves in a ridiculous scene of this kind? But: are there two dogs involved? Or is there one, the dog on heat, who feels desire, and then its impossible target, who feels no desire and by this very fact ceases to be a dog and becomes something else: something inert, a stone, a plant, a tree trunk shaped like a dog? So, inevitably, between the one who feels desire and the one who does not, it is always inevitably the former, because when he throws himself on a being that does not feel the same way, he is not making an error of taste, judgement, or opportunity: he is choosing the wrong species.

This was the tragicomedy which over the next fortnight the earliest and most loyal employees of the club were witness to. Nancy threw herself at Rimini. Distracted, Rimini looked elsewhere – as if in the distance he could hear one of those whistles inaudible to humans but which dogs find it impossible not to respond to. From adopting a sort of functional indifference that only allowed her to be interested in sporting matters, Nancy started to move in the sphere of unstable, bewildered sympathy that (for want of any other possibility) the urgency of desire often employs as a concealed way of approaching its prey without scaring it off. She greeted him enthusiastically: she no longer merely offered him a distant cheek, but taking him first by the arm, then by the shoulder and finally by the back of the neck, she pulled him towards her and kissed him so quickly that his kiss in return always arrived a moment late, and instead of seeming like a polite formula (which is what it was for Rimini) appeared more like a shy, confused response to her kiss. She started to talk more, about anything, with childish enthusiasm, as though she had been gagged for months. She seemed to say everything in spite of herself, as though giving away her secrets with spontaneous sincerity. Each sentence was a private chaos that effortlessly jumbled together a memory from her schooldays, gossip from her hairdresser, a few saucy lines from a fictionalised biography of Mariquita Sánchez de Thompson, praise for the gardener in the summer place she and her husband had in Punta del Este, the wig collection belonging to a close friend (recently restored to health by the removal of a brain tumour the size of a melon), the cold sweats of her menopause, a crucial dilemma – eurhythmics or ashtanga yoga? weights or flotation tanks? certain suspicions about what her maid got up to in her free time – and always, inserted as though by chance into all these preoccupations, a question or two about Rimini's private life, which Nancy always lowered her voice to ask. It was as if, however desperate her desire to know, she was sufficiently aware to change her tone in order to lend special emphasis to the true target of her pursuit.

It was not long before her tennis suffered the consequences. It was already bad; now it became unpredictable. She lost all sense of distance: she either ran too late or threw herself at the ball too soon. She accelerated when she should have waited, retreated when she should have advanced. Her best shots deserted her; as if she had lost all her memory due to an accident, her downwards sliced drive (which Rimini had baptised 'your scythe shot' the first time he had been its victim) disappeared without trace overnight from her modest arsenal of self-taught ruses. She lapsed back into faults she seemed to have corrected: she lost concentration, muttered to herself, wasted time: she would hit a ball into the net, for example, and instead of picking up one of the thousands dotted all around her, she would slowly go and fetch the same one, dragging her feet as if in some sort of funereal march. Everything she did – intentionally in about ten per cent of cases, driven on by the violence of her desire in the other ninety – had a sole purpose: to force Rimini to come to her side of the net and by making him come into bodily contact with her to correct her position, to rekindle that overwhelming moment of combustion. And Rimini did come round the net time and again to repeat patiently and devotedly the show of puppeteer and puppet. He corrected the tension of his pupil's torso, the strength of her forearm, the synchronisation of her feet, but remained completely indifferent to her plunging necklines, her glinting fuzz of hair, her transparent knickers.

Until one morning when, as they say, what had to happen happened. Rimini was mixing long and short balls, first keeping Nancy at the back of the court and then all of a sudden forcing her to come up to the net, where she was supposed to win the point, decisively if possible. Backed up against the wire netting, Nancy returned one of Rimini's deep drives with all her might, hoping only to send it soaring out on to the railway track, but then, first to her own amazement and then to Rimini's, the combination of despair and discouragement with which she hit the ball somehow managed to turn it into a lethal shot. The ball grazed the net, skimmed the ground and bounced right on the baseline tape, where with a huge effort Rimini just managed to intercept it. He did not have the time to hit the ball; he simply stuck out his racquet and stopped it. But Nancy had hit it so hard it did not need any further energy: the ball simply bounced back off the strings of Rimini's racquet, lobbed up into the air, and began a slow, unsteady return towards the other side of the net. On its way it ran into an opposing breeze, came to a halt as though it had run out of fuel, and suddenly dropped almost vertically, hit the net and fell on to Nancy's side. It bounced gently, as though merely to follow the rules of the game. But Nancy was not going to give up now. The force of her desire changed to despair (in other words, to self-regard) and drove her on so swiftly that while still admiring the strength of her own shot, she sped forward like an arrow. She ran as she had never run before, as though she wanted once and for all to rid herself of the tingling sensation that had been bothering her for days. She heard Rimini's shout of encouragement, heard the sound of her own rushing footsteps amplified by an echo, stretched out her arm, hand, and racquet as far as she could to reach the ball which, now in slow motion, seemed about to bounce a second time. She thought she was just about to make it, that she was going to return the ball when something – not being seized by a male as she would have liked, but the slightly lifted tape on the service line – caught her right foot, the only thing which at that crucial moment linked her body to the ground. She fell head-long. Rimini saw her trip, consulted an old mental archive of tennis accidents, realised it was nothing serious and giggled, the same care-free giggle he used to hear from his father – 'to reassure you' he would say in his defence whenever a furious Rimini took him to task for it – when he slipped and found himself flat in the clay dust during a game. Nevertheless, Rimini ran to help her. Face down on the court, Nancy could not see him, but she could imagine him jumping the net and felt the tingling sensation creep up the inside of her thighs. When he laughed a second time she hated him with all her heart. 'It was nothing,' said Rimini, helping her to her feet. Yet again, he was trying to calm her, but succeeded only in showing his lack of concern. Ready to play her final card, Nancy was willing to forget the hurt, how ridiculous she looked, the point she had lost. She showed him a tiny graze on her knee and lifted it slightly, as though offering it him. 'It's only a scratch,' said Rimini, picking up Nancy's racquet and handing it her. 'Leave it as it is, the air will help it breathe.'

The class was over shortly afterwards. Nancy, the spurned Nancy, dropped her monthly payment on to Rimini's racquet cover, waved goodbye, and hobbled over to the clubhouse, more desperately in need than ever of her morning's alcoholic consolation. Rimini sat for a while on the court bench, towel wrapped round his shoulders. He particularly enjoyed these quiet moments between classes, when the physical effort he had put into the game settled in his legs, creating at first a delicate feeling of pain and then slightly putting them to sleep, while a fresh, transparent breeze (the interior version of the one which on the outside dried the sweat on his neck, face and arms) seemed to blow through the spacious rooms of his mind. After a few minutes, he realised something was missing. He glanced at his watch, calculated, and concluded that Boni was skipping his class again, the victim of another of those nights of dissipation of which Rimini, due to his reluctance to report them, had ended up becoming an accomplice. He thought of leaving, but it was a beautiful sunny morning, cool and clear, the club was empty and the few sounds he could hear – water from the sprinklers, a rake being pulled across a nearby court, the intermittent buzz of a chain-saw – were so clear and perfect they seemed unreal. Rimini stirred. He drank a whole bottle of mineral water in one go. He looked up towards the terrace, where a portly waiter in an unbuttoned jacket was clearing Nancy's table, and in a wave of enthusiasm decided to go for a walk around the club. He slung his racquet over his shoulder and strolled about the courts for a while. He passed by the empty swimming pool (a man on all fours was busy scrubbing the bottom) skirted the football pitch and then went through the garden area, still decked out for a child's birthday party, walked around the outside of the car park, pursued by the rather sickly perfume of the jasmine bushes. He was about to go into the clubhouse when he heard a dull thud – a muffled blow – and was surprised to hear a familiar tune. It was a mechanical, speeded-up musical box version of *Für Elise*, like the one companies put on their telephone answering service for waiting clients. But this time it was a car alarm. Rimini went over to the wire netting, found a gap in the hedge, and peered into the car park. He saw the white Mazda, parked half inside a yellow line and half in the next-door space. Then he saw Nancy standing beside it, wearing her sunglasses and with one of her long dark cigarettes dangling from her mouth. She was beating at one of the side windows with her racquet. Rimini ran into the club, avoided a trolley full of white towels, and was spat out of the main door. By the time he reached the Mazda, Nancy, her cigarette doused by her tears, had taken the racquet out of its cover and was flailing with it at the wing mirror. Thousands of shards of glass glistened on the car seats, the floor, the dashboard. 'I locked the key inside,' said Nancy, hacking at the metal arm of the mirror with the racquet edge. She was still sobbing desperately, but her voice had a cold, completely impersonal assuredness. 'Inside,' she said again. 'The key, inside.' Rimini peered in and saw the key dangling from the ignition, swinging nonchalantly to and fro. 'How does it switch off?' Rimini asked. Nancy, clutching the racquet above her head with both hands as she was about to attack the car roof, turned towards him as if she had only just noticed he was there. 'What?' she said. 'The alarm,' he replied, 'how does it switch off?' Nancy shook her head vigorously from side to side as if there were something loose in it, or as if she had water in her ears, repeated her refrain yet again: 'the key, inside', and finally brought her racquet down on the car roof. Surprisingly, it did not budge. Rimini put his hand in through the window, pulled out the key and started pressing all the little buttons on it in whatever order he could think of. Eventually there was a hiccough, and *Für Elise* died a death. As if synchronised with the alarm, Nancy dropped her racquet and fell into his arms, while with a last dying plea she begged him to get her out of there.

He settled her as best he could on the rear seat. She was still crying as he used a towel to sweep away the fragments of glass, sat in the driving seat, and switched on the ignition. The previously dark dashboard was filled with thousands of tiny coloured lights, and there was an explosion of bleeps. For some time, Rimini drove like a robot, relieved to be in motion. He glanced back at Nancy a couple of times in the rear-view mirror: all he could see was a close-up map of her wounded knee, standing out in morbid realism against the leatherette upholstery. He soon discovered they were lost. They were travelling slowly down a very narrow tree-lined road. Two women were jogging along it. Rimini startled them by blowing his horn, and as they moved apart to let the car through, they shot him hostile looks. A stray dog mistook the Mazda's wheels for ankles, and chased them to the next set of traffic lights, where a school bus coming in the opposite direction flashed its headlights at him. Rimini realised he was going the wrong way up a one-way street. He steered up on to the pavement, and then across the grass, where his wheels started to spin. He avoided some trees growing in a zigzag pattern, as if put there for training purposes, and after getting up the hopes of an aged prostitute standing guard under a eucalyptus, he returned to the roadway. He had a strictly urban sense of direction: nature, even in its most domesticated guise as woods, parks or lakes, seemed to him a realm of subtle repetition, the ultimate maze. So he doubled back on himself, went along avenues and across bridges, and at some point, deafened by Nancy's continued howling from the back of the car, wished more than anything else in the world that the club entrance would reappear, with its old brown bricks, its banners, its green gates – the same club that only fifteen minutes before he had been so desperate to get away from. But in the end it was not the club that appeared, but the dome of the Planetarium, dimpled like a golf ball on its struts, with its outmoded futurist appearance. And it appeared not once, but several – too many – times, so that in the end Rimini searched in vain for the indicator – managing only to switch on the windscreen wipers, the fog lights, the demister and the air-conditioning – and parked. Nancy was now wailing in a weak, childish way, as if a creature trapped in someone else's body were calling for help. No, she said, she didn't want to go home – her words interspersed with heavy sighs: she wanted to see her psychiatrist. Fine, said Rimini. They were leaving the Rosedal when her swollen face popped up behind his seat-rest. She had changed her mind: she wanted to see her chiropractor. A few blocks further on, as they were passing a huge shopping mall, Rimini glanced in the rear-view mirror and saw that Nancy had her forehead pressed against the window. She had taken off her glasses and was staring calmly in a sort of dreamy ecstasy at a long caterpillar of trolleys that a uniformed boy was pushing along the pavement.

They took the supermarket in their stride, as though they were from another planet, where doing the shopping in tennis gear, with sweaty tops and shoes covered in clay dust, were the most common thing in the world. Rimini was behind, pushing the trolley. Ahead of him, Nancy, who had miraculously recovered her composure, strode along jauntily, one hand on the trolley as if to pull it along, the other poised in mid-air, pointing to or rejecting items as they swept past. So, without choosing anything, they went through 'Cleaning Products', then 'Meats' and 'Fruit and Vegetables' (an assistant stopped piling up sweet corn in a box to enjoy the sway of Nancy's short pleated skirt) until they reached 'Drinks'. When they got there, Nancy started to give precise orders, as though the systematic looting they were now indulging in had been planned beforehand rather than being the result of desperate chance. They filled the trolley with all kinds of bottles, from the most common: gin, whisky, vodka (she invariably chose the most expensive brands) to the most extravagant: cider and fruit punches, for example, or brightly coloured pre-mixed alcoholic drinks that seemed to glow from inside, and which Rimini had never even dreamt existed. Then, as Rimini was pushing the trolley towards the tills, mentally calculating the length of time or number of guests Nancy would need to polish off all this stock of alcohol, they took a detour via 'Snacks', where she filled all the empty spaces in the trolley with every kind of cocktail food. Studying the label on a fizzy Greek wine with great curiosity, the cashier asked if all the purchases were for home delivery. Nancy shook her head; her mouth was full of crisps. She had already finished one packet (spring onion and peppers) and was well into her second (smoky bacon flavour). She fished out her credit card and handed it to the cashier; her fingerprints stood out like holograms on the golden plastic.

Later, shortly after lugging fifteen kilos of alcohol through the underground car-park at Nancy's apartment building, Rimini himself experienced the groping eagerness of those greasy fingers. He found himself in a kitchen, stretched out on his back on a table and crushing the packets of crisps he had just emptied from the supermarket bags, while Nancy clambered all over him, pressing her body against his and pushing half of her salty hand into his mouth. It did not last long. Taken by surprise, Rimini withstood the first onslaught by staring up at some cobwebs growing in the corners of the ceiling, and only reacted when Nancy's free hand, after wasting valuable time struggling to cope with the intricate folds of his jockstrap, finally managed to discover the nook where his prick was curled up. Then, without warning – because urgency is the enemy of pleasure and Nancy's fingers, covered in tiny bits of crisps, were not exactly a model of gentleness – his whole body shook, he shuddered and his prick, which had not yet even seemed to have stirred, exploded in a hasty eruption, smearing the rough fingers that had aroused it with a few forlorn drops. It was almost unreal, like the times he came in the middle of a dream and felt no proper satisfaction – because they were so short they left no traces – but which, after shaking him awake, returned him to the arms of sleep in a state of pleasant relaxation. Except that this time he was not asleep, he was not dreaming, he was not on his own. He opened his eyes and saw Nancy's face right next to his, her eyes staring wildly and her clumsy, furious fingers thrust into her mouth, rubbing her gums with semen the way that Rimini had occasionally rubbed his with the last traces of cocaine. The sight horrified him, but he had no time to react. With the strength of a being possessed, Nancy hauled him off the table and took his place. She lay face down and clawed at her knickers until the outline of her sex was uncovered, then clung to the edges of the table like a shipwrecked sailor and began to shudder and shake, beating the wooden surface with her breasts. 'Now,' she groaned between her teeth, 'put it in me now.' Rimini went over and pressed timidly against her buttocks. Nancy rubbed herself against him, searching for a hardness that was nowhere to be found. Beside herself, she started groping among the shopping bags that lay scattered on the floor around the table. 'Anything, you bastard,' she shouted, clawing desperately at the air, 'fill my cunt now or I'll kill you, you son of a bitch.' Confronted with what seemed almost like a medical emergency, Rimini did not even stop to think. He bent down, felt in one of the bags and pulled out the first bottle he could find – pineapple fizz. He stuck the entire neck of it, cork, metal clasp and gold paper covering and all, into Nancy's vagina. He heard her give a long, low groan of pleasure and surprise; then saw how she shuddered and came, electrified by this foreign body that had suddenly been thrust inside her. Then, partly perhaps to prevent any pain, partly to make the pleasure last, she started to move extremely slowly, rhythmically sucking in and pushing out the bottle as she did so. Rimini stood leaning slightly over her, firmly holding the base of the bottle, inert and yet vital, like one of those bars acrobats use to perform their most audacious stunts on – a prop that is both nothing and yet is everything, because any slip could ruin the whole show. As Nancy slowly increased the intensity of her thrusts, he started to survey the kitchen. He saw the window-frame opposite him, and the greenish shadow of the climbing shrub growing over it from outside; the fake wooden panels on the walls, the gilded metal fittings, the patterned tiles, the Magritte poster, the marble work surface (probably fake too, with what looked like incrustations of candied fruit in it) where a battery of the latest electrical appliances was drawn up waiting to go into action; the clock, the profusion of flowers on the formica in the larder, the tea-towels with animal designs on them; the rash of magnets spreading all over the fridge door . . . ; and while he was casting his gaze over this domestic scene, he felt that he was jumping (like CDs jump when there is a fault) and found himself transported to one of those scenes in a pornographic film where all pretence of constructing

313

a plot is finally abandoned and it gets down to business, with the same delayed relief that the protagonists abandon the fictional characters the screenplay has created for them and surrender to the anonymous pleasures of copulation, where they are nothing more than mounds of flesh, organs, and fluids in a state of ritualised exchange. Yes, Rimini recognised the décor, the harsh lighting, the speed with which the everyday surroundings had been disrupted by the sexual passion . . . but of all these familiar elements, which reproduced almost exactly commonplaces he had seen in photos, magazines and videos, what most catapulted Rimini into the conventions of pornography was not so much the explicitly sexual nature of the situation he found himself in, but the capacity to stand back from it, the way he could linger over insignificant details: the formica in the larder, the different surfaces, while at the same time he went on responding, in his own way at least, to Nancy's urgent desires. That was what had always fascinated him about pornography: the kind of supernatural stereophonic quality it had, the proof of the actors' professionalism, which he thought was comparable only to the distance pianists achieved from their playing. That, much more than the size or thickness of the men's pricks, the skill of hands or lips, the multiple ejaculations, the management of time, changes, and speeds. It was as if Rimini was connected to two independent but parallel circuits, always allowing for the fact that one of them, the sexual circuit (by definition the most absorbing and self-obsessed of all human circuits) was the one least likely to accept the simultaneous co-existence of another one, however superfluous that might be. He was aroused, as sometimes happened when he returned home after a haircut, looked at himself in the bathroom mirror, and immediately felt an erection. So, while his eyes completed their scanning of the kitchen, Rimini took advantage of the fact that Nancy, tempted by the accidental contact between her sex and the table edge, had momentarily released the bottle neck, and stood behind her to wait for her body to come back towards him. When, after rubbing herself furiously against the table, Nancy pushed back once more, what she took between her legs was not the glass of the bottle but Rimini's palpitating flesh. The shock produced in her a perhaps slightly exaggerated animal howl, which Rimini quickly stored on the sound-track of the home-made movie he was making. While he thrust away, driven less by desire than by the images he could see inside his head which (like rhyme and metre for poets) seemed to dictate all his movements, his gaze still roamed around the kitchen, this time noting the plates drying on the draining-board which still had a few drops of water clinging to them, and then plunging into the kitchen sink, where it came up against a colander full of freshly washed lettuce leaves. Then he saw the small but constant drops that the tap (as though cautiously allowing a few drops at a time to a parched person) was still dripping on to them. He had a worrying portent: he thought he was not seeing all there was to see, that something vital was escaping him. From the other circuit Rimini could hear Nancy's hoarse bark and his own panting as the climax drew near, but he was already going over everything he had seen a second time, and now that he was casting a suspicious glance at them, he seemed everywhere to detect a presence that, invisible now, was perhaps . . . Nancy slapped the table with the palms of her hands and came, with a roar from beyond the grave. A few seconds later, Rimini more because he was dragged along than for any other reason, also came. He put the bottle down and turned his head, alerted by the sound of hinges. A door creaked slowly open; a hand tried in vain to pull it shut from the other side. 'The maid's bathroom,' Nancy groaned, her face flat on the table. The door swung fully open, and Rimini discovered a young woman sitting on a lavatory. Her eyes were rolled up and her legs were wide open, pressed against the toilet walls. The tip of a purple tongue peeped out between her lips. One of her hands was still on the doorknob; the other was digging between her legs under her uniform. Everything stayed as it was for a few seconds, as if her frenzied hand were the only sign of life left in the world; then she too came, with a few silent twitches. 'That's Reina, the maid,' said Nancy. She sat up, tidied her hair and straightened her glasses, and pushed Rimini away with a cold, impatient gesture. 'I'd like a sparkling mineral water, Reina. In a tall glass,' she said. 'What about the gentleman?' Reina asked as she stood up, bumping her head against the clothes-line above her. 'I don't know. Give him whatever he wants,' said Nancy, and left the kitchen. Reina came out of the bathroom, adjusting her uniform. 'Sir: tea, coffee, water?' she asked as she went by. But Rimini was no longer listening to her. Something on the bathroom wall had caught his attention: a vertical rectangle, with a small circle in the centre, was swaying between the lid of the water tank and the lavatory seat, as though the maid had brushed against it when she stood up. Rimini moved slowly towards it, almost paralysed by astonishment. 'Sir?' Reina asked again. Rimini took another few steps and went into the bathroom. It was a painting – a Riltse. And it was an original.

CHAPTER 4

The Bogus Hole is one of the studies from the 'Medical History' series
that Jeremy Riltse must have painted (or simply imagined) at some
point in 1991, the year when he was given up for dead at least three
times, in one or other of the nomadic workshops he compulsively sought
refuge in whenever the London nausea gripped him. It is a study precisely
because everything in it is perfectly finished: in the letter Riltse sends
from Hamburg to his dealer's major-domo – the person whom, after
his last quarrel, he chose to communicate through to both his dealer
and the rest of the world; a letter which is at the same time the only
actual evidence of any project called 'Medical History' – the painter
makes it very clear that he is proposing to invert the relationship between
study and finished work. Four such studies are known, but the finished
works – the only ones meant to be shown in public, as Riltse expressly
states – never materialised. It may be that they were lost – falling victim
to the journeys, the increasingly frequent mental lapses, or the precar-
iousness that characterised the artist's life at this time. It may also be
that they never actually existed, either because from the outset Riltse
realised he was never going to create them (and only mentioned them
for a tactical reason, to rekindle the flames of his reputation, which by
then were burning rather low), or because something happened along
the way which prevented or dissuaded him from carrying them out.

(Two biographies which disagree about everything else coincide in
stating that what wrecked the project was the chance meeting Riltse
had with Pierre-Gilles in Frankfurt central railway station in the bitterly
cold November of 1991. Pierre-Gilles, who distrusted planes almost as
much as he did banks, had arrived from Amsterdam and the twenty-
sixth Hot d'Or awards, where he had just been the unanimous winner
of half a dozen statuettes – among them the industry's greatest prize,
the Hot d'Or for the Top Producer of Pornographic Cinema in Europe
– and amazed the audience with the verses from Paul Eluard he had

chosen for his thank-you speech. Riltse had not left the station for twelve days; he was living the anonymous life of a tramp inside. During the day he went from café to café clutching an old lined jotter and a pencil, which he sharpened with his thumbnail, offering to draw the portraits of unwary customers. At night he slept in a corner of the left-luggage office, on one of those big carts for transporting cases, using sheets of newspaper and cardboard for blankets, and his little jotter as a pillow. Pierre-Gilles recognised him at once; not from his appearance, which the beard, the dirt and the flakes of psoriasis [as well as the passage of time, of course] concealed only too well, but from his way of coughing, which was still apocalyptical, and from his footwear – black boots zipped up at the side, Beatles style, to which for more than forty years Riltse had added specially high heels so that he could reach the only height he felt comfortable with. Pierre-Gilles saw him and recognised him and, according to the two biographers [who at this point call a truce and sing from the same songsheet] fell on his knees before him. He burst into tears and begged for his forgiveness [in unison, the two biographers wonder why], then declared his love for him, offering him shelter, care, money, a medieval castle in the Black Forest whose cellars had been refurbished to provide studios for his production company, a villa in Torremolinos, where he spent his summers accompanied by his following of over-endowed stars, whom he employed between shoots [to avoid the costs of laying them off] to work for him as personal trainers, domestic servants, gardeners, or chauffeurs. He offered Riltse everything, including all he had accumulated since the last time they had met, at the courts of justice in London, on that afternoon almost half a century earlier, when Pierre-Gilles, in a strait-jacket, handcuffed and guarded by two policeman, heard the judge issue an order preventing him from coming within a two-kilometre radius of Riltse, and heard Riltse, who was sitting only two rows away but was free, unencumbered around the wrists apart from the links of a platinum Movado, cackle sarcastically as his way of saying goodbye for ever. But now Riltse pushed a lock of hair away from his face and stared at him, stared from the depths of his glassy eyes at this huge man who, kneeling before him like a believer in front of his god, had just dipped the tip of his fur coat into a pool of water mixed with oil and urine, and patted him on the shoulder once, twice, three times, with a heavy, paternal hand, as if trying to calm a lunatic. Then he stood up and walked off, slightly unsteadily, smiling like someone who is already anticipating the effect he will produce when he tells the story of the miraculous little demonstration of absurdity he has chanced to witness.

A farce? A deliberate snub? Or did Riltse, alienated by the length of time had had spent out in the cold really not recognise Pierre-Gilles? Although they share the same questions, neither of the two biographers offers a satisfactory answer. It is true that neither of them makes much effort to do so: one uses the simple expedient of a full stop and new paragraph; the other writes two lines full of adverbs and a blurred photo [Riltse in the Bloomsbury Hospital] to separate events, before they both move on to London a year later to describe the main events of 1992: the [deliberately started?] fire at the cottage, tuberculosis, discovery of homeopathy, the purchase of Gombrich, the failed project for an electronic opera with Brian Eno – and this [the phrase, exactly the same in both biographies, gave rise to a legal dispute that is still going on] is all they have to say about the enigmatic series of paintings: 'Perhaps in order to destroy the memory of the unfortunate experience of "Medical History", Riltse does a U-turn, turns off all heating in his Notting Hill house, and decides . . .')

But why follow this intriguing but decidedly speculative trail when the supposed meeting between Riltse and Pierre-Gilles – which provides the occasion for the momentary reconciliation of these two warring biographers – is conspicuously absent from all the others? And why follow a psychological trail, when the organic one is so obvious? If the 'Medical History' series never saw the light of day, perhaps it was because it fell foul of the same element (or, more precisely, an unexpected development of the same element) which had originally inspired it: illness. *Aphtha, Herpes* and *Plaque*, the three studies which have survived, together with *Bogus Hole*, prove just how far Riltse chose that year of 1991 and this projected series to take an old, but extraordinarily persistent, idea of his – that art and organic imbalance are one and the same – to its ultimate consequences. The neologism Sick Art which was later to become so famous and so misunderstood, is first to be found in Riltse's papers from the mid-1940s, around the time of Pierre-Gilles' self-mutilation, perhaps inspired by it, or perhaps as its cynical artistic corollary. But when one sees the extraordinary patch of skin in *Plaque* that Riltse sliced from his thigh with no other aid than a blade sterilised over the flame from a burner, it is impossible or stupid not to immediately think of *Glans*, that other great mythical work in the painter's career, which has never been found, but has been the source of the wildest speculation right up to the present. It is true that there are essential differences between the two works (always supposing that the second of them really exists). *Plaque* shows a sample of diseased skin, but the illness already existed and had been diagnosed even before the artist decided to include it in a work of art. But in spite of Riltse's insinuations of 'painful blennorrhagic suppurations', which Pierre-Gilles responded to with a famous phrase: 'Riltse is the virus', there is no proven disease that can be attached to the glans of *Glans*, with the possible exception of its size, which according to comments made in letters prior to their argument, Riltse never really saw as a problem. When it reached Riltse's hands, the penis was basically healthy, as healthy as any dead tissue can be said to be, particularly after it has suffered the damage that a long postal journey – made even worse by being very badly packed – can cause to bits of the human body that were never designed to travel by mail. However, whether the work exists or not – whether it was engulfed by the flames in the cottage, or whether Pierre-Gilles paid a six-figure sum for it at a Clandestine Porno Art Network auction and then, as rumour has it, kept it hidden in a security vault in the Deutsche Bank – the idea for *Glans* is a first manifestation of Sick Art. And should there be any doubt, *Aphtha, Herpes, Plaque*, and the small, intense, implosive *Bogus Hole* exist to offer their retrospective authentification of the discovery.

The sequence of events seems clear. Riltse wanders around Europe 'collecting misery, danger, illnesses, anything I could use as raw material'. Every so often, when his stock reaches a certain threshold and the desire to work becomes irresistible, Riltse seeks out a basement, a squatted house, or any immigrant tenement and there, in his famous 'nomadic workshops', he starts producing the studies for the series. He creates the four we know today (and perhaps a fifth, the one that comes first in chronological terms: *Fingernail with Fungus*, that for some reason or other he chooses to destroy) and ends by imagining the conceptual framework for the series of finished works, the titles of some of which (*Prostate, Bladder, Rectum*) give us a rough idea of the direction in which he was heading. Sick Art, 'in the opposite way to homeopathy', proceeds from outside to inside. It is reasonable to think that after exhausting the possibilities of the skin diseases from which he was suffering, Riltse was intending to go straight to the insides of the body, to that invisible realm (the organic world) which he could not name without giving a long, voluptuous sigh of nostalgia. And the key to this transfer is *Bogus Hole*.

At the risk of offending those art historians who are so keen to sacrifice everything (as long as that everything has nothing to do with them) in exchange for a dose of eccentricity that they can use in their interpretations, it is a stroke of luck that Riltse's endeavour was destined to remain at its most superficial level. *Plaque, Herpes* and *Aphtha* were bloody, but were basically restricted to the skin: even so, they were enough to threaten Riltse's physical integrity. It is easy to imagine what would have happened if he had taken the next step. Stapling a psoriasis plaque, the yellow sore from the edge of a tongue, or the plum-coloured pimple that a virus forms on a lip to a canvas is itself a bold move, how much more so would have been the attachment of a piece of prostate, bladder, or rectum. Yet, however crazy it may seem, the physical risk implicit in the project stands in direct proportion to its aesthetic ambition. Contrary to Fonrouge, Peiping, or that pair of clowns Gelly & Obersztern, 'artists' who unscrupulously used the handful of occasions which good fortune had allowed them to meet Riltse to promote the cleaned-up version of Sick Art they claimed as their own – and which basically (underneath a clumsy façade of provocation) did nothing more than restore the ancient curative (and hence, religious) function of art – Fonrouge recovers his sense of colour after *Retinae*, Peiping 'paints' the *Gluten* triptych and says goodbye to a lifetime as a coeliac, Gelly & Obersztern install *Wise Blood* in the centre of Hyde Park and the rare kind of twin diabetes they suffer from goes into remission – contrary to this adulteration of the original concept, which links sickness to art in order to restore the health of the artist, Riltse conceives and practises Sick Art as a pendulum, a constant exchange, a celebration of reciprocity. If Riltse cuts out a sore from his tongue and pins it to a canvas, it is not to cure himself; it is so that the sickness on his tongue can change, transmute, adopt a different

321

state. And while it is true that the original wound is no longer there, that is no reason for the Peipings, Fonrouges or Gelly & Oberszterns of this world to think they have triumphed, because the sickness is still there, present but changing: now the sickness is the incision which has taken the place of the sore. ('What is curing an organ compared to causing its sickness in the first place?' the artist asks himself, paraphrasing Brecht, whom he has never read, but whose proletarian jackets he always envied.) The triumph of Sick Art is not, as this pathetic flock of evangelists would have us believe, cannot be the health of the artist, but the constant renovation of his sickness and his art. Sick Art as the economy of the double gift, or two-way contagion: the refusal to give sickness to art without giving art to sickness, and vice versa: 'to artify' sickness while at the same time making art sick. These premises define Riltse's project without exhausting its meaning; although they are radical, they are still too 'internal', too concerned with the practice of art, for someone who can only conceive a revolution in art in terms of a revolution in the institution of art. Between *Aphtha* and *Herpes* – May? July? – at some particularly conflictive moment in the period after being discharged by the Hamburg Hospital for Infectious Diseases and his emergency admission to the Hasselhoff Clinic in Geneva, Riltse writes to his dealer's major-domo, and through him to his dealer, the world in general and in particular to all the Fonrouges, Peipings and others of that ilk: 'Isn't the fact that artistic affairs are the exclusive domain of artists, critics, historians and all that gang of impostors who call themselves "specialists" conclusive proof that art is in decadence, a state of terminal decadence?' One may smile at the literal way that Riltse gives rein to his indignation, but how instructive for anaemic clowns such as us today are his enthusiasm, his refusal to compromise, and his success – above all, his success! The study is not the work. *Herpes* – the squared-off stretcher, 15 x 17, mixed technique, which nowadays hangs in the offices of the leader of a Satanic rock band – is not the final work; it is nothing more than a point – an impressive one, yes, but one that enjoys no special privileged position among the vast, shapeless and resolutely incomplete network of points that make up the experience that is *Herpes*, which among many other things includes the bottle of Rohypnol the artist finished half an hour before he started work; the Staedtler blade he used to extract the sample of tissue; the Black & Decker stapler for stapling it to the canvas; the piece of pullover sleeve he tried to staunch the bleeding with; the card of the only Viennese taxi firm which would agree to take him to hospital in the state he was in (naked apart from his old imitation camel hair duffel-coat, wearing sandals and with his mouth pouring blood like a tap); the emergency service's admission form with his shaky signature and bloody fingerprints; the sterile gauze used to stem the flow of blood; the butts from two cigarettes he managed to smoke while he was waiting, before he was caught in the toilets and threatened with being thrown out of the hospital; the dosage chart with the phone number of the young intern who recognised him, almost went down on his knees begging for his autograph and who, still on his knees and in the same toilets that Riltse had used five minutes earlier as his secret smoking den, sucked him off lengthily and uncomfortably until he produced 'the most satisfying drops of come of my whole stay in Vienna'; the bottle of smelling salts used to revive him; the medical report; the biopsy request filled out by the doctor; the results of the first blood tests ... (All that is *Herpes* – all that until now, because what is to prevent one of those tireless bloodhounds who are so used to rummaging in the rubbish bins of illustrious lives from uncovering some of the millions of precious items – Underground tickets, stained banknotes, two or three million red blood corpuscles congealed in a musty test tube – still waiting to fill in the gaps between the already named parts of the work?)

'A Pyrrhic victory', one of the biographies declares, with the disregard and scorn so typical of the genre. Possibly. But the profit-and-loss values behind this kind of judgement are so contaminated by the toxins of accountancy, and are so alien to Riltse's artistic project, that the mere fact of even considering them is a huge, unpardonable mistake, similar to reproaching Matisse for not giving depth to his figures by adding shadow to his colourful surfaces. This type of reckoning, where hostility and money show their ugly heads and merge into one, would be justified in the case of an artist so concerned with the balance-sheet as De Vane, or with absolute saving such as Bowitt. But Riltse is not De Vane, whom he despised, and still less Bowitt, with whom he once shared a confused episode in the weights area of a gym, involving leather straps, masks, and a large rubber object with two heads, but whose aesthetic precepts he considered to be 'immeasurably poor'. What Riltse is seeking to achieve in Sick Art is the exact opposite: the destruction of balance, of all balance, through disproportion. And disproportion, that lethal combination of heterogeneity and change of scale, is the force that allows him to break out of the 'perverse enclosure of art', to 'spill out' – the metaphor reappears time and again in his letters – into the 'common places of social life'. *Success* is the name (a self-fulfilling prophecy) of that Riltsean disproportion, the unavoidable evidence that *all* the biographies finally have to accept – even, or perhaps especially, those which waste so many ridiculous pages on calculating pluses and minuses. (As often happens with great artists, the truth is not be found in the biographies which top the bestseller lists; it appears like a lightning flash in more modest, secret publications, whose ink comes off on the tips of our fingers and which vanish again very quickly, before they succeed in inflicting their tiny but precious quota of harm: 'Perhaps Riltze's [*sic*] true work, his one real masterpiece, the one whose significance escapes us while the artist is still alive but which appears quite clearly once he is dead, is not to be found in his works but in that invisible but amazing vein of gold that joins everything up and gives it all meaning, namely his invention of success as *disproportion*, a monstrous creation that undermines all rational connection between cause and effect and, as with sickness in a body, leads to the suspension of all laws governing the system of exchange of human goods'.) What are the two and a half million dollars that the Satanic rocker paid for *Herpes* (already a disproportionate amount) compared to the quarter of a million offered at Sotheby's for the blade which left its author's top lip permanently disfigured? And what, when it comes down to it, is that compared to the eighty-five pounds that the owner of the boarding-house where Riltse was living accepted (after some lengthy haggling) as the value of *Spectre's Portrait*, the painting Riltse offered him in payment for four months' back rent? (In this sense, *Success*, a late high point in that laboratory of disproportion known as Sick Art, was not strictly speaking new; it was the reverse image of *Failure*, something Riltse had experimented with throughout the first thirty years of his career.) But fools say money comes and goes, and fools are right. If Riltse found success with *Success* (a feat that in many ways recalls Andy Warhol, Riltse's contemporary,

324

but whose dry, 'dehydrated' conceptualism, 'typical of capitalist protestantism' seem to be indirectly criticised by the bloody excesses and kamikaze compulsion of Riltse's work) it was not so much in terms of the monetary gains which – to the benefit of the partners he shared beds, urinals and the back seats of cars with for more than a week, and to whom he always (with the sole, romantic exception of Pierre-Gilles) automatically bequeathed varying amounts of his fortune, calculated according to the same formula: multiplying the length of their penises by the number of times they had fucked, then adding to the total a random number of zeros – he was never interested in, but rather due to the fact (almost unique in twentieth-century art) that when they come to the last ten years of his life, the books covering his career turn away from the specialists, who only appear gesticulating wildly in the distant background, like the members of the Italian co-production team in the travelling shot of the traffic jam in *Weekend*, so that the reader will not completely ignore them, which he immediately in fact does, with the result that they disappear again without ever being heard, and concentrate instead on testimonies from doctors and nurses, his medical reports and records, hospital lists, x-rays, notes from police stations, legal records – all those documents which according to Riltse himself (contrary to the general rule for artists, especially the Fonrouges, Peipings, etcetera, whose biographies consist almost entirely of 'a choir of artists' guild, who, like all guild choirs, know only one song, and only sing that completely out of tune') would eventually lead to his consecration as he wanted to be consecrated – not as the author of Sick Art, or as its chief representative – but as its main and most devoted patient, and even its victim.

But a victim's pleasure depends on the executioner. And not just any executioner: one who is worthy of the role, who plunges into the victim's wound as devotedly as the victim himself would if he could. Riltse tried both things, with some success: *Herpes, Plaque* and *Aphtha* are the works of a victim as much as an executioner. The artist is at one and the same time the mind that conceives the idea, the hand that carries it out, and the material that suffers. As far as we know, this autarkic conviction was enough to satisfy Riltse for a few months, largely because it was so convenient (a neglected virtue only properly appreciated in the great lazy artists), but there came a moment when it became repetitive and bitterly unproductive, with an ape-like sadness, like the jerking off that a masturbator who has already run out of semen inflicts on himself in front of the mirror. Just released from hospital after his latest illness (*Aphtha*), weakened in the extreme by the battery of drugs that the doctors (alarmed not only by the infection on his tongue but also, and more importantly, by the septicaemia that seemed to have been taking over his organism for months) have filled him with for several weeks, Riltse accepts (he has no other option) the offer made him by Lumière, a terrifying but completely harmless bear of a man whom he met and instantly seduced in the detox pavilion of the clinic where Riltse, giving his nurses the slip, had gone to steal some dopamine, and finds himself in the back room at the Song Parnass, the disco bar where Lumière lives and works as doorman. It is a difficult situation. Lumière offers him a bed, cooks for him, takes over the treatment that his still suppurating tongue requires, and yet on the dot of seven every evening (without fail, because Sachs, the bar owner, a hyperactive Swiss whose greatest pride, apart from the Song, is to claim to be the half brother of the Gunter Sachs who was Brigitte Bardot's boyfriend, demands absolute punctuality from all his employees) he abandons him to take up his post at the entrance to the bar, returning only at seven the next morning. This means that Riltse suffers twelve hours of hell each day, not so much from the solitude, which he finds acceptable and even (when Lumière, mortified at having left him on his own, redoubles his attentions, 'suffocating me with the slathering, naïve, gruffly devoted affection that bears have made the emblem of their pathetic sexual brotherhood') would like to see more of, but because of the noise from the Song, the incessant, monotonous beat of music of course, but also the sounds of crockery and knives and forks, laughter, drunken singing, loud thumps, fights, and general chaos that inevitably leads to police sirens, shots being fired and sometimes even tear gas – all of which the partition wall between the bar and the back room not only fails to deaden but somehow even seems to transmit and amplify, translating it into 'the unbearable language of vibration, shaking, and shuddering, which is not only audible but is felt through the whole body'. Riltse grows desperate. He cannot even think of working, but can think of nothing else either. *Herpes, Aphtha, Plaque* – already made, already lost – glow in his memory like febrile goblins. They seem to be talking, to be demanding something of him: but what? All at once he wakes up, unsure whether it is day or night, or if he has really been asleep. A reality check (the only one, or perhaps its opposite) comes in the shape of something pushing at his buttocks. He turns round slowly, and discovers Lumière clinging to his back: asleep, drunk, possibly drugged. He realises that the thing probing his back entrance is his friend's stiff, four times larger than normal, prick. And this insistence, which at any other moment he would welcome by opening like a flower, only succeeds in repelling him. They argue. In reality, the person arguing is Riltse, who disguises a certain logical fear born of the disproportion (the irony is justified but misplaced) between his physical weakness and his friend's virility behind passionate but unconvincing moral scruples; like a wounded old slave, Lumière bows his head and locks himself in the bathroom. A few days later, when the good slave tries timidly to renew his advances, Riltse, who in the meantime has not only felt sorry for his attitude but has begun to feel the thrust of desire too, quickly improvises an alternative. He piles up ten canvas stretchers and ties them together. Then he cuts a more or less round hole with the diameter of Lumière's member into the stack of canvasses. He fills this tunnel with an abundant supply of oil paint. After which, like a circus ringmaster brandishing a hoop in front of a trained dog, Riltse holds the strange object up to Lumière, challenging him to try it out. Yet, even though there is no cavity in the world, however unknown, stinking or threatening it may be, that has ever frightened him, this time the bear hesitates. And if, after a few seconds in which time stands still and Lumière and Riltse stare at each other, then at the smeared hole in the centre of the canvasses, then at each other again, Lumière closes his eyes and finally plunges his prick into the oily cave, it is less out of pleasure or audacity than because of something that he is perhaps feeling for the first time in his life, namely love: he discovers that for this weak, irascible old man, ruined by vices and sickness, of whom with difficulty he understands perhaps only ten per cent of what he is saying (and that consisting largely of insults or unkind remarks about him) he will do anything, even (and here the shade of Pierre-Gilles zooms past, spraying the romantic scene with sarcastic cackles) castrate himself. How long goes by between him sticking his penis into the hole and him coming: three seconds? Five?

His whole body shakes as though he is being electrocuted, or like a mountain incubating some natural disaster. Standing next to him, holding up the contraption the other man's penis is stuck in, Riltse could swear the whole building trembles. It is the most powerful and longest ejaculation that Lumière has ever experienced. *Ejaculatio praecox*, a contemporary account scornfully reports, undoubtedly more out of disappointment or jealousy than any clinical accuracy. Combustion seems like a more correct term. Combustion, incandescence, the idea (probably unheard of, and even today, despite the complete disuse into which it has apparently fallen, still very relevant) of a spontaneous pleasure free of all protocol or preparation – but the question is: does it really matter? Is it worth sharpening one's pencil to sketch the sexual physiology of a secondary character, one who anyway is destined (though this is also of secondary importance) soon to disappear from the scene, and not in the most elegant way imaginable, when right there, only a step away from him, the man who turned physiology into an art-form (and vice versa) is in his innermost being hatching the seed of all that is to come? Lumière ejaculates, and at exactly the same moment – the synchronicity is so astounding, the artist says, that 'it must have been recorded in some cosmic annal' – Riltse feels a stabbing pain in his rectum and also ejaculates, without his prick even having to go through 'the troublesome business of getting hard'. Riltse christens the miracle with the (admittedly somewhat pompous) term of 'instantaneous telefornication'. But by naming it he is trying to forget it, to move on to something else. Above and beyond the very special pleasure they give him (ideal apart from anything else for a still precarious state of health) the hole in the canvasses and the stabbing pain in his rectum are not merely signs but messages that succeed in renewing his sensibility, his creative vigour, and his inspiration, directing them towards that strange dimension just beginning to open up in front of him: inwardness. (Yet again, unless there are complex neurological factors in play, there is no valid reason to replace 'inwardness' with 'depth', a word Riltse confessed he 'hated more than anything else in the world'.) There is no true art which does not offer access to new dimensions of experience. This maxim does not come from Riltse or anyone else, and therefore is not debatable. In *Herpes*, *Aphtha*, and *Plaque*, once so devastating and now, only a few months later, already so out-of-date, the artist had got in touch with the changes to his outward, visible, phenomenological appearance. With *Bogus Hole* – the expression was coined by Lumière, perhaps the most poetic of his entire life, although the poor man never even got to read it on the backs of the ten canvasses, where his ungrateful love had written it – Riltse was preparing himself for 'the inner journey', for 'the inner exploration of the galleries of that secret lair, ready to turn my organism inside out like a glove'.

The first step towards going in is to go out. Riltse takes advantage of Lumière leaving for work (and with what innocent candour the bear smiled at him as he left, completely unaware of the future reaching for him with its cruel fingers) and flees Song Parnass just as night is falling. Protected by that confusion of light – the light of day dying, while thousands of others start to shine like glow-worms – that makes everything seem unreal, equipped with the small Polvani bag he has stolen (Riltse did not call it stealing, but collecting souvenirs) where he has stuffed the ten canvasses of *Bogus Hole*, after hacking them down to the size they would later be known in, because the originals are too big to fit. After that, who knows. The Prater, the bath-houses of the Prater, the Underground station at the Zoo . . . We have lost the tracks his footsteps left, but we can follow those of his mind. In a deliberate echo of the structure of the studies, Riltse imagines a new series: a triptych made up, he tells us, of the organs 'closest to hand'. The first target: his rectum. To be followed by the prostate and the bladder, then probably, the liver. What will he find in this Atlantis he has just spied on the horizon? But it is no easy matter. Driven on by the need for assistance – 'Executioners!' he writes on the back of a leaflet he must have found in the Prater, an advert for six hundred dishes offered by a Chinese take-away, 'while thousands of anonymous monsters roam the streets every day in search of victims, I went out to look for executioners' – he tours the hospitals that had taken him in during the 'superficial' phase of his art. He meets the same doctors who had looked after him then, who knew him and in some cases knew how famous he was, and even admired him. But his plan, which to him seems perfectly reasonable, even simple, the obvious culmination of Sick Art, proves more difficult to sell than he expected. Even for his admirers, Riltse was not exactly an easy patient, and the memory of his outlandish behaviour is too fresh for them to take him in again without demur, without a medical reason to justify it, simply because a new and equally bloody eccentric idea has occurred to him. Added to which, Riltse is extremely frank, and the wealth of detail with which he describes his plan, plus his wild appearance as he does so, has the effect of scaring the doctors off rather than persuading them to help. One by one, all those who agree to see him – less than ten per cent of those who had dealt with him in the past – refuse to cooperate, on the grounds of humanitarian ethics. Riltse, who feels like vomiting whenever he hears the expression 'humanitarian ethics', tries to involve them in an aesthetic debate, the only kind of argument, he reasons, that can prevail against their 'moral blackmail, the worst kind of all'. He manages to get a few of them – two, at most – involved in this kind of debate, both of them caught at a moment of weakness after a dreadful day in the hospital spent running from the operating theatre to the emergency unit, from open heart operations to traffic accidents, a moment when to go along with a lunatic is perhaps not advisable but is the easiest thing to do. But when Riltse succeeds in reducing the 'humanitarian reasons' to nothing, like fields of crops under the hooves of Attila, the doctors turn to legal ones – without a medical justification, an operation a thousand times less risky than the one Riltse is proposing could cost them their job, their title, and even prison. At that, they consider the discussion closed. All known doors slam in Riltse's face. His rectum though keeps calling him, and the intensity with which its piercing cries shake him is inversely proportional to the difficulties he encounters in satisfying them. He searches out less well-qualified doctors, in the hope that a bit of charisma and money (which he does not have) can persuade them in a way that sincerity failed to do with the others. To no avail: they all know who he is, all of them have received and obeyed the order not to have anything to do with him. Desperate, convinced that his dealer is orchestrating a plot to sabotage his work and force him to go back to London, Riltse is already thinking of leaving Vienna and heading for Prague, Budapest, or Warsaw – any lawless city where there might be people to do the job – until one night, the same night, thanks to one of those completely random occurrences that all the biographers delight in portraying as an ironic twist of fate, that Lumière (who for the first and last time is late for his post at the entrance to the Song Parnass) throws himself off the Praterbrücke into the Danube, his pockets full of stones and his stomach full of a bottle of sleeping tablets (which only goes to show what a mistrustful character he was) Riltse runs into the medical intern who, thanks to his 'expert oral hospitality', had remained associated in the most delightful way with the experience of *Herpes*. In reality, it is the other way round: it is the doctor who, caught up in his own thoughts, does not notice Riltse and stumbles over his feet as he lies – as he has done for hours – underneath the arches. His fall costs him a pair of glasses (the same pair he let slide down his nose in order to get a better look – with a touch of precocious old age that made Riltse quiver with pleasure – at the way the artist's penis was growing rigid) and a few minor scratches on his hands. Nothing that first his astonishment and then his delight at seeing Riltse again cannot remedy. Riltse is the one in need, and he, his mouth still savouring an acid memory of the other man's secretions, is the one who can possibly save him. The young doctor is all ears. He feels strangely happy: he realises that Riltse's plans are crazy, and yet decides to help him all the same. He has not yet decided what the price might be when the two of them make off down the subway steps, and then stop halfway. He stands there, legs slightly bent, while the artist kneels and does his best to return the favour he received for *Herpes* with an energetic, rapid sucking. It is easy to conclude, as does one of Riltse's biographers (perhaps identifying too closely with the scene in question) that this 'was not what could be called an erotic apotheosis'. But it is plain that the doctor is not seeking sex so much as glory, and if he suggests being sucked off as a condition for helping, it is not so much that he really means to demand it, as to enjoy the pleasure of having this 'sacred monster' at his feet.

However, he soon understands that the task is beyond him. After all, as Riltse conceived it, *Rectum* implies surgery, an anaesthetist, heart monitoring and some post-operative rest (which could be shortened but not avoided altogether) in more or less guaranteed sterile conditions. Far too great a risk for someone still doing their training, and whose ambitions have nothing to do with art but are aimed directly at scaling to the top of the pyramid of the medical profession in Vienna. However, in addition to the academies, the honours system, the regulations and the pantheon which make up that institution's public face, predictably enough the pyramid also has a secret, much less honourable face which only smiles surreptitiously, in dark basements, for those few initiates privileged to look upon it. Fortunately for Riltse, our young doctor is one of them. With amphibian dexterity, he glided, equally at ease among the shining offices of the university where careers are promoted and jobs handed out, as along the tile-lined corridors only dimly lit by flickering bulbs where illegal operations are carried out after whispered consultations, and newborn babies and chemical phials are sold for unbelievable sums. He now returns to this under-world, not to learn about the silent forces behind this counter-medicine as he has done in the past, but to enjoy the fruits of an apprentice-ship to which he has dedicated years of his life (in truth, many more years than those demanded of him by his formal medical career – which in Vienna is known throughout the world for its rigour, severity and for the sacrifices it entails). There, after sounding out nurses, midwives and surgeons with the utmost tact – because this clan-destine world, which perverts all the laws of official medical practice, nevertheless not only preserves but encourages one of them: discretion (probably in this context the least useful quality of all) with a single-mindedness that the official world would doubtless have envied – he discovers the ideal candidate. His name is Sandor Salgo. He is Hungarian, and nobody has ever managed to read the ancient bit of paper covered in stamps which he waves in the air then rapidly puts away again whenever anyone, simply to goad him, questions if he ever finished his university studies. But in the morgue he is almost as much part of the furniture as the aluminium sinks, and is famous for his skill in cutting up bodies, a talent probably acquired during his two years as an apprentice in a central Budapest butcher's shop. His speciality, for which he is universally recognised, is in the traffic of organs. Early one morning, still doubtful about it, our young doctor friend decides to put Riltse's project to the Hungarian. When he goes to wash his hands (a habit inherited from the aunt who brought him up, who apparently spent her entire life wearing gloves) he catches Salgo in the toilets, taking a shit with the door open. Not a very pleasant sight. Salgo, whom the doctor only knows by sight because a common acquaintance, after giving him a brief summary of his curriculum, pointed him out in the distance in a corridor, is a short, plump man, with hair all over his body. He grunts to himself the whole time, as if he always has something to complain about. His grey flannel trousers which now lie crumpled around his ankles, soaking up the wet from the toilet floor, are the same pair he wore a week earlier, when the young doctor first saw him, and will most likely be the same ones he wears for the next six months. Salgo raises his eyes from the magazine he is reading and spots him. Embarrassed, the doctor withdraws, with a sense of revulsion – although he noted that the magazine was *The Nation*, and this disconcerting fact (nothing he knew about Salgo suggested he was bilingual) leaves a slight sense of mystery in his mind. Salgo grunts and goes back to his reading; a second before he gives up and leaves, the doctor notices that what Salgo is reading with such intense concentration – in the same way that other people, in the best cafés of Vienna, read the stock exchange news or the obituaries – is the art page written by the critic Arthur C. Danto. Salgo is definitely the man for him.

We are in October 1991. (Pierre-Gilles must have been somewhere around, but Riltse's biographers pretend to be unaware of the fact so as not to spoil the dramatic effect of his subsequent bursting on to the scene.) The autumn is a study for the coming winter. At the young doctor's suggestion, Riltse and Salgo meet in a café one bright, cold afternoon. Scarcely able to conceal his joy, the doctor points to a table outside. As if by common accord, Riltse and Salgo turn towards it at exactly the same moment, their faces lit not so much by the sun as by the possibility of it. Artist and butcher. They look as though they have escaped from a circus: raging, impotent freaks who do not know whether to attack each other because they are so similar, or to fall into each other's arms because of all that separates them. Riltse is clutching the Polvani bag, where the tomato sauce from a badly closed bottle of beans has just irreparably damaged two of the ten *Bogus Hole* canvasses. To match him, on his knees Salgo has a dark, stiff Gladstone bag, in which lie a few worn carpentry tools. Acting in unison yet again, as if they had once been Siamese twins, they turn towards the young doctor and with a single glance (although in fact there are two) dismiss him from their talk. The doctor is not even upset. He seems to have foreseen this, perhaps even to have secretly prepared it, because he smiles, stands up and, without a word, leaves a generous amount of money on the table (nobody has ordered anything as yet) and walks slowly away. He walks backwards, still looking at them and smiling, with all the exultant indulgence and false modesty that gods show when they forgive acts of defiance in the beings they have just created, until he is caught out by the edge of the pavement, stumbles, and is almost run over by a motorbike with an advert for a dry-cleaning laundry on its petrol tank. And in the same way that the young doctor tiptoes away from *that* table on *that* afternoon, slowly growing smaller in the distance – so pleased with himself, so naïve, the poor fellow, that one can only feel sorry for him – so he slips out of the story, or rather, to be fair, he is let slip out by those telling the story, who take advantage of this fleeting moment of personal ecstasy in which the doctor, from the mere fact of leaving the couple he, and only he, has created on their own together, feels himself master of the world, to remove him from centre stage, banish and extinguish him (as one says of a fire or a species) once and for all. Because no sooner has the young doctor started to move away than the light of this icy afternoon starts to change, the sun that lit the sky fades, and everything is suddenly plunged into darkness as at an approaching storm. Everything – the café, the broad, tiled terrace, the square and its fountain – except for the table where Riltse and Salgo are sitting, still sizing each other up, which floats like a luminous bubble in the dark night of space.

Then all at once, as though obeying the same order, the two of them come back to life and split the money the doctor has left into two equal halves. In an eager torrent that he does not even interrupt to draw breath, Riltse pours out the idea of *Rectum* and his plan to achieve it. Salgo listens closely, grunting as usual, from time to time digging at a nostril with a filthy finger. When the other man has finished, he asks in a cavernous voice: 'How much money.' 'None,' says Riltse, opening the Polvani bag and taking out the first *Bogus Hole* he can find – luckily, not one that has been ruined with tomato sauce. Salgo sticks out his lower jaw a little, bites his lip and while Riltse is looking at him, irresistibly imagining the Beast in *Beauty and the Beast*, leans forward over the table, grunts at the approaching waiter to drive him away, and starts to examine the painting. After a while he points to it with the same finger had has been using to pick his nose with, and in an urgent but expressionless voice says: 'Five. Identical.' For a moment both of them remain silent and very still. Riltse cannot believe it; he feels literally as though his hands are touching the sky. 'There are nine of them,' he says eventually in a gleeful tone, handing the first one over. 'This is just an advance.' Salgo nods, opens his bag and stuffs the canvas, which is far too big for it, in between a metal file and a saw.

Riltse is impressed. Not only with the speed, the complete lack of hesitation and simplicity with which the bargain has been struck, but also by the figure of Salgo himself. He is so much on the outside, so material, that he is a complete enigma. 'A prehistoric creature. I had never seen anything so heterosexual in my whole life,' Riltse writes on a napkin which his dealer's major-domo reads a fortnight later, overcome by a tremendous fit of jealousy. 'But, when it comes down to it, I wouldn't dare say he is a man. To call him "Thing" seems to me not only wiser but more accurate. If God – that parasite disguised as a demiurge – ever decided to create a being from the bits that have accumulated in the linings of man's pockets, I'm sure the result would be something very like that: a Salgo. He also made me think of Kakfa's Odradek. I wanted to re-read it, and tried to steal the volume of his short stories from a bookshop, but I was caught red-handed. I wouldn't be here writing to you now were it not for the fact that one of the booksellers intervened because he said he recognised me, and they let me go. He must have problems with his eyesight, because he apparently confused me with some local third-rate hack who often goes in there disguised as a tramp.' Riltse is so impressed that, for perhaps the first time in his life, he does everything the other person tells him to. 'Everything' is an exaggeration: in fact, all that Salgo demands of him is that he wait. He is not sure what he has to wait for. Part of Salgo's explanations vanish in the air of secrecy surrounding the operation, which seems to justify the great number of incomprehensible, unfinished or simply inaudible phrases he uses, the rest are lost in his garbled way of talking, most of which is indecipherable although every so often there is a flash of fake rustic lyricism. But Riltse waits. How could he not, with *Rectum* almost within his grasp, and after that *Prostate, Liver*, and all the other works of 'Medical History' that he has already thought of and can already see, and whose tiny voices, glinting in the most hidden folds of his organism, are already calling out to him?

One night they have just thrown Riltse out of the Young Christians'

Association – nothing out of the ordinary: the usual hypersensitivity of believers, plus a minor incident in the showers with a conscript, 'worse still, completely tasteless, like one of those rice cakes you're crazy about, and whose crumbs drive your boss mad,' he writes to the major-domo – and in the street (where he has landed after being literally kicked out by a furious mob of budding Catholic priests) he bumps into a man in uniform, a doorman perhaps, a garage mechanic, or possibly a doctor (the light is poor so he cannot see him properly), who stops and helps Riltse to his feet. While he is brushing the dust from the coat, he slips something into one of its pockets. By the time Riltse realises what has happened, the man has vanished. He puts his hand in his pocket and pulls out a brand-new hundred-schilling note. He unfolds it, and inside finds a scrap of paper with a date, a time, and the address of the hospital in whose basement Salgo works written on it in rough, cave-like capital letters. His fate is sealed. Now Riltse has a double wait: on the one hand, he has to wait because, apart from searching for something to fool his stomach's hunger and for a roof over his head for the night, and apart from the banal scandals he gets mixed up in, which while they are happening seem to revitalise him but once they are over tend to plunge him into deep depression, the kind of spleen that accompanies a surfeit or an absurdity, he has nothing to do. On the other hand, he is waiting because now he has been given a date, with the result that waiting, which before was as virtually endless as a sea, has become a countdown. Counting, yes, counting backwards, thinks Riltse, but how? Where to start? He is still feverish, has not eaten for days, feels dizzy and his right hand – the one he tried to punch the conscript with – is a powder keg of pain. He can see *Rectum*. He can see it completely clearly, already made, *cosa mentale*, but he does not even have the strength to count the seconds separating him from it. So he slumps in an alley-way, still clutching his Polvani bag, and, foreseeing a long weary sleepless expanse stretching out in front of him, more to send himself to sleep than to speed time up, he starts to murmur (like someone singing a nursery rhyme to himself): one thousand, nine hundred and ninety-nine, nine hundred and ninety-eight, nine hundred and ninety- . . .

The question is: what is more important, the man who is on his own and waiting, or the man who is keeping him waiting, the man who will keep him waiting longer than he was hoping to, who will perhaps keep him waiting for ever? The decision is a dramatic rather than a moral one; in other words, completely amoral. We see the night sky thanks to the way the stars shine, and yet there is no more moving, more macabre and attractive, sight than the one that a star offers when it is extinguished in the midst of that huge black velvet dome which for century after century it helped to light. And at the crucial moment when we are present at the extinction of a star and an invisible but seemingly endless thread, which has travelled through so much space it leaps into another dimension and crosses time – complete eras – as well, appears directly to link the twinkling of the star with our astonishment, who among us remembers what that nameless dying object did to make our nights not a bottomless pit but a fresh, incomparable delight filled with hope? Why should we remember it anyway, when at the same moment that this star goes out there are millions of others which go on shining indifferent to its fate, and among them we find one, a single one which perhaps will cast a spell on us with its colour, its unique way of shining, with the pattern it forms with its neighbours, and by enchanting us confirms our forgetting of the one that is dying before our eyes? So it is with Riltse, so it is with the star and his cortege of biographers, lapdogs who in the name of 'life' deny the logic of life, not merely its multiplicity but the whole system of light, dark and new light – spurning any hierarchy, pure alternation, cosmic rotation – that undermine and renew it, and then drag themselves away, panting, always in pursuit of the same trouser legs. Man dies out in order for his work to shine all the more. Isn't that the ultimate law of art? And before dying out finally, like a fading star which twinkles less and less frequently but manages to shine all the more brilliantly, as though extracting one last source of energy from its own death throes, the artist, whose feet are already dragging on the pavement, who can barely raise his eyes from the gutter, somehow succeeds in sending out a few last signals, which we must capture. With the piece of paper in hand, as proud and terrified as a boy going into a grocer's for the first time on his own, clutching his mother's shopping list, Riltse turns up at the hospital on the agreed day and time. He finds a rusty iron door hidden behind the skeleton of an old deep-freeze. He knocks on it. The door creaks half-open; Riltse asks for Salgo. 'Who?' says a face on the far side that he cannot see. 'Salgo,' he repeats, 'Sandor Salgo.' Then he adds, as though it were a password: 'I'm Jeremy Riltse.' 'And I'm Christiaan Barnard', he hears amid laughter, before the door is slammed noisily in his face. Riltse knocks again. A few seconds later, an almost identical scene takes place, only this time with another, more aggressive voice, and another heart-transplant celebrity (Riltse thinks he hears 'Vamalono' or 'Fafalolo') in place of the famous South African playboy. Riltse grows impatient, knocks again, the door opens, and so on and so on. At a certain point, he jams the Polvani bag in the door jamb, uses it as a lever (trusting to the solidity of the *Bogus Holes*, two of which are unfortunately torn in the manoeuvre), struggles with the nth unwelcoming doctor who responds to his hammering, finally manages to get in, and starts shouting out aloud for Salgo. Nobody knows who he is talking about. 'I'm Jeremy Riltse!' he bawls, as if this were a magic formula that could make the Hungarian appear. They all know who Riltse is (which says a lot for the general cultural level of the hospital's medical team), but none of them will ever believe that this emaciated, stinking apparition in rags, burning with fever and trembling from head to toe – who also seems to find it as hard to say the consonants 'ltse' as he would to climb the Himalayas – could possibly be the most famous artist in England. Horrified, Riltse pulls back; for a single fleeting moment, he thinks of his dealer. His thought is as rapid and lethal as a designer drug, and not only uncovers and dismantles the plot against him, but at the same time annihilates the man behind it. Then, driven on by an almost divine fury, he steps forward again and, waving the Polvani bag where, as though alarmed at all the noise, the two damaged *Bogus Holes* peep dangerously out, he starts to shout the whole story (in full detail, and with a certain confusion in the chronological order) of the plan that has brought him here: *Herpes*, the urgent need for him to have a sample of his rectum removed, the conscript's face pressed against the tiled wall of the showers, the canvas he gave to Salgo as a down payment, Sick Art itself, the young doctor's help, *Prostate, Liver* and all the other works to come, the hundred-schilling note, the celestial touch of the doctor's mouth on his prick, how fierce the sun had been that afternoon on the café terrace, the unscheduled check-out from the Young Christians' Association ... But we are, in a manner of speaking, in a hospital, in

338

the basement of one of the busiest hospitals in Vienna, and the doctors have much more important – if not necessarily more entertaining – things to do than help rescue a filthy lunatic from the limbo of violent hallucinations in which he is floating. In short, at a discreet signal from one of the doctors, two massive male nurses step resolutely forward like chess pawns or foot-soldiers, and enfold Riltse in their muscular grip, while a third nurse pushes up his sleeve and after two or three failed attempts injects in his vein enough sedative to calm a horse.

This – dirty, drugged, his eyes rolled up and with a greenish foam bubbling from his lips, but above all with his heart and his dreams shattered by a perfect stranger – this is the Riltse received once more by the streets of Vienna. The welcoming menu includes a hailstorm, forty-eight hours of non-stop rain, a historic snowfall, and a week of Arctic temperatures which force the city authorities to declare a state of emergency. This is the Riltse who, all but petrified by the cold, balances like a demented acrobat on the eastern parapet of the Praterbrücke, putting the heel of one foot directly in front of the other, as though he is measuring the bridge, and then suddenly, as though still unconsciously following in Lumière's wake (this was the spot where a few days earlier he had ended his life – 'Marx, always Marx, history is condemned to repeat itself . . .'), Riltse plunges into the void – who knows whether accidentally or by design: Riltse says he was distracted by seeing in the sky 'a cloud that reminded him of the third plate in the Rorschach test' – and begins a new, shorter countdown. For days now, hordes of teenage children, sent home from school, have been tracing circles, figures of eight, and elaborate spirals two or three bridges further down, but as Riltse's body goes limp, anticipating the combination of resistance and elasticity it will meet from the waters of the Danube, to his complete amazement he instead comes up against a thick, solid sheet of ice which breaks his fall impassively, although right next to him the Polvani bag, which he must have dropped on impact, opens a small crack in the ice and starts, like Lumière, to sink, still carrying its precious load. All the remaining *Bogus Holes* disappear into the black depths. And this is the Riltse that Pierre-Gilles bumps into in the central train station – the shadow of a man, a desperate genius who is nothing more than a vulgar caricature of the great work he has conceived: one *Bogus Hole* in Salgo's possession, the others at the bottom of the Danube (where, years later, a new generation of Riltse fans, keen to restore to art the sense of adventure they say it has lost, will dive in frogmen's suits to try to recover them) and *Herpes, Aphtha* and *Plaque* all scattered by the forces of the market. Almost all that remains of Sick Art is in Riltse himself. It *is* Riltse.

This is the Riltse we are leaving. And the only thing that can make this farewell less sad is the knowledge that we could have left him earlier but chose not to. Earlier: the moment when for example the artist, busily tearing another limb off the monotonous millipede he had dreamt up to compensate for the agony of waiting – 'seven hundred and twenty-three, seven hundred and twenty-two, seven hundred and twen . . .' – was unable to guess that at that very moment on the far side of the city, Sandor Salgo was stuffing all his worldly possessions into a suitcase – pride of place obviously going to the *Bogus Hole* (although the legal status of how he came to acquire it might have been debatable) – and was fleeing Vienna. This was not the first time. Budapest, Moscow, Zagreb . . . all the cities where he had carried out his shadowy profession had seen him vanish like this, hastily, with only what he stood up in, as they say, and as surreptitiously as he had arrived. A damaged liver, a break in the chain of keeping an organ frozen, negligence in calculating the compatibility between donor and recipient . . . Who knows which? The fact is, somebody made a complaint, in some public office or other a computer spat out a list of atrocities committed by Salgo, and the criminal's network of informers worked to perfection once more. While the police were starting to organise raids and his arrest, the organ trafficker was travelling through the outer suburbs of Vienna on board a taxi driven by a former East German, a timid but optimistic client of his whose corneas (supplied by Salgo at a ridiculous price) would soon begin to cause him problems.

There it goes then, disappearing into the fugitive night: the only *Bogus Hole* to have survived all the disasters. Is Salgo aware of what he has in his suitcase? We have to be careful about that copy of *The Nation* and the name of Arthur C. Danto, as careful as we are about any titles of nobility (flattering but inadequate) we find bestowed on us in our dreams. They could all be lies, but not the rapid and unhesitating way that Salgo (who without those titles is once more what he always has been, an insensitive, starving brute) accepted the canvas as his only form of payment and later, in his haste to flee, when he had to choose the most precious belongings from all he had accumulated in Vienna, or at least the ones that he could turn most easily into money, he once again had no hesitation in including it in the reduced amount of luggage he took with him. No, those actions do not lie. But nor does the state he condemns the canvas to travel in, squashed between a mustard-coloured jumper and two moth-eaten woollen vests, while the buckle from a nearby belt, emboldened by the jolting taxi, starts to examine the orifice that had once so delighted Lumière. No, Salgo does not know. He does not have the slightest idea. He has never been able to read English (he can only write Hungarian with difficulty), the name of Arthur C. Danto means nothing to him, and if a more careful observer than us had taken the trouble to study the magazine page he was so engrossed in when the young doctor bumped into him, he would have discovered, only centimetres away from Danto's signature, a half-page advertisement for Turbulence, with two twin naked nymphs kissing each other on the mouth under a blazing sun. This would have explained not only the beast's rapt attention, but the enthusiasm with which his stiffening prick was poking out from under the edge of his white coat – a detail which our young doctor (usually so sensitive to this kind of effusive display) can only have missed due to the excitement caused by thinking he was in the presence of a true connoisseur. What little Salgo does know is thanks to the desperate urgency of his flight. Yes, he takes something rather than nothing in his case – something that to him is a piece of nonsense, a waste of time or an unfathomable mystery, but something which the respect, admiration or greed of others has given an unexpected value, something that means he can take it instead of something else, something which he therefore should not get rid of, at least until he has found out what it can be useful for.

Obviously, this romance was not meant to last. If *Bogus Hole* survives the first upheavals it is because Salgo, even in his flight, has some money and is operating in known territory, where he has contacts and people who owe him favours, so that he can completely forget about the canvas. So, still inside the same case, still squashed up against the other victims of confinement, *Bogus Hole* goes from the boot of the taxi to the luggage compartment of a long-distance bus (where it acquires the persistent odour of oil and gasoline that will give it added value in years to come) and from there to the inside of a Volkswagen van that has a few problems with its steering and where if it could, if the leather of the suitcase and layer upon layer of disgusting clothing (which not even the most destitute tramp would wear for a single minute) were not in the way, it could contemplate (a poor but incredibly romantic compensation) how the black Austrian night sky, until then dotted with thousands upon thousands of silver glints, suddenly begins to fill with clouds, distant flashes and towering scars of light. Something is going on close to the border. The rain has already started, the windscreen wipers are broken, the driver of the van is scared. Pulled up on the verge, the two men talk it over – as far as anyone can talk something over with Salgo, for whom anything more than three words strung together is a paragraph, and a paragraph is the most graphic illustration of the impossible. They decide on another change of vehicle, the last on Austrian territory, to avoid any unnecessary risks. Half an hour later, by which time the rain has ceased and the clear, pure black of a calm night is chasing away the last vestiges of cloud, a metallic grey Audi 4 pulls up almost without a sound next to the van and waits with its emergency light on. At the back there is a slight click and as if by miracle the boot opens. Salgo drags the suitcase over to the car (one of its edges digs a groove in the mud at the side of the road, something that will later give the investigators sleepless nights) and hesitates, standing next to the Audi's expectant jaws. 'Get a move on!' someone shouts from the van. Grumbling at the weight, Salgo lifts the case and clumsily or carelessly drops it into the boot, then pushes it towards the far end, which it takes an extraordinary length of time to reach. Then he himself clambers in, lies down on the synthetic mat, turns his back on us with a shy, inexplicable gesture, clutches the case like some sort of nocturnal talisman, and the top of the boot slowly closes over him. That is the closest the Beast Salgo ever gets to the *Bogus Hole*. And that is how he crosses the border, clinging to the wet leather of the case and lulled to sleep by the car's futurist vibrations, while outside, at an interval of only two minutes (the time it takes the Audi to travel between the two posts) two migration officers, one Austrian, the other Czech, both of them absorbed in their reading of a back issue of *Fleisch* (another side-line of Pierre-Gilles' production company), confirm the Audi's number plate out of the corner of their eye on the tiny monitors they have in their cabins and, as they are raising the barriers, give the driver (whom the tinted windows reduce to a glinting shadow) the usual lackadaisical salute.

There is only one advantage to Czechoslovakia: it's not Austria. The rest is one long headache. If he wants to stay ahead of the coordinated efforts of the two police forces, Salgo has to move fast. He needs money, a plane ticket, a new passport. Luck is against him. Like a comic-book Midas, every contact he touches disintegrates in his fingers. Some are in jail; others, now out, have been rehabilitated and threaten to turn him in; one has abandoned wife and three children and is wandering around India creating a *jibuthi* 'much better than Sai Baba's'; another weighs twenty-three kilos and is gasping for breath in a public hospital. Reluctantly, Salgo plays his last card and gets in touch with Teun Van Dam, a tall outcast with a face full of freckles who was once his best friend and colleague in the organ trafficking business, but then, in a drastic moral conversion that Salgo has never been able to come to terms with, gave it all up and invested his earnings in a hi-tech artificial limb factory for which he is now famous. Van Dam is prosperous and decent; like all former delinquents, he underplays his prosperity and overplays his decency, but unlike Salgo, who feels nothing but resentment at his ex-associate's new life, Van Dam feels towards his own past – and therefore for Salgo – an almost Christian sense of understanding, in which tolerance co-exists with an extravagant belief in scientific progress, and the illegal traffic in livers, kidneys and human hearts is not in itself reprehensible because of the moral outrage involved, but for the degree of backwardness it shows when compared to the advances of what Van Dam calls – with an expression that can already count with the enthusiastic approval of half a dozen European conferences – the organic replacement industry. So this is the person whom Salgo calls, and after four wrong numbers which provide him with the entrepreneur's four last moves, he eventually finds him in his office. Although the jovial friendliness he is greeted with disturbs Salgo, who may be a beast but, as so often happens with beasts, has a very good memory, and however successful Van Dam may be now, this can never erase just how greedy and duplicitous Van Dam had been as a trafficker, he finally accepts the temporary asylum the other man offers him, a weekend house on the outskirts of Brno. This is a small but absolutely enchanting 'dacha', as Van Dam likes to call it, a place where he takes (the last remaining trace of his previous illicit life) the tiny, fierce Asiatic secretaries he chooses for lovers.

Everything is fine: the thick carpets, heated pool, jacuzzi, the giant screen, the stealthy generosity with which each night someone replenishes the fridge he has raided, even the nocturnal antics of the young Vietnamese girl whom Van Dam, with typical poor taste, has contracted specially for the occasion. If these antics fail, it is because Salgo (who inside is bursting with desire) is unable to decipher them, and prefers to put the mysteriously open windows, the swirling veils of curtain, the moonlight picking out two very similar initials on the wall (his name?), the silent way the girl has of gliding over rather than round the furniture in the living-room, enclosed in a bubble of light – all the kitsch props that Van Dam has been able to dream up (simply in fact reproducing the same tricks that he employs twice a week with his harem of exiled rice-growers) – down to some superior magic power which Salgo is grateful to but does not dare accept because he is so abashed by its sacred nature ... Everything is fine, but by the end of three days, there is nothing much to choose between prison and asylum. Salgo feels suffocated. He has nightmares. He starts to feel persecuted. He sees the graceful Vietnamese goddess, who appears before him each night, naked and with her pubic hair completely shaved off (detail which at a less anxious moment would in itself have been enough to empty the Hungarian's testicles of their last drop of sperm), as a spy, an undercover Czech police agent, the phantom emissary of some client who finds himself panting far too much because he has been given an unsuitable new lung and now wants revenge. (A trivial irony: only the name of Riltse – the only one with any real reason to appear, is completely absent from this spring-like blossoming of Salgo's paranoid ideas.) Alarmed, Van Dam pays him a visit. Salgo forgets all his suspicions and pours out all his needs: a fake passport, plane ticket, and so on. Once he has managed to understand him, Van Dam lights a woman's cigarette with an enormous plastic lighter (the same one with which Salgo tried in vain to light one of the burners in the kitchen) and thinks about it, shrouded in a veil of perfumed smoke. 'Hmmm ...' he thinks, then says: 'How much are we talking about?' Salgo hesitates.

Van Dam fixes his eyes on him, and it is the first time, really the first, that he feels something akin to a sadistic pleasure towards his old friend. Salgo stares down at his bare feet. 'You're not new to this, Sandor: how many lives do we have to hide? Ten? Twenty?' says Van Dam, cupping his hand under the caterpillar of ash threatening to fall from the tip of his cigarette. And then, pow! Salgo has a brainwave, as they say, runs over to his suitcase, throws out all his junk and comes back to Van Dam clutching the *Bogus Hole* to his chest. Taken aback, Van Dam raises his cruelly plucked eyebrows. Salgo looks down, sees he is showing him the back of the painting, and hastens to turn it round. He does not even see the spark of greed that Riltse's signature, clearly visible on the back of the canvas, has lit in Van Dam's eyes.

Farewell, Salgo. Farewell. This is the moment when the little green light (Salgo) and the little red light (*Bogus Hole*) which have travelled together inseparably (in a manner of speaking) from Vienna to Brno, now remain motionless for a second, probably saying goodbye, and than start to move apart. The picture changes: it is like one of those ticks that TV presenters use to show that they have finished an item of news and moved on: the little red light now moves only a few centimetres to the left, to the north-west (Prague); more ambitious or more desperate, the green one shoots off up and to the right, to the north-east (Lodz), leaving on the paper the bright trace of a Christmas firework. And while Salgo, thanks to that talent for amnesia that comes only with stupidity, forgets everything (the basement in the Vienna hospital, the half-dozen trafficked organs that gave him a living for two years, his meeting with the young doctor, Riltse, and, of course, that comical hole in the shape of a painting which, by the way, took advantage of its brief co-existence with the mustard-coloured jersey to stain one of the armpits blue) and finds that – thanks to a course at the Lodz film school which he mistakenly (another language he has not managed to get to grips with) takes to be a recruiting session for nursing staff – filming organs is easier and less dangerous than trafficking them. So he embarks on a brief but successful career as a surgical documentary-maker, and this takes him from Lodz to Warsaw, from Warsaw once more to Moscow, and from Moscow – from the Moscow Hyatt, where he is put up in great luxury as the guest of honour at the XIII World Congress of Scientific Documentary Film-makers –

following a confused episode involving the kidneys of a youngster decapitated in a road accident, which the Moscow police claim to have found wrapped in tin foil in his mini-bar – to Minsk jail, a real walled fortress where its chief inmates, a posse of Russian mafia bosses, serial killers and child traffickers, give him the welcome he deserves. So Salgo's light, that green heartbeat which so gaily crossed half of Eastern Europe, dazzled by the charms of a new life, flickers for the first time, weakens, and starts to go out, this time for ever. But while Salgo forgets and is forgotten, the *Bogus Hole*, which, following its brutal abduction by the Hungarian beast, thanks to Van Dam once again finds itself back in an atmosphere that is closer to the sensibility which first created it, settles down into one of those quiet, peaceful interludes in which art delights, but which so infuriate second-rate biographers.

The painting remains in Prague, in the penthouse Van Dam bought for next-to-nothing from a child prostitution tsar in serious legal trouble, hung between the Freud and the Hockney (who seem rather troubled by it) in the private gallery that takes up the entire upper floor of the apartment. However settled the painting may be, it enjoys a busy social life, and receives all kinds of visitors. For a few months at least, it is the main attraction in the parties that Van Dam throws to help him survive the rigours of the Czech winter, and the only reason why the artificial limb magnate breaks his own (and until this moment strictly observed) rule (even after his much commented purchase of the Bacon) forbidding the parties taking place on the lower floor from ever spilling over into the upper one, where he keeps his collection. As befits any true star, the impact the painting makes is uneven, although perhaps this is due more to the wide variety of people who attend Van Dam's *soirées*, where it is common to find art collectors discussing international politics with surgical appliance manufacturers, and former prostitutes who now grace the catwalks as models drinking toasts with football players who have just been sold to clubs in Spain or Naples. However odd it may seem, many experts study the painting and, when Van Dam is present, are loud in their praise, but as soon as Van Dam turns to snatch a drink from the tray, almost decapitating Ute Ulme, the giraffe-model, in the process, those same enthusiasts cast each other mocking glances and together stifle their dismissive snickers. And vice versa: many *mannequins*, designer boutique owners, chefs and even some diplomats or government officials, who would not necessarily seem to have any affinity with contemporary art, come to a halt in front of the painting, mysteriously attracted to it. A minute earlier, their jokes, laughter and loud greetings had drowned out the party music, but now they fall silent as if the Riltse, rather than being an object of passive contemplation, as they say, emitted some kind of radiation that paralysed them. To anyone familiar with Riltse's aesthetic beliefs, this strabism is perfectly predictable; for Riltse (for the ultimate aim of Sick Art: to inject art into non-artistic organisms) it is the logical consequence of his work, the only one that faithfully reflects his art's proposals, and the only one that he as its creator is willing to accept. But to someone like Van Dam – who is literally drowning in money (and who only agreed to keep the painting thanks to one of those mistakes that so delight the hyenas of art history, because when he read the name of Riltse on the back of the canvas Salgo was holding up, he had immediately associated it with a painter to whom his favourite magazine *Goodbuy* had devoted ten pages in a special edition about new areas for investment, describing him as an artist 'with prestige but not yet incorporated into the mainstream of the international art market' – a painter who, and this was the treacherous detail that explained the *sotto voce* glee of the connoisseurs in Van Dam's parties, was not Riltse but Pilsen, the Mexican Arturo Pilsen, said to be the bastard child of Frida Kahlo and Leon Trotsky) – to someone like Van Dam, who like any self-made man was extremely susceptible to any hint of social stigma, especially unfavourable comments by people he himself calls, putting the expression into imaginary inverted commas 'the specialists', the fact that his new acquisition should divide opinion into two opposing camps could not help but be disturbing.

He at once reacts (typically) by thinking he has been swindled. This means the end of the social whirl for the *Bogus Hole*, with its champagne bubbles, evening gowns, and commentaries, and the start of a painful calvary. Throughout an exhausting month, half a dozen experts – the most expensive, of course, and the most unscrupulous – pass through the penthouse and submit the Riltse to all kinds of examinations and tests. Van Dam, who knows that his cheques can hire knowledge but not necessarily silence suspicion, invents a whole series of unlikely explanations as to how the painting came into his possession.

The verdict is not unanimous, but is unanimously negative: those experts who do not say the painting is a fake say it is dreadful, and therefore unsaleable, whereas those who consider it wiser not to speak so categorically of it decide it is so crazy that it would be hard for it to find its place, *any* place, on the market.

Van Dam grows depressed. This is not the first time something like this has happened to him, but to his nouveau riche mentality, which refuses to learn from experience because that would automatically mean he had to face up to being nouveau riche, something he is not prepared to do, as he says 'for all the gold in the world', it is always as if it were the first time. His blindness is as complete as his disarray, and the anger with which he reacts to the series of verdicts from the experts (which they have agreed upon even before they see the painting, in private meetings where they snigger and wreathe themselves in pipe smoke, as another of the private jokes that every so often – filled with a sense of the purity of art which seems mysteriously to desert them whenever they are hired by a real collector in difficulties and put their signatures to the most outrageous estimates and authentifications – they claim is their way of gaining some revenge for art 'in its always unequal battle against the despotism of money') is not the reaction of someone calling them into question (as he would be entitled to do, given the huge number of irregularities which invalidate their opinions), but rather of someone pathetically accepting their judgement. Unsettled by their opinion, but as yet undecided about what to do with the painting, he wraps it and puts it in the boot of his car, and almost without thinking calls one of the girls from his Asiatic harem, the first he finds in his address book – because in the state he is in, all Vietnamese names sound the same, and he finds it impossible to put a definite image to a face, a body or fornicatory skill to any of them. He invents a lightning visit to an artificial limb manufacturers' congress ('The End of Bones: Nightmare or Utopia?') and seeks refuge in the dacha near Brno, in the hope that a few days of carefree debauchery will release him from his anxious bewilderment. He is mistaken – completely mistaken. But by being mistaken, and by one of those tours de force with which destiny, inexplicably obliging to the susceptibilities of the nouveaux riches, is in the habit of compensating them for the difficulties their pig-headedness get them into, he solves his problem.

All at once, everything in the dacha seems to remind him of Salgo. He finds the clump of hair blocking the shower, the crack in the soap dish, the unscrewed coffee jar top, the cemetery of yellowing fingernail clippings buried in the plush of the living-room carpet, and wherever he goes, he imagines he can see the phantom of the Hungarian swindler doubled up laughing at him. This is too much. He is no longer depressed: he is beside himself with rage, and can only think of revenge. This is his state of mind (thinking of how to get revenge) when the Vietnamese girl appears in the doorway to the breakfast room and strikes a calendar pose. She is wearing a pair of Van Dam's silk pyjamas; the unbuttoned shirt shows the firm golden flesh of her stomach and part of the white areolas round her breasts; a wisp of pubic hair pokes as if by accident above the top of the trousers, which are too big for her skinny boy's hips. The obvious signals are there, as she faithfully repeats the sexual protocol Van Dam himself established in order to be aroused, but now, just as an amnesiac is completely indifferent to the most intimate faces, names, or voices, they leave him cold. Because he, Van Dam, sees something very different: he sees the reddish stain that is an outrage to the shiny sand colour of the pyjama top, sees how it ignominiously splashes the embroidered italic monogram, and the brutish image he has of Salgo spilling the tomato purée all over himself as he eats it straight from a tin turns his stomach. But the Vietnamese girl, whose professionalism prevents her from noticing anything that is outside the realm of desire, gracefully slides out of her beauty queen pose and starts to tiptoe over to him. What she does not realise is that the hem of one arm of the pyjamas gets caught in the doorknob, and tears. Bingo. 'Stupid peasant woman,' says Van Dam, standing up very, very slowly. 'Paddy-field peasant, chink shit, heap of nothing, slit-eyed foetus, slave.' Instinctively, as these insults strike her like stones, she pulls the pyjama round her, tearing it still further, but she is not really the cause: that is the abominable figure of Salgo, whom Van Dam, if he could somehow see beyond the pure present of his humiliation, would doubtless blame for all the ills he has to suffer, from his persecution by the Dutch tax authorities (the only reason behind his residence in the Czech Republic, 'that kiddies' play-room run by poets and do-gooders in general', which he loathes with all his heart, but whose virtues as a tax haven suit him down to the ground, to the arterio-sclerosis that took the life of his second wife, after plunging her in the most atrocious pain imaginable – and yet whose body was useful for him to try out the (somewhat experimental) prototypes for organic replacement.

This is the prelude to an atrocious, endless night. After the verbal abuse, which reaches unheard of depths ('rotting cunt, aborted foetus, human pustule') and grows and grows, there comes the session of unbridled sex, which Van Dam has no intention of depriving himself of, but now adapts to the needs of his current fury. The slaps, the blows on buttocks, the twisting of limbs begin. Confusing this violent treatment with the brutal but controlled rituals Van Dam has accustomed her to, the girl seems to be able to bear them without any great difficulty. She is trained to soften their painful effects and translate them into the rhetoric of sexual arousal, and above all to suffer them in silence, because of the near-slave regime (a single no, a word of protest, and any of the harem could instantly be deported) that Van Dam imposes on them. But he quickly leaves behind this titillating foreplay, whose marks glow for an instant on the girl's skin and then vanish like mirages. And the girl quickly moves from a lazy acceptance to a state of complete terror when Van Dam first of all ties her feet and hands to the frame he has had specially designed by a blacksmith friend, and then displays the collections of whips, sticks, thongs, rubber dildos, knives, metal clips and hole-punchers that a client (an old friend of these pages) once used to pay him for a hi-tech prothesis that would allow him to renew genital activity after decades of extravagant but unsatisfactory subterfuges. Van Dam has never dared use them before, horrified (even though he is someone who when it comes to erotic experiments has never baulked at anything) at the possibilities the mere sight of these implements suggests. What follows – cuts, blows, mutilation – would not have been out of place in the most vicious libertine's imagination. Unable to move, the Vietnamese girl starts to howl with pain as soon as she gets a glimpse of all that awaits her; she writhes on the frame, digging the ropes still further into her wrists and ankles; she passes out. Over the next few hours, the same cycle is repeated time and again with the monotony of a macabre ritual, the only variation being the intensity with which Van Dam, still blinded by the image of Salgo (his *bête noire*), carries out his torture programme, which grows all the time and appears to have no limits. In the early morning, after suffering several bouts of truly sexual violence, close to martyrdom, bleeding and perforated (literally) by the set of stainless steel bits that her executioner eventually added to his arsenal – hand-made tools Van Dam himself designed for the 1978 Copenhagen Universal Pornography Exhibition, powered by a miniature battery which adds sudden electric shocks to the lacerations the bits make in the skin – the poor girl gives a faint sigh and loses consciousness one final time. There is nothing Van Dam can do to bring her round – and he tries everything, because the revenge-hungry animal he has become can tolerate the idea that his prey might resist or despise him, might put up a fight or even pay him back in kind, but never that it could escape – nothing can bring her out of the deep well in which she has taken refuge. Van Dam leaves the torture chamber, collapses on his back on the sofa-bed, and falls asleep, half-naked like a gladiator, his body covered in leather thongs, two rubber dildos forgotten round his waist, a steel prick, its point covered in blood, still in his hand. He falls asleep, so deeply that at half-past six in the morning, when the girl recovers thanks to heaven knows what inner Vietnamese strength, wakes up, unties herself and runs out of the house, taking the Mercedes, which, after all the blood she has lost, and given the fact that her driving experience until now has consisted entirely in the occasional rickshaw or borrowed scooter, she only manages to get out on to the road after crashing into one of the two ancient elms standing guard over the Brno dacha, Van Dam wrinkles his nose, swats an invisible fly from his cheek, turns on his right side, smiles like the radiant, diaphanous baby he once was, and carries on sleeping.

Everybody stand by. The little red light is on again, the *Bogus Hole* rouses itself and is moving across the map once more. Predictably enough, its first steps are short, stumbling ones; they come and go, trace circles, set off in one direction and then another as they follow the erratic progress the Vietnamese girl makes in her escape on board the Mercedes. Then at a certain moment they stop (the German border), jump forward (the girl opens the boot to get her luggage, sees the wrapped-up painting, tears the wrapping, recognises the work that caused such a scandal in the last social gatherings at Van Dam's penthouse) and almost without thinking decides to take it with her.

She abandons the Mercedes next to a stinking poultry farm, and after a short interruption that is long enough for the girl to pay the sordid carnal tribute demanded of her by the border guard to let her through, the painting continues on its way to Munich, only a few blocks from the mattress-makers from where a fortnight earlier the latest model of water-bed had been despatched to Brno, where the still sleeping Van Dam is unaware that the tip of the steel prick is busy causing it irreparable damage. After that, the painting's path follows a long vertical line (an old Volkswagen van full of spaced-out hippies and aggressive ecologists who have only one thing on their mind – the sun) down to the Yugoslav coast and then, following kilometre after kilometre of coastline, it comes to a halt in the south of France, in Cannes, in the warm month of May, with lilacs in bloom and budding starlets parading along the Boulevard de la Croisette breasts in the air, and Hollywood film-stars stubbing out their cigarettes on the carpet that the Festival Palace flicks out like some huge red amphibian tongue, while an army of paparazzi fires off shot after shot.

It is easy to imagine the Vietnamese girl wreathed in clouds of marijuana as she clings to the canvas (she was bold enough, or careful enough, to free it from its stretcher) and puts a hesitant sandalled foot on the running board of the van as the early spring sun filters through the tops of the palm trees and blinds her sleepy eyes. She has never been in Cannes; she does not know a soul, she had only just started to stutter out a few words of Czech and now has to face yet another language – and one which, unlike Czech, will not tolerate being badly pronounced. But who cares about these tiny details? She is very young – only seventeen, and at an age when any foolish youngster in the western world is trembling as they buy their first cigarette of drugs, she has already survived the most violent mishaps. Furthermore, she is beautiful and exotic – a fact which in her first days in Cannes gives her the idea (after seeing on a TV set in a bar the particularly bloody scene from *A Man Called Horse* in which Richard Harris is literally raised in the air by the hooks the Indians have placed in his nipples) of convincing her saviours by sign language that the marks Van Dam left on her body are in fact ritual inscriptions typical of her native village – and the fashion for all things Asian, women but also cuisine, clothes, tourism and of course cinema, has somehow, inexplicitly but blatantly, become the main theme of this year's film festival. It is easy to imagine the pleasure of the meat-hunters as they watch her pass by with the irresistible ungainliness of as yet unformed beauties along the streets of a city that is ostentatious to the point of vulgarity. Men with big, jewelled hands and shirt-collars worn over their jacket lapels try to intercept her. So recently rescued from hell, she rejects their offers, even though the least generous of them would allow her easily to resolve her most pressing needs. None of this is new to her. Back in Saigon she has seen the same predatory gleam in men's eyes, and heard that low but persistent whisper she now has to listen to two or three times on each block she walks along, a mixture of desire, insistence, and threat. She wanders around all morning, then fetches up at a beach far from the centre, one of the popular spots that the city's international pomp has not yet completely ruined. There she discovers a group of young women enjoying their picnic lunch in the sun. She sees them, they see her, and invite her to share their food. There is no need for any of them to speak: like vampires, they recognise each other thanks to a secret but silent shared language, the keys to which are an old scar, a bruise, the tiny patch of dead skin left by a burning cigarette. An hour later, the same pimps who were whispering money in her ear watch her stride victoriously back into town. She is more beautiful than ever because, of all the states that beauty can combine with, none is so advantageous as indifference, and she now enjoys the protection of the court of blossoming young women she has just joined. She soon has a house – a small hotel in a discreet neighbourhood that she shares with the others, but where she has her own room – and work: 'Luxe, calme et volupté' is a hostess agency run by a fat Fanny Ardant looka-like, and in the not-too-distant future, they promise her, she will have her legal papers.

There is a knock at the door. What about the *Bogus Hole*? a tiny imp's voice asks. OK, OK. Everything is happening so quickly. Everything is going to happen so quickly. To begin with – the fate of a pariah, as though the clandestine existence the girl is finally leaving behind were contagious – the canvas simply vegetates. It spends a few uncomfortable weeks curled up like a stowaway in the cardboard box which a few days after she had arrived at the 'Luxe' the Asian girl kicked underneath her bed just in time, a few seconds before Fanny Ardant, on one of her tours of inspection, knocked at her door and as usual burst in without waiting for a reply. Yet compared to the promiscuous imprisonment the painting suffered at the hands of Salgo, these weeks of confinement seem almost like a holiday in a seaside resort. The Riltse is still a prisoner, but it does not have to share its cell with anything, and although the bed support it is leaning against in its box is the favourite meeting place for fluff, insects, hairgrips and even false nails (a fashion accessory that Vietnamese girls are apparently very fond of, partly because they help disguise the disastrous state of their real nails, and partly for the role they play in their loving arts, where they are employed with tremendous skill) which usually all seem to end up in the middle of a cobweb, the room is fresh and sunny, with windows opening to the south, to the sea, from where blows the breeze that (each time the girl leans out to fill her lungs with air and thank the obscure deity she prays to each night for this change in her fortune) pulls all the fluff and hairgrips and false nails from the web and deposits them under the bed. One afternoon, in the quiet *intermezzo* between two clients, she searches in vain for the pewter ear-ring that she will later discover, to her astonishment and fury, in the jewel box of her neighbour, a girl from Cape Verde, who has to stoop every time she enters a room. She pulls the bed out from the wall and finds the box. She stares at it as if it were not hers, and in the joy of discovering it again – the joy of forgetfulness, the only force capable of making everything it touches seem new again – opens it and takes out the canvas. She pins it to the wall and sits for a few moments studying it, as though calculating the aesthetic effect it could have on the room and on her own spirit if she could leave it hanging there. Three, four minutes at most, but for Riltse's canvas this extraordinarily intense burst of freedom is the equivalent of the few, miraculous drops of water a good Samaritan drips on to the tongue of a traveller lost for days in the desert.

The girl soon enjoys considerable fame. Despite herself, she realises that the need to respond to Van Dam's extravagant demands was, as well as being torture, the best training she could have had. It is rare for her room in the Luxe to be empty, and even more rare to find in the queue of men visiting her any poor, badly shaven clients who when it comes time to pay have to scrape the bottom of their pockets for the banknote to complete their payment – although this kind is frequent in her colleagues' appointments books. The men who ask for her (because they arrive at the Luxe with her name on the tip of their tongue, willing to wait if necessary in the small room set aside for that purpose, but never to exchange her for another girl, however much Fanny tries to build up their reputation) are solvent, very self-assured, usually discreetly elegant. The most obvious indication of how powerful these men are is their even-handed treatment, as if between equals, of the young Vietnamese girl, and the way that they consent to talk of money only when it is absolutely necessary, in a private *tête-à-tête* with Fanny (never with her) and using cheques or credit cards (never cash). They display all the pleasant flirtatiousness, the same conversation, and the same kind of personal curiosity they deploy when meeting women from their own circle in the cocktail parties they have just left, in a state of indescribable excitement, to treat themselves to a couple of hours of physical ecstasy. Soon, the girl's name and talent become an open secret, and the atmosphere of the festival, which is both enclosed, like a self-contained world of its own, and at the same time is phenomenally cosmopolitan and outward-looking, acts as a tremendous sounding-board for her. Her status changes. She no longer receives clients only in the Luxe; she is also sought after to accompany the same rich and successful men to cocktail parties, openings, and private functions; they pay to introduce her tiny body inside four walls. Fanny accepts this, even though it breaks the long-standing house rule of conducting business only there. This is a crucial decision, although not so much for the girl herself. For her this means at most that she is extending the radius of her imprisonment from her room at the Luxe to the whole of the city, its luxurious suburbs, even to the yachts swaying gently in the harbour, where the debauchery, blessed by the immunity that being on water provides, goes on for days and nights without stopping. But soon she will be back in her confinement at the Luxe, only this time in a much smaller room than the one she has been in until now, and 'with a furrowed brow' according to the tango expression she will have learnt from the man who is both her victim and her executioner. No, it is a crucial decision for the *Bogus Hole*.

Because the film festival comes to an end, and with it the heady days, the glamour, the monstrous fever that unites money and art. A few weeks later, when the Vietnamese girl has only just finished sorting out all the treasures from her fishing expeditions – yielding, at Fanny's insistence, a modest percentage of them to her colleagues, in order to temper the jealous hatred in their looks when they are in the dining-room, the showers, the room where they wait for their medical check-ups – a new circus hits town. The advertising market festival erects its tents on the ruins of the previous one. Parties, receptions, banquets: everything starts all over again – and naturally, that 'everything' includes the deliciously exciting burning sensation that fills the Vietnamese girl's still warm dance card. Yet at the same time everything is more vulgar, more restricted, more ostentatious. This is because the stars of advertising, unlike movie stars, whose fame, however ill-deserved, tends to shine to the furthest regions, twinkle only in their own little world, where at best they merely co-exist with the brands of clothes or revolutionary sweets to whose names they will be forever linked, and out of this alchemy of art and money, all that is now left is money. None of this appears to affect the most popular girl in the Luxe, who once again starts her exhausting routine and again makes use (this time more than ever, in fact) of the right to roam that Fanny has given her. She goes to preview theatres, luxury restaurants, bars, night-clubs, hotels, walled palaces and yachts on the arms of Japanese, Swedes, or Mexicans. Everywhere the regular staff, from managers to waiters, not forgetting the croupiers, the cloakroom attendants and the security men, celebrate her return with deep bows, and a stealthy kind of complicity, the sort of cooperation that unites people who may be very different, but are victims of a common enemy. She ends her nights with one or more of her clients in hotel bedrooms the size of a whole apartment, with heated swimming pools out on the terrace, curtains opened or shut by remote control, and fridges stuffed with luxuries which in money terms would be enough to keep a Vietnamese family (her own, for a start, from whom she only rarely receives any signs of life) for two years at least. She goes out almost every night. She attends product launches, beauty contests, jingle competitions. She is intro-duced to bankers, stunt men, fashion designers, public relations managers. After a while, boredom sets in. She has had her fill of oysters, perfumes, images; the only thing that catches her attention (because of her situation and lack of experience, she sees everything with the eyes of a foreigner) is the delegation from Argentina. Now that she is more or less familiar with their faces, she remembers they were the first to arrive, the ones with most luggage (she was soon to learn that half of their suitcases were empty), and the only delegation which insisted (threatening to leave the hotel on the spot) that they should all be put up on the same floor and in adjacent rooms. It is also the most numerous delegation, the one with the fewest women, the noisiest, the one most likely to protest, the first to rush at the buffet tables. But out of all this disturbing group, the person who most intrigues her is an older man with a fair moustache, face dotted with freckles, and hair always unkempt, as if he had just got off a motorbike. As far as the Vietnamese girl can tell, he speaks the same language as the Argentinians: he uses the same tone of indignation and hurt pride as them, and therefore must be another member of their delegation, and yet he always turns up to the events on his own, either too early or too late. He bursts into the room wide-eyed, teeth clenched and chin thrust forward like a ship's figurehead, and stands (when the rest are all sitting), or sits down (when all the others are standing up). He smokes cigarettes which he rolls between two fingers to dislodge some of the tobacco, and seems to be in the state of constant tension of someone who is expecting a signal, in the midst of a crowded meeting, to detonate a bomb that will blow them all up. He emerges from this impatient waiting attitude only to shout rude comments about the speech someone is delivering, the film being shown, or the prize about to be awarded. The girl sees him on several occasions. She sees him once in a corner of the main hall of the Festival Palace, cleaning some dog shit off his shoe with the fringe of a velvet curtain. (He always seems to wear deck shoes, even with a tuxedo.) Early one morning she thinks she spies his shadow busily trying to operate a cash machine. She sees him in the most expensive restaurant in Cannes, scribbling some drawings for the astonished owner, while at the same time scratching his bare right foot with a silver fork; then sees him again at the grubbiest stall on the railway station, eating a stack of *crêpes* with a greasy hand while intently studying the business section of a London daily. The girl, who knows and has been in all the hotels, has never seen him entering or leaving any of them. She checks, and someone tells her that the Argentinian stranger is not staying on dry land, but on the yacht *Evita Capitana*, in which, taking advantage of the fact that he was involved in the Buenos Aires – Punta del Este race (where his performance left a lot to be desired) he decided to cross the Atlantic single-handed.

So then the inevitable happens: the Argentinian man (who according to her had not even looked at her until then) comes to hire her. When he arrives at the Luxe, as dishevelled as ever and with his jacket lapels covered in cigarette ash, he refuses the drinks, music and conversation – all the pleasant preambles that Fanny likes to greet her clients with, rushes upstairs and, as if he were being pursued by the police, locks himself in the girl's room. Once inside, still wearing his jacket, the Argentinian takes out a cigarette, rolls it between his fingers for a moment, lights it (the flame catches on the tobacco shreds clustered around the tip and appears to immediately consume half the cigarette), sits on the floor, pulls a couple of sheets of paper out of his pocket and in a deep, fine, masculine voice (a combination of baritone and army officer) almost sings as he recites the poems from his next book, *Drug*. For the next six days, he does exactly the same: he reads to her, recites people's poems from memory, in languages he knows nothing of but which he pronounces perfectly, sings – Wagner and Schumann *lieder*, the whole of *Der Rosenkavalier* – and impresses her with his encyclopedia of useless knowledge, compiled over his lengthy career as a market researcher and publicist (facts from which he always manages to extract the tiny detail, the statistic or percentage which – completely insignificant in themselves – nevertheless, properly considered, serve as the key to explain the fall of the Berlin Wall, the shape of African women's breasts, AIDS, the First World War, or Sony's irresistible rise). Sex is the last thing on his mind. He can spend an hour and fifty minutes explaining a theory – for example, in order to please the girl, a theory about the vital role played by the irrigation systems in the ricefields in the Vietnamese guerrilla's defence strategy and the defeat of the US forces – and devote only the last ten minutes left to sexual gratification (which also tends to be somewhat strange: ten minutes of anal massage, for example, or masturbating standing up while she jabs him in the nipples with the point of his Montblanc fountain-pen, or a quick 'navvy's fuck' as he calls it, his trousers down round his knees, the belt pulled tight round his neck. After six days, the Vietnamese girl is obsessed with one sole question: who is this man?

It must be love: there is no other answer. Fanny is the first to tell her so, when she starts surprising her in those absent moods which seem to come upon her for no apparent reason while she is taking a bath, or coming down to the dining-room, or standing next to a window, or raising a cup to her mouth. For a few seconds she stays stock still, as if in suspense: she has literally ceased to exist for the world around her. The girl herself only realises it one evening when, after having put up with the reading of some erotic sonnets and listening (without really understanding, because the Argentinian's English is as bad as hers) to a complicated explanation about the relation between the sterility of bees, polyester, the huge increase in allergies and the international drugs companies' lobbies, to her own great surprise finds herself doing something she has never done before: telling him the story of her life. It doesn't take long: it's a short life, and her many adventures can be easily reduced to two or three recurrent themes. But at some point, towards the end of his time with her, she pushes the bed away from the wall, digs out the cardboard box and shows the Argentinian the *Bogus Hole*. She probably hopes that seeing the painting will give the episode about her fleeing from Van Dam's orbit a convincing realism that her words, to judge by the Argentinian's expression, have completely failed to do. The effect is instantaneous, but not exactly what she was expecting. Like a seasoned addict suddenly discovering a weakness he never knew he had, and compared to which all his previous vices now seem trivial or child's play, the Argentinian unzips his trousers and pulls out his penis, which has gone hard at the mere sight of the painting. Two seconds later, and he is kneeling on the floor behind the Vietnamese girl, exploring the depths of her flesh while he thrusts away (faithful to the logic of the deranged genius who conceived it) at a *chef d'oeuvre inconnu* of contemporary art. Let us call a halt there, please, before the biographers use a bastardised version for their salacious displays. The Argentinian has, as they say, instantaneously seized the secret meaning of the Riltse; he has seized it before realising it is a Riltse, or perhaps even that it is a work of art. In fact, it is not him, but his penis, 'my reading prick' as he calls it in the opening sonnet of *Drug*, a lengthy and occasionally very entertaining disquisition on all the blind things that have suddenly started 'reading' in the modern world. And what is this miraculous under-standing, this tele-comprehension, which 'lowers' the aesthetic experience to the depths of the organic, if not the perfect conclusion, evoking as it does (in one of those echoes that would be sickening if they were not true) the instantaneous ejaculation with which Lumière christened the *Bogus Hole*, the original source of the rectal arousal and discharge that led Riltse to the most radical expressions of Sick Art? Oh, to have been Riltse, to have been in his skin to discover whether at this decisive moment, when the Argentinian, after plunging into the Vietnamese girl's slit, spills his milk around the edge of the hole of the *Bogus Hole*, whether he, Riltse, did not feel a second time the sacred stab in his rectum, thereby confirming the tele-transmission of his art!

Whether they know it or not – and everything points to the fact that they do not – the girl and the painting have their days numbered. Separated from its creator, the *Bogus Hole* has one natural owner, and that is the Argentinian. There could be protests, or the painting's legal status could be invoked (from its inception, this is one long list of irregularities) but this kind of genital recognition – far superior in its spontaneity, immediacy, and rejection of all premeditation, to any kind of recognition born of aesthetic perception, taste or knowledge, in the same way that in Brecht's play the chalk circle serves to determine who is the real mother – will brook no argument. Things start to move more quickly. The Argentinian turns the canvas over, sees and recog-nises Riltse's signature. The girl, who for the first time, thanks to this eccentric client who always pays, according to Fanny, in banknotes from six different countries which she immediately converts to French francs thanks to her infallible mental computer, has seen her own life flash before her eyes, begins to drop her guard, to languish, to start to feel compassion, to dream of being someone else. She laughs at the slightest thing. The sight of his untied shoe-laces, still wet from the last puddle they were dragged through, moves her to tears. His erudi-tion – one whole evening is devoted to etymology – astounds her. His gifts – modest and out of fashion as they are, with that shamefaced, apologetic look that stolen things have – touch her deeply. But he is married. He, who has never had the slightest problem confessing it, has no difficulty now in dismissing the problem with a sarcastic laugh. He'll get divorced, he says, or maybe he'll kill her. Of course, the girl does not believe him, although she is impressed by the determination with which he announces these crazy schemes. Fine, he says – his enthusiasm increasing in direct proportion to the viability of his ideas – he'll take her to live with him in Argentina, as his maid. He seems to have it all planned: the advantages of this hidden bigamy, the navy-blue apron with white polka dots, the cap – which he will ejaculate over when she is off duty, and is dancing drunkenly, like a being possessed, in a disco in the Plaza Italia or Flores ... The Vietnamese girl pulls back. 'Argentina': the mere mention of the word makes her shudder. Has she fled from Saigon to end up in Argentina? And, as so often happens, sensing her hesitation only arouses him still further. He raises the stakes, as they say, and changes the domestic panorama he is offering – easy for him, but too demanding for her, however false her position – for one in which they lead double lives, she has proper papers to stay in Argentina, a job, an apartment in a residential neighbourhood, even a maid of her own, with a navy-blue apron and white polka dots, and a cap ... but he does not seem to understand: the problem is the country, Argentina, that 'uttermost land' as he himself calls it at close of day one particularly sad evening. Some difficult hours follow: after the daring moments of rapture comes remorse. Something changes in the Argentinian; his tolerance, which before bordered on indifference, disappears; he is possessed by a kind of evil rancour. Everything becomes more related to sex – as if their love, which exists and is true, could only grow thanks to violence. One night in the Luxe, at the height of his despair, he tells her he will not lose her before he has 'broken her arse' – a prerogative she has offered him since the first day, but which, horrified, he has always refused. Now, however, it is the girl who refuses. No, she says, she won't allow it. But the question is: *can* she refuse? The Argentinian has always paid, even when they were carried away by love to one of those realms where money, they say, has no right to exist; and the mere fact of there being this economic contract would seem to authorise him to ask for, and above all to receive, everything he wants. They argue. All of a sudden, she bursts into tears and starts to tremble, like a flower a single drop of water has fallen on. So then he, with the gallant behaviour that comes from the worst kind of disdain, settles her down as he pleases, calms her, and when she is no longer crying (or rather, when all that is left is the trembling, like a damp, orphaned flower, that so encourages the pleasures of the flesh) he tries to obtain from in front what she would not let him achieve from behind, and thrusts his penis in her mouth.

Up to this point, so much is clear. After that, whether it was with her teeth or her nails . . . the fact is that all at once a scream disturbs the calm of the Luxe, and when Fanny bursts into the girl's room, the Argentinian is lying naked on the floor, hands between his thighs, trying to stop the bleeding. Fanny's contacts, the good reputation her establishment enjoys, and above all the many prominent physicians who figure among her clients, help resolve the medical emergency in a discreet manner. But what about the legal emergency? The Argentinian could talk, and there is always (even in Cannes) a susceptible or hypocritical judge who might try to use a sordid story like this to boost his career and win a transfer to Paris. And if he were to talk, it could mean closure, jail, ruin! The interested parties meet in the Luxe. Fanny, who has taken the precaution of locking the Vietnamese girl in the basement, where she will work from now on, takes the initiative and offers the Argentinian, who remains standing throughout the whole meeting, right hand in his pocket, stroking the bandage he can feel inside, whatever compensation he thinks adequate. But he does not want money, or a lifetime's voucher he can spend in the Luxe, or the privileges that Fanny can secure for him in the most select circles of the city just by lifting the phone. He wants the *Bogus Hole*.

He wants it, and he will get it, because Fanny, who only discovers the existence of the painting when the Argentinian drags her to the Vietnamese girl's former room and points it out to her on the wall, can scarcely believe that this piece of rubbish, which did not even cost her a cent, will allow her to escape from one of the most dangerous episodes of her entire career as a madam. So the Argentinian ends up taking the canvas with him back to Buenos Aires in his only suitcase, where it is crammed in with the same kind of promiscuity it had suffered during Salgo's flight from Vienna, except that this is a rather more refined incarceration, because the dresses, shawls, jackets, leather boots and bags it has to share space with are all high-class items, costing fifteen hundred dollars each at least. But if the Argentinian takes it with him, it is not because he intends to keep it for himself – he knows Riltse, of course, and apart from the erection he got when he first saw the painting, which he prefers to put down to some kind of empathy or chemical reaction, he is left completely cold by pictorial representation, whether created by Riltse or anyone else, considering himself incapable of being moved by any kind of expression apart from words and music. No, it is in order to 'shut the mouth', as he says, of Nancy, his wife of twelve years, the owner or more correctly the inheritor of the fortune that has allowed her husband (amongst other things) to write poetry and publish it, to head an advertising agency which in five years only produced two images, two modest column fillers that the client, a whisky importer, was so angry with that he withdrew them from circulation the day after they had appeared, to sail and compete in regattas, to travel to Cannes on his yacht, to spend a fortnight in the 'Luxe, calme et volupté' and, to return full circle, to bring back the quantity of clothes, make-up and perfumes that his wife makes an essential condition of his leaving the country without her. He has everything planned: he already knows what he is going to do, how he will use the Riltse to silence his wife, who is always to keen (despite the care he takes to fulfil her demands) to accuse him of wasting money, and is always so suspicious in general. With luck and a favourable wind, he will reach Buenos Aires two days before their thirteenth anniversary. That should give him just enough time to have the painting framed and wrapped up and, on the night of their celebration, have it brought to the table with mock surprise by the maître d', who will set aside for a moment their first courses that have arrived too soon – salmon carpaccio or prawn cocktail, his two classic dishes – and present it to her as if it has just fallen out of the sky. Yes, the Argentinan is only just leaving Cannes, but he can already see it. He can see the smile of astonishment and enthusiasm that the still wrapped painting brings to his wife's face and then, once it is revealed in all its glory, the disappointment and irritation that quickly transform her expression. But he can also see how surprised and relieved she will be when he, anticipating the reproach already on her lips, tells her how much he paid for it – not a cent, nothing at all – and the gleam of almost murderous satisfaction that spreads over her features when she learns what Sotheby's or Christie's will one day offer them, whenever they decide to get rid of it. As he steers *Evita Capitana* with one hand, and with the other raises the rim of his pullover up to his chin, what he does not see, so dazzled is he by the future horizon he has planned, is the slice of the *real* future that has slipped unnoticed in among his visions – not to destroy them, no, but simply to modify them with an intimate scene (like a bucolic indoors portrait) in which Nancy, the beautiful mature woman, who has already relegated his gift to the maid's bathroom – where she says it will no longer annoy her, is lying exhausted and asleep in the arms of Rimini, the young man who does not sleep but thinks of the *Bogus Hole* with a sort of emotional covetousness he is completely unaware of, while two of his fingers brush away a lock of hair that threatens to wake her up, stroke her cheek, an ear, and then find themselves unable to resist following the thin white line like an ant's trail they have discovered at the edge of her scalp, a line her surgeon's masterly hand has traced over the years.

CHAPTER 5

They never again reached the heights of that first occasion, but their encounters, governed by the days and times that Nancy had classes, gradually took on the regular rhythm of a diet or medical treatment. They met in the club lobby before the class, and greeted each other in a conventional way, with that mixture of intimacy and embarrassment that characterises teachers and pupils sharing a physical activity. But as Rimini brushed her creamy cheek with his lips, and took her to task for arriving a few minutes late, Nancy, who usually avoided touching him in public, dug her purple fingernails into his forearm. Rimini immediately found himself following her towards the women's changing-room, as deserted as the rest of the club at that time of the morning, and two minutes later they were humping away against one of the wooden lockers. She had her back to him, her arms outstretched and her head practically submerged in her own locker, while Rimini stood with his hands round her waist and worked away in that absent-minded way of his, staring all the while at the freckled, slightly wild-looking face of her husband that smiled at him from a photo stuck to the inside of the door. Or they met after the class, when Rimini, let down yet again by Boni, started to wander round the club and, trying to conceal the irritation he felt at his pupil's lateness, just happened to glance over at the terrace bar, where Nancy, glass in hand, was standing at the table and dazzled him with a passionate gaze in his direction. He would continue on his way and so would she, as if resigned to the fact they were on different orbits, but he was only pretending to be wandering about, and she was only making as if to leave, because a few moments later (synchronised in a way that, if they had paid it any attention, would have astonished them) they would collide in one or other of the places they had chosen for their skirmishes – her car, hidden in the shade of a huge *palo borracho* tree, which offered the choice between comfortable reclining seats at the front and the uncomfortable back seat, or the corrugated-iron shed, discovered by Rimini, where the club rather carelessly kept (even he had been able to prise open the padlock) all its maintenance tools.

Those two urgent flashpoints – Nancy's nails digging into his skin, or her eyes stabbing him like a pin through a bee – were all that had survived from the original eruption. The rest – so brief they did not even break sweat, was a physiological need they despatched twice a week with professional indifference, as though they were taking part in some statistical survey. Rimini was under no illusions. Apart from the hint of pride he felt at being able to respond more or less adequately to a situation where he was no more than a completely inexperienced object, he knew that his performance was merely satisfactory – for which he secretly thanked the monotony of their encounters, limited as they were to the most perfunctory forms of coupling – and he also knew that the frenzied peak Nancy had reached that afternoon in the kitchen had nothing to do with him, his personal charm or his sexual abilities, but was something that was there long before he was, which went far beyond him, and that had only chosen him by sheer chance. Yet he accepted his role without complaint, like someone who too late discovers the extras involved in a contract he has read too quickly and has already signed. It was as if these periodic doses of satisfaction, which seemed more like relief than pleasure, were part of his job as a tennis coach, similar to other much more obvious ones like a warm-up or stretching exercises, or theory – which however had never entered his head and which nobody, least of all Nancy, demanded of him. So he did not fight it, and let himself be carried along in the same way that other people – on a journey, for example – put up with music they would never have chosen but which, precisely because of its vulgarity, lack of ambition, or simplicity, produces the perfect narcotic effect they need in order to be able to fall asleep.

One afternoon he returned to his refuge on the twenty-second floor in Núñez – exhausted not only from a quick gallop with Nancy on the back seat of her car, but also because Boni, as happened from time to time, had converted his hormonal chaos into aggressive energy and had pushed him to the limit – and found all his hypotheses proven true. His predecessor, the tennis coach he had replaced, was lying on a mat in shorts with his robot's leg up on a weights machine while the trainer knelt beside him and massaged his good leg. When he saw Rimini, he became nostalgic and asked after his former pupils, listening carefully to the reports. He applauded the progress Damian had made (progress Rimini had quickly invented to give himself airs), made excuses for Boni (for whom he had a weakness), and added his own sympathetic comments about the 'ladies', admitting he missed their hopelessness almost as much as their end-of-year presents. When Rimini reached Nancy – he had left her to last on purpose, calculating that by doing so the coach would understand how important she was to him – the other man looked up at him in astonishment. 'Nancy?' he asked. 'Is Nancy still going?' Rimini nodded. 'You must be worn out. How often?' 'Twice a week.' 'Ah,' the coach said, 'You're lucky. I had her four times.'

That, and the knowing look the two other men exchanged, was enough for Rimini to realise just what he had inherited. But this suggestion, which for him was a fleeting but complete enough version of the truth, and therefore needed no further comment, was for the coach simply the aperitif. The main course came next: the examples, a complete illustration of what had happened, which he related without thinking, without even having to make the effort of remembering, as if his intimacy with Nancy were not stored up in his memory but in a much closer and more convenient file, that he could access by stretching out his hand: Nancy lathered in soap in the showers, her face pressed up against the tiles; Nancy with the grip of her new titanium racquet between her legs; Nancy on all fours, her towelling wristband stifling her cries; Nancy up against the wire-netting; Nancy dangling from the parallel bars in the gym; Nancy with her mouth full; Nancy spattered with . . . and while he was creating a portrait of Nancy in his own words (underlined by brutally graphic descriptions such as 'human suction pump', 'bottomless pit', 'sick in the cunt') and the trainer slapped his knees and celebrated this picaresque adventure as if this were the first time he was hearing it, although it was perfectly obvious he had heard and repeated all the details a thousand times, Rimini could feel a burning sensation at the back of his eyes; his mouth went dry, his lips felt swollen, and something dark and heavy filled his throat. He kept a tight hold of the tennis bag he still had slung over his shoulder, as if that were the only way he could stay upright. When he realised the burning came from tears, he excused himself – the two men's laughter drowned out his words – and ran to shut himself in the bathroom. And it was there, in his fugitive solitude, that he fully understood what the sudden onset of emotion had signalled: all those anecdotes, apparently meant to condemn Nancy to a hell of vulgarity, in fact only absolved her. And he, who previously if he had been forced to do so, would have described her with the same scorn as the tennis coach, now all of a sudden felt they were not talking about the same person, as though the original Nancy – whose name had been enough to unleash this incredible flow of obscene betrayals of confidence – had, simply by coming into contact with all this derision, given birth to two different women. One of them, defenceless, was still struggling in the hands of her executioner, while the other, somehow purified, was beginning to make her way into the only part of Rimini where nobody (least of all Rimini) could have suspected she might gain access: his heart.

No, he did not love her, because any kind of love would have driven him to demand she change, to want to redeem her, to assault her duplicity in the hope that one of the two women she was would defeat and suppress the other. And the emotion Rimini began to feel whenever he saw her, that sort of intimate, inadmissible quaking which, had they noticed it, the tennis coach and the trainer would doubtless have dismissed as a passing hallucination – so convinced were they that Nancy, the insatiable, vain Nancy who made them laugh so much, could produce any effect in a man barring real emotion – this emotion was born precisely out of that duplicity, from that unbelievable contrast – like that rare kind of beauty which is born and flourishes in the foulest of pigsties and which, if removed and transplanted somewhere else that is more responsive to its needs or at least less hostile to its nature, its 'natural' surroundings as they are normally called, would not survive a single moment. The Nancy that so moved him was not 'another' Nancy, but the same one as always: the empty Nancy, stripped of all feeling by her own spitefulness, her rancour, her rapacious attitude towards the world – the same Nancy who for the tennis coach meant only erections, scorn and violence. Yes, perhaps Rimini felt sorry for her. And perhaps the way that Nancy remained faithful to herself, the way she had of persisting in her vulgarity, was what had brought about the change in Rimini. No, he did not love her; bit by bit he was becoming her saint. And just as when a saint kisses a wound, he kisses injustice, the calvary and therefore the purest reserves of humanity that are manifest in sick features or skin, so Rimini was redeeming – through the silence of his secret kisses, because one of the solidest bases of the emotion he felt was the impossibility to communicate it – the avidity, lack of respect, and overbearing attitude that Nancy treated him to twice a week.

This was the same power of disassociation that had so surprised him a fortnight earlier, that afternoon in the kitchen, but raised to a higher plane, where his egocentric distractions had been replaced by a vague but persistent wish to do good. Whereas before Rimini let himself be swept along, allowing inertia to take the decisions neither he nor his body dared take on their own, now he was ready to take responsibility. Now he was there, in the most moral (most generous) meaning of the term. And he was there not because he was responding to the urgency of desire, which after all would only have meant substituting one kind of inertia for another, but to smuggle an extra, anti-carnal dimension into the carnal economy they were part of, a dimension in which, without her knowing it, Nancy displayed her naked, scraped-dry soul to him, and Rimini, instead of turning away and avoiding the spectacle (horror, pure unimaginable horror), looked straight at it. By simply doing that, by being there, he not only understood how naked she was, but also offered her protection, helping – if only for the few frenzied moments of their coitus – to alleviate the glacial cold she must be feeling in her world. But Nancy was not allowed to know this. Rimini took the discretion shown by those philanthropists who will only donate money if their anonymity is guaranteed and raised it to an almost incongruous level: in his case it was not the identity of the donor that he wanted kept secret, but the donation itself. That was his only privilege.

He was there. He contributed by being available, and he had that rarest of gifts, the ability to be invisible and accidental. It was almost a tautology: to be there, Rimini did not need to do anything but be there. What was most extraordinary was that for his donation to reach its destination – and, unlike donations in general, which never pass from one side to the other without being damaged or losing something on the way, without giving rise to some kind of doubt, suspicion or misunderstanding – the donation he was offering, as it had no need to travel, was guaranteed to arrive intact, and did not even have to appear like a donation. There was nothing personal or unique about it; anyone could take it for something else entirely, at any moment, and with every right in the world – and, since it was undefined, it placed no obligation on the person receiving it; there was nothing to pay.

Inertia does not produce change. In fact, it does not produce anything. At most, it allows something to happen: decay, for example, or entropy. Change though does produce things: inertia for example. But who would be so bold as to affirm that the difference between something changing and something deteriorating, between a sign of change and one of deterioration, is really different? Unmoving, solid, Rimini was there for Nancy in the same way that his racquet was always there, at the net, bringing out blisters and callouses at the base of his fingers, returning (only returning, not speeding up or aiming elsewhere) the balls that Nancy hit at him with a groan, with an effort that seemed always to leave her on the point of collapse, as if she had to re-supply herself with energy from zero at every stroke, to find fresh strength in a distant and almost exhausted source. Rimini fulfilled his role: something that was already quite a lot for a convalescent. He made no attempt to go any further; he did not want to add or achieve anything. He did not expect anything from Nancy she herself did not want to give or ask him for. And Nancy, who in more than one sense had reached a strange state of perfection, so much so that satisfaction – that mechanical exercise she took part in with Rimini every Tuesday and Thursday – had done away with all her ideas of enjoyment, happiness, pain, loneliness, all the unanswerable dilemmas that usually prevented her from living or made her life a misery. Nancy also stayed in the same position, the only one in which she could claim to be a good pupil, because on court she still ran in a straight line (which explained the scabs on her knees), did not keep her eye on the ball (so that she kept hitting it all over the place), and insisted on never bending her knees (which meant that two out of three of her shots ended in the net).

And yet, like all forces without energy, inertia does allow for subtle movements, tremors that appear, make themselves felt for a moment, and then subside, until the chance stimulus that produced them happens again and they reappear, in a cycle that follows a pattern which, considered individually, never results in any change in the world they impinge on but which does leave the distant echo of a sound that could be taken as the memory or the prophecy of change. In the same way that a lazy traveller falls asleep on the deck of a ship until all of a sudden he is woken by a shaft of light or the cry of a gull, then looks around him and, still half-asleep, at the same time as he recognises everything he sees – the sea, the infinite horizon, the sky – senses that something subtle but indescribable has changed, but only when he tries to stand up and finds himself staggering does he notice that the deck is tilted over, and thus realises that what has changed in the view around him is not exactly part of that view but is in the 'before' from which he was contemplating it, which is now affected by a fresh instability (brought on by the waves, an instability he had not been aware of when he fell asleep), so at some point Rimini sensed that his 'being there' for Nancy, simply by reason of its obstinacy, had permitted something to tilt, to shift sideways in a way that threatened to lead to something else . . . for example, after their exertions in the shed, Rimini would bend down and tie her shoe-laces. Or in the car, aching from the contortions that the back seat had obliged him to perform, he would pick up her old parking slips. Or he tidied her clothes, smoothing out the creases with his hands. Or he pulled out the collar of her tennis top, which had bashfully curled up inside. Or, lying on the sloping lawn beside the pool into which, thanks to a completely surprise telepathic inspiration, they had dived before their class, he cleaned bits of grass off her back. Or he carried the bag that a few minutes earlier she had pushed under her waist so that their bodies would be at the same height, and deposited it in the car for her. Or he bought her cigarettes in the machine at the bar. Or he paid (with money she had given him) for the drink she had left half-finished on the terrace table.

As the days went by, Rimini's functions multiplied: he was her chauffeur, her message and errand boy. It was a gradual process, which Nancy accepted quite naturally, as though the presence of this shadow that was beginning to follow her everywhere was not so much a sudden privilege as the recognition of a right she had always had, and only been deprived of as the result of a terrible injustice. But, contrary to what might have been expected, this increase in his functions, which also increased the areas of Nancy's life that Rimini came into contact with, did not reduce the distance between them, or even help to disguise it with the kind of casual froth – light-hearted banter, shared intimacies – that often serves to lubricate this kind of relationship. When Rimini saw her in action outside the club (which by this point had been reduced to a stage-set that was so convenient it seemed to have been especially designed for the two activities they practised there) he realised how far Nancy was a social invalid, someone left completely helpless by the slightest involvement with someone else. It was as if she knew only a strictly limited range of the language necessary for the everyday exchanges she encountered – giving orders, protesting, grumbling (all of them characterised by the same hostility, the same physicality), whereas all the others – precisely those most employed in the commerce of daily life – asking, doubting, agreeing – were completely beyond her grasp, so alien to her that not only did she never utter them, but she was totally flummoxed by the fact (quite a common one) that other people used them with her. (And how quickly she went from bewilderment to fury whenever someone – a cashier, taxi-driver, or bank clerk – repeated the question which she, unable to understand it because to her ears the words sounded as though they had been spoken in some foreign language, had deliberately ignored – as though whatever the question was, the other person's insistence forced her into a position in which she felt humiliated).

So a visit to the hairdresser, a shopping excursion, or a session in the gym – all of them activities whose regularity should have made them perfectly familiar to her – ended up being (for her, and now also for Rimini, who followed her every move) the source of extraordinary potential conflict. Every contact – a doubt about a size or a price, a delay in processing her credit card payment, losing a parking slip – contained a thousand possibilities for disaster. Isolated by the vehemence, the voracity and the demanding nature of her capricious needs, which turned the slightest difficulty into an intolerable insult, and which were the defining characteristics of her behaviour, Nancy was rude, domineering, and at the same time displayed a regal disdain. Rimini had already suffered from these defects twice a week and in double measure, both on the tennis court, where any suggestion he made about her technique gave rise to a snort, an argument or even a refusal to go on with the class, and in the shed, the car or the sloping lawn next to the swimming pool, where Nancy (as on that occasion on the kitchen table) was the one whose needs determined the rhythm and content of their sexual couplings. Now, however, he unexpectedly felt a kind of vengeance when he saw the same scorn being poured out over shop assistants, shampoo girls, lift attendants, waiters. What was hard to understand was why there was never any reaction. Rimini at least had the excuse of sexual release. Perhaps the condition of being a 'client' was a limiting factor, reducing the tension in a situation before everything got completely out of hand, partly due to the submissive attitude every employer instills in their staff when they are training them to attend customers, partly due to the expectations Nancy created whenever she showed the contents of her bulging purse, and the completely careless way she threw her money on to the counter.

After a while by contrast, Rimini, who lacked any social graces, found himself becoming attentive, affable and resourceful, capable of putting up with everything, like a diplomat or public relations expert, if this meant avoiding any friction. Nancy sniffed things out, poked them, tried them, praised, paid, or signed; Rimini was the one who did the talking, asked questions, negotiated, complained or gave thanks. He was the one who ensured that these transactions did not degenerate into bloody battles, but kept a reasonably human aspect. Seen from afar, even without knowing them it was obvious they were lovers, or that the invisible link between them (because in public they avoided all physical contact and hardly even spoke to each other) was a sexual one. As Rimini occasionally discovered when he turned back to the till where they had just paid and caught the cashiers whispering to each other, this produced a confused reaction that was a combination of disgust, envy, and excitement, but there was also something in the image they projected, possibly their increasingly smooth interaction or a certain hygienic air they had which made them seem like a foreign couple, or one of those unequal pairs who are joined together by some basic needs, such as, for example, a female ambassador in a foreign country and her local male secretary; as a foreigner, she will always be slightly apart, and yet at the same time she is the one who takes all the decisions, while he is on the look-out at the border of their situation, one eye looking inwards, the other out, always attentive and busy, as if trying to compensate by all his initiatives for the lack of movement by his employer. And as always happens with this sort of couple, who become stuck in all the protocols surrounding them, Rimini and Nancy did not progress: they stayed at the same point. She was a queen in exile, the queen of a minor kingdom, created thanks to one of those strokes of luck – a diamond mine, the discovery of oil – with which nature blesses countries previously condemned to misery – and exiled in an even more wretched country than the one she had left behind. He was her slave.

One radiant morning, they had gone, still dressed in their tennis clothes, to a suburban supermarket attracted by one of those spectacular offers, full of amazing prices and exclamation marks, that seemed to have an almost religious fascination for Nancy. Rimini, who was pushing a fully loaded trolley, lifted his gaze and saw her standing at the check-out, her crotch pushing gently against the aluminium counter edge. The contrast between the white of her pleated skirt, her tanned thighs, and the metallic grey of the counter gave him a confused feeling. He thought at first it was embarrassment, or a sense of shame, or the sign that he was repenting, trying to blot out everything he had lived with Nancy over the past months. But it was desire. And if he understood this, it was not thanks to his own powers of introspection, which would have called for an honesty far beyond his capacities, but because he saw it reflected in Nancy's eyes, which were staring at him in a puzzled way. Before he could disguise it, Rimini realised he had blushed.

They left, and loaded the car. Nancy wanted to drive. Rimini dropped the keys into her open palm and walked round the front of the car, staring at her the whole time as though watching over her. They travelled a few blocks in complete silence. They were going down a narrow tree-lined street when Nancy stamped on the brakes, pulled the wheel to the left, and drove into a hotel car park. It was almost deserted, but it took her half a dozen manoeuvres to park alongside a Ford Falcon family saloon: so close that Rimini had to be careful not to scratch the door when he got out. He squeezed his way out in fact, and as he did so could not help taking a quick look inside the other car, doubtless attracted by past memories Falcons held for him. On the back seat he saw a whole collection of polystyrene containers, arranged in order of size, some of them square, others round or rectangular. They all seemed to be floating on a bed of powdery snow. Despite the fact that he had important (or at least urgent) things to think about – the meaning of this sexual digression he was about to embark on with Nancy, for example, which disrupted in such an extraordinary way a routine that had always seemed inflexible – the image of that snowy landscape, like those tiny villages enclosed in snow globes that are always at the mercy of the silent storms that hit them whenever someone turns them over or shakes them, stayed with him all the way across the parking lot. They followed some neon arrows down a corridor, then pushed open a door and came out into, or rather entered, a reception room where everything – floors, walls, ceiling, even the pedestal supporting a plaster Venus caught in mid-flight – was covered in carpet. Surprisingly, Nancy took charge: she asked for the cheapest room, and only accepted the TV remote control after being assured it was included in the price. Rimini meanwhile had called the lift and was trying to recognise the song competing with the noise of the waterfall in the background. Roberto Carlos. Roberto Carlos in Spanish, with the weak 'r's and the pronounced 's's that Rimini (who as an adolescent had heard them incessantly throughout the whole of one summer, one of those periods of doing nothing, torrid heat, and reclusion that he had taken advantage of to masturbate up to four times a day) seemed to have kept in some particularly inaccessible or useless corner of his memory. Yes, it was Roberto Carlos, but what was the song: 'Details'? 'Words'? He opened the lift door, allowed Nancy to leave first, and as he looked down at her feet, with her trainers caked in clay dust, and the pom-poms on her socks slightly askew so that it looked as if they were sprouting from her ankles, he saw a few bits of polystyrene stuck in the groove under the door. He found still more upstairs, sprinkled like a trail all along the corridor carpet. Nancy went into their room. Rimini dawdled outside for a moment, and followed the white trail with his eyes. Three doors down, a couple were arguing, bathed in a blood-red light. The woman was tall, masculine-looking, with slow, heavy gestures; the man was bald and slightly-built. Rather than talking, he seemed to be buzzing around her like a frantic wasp. When they realised they had been seen, they suddenly fell silent, and turned towards

Rimini, who, without thinking, dismissed the woman and fixed his gaze on the man. He saw dark eyes lined with black circles, saw the sudden way that the anxious gleam in them changed into a grimace of astonishment and shame, and all at once the Ford Falcon, the containers on the back seat, the balls of polystyrene, converged as though attracted by an invisible magnet on a central point, and made sense: it was Rodi, Sofia's father. The polystyrene king. Rimini was surprised yet again at his small, perfectly proportioned body, like an acrobat's or jockey's. Before he followed Nancy into their room, Rimini saw him raising a hand.

They went at each other standing up, without undressing or switching a light on or off, with an urgency Rimini had not felt since their first time together and which helped him forget for a few moments at least the image of Sofia's father. Ten minutes later – Nancy was having a shower, Rimini was getting more than his fill of a multi-racial orgy in black-and-white – and there was a knock at the door. Thinking Nancy must have ordered something to drink, Rimini lifted the cover of the peep-hole, and was greeted by Rodi's face, tense yet grinning like a puppet. They stood there for a while, staring and sizing each other up through the tiny window that was like a defect in the wood. Rodi was trying to say something, his body jerking as if in response to sudden impulses that had faded by the time they reached the surface. Rimini was overwhelmed by the same endless irritation he had felt for years without ever being able to resolve it. He remembered how he used to be driven mad by Rodi's impatience, his constant scatter-brained inability to concentrate on any one thing and complete it without changing his mind on the way. He remembered long car journeys to the coast: trips that could take six, seven, or even eight hours, and which Rodi, who insisted on driving the whole way and would never allow himself to be replaced, somehow managed to transform into one long calvary because of all his compulsive tics. He would switch on the radio and then twirl the dial first in one direction and then the other, without pausing for more than a couple of seconds on any single station, just long enough for any music, however innocuous, to sound hateful, before finally switching the radio off again with a brusque, dismissive gesture, as if the producers of the twenty or thirty stations he had flicked through were to blame, rather than the lunatic speed he had listened to them. Then, five minutes later, just when his travelling companions were beginning to enjoy the newly regained silence, he would enthusiastically switch the radio on again, as if in the hope that everything might have changed in that short space of time. Or he would suddenly accelerate as fast as he could, wrench the wheel and overtake a lorry whose slow pace he had been cursing out loud for the previous quarter of an hour, only to take his foot off the accelerator immediately as though taken aback by his own audacity, slow down again and continue at the same speed as he had been going before, once again starting to curse the lorry driver who by now of course had taken advantage and overtaken them again. Everyone who travelled with him, his wife included, inevitably emerged from these torture sessions with their nerves in tatters, feeling nauseous, and secretly swearing to themselves they would store up the memory of all they had just suffered in order never to have to go through it again.

Rimini wrapped himself in a towel and went out into the corridor. Rodi, in underpants and a white t-shirt, with his shirt unbuttoned at the bottom, flung himself on Rimini and, clinging to his body, hugged him with animal determination. Rimini was aware of his short arms feeling around blindly, as though searching him for weapons. They stepped back. Rodi was short of breath; he kept glancing up at Rimini and tapping his arm as if to make sure he was real. 'Disappeared,' said Rodi. 'We never see you any more. You were so lucky to have us as your in-laws ... How long was it: thirteen years? All that time, my God! And we loved you so much'. For a split second, Rimini could identify with this emotion that impelled him to try to say everything at once and so excuse his chaotic jumble of words. He looked at Rodi, almost naked, shrunken by age and yet still so lively, so full of the empty, directionless adolescent energy that, at sixty, led him to fling himself into the most extravagant existential adventures, from reiki and the tea ceremony to tai-chi and nudist therapies, taking in spiritual retreats, corporal expression and reflexology along the way. Freed from the protocol of father and son-in-law that had usually conditioned their relations, Rimini felt almost affectionate towards him. But on second glance, it seemed to Rimini there was something more, that the emotion whose childish purity had touched him was contaminated by another, more selfish sentiment which that emotion (however genuine) was in some way helping to conceal: it was fear. Rodi was terrified: his ex-son-in-law had just found him in a hotel with a woman who was not his wife. Seen in this new light, and as everything that had been blurred a moment earlier became clearer, as the agitation, the smiles, the joyful anguish, the little taps on the arm and the moist gleam in Rodi's eyes lost their spontaneity and turned into techniques of dissuasion, of keeping him quiet or bribing him, all of them aimed at silencing him, Rimini, who until then had remained more or less neutral, the witness to a strange situation rather than someone involved in it, felt himself sliding slowly towards an abyss of melancholy. He remembered how often Sofia, in a state of extreme anger and disillusion, had confessed to him her suspicion that her father was leading a double life. She mistrusted his secretaries, the women in the factory, the young girls he employed to promote new polystyrene lines. All the group activities he devoted his free time to – all the time he refused to spend with his wife – activities he always flung himself into with unbounded enthusiasm, as if, after searching in vain for years, he had at last found the panacea for all his ills – only to drop them casually a fortnight later, no longer in the slightest bit interested, and blaming his abandonment on trivial details, such as a problem of timetables, a falling-out with someone in the group, a tiny physical problem which, transformed by Rodi's own peculiar alchemy, changed from cause to effect – all the disciplines and practices he pursued so fanatically (all of them linked to the 'interior world' which he always complained was in such a bad shape) all the groups he formed part of (full of lonely, suffering women and charismatic women teachers, experts in the most hidden secrets of body and soul) – all this world of seminars, courses, workshops, marathons (whose 'despair factor,' as she called it, Sofia was perfectly familiar with, since she herself devoted all her time to them) – for her (and for her mother, with whom, sometimes even with Rimini present, she shared her suspicions) this was nothing more than a decoy, a smokescreen, or possibly the true core of a clandestine life. And now that the truth had come to light, or at least to the sinful glow bathing the two of them in red in this hotel corridor, Rimini, who had never before been particularly interested in uncovering it, partly because even the more pathetic forms of being an adulterer seemed to him ill-suited to this fearful little man who instinctively shied away from anything new, who preferred to go on wearing his old, patched-up pullovers (running the risk that his clients would take him for a tramp) rather than to have to go to a shop and buy new ones, and partly because he dismissed Sofia's suspicions as a kind of universal feminine axiom, now discovered for himself how sad history can be when it becomes ironic. Because the truth that Sofia and her mother had searched for over so many years, and for which at the time (when Rimini was still part of their lives) they would have been willing to make any sacrifice – that truth was doubly superfluous: it came out now, when it was too late, and it was revealed to him, who had never gone looking for it, and who no longer had any link with the world it could dynamite. While Rimini was beginning to wonder whether this perhaps explained the catastrophic fate of human truth – not that there was no such thing, but the fact that the truth always appeared at the wrong moment, when the mystery it was meant to solve had already been forgotten, and never fell into the hands of those who were searching for it or needed it – he heard a strange sound, the rub of leather, a muffled clinking, and suddenly saw the woman coming impatiently out of their room, wearing a chain round her neck, her bare bosom criss-crossed with black thongs, and a slender rubber whip quivering in her hand. Separated from Rodi, she no longer looked so huge. Rodi did not turn round. 'Ah, I have to go; that's life,' he said, taking a business card out of his shirt pocket and almost forcing it on Rimini. 'Come and see me. I might have something for you. I know you've been having a few little problems . . . Sofia is one thing, we're another. We love you, you know. We love you a lot. We always ask ourselves . . . Or drop in at home. That would be really nice.' He put both palms flat on Rimini's chest as though massaging him, then walked off backwards down the corridor, still looking at him, while the woman disappeared again into the room. Rimini had the impression he was crying. 'Drop in sometime, why don't you? Promise me you will. Just drop in,' he said, as his small, bare, aged child's feet slid back along the turquoise carpet.

CHAPTER 6

The next two nights Rimini slept badly. He could not find a suitable position; he tried the usual ones but they seemed unreal, uncomfortable, like clothes two sizes too small, while any new ones kept him happy for a while, but then after a few minutes he emerged even more irritated, and turned over again. When finally he did drift off, the layer of sleep was so thin and slight, and he was so conscious of its fragility, that he slept in a state of permanent tension, moving as little as possible, as though he was lying on a sheet of glass. On Thursday, he woke up in the early morning, with all the covers off. His whole body ached, and he was stiff with cold. Almost as soon as he opened his eyes he repeated out loud a phrase from a dream he did not remember having: 'Loving is what bodies do, and we now are no more than phantoms.' A lost fragment of some translation or other, he thought. He decided to take the morning off, and not go to the club, but made the mistake of admitting it over breakfast. The trainer talked him out of it with one of those terrorist gym arguments he used to quash any revolt born of weakness. To mitigate his harshness, he served him a double portion of cereal. Then came the morning exercise routine, which Rimini went through mechanically. For the first time, he cheated: he took advantage of the trainer concentrating on his exercises to shorten his own, to leave parts out, to falsify the count. At one point he stopped and looked alongside him: instead of seeing and recognising the trainer, or not exactly seeing him but instantly accepting the idea he had of him before looking at him, what he saw (as though on an anatomical chart) was pure muscular structure, tendons and ligaments wrapped around an invisible frame, a play of shapes and lights, contractions and dilations, all of it accompanied by a monotonous music from the lungs. This vision, as bloody as a butcher's table, made him retch; he turned over quickly on the mat to hide it. Something in the obedient machinery of his life had gone wrong.

At the club, the crisis hit. Befuddled by his tiredness, which made moving slow and painful, Rimini had to hurry. He abbreviated his preparations as much as he could and, nerves on edge, made it in time for the first lesson. But Damian was late, and this forced Rimini, who was still keyed up and on edge, to do all he could to slow down, and adapt to having nothing to do. Just as Rimini was about to call the class off, Damian finally turned up – which meant another change of rhythm – and he was even more irritable than usual, so that for an hour and a half (it was the start of the month, and Damian threatened not to pay unless Rimini gave him the full lesson) he chewed gum and sang, two liberties Rimini never normally permitted his pupils. Towards the end of the class Rimini, still feeling annoyed – which explained the unusual aggression with which he forced Damian to chase the most demanding shots – reduced the speed he was returning the balls in the rally, told him they were going to practise volleys now, and drew him in towards the net by dropping each return a bit shorter. Damian grew more confident; he came up to the net hitting the ball as hard as he could, and Rimini responded with low, not particularly strong but well-directed drives that forced him to the sidelines, shouting to him that he should keep them covered. The youngster blocked three passing shots on the run, one to his right, the next to the left, the third to his right again, but just as he was preparing to hit the ball back on his left a second time (as that seemed to be the logical sequence of play) Rimini hit a monstrously fierce drive straight at him, as if the trajectory had been drawn by a ruler. It hit Damian right between the eyes. Still grasping his racquet, he fell on to his backside, stared in complete astonishment, and then fainted. Rimini leapt over the net and bent down to help him. The chewing gum was poking out of a corner of his mouth like a timid pink insect. Five minutes later, Damian was sitting on the bench in tears, pressing a towel with ice cubes in it on to the reddish bump that was already starting to swell in between his eyebrows. Trying to suppress a desire to punish him still further, Rimini was glancing vaguely at the club terrace when he saw – at first with surprise, then with a disturbing sense of anxiety – how his next two pupils (Nancy and Boni) were coming out together into the sunlight (it even seemed to him Boni was carrying her tennis bag) and then sitting down at the table where Nancy usually had her drink in the sun. He saw them exchange a few words and then fall silent, wave away the waiter who had come over to serve them, and finally point towards him, Rimini, or something close to him. Rimini got rid of Damian as quickly as he could. Everything was happening so quickly, and yet the hurry he was in had nothing to do with time. Nevertheless after the boy had left, a wounded unicorn dragging his bag and his racquet along the ground, where they left two long furrows, the first thing that Rimini did, after signalling to Boni to come down to the court, was to consult his watch, make a mental calculation, and convince himself that seeing the two of them together at this hour of the morning – they usually ran into each other between classes, never before – was not so much a novelty as an aberration.

Boni was the opposite of Damian: he could hardly move. He dragged himself round the court like an invalid, head down and sunken-chested, and instead of running simply stuck his racquet out not so much at the ball (which he would have done if he were really trying to return it) as in the general direction (calculated more in function of his laziness than of its real trajectory) of where it might possibly bounce. Then, as he swished the racquet and only succeeded in creating a small breeze, while the ball continued on its way and crashed into the wire netting at the back of the court, he would raise his eyes to the heavens, give a strangled cry of self-reproach, and stand leaning on the net for a few moments, head drooping to one side as he wiped off the beads of a sweat that existed only in his imagination. It was during one of these uneasy moments, which the adolescent of course knew how to fake like an expert, and which Rimini tried to avoid by hitting him balls on the volley, as though he were aiming at one of those human-shaped targets in an old-fashioned fairground – it was then that Rimini, who had just suggested they change ends (in the slightly malicious hope that having the sun in his face might wake Boni up) caught sight of the purple mark on the side of his neck. As they crossed at the net, Rimini tried to make a joke of it: 'You must have had a wild night,' he whispered. Boni said nothing, but changed ends with his racquet draped over a shoulder like a shovel. Rimini spent the last ten minutes of the class wreaking vengeance for the shock he had received. First of all he put up high lobs, which forced Boni to look into the sun and blinded him. Then he hit hard, low drives right into the corners. And once the class had finished, he forced him to pick up all the balls scattered around his side of the court. Still dazzled by the sun, Boni looked round and saw himself surrounded by a sea of yellow: all the balls were on his side. 'When I get back I want to see every one in the basket,' said Rimini. Boni looked at him beseechingly, but Rimini was already striding away towards the clubhouse.

He leapt up the steps three at a time, ran across the terrace, and went into the bar in search of Nancy. The room was empty. He emerged into the lobby, where an electrician was busy with a bunch of cables at the top of a ladder. Out of the corner of his eye, Rimini saw his name had been mutilated on the noticeboard: the two first letters of his name had come unstuck and were lying at the bottom between the baize and the frame. He poked his head into the ladies' changing-room: it was empty and shiny from a recent spraying, so when he heard the sound of a door closing, he returned to the bar. Still no one. He began to be worried: he felt as though as soon as his back was turned, things began to move, but when he looked at them, they came to a halt again. He went out on to the terrace, shaded his eyes with his hand, and looked all round the club: the paddle tennis courts, the *pelota* walls, the tool-shed, the pool, the tennis courts, delaying as long as he could the moment when he came to his own court, where he expected to see Boni still picking up the balls one by one, like some elegant stork. But the court was clear: the balls were all in the basket, and Boni seemed to be in animated conversation with Nancy. She was standing with her back to Rimini, one hand raising the hem of her tennis skirt to scratch her thigh, while Boni sat on the bench, staring down as he drew geometric patterns in the dust with his racquet grip. Rimini blinked; he had to close and open his eyes, then look at the pair again to be sure that what he was seeing was really happening. Could it be possible? Mentally, he went over the different ways of getting from the clubhouse to the court: it was very odd that he and Nancy had not bumped into each other. He leapt down the steps, not taking his eyes off the two of them for a second. He sensed that Nancy stiffened, as though realising he was coming towards them. Boni stopped doodling on the ground, stowed his racquet in his bag, and walked out of the court by the path that ran parallel to the train tracks.

Rimini hesitated: should he follow the attacker, or assist the victim?

He thought about following the boy and questioning him, but when he saw Nancy smoking one of her mile-long cigarettes and practising shots in the air without a ball, the shameless look of repleteness on her face made him decide to go into the court instead. He stammered a greeting, sat on the bench, picked up a towel and then dropped it, and rummaged in the bottom of his bag without really looking for anything, just to buy time. He turned and saw that Boni was disappearing in the distance, and sprang to his feet, rushed at Nancy, then tried to kiss her. All he succeeded in doing was to tear a button off her top. He kneeled down to try to find it, pretended to be searching the ground, then all at once flung his arms round her legs as though begging for mercy. Nancy pushed him away with her racquet. 'Please, do me a favour. Don't be so ridiculous,' she said. 'Let's go to the shed right now,' said Rimini. 'No.' 'To the car; let's go there.' 'No.' 'To the lawn then.' 'No, not today,' she said, 'I'm exhausted.' She crushed her cigarette on the ground, stole two balls out of the basket and, rejuvenated, light, ran to the back of the court, where she started doing little warm-up jumps and bouncing the balls, as if to challenge him. In a rally a few minutes later, Rimini suddenly changed rhythm and took advantage of a low, deep backhand he had hit to come up to the net. But this time, Nancy did not stay on the baseline waiting for it; she ran forward, met it in mid-air, and lobbed it back over his head. Taken by surprise, Rimini tried to reach it with a backhand smash, but was blinded by the sun and missed the ball completely. It sailed blithely on towards his baseline, but Rimini's wounded pride would not let him give up, and he somehow managed to catch up with the ball. But it hit the tape, which was sticking up slightly, and bounced off at an angle, so that Rimini missed it a second time. As it bobbled away to the back of the court, Rimini tripped over the tape and found himself face down in the clay dust.

Nancy was inspired. It was as though she had woken, starving, from her prolonged lethargy, and was pure concentration: she ran everywhere, and fought for every ball as if she were playing a championship final. Disconcerted, Rimini started to interrupt the lesson. He stopped rallies to correct the slightest thing, with the same concern he had previously shown for keeping the rhythm of the game going. At his third or fourth comment, delivered with stinging sharpness, as though

384

he were speaking to an idiot, Nancy counter-attacked. She objected to every correction he made, invoking principles taught by his predecessor, and after a few minutes moved on from this technical argument to more personal comments, where the problems were ones of 'atmosphere', 'communication', or even of 'skin'. Nancy was smiling as she made her remarks, with a thoughtful expression that seem to be taking her far, far away. Rimini did not have to give it much thought to realise exactly where: it was a distant country he knew well. He had a vivid memory of the partial views of it his predecessor had shown him that afternoon in the Núñez apartment. And now, as he observed Nancy's flushed cheeks and the secret glow of contentment in her face, they all flashed through his mind once more, like postcards from a world of delights which on that occasion had sickened him, and now wounded him mercilessly: 'pumpkin belly', 'human leech', 'carnivorous plant', 'suction pump' . . . the class went on a while longer, but on its own, without them: Nancy never really recovered from the daze she was in, and Rimini never managed to get out of his hell. The spectacle crucifying him had too many layers; every time he stripped one off, hoping to feel better, another immediately surfaced, even more obscene and repulsive than the one before: now the coach, Nancy, and Boni (displaying all the typical enthusiasm of a newcomer), were intertwined in a whole series of ghastly circus-style contortions. Rimini could not stand it any longer, and said the lesson was over. Nancy looked at her watch and, still smiling, pointed out that there were twelve minutes to go. But Rimini was no longer there to hear her.

He reached his Núñez apartment in a desperate state. There was a pulse beating in his temples, his mouth was bone dry, and he was shaking so much it took him five minutes to fit the key in the lock. When he finally managed to get in, the brightness of the empty apartment enveloped him in a sandstorm of light. He collapsed on to the sofa and sat without moving for a few minutes, staring at the misty glare that veiled the horizon. Then he picked up the phone and dialled Sofia's number. While waiting for an answer, he went over everything in great detail in reverse order, as though he were rewinding a tape: the tiny doll's feet padding away from him along the carpet, Rodi's trembling voice trying to bribe him, the woman standing in the corridor calling him back, whip in hand, the t-shirt under his shirt – yes, he thought, I'll tell her everything, just like that, without thinking about it, without dressing it up, as if he were sending her an anonymous message. Someone answered, throwing Rimini into confusion. He was so caught up in what he had decided to say that he was upset at being interrupted. He heard the end of a sentence: '. . . spend the night in the clinic', one of those fragments of private lives that you sometimes hear over the phone, and then a voice snapped: 'Hello; hello?' Rimini waited. 'Hello?' the voice repeated. 'Sofia?' said Rimini. Silence. 'Rimini? Is that you?' He was about to say yes when he heard three sharp thuds, as if the phone was falling down stairs, and then, for several moments, evidence of an urgent negotiation: the mother was trying to convince Sofia to let her talk – 'I'm sorry, but you're in no state to . . .' then Sofia resisting: 'You even less, mama,' then the sound of a struggle over the handset, more thuds, hysterical shouts: 'Leave me on my own! On my own, I said!' a door slamming, then everything falling silent. There was a long sigh, a startled gulp, and Sofia's quavering voice came on the line again: 'Rimini, I can't believe it. It's a miracle. I was just about to call you. I needed *so* much to talk to you. How did you find out? Was it Victor who told you? That's odd: we spoke half an hour ago and he didn't mention it. It's incredible. Life is incredible, Rimini. Do you know who papa was talking about only a minute before he had the heart attack? You. He was saying how much he missed you. The poor man. He was almost in tears. He told me he wanted to see you. He missed you.'

CHAPTER 7

It was only in the taxi, when the play of light in the tops of the plane trees, the width of the avenue and the discreet, functional elegance of the buildings (with the ancient optician's filling a whole corner) took him back to that area of his life stored in his files as 'German Hospital', a solid, unmoving image although it spanned several distinct periods, all of them linked to sadness and death, that Rimini realised he had not changed out of his tennis clothes. He had put the phone down and gone out, pausing only to pick up his keys and some money. Now as he looked down at his trainers and his uncovered legs – which the leather seat of the taxi made seem doubly naked – his sweaty wristband, his cotton shorts and towel, he could not help feeling uncomfortable, as though he were going to a funeral dressed as a clown. He felt like turning back, but stuck his head out of the window, saw he was already close to the clinic, and changed his mind when to his surprise he began to feel proud of how incongruous his clothes were. They were not an insult, but a token of how worried he was; he had heard the news of Rodi's heart attack when he was least expecting it, and it had affected him so much that he had not hesitated in dropping everything there and then and going to join Sofia and her mother in their vigil at the hospital.

Sofia was waiting for him at the door. Her hair was long and unkempt, with a broad dark stripe down one side, as though she had decided to dye it, reconsidered halfway, but had not been bothered to return it to her original colour. She was very pale, and when she ran to fling her arms round his neck as he was stepping out of the cab, Rimini was overwhelmed by the heavy perfume from her make-up, a sweet, warm sickly smell that was too much for him. He pushed her away, and looked at her: she was in tears. It seemed to him that her face was no longer human, was not bones, flesh and blood, but a kind of pink dough made of creams, powders and lotions, all of which seemed to be dissolving by the second. 'Thanks for coming. Thank you, thank you, thank you,' Sofia whispered in his ear, grabbing him again and kissing him on the chin, neck, and ear lobe with quick, desperate kisses that went up, down, and back up again. 'I was dying to call you, but didn't dare. After all that happened, I thought you wouldn't ever want to see me again. I'm sorry, Rimini. Please forgive me. I don't know what came over me. I've got a blank, you know. I don't remember a thing. I remember the hotel, the taxi, and then – nothing, a complete blank, until I'm back at my place and I look down at my hand . . . (I'm crying because I still can't believe it: it's as if I was talking about some other life, some other person) and I find I'm holding that lock of hair . . .' Rimini stroked her back to calm her down, pushed her away once more, and, adopting a dry, professional tone, asked her how her father was. Sofia fell silent, looked at him without really seeing him, then blinked several times in succession, as if she were coming out of a trance. Then she smiled, and stroked him gently, softly, in that understanding way of hers that Rimini knew so well, as though she magnanimously accepted his reasons for changing topics, and yet wanted at the same time to show him she did not agree, and even found them childish, born not of a real decision but out of fear, in other words from a desire Rimini would not yet permit himself to admit to – which made them easy to refute. Yet again, Rimini realised just how far the capacity to understand (with all its prodigious ability to seize, absorb, and assimilate) was Sofia's true talisman, the antidote which allowed her to recover so speedily and effectively, to leave behind all the bungling, disasters, and madness and convert them into massive, doomed feats of daring which served more than anything to prove just how uncaring and stupid the world was. But instead of, as she usually did, rounding off this penetrating diagnosis with her description of what he needed to do to remedy his failings, this time Sofia simply smiled once more, shook her head a couple of times as though dismissing all the arguments swirling through her mind as too trivial and, taking his arm, steered him towards the clinic entrance.

Rodi was not well. He had been in intensive care for two days, and the prognosis was not good. As he was going up in the lift with Sofia, Rimini, feeling slightly guilty, asked exactly when the heart attack had happened. 'On Tuesday evening,' Sofia told him. Everything she knew in fact was through her mother. That evening, Sofia was in Adela H., working as hard as she could for the opening. Rodi had got back from the factory later than usual. He was exhausted, said he was aching all over 'as though he had been given a beating', and was in a state of great anxiety. He took a tablet and had a bath, something he rarely did because he thought it was a woman's habit. He went to bed, and asked for his dinner to be brought there. He hardly touched it, complaining he had a bitter taste in his mouth. He dozed off for a quarter of an hour. At around ten he sat up in bed as if he had just remembered something important, and began talking about Rimini, recalling him, even reproaching himself for the careless way they had allowed their relationship with him to fade out. Sofia's mother had let him talk. It all seemed a bit peculiar, but she was pleased to see him enthusiastic about something at least. They watched a bit of television at random. As usual, Rodi would pick a channel and then five seconds later flick to something else with the remote control. When his attention was caught by an image, he sat staring at it in absorbed silence, until something he saw or heard in the programme reminded him of Rimini and his concentration would wander, he lost interest, and started channel-hopping again. Half an hour later, when his wife, worried that his anxiety did not seem to have diminished, came in with a glass of water and a second tablet, Rodi was euphoric: he pointed the remote control at the TV set, where the titles for *In the Event* were showing, followed by a documentary on the early years of the painter Riltse. 'We have to tell Sofia!' he shouted. 'And Rimini!' he shouted. 'Rimini as well!' So as not to bother him, his wife went out into the living-room. She left a message on Sofia's answering-machine and just in case, wrote down the number at Adela H. When she went back into the bedroom, she found Rodi sprawled over one side of the bed, unconscious. That had been the first attack. He had another two, which by some miracle were not fatal, in the ambulance on the way to the hospital.

No, Rimini did not know anything about Adela H., and he had not seen or heard anything about the documentary on Riltse's youth. Sofia cast him a mistrustful glance, as if there was something suspicious about this double negative. The lift came to a halt. It was only when they were in the lobby – one of those precarious, never finished spaces hospitals always use to signal an entrance to their most sensitive areas, and so dissuade the public from visiting them – that Sofia noticed Rimini was in his tennis gear. Somehow, however outlandish it looked, it seemed to chime in with the nurses' white aprons. She again asked him how he had heard about her father. Rimini hesitated. The date, the meeting in the cheap motel, Rodi's desperate confusion, the probable fear that Rimini would give the game away, and then, as if all that were not enough, the session with the woman in thongs – it all fitted. He had a mental picture of Rodi naked, sinking into the steaming hot bath, the bruises and whip marks wavering and dissolving under the watery magnifying glass, his penis shrivelling until it was almost invisible, a distant, mocking reminder of the proud organ which forty-eight hours earlier had forced its way into one of the holes (probably the least likely) of that terrifying woman. 'What made you think of calling me?' Sofia asked. Rimini shrugged and smiled, with a lack of conviction that looked like modesty. Sofia looked at him long and hard, with amorous determination: the look she always used when she intended to get to the bottom of something she suspected his silence was concealing, and not merely get to the bottom of it, but uncover it, interpret it all, not as he had done (always supposing he was aware he was hiding something, and had the courage to bring it to light and face up to it) – but in the way only she was capable of, she – who in a few years might no longer be mistress of his body or his heart – would always be in charge of, something Rimini could not ever refuse her, simply because it did not belong to him: the keys to his soul, the master keys to all his secrets. And after she had surveyed him in this way, she stood on tiptoe, took hold of his head, and, when her face was so close Rimini could not focus on it, before she kissed him she reassured him that it was not really necessary for him to tell her, that she knew he would never use the word 'telepathy', but there was no need to, because that was exactly what telepathy was, being able not to say anything, to allow words to vanish into something else, something huge, bigger, much bigger than words, something that had room for everything, even a house, the house where they had lived and were still living, where they would always live, no matter what they did.

She kissed him, then waved to the two nurses staring at them from the far side of the glass partition. She pushed open a swing door and dragged him into the base camp she and her mother had set up for the length of their vigil, a small, narrow room cluttered with half a dozen metal saline drip poles, pile upon pile of cardboard boxes, a trolley converted into a perfectly made bed – Rimini recognised the old Uruguayan blanket that twenty years earlier, on a windy March or December evening, had allowed them to frolic on the beach without getting their backs scratched with sand, and rows of sagging shelves weighed down by an arsenal of hospital accessories. Still numbed by the scene in the lobby, the misunderstanding, and the kiss, Rimini let Sofia take the lead, and reacted only when he felt the rough material of a dressing-gown between his fingers. 'What? No way,' he managed to say, but then looked down at his feet and saw they were already covered in sterilised plastic bootees. 'It'll do him good to see you,' Sofia said, putting the gown round his shoulders than dodging behind him to fasten it. 'He's got an oxygen mask, so he can't talk much, but just seeing you will be enough. He's going to be so pleased.' 'But he's in intensive care,' Rimini protested. 'We members of his family can go in. We're allowed two hours' visiting a day,' said Sofia. 'And you, like it or not, are part of the family.' 'I don't know,' he said, 'I'm easily upset. Remember when . . .' 'Don't worry. You won't see a thing,' Sofia inter- rupted him. She took a step back and surveyed him from head to toe, as if she were just about to send him out on to the catwalk at a fashion show, until the door opened and banged into her side. A doctor with a freshly shaven chin appeared, apologising. He was wearing a mask round his neck like a collar. 'Are you going in?' he asked Sofia. Sofia shook her head and pointed to Rimini. The doctor looked at him and held out a limp hand. 'This is Rimini,' she said. When the doctor heard his name, Rimini could feel his hand coming to life. 'Ah, the famous Rimini. Good, very good,' he said, shaking his hand vigorously, as though evaluating an unorthodox but promising treatment. 'Will you take him?' Sofia asked. 'Yes, of course,' said the doctor. 'This way, please.' Rimini turned sideways to get past her, and as he did so, cast her a final, doubtful glance. 'Just a moment,' she said, after studying him one last time. She stretched her hand out towards a pile of hospital clothing in a basket, and handed him a mask. Then, in a theatrical swoop of her voice, she whispered an inaudible 'thank you' to him.

The doctor led him down a corridor lit with neon tubes. Rimini felt weak, cowardly, tense. He had the almost supernatural clarity of

391

someone who after a couple of sleepless nights goes out into the street and sees lights, colours and shapes with an almost painful sharpness. The doctor was talking to him over his shoulder, in a voice that Rimini thought was far too loud for the crop of dying patients he surmised must be lying on the other side of the green-painted partitions. The doctor was praising the therapeutic value of feelings, which, in his experience, could be as effective as any clinical treatment. Rimini heard him in the distance, only half-listening, just as he heard the coughing, the sounds of the machines, the rustling of sheets, although most of his attention was on a kind of continuous low hum that seemed to be following him along the corridor. When the doctor came to a halt at a door, waiting for him, Rimini sensed that the hum had suddenly stopped as well, as if it were a sound the other man gave off as he walked along. But then he looked up and saw a burnt-out neon tube on the ceiling. The doctor opened the door, pointed for him to put the mask on, and ushered him in.

There was no blood, no needles, none of the things Rimini most feared. Rodi was lying on his side in the bed, holding the oxygen mask a few centimetres from his mouth. Rimini thought he was asleep. Sensors ran from his chest to two monitors hanging close to the bed, and a big bandage covered the vein in his forearm through which they were feeding him. Rimini went cautiously over to the bed, taking long slow steps like an astronaut in a gravity-free atmosphere. As he put one foot down, he was startled to hear a squeaking sound. He looked at the bottom of his foot: a granule of polystyrene was stuck in one of the grooves in the sole of his trainer, outside the protective covering. When he looked back at the bed, he saw Rodi staring at him with wide-open eyes. Rimini smiled, and started to smooth down the bedclothes, imitating the movements from a transition scene in a programme about medical emergencies. He rescued the blanket from where it lay crumpled at the bottom of the bed, lined it up carefully with the sheet, and then drew both of them up to Rodi's chin. He was rewarded with a grateful smile. He was still staring at Rimini; he had the shiny, protruding eyes of a fish just taken out of water. Then, with a sudden gesture that alarmed Rimini, his arm shot out from under the covers, which lifted for an instant and then fell in a heap on the floor. Rimini was treated to a fleeting vision of his naked body – two skinny legs drawn up on the bed, with large hairless patches and varicose veins on his calves – and quickly looked away. Rodi complained about the heat: he was burning up. His voice was a hoarse whisper, lacking any strength or definition, as if it were nothing more than air. He unbuttoned the front of his pyjama top and, settling on to his back, showed Rimini the landscape of his shaven chest patched with electrodes. He grabbed one of Rimini's arms with a strength he would never have dreamt him capable of, and forced him to lean closer. 'Rimini,' he said. 'Rimini,' he repeated, as if that one word summed up all that the situation required he say, but which he had no intention of saying. 'Now you're here,' he said, 'you'll do me a favour, won't you?' Rimini stared at him in silence for a few moments, and only nodded his head when Rodi tapped his cheek as if to wake him up. 'Take down this phone number, will you? 981-8725. Nine – September, the month Sofia was born. Nine minus one: eight. And one – the one you took from nine. Eight again, then take away one again: seven, two and five, in other words, seven minus two. Repeat it for me.' Rimini did as he was told, and every time he hesitated, every time he confused one of the numbers, Rodi's fingers gripped his forearm like a mechanical claw. When he had finally memorised it, Rodi muttered an inaudible thank you, smiled once more, and pulled him down towards him again. By now most of his strength had gone – the anxiety of watching Rimini learn the number off by heart seemed to have been even more exhausting for him – but he seemed contented, as if by passing this test Rimini had not only proved he had a good memory, but had advanced a number of squares on the board of his trust – exactly enough, apparently, to enable him to take the next step. 'Rimini. Listen to me,' he said, raising his head and leaving a few hairs on his pillow as he did so. 'Now you're to go, you're to go out into the street and call that number. What was it again?' '981-8725,' said Rimini. 'That's right. You're going to call – what time is it now?' 'Two o'clock. A quarter past two.' 'Perfect. You call, and a woman will answer. Her name is Ida. Like Ida Lupino. She's the woman you saw me with the other day. You're going to tell her you're calling on my behalf, on behalf of Rodi, to say that I won't be able to go to paradise today. Say just that: Rodi won't be able to go to paradise today. Tell her I had a problem, that she shouldn't worry, that everything's fine, and that I'll get in touch with her. That's all. If she

393

asks what kind of problem, you've no idea. That I'll be in touch soon. I asked you to give her the message: that's all you know. Now repeat after me: "Ida, I'm calling you on behalf of Rodi . . ." Go on, say it.' They said it together, Rodi nodding at the end of each sentence. Rimini felt an age-old sense of distress. 'Good. Very good,' Rodi sighed, finally at peace. He let his head drop back on to the pillow, and closed his eyes. Rimini looked at him. It seemed as if he were distancing himself quickly, very quickly, from everything: from himself, from the room, even from his own body. Rimini thought he was dying, and had to fight an urge to run away, as if afraid that someone would come in and, finding him there, would accuse him of speeding up Rodi's death. He was about to sneak out when he felt his arm being pulled at. 'Rimini,' the voice emerged slowly and painfully from the depths. 'I've been thinking a lot about us. About our meeting in the hotel. It means some-thing, I'm sure of it. I don't know what exactly, but then I was never very good at finding the meaning of things. I could have asked Sofia – she's an expert at that kind of stuff, as you know – but I was a bit afraid, I thought I might say too much and she'd find out all about it . . . but something put you in my path. Something wanted you to be the one to know. The only one, Rimini: you're the only one who knows. Ida is the love of my life. I've known her for thirty years, and there's nothing, absolutely nothing, she doesn't know about me' – his grip tightened – 'Listen to me. Listen carefully. Some days I wake up and I'm trembling. I open my eyes and I'm trembling; when I realise what's going on I know it's because I'm going to see her, and I go on trem-bling all day long until we meet. It's been going on for thirty years now, three times a week. And on the days I see her, I can't do a thing apart from wait for the moment when we get together. I say I'm at the factory, but either I drive the car around aimlessly, or I go to the cinema. I'm always terrified. I start thinking about all that has to happen for the two of us to get together, and it seems impossible something won't go wrong, that there won't be a problem – and I'm happy, Rimini. Happy as a sand-boy, idiotically happy. Happier than the happiest person on earth. Everything I possess is like a weight on me; I'd happily give it all to the first person I meet. The factory, the cars, the house in Valeria. All of it. I'm sixty-eight, Rimini. Do you know what people my age do? They say goodbye. Every day there's something to say goodbye to for ever. But me . . .' – clinging to Rimini's gown, Rodi had lifted his head and was very close to him, speaking now with a despairing fury – 'me, I think of Ida. I think: I don't mean I see her, or even glance at her photo. I think of her, and look what happens. Do you believe in miracles? Take a look at this.' Rimini saw him plunge his hand into his old baggy cotton Y-fronts, and pull out his penis, tiny and stiff like a plastic toy. Rimini could hear a rapid bleeping sound: one of the monitors was registering the excitement. Rodi groaned and collapsed back on to the bed. 'Calm down,' said Rimini, getting to his feet. 'Stay calm.' 'No, no,' Rodi protested. Rimini began to be alarmed. 'What?' he said. 'What's happening?' 'Too late.' Rimini offered to call the doctor. Rodi screwed up his eyes and shook his head. 'Once it's started,' he said, 'I have to go on.' Rimini stared at him, trying to interpret the meaning of his twisted mouth; when he heard the rustle of the bed sheet, he realised exactly what it was Rodi had to go on with. The bleeping started again: the peaks on the monitor became steeper, more irregular. 'What are you doing?' Rimini protested, watching the erratic lines on the screen. 'Calm down, Rodi, I don't think this is a good idea . . .' 'A good idea!' Rodi shouted, a moist glint showing at the corner of his eyelids. The rubbing stopped, but his body was still tense and rigid. By now he was crying disconsolately. 'Please,' he said, clinging to Rimini's arm once more. 'Help me.' 'Yes, of course,' said Rimini, bending over to receive instructions. Without meaning to, he leaned a hand on his chest. Rodi took a deep breath and for some inexplicable reason held it and held it until a coughing fit forced him to breathe out again. His face was already a deep purple. 'I'll call the doctor,' said Rimini. 'It must be one of these buttons.' 'No, no,' Rodi implored him. 'What I need is a hand, Rimini. The touch of someone else's skin. Lend me your hand and everything will be fine, you'll see. Just for a second. Please, your hand. Your hand will set me free.'

CHAPTER 8

They found him in the Núñez apartment. He put up no resistance: he would not have had the strength. When the two officers came in and stood next to the bike machine, one on each side as if they were guarding it, dazzled by the gleaming whiteness of the room, the still warm remains of all that was left of his energy had dripped on to the black leatherette of the weights bench. In unison, the two policemen turned their backs on the window, less out of a sense of shame or disgust than to protect themselves from the glare. Rimini took advantage to bring a cloth from the kitchen and carefully wipe up the stains. Once they had recovered, the two men showed him the legal warrant – which Rimini did not even bother to read – and asked him where the Riltse was. Rimini merely nodded towards it, and went on rubbing the same area of the floor in slow circles. The painting was hanging over the bench, held up by two weights bars, as if ready to be chopped in half by a karate blow. One of the policemen studied it from a distance, as cautiously as someone examining an unknown package that might be dangerous. He took a photo out of his pocket, and compared it with the original. He was not convinced. 'Where's the signature?' he asked. Rimini stood up, cloth in hand, turned the canvas round, and showed him the back. The policeman had difficulty following the brush-strokes. 'Spell it out for me, would you?' he asked. 'R-i-l-t-s-e,' said Rimini. As he did so, the policeman crossed each letter off on the back of his photograph. When Rimini handed him the painting, two final drops dripped from the edges of the hole, traced two parallel lines down the thick paint on the canvas, gathered at the bottom edge, and fell off in slow motion. 'Is it still wet?' the officer asked, holding it up to the light. His colleague bent down and scooped up a sample. 'It's fresh all right,' he declared, 'but it's not paint,' he said, looking down at the tip of his forefinger. His mouth twisted slowly in an expression of disgust. Rimini went back to his cleaning. He had to leave everything spotless for when the trainer arrived, he told them. The policemen looked at each other in bewilderment. 'You're under arrest,' they said.

Once, said Rimini, scrubbing as hard as he could at the edge of the bench, in the days when he used to masturbate two or even three times a day, usually at nightfall, because he had been taking cocaine and the girlfriend he was seeing (whom he later started living with, and who later still died in a traffic accident at the intersection of Corrientes and Ayacucho, as she was leaving a seminar where he had been working as an interpreter – shortly before a rare illness started wiping the small but surprising linguistic encyclopedia he had been building up all his life from his brain) was about to arrive, and he had not wanted her to find him in the anaesthetised state that cocaine usually induced in him, once, as he was about to ejaculate, he had lost control of his prick (something that happened only very rarely) and instead of splashing the tiles with his sperm as usual, he spilt a few drops on to the toilet seat – an old, wooden seat that the owner of the apartment had always refused to replace. One of the policeman leaned over, took him by the arm, and helped him up. The other, who was holding the painting well away from him as if it stank, read out the warrant. Rimini nodded and explained, as he was folding the cloth carefully into four, that no sooner had he come on that occasion than he had wiped up the splashes with a floor cloth he kept hidden behind the toilet, the spots on the floor and on the seat which, although he had been so worried about them, disappeared completely after a few minutes of careful scrubbing, and to his amazement and delight, his girlfriend (to whom he had never paid the kind of tribute a deceased girlfriend deserves – he had never visited the cemetery, for example, or her family, there was nothing left of her, she was gone for good, as though she had never even existed) had never realised a thing, either about his cocaine addiction – the traces of which she discovered whenever she kissed him and ran her tongue over his gums, but dismissed as some kind of anaesthetic prescribed by his dentist – or his wanking. But the next day, on his own again, when after snorting his fifth line of coke he went to the bathroom to have his first wank and (lesson learnt) lifted the toilet seat, he discovered he had obviously missed one of the spots on the inside, and this, after almost twenty-four hours, had corroded the wood and left a white oval about the size of a five-cent piece: an indelible mark, he thought, one impossible to remove – and so it proved when, armed with the floor cloth and then all kinds of cleaning products, it stubbornly refused to budge. They told him he was under arrest for allegedly stealing a work of art. He could call his lawyer and take some clothes with him. Rimini turned his head towards the window, apparently searching for something on the whiteboard of the sky. Then he lowered his eyes, thought for a few seconds, and asked: 'Would you like some coffee? Tea? Gatorade?'

He slept solidly for four hours on what looked like a narrow fakir's mat, curled up against the damp cell wall. At about ten that evening he raised his head, asked a question in the loud, sing-song voice typical of sleepwalkers: 'With hydromassage or without?' and then laid his head again on the pair of trainers he was using for a pillow. At eleven, he woke, and ate in silence with the pickpocket who had been brought into the cell while he was asleep, a young man in a tracksuit with very expensive shoes, who spilled soup all down his chest. Then he fell asleep again. At two in the morning he was awake once more, clear-headed, brimming with energy as if he had been given a blood transfusion. The pickpocket had disappeared. He paced up and down his cell. When he knew even the cracks of every tile on the floor by heart, he started to do exercises. He began with the first routine the trainer had given him, the most rigorous one: he multiplied each series by six, and performed them without a moment's rest, to the admiration of the orderly who passed by trailing battered boots and carrying trays full of plastic coffee cups. Later, probably on the orderly's recommendation, a guard came in and handed him a broom so that he could sweep the patio at the back of the station. Within twenty minutes, there was not a single scrap of paper left.

They got him some bleach, and Rimini turned his attention to the bathrooms and the kitchen, where the orderly prepared coffee and always burnt it. Slowly, as though as he grew tired from the work a thick veil were being torn, Rimini began to glimpse a few scattered pieces of the mystery the last few days of his life had become: a neon sign with all the vowels missing, a rubber mask, a fallen body . . . They were not exactly memories: Rimini could see them too clearly – they did have the kind of detail that the most intimate images or impressions have, and yet he had difficulty recognising them as belonging to him, because they did not have any of the stains, veils, or areas of shadow that usually cloud our personal recollections, and also because they did not seem to come from inside him, from his memory, but from outside, from some anonymous archive or lost property office. Later on, while he was having coffee with the orderly, he saw a policeman pass by with a supermarket trolley loaded with stereos, speakers, rear-view mirrors, weapons, women's handbags, bags, briefcases, trainers, electrical goods. On top of this mound of treasures, wrapped like all the other objects in a plastic bag, and leaning against the front of the trolley as though it were at the head of the procession of recovered goods, he saw the Riltse painting. As soon as he caught sight of it, the picture naturally became part of the series of memory flashes that had taken him by surprise an hour earlier. He saw the painting and watched as it was carted away. When the policeman, the trolley and the Riltse had disappeared behind a door, Rimini lowered his head and burnt his lips on the coffee yet again.

He was paralysed by a tremendous sense of tiredness. It was nothing to do with feeling sleepy, or with the fact that he had polished off in two hours what it normally took the most experienced cleaner six hours to complete. It was an age-old, historic tiredness, which converted the few decades he had lived into geological eras, and the past few days into centuries. Perhaps this was the real mortal tiredness, the only one that could justify the expression 'I'm dead' – the kind of tiredness that old people embarked on as they were approaching the end, or which led them to wish with what little strength they had left that the end would come. Yes; he was an octogenarian – and he remembered one of the final scenes from *2001 – A Space Odyssey* in which, totally unexpectedly, thanks to a simple editing cut, the astronaut's journey and the psychedelic acceleration it entails give way to a silent panning shot of a large room with white walls that are so bright they look as though they are filled with light. In the centre of the room there is a bed, and in the bed there is a man, sitting without moving, wearing a dressing-gown and covered up to his waist. We see his face only in the next shot, when the camera moves in and we see the maze of wrinkles into which time has converted him. For the first time, Rimini felt he had a life – that at last he had the richness, variety, complexity, and ballast that he had previously searched for in vain in his own experience, and

399

yet found flourishing with luxurious exuberance in almost everybody else's. And it was precisely at that moment, when he could say 'my life' out loud without lying, that he also discovered that it no longer belonged to him, that this life had been left behind, and now that it was lost was threatening to engulf him. He had a life, but understanding that risked killing him. As with everyone else, it had taken Rimini a long time to understand how illness or chance events could bring people's lives to an end. Now to these two possibilities – and perhaps all the mystery came from the fact that there were only two of them – he was forced to add a third: tiredness. He felt as if he could not hold anything, not even the plastic cup in his hand. He tried to leave it on a shelf; his hand did not respond, or trembled, and he spilt some scalding hot coffee on himself. He did not cry out – he was too tired even to feel pain. The orderly prised the cup from his fingers and pressed a damp cloth on the burnt area. Rimini looked at him. In a film, he could have been one of those minor characters, a distant relative of the main protagonist (an uncle who dies prematurely, a cousin living in another country) who, despite the tenuousness, the lack of continuity and of involvement of that kind of relationship, or precisely because of them, has left in him an indelible impression, the causes of which have been lost but whose effects linger on, preserved by a kind of magic aura that it is impossible to tell whether it originated in the relationship itself or was added later, with the passage of time and memory. The orderly had a thin, abnormally snub nose, and wore a brick-coloured toupee, which hung down over one ear and which he kept adjusting, pretending to be combing it. Rimini felt he had never been in such an intimate situation with anyone. He was tired. He was dead. He could remember.

He had fled the hospital. He could still hear Rodi's dying gasps, the sticky mess between his fingers, when he found himself outside Nancy's apartment building. It was mad to turn up like that, out of the blue, without even tennis as an excuse . . . He was about to press the intercom buzzer when a wave of terror struck him. He was starting to change his mind. He saw that the lift, which until then had been stuck on Nancy's floor, was coming down. He waited, filled with a strange presentiment. The lift reached the ground floor; the door snapped open. It was one of those concertina doors which fold and sometimes, if they are not treated properly, bounce back and stay halfway across, blocking all exit. Bewildered by the light refracted from the glass entrance to the chrome fittings, from the chrome to the mirrors in the lobby, Rimini could only see the outline of a man carrying a big, awkward machine and struggling to push the lift door open with his shoulder. He eventually stuck his heel in the gap and pushed the door fully open; when he saw someone was waiting to come in, he left it as it was. Rimini looked down, and recognised the machine – a green IBM golf-ball electric typewriter – then glanced directly at his feet: deck shoes, with some of the stitching coming apart, and the laces undone. 'So then . . . ,' he thought, but before he could go any further, the sheer number of disparate, distant elements he would have to bring together if he really wanted to think it through raced across his mind, and he gave up. There was no time. He turned to one side, and dropped his head on his chest, as though this were his secret method of becoming invisible, then stepped aside to let the other man out. And, even though he screwed up his eyes and shrank as far as he could into himself, Rimini could not help discovering the same tanned, light-complexioned face, with unruly eyebrows and nicotine-stained moustache, which twenty years earlier he had seen bending over a mirror and snorting the lines of cocaine that, in response to Rimini's flustered reaction, he claimed was a remedy for his chronic sinusitis. But the man who held the front door open with one foot as if inviting him in, and who brushed against him with one of the corners of the typewriter, not only did not look at him as he went by: he did not even consider him. He merely offered a distant echo of the memory that had just struck Rimini, by sweeping the space he was filling with his nose. That was it: he sniffed at him, with all the insolence that the sense of smell is capable of – the only one of our senses which registers the world indiscriminately, without choosing or thinking, without any moral judgement, reducing everything that has a smell to a state of complete passivity – he sniffed him, and walked on.

Rimini went up in the lift, rang the bell, knocked at the door. Sleepy-eyed, Nancy opened it a little way. She was in her dressing-gown, with no make-up; she still had sheet-marks on her forehead and cheek, her eyes were puffy and in general she had the air of a diva just surfacing from a disastrous night. As she slowly realised who her wild-eyed visitor was, Rimini put his shoulder to the door, burst the security chain open, and literally took her with him as he charged across the hall, ending with her pressed up against the quilted wall. Nancy put up a half-hearted struggle, as theatrical as her hung-over features, but then gave in, went limp, and almost fainted in his arms. Rimini rebuked her for the way she had been so distant, cold and ambivalent towards him in the previous few days, the way she had kept appearing and disappearing simply to torture him, while at the same he was lifting her up against the wall. He threw some of the paintings on to the floor, and with a crazy, strange precision, placed her at exactly the height he wanted. He paused for a moment, then penetrated her with one long, slow thrust. Corpse-like, Nancy did not react, until a corner of a Fader painting started digging into her shoulder, and she begged him to take her to the bedroom.

He made love to her with all the patience and devotion of a gold-smith, just as carefully as he had spent the past few months being her shadow and protecting her from the world. He made love to her comprehensively, crazily focussing on every last detail, alert to the slightest signs he encountered while exploring the inside of her body, like a bomb disposal expert. He made love to her so that she would never forget him, to make her his slave. And when he suddenly arched his back and came, light years after she had finished (she was chewing her fingernails, staring up at the mouldings on the ceiling) Rimini rolled off, but kept one arm around her: as a professional lover, he was very aware of not only how relieved she would be to get his weight off her, but also of how bereft women feel after sex, when satisfaction gives way to lonely emptiness. Flinging his arm off as if it were a towel, Nancy got up, wrapped herself again in her dressing-gown, looked for something in her handbag, and, while she was making him out a cheque for 500 pesos (an amount that more than covered her remaining lessons that month, which of course she would not be having, as well as all the extra services he had been rendering her, including the one he had just performed, undoubtedly for the last time) told him in a flat, emotionless voice that she no longer needed him, that she had more than enough with Boni's impetuous penis, and that he should take the cheque quickly, before she changed her mind. She was going to have a shower; she did not want to find him still there when she came out.

Rimini lay in bed, completely stunned, until the sound of the shower woke him from his daze, and he stood up with martial determination. He knew what he had to do – it was as if a voice were giving him an order. He looked for the trainer that had fallen off, and as he bent down, caught sight of a framed photo in which Nancy was balancing on a pair of skis while in the background her husband, oblivious to the cold in a t-shirt, was striking a body-builder pose. Rimini felt calmer: he realised that the meeting downstairs at the door to the building had not been a hallucination, nor his memory playing tricks on him. He went into the kitchen, opened the door to the maid's bathroom, took down the Riltse and wrapped it in newspaper. Then he took a swig from a bottle of flat champagne, put all the paintings he had knocked down back up again, and left the apartment.

It was at this point, when Rimini emerged into the street with *Bogus Hole* under his arm, that the image was interrupted, and a glaring white light invaded the whole screen. A few seconds later, when the first heads were turning towards the projection booth in the hope that by identifying the source of the problem they could somehow resolve it, the film jerked back into life, showing a clear blue sky, trees, a road surface with the tail-lights of a car disappearing up it, then the front of a cheap motel, its green neon sign lit, but with all the vowels missing. Rimini was there. It was him, there could be no mistake; he was on guard, still in his tennis clothes, crouching like a pariah in a doorway. How long had he been there, waiting for a woman who was not expecting him, a woman he had only seen for a split second in the garish red light of a hotel corridor, a woman, if he should ever get to see her, to whom he had nothing to say, apart from: Leave here, Ida, go home, Rodi is not coming to paradise today, not today, tomorrow, or ever again. He was there; he wanted to see her. It was something he had wanted to do ever since he had been in the intensive care unit, and Rodi had tried to get him to remember her phone number. No, he had thought, I don't want to talk to her. I want to see her. On his death bed, Rodi dedicated his last drops of passion to the love of his life, while that love of his life lived, simply went on living, protected by her ignorance – and Rimini was the only person on earth who could connect those two parallel worlds and put an end to the scandalous indifference. He had not been entrusted with an errand, but a mission, and missions were fulfilled in person. So Rimini went back to the hotel at the time he had been there with Nancy a few days earlier, and waited, waited while night fell and he dozed off crouched in the doorway, until the arm he was leaning on went to sleep and he started to shake it back to life. He looked towards the hotel and saw nothing, but glanced sceptically towards the avenue, and thought he could make out a woman stepping off a bus. He got to his feet. Drawn by some invisible force, he started to walk slowly towards the corner, towards the woman, who was headed towards the hotel. He surveyed her with growing excitement. She was round, stocky, or perhaps merely had on too many clothes. She was wearing a flowery headscarf and walked with short, quick steps, almost skipping along, clutching a small leather suitcase to her. Rimini had closed the gap between them: only the street separated them. As he crossed it, he could see the old-fashioned cut of her clothes, how worn and faded they were. Ida stopped a few metres from the hotel and looked anxiously around her. She was looking for Rodi. That must be how they met each other, thought Rimini. But Rodi had not arrived, and this simple fact, which could easily be reversed by just waiting a little, seemed to strike her as a terrible omen. She looked at her watch, inspected both ends of the street once more. Then, with a mixture of impatience and disappointment, she leaned gently against a wall and began to wait. She could have been a widow, a mother overwhelmed by a series of family crises, a nurse who gave injections at home – anything, thought Rimini, apart from that rapacious Amazon who had peered out into the corridor in search of her prey. Rimini felt weak, weakened by sadness, but went on across the road. He called out to her by her name. Ida glanced at him suspiciously, then looked all round her again, urgently and hopefully, as though this stranger who had just shouted at her was a threat but also someone she ought to listen to, the messenger from something that was bound to arrive, something she was waiting for heart in mouth – the only miracle that for thirty years now had succeeded in rescuing her from her deadly life as widow, care-worn mother, or domestic nurse. Yet the street, the parked cars, the trees, the shops on the block, everything she could see discouraged her, precisely because she could see all of it so clearly, precisely because it was so empty, because the man who blotted everything else out for her had not come, was not coming, would never come. When Rimini, who knew this and was beginning to feel the weight of this knowledge intolerable, shouted at her again, Ida clutched the suitcase more tightly to her, turned on her heel and started to walk away, at first slowly, trying to look natural (as if something trivial had led her to change her mind) and then, when she saw Rimini following her, with ever quicker steps. 'Ida!' shouted Rimini. Frightened, the woman gave up all pretence and bolted. She ran and ran, until a few metres before the street corner, her shoes, which she was crushing like a pair of slippers as she sped along, betrayed her, and she stumbled over something or slipped, or twisted her ankle, and ended up face down on the pavement. The suitcase flew out of her hands, banged against the stunted trunk of a tree and, as it hit the ground, fell open to reveal a whip, a rubber mask, a leather bra, thongs. Rimini bent over to help her up; she drove him away with her shrieks. Two men crossing the avenue turned to look, and then started towards them. Rimini backed off. He had a last view of her: still on the ground, still shouting, Ida was trying to recover her modest transgressive treasures. The more she tried to stuff them all back at once, the more the suit-case resisted. The whip got caught up in one side, bent and then sprang back, hitting her in the face. This time she cried out in pain. Her fall had pushed up her coat and skirt, and as Rimini stared at the milky-white skin of her legs, he was horrified to see she was wearing no pants. He had to look again to make sure he wasn't dreaming – but yes, it was her white, completely naked buttocks he could see, in the middle of the street at nightfall, as out of place as an armchair or a standard lamp in the countryside. So it was this – incongruousness – that was the secret of thirty years of happiness, Rimini thought, as he ran away from the scene: a sort of anti-illusion, a charitable swindle, degrada-tion even . . . like women who wear shoes without stockings, he thought – leather next to skin, fabric against flesh. As he was running, an image flashed through his mind, as vivid and magnified as a reproduction of the detail of a famous painting: a lace border peeping out from the bottom of a worsted skirt – the drab skirt worn by a primary school teacher.

Then, as if memory were ruled by its own set of laws, according to which the tiniest elements are capable not only of raising but of dislodging, moving, and transporting the heaviest and most dense of objects with complete ease, this sliver of recollection, based on something as slight as the contrast between two materials and the mistake made in calculating the length of hems, immediately brought back to Rimini the one true, erotic epiphany he had experienced in his childhood – the whole immense weight of it: not just the name of the person involved (Señorita Sanz), not just her glassy bright blue eyes, or her youthful, pale, unhealthy-looking doll's skin, or the blood-red lipstick she smeared on her mouth; not just the way she sat on the edge of her desk to give her classes, turned slightly in profile to them and with her legs crossed, hands cupped round knees, the tip of one foot resting on the floor while the other, with the flat shoe dangling from it, hung in mid-air; but also entire rainy, sleepy mornings, the damp wood of his desk, the floors covered in sawdust, the fumes from the gas fire, and above all, someone's revelation (which for some reason, that had nothing to do with scrupulousness, nobody at the school had ever challenged) which explained this repeated morning exhibitionism: Señorita Sanz lived a long way away, took sleeping pills, had problems waking up, survived on the hours of teaching she did, and could lose her pay if she was late; so she was constantly battling against time, and every morning, to make up the two or three precious moments the sleeping pills had stolen from her, she put on her clothes straight on top of her nightdress.

As childhood is only interested in living and reproducing life, it is blind and cruel. It only acknowledges anything that gives it sustenance, and only recognises that as sustenance; everything else, everything related to the 'life' of that sustenance, the life it has when it is not supplying the needs of childhood, is not just irrelevant, it gets in the way. Once it had become public knowledge, once the twin parliaments of school existence – the toilets and playtime – had begun to debate the question, the drama of Señorita Sanz's social life might have been expected to lessen the erotic effect of her negligent way of dressing. If this was not the case, but in fact quite the opposite, leading to her being surrounded by a kind of sordid, voluptuous fog in which money (or rather the lack of it) and the figure of a man who was always away travelling – whom Rimini and his classmates imagined to be something like the cartoon figure of a yeti, a hard drinker and sexually rampant, but someone more interested in wasting his energy on natives in exotic lands than on this blonde, almost transparent woman waiting patiently for him at home – were essential factors, it was because the outside world impinges on childhood only if it obeys its rules and serves its own ends, because compassion, pity, and understanding – any of the logical emotions that this world should have aroused in the admirers of the hem of Señorita Sanz's nightdress – were admitted only if they could be incorporated into the erotic trance they were meant to dispel, and finally because childhood will only permit what we call an explanation when it adds something, when it is travelling in the same direction as the effect produced by the phenomenon it is meant to be explaining, to the extent that if the explanation, as in the case of Señorita Sanz's lacy hem, modifies, diminishes or tries to subordinate that effect to some higher purpose, childhood will always manage to skew it towards its own interests and make it part of its original intention, and if not, if it contradicts that original intention, then childhood will dismiss the new explanation completely, and carry on as though it had never existed. With the result that the sadism of childhood, which is not only the enjoyment of inflicting pain, but above all the use, in order to inflict pain, of the same moral reasoning employed to argue that inflicting pain is bad, is nothing more than morality transformed into sustenance for instinctive desires. That the origin of the excitement caused by Señorita Sanz's lacy hem might have been economic hardship – and not, for example, Señorita Sanz's intention to arouse the schoolboys with a disturbing spectacle – only served to increase and deepen that excitement, inasmuch as it brought in certain social (and therefore non-scholarly) dimensions that would otherwise have been difficult to attain. The fact that Señorita Sanz was poor was not a mitigation – it was another reason (one of the best) to carry on sneaking a look at the strip of nightdress peeping out from under her skirt, that tiny but irresistible scrap of intimacy that Señorita Sanz paraded in all innocence among their ranks. Like her unfinished early morning attempts to comb her hair, which left one half properly smoothed under slides, but saw the other half left to its own devices; the buttons done up wrongly; the untied shoe-laces; or all the things – her watch, text-book, coloured pencils, illustrations – which she only realised she had forgotten in mid-class, causing her not merely to blush but casting her into a state of crushing embarrassment that she could recover from only in fits of reasonable but exaggerated anger directed at the two or three inevitable trouble-makers in the class – that timid strip of material, as well as being such a powerful sexual talisman, was a kind of threshold, the window which Rimini and his companions could gaze out of (prisoners as they were of the entirely interior world of the school) and glimpse the outside world, all the effervescence, noise and movement that the morning school bell cut them off from. Chained to their desks, they could travel. They eagerly followed the trail of her shoe-lace in the sawdust, discovered the ear lobe missing its ring, the empty glasses case, the fountain pen she had forgotten to bring a fresh cartridge for; they were in ecstasy at the way her night-dress brushed against her knee, and leapt out of their world to land unseen in this world within world – the only one in reality that really interested them – the world of the street, the building, the flat, the bedroom, the unmade and still warm bed where Señorita Sanz lived. And from the bed, the ultimate goal of this expedition, where all of them imagined her asleep, in her nightdress, tossing to and fro in a drug-induced sleep punctuated by nightmares, they would start to investigate the more lurid details of the surroundings: the sauce or oil stains on the bedspread, the shoes caught up in a trap of fluff and cobwebs under the bed, the dirty plates, glasses and cups scattered all round the room, the open drawers, the TV and the light left on at all hours, the chaos of make-up on the bathroom shelf, the burnt coffee-pot, the always drawn blinds, the old newspapers scattered over the floor – a complete picture of her world that they would stay engrossed in, intoxicated by the realism of all these details but also, no doubt, by the sickly sweet smell of the gas stove in the room, a smell which for years Rimini associated with these morning hours, and from which they emerged only when Señorita Sanz, tired of asking them politely – with that kind of woozy amiability that tranquillisers induce – to get out a sheet of paper and write their name and the date in the top left-hand corner, the only response to which was the nodding of their dreamy heads, started to bang her desk with the board-duster and, literally beside herself, as though something inside her had snapped, began shouting at them, changing what had been an invitation into an order, a threat, a punishment – which she immediately regretted, collapsing into her chair exhausted from the effort of getting so angry – and like all the rest of them becoming conscious of where she was, taking out a crumpled handkerchief and pretending to blow her nose to hide the fact that she was crying. They came and went every morning, as regular as addicts, for their fix of her lacy hem or her stockings (which were often odd), and whenever she was absent – something they feared but which happened only infrequently, and which Rimini could tell was on the cards as soon as he saw the headmaster standing at the classroom door supervising the pupils' entrance, with that serious, vacant look of someone about to give bad news – an irremediable gloom descended on their morning, they lost all interest, and the school day ahead of them, even with the consolation of the free hours, the extra gym class or the excursion to the library, became an endless torment.

Señorita Sanz. Rimini once more found himself fascinated by her fleshy, half-open lips, hesitating between astonishment and the desire – but not the strength – to speak, that startlingly white, almost blue skin of hers, sprinkled with the most extraordinary variety of birthmarks Rimini had ever seen, ranging from some that were perfectly smooth, and looked as though they had been painted on, to others that stood out like warts – like those on the backs of her hands which Rimini caught sight of whenever Señorita Sanz treacherously seized the sheet of paper where he had been struggling to copy (badly, so affected was he by the distance and his own nervousness) what the boy sitting next to him had written – the overall impression of thinness her body gave, even though its real shape (hidden under all the layers of clothing she always wore, giving Rimini only a wintery image of her) remained a mystery, and her exceptionally small-sized feet, more like a little girl's – a girl smaller than those she taught every morning – or a doll's, than those of a woman how old? Twenty-eight? Thirty? Thirty-five? (But how irrelevant, how useless it was for adults to measure themselves out in years when for a child adulthood, that walled kingdom of 'the biggies', was a realm that began slightly further on, at seventeen for example, exactly when school finished, and then stretched out homogeneously, all of a piece, to the horizon.) And yet his yearning for Señorita Sanz had nothing to do with her characteristics, her attributes, or even her features, which Rimini allowed himself to indulge in both because he was looking back with hindsight and because he was encouraged by the presence of the orderly, someone who was completely foreign to the story he was hearing but who, confronted with other evidence – a photograph from those days, for example, or another eyewitness's version of events – would not have been surprised in the slightest to discover that what he was saying was simply a fantasy or a lie. In fact, thought Rimini, if there was a secret to that attraction, if there was something he could name and locate to explain why Señorita Sanz's lacy hem had held him in thrall for a whole year, it was an idea: the idea of imminence – the idea that a woman was not something in particular (which meant that categories so prized in the adult domain such as beauty, grace, kindness, or intelligence immediately became worthless), but was someone always *on the brink* – in Señorita Sanz's case, on the brink of exploding, getting hurt, howling, bursting into tears, or collapsing. That's what she was: the edge of suspense. More than once when he saw her facing some insubordination typical of a primary school class, some vandalism or sabotage, or the whispering that spoke of a plot being hatched, or when she was tormented by one of those dramas beating in her breast, a drama born of that same sordid, solitary world of which the lacy hem was an ambassador, teetering on the edge then, when her downfall was a matter of seconds (as was evident from the rashes, her problems breathing, the violent way she rubbed her hands together), Rimini had been gripped by the delicious yet terrifying sense, doubtless stimulated by the title of a book he had discovered in his mother's library, *The Broken Woman*, that at any moment he would see Señorita Sanz's body literally fall to pieces, completely dismembered, like a puppet destroyed by a madman or a stick of dynamite, and the trance he fell into at that point, frightened but determined to guess what disaster was about to engulf her, produced in him a state of crazy excitement, very similar in many ways to what he felt at the end of each episode of his favourite TV serial, when the superheroes he worshipped were left helpless in the face of a horrible – a twisted and horrible – death: submerged in a giant vat full of acid, devoured by starving pythons or sawn in two by giant rotating blades, while a worried narrator (whose ironic undertone it had taken Rimini twenty years to discover) asked out loud the same life-and-death questions that Rimini was posing himself silently, still in his school uniform, sitting on the carpet of his bedroom. And yet, despite the frequency with which throughout that year Señorita Sanz had seemed to be on the brink of breaking down, she had always managed to stop just before it happened, to postpone indefinitely what had seemed inevitable. She did not break down on the morning stage of the theatre that was school, in front of a huge audience of anxious spectators – something which disappointed Rimini but somehow only served to increase to the maximum his desire to see it happen; although considering what did happen afterwards it is possible to think that the source of that self-control had less to do with Señorita Sanz herself, or her will-power (which she seemed to lack completely), or her sense of shame (which, given the states of emotional crises she suffered, would have been of little use) – so much as the ecosystem of the school as institution, which by virtue of its completely self-sufficient nature filtered out or somehow subdued any extraneous psychic disorder. But towards the end of the school year, in keeping with the more relaxed atmosphere that seemed to go with the increasingly hot mornings and longer days, the school (in one of those rare initiatives with which forty years ago, schools apparently accepted – grudgingly – the possibility that beyond their ancient walls there might be some signs of life too) decided to send Rimini's class on an excursion into the real world, or rather into one of those select mini-worlds – a sweet factory (the other choices on the menu were a municipal library with creaky floors and dusty stained-glass windows, the museum-home of one of the nation's heroes distinguished by a wart on his Adam's apple, the Planetarium and its glamorous urban science-fiction design and, two or three years later, a theatre also belonging to the municipality in which hordes of pre-teenagers, separated by everything – social class, family situation, level of education, uniform – banded together for an hour and a half to pelt the poor Don Juans, Juliets or Victorias trying desperately to come through their stage dialogues unscathed with all kinds of unlikely objects) – into which the school divided the real world when it deigned to recognise its existence.

The night before, Rimini had barely slept. He tossed and turned in his bed, writhing impatiently, and at first light, two long hours before he was meant to be awake, he leapt out of bed and in a flash dressed himself in the clothes that to his mother's astonishment he had already chosen and hung from a chair-back. What had kept him awake was not the promise of coming back from the excursion with his stomach and pockets full of sweets. It was the fact that, for the first time, he would be seeing Señorita Sanz outside school. If he had thought of this possibility before – something he had never done, because it seemed so far-fetched – it would have seemed to him impossibly daring. He had no idea whether she really existed or not outside the school! And yet now he was going to see her talk, in everyday language, with strangers, he would see her in unaccustomed places, watch her taking the lead in unheard-of dramas ... Would she resist, or would she crumble to dust as soon as she came into contact with this foreign atmosphere? They all met at the school gate, where a bus was waiting for them, engine running. It was a long journey, because the factory was on the outskirts of the city, in a neighbourhood of low houses patrolled by dogs. Five minutes after they had set off, the schoolchildren, roused by the kind of increased alertness that extraordinary adventures create, erupted into a euphoric contest of shouting, cursing and athletic prowess in the aisle of the coach. Seated in the second row, Rimini had nothing to do with any of this. He spent the whole journey with his eyes fixed on the row in front of him, where, the minute she had got on the bus, Señorita Sanz had collapsed in an obviously exhausted heap. Her eyes were red, and after she had made an assistant responsible for the children's behaviour – the same bent, useless old man they ran rings round during their breaks – she quickly fell fast asleep, her head on the window and still grasping the small imitation snake-skin handbag she was carrying. She woke up, with one side of her hair flattened by the glass, and a trickle of saliva at the corner of her mouth, only when the driver was already pulling up in the factory car-park. Rimini realised the kind of trap they had fallen into almost as soon as the visit began. They had associated the term 'sweet factory' with a fantastical, ideal world, a kind of super sweet shop whose treasures, unlike those of normal shops, would be free and just for them. They had been thinking of 'sweet' rather than 'factory', whereas what the excursion soon turned into was a long, tedious procession through a series of sheds where gangs of taciturn workmen operated a string of noisy machines that processed raw materials which nobody, not even the stubbornest sugar addict in the class, would have linked to the tiny brightly coloured drugs they were able to buy legally any day of the week on the street. On top of all this, their squad was led around by a guide in a grey dust-coat, clearly chosen because of his garrulous and histrionic nature and his easy smile, all of which only made the torture even more unbearable. He had a high-pitched voice which at moments of enthusiasm bordered on a falsetto, and alternated the most improbable technical details (so improbable that as he was speaking the men on the machines glanced mockingly at him behind his back, then shared their mirth with the school-kids) with carefully inserted moments of 'participation' intended to liven up the farrago of his industrial explanations – inviting them to solve riddles, complete jokes or tell personal stories of their involvement with sweets – all of this done in the language of an entertainer at a children's party, as though his work as a guide were merely a prelude to his imminent leap into the theatre or TV studios. Within minutes, the excitement the visitors had tried to work off on the coach was buried under a thick blanket of boredom. They advanced like robots, looked at everything leaden-eyed and, apart from the two or three inevitable toadies anxious as ever to ingratiate themselves with any human being ten centimetres taller than them and with the slightest sign of hair on their cheeks, they resisted the guide's blandishments and only responded timidly to thank him for the minimum amount of pastilles or rubbery sweets they were handed every so often – the only bribe capable of preventing them from deserting en masse. For a while, Rimini remained alert by spying on Señorita Sanz: she was there with them, but was always to one side, slightly apart from the group, and whenever the guide came to the end of one of his incomprehensible technical explanations and, with an exaggerated wave of the hand, like an overgrown boy-scout invited them to carry on to the next marvel the factory had to offer, she was always the last to move, as though, completely oblivious to the guide's instructions, she reacted only thanks to a tardy herd instinct, when the fear of being on her own became more powerful than the inconvenience caused by having to stir herself. But it was only the empty carcass of her body that accepted being part of the herd; everything else – her soul, her senses, her imagination – was a long, long way off, not in a well-defined point in time and space (which would at least have placed her absence somewhere) but at the confluence of all her struggling impulses, which pulled her this way and that and seemed to plunge her into a state of desolate indecision. She walked

413

slowly, but what seemed in her like a lack of interest, weariness or boredom was in fact the inertia of someone who has not the slightest idea of what to do, someone who, feeling threatened by all the possible alternatives, cannot bring themselves to choose one of them, and thus risks losing all of them, or someone who, as soon as they have chosen one course of action, snatching it as forcefully as they can from the mess of confusion surrounding them, immediately changes their mind and gives up, unable to choose a different one because the world by now has moved on. Rimini saw her raise a hand to her mouth, as though stifling a scream or seeing something revolting, then letting it drop lifeless down by her side, only to clasp her other hand with it a second later, then thrust it into her pocket, take it out again, lift it to her hair, straighten a curl that had not moved – like a caged animal.

In mid-morning they were given breakfast. They gathered in the factory canteen, a large room with big windows overlooking the parking lot where their coach was waiting for them. While their guide strolled among the tables explaining the brand's history, describing a curve that over the past thirty years, he said, had gone up and up, with the result that its logo (a smile with a tongue licking it) and its products were flooding the shops of several neighbouring countries, two dinner ladies in kitchen aprons handed out plastic aeroplane trays on which stood an orange fizzy drink and a tiny filled biscuit. It was not five minutes before the entire class, after giving short shrift to everything on their trays, suddenly seemed to wake up again – revitalised by the breakfast but above all by the changed situation, which had not freed them from the guide but at least from the wandering yoke of the visit, and in a matter of seconds had changed this industrial canteen into a battle-field. Desperate for the toilet, Rimini had to creep out, avoiding all the things being thrown. He peed standing up, reading the hygiene instructions plastered on the walls of the toilet, and scrupulously avoided following any of them (after all, he was a stranger here). As he was coming out he saw Señorita Sanz with her back to him at one of the two public phone booths that, as the guide had proudly informed them, the firm had recently installed for its employees. Rimini stood rooted to the spot. He felt that good fortune, which until then had been so against him, was finally coming his way, and was offering him, and only him, the chance to be present at one of those scenes which all the boys in the class had probably dreamt of. The sense of privilege overwhelmed him, as if he did not deserve it. Then, under the spell of the asymmetry of the situation, which allowed him to see without being seen, he felt as if his body were slowly growing to giant size, while just as slowly Señorita Sanz's body was growing smaller, until at a certain moment it seemed to him that if he stretched out a hand (as he recalled seeing in a science-fiction film one Saturday afternoon, featuring a huge angora cat in his role and a microscopic, almost inaudible man in the part of Señorita Sanz) he could play and do with her as he wished. He was filled with a new and intense sense of excitement, as unknown to him as the kind of adult intimacy he was witnessing. And everything which until then had aroused him, all the early morning carelessness – above all, her lacy hem – which transported Señorita Sanz and a panting Rimini along with her, to the warm voluptuousness of her bed, to leave her lying there open to his gaze, more naked than if she had really been naked: all that seemed so childish, so superfluous and tepid, compared to what he was witnessing now. Yet, instead of reaching out one of his claws and tearing her dress, thereby uncovering the whitest, most delicate shoulder this sweet factory entrance hall had ever seen, Rimini cocooned himself from the noise coming from the canteen, where his classmates, some of whom had even clambered up on to the tables like climbers on a mountain top, and were pelting each other with the ammunition they had hidden in their pockets expressly for an opportunity like this, and tried to concentrate on the phone conversation. For a long while he could not hear anything. Scarcely taller than the phone itself, Señorita Sanz stood there in silence with the receiver glued to one ear, her body taut, apparently held together by the voice she could hear at the other end. Every so often, she nodded, and then, following several rhythmic nods, she would continue to look down and start to stub out a non-existent cigarette with the tip of her right shoe. Two or three minutes must have gone by, when the hubbub from the canteen suddenly died down, as though someone had just shut the door, and Señorita Sanz's body started to shake. Seen from behind, where Rimini was, it was hard to tell whether she was laughing or crying. 'Please . . .' he finally heard her say in a quavering voice, while she tried to halt the air with her open hand, in one of those apparently purely rhetorical gestures aimed at stressing the speaker's intention, but which when they are performed, as if the other person could see them, are really an attempt to abolish the distance into which they are fated to disappear. She was crying – and the shame she felt at crying was as painful as the reason that had caused it. 'Please . . .' she said, 'tell me what you want me to do. Tell me, and I'll do it. Whatever it is. If you want me to come crawling, I will. I'll do it. I don't care. I don't care about anything. I've got used to being dead. But please, don't leave me. Forgive me. Yes, please forgive me. I won't do it again. But how can I tell if they give you the messages? If you would only answer me occasionally. See? Now we're talking to each other, I feel better already. I need so little. Your voice warms me. Are you listening to music? It sounds nice. What is it? Ah, she has good taste. Wait. What are you wearing? I want to know; I can't see you, but I can imagine you . . . which, the green one with diamond shapes? I prefer the blue one, but yes, it suits you. See how easy it is? You live with her, you go out, you have fun, you've got kids, you go to the club, you go on holiday. And with me you can do as you like. Anything, whatever you like. If you want to beat me, you can. If you want to . . . no, wait. Don't hang up. Please. If you hang up, I don't know what I might do. No, I'm sorry, I didn't mean that. You don't understand: I'm not bothered about being happy. I don't want to be happy. What's the point? All I want is for you to tell me what you want me to do. Whatever you like. If you want to see me on my knees, I'll go down on my knees. If you want me to wait, I'll wait for you. There is a point to that. If you want me to give up everything . . . No, wait. Let's carry on a bit longer. You're so close to me. Tell me: do you miss me? Don't hang up! Tell me you think of me, that you love me, that I'm the love of your life. Please. I beg you. Don't hang up. All right, I'll hang up. Yes, right now, but first tell me you love me. Say: "I love you." Just three little words . . . What are they to you? Even if it's not true, I want to hear you say it. Please. Ah . . . my love, my love, my love, my love . . . No, I can't do it. You're going to have hang up. I could stay like this for the rest of my life. Go on, you hang up. Please. I love you. Yes, now. Do it: hang up. I love you, love you, love you. Hang up, for God's sake . . .'

She stood there, head down and with her ear pressed to the receiver, holding her breath as though she thought the call was not over, and she was trying to save its dying remains. 'Hello,' she said timidly after a few seconds. 'Hello?' she repeated, then again 'hello?' her voice weaker each time. Then she hung up and turned round – her face was contorted from crying – and headed for the toilets. Rimini felt that if he had not got out of the way, she would have knocked him over. And that was the end of his first erotic epiphany. The first ending, in fact, because just as every event always happens twice – the first as occurrence, incident, mark, the second as awareness and recollection of that event – so all processes have two endings, and nothing which has had only one full stop, however drastic and categorical, can really be considered over and done with. In this case, as often happens, a considerable length of time elapsed between the first and second endings: enough, at any rate, to insert between the two of them not only a considerable weight of experience that had nothing to do with Señorita Sanz, but also, and above all, the distance brought by forgetting, which drastically reduced the relation between the two. If the second ending had not had the impact on Rimini that it did – as strong and deep as the one that morning in the sweet factory – it would probably not have stayed in his mind as a conclusion – that padlock finally closing off a room whose door (even if we did not hear it) kept on banging – but as one of those pieces of information that reach us when they are no longer of use to anyone, at best something which rounds off (without even bringing it back to life) an already vague recollection with a purely anecdotal detail. Because that Friday, the Friday of the factory visit, Rimini went back to the school and his other, afternoon, teacher, went back to the dining-room and its endless queues, its smell of frying, its steaming plates, to the gym class (which he tried to get out of by claiming he had a pulled muscle) and he saw how the mean fabric of school life, which the factory outing had torn apart (leading him to believe that nothing would be the same as before) was repaired and quickly, miraculously restored, without anyone or anything even taking the trouble to recognise that it had been torn in the first place. Then came the weekend, with its classic array of mindless activity, then the weather started getting really warm, and the last weeks of term fizzled out in exams, school ceremonies, and holiday preparations. After which there was the happy diaspora of summer, and then in March, when Rimini went back to school – exhausted, because he had not slept a wink all night, but in a state of great excitement, with his new shoes and the half dozen tales of holiday derring-do on the tip of his tongue (all of them invented, ready to amaze his classmates) – he was so caught up in trying to absorb all the novelties that would govern his life for the next nine months that he did not even realise Señorita Sanz was not there. It was not so much that he had forgotten her: he had cut her out of his life, just like that – not in a premeditated way, because nothing is more natural in childhood than ostracism, but definitively, with the same steady determination that someone who has climbed a few millimetres higher on the pyramid of wealth cuts out from his life, his conversation and even from his past, all the habits he used to have when he was poorer. That was that until six or seven years later, when nobody – apart from the most discerning of his close relatives – would have said that this adolescent, who already spoke four languages and practised a particularly complicated form of coitus interruptus with his girlfriend, was the same person as the shy, anxious boy peering out (with a grimace of pain) from a fourth-year photograph on the right of Goberman, who is ever so sneakily stamping on his foot with his boot, and Rimini, while he was talking to Sofia under the stairs in the courtyard, the desperately uncomfortable hiding-place where, to the dismay of all their classmates, they spent the whole of their breaks entwined together, saw the light and at the same time received the *coup de grâce* he did not even know he had been waiting for ever since that sweet factory visit at the age of nine. In fact, they were not so much talking as arguing, with the passion and obstinacy so typical of new couples in love, who on principle adopt anything that will provide them with an intense reaction, provided that it is reciprocal; they were discussing the topic that most intrigues and fascinates new couples in love, namely what life and the world were like before they fell in love, not life and the world in general (which they could not have cared less about), but what they were like, where had one of them been when the other was in such and such a place, what had one of them been doing when the other was doing this or that – the details of their parallel lives which seemed to them completely incredible and fascinating, because, reconstructed from their present (in other words, from their love, which was so absolute they could not understand how they had ever managed to live without it) these details seemed so strange as to make them unrecognisable, as if they were episodes from other people's lives, yet at the same time succeeded in attracting and casting their spell over them, in the same way as their behaviour during a session of hypnosis or sleepwalking might have done. Of course, within this wide margin of the past that they so frequently excavated, what interested them most was not the effect of simultaneity in itself (this had its intensity, but was only short-lived) so much as the moments when their parallel trajectories, sent spinning from their orbits by some chance event, came closer, met, and brushed against each other – not that these shared moments could be called love, or even love-related events which had never been recognised as such and had therefore been completely ignored, abandoned, aborted – until they moved apart and went on along their own individual paths again. But, being prisoners of the past, these moments (even when an exhaustive memory could recall every detail of them) were far from unanimously accepted by the two of them. That afternoon, for example, initiating a difference of opinion that they soon converted into coquettishness, acting it out in public like one of those intimate scenes, poised between affection and hostility, that couples proudly put on display as the seal of authenticity of the love they have for each other, Sofia claimed they had been in the fourth year together, and that her first memory of Rimini – shoe-laces untied, trousers torn at the knees, a school-bag stuffed with books and notebooks he pulled roughly down the stairs – came from those days. Rimini listened, unconvinced. He could not say no or yes, but for some reason the impossibility of saying yes seemed more plausible than the opposite. He was in love with Sofia; if that was the case, and if they really had been in the fourth year together, how could he have forgotten it? It must be a false memory, a transposition, one of those super-imposed images where memory, driven by a specific purpose in the present, uses the same element – a person, a context – to link and confuse two distinct periods. Sofia insisted: she could not remember the room number, but could see the floor, the parking lot its windows looked out on to, the patches of damp in the corners of the ceiling. Rimini gave a mocking smile, pushed her away from him and then clutched her to him, burying her under an avalanche of kisses. Anyone could remember that, he laughed, from any year and any classroom. He tried to provoke her, demanding more precise details: where she used to sit, for example. At the back, said Sofia, at the back, as always, and close to the wall, not near the windows. 'As always,' Rimini said, and shook his head in disappointment. He wanted precise details, she was offering generalities. But for Sofia, that was not the real problem. In her view, Rimini found it impossible to remember her personally – not just her, but any of the girls he had shared years with at primary school – not because he did not want to, or due to some lapse of memory, but for the simple reason that, in the fourth year, the boys saw the girls as little more than extras or objects, with which they shared a certain obvious existential inferiority which should have obliged them to go about unnoticed, an obligation they ignored by adopting the habit (unthinkable for any of the boys) of wanting to be seen, of getting in the way, of straying into view all of a sudden and demanding attention, which obviously forced the male population (Rimini included, however much Sofia loved him, as a representative of that population) to redouble their efforts to forget them, in the most drastic cases directly blotting them out from their past records, or simply lumping them together as a kind of pervasive, extremely vague, presence, where there was no room for individual identities and which existed basically as a nuisance or a threat. Rimini laughed, as if he had been caught in flagrante. 'Yes,' he admitted, 'there was a world of details – the map of Argentina with the ink-stain covering the Chaco, the rough surface of the blackboard, the crack in the last window – and then there was you, "the girls", like a string of clouds floating across the sky . . .' 'And there was Señorita Sanz,' said Sofia. 'Yes,' he said, still laughing. 'Señorita Sanz,' he said again, and as he did so, felt that the memory of her engulfed and isolated him. 'Señorita Sanz,' she went on, 'who on that day of the Georgalos visit started crying on the phone.' This revelation was so sudden that Rimini felt betrayed or violated. It was as if something very close to him had been stolen. In self-defence, he thought that this still proved nothing. Perhaps Sofia had found out thanks to someone else in that year, a witness whom Rimini, caught up in the scene unfolding in front of him, had simply not noticed. But now this was equally unimportant. Dumbfounded as he was, Rimini nevertheless went back and reconstructed the factory entrance, the exit from the toilets, the wall with the public telephones, the corridor which turned a corner and led to the canteen, and although he could see no one – no one apart from himself standing there, heart in mouth, and a strange burning sensation growing between his legs, and Señorita Sanz, the newly discovered adulterer, bathed in tears and more irresistible than ever as she tried to tear her lover from the married paradise imprisoning him – he realised it was too late, that the scene (even though apparently intact) had changed for ever: now that Sofia had shown she was aware of it, he knew there was someone else there, not necessarily a person with name and address, a body (Sofia's or anyone else's), but simply another pair of eyes, and that was more than enough. The scene was different. Rimini, who had been able to enjoy it thanks to a stroke of good fortune – that of seeing Señorita Sanz without her realising it – suddenly discovered that in the real scene (not the one he remembered but the one he had just found out he was part of) he had played a role remarkably similar to that played by Señorita Sanz, and that other people had enjoyed his astonishment in exactly the same way as he had enjoyed Señorita Sanz's collapse. It was exactly the kind of discovery against which he had no defence, and which, however slight it might seem, could literally blow him away. If he did manage to survive, and not only that, but to close the strange door which, although he was unaware of it, had stayed open for eight years, it was because Sofia, possibly sorry for the commotion she had caused in him (obviously effective, but spoilt by childish spite), went further, much further, with that talent certain women have for curing the wounds inflicted by cruelty with still worse cruelty, and commented (leaving behind the explosive effect of her first revelation as if it did not matter, like someone tossing aside a lethal weapon) that the year after the factory visit Señorita Sanz had not returned to the school. Rimini detected a slight note of hesitation in her voice, and looked at her. 'That's true,' he said, 'now you come to mention it . . .' He could sense a dark shadow gathering above his head.

Everything Sofia knew, in fact, was thanks to her mother, who was an English teacher giving classes in a private institute in Belgrano, and had by chance taught Señorita Sanz. At the end of six months, from August to February, Sofia's mother could not have said they had become friends, because the size of the group made personal contacts difficult, and Señorita Sanz, who usually came late and was the first to leave, seemed always to be in a hurry and never took part in those occasions outside the class when teacher and students, freed from the classroom protocol, tend to explore less formal aspects of their relationship, but did feel they had established a certain trust in each other, a trust based above all on the patience and dedication Sofia's mother showed in supervising her student's learning. Señorita Sanz did not make much progress, or at least not as much as was desirable, and not because of any lack of interest or ability, but because of the great difficulty she had in concentrating, following the lessons, and focussing on the exercises. She always seemed to be somewhere else, but her absences seemed to have less to do with day-dreaming than because she was always tense, on edge, as if less concerned with the beauties of the outside world than that there, sitting under the neon lights, she was losing herself in the difficulties, accident or terrible threat that hung over her, and the attention she found it impossible to give in class, where everything encouraged her to do so, must have evaporated completely when she was on her own at home, as her exercise books invariably showed in the following class: the homework had never been done, and the pages of set reading from text-books she had been asked to do were always so impeccably clean and new that it was obvious she had not even bothered to glance at them. Sofia's mother never discovered what exactly it was that kept her in this anguished state, always on the brink of bursting into tears or running away. 'I've got problems,' Señorita Sanz once told her in one of the personal moments that, taking pity on her, Sofia's mother offered her even during the class. So great were the timidity, awkwardness and lack of social graces that Señorita Sanz displayed, that this generic formula: 'I've got problems', usually employed reticently, in order to satisfy the other person's curiosity while at the same time denying him the gory details he was hoping to hear, in her case sounded as intimate, dramatic and eloquent as the most detailed confession. As the heat grew in December, and with the approach of the festivities and (an essential element, as the class was entirely made up of teachers) the end-of-year exams and reports to be written, which threatened to consume whatever remained of their reserves of energy, the group quickly dissolved. Sofia's mother, who had taught for years in the institute and so was not surprised at the speed with which they all disappeared, was nonetheless taken aback when one afternoon in the general office, where she had come to pay (late as usual) her last instalment for the year, Señorita Sanz suggested they go on with the course – even though Sofia's mother knew that on top of her personal problems she was under the same kind of academic pressure as the rest of the class. She had to explain it was impossible: apart from the general desertion of the class, which in fact had merely brought forward the end of teaching by a few days, the course was meant to finish by mid-December. When she saw how badly this explanation affected Señorita Sanz, by way of consolation she added that she would only have to wait two months because, like all the other annual classes, this one would begin again in March; she suggested she might take advantage of the free time in the summer to clear her head and replenish her energy, something which, as far as she could tell, might be equally or even more important than learning a foreign language . . . But Señorita Sanz did not hear her. She had listened as far as the words 'free time' and then, as if they had shaken her up badly, she lowered her head and, standing there in the institute office, in the presence of the bursar, who was sorting through some invoices, and the office boy, emptying a cupboard of files, she began to cry her heart out, alternating her sobs with dreadful moans, as though Sofia's mother had just given her an unexpected, terrible piece of news: being thrown out of her home, the death of a loved one, a fatal illness, something that left the person hearing it in a state of utter despair. It was not Sofia's mother, who was too busy trying to comfort her, but the institute's bursar who – feeling sorry for this poor woman who had burst into tears in front of her without the slightest sense of shame, not because she was shameless but because she simply could not help herself, as if the news that these two months which she had hoped to devote to studying English and would now be empty for her, was the final straw – had a sudden brainwave and mentioned the idea of an intensive summer course. To Sofia's mother that seemed like salvation; at least that was what she had thought then, as she ceaselessly stroked Señorita Sanz's hair, damp from all the tears. The courses lasted two months, did not require any prior knowledge, and although the inscription period was over, they could always make an exception.

Sofia's mother never had a more dedicated, attentive, or persevering student. In a little under two months, at a rate of five classes a week (she did not miss a single one) Señorita Sanz had not only surpassed her performance in the whole of the rest of the year (which was no great achievement) but also that of the best students in her class. She was so dedicated, so anxious to learn, that Sofia's mother was forced to stay behind afterwards, when all the others had left the institute, to give her extra reading passages and exercises. Señorita Sanz always welcomed these like a puppy receiving a reward, and handed them back perfectly completed long before the deadline. Yet the most satisfying aspect of this was not her amazing appetite for work, nor the way her knowledge of English improved with every day, nor even the enthusiasm with which she approached each new stage of learning, which drove her to invest even more effort than was demanded of her: it was the way in which this dedicated attitude (less like that of a student than of a missionary, for whom there is nothing in the world that can come anywhere near replacing the cause she has embraced) had apparently eradicated all the problems that had made her suffer so throughout the year. According to Sofia's mother, she was a changed woman – she was unrecognisable. Even her appearance had changed. Whereas before colour only came to her cheeks very occasionally and by accident, whenever she could not control something or felt embarrassed, now she was positively beaming, and looked so fresh and youthful that it made her old-fashioned wardrobe seem out of place; at the same time, her gaunt, frail body looked stronger, as if she had put on a few kilos. That was why, one Monday morning in mid-February when Sofia's mother closed the classroom door, turned towards her students and noticed that for the first time her place was empty – the only seat that, as she then realised, it had been important to her to see occupied every day – she was filled with a strange foreboding. Señorita Sanz was also absent on the Tuesday, the Wednesday, and every other day of a week that became unbearably long. She did not send any word, and none of her companions, with whom she had little contact apart from saying hello and goodbye, and sometimes in between asking them a technical question about the course, could enlighten her. The next Monday, Señorita Sanz's seat and desk were still empty. Terrified, it flashed through Sofia's mother's mind that the amazing improvement she had witnessed over the previous month and a half might merely be one of those brief periods of health and strength that some sick people experience before they are plunged into the final disaster. She gave the class as best she could, strictly adhering (so as to avoid further worry) to the outline she had prepared at home, but even though her reflexes worked well and hid her troubled spirit behind a screen of professional competence, more than once during the class she raised her head as though rousing herself from a deep slumber and caught all her students staring at her, waiting for the answer to a question she had not even registered. As soon as the class had finished, she went down to the office and asked for Señorita Sanz's file, then dialled the number, ignored the intrigued look on the bursar's face. Nobody answered. She wrote down the address without thinking. Five minutes later, struggling to read her own handwriting, she read it out, heart pounding, to the taxi-driver who was staring at her through his rear-view mirror. It was at the other end of the city, in a neighbourhood of low houses, cobbled passages, and empty lots. Señorita Sanz lived in a five-storey block, one of the few modern buildings in the area. The street door was open. Sofia's mother went in, took the lift, and, after ringing the bell to no effect, knocked on the door. A few seconds went by before someone opened it. Taken aback, Sofia's mother recoiled a few paces: the woman opposite her was an exact copy of Señorita Sanz, but she smoked, was ten years older, and had her hair bundled up in a headscarf. Not only that, but everything that in Señorita Sanz was hesitation, vulnerability, daintiness, was here hidden under a thick coating of tough ill-humour. She leaned on a broom, screwed up her eyes (a cigarette dangling from her lips) and studied Sofia's mother with scornful curiosity. Sofia's mother explained who she was. At that, the woman turned on her heel and took up her cleaning again without even closing the door – not so much inviting Sofia's mother in as ignoring her completely. Feeling awkward, she watched the other woman working for a while in the small, empty apartment: she swept the floor energetically, almost furiously, angrily pushing aside the few remaining pieces of furniture, as if they were in her way. Sofia's mother looked for anything that might remind her of Señorita Sanz. She could not see a thing; all that remained was the stale, enclosed atmosphere, that persisted even though the windows were open. She finally screwed up her courage to ask, but no sooner had she opened her mouth to speak than the woman, as though guessing her intention, broke off her work again and turned towards her – not out of deference, because it was more than obvious that not only Sofia's mother but anything

425

relating to this apartment (and, by extension, to the person who had lived there) was a source of annoyance to her, a weight she would never tire of complaining about – but so as to leave no doubt as to the hostile intent of what she was about to say, to ensure that Sofia's mother would never again cross her path: in a flat voice, without the slightest sign of grief or pity, but full of drama, she told her that Señorita Sanz, whom she described as 'that great idiot of a sister of mine' had died a week before in a clinic in Saavedra, either before, after, or during the abortion she had finally decided to have, in order to try to keep the man who had got her pregnant – and the only one, as far as she was aware, who had touched her in her entire life – a married professional with children who, when he had heard of the trap he had fallen into – a typical trap laid by women who knew that otherwise no man in his right mind would go near them – had warned her that she should have the child if she wanted to, but that if this happened she would never see him again, not even in photos, and should forget him once and for all.

CHAPTER 9

At dawn they woke him and took him to a freezing office, even smaller than his cell, where a stranger in a suit and tie shook hands with him with routine politeness and pushed towards him an open cardboard box, like a shoe-box, with the number 19 written on the front, which the same policeman who had taken his fingerprints the night before got down from an ancient wooden stand divided into compartments. Rimini recognised the watch, belt, shoe-laces, wallet, and bunch of keys, and this hoard which twenty hours earlier when he had been obliged to give it up by the man signing him in had seemed a priceless treasure, now looked to him pathetically poor. He stared at it for a while, without moving and without really seeing it, like someone watching the lazy circling of fish in a fish-tank, and if the lawyer, annoyed at the early hour, at the time Rimini's indecision was causing him to waste, and at the obviously completely useless kind of client Rimini was for him anyway, had not butted in as brusquely as he did, turning the box over like a cup of dice and throwing the personal effects on to the desk, Rimini would quite happily have left them there, pleased to think that such a modest heritage could hardly find a more appropriate home than the four cardboard walls, or a more responsible keeper than the policeman who had by now turned his back on them and replaced the box in its compartment.

'Is everything there?' the lawyer asked. Rimini nodded, signed a form on the dotted line the lawyer was pointing to with a nicotine-stained finger and then, instead of putting them on (which might have been expected, at least in the case of the belt, the watch, and the shoe-laces) he put everything slowly away, as if there were lots and lots of them, until his trouser pockets were bulging uncomfortably. Another form appeared. The lawyer said: 'Here' at exactly the same moment that Rimini once again saw the yellow-stained fingertip pointing at an empty space on the sheet of paper. It was as if the voice were springing out of the end of the finger. Rimini looked at him with a mixture of surprise and suspicion. 'It's the way out,' the lawyer explained. Like all specialists, he allowed himself the luxury, in the presence of the uninitiated, of replacing complete sentences that took time and energy and risked not being understood, with stray phrases which sounded like imperious spokesmen for all that had been left out. Rimini signed without fully understanding what he was putting his signature to. He was regaining his freedom in the same resigned way as he had lost it. Everything looked new to him, as if it were one of those dream sequences in which all the objects are shiny and untouched, as if they have been bought at the last minute for the scene and suggest this may be a joke or a trick. The lawyer folded the form like a handkerchief and put it in his pocket. 'Let's go,' he said, taking Rimini gingerly by the elbow and steering him towards the door, where an alarm had just started to go off. They went out, crossed the police station entrance, where a woman in slippers and housecoat was sitting waiting, holding a cold drinks can to a black eye, and before the lawyer could open the street door, Rimini managed to escape from him for a split second and to call out weakly, as if he were still asleep: 'The Riltse!' but then, without him realising exactly how – probably because of the force of the stupefied look the lawyer gave him – he found himself outside.

Outside was the street, cars with their doors taped up, the ID-card photo booth, the local bar where the metal shutters were just coming noisily to life, the same signs of everyday activity that Rimini must have seen the day before, when he was brought here in the patrol car, but which now, eyes stinging, and dazed less by a lack of sleep than by the speed and ease with which he had been rescued, he seemed to be seeing for the first time. Sofia was there, on the pavement opposite. She moved away from the wall she had been leaning against, slipped sideways between two car bumpers, and came across the street towards him, towards them, with her flaming hair and that halo of light all around it that left her face in shadow, as if she were against the light. She was the last thing he had expected to see. And yet as soon as he saw her, he felt yet again that for her to be there was as natural and predictable as the red glow of dawn,

428

the cool breeze or any of the other impassive signs the world offered
to persuade anyone who might have forgotten it that they were still
alive. He saw her, and everything fell into place, like the scattered
pieces of a jigsaw that, as in a film played backwards, effortlessly reformed the original diaphanous landscape. Tartan skirt, dark roll-
neck jumper, leather jacket with a sheepskin lining: Rimini could
have sworn she was wearing the same clothes as – when? The last
day of classes, twenty years ago? Even further back? The evening
when, stuck uncomfortably but happily between the edge of a coffee
table and a double sofa, they took advantage of a lapse in Rodi's
supervision to explore each other for the first time on the living-
room carpet, at the beginning with the starving urgency of shipwrecked sailors, then almost immediately with the clumsiness of
guilt, while all the time Yves Montand (thanks to an unexpected
scratch in the vinyl) repeated over and over again the same verse
from 'Les feuilles mortes'? Did it really matter when? If the past were
this calm, flat, endless sea, and Sofia its only representation, so much
so that it was enough to say her name to conjure it all up, what did
facts or dates matter? And in this sense, could he say that Sofia was
really 'outside'? Was she something in the outside world? Or was she
part of him? Why, as she came closer, did everything around her,
the background and the accessories that situated her and made her
real, why did all of that suddenly start to waver like a reflection in
water, and then disappear, leaving her as the only thing he could see,
intact, alone in the midst of nothing?

He watched her cross the road, step up on to the pavement. Yet
again he was astounded at the assured, almost suicidal naturalness of
Sofia's behaviour in such an extraordinary situation. She did not allow
it to overwhelm her, and yet did not try to underestimate it, as if its
extraordinary nature, which to Rimini was of central importance, to
her was nothing more than a casual factor that would only serve to
enhance her dominion. Yes, now he understood, he thought: Sofia –
this living, organic Sofia, who was so present that even if she were
removed, the physical space she occupied would still be filled – was
made of the same stuff as Señorita Sanz, as the hem of her sea-green
nightdress, as the classroom that the gas fire still filled with fumes, as
the sleepy faces of his companions, as he himself, the childish version

of Rimini, his grey flannel trousers patched at the knee, his shoe-laces always untied, spying with macabre delight on the trembling back of a school teacher betrayed by her married lover – the same stuff of which all the spectres from the past that had visited him one by one in the police station were made. A flat, dimensionless material that went on and on and above all was indestructible: the stuff the dead are made of.

The lawyer stepped in front of him, held out his hand to Sofia and said: 'He's all yours.' He sounded relieved, as if he were handing over a small but rebellious animal with tiny but very sharp claws. Before leaving them, he turned back towards Rimini, gave him one last look – either because he was concerned, or out of a sense of professional scrupulousness – then looked over at Sofia and added in a worried voice, as though a troublesome little cloud had just ruined the sky of his relief: 'Give me a call if there's anything I can do.' Sofia said nothing; she did not even nod. Now that she was closer, and the halo of flames around her head had quietened down, Rimini discovered that her hair, which the last time he had seen her in the clinic had been a honey-blonde colour, as he remembered it always being, had now gone grey, a light, uniform grey, like ashes. She took a couple of steps forwards – Rimini could sense the lawyer vapourising in the dawn air – and they hugged each other, or rather Sofia completely enveloped him in her arms (something that was hard to explain, since not only was Rimini twice her size, but her sheepskin coat must have considerably reduced her room for manoeuvre) as if she were finally reclaiming something that divine injustice had robbed her of. Then, in the tumult of their embrace, gripped by the vice of dampness and warmth from her breathing, locks of hair, the leather of her coat and its sheepskin lining, her woollen jumper, her forearms, Rimini heard her weak but crystal-clear voice gently, charily making its way towards him – prepared to fall silent rather than to seem like a threat – whispering a single word: 'Enough', as if to calm him, and then, as she slowly shook him as though to wake him up, she said over and over again; 'Enough, enough, enough', until Rimini felt that the voice was growing more dense, was precipitating, changing its state until it became a chemical substance, less a voice and more a dose, which entered directly into his bloodstream and started to move unhurriedly through his veins, guided by a single blind desire: to reach his heart, take it over, impregnate it.

PART FOUR

CHAPTER 1

*How long has it been since I watched you sleep? How long since you
offered me that spectacle? (Just now, a drop of water – I've had a shower,
it's a quarter past twelve, I'm going to be late, you've been sleeping now
for thirty hours non-stop – ran down my arm, gathered at the elbow, as
if hesitating, and then fell and exploded on your cheek, about two millimetres above the mark the sheet has left there. It split into lots of smaller
drops, one of them went on down and down the skin of your huge face,
until it disappeared into a corner of your mouth. Immediately, your tongue
poked out, like an animal from its cave, but it was too late: there was
nothing left to drink.) As you see, I still like to write. And I still like paren-
theses. I can't help it. It can't be helped, Rimini. We can't help it – that
could be our slogan. I keep putting sentences inside sentences, and you
keep on . . . Is it too soon? You'll say it is (though you don't say anything,
you're silent, so I can talk to you for hours, as if I were a hypnotist, then
I can wipe it all away and when you wake up you won't remember a
thing). But Rimini, I at least keep on <u>seeing</u>. And what I can see now
(what little you are going to find out for now of all that I see as I watch
you sleep) is that, even though for years you have been sleeping without
me, far from me, against me, you still sleep with your arms squashed
under the pillow (I'd love to see your horrified face when you wake up
and can't feel them, and for a split second think they're no longer there,
that someone – me, for example, the monster-woman, the knife-woman
– tore them off you while you were sleeping, but you're wrong, Rimini, if
I wanted your arms, I would turn them to stone), you still sleep with
your socks on, still rub one foot against the other in your sleep, still soak
the tip of the pillow with saliva, still talk in your sleep (by the way, did
you know that in your dreams you talk a stilted but perfect French?) you
still toss and turn and pull all the covers over to your side (nothing we
can't sort out with a bit of effort), you still cover your eyes with your
forearm, as if overcome by grief or blinded by the sun, you still sit up*

straight in the middle of the night, completely asleep but with your eyes open, in a panic – just like you told me you used to do as a boy (but you're a grown man now, so you don't get out of bed and walk around the apartment, you just stare at two different points in the darkness – the ceiling fan, for example, and my knee, which the folds of the sheet make look as though it's sculpted in stone – and when you've looked from one to the other several times, when you've exhausted the terror that gripped you, you collapse back on to the bed in a single movement, like those reclining seats that tip back, and it's as though nothing had happened). The anatomy lesson. You still tremble, Rimini. My poor little Rimini. My shipwrecked sailor. But it's finished, it's all over, you're back home now. I spoke to the lawyer: they gave him the painting and the woman has withdrawn charges. We had to give her a few pesos as well. My lawyer did not want to. He doesn't like you. (He even seems to think my father died because of you.) He said he had never met such a vulgar woman in his life. How could you fall so low? I knew that without me you were lost – but that lost? (A woman in her fifties covered in gold jewellery – yes I know, I never actually met her, I never had that pleasure.) A . . . what do they call them? A personal trainer? I'm talking about the person who called me to tell me. And you . . . seeing you coming out of the police station in those trainers . . . I wouldn't have been surprised if you had become an alcoholic, a cocaine addict, a male prostitute. But to stoop to sports???) I could have left you rotting in jail, you know. Don't imagine I didn't think of it. Not out of vengeance (you hurt me, I hurt you: we hurt each other exactly the same amount, as only happens between two people who can't help it), but out of love. I saw myself visiting you in your cell, taking you things like in the movies. As though you were in jail for me. A crime of passion. As if you had killed my lover, or my husband who beat me, or my boss who had raped me. I know you stole the Riltse for me, out of love for me. (But those aren't things you can explain to my lawyer.) I'm telling you this now, while you're asleep, because I know that when you're awake you're never going to admit it. (Real men keep their secrets!) I also considered (you'll say I'm mad) taking her to court. Of getting hold of that cow and prosecuting her. Because what you did was not robbery: it was an expropriation, an act of justice. She was the thief. Those who buy Riltses are the thieves. It doesn't matter who they are. Riltse is ours. I looked up that painting in the catalogues; I couldn't find

436

it. Afterwards, fool that I am, I realised my books only go up to 1976, the last days of our youth, and that I don't have anything from any later. Now I'm looking at you asleep, for the first time I'm amazed at how you haven't changed. Yes, I know it's nothing new: you were always Dorian Gray. But when we were together it's something I could never understand. We loved each other = we were the same = we did not grow older. Neither of us. (And yet my father died, he died with that smile on his face, the smile you left him before you ran off, and the next morning I woke up with grey hair.) So now you are Dorian Gray, and I'm the picture. Would you have liked us to change? Is that what you wanted: a flexible love that could change to something different? Well, it's happened. 'She could be your mother.' Sorry, I had to answer the phone. It was Victor, from the hospital. I told him. I said: 'You'll never guess who's sleeping in my bed.' Do you think he was surprised? Nobody is surprised. (We come from so remote a time, Rimini. We're millions of years old. Our love is geological. The separations, encounters, fights, everything that happens and is visible, everything that has a date, like 1976: all that is as insignificant as a cracked floor-tile compared to the quaking that has been making the centre of the earth tremble for thousands of years.) Victor is dying. I think someone was holding the phone so that he could speak. He missed you as well. He asked whether we were going to throw a party. I said we weren't. I told him he had to get well for the opening of Adela H. I have to go now. The women will kill me. There's coffee in the pot, and clean towels in the bathroom. I'm leaving you the box with all the photos. It's still intact: it's been waiting years for you. No, I didn't have time to get another set of keys cut. (Now I come to think of it, I'm not sure I want you to have another set.) Are you here? Is it really you, arguing in your dreams in that bed of mine? Farewell, my sleeping beauty. Farewell, my Prisoner.

CHAPTER 2

He woke up at the slightest thing: a dripping tap, galloping noises from the central heating pipes, the straining sound of the lift five floors below whenever some night-bird called it. And of course, Sofia's breathing. She did not snore. It was a study: it suggested snoring, but never actually became it, like those studies for paintings which promise figures, shapes and colours that eventually languish and are forgotten. Sofia breathed with extraordinary intensity and depth, as if her lungs could never get enough air. At first, startled but still asleep, Rimini thought that if he turned round in the bed he would find some kind of enraged animal, with flashing eyes and two trails of vapour rising from its nostrils. But he got used to it, and over the next few nights the sight of Sofia's face, flat on her back, completely relaxed, breathing such enormous quantities of air in and out, with the only noise the slight whistling sound that appeared in the background and modulated the relaxed opacity of her respiration – that sight came to be the spectacle with which the world rewarded his first waking moments. Because Rimini woke up and, after a few seconds of utter confusion, would immediately leap, completely wide-awake, into a state of alertness, such a smooth, homogeneous state that it seemed it must have been the laborious fruit of year upon year of not sleeping; almost at once, like someone who remembers a task he left half-finished and feels guilty about, he felt the need to get moving, to do something, to use up the extraordinary amount of energy he had woken up with. So, before he slid out of bed and went to sit, wrapped in Sofia's dressing-gown, at the dining-room table, surrounded by his files and pencils, in order to write details about the photos (a task he had set himself soon after he had gone back to live with Sofia and which had spread from these early hours of the day to take up not only the whole morning but the greater part of his day, because there were so many of them, and because so many memories came rushing back to him as he looked at them) he spent a long time watching Sofia sleep, studying her. He was as still as her or even more so, because it was normal for Sofia, throwing off the covers or reacting violently to the stimulus from a dream, to change position, suddenly moving closer to him or away from him, or sometimes totally disappearing from view – when, for example, she became completely wrapped up in the bedclothes – or sometimes coming so close to him, to his face, that he was forced to squint; whereas he, taking his responsibility as an observer seriously and fearing that any movement he might make could affect and thereby spoil the spontaneity of the phenomenon he was observing, forced himself to remain still, to hold his breath and even to put up in silence with the most uncomfortable positions, the most outlandish tangle of limbs, if only to preserve the integrity of his mission. He watched her sleeping while he himself was waking up, as if his eyes were drawing out of her, from the deep, dark well in which she lay, the substance he needed to clear his head completely. At first he regarded her with a distant, conventional kind of tenderness, in the way that one looks at anything guaranteed to arouse tender feelings – the photo of a pet, or a child, or a child with its pet; but then, once he had gone beyond this initial phase, he began to concentrate, and his contemplation took on an inquisitive, expectant quality: he watched her expecting something to happen, like someone on guard duty. Time and again, each morning, along with disappointment (because if on occasion Sofia deigned to respond to Rimini's expectations, it was with a sleeping person's typical reflex movements: turning over, kicking him, scratching herself, seizing a bit of the sheet, but never the revelation he seemed to be hoping for) Rimini discovered that what kept him there gazing at her sleeping body, what intrigued and at the same time fascinated him – so much so that he could spend an hour or more next to her, long enough for the dark night he had begun his vigil in to give way to the light of day, and the silence start to be filled with the first timid sounds – was not so much the possibility that she might emit some unexpected signal from her sleep, one that might give voice to the secrets she hid while awake, but the natural, completely unconcerned way in which, fast asleep, Sofia nevertheless managed to be there, a few centimetres from him, lifeless, so unprotected that he had her at his complete mercy, and yet at the same time could be so far away, at a distance no longitude could measure, immersed in the world of her sleep, that sphere which Rimini could disturb, by caressing her or kissing her, and also destroy by waking her up, but which he could never, try as he like, share with her.

Sofia was right: nobody was very surprised. First and foremost, Rimini himself. As he left the police station that morning and saw Sofia, it occurred to him, with a sort of astonished perplexity, how easily and quickly the world brought changes to his life which if he had decided to make them himself would not only have taken him centuries but would have demanded a determination he knew he could never have mustered. But that had been all: a flash of lucidity which shone and blinded him (the white flash erasing the figures of Sofia and the lawyer), and then vanished as soon as Sofia folded him in her embrace. He accepted his new life without complaint, with the resigned docility of an orphan, and his new life welcomed him hospitably and in a kindly fashion: it was not entirely disposed to forget his transgressions, but was willing to disarm them by reducing them to the category of youthful peccadilloes, which may have been serious but were stupid and meaningless and which never (as the fact of his having returned demonstrated) really represented a true threat. And besides, everything looked so familiar to him . . . he did not know Sofia's apartment, but it was enough for him to go in and smell the air (a thick, sweet smell that anyone else would have said was caused by a stale atmosphere, but which Sofia insisted was the warmth of the hearth) and to notice the predominance of wood – a light, finely grained wood, old oak – the only material Sofia considered sufficiently experienced to live with her – to feel he knew it all by heart, and that if at that very moment a power failure had plunged them into utter darkness, he would have been able to find his way around blindly, guided merely by what his memory told him. Faithful to her principles, which dictated that she stuck to everything that had some history attached to it, Sofia had not thrown anything away. Rimini allowed himself to be enveloped in this general, atmospheric déjà-vu. It did not take him long to identify all the holy relics he was once again part of: the dining-room table, the chairs, the bookshelves and the cane sofas – which Sofia had somehow managed to inherit from Rimini's grandmother with the apparently irresistible argument that Rimini wanted them more than anything else in the world, but was unaware of it – the big, fluffy white

rug like a polar bear flattened on its face, the old wheeled table, originally a drinks trolley, which Sofia still used for her phone, the standard lamps with their imitation parchment shades, the eiderdowns –
one covering the bed, the same bed, the other on the living-room sofa
– the cork drinks mats, the prints of plants and birds in the kitchen,
the valve wireless, still miraculously working . . . And all this, which
used to belong to him, and which he had rejected and forgotten, all
of it welcomed him back unconditionally and without rancour, even
with some sympathy, just as a sick person is welcomed back home after
spending several weeks in hospital. And when Sofia flung open her
wardrobes for him, this time adding a touch of solemnity to the naturalness of her gesture, as though giving him access to a secret chamber,
the innermost sanctum of her power, and Rimini started to fit the
clothing that had survived the wanderings of his last few years into a
space she herself had cleared – two or three worn-out, almost identical changes of clothing, of which Sofia had taken the trouble to remove
the very last one, the one he had been wearing when he left the police
station, and had immediately donated to the Orphans' Society, a charity
she regularly contributed to – convinced as she was by a kind of animist
faith, which Rimini was already familiar with, that clothing, personal
effects in general, and above all places, were all marked by the circumstances they were used in, and so retained a kind of magical aura of
those circumstances that was filed away in a state of readiness, to be
released again when the conditions were right – it seemed to him that
among Sofia's clothes there was absolutely nothing he had not seen
before in the wardrobes of the last apartment they had shared, nothing,
not a single item of clothing, or fabric, not a colour or fashion – and
beginning, logically enough, with the scent that seemed to envelop
them all: lavender, bags of lavender slipped in between the pullovers,
hanging from the rails, scattered in the socks drawer – a scent that
seemed to leap out at Rimini as soon as Sofia had opened the doors.
No, he was not coming back to a home, nor to the love of a woman
or even to a past – because the home, the love of a woman, and even
the past, are not completely immune to the actions of time. He was
coming back to a museum: the museum in which he had been born,
which had educated him, which he had been stolen from and which
over the years had not only refused to fill his place with another piece,

but had kept it empty, against all the odds, in the same way that the site of a miracle is preserved, in the hope, or rather the certainty, that sooner or later he, Rimini, would come and fill it again, and the miracle would happen once more.

He spoke to his father. Not only did his news not come as a surprise, it seemed to relieve him, as though he too had an interest in the museum, and the return of the piece brought a long period of uncertainty to an end. Later, in order to explain a calm acceptance that might have seemed suspicious, Sofia admitted she had already mentioned something about it to him. With that strange mixture of surprise, scandal and pride aroused by harmless forms of betrayal, Rimini realised that neither his father's exile in Montevideo, nor Sofia's erratic existence, nor his own absence – at the same distance from both of them – had ever prevented his father and Sofia from staying in touch behind his back. It was then that he, who years before had thought about it and reached the conclusion that his break with Sofia was like an entire planet exploding, in such a tremendous and massive explosion that it was unthinkable that the fragments (Rimini and Sofia first and foremost, but also Rimini's father, Victor, and all those who in some way or other had been part of it) could possibly come together again, still less reproduce the kind of bond that had existed before the explosion – Rimini discovered how far all that had been an illusion, and how far he had been the victim. Because it was obvious that either the planet had not exploded at all, and instead it was Rimini who had simply cut himself off from it, the only one who had done so, which helped explain why now on his return he found everything exactly the same as before, or it had exploded, but the fragments, after travelling aimlessly through space for a while, had finally reconstituted the original planet and welded together again, and it was only because Rimini (who of all the pieces had perhaps been the one which had travelled the least distance) had been so slow that by the time he arrived, all the scars on the planet had healed.

No, he was no Ulysses returning to Ithaca after surviving the Cyclops, Circe, the sirens' song. He was one of those weak, stubborn creatures, ruined by a particularly perverse illness – alcoholism, for example, or memory lapses – who from time to time, with a regularity their family members know well, as well as the signs they have learnt to decipher in order to know what is going on, suddenly uproots themselves, and with their loved ones' consent or otherwise – because they have already tried to dissuade, oppose, or lock them up, all to no avail – they disappear without trace, only to reappear a few days later exhausted, with the scratches from their excursion still evident on clothes and body, knock at the door – God knows what ditch they lost their keys in – and when it opens raise their eyes to the face they love, ashamed but full of a feverish longing, hoping to find the exuberant, dramatic welcome they thought they had merited by disappearing, whereas what they get, at best, is a wan smile like something from a manual of how to give charity, slaps on the back, encouraging words said loudly enough to hide the sound of the lock turning twice in the street door, or simply a resigned twist of the mouth, an accumulated rancour, and a list of all the obligations that have accumulated since they took flight and which are now waiting to be fulfilled. No, there was nothing epic about his return; not even an epic of failure or revenge. And yet, after his initial disappointment, Rimini felt it was better that way, that in the lack of surprise and emotion there was also something sweet, a balm that soothed the dangers of intensity and stayed with him, buoying him up, as he progressed towards a life that was at the same time both new and old, in the same way that in his childhood, just before an operation, the half pill his mother gave him was enough to help him cover the most difficult stretch – the journey from his room to the operating theatre on a trolley – with an almost voluptuous veil of indifference.

And there was an unexpected consolation. That curiosity – curiosity! not even delight, astonishment, or turmoil – that he failed to find in his own father, or Victor, or, of course, in Sofia, and not even in those who had never before seen him in person, satellites who had moved into Sofia's orbit while he had been away and for whom Rimini, however much Sofia had talked about him, was not someone coming back, but a complete stranger, an apparition, a first time, was something Rimini eventually discovered among the women of Adela H. Apart from the bricklayer and the gas fitter involved in the refurbishing of the premises (the woman architect had been unable to find any female equivalents for them, although she had been successful in discovering women to do the electricity, the painting and the carpentry), Rimini had been the first man in Adela H. Partly because of this, which already gave him a slightly mysterious air, partly because of the expectations that Sofia's comments about him had aroused in her companions, and partly also because the first time he had entered the building, confused by the contrast between the bright daylight outside and the gloom inside, he had not seen the steps going down, had stumbled and, had it not been for Sofia's steadying hand, would have crashed headlong into a pane of glass two women were carrying, Rimini's arrival could not have been less inconspicuous, and it would have been comic, side-splittingly comic, if the women had not 'dampened it down' with the blanket of their remote eyes – the same way that Rimini, seeing them in Adela H., or going with them to do the shopping, or in the fortnightly meetings Sofia held in her apartment, when Rimini received them, served coffee and cakes, read out the agenda and took minutes, realised that they regarded the whole world. How many of them were there? Eight? Ten? Twelve? The numbers were always so fluctuating, the faces always so similar, and the group effect so strong, that he never really found out. That first evening, the evening of his presentation in society, as Sofia put it, surrounding the words with ironic emphasis to break the ice after the initial near-disaster, Rimini smiled at and kissed half a dozen women grouped round him in a semi-circle, as he heard and immediately forgot the names Sofia called out, and after he had gone round them all, stood there with his hands over his groin (as if he were naked), lowered his head and allowed them to judge him in silence, at their leisure, while a drill screeched in the kitchen. He was approved.

In fact, Rimini felt he had not so much been approved as adopted. Once their initial curiosity had been satisfied (the length of time it took for them to corroborate with him, around him, that what Sofia had told them was true), they invited him in, told him to make himself comfortable – not an easy thing to do, given the fact that the only seat that had not just been freshly painted was being used as a step-ladder by a woman in dungarees who was standing on tiptoe to wrap insulating tape around some lengths of cable – and started talking to him in low voices, always from very close up, so softly and slowly that they all seemed to have learnt the same method in an etiquette class. He was the one taken by surprise. For some reason, this was not the way he had expected to be greeted. He knew about Adela H., just as he knew about the existence of the group Sofia had been working with for the past two years, the association of Women Who Love Too Much, which had ended up replacing (to Sofia's eternal satisfaction) the endless series of seminars, labs, and workshops on which she had spent most of the previous twenty years of her life. But that was not all. If Sofia did not explain a great deal to him, it was not out of discretion or reticence, but because Rimini did not dare ask, or because Sofia thought that in this way, by taking everything for granted, Rimini could become part of the project (as she liked to call it) in a clear, transparent way, thereby sparing them the always troublesome business of a transition. It was true that the name of the group intimidated him a little, and when Sofia showed him the group's logo with the design one of the women had come up with for all their stationery, he found it hard to hide his unease. 'Isn't it perfect?' Sofia said, curling up beside him, admiring the way that the initials plunged into a tiny, bleeding, purple heart.

Despite all this, their reception disconcerted him. They were polite, friendly in an almost unctuous way. They talked in a delicate, caressing manner – and not just when they were speaking to him (to whom, after all, as the man in Sofia's life, they owed some special consideration), but with everyone, always: when they were talking among themselves, giving orders to the people roaming round Adela H., or arguing (if it were possible to remove all the weight of aggression implied in that word) over some urgent question about their cause in a group meeting. For them, raising one's voice seemed to represent a combination of wastefulness and vulgarity, a waste of time and an outrage. The same was true of their movements and gestures, the special way they had of managing their physical presence: everything had to be gentle, soft, fluid. Wrapped invariably in tunics or loose-fitting dresses, they seemed not so much to walk as to slide or glide along, a bit like those geishas who, when one looks at them only from the waist up, seem to be in perpetual movement, as though they are on an escalator. And they seemed to extend this control over their bodies to the space around them, to objects and to other people's bodies, with the result that between them and the world all possibility of violence or chance encounters had disappeared, even the possibility of any unplanned exchange, to such an extent that, inspired by this kind of unfailing

445

choreographic instinct, doubtless the fruit (Rimini thought) of the
dozens of different exercise disciplines that had merged and fermented
within them over the years, not only was it extremely rare to see them
stumble or bang into things, but, thanks to a magical or technical effect
– like the one that happens when we suddenly turn down the sound
on a television set and the images go on in silence – they seemed not
to make any noise: no noise, in any case, that went beyond the intimate threshold of brushing against something, and to have become
strangely bodiless. And yet, beneath this fluidity, which Sofia had
explained to Rimini as being related to one of the passions the whole
group shared, namely the passion for 'connection' – by definition,
opposed to all those forces which tried to interrupt the continuity of
life – Rimini soon discovered that when he looked more closely at this
cushioned world free of all violence and threat of collapse, he could
discern the unmistakable signs of effort. How hard they worked! How
disciplined they were! he thought, and the only part of the picture that
disturbed him, the shadow of unhappiness or bitterness he occasionally imagined he glimpsed flitting across the faces of these women who
were normally so in control of themselves, stood out against this hard-
working background and took on a deeper meaning. They worked:
they worked full-time, twenty-four hours a day, because the task they
had dedicated themselves to, that of harmony between body and world,
did not pause for a rest even in sleep, and work, apart from the state
of grace or insubstantiality it afforded them, devoured them entirely,
like torture or an invisible illness. They were weary, and perhaps it was
this weariness that produced the stuffy, slightly old-fashioned atmosphere present not only in their clothes, their tastes, or the verbal
anachronisms that occasionally crept into their sentences, but even in
their bodies, in the crow's feet of wrinkles round their eyes, the lines
beside their nostrils, their untidy hair which always looked as if they
had just got up, in the lack of interest, almost disdain, that they professed
for all make-up, as well as in the drugged distance from which they
surveyed the world, apparently respecting it in a tolerant way that at
first glance did not exclude a certain curiosity, but which in reality
meant quite the opposite, since they disqualified it totally, denying it
any chance to surprise them, as though they were not the ages – thirty,
forty, fifty years old – that appeared in their official documents, but

instead were hundreds or thousands of years old, the superhuman age boasted of by those who say they have seen everything.

That first evening, one woman in particular caught his attention. Unlike all the others, who had stayed in their semi-circle and obliged him to move forward to greet them, she had taken two steps towards him, almost intercepting him, and grasping the hand he had decided it was easier to leave hanging in mid-air, as he still had another five or six women to say hello to. She kept his hand in hers for a while – much longer than the fleeting contact her colleagues had preferred to offer – smiling with one side of her mouth as she stared at him with her grey, watery eyes that looked as if they were about to fill with tears. Then, after a few moments, during which Rimini felt she was expecting something of him, something which he, bewildered by such close attention, was unable to decipher, she drew him to her and, thanks to a mysterious series of manoeuvres and pressures, somehow managed to get him into an intimate clinch in which they kissed each other at great length, like two old friends finally meeting up, while at the same time giving the impression that it was he, Rimini, and not her, who had chosen this level of intimacy. 'My love,' he heard her whisper in his ear. 'How long it's taken you!' Then he felt the woman pushing him away, as though putting an end to an insistence that Rimini did not feel in the slightest, and there she was staring at him again with her cloudy eyes, contented but troubled, as if their re-encounter had closed a debt she had always considered it impossible to repay. 'You see, Isabel?' Sofia said triumphantly. 'And you said he wouldn't remember!' 'Isabel,' thought Rimini. He was already moving on to the next woman, going through the stages of a ceremony he knew nothing about but had caught an absent-minded glimpse of on television – an ambassador presenting his credentials, or a kissing of hands in the Vatican, and together with the name he had just heard (which, to his surprise, was already ringing bells in some distant corner of his memory) he had an after-image of the face he had left behind: white skin, drooping eyebrows, the almost transparent grey of her eyes – and suddenly he remembered who she was; all he had to do was imagine her somewhat younger, put the colour back in hair that was now a dull grey, clear her voice of the harshness the years had created, and nothing more, because all the rest – the Indian blouse, black velvet slippers, her firm body that always seemed so much more youthful than the rest of her – was exactly the same as before, and he could see her where he had last seen her, sitting on the sofa in the Calle Vidt apartment, a plate of strudel balanced on her lap – that unmissable treat, cooked by her own fair hands, which she delicately lifted mouthful by mouthful, keeping the other hand beneath the fork to catch any crumbs, to the waiting mouth of Frida Breitenbach. And then all the faces became familiar to him, as if they had been illuminated by the echoes Isabel had managed to stir in him, and emerged out of the darkness. He thought he recognised some of them, and even allowed himself the pleasure of mentally putting names to them, using the old, painful names that began to revive in his mind: Milagros, Rocío, Mercedes. He saw them all, plate of strudel on their knees, taking turns to keep the fangs of their leader occupied. He heard all of them, without exception, in one or other of the free zones of the apartment (a corridor, the cloakroom, the lift or the street door, which was always kept locked and which they took advantage of whenever they had to go down and show someone out) whispering the details of their latest turbulent love lives. That 'latest' was just a way of putting it; it would have been the same if they had been talking about their 'first' loves, so hard was it with these women to distinguish between their mature and their adolescent passions: desperate, hopeless affairs which left them bereft – the victims of love, as Frida said to their faces, in a slightly mocking tone of voice which later, in private, when the bulk of her guests had left and only a circle of her closest friends continued the evening in front of the gas stove, snacking on the remains of the feast – Sofia was one of them, of course, and so was Rimini – became pitiless scorn, that was brutal but far more appropriate than mockery to accompany the expressions she used, now they were no longer there, to describe them in a cascading verbal torrent: 'fourth-rate lambs', 'sacrificial flesh', 'professional widows', and so on, insults that the others (thought Rimini) were only spared because they were still there and because they believed, with a credulity that she could do nothing to discourage, that the fact that they had been selected by Frida as the chosen audience for her vitriol meant that they would never be on the receiving end. It was when they were fleeing Frida's sarcasm, or simply her watchful eye, that the Milagros, Rocíos, or Isabels, using the slightest, most unlikely excuses, left the living-room and took advantage of anyone they chanced to meet to comment (naming no names, in phrases whispered because of their urgency and the threat hanging over them) on the latest abandonment, the latest betrayal, the latest sleepless night or unanswered phone call, the latest dreams to have gone up in smoke; and it was during these hidden, almost conspiratorial skirmishes that Rimini usually came across them on his way to the bathroom, or when he was carrying a couple of bottles out to the kitchen and stumbled across them in twos or threes, heads together, bodies bent forwards as though they were trying to protect the secrets they were sharing. As soon as they saw him, they smiled guiltily and immediately disbanded their meeting, separating or returning to the task that had originally been their excuse for leaving the living-room, as if they saw Rimini not only as an unwelcome witness, an intruder, but also as the informer who could betray them.

Even though the words she had whispered in his ear worried him, forcing him to think whether there might perhaps have been something more between them than the rather forced intimacy of Breitenbach's inner circle, it was thanks to Isabel and the eagerness with which she had broken the protocol rules that Rimini understood just how far the warmth of the welcome was personal, directed at him in particular, and was to some extent an expression of gratitude. He discovered that if his return was a matter of celebration for the women of Adela H., it was not just because it renewed something that had been broken off, healing the wounds of that hiatus and so giving fresh impetus to the belief (so important for a certain kind of belief in love) that where feelings are concerned there is no possibility of establishing rigorous boundaries, there is no end, nothing ever really comes to an end, everything is up in the air, open, waiting for something, and even when a relationship broke down, in the sense of it falling apart, sending each of those involved flying in opposite directions, so that everything they have shared is torn in two, divided into two irreconcilable halves – even then, however much either or both of those in the relationship celebrated the break-up at the moment it occurred, justifying it with facts, causes, convincing arguments – neither of them will ever be in a position to know with any certainty whether what they say is the end is in fact that, or is simply a gap leading to another phase, a latent one, for example. There was something more: Rimini's return was a test case, the first really definitive one, proving that the cause of women who love too much could have a happy ending – different (not to say diametrically opposed) to what usually happened, which, as all the Isabels, Mercedes, and Rocíos, and even Sofia (before this dramatic reversal of fortune) demonstrated, was nothing more than a vast catalogue of disasters. Until then, until the moment that Sofia told the group that Rimini was returning to the fold, their cause – as the founders of Adela H. called a passion they were no longer willing to hide or feel ashamed of, and yet did not want to limit to a purely personal experience – had solely consisted of one long calvary, which might offer them satisfying depths of feeling but seemed guaranteed always to reach the same tragic, disturbing conclusion. Theirs was not just a mystique of suffering, it was one of defeat. Loving too much could never have a happy ending. But it was this inexorable failure, with the sense of sadness and desolation accompanying it, that gave their cause its true meaning – as if in their anguish, despair or any of the other maelstroms these women were condemned to fall into as a result of their disproportionate capacity for love, and from which they surfaced a short time later, swept away by grief but still holding aloft, more aloft than ever, the banner of their cause – although this was not always the case, to judge by the number of attempted suicides, the stays in hospital, the therapeutic treatments or all the pills (consumed in terrifying quantities, because by this time that was the only way they were going to have any effect) that were often the real reason for the remote way they had of looking at the world – it was as if by plunging into this inferno of the feelings they could reach out and touch the truth.

But now perhaps they could have everything, as Sofia had stressed to them in one of the group's first meetings after Rimini's return. To have everything: the excess of love, the calvary, the truth – and happiness. And to have it all without having to yield in any way – that was the most important thing, the reason for the sense of pride which at that same meeting, held in the dreadful damp and cold of the still unfinished kitchen in Adela H., had given these women back all the vitality and emotional energy that they seemed to have lost. And on this point, however much they regretted it, all of them (and not just Sofia, who after all, thanks to the years of the stable relationship she had enjoyed with Rimini, was the only one who could pride herself on not having been one of Frida's targets in this way) had to give up the bitterness and rancour that had been intensified rather than alleviated by Frida's death, and accept the fact that the Breitenbach message – an extreme message, which they, seeing it as part of the lengthy campaign Frida had fought against anything that smacked of female weakness, had always rejected – was not in the least absurd, and in fact had hit the centre of the bulls-eye where throughout the years all their feeble, hesitant, clumsy arrows had come to nothing. It was by taking the excess of love to excess that the women who loved too much could achieve what they set out to achieve, to seize it and open the way to some kind of happiness in love. This was the way to do it, not by trying to limit that excess of feeling or reining it in, not by hiding it behind all the presentable façades that would give it a social existence, but at the price of ultimate betrayal.

Just how far they had accepted this truth became clear that same evening when, seated on benches they had made out of piles of bricks, and trying to combat the cold with the builders' heater, two of the women in the group even questioned the only thing which until then (two years after Frida's funeral, which had been the starting point for Adela H.) had remained intact: its name. If that was how things stood: if Rimini's return did in fact prove that failure or bitter loneliness were not essential but accidental aspects of their cause, and if loving too much, in addition to being what it had always been – an unrequited waste of time and energy, synonymous with the most complete emotional bankruptcy – could also be an engine, a formidable power of attraction that was all the more powerful for being so intransigent, then the choice of Victor Hugo's youngest daughter as their muse was not only a mistake, but a serious ideological miscalculation. Now, in the group's post-Rimini era – a definition which Sofia herself used that same evening, without of course realising how much discussion it would arouse, as she was clearing off the wooden plank they used as a table for their plates, knives and forks, portions of strudel and shots of Cointreau – all the sad adventures of the unfortunate Adèle seemed to belong to an already buried past: not only her passion for Lieutenant Pinson, whom she had met at her own home, during one of the famous spiritualist sessions organised by her father – the unique, all-devouring passion for which Adèle, after rejecting the only man who truly loved her (poor Auguste Vacquerie, who had every intention of marrying her), threw up everything, including her sick father, who was only to see her again much later, when she was quite mad, and found himself obliged to confine her to the Saint-Mande asylum, where she spent the last forty years of her life playing the piano, gardening and writing her diary in code – and her mother, whose name she had inherited, and her two brothers – Charles, a translator of Shakespeare, and François-Victor, a budding photographer – and even Guernsey, the tiny island where her father, France's greatest poet, had been forced to seek exile after Napoléon III's coup d'état. Adèle left all this behind to set off alone on the strangest and, given the period (the second half of the nineteenth century), least advisable journeys a barely thirty-year-old woman could have undertaken: first to Halifax in Nova Scotia, Canada, where she had heard that the regiment Pinson was serving in had been stationed, and then to Barbados, still in pursuit of Pinson, who, even though she went around using his name as if she were his wife, she even failed to recognise when they met in the street; no, not just that – the Pinson affair, that doomed love that led her to lie, dress as a man, change her identity, to pretend that she was Leopoldine, her dead sister, to hire a hypnotist in order to try to get her beloved to confess in a trance to the love he stubbornly refused to admit to when wide-awake, all this so as to live up to the slogan that neither failure, nor suffering, scorn, or even the profoundest mental disorder could make her renounce, and only death could get the better of: 'love is my religion' – but also the huge gulf between her sacrifice and the way she remained anonymous, between her musical talent and the agonisingly few traces left of it, between the intensity of her life and the disdain that history showed for it. Adèle, Adèle H., forever eclipsed by the tragedy that befell her sister Leopoldine, who drowned with her husband in the sea at Villequier. Adèle H.: whose death in 1915 was silenced for ever by the tumult of the First World War.

The debate was lively but short-lived: like one of those sudden fires that flare up in a tranquil landscape and threaten to change everything, but then die out as quickly as they first appeared. Nothing changed, partly because of the difficult conditions in which the meeting was held – it was not a moment to sit around discussing things, when they were in such a rush to get the opening organised; partly because of the apathetic state of most of those involved – who, apart from Sofia, Isabel, and then two women who objected, knew nothing at all about Adèle H., and were therefore left completely cold by the discussion; and in part thanks to the firm, subtle and apparently disinterested way (doubtless learnt from all those years of association with Frida Breitenbach, that past mistress of manipulation) that Sofia defended the need to keep the original name, arguing amongst other things that it already appeared on the huge sign at the door, written in a neon imitation of nineteenth-century italic handwriting, and on the smaller posters that had been ordered two months earlier and were just about to arrive, and that it was all over the menus, napkins, matchbooks, glass mats, plates, wine glasses, not to mention all the stationery they had used for the inserts with which for weeks they been flooding the publications destined for lonely women. And yet when Sofia, red-nosed and slightly hoarse, came back from Adela H. that night and told Rimini what had happened, he realised that however justified these practical excuses might have been, they were not the whole story. Just as on every day since his return, Rimini had spent the whole evening sifting through photos, the same hundreds of photos they should have shared between them when they separated, and which Rimini – who found himself unable to bear to even look at them, afraid that they would sweep him into one of those emotional whirlpools he was always frightened of drowning in – had conveniently 'forgotten', without meaning to but quite deliberately, at Sofia's apartment, and which she had kept for years in two big cardboard boxes, protecting them from everything, from accidents when she moved house, for example, but also from the unhealthy, threatening curiosity of some of her men friends, but above all from her own resentment, which had more than once tempted her to take out on them all the revenge she could not wreak on Rimini himself. He had been looking at them, trying to put them in chronological order, and even though he had not made much progress – because whenever he picked up any photo, instead of limiting himself to the few details that would have helped him give it a date: the age of the people portrayed, their clothes, the cars, where it had been taken (and not to mention the date and time that was often printed on the back of them) – he allowed himself to be drawn into the tiny, private signs they contained, which only he and possibly Sofía could recognise – signs that took him to a strange, pure form of the past, where time's internal folds disappeared under an oceanic blanket of emotional continuity – after a few hours, almost without realising it, he had started to give the photos a number and to write in a notebook, under the corresponding number, all the impressions that looking at them again in this way produced in him. He had been, as he told Sofía when he saw her come in, raising his eyes and brushing aside the mist veiling them so that he could see her properly, floating for hours on end in the past. Perhaps that was why (her story about the controversy over the name surprised him with one foot in the present and the other still in the site of his excavations, from where it was obvious it was not easy for him to escape) he immediately pushed aside the practical reasons and set about looking for the real ones. He started searching among the photos. He had seen one in passing that he had not considered important, but, instead of fading, the image had left a trace, that sort of mnemonic poison which later, when some unexpected stimulus acts on it, suddenly brings an image we thought unimportant back to life, filling it with a strange sense of premonition. He found it: it was a bad photo taken in a square. An adolescent couple had their arms round each other on a stone bench, against a background of tangled *ombú* or *palo borracho* branches. These branches were in fact more in focus than the figures, which were blurred not only because the photographer had miscalculated, but because of the speed of the gesture with which the boy – if it was a boy – was trying to console the girl (if it was a girl) as he struggled with about half a ton of sheepskin draped over the arm of his suede jacket. It was Barrancas de Belgrano, in winter, Rimini started to say as he handed her the photo: *Adèle H.*, one of the first films they had seen together. The very first, he thought. They had arranged to meet outside the cinema in Avenida Cabildo, a building that has now gone and even then was run-down, spotted with damp and smelling of cat's piss, which managed to survive only thanks to a documentary film about a legendary American rock festival and of course the successive generations of young people who for years had been packing the late night shows to see it, audiences who could not have cared less (partly because of their fanaticism, partly because of the state of collective trance they fell into) about the progressive deterioration of the copy of the film they were seeing: its jumps, blanks and emergency repairs had long since ceased merely being obstacles to the narrative and had become an arbitrary, but not always ridiculous, selection of songs and even entire groups, to a point where what distinguished the generations of youngsters visiting the cinema was not only their ages but the different bands that the ruined film had allowed them to see. It was not just the first film they were seeing together; it was perhaps the first time they were going out together, the first time that – too bold, too innocent – they were transplanting their modest, shy, still imperfect love story from the world of school, where it had been born and where, for good or ill, it functioned more or less naturally, to the jungle of the outside world, which simply because it was so unknown to them would undoubtedly be hostile. No sooner had they appeared at the box office than Rimini, who in order to cut short the purchase of their tickets as much as possible had got the exact amount of money needed in his hand, found himself being stared at hard by the assistant. Without meaning to, Sofia saved the situation by suddenly coming forward out of the background where she had been waiting and, leaning over to see what time the film started, pushed her beautiful precocious smoker's hand between the executioner's gaze and his victim's helpless body. The battle was won, but not the war. A few moments later, when he happily or at least with great relief handed the tickets to the usher and moved on, carried forward by a rush of optimism, hoping to go straight into the darkened theatre, he found himself held back by the usher's arm, which had dropped like a mechanical barrier, and by his neutral, equally mechanical-sounding voice asking how old he was. I'm an adult, Rimini protested, feeling his face flush bright red. How old are you? the man insisted. Sixteen, Rimini said. He tried to hit back: do you want to see my ID card? Yes, said the usher. Then, already humiliated and so with nothing to lose, Rimini allowed himself to snort violently, in a gesture of civic indignation he had probably learnt from his father – who never went past any window, toll booth or customs post without provoking some kind of scandal, a miniature private revolt, the tell-tale signs of which (unnoticed by the rest of the world) he cherished as trophies from an unceasing struggle – and searched for his card as slowly as possible, demonstrating to the usher the precious time he was making them lose because of his suspicions. When eventually he found it, after feeling an alarming number of empty pockets and noticing how his confidence and self-assurance (doubly felt, because he knew he was within the law and yet had been mistreated) were seeping away, he thrust it at him angrily, almost stamping it on his face. By then the usher had lost interest anyway. He ignored the card and simply tapped Rimini on the shoulder, pushing him towards the entrance and snapping his fingers impatiently for the other few spectators in the foyer to come forward, tickets in hand. It was over, they were inside, and could sit where they liked without any neighbours, and yet Rimini was still stunned by the rush of uncertainty that had so affected him. He sat there, so cut off from everything that all Sofia's kisses, caresses and excitement vanished like spirals of smoke. This mood only faded a few minutes later, when the lights in the cinema began to go down and, as if too impatient to wait for everything to go completely dark, the screen suddenly filled with the colours of the landscapes painted by Victor Hugo. 'The story of Adèle H. is a true story. It deals with events that really happened, and with people who really existed'. From the appearance of this prologue a few seconds after the Hugo watercolours, to the scene in which Adèle, alone in her room in Halifax, starts to write in her diary, they followed the film in silence, curled up against each other, as if the darkened cinema were a hostile, stormy sea, the first example of an imaginary shipwreck that they played out time and again over the following years.

Adèle disembarks in the port at night. She is the only woman among a ship-load of men. Searching for somewhere to stay, she tries the Hotel Halifax, but it is so crowded she takes fright and runs out. The cab-driver leaves her at a small family boarding-house, where she introduces herself to the landlady, Mrs Saunders, as Miss Lewly: the first in a whole string of false identities she will assume throughout her life. She goes to sleep. The next day, she goes to see a public notary and gives him the task (raising her voice a little, because Doctor Lenoir is, as they say, a little hard of hearing) of finding an English lieutenant by the name of Pinson, of the 16th Regiment of Hussars. She makes up a story (this too is the first of a string of them) and tells him about a niece of hers, a very romantic niece – not her, she says twice in quick succession, because she has not the slightest interest in this lieutenant

– who, head over heels in love with Pinson, has found herself separated from him, against both their wishes, due to the sudden transfer of his regiment to Halifax. A few minutes later, she suddenly comes to a halt outside a shop, the Whistler bookshop where, accompanied by a beautiful young woman carrying a pair of lapdogs, Lieutenant Pinson (Rimini and Sofia both know it is him: they were aware of it before he turned round, simply from the way in which Adèle is looking at him and her eyes seem to turn pale, to lose all their colour and become literally transparent, like a blind person's) is saying goodbye to the bookseller. In order to avoid being seen, Adèle moves quickly away from the shop window. She waits for Pinson and his companion to leave and walk off before she too goes into the bookshop. She invents a plausible excuse – she needs money, she has to draw up a 'will' and so will need much more than a few sheets of paper; an entire ream in fact – in order to strike up conversation with the bookseller. Wasn't the man who just left Lieutenant Pinson? That's right, he's a good client: he hasn't been in Halifax long, but he already has something of a reputation, says Mr Whistler. At least, that's what they say. Oh, yes? And what else do they say? Adèle asks. They also say he has heavy debts, but here he always pays cash. I'm sorry, Mrs . . . Miss. Miss: are you a relative of his? Yes, says Adèle, he's my brother-in-law, but we don't see much of each other: I'm not on good terms with my sister. Before they say farewell, the bookseller (who is obviously interested in Adèle) offers her the service of his travelling library. Adèle promises to think about it.

Night falls. Adèle returns to the boarding-house; Mrs Saunders invites her to share the evening meal with her; her husband has had to go out: he's been hired as a waiter for the banquet in the Officers' Mess. Already at the top of the stairs, Adèle stops and asks if British officers will be going. Of course, Mrs Saunders tells her: the banquet is in honour of the Hussars regiment! Adèle looks thoughtful. Well then, she says, as if thinking out loud to herself, my cousin will be there. You have a cousin in Halifax? Yes, Lieutenant Pinson. A sudden idea brings a gleam to Adèle's eyes. I call him my cousin, but in fact we're not related. We were brought up together: he's the son of the local vicar. In fact, he's been in love with me since we were children. Not that I ever encouraged him in the slightest. It's been so long since we've seen each other! Perhaps this would be a good occasion for us to meet again. If I gave you a letter for him, could you make sure he gets it? Adèle shuts herself in her room. Our separation has destroyed me, she writes by the light of an oil-lamp; I've been thinking of you every day since you left, and know you suffer as much as I do. I never received any of the letters you sent, and I'm sure you haven't received any of mine either. But now I'm here, Albert, on the same side of the ocean as you, and everything is going to be like it used to be. I'll soon feel your arms around me. I'm very close, Albert. Waiting for you. I love you. Your Adèle.

Later that evening, Mrs Saunders is admiring Adèle's sketch book. My brother did them, Adèle tells her. This is a beautiful portrait, says the woman. Is it you? No, it's my elder sister. Does she live in Europe? No, she died a long time ago. My goodness, says Mrs Saunders, I'm so sorry. Leopoldine drowned a few months after our mother drew this portrait. She was nineteen, and newly wed. They had gone out boating together. Her husband died with her. Our father was away on a trip. A long way away. He found out by accident: he read about it in the newspaper. He was driven almost mad by grief. What about you? Mrs Saunders asks. You must have been very sad. Adèle does not raise her eyes from the portrait of Leopoldine. She was everyone's favourite, she says. How adorable she looks! Adèle opens a jewel box and takes out a necklace. This belonged to her. I keep it with me always. Mrs Saunders studies it, then tries to put it on Adèle. She moves away quickly. No, no she says, I could never wear it. I understand, Miss Adèle: I've always wanted to have brothers and sisters myself. No! says Adèle, intimidating the good woman with her violent tone, you don't understand! You don't know how lucky you are to be an only child! That night, when Mr Saunders returns from the banquet, Adèle fires questions at him: did he see her cousin, how was he dressed, what did he talk about? And the letter, Mrs Saunders wants to know. Did you give him the letter? Yes, of course, says Mr Saunders. Well, what are you waiting for, says his wife: give the reply to Miss Lewly here. No, says Mr Saunders, there was no reply. The lieutenant read the letter, but had no wish to reply. Oh, that doesn't matter, Adèle says, hiding a look of discouragement, I wasn't really expecting one. As Adèle goes to climb the stairs, Mrs Saunders questions her husband about the menu. General Doyle's chef drew it up. There was turtle soup, curried chicken ... They hear the sound of Adèle's door closing on the floor above. You know, that letter, says Mr Saunders – the lieutenant did not even open it. All he did was glance at the envelope, shrug his shoulders, and put it in his pocket. That's odd, isn't it? For a man in love ... The scene fades to black; when the light returns, we see Adèle tossing and turning in the midst of a nightmare: she is in her nightdress, lying on her back on her bed, but there is water everywhere, as if the room were sinking, and she is struggling desperately to keep her head above water.

The next day she calls at the bank, where a clerk gives her a letter. Adèle looks disappointed. She was expecting something more, a money transfer. The clerk shakes his head: perhaps in a couple of weeks. Back in her room, Adèle cuts in half a sheet of paper she has taken from the ream. She writes: Dear mother and father, If I left without warning it was to avoid yet another of those arguments which in our family tend to flare up over the slightest little thing. If Lieutenant Pinson were to leave his post now, it would ruin his entire career. So I cannot leave him. As you well know, I love him, and he loves me. We want to get married. But I will do nothing without your approval, and I am waiting for a reply from both of you. With all my love, Adèle. PS: Father, you owe me the monthly allowance for May and June. I know part of the money is being sent via the British North American Bank, but I'll need the whole amount: life in Halifax is very expensive.

While she is waiting, Adèle kills time strolling along the promenade. She passes by an officer, turns round and catches him up. She taps him on the shoulder. The officer comes to a halt and looks at her in astonishment. Embarrassed, she lowers her eyes and walks away. She shuts herself in her room. We must consider all the little things of our lives as being important, she writes in her diary. I know we have to fight our own moral battles. Thousands upon thousands of miles from my family, I see life differently. I can learn everything on my own, but to love I need him.

At this point Sofia started to shake, as if she had had an electric shock, and began silently crying. She cried so much and for such a long time that soon, when Rimini, whose forearms were already soaked from all the tears as he hugged her, became aware that this was not so much a happy accident – one of those episodes which, despite appearances, help to speed up a closeness that timidity, a sense of shame or a lack of confidence often hinder – as something else, something of an order he did not understand, but which demanded he take an immediate decision: Sofia's eyes were so puffy from her tears that she could not even see the film, because whenever she opened them she felt a burning pain that forced her to shut them again at once, and when she did manage to keep them open for a few seconds, the tears were so dense that a curtain of water prevented her seeing anything on the screen. It was a record crying bout – forty minutes on the watch – from the words written by Adèle H. that had started it all off, to the moment when, in Barrancas de Belgrano, where Rimini, after dragging her out of the cinema, had managed to lead her, and a few seconds after the photographer in the square had caught them on the bench and taken the photo that Rimini was showing her now, a couple of gypsy women appeared from nowhere, from the tree trunks, the bandstand, or any of the hundreds of lairs they had all over the square, and bewildered them with vaguely magic gestures and threatening whispers, offering to tell their fortunes, giving them little nudges on their chests and shoulders, until Rimini and Sofia realised they had been pushed apart, and she was on one side of the path, standing in the soil of a flower-bed with the gypsy woman almost on top of her, looking as though she were dangling from her clothes, and Rimini was on the other side, trying to grab back the hand where his gypsy had started to read the clues of his imaginary future. It was only thanks to the terror caused by this pair of multi-coloured monsters – for whom fortune-telling was not so much the heritage of their race as a piece of business they seemed to know by heart, the minimum dose of exoticism needed to achieve, as quickly as possible, their true aim, the only one that really interested them, namely to ask for money – only that kind of terror, Rimini recalled, was capable of tearing Sofia out of her trance and making her stop crying. Rimini managed to shake off the gypsy clinging to his arm and went to rescue Sofia, who was searching for a coin in her pockets. As they ran off back up towards the bench where the photographer was now waiting to sell them the photo, Rimini looked carefully at her face, as though to make sure the episode with the gypsies had left no trace, and saw that her cheeks were white, blooming, shiny as a street in sunshine after a shower of torrential rain.

But Sofia was not convinced by his reconstruction of events. In addition to her facility for tears, which had not changed and which she always defended as the proof of her supernatural sensitivity, all the elements of the picture he drew were familiar to her: the film about Adèle H., of course, the cinema on Avenida Cabildo, her first date with Rimini, the usher asking to see his ID card, the square, the gypsy women – but not in the order that Rimini had given them, and certainly not in the same time-frame. Take the photo, for example: yes, it was her, Sofia, and the bench was a light-green colour and had a curved back, yes, and it was the square in Barrancas, yes, and the boy embracing her and apparently trying to hide her face, as though protecting her from the photographer's lens, was wearing a suede jacket – but she could have sworn it was not Rimini, whom Sofia could not recall ever having been in Barrancas with, but his immediate predecessor, a boy called Moacyr, the wayward child of a Brazilian diplomat, who was considerably younger than her but much more experienced: at thirteen, his curriculum included a number of enviable achievements like having been on a plane, having gone to two or three massive rock concerts, having had a couple of adult relationships (sex included), knowing about a wide range of drugs, putting up with a beautiful, alcoholic mother and being a distant relative of one of the founders of the bossa nova. In the photo, Sofia thought she remembered, he was trying to convince her of the virtues of free love as practised in the palatial mansion he and his father, together with a host of chauffeurs and servants, lived in at the heart of one of the city's most exclusive neighbourhoods; the same one where as a little boy Rimini (as he had once confessed to Sofia), who had just learnt the art of riding a bicycle, had crashed face-first into a flag-pole where the Argentine flag was flying.

They could not agree, but it did not seem to be that important, so far removed were they from the atmosphere in which this kind of argument could produce a negative effect. Sofia in fact celebrated the misunderstanding as a victory: she saw the detailed comment that Rimini had written at the bottom of the photo as convincing proof of his good health. Not only had Rimini come back: his memory had come back too. This restoral of memory in someone like him, who for years had been convinced that his only chance of survival lay in his ability to forget, and thought that he had no emotional future if he could not first rid himself of the weight of the past, seemed to her an amazing feat, probably the only real miracle, so much so that Rimini's physical presence in her apartment, her bed, among all her things, even in Adela H., even doing what he did – first and foremost slowly re-establishing the sense of balance that had been missing for years, and subsequently providing (by the mere fact of being there) in all the places where his absence had been so obvious, the evidence that men could in fact come back, being the living proof of that evidence – all this paled into insignificance for Sofia – she was proud of it, but could if necessary do without it. The real key to his return was the return of his memory, that was the foundation, everything – just as rejecting memory, losing or postponing memories, letting them slide away and forgetting them was the key, the nub, the model of all loss and absence. Besides, wasn't that exactly how the excess of love usually first showed itself: by standing out against a background of amnesia as an excess of memory? The forgotten anniversary, the missing detail, the context in which something happened that cannot be summoned up: wasn't this exactly how all tragedies began?

It was only on that strange evening, full of tiny, unsettling portents, when Rimini had quite spontaneously thought of bringing the story behind a photo taken in a square to light, that Sofia was finally sure he had come back to her. She saw him remembering; she witnessed the conviction and naturalness with which he showed these images – so full of life that nobody would have believed that they were more than twenty years old, and still less that seven of those twenty years had been spent buried in a basement – and his absorption in this task somehow made him more real for her than everything else she had been clinging to as proof that she had won him back: his smell, his sudden flushes, the sound of his footsteps, the abrupt way he had of opening a window or pushing back a chair, the flash of fear that still appeared in his eyes whenever he looked at her – all these signs, compared to the weight of his evocation of the photograph, seemed light, trivial, provisional, in comparison. That was why she let him go on talking, silencing all the objections that occurred to her while he was showing her the picture. And if she decided to mention them anyway, creating a gap of uncertainty between them that soon disappeared when they burst out laughing, it was only because she was absolutely convinced he had returned. Protecting memory from a few corrections which could not in any way endanger it – that was to be unworthy of it rather than to honour it. Memory was the only guarantee. Everything else was air or dust, which sooner or later would come to nothing.

As Rimini was to discover shortly afterwards when, interrupting a meeting to serve coffee, inform them of a telephone call, or the arrival of someone else, or when he gave Sofia a cheque for her to sign, he would catch a small part of the debates raging in the group, this famous resurrection of memory had, on the list of objectives for their cause, quickly replaced the aim that until then had seemed to include them all: the return of the man. It may have been a simple problem of means and ends, but for a while, whether he came in at the start or end of a meeting, took them by surprise or gave them time to pretend, lower their voices, or change topics, Rimini hardly heard them use any other expressions than: 'archive', 'mnemonic capital', 'administration of the past', or talk about any problem other than the ways of (according to the strange turn of phrase once uttered by Sofia in his presence) making a memory for men. Everything else had faded into the background: techniques for winning someone back, seduction, sexual wiles, emotional mimetism, blackmail – all this was ephemeral, insufficient, ineffective, as was more than amply demonstrated by the examples of false returns that the emotional lives of the women of Adela H. were full of: men who came back after days, months, or years of separation, supposedly for the most tried and tested reasons – contrition, the need for shelter, desire, a longing for intimacy and communion – and were received with the welcome typical of all reconciliations: a combination of unconditional acceptance, outrageous romanticism, daring, tolerance, a permanent willingness to negotiate and a wish to please – and who, days, months, or years later vanished into thin air again, squandering the capital accumulated and leaving the well that had given them water dry and sterile. But fullness, tying together, permanence, gravity – everything that the conventional methods of achieving reconciliation could achieve only incompletely and for a short time (leading to the inevitable heartbreaks) – could be made possible by memory. To make a memory for men, as Rimini heard Sofia tell a handful of bemused journalists at the opening, while the huge, pale face of Adèle H. was being projected on all the walls of the bar; just as men had spent centuries making babies for women. In some cases, like that of Rimini for example, it would be enough to bring the already existing memory back to life, wake it from the sleep in which it had been vegetating and stir it up by all possible means until it had recovered the dynamics, the reflexes, the passion for detail and the sweet, obliging, comfortable domesticity that made it irreplaceable when it came to cementing love; in others, where it had been completely destroyed by the length of time spent apart or negative feelings, it would be necessary to implant it. As happens with some types of plants which, when they are transplanted, wither and die, but seem to come miraculously back to life as soon as their roots come into contact again with their original soil, not so much for biological reasons – because the properties of the earth into which they were transplanted were not after all that different from those where they first saw the light of day, and if there were differences, these could always be overcome; and yet inevitably, the transplant would fail – but because that simple contact is the spark that is enough immediately to reconstruct, in all its complexity, the vital fabric it had grown in up to that point, those subtle surroundings in which certain properties of the earth, air, light and humidity are decisive, although if, and only if, they are combined with one essential factor, time, the length of time that the plant spent in contact with all of them, receiving their benefits but at the same time influencing them – according to Sofia, that was exactly what happened with lost men. According to what Rimini read in one of the first set of minutes of Adela H. that he had to transcribe, the memory of love was the smallest part of love, the veins from which it was possible to construct the whole leaf, the leaf with its flower, and the entire plant; and not just the plant and its position in the soil but all the ecosystem of which the plant was, when it came down to it, the fruit. The fickle or indifferent man, the adulterer, the uncontrollable faun, the dodger, were all problematic, difficult cases, uncertain challenges; but the amnesiac man – he was the blind spot, the quintessence of refraction. To the man who loves and forgets – so deceitful, so common – they definitely preferred the man who hates but remembers, the man who hoards every memory because it feeds his hatred and the last thing he wants to do is to forget, because he wants to go on hating to the end. The former ends by destroying love; the latter at the very least shows a stubborn willingness to be present and to persist, and perhaps even, who knows, offers the possibility that he might fall once more into the nets of love – if, in the midst of his revisionist fury, some pleasing recollection (a protective gesture, a spark of warmth, a scene that makes him laugh) catches him unawares and makes him a target for love's arrow once more.

The opening was a success. Sofia and her retinue of women were the heroes of the night; in his subdued, subservient way, Rimini was the star. Three times more people came than they had been expecting, so that Rimini was obliged to leave in the middle of the party to restock the fridges. When he returned, pushing a supermarket trolley full to the brim, and with his pockets full of bottles too, Sofia intercepted him at the service entrance and, softening her voice at the last moment, threatened to sack him if he went off again like that. They had been looking everywhere for him. A fresh wave of guests had just arrived, and the most radical among them had stopped her and demanded, in the furious tones of a union demand, that she release him from the basement where she kept him and lent him to them for a while. When Sofia had been unable to find him, the women had threatened not only to leave, but to denounce Adela H. to the small but powerful circles of experimental therapies. It took Rimini some time to work out that the fairground attraction she was speaking of was him. He could have saved himself the trouble. Sofia took him by the hand and almost dragged him into the main room, where he immediately made out a group of thin, ash-grey women with scarves tied round their necks, wrists and ankles (as if they were gift-wrapped) who formed a sighing chorus with plastic cups (there had not been enough glasses either) into which someone had poured the last drops of some last bottle or other. 'Girls, *voilà*', said Sofia, gently pushing him towards them like a shy child being introduced to the gaggle of babysitters who were to look after him. The women turned towards him, also in chorus, and as Rimini, simply to relieve his anxiety, started to fill their glasses, they stared at him in wide-eyed nostalgia and amazement, as though he were the last living specimen of an extinct species or the first of one that was about to come into being. All this lasted only a matter of seconds, before the hypnotic effect wore off and the women came round and started giggling nervously, blushing as they realised that the hypnotist had taken advantage of the trance to take all his or their clothes off.

It was only then that Rimini fully understood. He was in a place crammed with people, where – apart from Sofia, Isabel and the other members of the group (whom he tended to confuse anyway) – he did not know anyone, but where everybody knew him. The only word he could think of using to describe this huge asymmetry was 'fame'. Rimini was a celebrity. And in spite of his fears, born from the envy and pleasure he got from following the hard knocks that fame gives celebrities in the papers or on TV, the situation was not at all unpleasant. It was like floating. Then he thought of the ecstasy that seems to grip rock stars when they dive into their audience and are carried, spread-eagled on their backs, by hundred and hundreds of anonymous arms. The fact was that, left to his own devices by the brigade of young women meant to be helping him (dancers, educational psychology students, playschool teachers, most of them more or less rebellious daughters of the same women they were supposed to be serving), who, however confusing they found it, had taken advantage of Rimini's popularity to abandon their posts and gather in the kitchen, where they snacked on the remains of the food, or in the toilets, where they smoked (the only smoke allowed in the main room was from the joss-sticks) and talked about men, Rimini had to struggle to make himself available wherever anyone needed something, and so had neither the time nor the energy to stop and enjoy, even for a few minutes, the new persona that the women's fleeting but definitely suggestive glances had created. He came and went tirelessly, until all of a sudden he thought he felt a pressure somewhere on his body – on the nape of his neck, his back, his cheek, as if a delicate, invisible finger was touching him, or someone had gently tugged at a string. When he turned round, still without stopping, the heads filling his line of vision started to tremble and drift out of focus – all except one, that of the stranger who had caressed him with her eyes from afar and who was still staring at him, her features standing out clearly through the haze. What these looks shared, apart from their interest in him, which obliged them to stare longer than necessary, was a certain superiority. They stared at him in order to confirm in his face, his gestures, his way of moving and dressing, what they already knew about him, but also simply to let him know that they knew, even though they were careful to hide any trace that might reveal what exactly it was they knew. It was a purely abstract situation: the height of non-reciprocity. What was important was not so much the secret – what could a stranger know about Rimini that he did not know himself? – as the idea of having a secret in itself, the unequal balance of power, the ambiguity (somewhere between black-mail and lascivious curiosity) that these looks conveyed as soon as Rimini gave them legitimacy by returning them.

The evening was well advanced when this asymmetrical situation, which by its very abstraction seemed destined at least in theory to go on for ever, came crashing down. By now there were fewer people in Adela H.; it was easier to breathe. A short while before, when the room had been completely packed, Sofia had taken advantage of a slight lull to get up on the stage where, trying out the spotlight (the only theatrical accessory the group's funds had been able to afford) on herself, with the result that she gave a high-pitched giggle, as though the light were tickling her, she announced the programme of events to follow. As expected, this caused a bit of a rush for the exit, which proved enough to clear the air and gave the rest of the audience more room. Many of those who left were faithful to the cause, but argued that it was already late, and that if they stayed they would only get to bed in the early hours, and they did not want to appear half-asleep the next morning to their small armies of suffering women, or put them off with the sad spectacle of black circles round their eyes, migraines, or stiff bodies. To stay would be betraying the self-discipline they led their lives by, contradicting all the reasons that had brought them to Adela H. that evening rather than anywhere else. A lot of others left for frivolous reasons, thinking they had already seen the best. After they had gone, the music changed, the windows were thrown wide open, and the audience started to collect in more intimate groups. Some of them went on talking quietly; others, fanning themselves with the menus, watched in silence as poor Adèle dreamt yet again she was Leopoldine and drowned on the big white back wall. Others still, now that they had the opportunity, started studying the installations for the first time; they soon noticed that, just as the change in atmosphere had led to the lively Greek tambourines (a souvenir Isabel had brought from a workshop in Paris, where she had happened to coincide with the first night of *Zorba the Greek*) being replaced by mournful Sephardic songs – faithful to the idols of her youth, this had been Sofia's idea – it was also time for something else to drink. 'Cointreau!' Sofia ordered, and Rimini rushed down to the basement, where the group kept an exclusive stash of alcohol for its more intimate occasions. He was coming up the narrow concrete staircase with two bottles of liqueur in his hands when at the top he saw a young woman – probably the youngest he had seen all night, so young that she seemed to come from another world. She shut the door behind her, and came down towards him. To Rimini, it seemed as if she were naked or was wearing a perfectly flesh-coloured costume, so real it was terrifying, and that the black rope hanging from her neck and wrapped round her body like a spider's web was in fact that: a phone cable. She leapt on him like an Amazon, clinging to his waist with her firm, well-trained thighs and starting to kiss him fiercely, tenderly, desperately, as though trying to smother him in kisses. In between her assaults, she whispered frantically in his ear: 'Yes, I too knelt before Riltse's rose in London.' 'Yes,' she said, 'I too detest Austria with all my heart.' 'Yes,' she said, 'I too had a raging fever in Vienna and allowed a doctor at the British Hospital to examine me.' 'Yes,' she said, 'I too had an allergic rash in Rio de Janeiro and smeared my face with useless creams.' 'Yes,' she said, 'I too listened to the rain on a corrugated-iron roof while I was having an abortion.' 'Yes,' she said, 'I too was blinded by my tears when Rocco and Nadia met on the cathedral roof.' It was a miracle they did not fall down the stairs. Stiff with shock, Rimini managed to sustain the girl's weight and kisses, but he dropped one of the bottles; its neck smashed against the edge of one of the steps and the liquid started to seep out. 'Marry me,' the girl hissed, her moist lips and teeth brushing against his neck. Rimini laughed and pushed her away to get a good look at her. He wanted to see if she was real; if he could still look a real woman in the eye. Her skin was very smooth and white; she had a moustache of beads of sweat on her top lip, and a tiny crater between her eyebrows, the souvenir of one of the slyest attacks of chicken pox he had ever seen. Rimini was on the verge of tears. He hugged her to him. 'Don't be a coward: marry me,' he heard her say again, as her young chin began to nestle into his shoulder as though it were a cradle, the age-old cradle that had always been there for it.

How many years had it taken him to overcome that cowardice? Twenty? Thirty? Was he going to throw all that away for a woman who could reel off the two or three most important moments of his life, without a single mistake, and whose very youth was enough to excuse her? He felt so ancient that the image of the old, dying astronaut in *2001 – A Space Odyssey*, seemed to him like a personal souvenir, another of the photos on which every day he wrote the autobiographical details that Sofia no longer even bothered to read. He wrote: 'Rimini on his death bed, solemn and happy, after receiving and rejecting the final offer of emotional redemption in his life'. Some time later, in mid-show (a Penthesilea, overweight but brimming with enthusiasm, had just finished declaring her love for an invisible Achilles, hidden somewhere on the bar between the whisky and tequila), and as the ambush on the basement stairs was starting to settle into the version that he was to remember it by for the next twenty years, Rimini, who was weaving his way, bent low, among the tables so as not to spoil the audience's view, turned and recognised his acrobatic suitor up on the stage, silhouetted against the backdrop by the spotlight, reciting a passage from *La Voix Humaine*, or rather shouting it into the telephone handset she was holding up level with her eyes, as if it were the severed head of the man who yet again had abandoned her, which ended in a desperate knot in the telephone cable that Rimini suddenly discovered was wrapped round her neck like a lethal scarf, and snaked all over her body. When he reached Sofia, who was watching the performance open-mouthed, he said: 'She's a student of yours, isn't she?' Sofia nodded. 'How old is she?' asked Rimini. Sofia deigned to lean her head towards him, but kept her gaze fixed on the stage: 'I don't know, it's incalculable,' she said, or that is what Rimini surmised from the lengthy alcoholic yawn that issued from her mouth. She was so drunk that when the girl finished she could not even applaud: she raised her hands in the air, stared at them with one of those huge efforts of concentration that drunks so often movingly display and then, as though to spare them unnecessary humiliation, let them drop lifelessly into her lap. The young girl left the stage, to be replaced by an older woman whose age was at least calculable. Rustling some deliberately aged sheets of paper next to the microphone, she pretended to be reading out: 'Dear mother and father, I have just married Lieutenant Pinson. The ceremony took place on Saturday in a Halifax church. In future you should write to me as: "Mrs. Pinson, 33 North Street, Halifax, Nova Scotia"' and for the next quarter of an hour, gave an abbreviated version, delivered with monotonous intensity, of Adèle H.'s letters. And when the hundred shadows that had followed this performance without moving all suddenly stood up and raised their hands skywards, to that sky where the blades of the fan circled tirelessly round and round, letting out whoops of joy as spectacular as a firework display, Sofia wanted to be part of the celebration. She began slowly and carefully to get to her feet; she wanted to shout, to add her voice to the general roar, but as soon as she opened her mouth it was filled with a bitter taste from the pit of her stomach. Her legs gave way: Rimini managed to catch her before she fell. Sofia lay there in his arms, face up; as he leaned over to examine her face, they looked like a statue to a dancing couple. Isabel, Rocío, Mercedes – somebody must have seen them, one of the bacchantes dancing in a trance around them must have spotted this tiny fairy-tale tableau they were frozen in, because all at once there was a shout, then someone said their names, fingers started pointing at them, and the beam from the spotlight, which had still been focussed on the stage where Adèle H. had left it, moved away, lit up the bodies crowded round to observe the scene with a vibrant white glow, and finally picked out the couple, endowing them with the magic halo that was all that was needed to make the enchantment complete. The shouts and applause became deafening: the throng of women closed in. Now they were not so much bacchantes as Amazons – the Amazons the plump Penthesilea who had spat out her passion for Achilles half an hour earlier had not wanted to allow up on to the stage for fear of it collapsing – who were now literally beside themselves (carried away less by the alcohol than by the build-up of excitement all night and the sense – so typical of drinking sprees, and so suspect – that they were living a unique, unrepeatable moment that would change every-thing, were busy taking their revenge and closing ranks to celebrate the allegory that an unconscious Sofia was embodying in the arms of her man. One woman had climbed on a chair and was suggesting someone paint them; another, more impatiently, flashed her camera at the motionless dancers. Rimini looked down at Sofia and saw how pale she was, with dark lines round her eyes, and almost purple lips. She even seemed to be trembling. He lifted her and carried her out, while the spotlight strained to follow them and someone began to sing a version of 'My Man' in Italian.

They were still the prince and the sleeping beauty in the street, in the taxi – egged on by the driver, a sentimental ginger-haired man who confused them with a newly married couple – and on the stairs of Sofia's apartment block where Rimini, trying desperately not to wake her, trod on the long belt of her dress he had undone in the taxi to make her more comfortable, and almost sent them flying. 'Not so much light, not so much light,' groaned Sofia. Rimini thought of going straight to bed, less out of a fit of romanticism than because that way he would have not have to carry her so far, and that is what they did, after a brief detour via the bathroom, where Sofia vomited three times in a very civilised way, bringing up most of the alcohol she had imbibed that evening. Then Rimini carried her into the bedroom, undressed her and himself, and the two of them dived into the cool paradise of their sheets. He listened to her breathing for a few seconds, stirring in her sleep, and before he knew it they were stuck to each other like leeches. They made love almost asleep, still pressed against one another, in drunken, lazy movements. Rimini was not even sure if he had penetrated her. He finished quickly, more quickly than her in any case, and as his body shuddered he was strangely but utterly convinced that this load of semen that he had shot blindly out without knowing exactly where, was going to be the last ever. He felt an immense, universal sense of relief, similar to what he had occasionally experienced after a fierce storm, when the rain stopped and the roar of the wind dropped to a gentle, friendly breeze. He thought of Lucio; he would have loved to be able to measure his height by putting the edge of his hand against his own body, as he had seen lots of fathers do. He could not even remember his face any more. He could feel fingernails digging in his back, pulling him down; Sofia was finishing. In among her gasping groans, he thought he heard her say something, or name someone: one of those trails that the language of sleep leaves when it crosses the sky of the waking world; after that, nothing.

Rimini soon realised he was not going to sleep; yet again he was amazed at the attraction that sleeplessness had for him. Everyone else but him was asleep, and that banal exception made him feel strangely superior; it gave him immunity, time – not only the time he was stealing from his own sleep but all that which in a kind of vampire-like swoop he was taking from everyone else's. He felt as if he were winning a race, as though these moments awake were one of those unique, absolutely privileged opportunities which, if properly seized, can make an indelible difference between the chosen person and those who are still fast asleep. He moved away from Sofia, sat up in the bed and stayed there for a while, staring into the darkness, stunned by the infinite number of possibilities that seemed to be fighting each other to fill these unexpectedly free hours. He began to weigh them up one by one, in order, so he thought, to behave responsibly in his privileged position, but soon discovered they were all equally interesting and valuable. He ended up making the easiest choice: he put on a dressing-gown and sat on the rug in the living-room to sort some more photos. The work for the opening of Adela H. had interrupted his task just as he was dealing with 1976; he had only had time to write the year in white pencil on the black cardboard sheets he used for an album. He tipped open the slimmest of the eight enormous manila envelopes, and the photos cascaded on to his lap. He spread them out more or less at random on the rug so that they were all visible, and then separated and put to one side the ones with serrated edges, which meant they had been taken with an Instamatic and therefore belonged to the seventies. All of a sudden, while he was glancing at them in general, in that tentative way we adopt in order to soften the impact of the moment when we really devote ourselves to something that is going to demand all our attention, he had the impression that something in him, in the photos, in the relation between him and the photos, had changed in a subtle but definitive way. Nearly all the photos he put to one side had lost their colour. They had never been particularly good, not even when they existed alongside the happy moments they were illustrating; they were old, but the cars, houses, furniture, clothes – all of that looked new, brand new, as though the photo were capturing something that was happening for the first time. On top of that, now they were yellowing or had taken on the dirty, greyish-red tone of the light used by photographers in their dark-rooms. But this chromatic degradation was what least disturbed him: after all, wasn't that what happened to photographs? And wasn't that the basic reason behind the survival of something so primitive as photography: the wish to see how that scrap of paper, in theory called on to immortalise a face, or body, a place or a moment of love, also deteriorated, grew old, was mortal? No: what disturbed him was to look at ten or twenty photos and to realise that, apart from him and Sofia, whose appearances were blemished by time and distance but were still undeniably them, he did not recognise a soul. Even the places where people were posing – a balcony terrace with trees in the background, a bookshop window, a beach tent, a plate-glass window reflecting the sun – were unknown to him. The two of them were always in focus, but the rest – the surroundings, the people they were sharing the picture with, all the objects, even the dachshund which, in a photo that had so many stains it looked as if it had been taken by a psychedelic photographer, was sniffing at one of Sofia's bell-bottoms – seemed to grow cloudy, to withdraw and be hidden behind a dark veil. Rimini searched for his parents, for Sofia's parents, for a young and healthy Victor waving to them out of their innocent past. He saw faces, ages, gestures, clothing, and paused over them in gleeful expectation. Then, when nothing leapt out at him – and only that moment of instant recognition could satisfy him – he resigned himself to glancing at them in an offhand way, like someone giving an audition to actors who could take the supporting roles in a play. He and Sofia were there, transported to a bogus world, specially constructed for the photo, or sent by mistake to a parallel world where all signs of familiarity had been eliminated . . . How could it be possible? He went back to the album and, like someone desperate to find dry land, began to glance at the years he had already sorted out. He looked at the photos, literally devoured the descriptions he had written. Yes, he had seen them before. Yes, he recognised it: it was his own hand-writing, but who were all these smiling people raising their glasses to the camera? Where did that Fiat 600 come from? Who was that woman in dark glasses and a turban flexing her puny biceps for? He read: 'On the dock, with Lucrecia and Cinthia, ten minutes after having mussels *à la provençale* for lunch, and five before travelling in an ambulance for the first time.' He rubbed his eyes, and forced himself to read it again. Lucrecia? Cinthia? Ambulance? It was more than enough trying

473

to decipher what he had written, never mind the insinuations . . . What kind of trance had he written those lines in? He stood up and looked around suspiciously, as though afraid that in those ten or fifteen minutes of confusion everything might have changed. Solid in the half-light, the objects in the room calmed him. It occurred to him that Sofia might be able to sort it all out. He went back to the bedroom and sat on the edge of the bed, but did not dare touch her until he had stopped trembling. Sofia grunted, rolled over in bed, throwing off the covers, and went on sleeping turned towards the other wall but in exactly the same position in which Rimini had found her. He took the duvet in his hands to cover her over again, and then saw a dark line coming out of her sex and running down the white sheet. He bent over and touched the sheet with his fingertip. It was blood. He moved his face even closer, and saw the blood oozing from the slit between her legs – at first it was a sudden gleam, as though the skin had suddenly grown moist, then there was a bubble, a tiny balloon that was not yet fully inflated but which had already burst, and finally there was a line, a shiny, red line that left its mark on the skin and ended up as part of the big stain Rimini had just discovered on the sheet. Rimini opened his dressing-gown and saw his penis was also dripping blood. He retraced his steps from the bedroom to the living-room, rubbing out the trail of drops he had left on the floor with his feet. Then he returned to the bedroom, got back in next to Sofia, and fell asleep. He dreamt of a town of poor, low houses, deafeningly noisy, where policemen were directing the traffic with loud whistles and there were at least half a dozen opticians and spectacles shops on every block. Optica 10, he read – or perhaps, in the same dream, he was already remembering it. Optica Luz, Optica Carron, Optica Mía, Optica Universal, Optica Exprés, Optica Jesucristo, Optica Nessi, Optica Paraná, Optica Americana. He saw his two naked feet on an artificial grass lawn surrounding a pool on the roof of a sun-drenched building. When he awoke, feeble daylight was filtering through the blinds. Nothing had changed. Still bleeding.